TEXAS SHORT STORIES

EDITED BY

BILLY BOB HILL

Browder Springs Publishing
Dallas

For information address:

Browder Springs Publishing
P. O. Box 823521
Dallas TX 75382

Cover art: Dana Adams
Book design and editing: Jane L. Tanner

This book is the second of the American Regional Book Series from Browder Springs Publishing. The first is Paul Ruffin's award-winning poetry collection, *Circling*.

Library of Congress Catalog Card Number: 97-70021

ISBN 0-9651359-1-8

FOR

ROBERT NELSON HILL
(1903–1996)

Contents

Contents

INTRODUCTION

In the spring of 1954 I got The Call, as they used to say, but it was not the call to preach the gospel, exactly: under the big live oak tree in the side yard of the house we lived in then in Mineral Wells, Texas, I got the call to tell stories, and I solemnly committed myself to a life of lies in the interests of the truth.

That following summer I got a job at the Queen Roofing Company in Mineral Wells, where I learned something about what is probably the primary requirement for being a writer, and that is the long patience about which I have since read so much.

Two specific jobs from that summer stick out for me: reroofing all the dozens of government duplexes in southeast Mineral Wells, out along the back road to Memorial Football Stadium, at $1.10 an hour straight time, ten to twelve hours a day, six days a week. I wasn't much of a roofer, but I was killer as a roofer's helper, and I could carry packs of shingles up a ladder all day long. That's where I broke the u-bolt in my back, I'm pretty sure, a break I didn't even discover for almost thirty years and didn't have repaired for almost thirty-five. But I sure learned a lot about long patience.

The other job I remember well from that summer was replacing the tin roof on a church—surely a Baptist church—in DeLeon, Texas, which is almost straight south of Desdemona, Texas, and which you got to in those days by heading south out of Mineral Wells on 281 past Stephenville to State Highway 6, where you turned right and headed west/northwest for seven miles or so. After long days in the blistering summer sun first ripping the old corrugated iron roof off that church and then laboriously replacing it with 1 x 6 shiplap followed by asphalt shingles, I rode home those several early evenings lying up on top of whatever refuse and equipment we had loaded into the back of our work truck, those miles from DeLeon. We crossed what is now Interstate 20, but was then U.S. 80, that

ran south of Mineral Wells, out past Seven Mile Park. We would head out
from work on the church just at twilight, when the air was beginning to
cool in the long dips in the road and the sweet smells of the country rose
from the earth. Those trips back home at dusk brought me such sweet pain
then, at seventeen, I felt I could not bear it. What beautiful country! I thought.
How wonderful it is to be alive!

That was a long time ago, but Paul Christiansen's story "Buried Horses,"
the last in this fine volume edited by B. B. Hill, brought back so many of
those sensations from my youth, in all their painful sweetness, both made
sweeter and more painful too by the passage of the years. Through the
virtual reality—the original virtual reality—of fiction, I got to take another trip back home.

These "lies in the interests of the truth!" What hunger do they feed in
people that makes us go back to them again and again over the centuries?
What do they provide us that we want—and maybe even need—so much?
Is it because we want the world transfigured, and imaginative utterances
such as these serve to do that for us? Do they provide what Robert Frost
promised of poetry, a "momentary stay against confusion"?

And yet, though stories do clearly help us carve out meaning from the
incorrigible chaos of life, reading fiction hasn't always been universally
considered a positive activity; indeed, it has often been considered quite
the opposite, even, sometimes, just a step away from sin. If books can
improve us—and of course they can—then we are logic bound to agree
that they can also harm us. In our culture, it is a chance most of us are
willing to take, though, most of the time.

In a chapter called "Forbidden Reading," in his fine book A *History of
Reading*, Alberto Manguel tells a story about Anthony Comstock, the
founder of the New York Society for the Suppression of Vice, which
Manguel calls "the first effective censorship board in the United States."
Comstock founded his society because he was convinced that "'immoral
literature' perverted the minds of the young, who should busy themselves
with higher spiritual matters."[1] In fact, says Manguel, Comstock's passion
was based in great part on his suspicion of reading all by itself, regardless
of the text: "'Our Father Adam could not read in Paradise,' he once af-
firmed."[2]

---

[1]Viking, 1996, p. 287.
[2]Ibid., p. 284.

This concern wasn't new with Comstock, of course. Plato allowed poets in his Republic only on the condition that they write nothing more than hymns and/or praises of famous men, and Manguel cites evidence of such suppression in the Orient as far back as fifteenth-century China.

Since "The Tales of the Magicians," which date back to +/- 4000/3000 B.C.E.,[3] to, say, "Linda's Daddy's Loaded," by Matthew Klam, a story I just read, in the January 13, 1997, issue of *The New Yorker,* people have been telling stories, lying in the interests of the truth, mostly about other people being people, trying, at some level, to organize life into a manageable package and, in the best of stories, revealing—over and over again—that there *is* someone inside those other skins, those cases that keep the insides in and the outside out. And during all these centuries, these story tellers have had an eager market for their wares.

Both the Old and the New Testaments are filled with short stories, most of them intended—one assumes—to glorify God. The *Iliad* and the *Odyssey*, which date back to between 900 and 800 B.C.E., are treasure chests full of story gems, the one a salutation and farewell to a time and manner of life gone by, and the other a salutation and welcome to a new way, a way dominated not by lechery, gluttony, sloth, wrath—a lot of wrath—envy, and pride, but rather cleverness, glibness, trickery, imagination, dissembling, eros, and intelligence. Achilleus is a hero, but he's also a pain; Odysseus is a hero, but he's also a con man, quick with the lip: the first modern man, it is often said. And what adventures he had!

Stories abound in most, if not all, cultures. Those in *The Thousand and One Nights* come from Egypt—Arabia, North Mica—from the 13th century, and can be bought on tape now, translated into and read in English, all these centuries later while we drive back and forth from home to work, or down the road to Kilgore for a little fresh air. The Medieval Age in Europe supplied us with fabliaux, exempla, and romantic tales. In Italy, Boccaccio ground out *The Decameron*, in England, Chaucer *The Canterbury Tales.* Both appear to have recanted, toward the end, by the way, won over to the certainty that what they had done was a sin.

Both the ballad and the 18th century essay exerted their influences on the development of the story to what it has become in modern times, though convincing most people of that connection is often easier said than done.

---

[3]A. Walton Litz, *Major American Short Stories*, 3rd. ed., Oxford University Press, 1994, p 3, as well as countless other places.

All one has to do to see that connection, by the way, is to go back and read once again the Scottish and English border ballads and the essays of Addison, say, in *The Spectator.* European novellas contributed their part to the development of what is now the short story, as did the synthesis growing out of the thesis of the romance, on the one hand, and the antithesis of the realistic novel of later times, on the other.

All of a sudden, as if from nowhere—and in a sense, it was perhaps partly from the Great Void, though certainly not wholly from it—came Gogol (from under whose "Overcoat," it is often repeated, come all modern short stories), and, roughly at the same time, come Irving, Hawthorne, Poe, *et al.* The step from there seems small—but may be one of the biggest steps of all—to Anton Chekhov, Stephen Crane, Sherwood Anderson, Ernest Hemingway, Scott Fitzgerald, William Faulkner, Carson McCullers, Eudora Welty, Saul Bellow, Flannery O'Connor, Katherine Anne Porter, James Baldwin, and all those other old standards we know so well and love, for the most part, sometimes even revere as icons of the modern age.

Then—once again—something happened to the genre, and the perpetrators, the suspects brought in for questioning, were the B-Boys, the Bad Boys of the modern/contemporary short story, Borges, Barthelme, and Barth—and you can add Coover to the list, as well—all happily, joyfully creating a kind of post-modernist confusion compared to what had been for most all the centuries before a matter of beginning, middle, and end: an investment in time with a clear psychological payoff mostly, pleasurable mostly, though absent, sometimes, from the stories of, say, Chekhov, and his followers.

These latter-day trouble makers rebelled against business as usual and chose to write stories a little further along the continuum of total predictability, on the one end, toward total unpredictability, on the other. All art dances this particular dance, in fits and starts, of course, from easy to hard, from the known to the unknown, from the same to the different. Again, the reaction to the status quo—the thesis—manifests itself in a pendulum swing that Hegel would call the antithesis, that simmers into the synthesis which then, in time, constitutes the new thesis, which spawns a reaction that *etc. etc.*, as Barth would say.

Why keep telling the same old stories over and over again, reasoned these bandits? Why not create some excitement by mixing things up a little, by varying from the Aristotelian formula of beginning, middle, and end, preferably ordered in a 2-3-1 pattern? (*i.e.*, Something important at the beginning, the least important thing in the middle, and the most important thing at the end—see Paul Fussell's *Poetic Meter and Poetic Form* on this.) Why not create, as Barthelme does so splendidly, a verbal collage? Reading Barthelme's "Indian Uprising," to take just one example from many—from a Texas writer, too—requires a different investment than reading a 'regular' short story; a different investment even than reading a Chekhovian 'slice of life' story. It requires more of the Apollonian and less of the Dionysian in us; it requires us often to abandon all hope of entering any sort of 'fictive dream,' as John Gardner called it, and entering instead something like Barth's funhouse. *"The reader be damned,"* says Samuel Beckett: *We are not interested in any 'fictive dream'; we are interested in something quite different, oriented toward our needs as artists, not the readers' needs as readers.*

Reading this new kind of story required a new way of looking. This kind of story presented a more disjointed narrative. It required us to break a new code, in a sense, not unlike, for example, what much of the poetry of e.e. cummings and others like him required of us when it was new. Many of these new fictions—like those poems—read as if they had been written out in a 'normal' way, then placed in a fire box with a fragmentation grenade, exploded all over the place, and then pasted haphazardly on the page, by a half-crazed writer laughing hysterically as he played with the paste, sniffing and pasting, sniffing and pasting.

The legitimate utterances of this kind may give that appearance, but they are not as haphazard as they appear. As in most art, pattern—which means repetition—is discernible in these stories, but one has to read with new eyes to discern it. This, of course, was part of the plan: to make it new; to cause us, as readers, to read with new attention, new eyes.

A further striking characteristic of many of these new stories—in addition to the absence in them of an obvious chronologically and psychologically oriented, followable narrative line—is their apparent absence of a proper ending. These open-ended fictions—we know them when we see them because we have to turn the page to see if the story is over, because it does not announce itself as ended—are often about the story itself, the difficulty of writing it, or the hopelessness of ever saying or naming in any way that could prove adequate to the story, the story teller, the truth, or the reader. Lies gone wrong, so to speak, dancing instead of walking purposefully on the way toward the truth.

One response to this new kind of story was, I suspect, a falling off of readership outside of the classroom—and, perhaps, a resulting boon to escape fiction, that fiction designed not for interpretation but simply for, well, escape. The post-modern—contemporary—short story seemed to be turning into something like the modern or post-modern poem: something so derivative, to use Marianne Moore's words, as to be unintelligible. Why read it if you need a pony to understand it? And, of course, all the while film was also exerting its disruptively enhancing influence on modern fiction. Funhouse indeed!

If the purpose of an imaginative utterance as distinct from an informational utterance, to use Paul Valery's thinking here, is to recreate experience—to dance, so to speak, but not on the way to the store; to dance just to dance—and the purpose of an informational utterance is to transfer data, information—to walk to the store to get something—then shouldn't an imaginative utterance be close enough to the predictability end of the continuum to provide for the reader at least a modicum of relatively thoughtless pleasure? To give him at least a crack in the door so he can pry it open and go into the room? To give him at least a chance to enter into a 'fictive dream?' To the later Beckett, as to others like him, the answer seems clearly to be no.

If the function of art is first to please, and second to inform, then are these functions perverted when the art passes that secret, unknowable, moving point in the continuum at which the optimum level of unpredictability lies? Or is it, as the writers of these fictions might maintain, their job to keep just a little ahead of their readers, to keep them at the stretch? And, anyway, they are sure to add, "Who says it's my job to please, to entertain, or to inform? Tell that to the Marines!"

Well, it ain't science, this fiction game, no matter how we may try to make it science, as people like Brander Matthews did with the short story earlier in our century. It *is* an art. And the artist who is quick on his feet never forgets for long the story about Picasso and the portrait of Gertrude Stein:

"It doesn't look like me," she says.

"It will," Picasso responds.

And, of course, he was right. It *does* look like her, now. As Vivian says in Oscar Wilde's "The Decay of Lying," "Life imitates art far more than Art imitates Life."[4]

---

[4]The *Works of Oscar Wilde,* cited by Ellmann and Feidelson in *The Modern Tradition,* Oxford University Press, 1965, p. 20.

In the same way, "Indian Uprising" is no longer unintelligible, nor, for the most part, is the rest of Barthelme's work. Remember how you felt the first time you read one of his stories, on your own, without any help? You either yelled for joy, and immediately got it, or you laughed a little, uncertainly, scratched your head maybe, "felt" it was right, but then went back to it later and began to try to puzzle it out. I belonged to the latter group, being a slow learner who didn't learn even to tie his shoelaces until he was eight or nine. In fact, I truly didn't get Barthelme until I heard him read once, in San Antonio, at a meeting, and then suddenly it was all so clear.

Sort of.

The casual reader—the nonacademic reader—however, doesn't have the time or the training for that kind of puzzle, it seems to me, and so, as I have said, I think the serious short story—and again, this seems to me to have happened suddenly, though of course it didn't—suffered—or enjoyed—a kind of lapse in popularity during the 1950s and '60s. But then, as it seems always to do, the pendulum swung back again, and the multitudes of young writers had a new model to follow, not the model of skewed coherence manifested in the stories of the Bad Boys, but a model that hearkened back to an earlier time in the development of the genre (which I think it deserves the name of, although you won't usually find it listed by itself anywhere as such). And with this pendulum swing came what many now call a renaissance in the short story in our time, a contention debated by others, including Tobias Wolfe, for example, in the Introduction to his anthology, *The Vintage Book of Contemporary American Short Stories*, 1994, who says in effect that the new wave of short stories, after the Bad Boys, merely continues in the older tradition of the genre.

However, if indeed there has been a renaissance in the short story in our country, Raymond Carver is the writer usually given credit for it. What Carver brought back to the form was a kind of up-to-date Chekhov: old wine, new bottles. Carver, like Chekhov, wrote stories in a voice familiar to us, about characters and actions we understood, in a way that didn't require us to bring our Scrabble or acrostic talents to bear. His stories do require from us, however, a similar, if not identical, problem solving ability, and that is the ability to add character, setting, and plot together and, with those parts, come up with a theme. That is, his stories, like so many of Chekhov's, may seem like nothing more than sketches—indeed, some of them *are* nothing more than sketches—but when we ask ourselves, *What happened, who did it, and where and when did they do it?*, the answers we come up with ought to help us articulate an answer to a further question, an answer that may stay with us the longest of all, and that question is *What does it mean?* In other words, do we get it, the way we get a joke when we do? It's easy with a joke; if we get it, we know because we laugh—or groan. If we don't get a joke, we are puzzled. We usually don't blame ourselves, though; we usually blame the joke, or the teller. Same with stories. By the way, if you want to read a story interesting on many levels, read Carver's "Errand," about the death of Chekhov, one of a series I am told he planned to write on the deaths of famous writers, a series cut short by his own death.

Raymond Carver died prematurely, at fifty, from cancer (as did Donald Barthelme, at fifty-eight, from the same cause—both great losses), but his stories live and delight their readers probably in the same proportion as those same stories serve to damage other writers. He is easy to imitate, as a writer friend of mine points out, and, because his stories—like the puzzling stories of the Bad Boys—don't always announce their themes as clearly as more traditional stories, it is harder to detect the good imitations from the bad ones. If Barthelme was the most imitated writer of the sixties and the seventies, then surely it has been Carver in the eighties and nineties.

I think of the problem with much contemporary fiction as being similar to the problem we sometimes encounter with nonrepresentational painting. If we have experience with the object represented, we can tell, when we look at a representational painting, whether the representation is skillfully done or not, because we have learned to see with eyes trained in perspective, color, shadow, and so on. But a nonrepresentational painting takes much of that away from us. It too asks us to look with new eyes—it does not wish, purport, or pretend to imitate anything found in nature. We are thrown back on our sense of pattern, of color, of proportion, of . . . of art without a subject, in a sense, or of art with itself as subject, perhaps. We are asked by this kind of art to add it to what we already know the world to be like; to increase the boundaries, so to speak; to rearrange the—if I may use this word, which I almost hate to do—the paradigm. That is, we are asked to place something new and different on the table of the known.

But painters aren't stuck with using everyday language as their medium the way story writers are. Everybody who knows the language can read the story. He may not be able to explain the difference between representational or nonrepresentational stories, as he may not be able to explain the difference between open-ended and closed ended fictions, or escape fictions as distinct from interpretive fictions, or metafictions as distinct from mimetic fictions, or conventionally coherent narratives from those in which the coherence is skewed—he may not be a very sophisticated, grown up, mature reader, in other words—but so what? It's his language, too.

In his *Major American Short Stories*, Litz writes of author John Barth, "As an undergraduate at Johns Hopkins University, he earned part of his tuition by shelving books in the classics library, which included the stacks of the Oriental seminary; and his recollection of those hours tells us much about his narrative aim." Then he quotes Barth:

> One was permitted to get lost for hours in that splendiferous labyrinth and intoxicate, engorge oneself with *story*. Especially, I became enamored of the great tale-cycles and collections: Somadeva's *Ocean of Story* in ten huge volumes, Burton's *Thousand Nights and a Night* in twelve, the *Panchatantra*, the *Gesta Romanorum*, the *Novellini*, and the *Pent-Hept* and *Decameron*. Most of those spellbinding liars I have forgotten, but never Scheherazade. Though the tales she [Scheherazade] tells are not my favorites, she remains my favorite teller. . . . Like a parable of Kafka's or a great myth, the story of deflowered Scheherazade, yarning tirelessly through the dark hours to save her neck, corresponds to a number of things at once, and flashes meaning from all its facets. For me its rich dark circumstances, mixing the subtle and the coarse, the comic and the grim, the realistic and the fantastic, the apocalyptic and the hopeful, figure, among other things, both the state of the fictioner in general and the particular endeavors and aspirations of this one, at least, who can wish nothing better than to spin like that vizier's excellent daughter, through what nights remain to him, tales within tales, full-stored with "descriptions and discourse and rare traits and anecdotes and moral instances and reminiscences . . . proverbs and parables, chronicles and pleasantries, quips and jests, stories and . . . dialogues and histories and elegies and other verses . . ." until he and his scribblings are fetched low by the Destroyer of Delights.[5]

---

[5]Pp. 687–90.

It may seem ironic, if not perverse, that such a statement should come from the pen of one of the writers I have tagged as being responsible for writing stories which sometimes don't seem to have a primary interest in story at all, but I don't think it is. The service done to fiction by writers such as Barth has been an invaluable one; these writers have helped break the story out of an unhealthy predictability by bringing to the form new ways to look at old stuff, by moving the marker a little bit further along the continuum toward total unpredictability, and the stories of others written after the Bad Boys would not—could not—have been what they have been without this service. It is clear that the serious short story has been forever changed because of them.

It is often said that there are only two stories to write: stories of love, and stories of adventure. I remember telling this to my oldest friend as we walked across his pasture where he lived just outside of New Braunfels, on the way to put up a horse or feed a horse or do something with a damn horse. I don't know why I was talking about such things, but I hope it was in answer to some question he had asked me; I hope I didn't start it. We walked on for a while in silence—which my friend is not uncomfortable with—and then he said, "I think there's only one story."

"Oh," I said. "What's that?"

"Adventure," he said.

He was right, I think, as he usually is. There is, finally, only one story, and that *is* adventure.

And so, Billy Bob Hill's present collection of short stories by and about Texans contains fifty-four adventure stories, all of them competent, most of them very good, and many of them—such as James Hoggard's "Patterns of Illusion," Marise McDermott's "Ancient Infant," and Betsy Berry's "The Reception," simply excellent—stories good enough to find a home in any of the most prestigious publications which make space for short stories in English. They show a more complex—and a more accurate—Texas than the Texas shown in most movies or in escape fiction.

Many of these stories-just less than half—are first person narratives that reveal their kinship with the oral tradition from which story springs, as are, indeed, many of the third person narratives. (That distinction, incidentally, is nowhere near as important as we were taught back in school, since "he" and "she" often prove to be really "I" in disguise.)

Some of the stories go back to the nineteenth century for their setting, such as Ernestine Sewell Linck's "One Woman's Trail of Tears," and Jan Reid's "Second Saddle." Others take place in the recent past, from the 1930s through the 1950s, including Mark Busby's "The Promise," D. R. Meredith's "Retrospective," James Ward Lee's "Rock-Ola," Clay Reynolds's "Goodnight, Sweetheart," and Judy Alter's "Sue Ellen Learns to Dance." Most take place in a kind of eternal present, such as Paul Ruffin's "Devil Fish," Jerry Bradley's "McLife," Michael Verde's "Weasel Loves," Greg Garrett's "Black and White," Albert Haley's "Horse on the Highway," Jo LeCoeur's "Wheelmen," and Terence A. Dalrymple's "Heartbeat." Some of these depend upon a narrative stance which reflects the peculiarities of how Texans speak. These latter stories are ones which harken back, usually nostalgically, to the rural past of the Texas that their authors, or their parents—and I—grew up in. Others are stories which only incidentally take place in Texas, that exist in the eternal anywhere, so to speak. Even these stories, however, have the look, and smell, and taste of Texas, if maybe not the sound.

No stories in this volume present the kinds of challenges presented by the nonrepresentational stories of our recent literary past in this country, stories of skewed coherence, say, stories which say with Beckett, "The reader be damned!" The closest are probably Pat Littledog's "When Luck Ran Out," Ruben Degollado's "Not the Truth (I John 1:6-9)," and Camilla Carr's "Massacre." A great many of them are, however, clearly the sons or daughters of Ray Carver and, if there is more of a danger in following him than there is in following a more conventional writer, it lies in depending less on oneself and more on one's reader to fill in what comes beyond the equal sign after *What happened, who did if, and where and when did they do it?*

If writing imaginative utterances is a game, like tennis, say—and, of course, it is—then the Scylla of being a bully and telling your reader too much—running around the net and hitting the ball back after serving it—is mirrored by the Charybdis of acing the reader every time and not allowing him even a slim chance to return the serve. Nonrepresentational stories often do this by pushing too far along the continuum toward unpredictability. The gang of Carver often do it by not being sure themselves what all the parts of their stories add up to, and leaving it to the reader to figure it out without sufficient or appropriate evidence. These are stories which are probably not truly short stories, but are instead slices of life, often, or, as I have said, sketches, perhaps, or maybe just scenes, many of them so slight that deriving meaning from them constitutes an exercise more in imagination than interpretation. And this may be just what suits a given reader. I say these things only to make distinctions, not to establish a hierarchy of value. They are imaginative utterances that reveal a sequence of events, but do not provide for the causal connections usually required for these events to constitute plots. Coming to the conclusion that one does not have enough evidence when he reads a story requires both experience and confidence as a reader. We should not be too quick to blame ourselves, any more than we should be too quick to blame the author. In other words, we should be tactful readers. But we have the right—probably even the responsibility, if we truly want to be tactful readers—to ask of every story, "So What?" I urge the readers of this collection to do that as they read. Good stories are not hurt by analysis; only bad stories are. Some of the stories in this volume which tease us in this way include Pat Carr' s "Wakefield O'Connor," H. Palmer Hall's "An Evening On Mustang Island," James Hoggard's "Patterns of Illusion," "Chuck Taylor's "Give Peace A Chance," and Chuck Etheridge's "Thunderbird." All good stories, and all teasers.

I also urge readers—when they are between stories—to think about some other questions as they read this book: *Why do you read? What do you read?* and *How do you read?* These questions are not just appropriate for English classes. According to Manguel,[6] there were 359,437 new books added to the U.S. Library of Congress in 1995 alone. I am unsure about that number, incidentally; I don't think it represents the number of books published that year in the United States, which is usually pegged at about 50,000/60,000, and, according to my colleagues in the publishing game, is said to have reached roughly 70,000 in 1996. But in both cases, high and low, the numbers represent the same problem: we can't read 'em all, 50,000 or 359,437, so how do we decide which ones we can read? How we decide what we read is dependent on why we read, which, in turn, leads us to ask how we read. In other words, we end up, as we do in most transactions in life, in the land of interpretation.

The whole question of literary interpretation is up for grabs these days—again—only this time it isn't primarily the concerns of the Vietnam War or civil rights for black people that intrude themselves into literature classes, but similar, if less focused, social concerns. Is every book by a white male a defense of the status quo? Does every book by anyone not a white male

---

[6]p. 135.

deserve to be moved up an arbitrary affirmative-action notch simply by virtue of its not having been written by a white male? I certainly don't think Ralph Ellison would have agreed, nor, say, Flannery O'Connor. This is neither the place—nor am I the person—to argue such matters in a sufficiently significant way, but these questions should not be turned over to the ideologues of either the right or the left. They are questions of importance to all of us, because all of us have a stake in our culture, such as it is, and such as it will be. Suffice it to say with Umberto Ecco, that for me, "The limits of interpretation coincide with the rights of the text."[7]

Women and minorities are well represented in this volume. Roughly half the authors are women, and stories like Betsy Berry's represent the excellence they offer. It's harder to tell about minorities by name alone or even, in some cases, by what the stories are about. In other cases, such as Ivanov Y. Reyez' "Eggs," Phyllis W. Allen's "Mama Minnie And Me," Talibah Folami Modupe's "Is the Other Man's Ice Really Colder," Susan San Miguel's "La Llorona of Leon Creek," and Carmen Tafolla's "I Just Can't Bear It," it isn't hard at all. These voices should be heard, and these stories should be good stories as well, as they are in this volume.

All of these stories—these lies in the interests of the truth—bring us something we are looking for, thirsting for, hungering for; something that—to quote John Updike—provides us "experience stripped of confusion."[8] And life *is* confusing as it unfolds before us, so confusing that alone, without stories, we usually try to make sense of it by resurrecting the past, or by planning for the future; that is by concentrating on any time but right now, because right now is too often simply more than we can handle, the sensory in-coming is simply too much; better afterburn from the past or reachback from the future than the intense, unmanageable, confusing jumble of the present.

Reading this book made me nostalgic for both my youth and for Texas. As I have said, I grew up in Mineral Wells, in Palo Pinto County, knowing there were 254 counties in the state of Texas (a hundred more, I was to learn later down in Austin, than Shakespeare's sonnets; and, don't forget, two hundred more than the number of stories in this collection), and knowing—before, I think, it was uttered this way—that Texas was Number One.

---

[7]Cited by Manguel, p 93.

[8]John Updike interview, *The Writing Life, National Book Award Authors,* Random House, 1995, p. 33.

Reading these stories now during a bleak winter holiday season out in a desert far west of where you probably are, took me back home, both in time, in some cases, and, in most, in space. It was a good visit, even when it was sad, and one I treasure, as I know you will, tactful reader that you are.[9]

John H. Irsfeld

The University of Nevada, Las Vegas
out of Mineral Wells, Palo Pinto County, Texas

---

[9]Anyone interested in reading further about the short story as a form is encouraged to look at the work of Professor Charles E. May, of California State University, Long Beach, especially *The New Short Story Theories,* Ohio University Press, 1994, and *The Short Story: The Reality of Artifice,* Twayne, 1995. Excellent stuff. He is currently working on a full-scale theoretical/critical history of the short story, due to be published by Cambridge University Press as part of a turn-of-the-century celebration.

TEXAS SHORT STORIES

HIS BROTHER'S KEEPER

JACK O. HAZLERIG

He was lucky to get a seat on the bus out of Ft. Smith, it was so crowded. As it was, he was one of the last to get a seat, and he thought for awhile that they would all be taken before he got on. He didn't know if he could take it, standing up in the heat of the crowded bus on a late summer afternoon, the bus swaying and lurching and the other standees bumping against him as the bus moved.

Not that he was a weakling; far from it. He had grown up on a farm and had finished months of training in the infantry and was in good shape, but he had just got out of the hospital that day—appendectomy—walked the mile and a half from the post hospital to the company, picked up his gear and walked another half mile to catch a bus to town. Since he was in a replacement company waiting for orders to go overseas, he had to take everything, which meant that his duffle bag was full, and very heavy for a man on convalescent leave. By the time he reached that seat, he was very happy to sit down, and only a little sorry for the people still standing. Also, he was glad that they were men, for if they had been women, he couldn't have kept his seat. In those days, men offered women their seats. There were some women standing, but they were so far in front that offering them his seat was impossible—they couldn't have made their way to it.

The bus just kept filling up, getting hotter and hotter. The smell of perspiration began to grow strong, mixing with the smell of manure on some farmers' shoes. He wanted the bus to start so the air conditioning could have a fighting chance. He heard a familiar voice say "Hello, Chip," and realized that the man in the seat next to him had been in the hospital with him. He had been shot in the gut in Korea and was being sent home to recuperate. He was out of the war now, still in some pain, but would be all right. Chip Farrington still had his baptism of fire to face, or, as Bill Mauldin's Willie had put it, he hadn't been kissed yet.

"How long do think it will take to get to Texas?" Chip asked.

"I don't know. This is a slow bus. I change right after we cross the line."

When they got underway, a tall black soldier standing in the aisle rested his hands on the seat in front of Chip and leaned over. In a little while sweat ran off of his face and dripped onto Chip's head, and he snapped, "You're sweating on me."

His head jerked back and he apologized, and Chip felt awful. After all, it wasn't as if he had sweated on him on purpose or had any choice. Chip mumbled something apologetic, but apologies in a situation like that sound awfully hollow. The black soldier looked as if he appreciated it, though, and said it didn't matter. It did matter, though, and they both knew it. When a white man spoke harshly to a black man in those days, it mattered. Sometimes it mattered a lot.

Now that the bus was moving, the air conditioning had kicked on and was cooling the bus off. The smell of sweat wasn't as strong now, but it was still there, mixed with the smell of manure.

The Arkansas countryside whipped past the window: trees and low hills, and now and then a field of corn or a farmhouse and barn. Chip had that strange feeling that he always had on a bus, the feeling of strangeness because he wasn't out in the fields working or at the barn taking care of livestock. He always felt unreal on a bus, suspended between two worlds. As dusk fell, the strangeness abated; now, he just saw blackness outside as they rushed past. In about twenty miles, the bus stopped at a little town. When the door opened, there was a rush of fresh air which really helped drive out the staleness. Several people got off, and there was a general shifting about as seats were vacated and filled up by others.

Chip and Jimmy, his friend from the hospital, carried on a desultory conversation, but it never really got going.

The bus kept stopping to let people off and take others on, but more people got off than got on, so fewer and fewer people were standing. But before long, most of the people standing were black. In those days, blacks sat in the back of the bus, and since there weren't many seats in the back, the blacks got the worse of it.

2

By the time they got about sixty miles from Ft. Smith, fewer people were getting off, because lots of country and small town people would get on the bus at a place like Ft. Smith to go a few miles to their homes. By now the people who were just going a few miles had got off and the people left were likely to be going a couple of hundred miles.

Some of the blacks were fairly old; the young black soldier stepped back and let his elders have the seats. He must have been getting pretty tired of standing by now. There were still numerous blacks—about half of a bus load—standing; many of them were women and several were old, much too old to stand for hours on a moving bus. Their faces showed no emotion. They just stared patiently ahead, never meeting the eyes of a white person. Chip was fairly near the back of the bus, and no black person was allowed to sit in front of a white person. The white person sitting in the rearmost seat, therefore controlled where the line separating black from white seating was located. It wasn't long before a couple of seats opened up fairly far forward. None of the blacks moved toward it, of course, and a strained silence developed. Then a white man sitting behind Chip got up and said, "Excuse me. Let me move up there and somebody can have this seat." He didn't need to say "Some black person can have this seat." That was understood. Chip looked back; there were other white people behind him, so there was no point in moving forward.

Chip dozed off, feeling sorry for the people standing but glad that he had a seat. On other bus trips, he had sometimes stood for long distances, but on those occasions he hadn't been recovering from an operation. He woke up now and then when the bus stopped to let someone on or off. As it got later, no one got on. He woke up when they got to Texas and watched the east Texas woodlands slip past in the lights from the bus. Although he could see little, he could visualize the pine woods alternating with patches of hardwoods, with now and then a tree farm with a solid stand of pine. The woods would be alive now, although very silent, as night creatures— foxes, raccoons, possums, rabbits, mice, and woodrats—slipped about, looking for food and trying to avoid becoming food themselves. Occasionally there would be a little squeal as something got caught, but mostly it was silent. Owls would be gliding silently through the trees looking for an unwary rodent. There might be the deep baying of hounds as men—boys, young men and old men—hunted varmints. Chip's Dad would want him to go fox hunting with him and his buddies.

It would be good. They would meet at some place on a back country road, a road so obscure that you could count on nobody driving by, a road so obscure that leaves would sometimes collect in the ruts. They would collect wood and build a fire and cook supper. They would sit on the ground and eat fried steak or pork chops, french fried potatoes and store bought bread, and wash it down with very strong black coffee. The hounds would be working through the nearby woods, occasionally baying deeply as they tried to warm up a cold trail. Once in a while the trail would get warm and the men would get excited as they interpreted the baying of the hounds. One of the men would bring out a half gallon Mason jar of homemade blackberry wine and set it beside the fire to warm up. They would all take a drink out of the Mason jar; refusing to drink from the same jar as the others would have been bad manners. When the level of wine went down a little, one of the men would bring out a pint of whiskey and refill the jar. He would continue to replenish the jar until his whiskey was gone. They would sip the mixture all night, nobody getting even slightly tipsy. That was one of the other great offenses one could commit.

Chip was brought out of his reverie by a stop where a lot of people got off. Jimmy was saying "I change buses for Houston here. You take care of yourself." Chip mumbled something and they shook hands and Jimmy left. The bus driver went inside and stayed for awhile. About half the seats were empty, and there were several black people standing, but none of them moved to occupy the seats. Many of the blacks, especially the older ones, looked exhausted. Their faces were nearly expressionless, though, except for a look of infinite patience. The bus driver got back on the bus and worked his way down the aisle counting empty seats. Then he worked his way back to the front, counting people standing. He was a nice looking, clean cut man, probably about Chip's age or a little older. When he got to the front, he took a deep breath and said, "Folks, there are enough seats on this bus for everybody to sit down. Will you people," here he looked at the white people in the back part of the bus—"move forward so these other folks can sit down?"

You could almost feel the wall of resistance rising from the whites on the bus. They were being asked to vacate their seats for blacks. Someone

4

muttered "I ain't givin' up my seat for no nigger." Someone else muttered "Yeah. We oughtn't to even let them get on the bus." The blacks looked straight ahead, being very careful not to meet anyone's eyes, especially a white person's eyes. It was a survival technique they had mastered generations ago. Chip began to get set to try to help the bus driver if things got rough, as they well might. He wished he had been at his best and not recuperating from an operation. He wondered what a sharp punch in the abdomen would do to his incision. It would hurt like blazes, of that he was sure. He wouldn't be able to do much to help. But there was one thing he could do, and that was to move forward and hopefully by example encourage others to do so.

Just as he was getting up, an old lady carrying a furled umbrella also got up and moved forward. She was not very big, but she stood up straight and walked with a brisk step. "Come on, folks, let's move forward," she said as she took a seat way in the front. Nobody followed their example right away, though.

When Chip settled into an empty seat a little forward of halfway, the man next to him said, "Well, kid, how does it feel to give your seat to a nigger?" That put Chip on the spot; he didn't like the man or what he said, but the situation could become very explosive, and he didn't want to make it worse by getting into an argument about race relations. He just forced a smile and shrugged his shoulders. Finally, a few other people moved forward, and then nothing. The remaining whites looked as if they had settled in and intended to hibernate. The bus driver tried again, "Come on, folks, move forward and let these people have a seat. They've been standing a long time." There was a pleading note in his voice.

Nobody moved. Some of the men seemed to press into the backs of their seats as if to make themselves immovable. It didn't look good. The bus driver moved up and down the aisle, asking people—white people—to move forward. One of the old black men tried to defuse the situation: "That's all right, Mr. Bus Driver. We used to standin'." But this chance to back down just made the bus driver more determined. "There's enough seats on this bus for everybody, and it's not movin' until everybody's seated." He stormed to the front of the bus and turned to face the passengers. He looked angry and determined. Chip admired his willingness to face half a busload of stubborn, angry people, but he wished he were bigger.

5

Chip was trying to sort out his feelings. He had grown up in Texas at a time when prejudice was so common that a person who wasn't prejudiced was looked down on. In the army, he had shared barracks, mess halls, and showers with blacks and was accustomed to it. He wasn't free of prejudice, but he was accustomed to associating with black people on a basis of equality.

People did begin to move forward one or two at a time. Some of them looked furious; others looked embarrassed. Some of them would mumble and growl, but there were no confrontations. The bus driver was now going up and down the aisle asking people to move, sometimes begging, sometimes scolding. When a seat was vacant, he would encourage a black person to take it. Finally, he had everybody seated except the tall black soldier. And there was one vacant place—beside a white woman.

The bus driver looked like he was about to burst into tears; if he asked a white woman to share a seat with a black man, it might set off a riot. He didn't know what to do, but he didn't seem to be able to give up. The soldier urged him to go on, saying that he would stand. It was obvious, though, that the black soldier was exhausted. He had stood for hours, bracing his body against the sway of the bus. The bus driver swore under his breath and started to the front of the bus, moving fast. Chip didn't know what he was going to do, but he reached out and poked him in the arm to get his attention.

"Driver, if the lady will trade seats with me, the soldier can sit with me."

A look of great relief spread over the bus driver's face and he went back to the woman and said, "Lady, would you mind trading seats with this young man? Then we can get going."

She was about forty or forty-five years old, nicely dressed with a prim white blouse. She set her chin, looked straight ahead, and said "This is my seat. You have no right to move me."

"As a matter of fact," the bus driver said, "I have."

As Chip got up to trade seats, the man next to him said, "So, kid, you goin' to set with that nigger? You a nigger lover?"

"We're wearing the same uniform, in case you hadn't noticed," Chip snapped. "And he's been standing up ever since Ft. Smith."

"So, you are a nigger lover."

6

That was too much for Chip. He was tired and his emotions had been in a whirl. Besides, he had seen numerous people—black people—stand up in the swaying bus for miles when there were empty seats. And he was embarrassed—embarrassed because these people refusing to do the decent thing were Texans, his people. Without any volition on his part his right hand made a fist and started swinging for the man's jaw, but suddenly his forearm was caught in a grip that admitted no argument.

"Take it easy, soldier," the bus driver said. "Just ease on back here." His voice was soft and soothing.

The bus driver went back to try to get the woman to move, and she still resisted. The old lady with the umbrella called back, "Come on, Miss Priss, trade seats with the soldier boy so we can get going. I've got a new grandbaby and I want to see him before he's grown."

Chip stood there a little while and then said, "Come on, Ma'am, you're being silly. Move up and let's get going. I want to get home and see my parents."

That was an appeal she couldn't resist. It was unpatriotic to keep a soldier from going home to see his parents. She got her things with sharp, quick, angry movements and went forward. The bus driver's "Thanks" was the most heartfelt Chip had ever heard. He sat down, but the black soldier waited to be asked. He was very embarrassed. Chip tried to apologize for his fellow whites, but the black soldier said never mind. Chip knew, though, that he was deeply wounded. It was difficult for them to carry on a conversation; there was too much tension left over from all of the trouble between blacks and whites, the knowledge that his ancestors had been owned by white men. He had no way of knowing, of course, that Chip's ancestors had been too poor to own slaves. It probably wouldn't have made much difference.

Slowly, though, they began to thaw out. They talked a little about the army (neither of them liked it) and about the likelihood that they would go to Korea (they were both likely to go). They tiptoed verbally around various topics that they might have discussed, each afraid of saying the wrong thing and each wanting desperately not to offend the other. Even so, they began to relax. Fatigue helped; soon they both began to nod off.

When they got to Sherman, Texas, they were told to get off and wait for another bus that would be along in about forty-five minutes. There was a lot of grumbling from the whites; Chip thought that they were delighted to have something safe and conventional to complain about. The bus station was dull and dingy as only a bus station at three o'clock in the morning can be. The passengers swarmed in to grab the few seats. Some arm rests had been knocked out of some of the seats so that they formed benches long enough to lie down on, and these were quickly seized by some of the white men, who immediately stretched out and went to sleep. Chip and the black soldier went outside and sat down on the curb.

Chip got out his cigarettes and offered one to the black man and took one himself. The air was cool and pleasant and it was good not to have to adjust to the constant swaying of the bus. Chip felt good because he was nearly home. He would leave his duffel bag at the station and walk the mile to his parents' home. They didn't know he was coming and would be surprised and elated when they heard his knock on the door. After the greeting, Dad would frown and ask "Did you walk all the way from the bus station?" They would try to convince him that walking alone at that hour was dangerous, but he knew that they would have been ashamed of him if he had been afraid.

He and the black soldier talked desultorily, Chip looking up when a car went through the intersection at the end of the block. The occasional car going by made him feel vaguely uneasy. After a little while, Chip remembered the reputation Sherman had for being antagonistic toward blacks and understood his uneasiness. It went back to the early part of the century. The stories were vague and muddled, but they all agreed on a few points: there had been a trial of a black man accused of raping a white woman, a riot had broken out and the prisoner had been taken from the jail and dragged to death behind an automobile. Then the rioters had raged through the black section of town; the blacks had hidden in their houses, the menfolk and some of the womenfolk clutching whatever weapons they had, twelve gauge shotguns and .22 caliber rifles, mostly, but some of them with axes, shovels, and clubs, desperately determined to protect their families. By daylight, the rioters had gone home and all of the blacks had moved out. Since then, no black person lived in Sherman, and it was generally understood that it was very unwise for a black person to let the sun set on him there.

"My God!" Chip thought. "I've got to tell him. I can't just let him sit here unsuspecting, like this."

"Look," Chip began. "There's something I've got to tell you. I just remembered it."

"Well?"

Chip took a deep breath and began: "There was some trouble here a long time ago and a man was killed. A black man."

"That don't have nothing to do with me."

"Yes," Chip responded. "It does. Ever since then they haven't—the people here haven't—Look, a black person can't spend the night here. It's dangerous."

There was a long strained silence. Chip could tell that the man next to him had grown stiff; he could hear his breath coming hard. Out of the corner of his eye he saw that the man's nostrils were flared. "I'm sorry. I had to tell you; I couldn't just let you sit here when something might happen."

"What do you reckon might happen?"

"I don't know. Nobody knows you're here."

"The man in the bus station knows."

"He isn't likely to do anything. Being in the bus station is sort of like being on the bus. You don't have to worry about him." Chip thought about that for a while and then said, much less certainly, "At least, I don't think you do."

"He was making a phone call as we came through."

"I see what you're thinking—that he might be calling to tell someone that we're out here." Chip thought about that and then said, "I don't think so. We've been out here fifteen minutes. It's a small town. If he'd called anybody, they'd be here by now." Chip wasn't all that sure, but felt the need to be positive.

"What you think I ought to do?"

"God, I don't know.

"Do you reckon I ought to go inside?"

"Look," Chip said. "There are two of us here."

"You ain't in this. You're white."

Chip held his khaki clad sleeve up to the other soldier's sleeve and said, "Our uniforms are the same color."

"That don't make our skin the same color. You ain't in this. No need in you getting in trouble, too."

"I think that if I'm here it might hold back anybody who wanted to cause trouble."

"You don't even know my name."

"Oh," Chips said. "I don't. What is your name? Mine's Chip. Chip Farrington."

"Mine's Charles Miller."

"Glad to know you." Chip extended his hand and they shook, Charles murmuring "Likewise."

"Don't you see, I'm in it. I can't run away and leave you alone."

"Well, you reckon we ought to go inside?"

Chip thought before answering. "I don't really think anything is going to happen. We're waiting for a bus. Anybody can see you're just waiting for a bus, and that you'll leave town in a little while. Also, it's about two o'clock in the morning and most people are asleep." Again, he sounded a lot more certain than he was. "I tell you what. We'll each watch one end of the block and if anything looks suspicious, we'll go inside."

"Bullets will go through that plate glass like nothing."

"Right. But they're not as likely to shoot into the bus station." Chip wished that he was as sure of that as he tried to sound.

They lit cigarettes and sat there, each watching his end of the street. Neither felt like talking, but after about ten minutes, Charles, his voice flat and emotionless, said, "I think the same car has gone by the end of the block five times."

Chip looked to the right at Charles's end of the block. In a few minutes, a car drove by slowly. When they lost sight of it around the corner, they heard it accelerate. The tires squealed as it rounded the next corner. Both men stood up at the same time and started for the door, but they heard the squeal of tires and saw the car pull into the intersection on the left and stop.

"There's another one at the other end," Charles said. His back was ramrod straight and his face was set. "This ain't your fight. You can still quit."

"I'll tell you the truth," Chip said. "I wish I could. I don't know why I can't. But I can't. So I guess it's my fight, too."

10

The two cars were now coming slowly down the street from opposite directions. They stopped side by side opposite the bus station. Someone in one of the cars called out, "Do you guys see what I see? Don't that look like a nigger over there?"

"Sure does. And look at that white guy. Don't he look like a nigger lover?"

The two soldiers went inside. The black passengers were huddled in the back of the room where they couldn't be seen as well. The white passengers didn't offer any help. One of them said to Chip, "Son, you oughtn't to meddle with these things. You can get in lots of trouble."

Chip turned his back without answering. The ticket agent hung up the phone and looked out at the men outside. There were about ten of them, late teenagers or very young men, and they were now on the sidewalk looking in. One of them had a rope. The ticket agent went over and opened the door and said, "You guys go home and sleep it off. We don't want no trouble here."

"We don't want no trouble, either," one of them said. "We just want that nigger."

"Well, this is bus company property, and you're trespassing. Get out. Go home."

A man in a bus driver's uniform came out of a room behind the counter and went out the door opposite where the teenagers were. He got in a bus and started the engine and began letting it warm up. The ticket agent came over. "We're going to start this bus ahead of schedule. Be ready to get out there and get on it. Once on the bus, you'll be a little safer. I think." He wasn't a big man or a young man; he looked worried, but he clearly had spunk. "I called the local police," he said. "I don't know if they'll be much help, so I called the highway patrol."

"Some of those men are coming around the building," Charles said.

Sure enough, about half of them turned up at the loading dock. They spread out in front of the door as if they didn't intend to let anyone get by. Chip took comfort in the fact that both he and Charles were big; he wished that he hadn't just had an operation. "How many of them can you take?" he asked, more to be saying something than anything else.

Charles thought about it for a minute and said "One for sure, maybe two. What about you."

11

"I've been in the hospital, but I think I can take one of them. With luck I could keep another one busy."

"That still leaves too many of them."

"Yeah. Say, Charles, if they—if we—if they kill us, I just wanted to say, I'm glad I met you."

He actually smiled. Then he said, "Me too. You're the first white man I ever thought was a buddy."

"Well, I'm no saint. I grew up just as prejudiced as these people." Chip nodded to the group of whites standing around the bus station.

"I don't believe it," Charles said. "If you was, you wouldn't have done what you did tonight."

Just then the ticket agent got on the loud speaker and announced that the bus was loading. The whites started moving toward the door, some of them pointedly not looking at the two soldiers, some of them looking at them with anger, and some of them looking with wonder and concern. The man who had spoken earlier came over and said, "Look, I don't like what you're doing, but I was in the army myself, and I'll stand by you. Get over here in the middle of these people and maybe we can get you to the bus."

Chip and Charles looked at each other doubtfully, and the man said, "Come on, both of you."

They moved over toward the door. Most of the whites hurried out, as if they were running from something, but a few of the men formed a little group around them and escorted them out the door. The old lady with the umbrella joined them, muttering. It was a very small group, even with the old lady. The boys from the other side of the building had come around to join their friends. One of the locals stepped forward. "You people go on and get on the bus. We got no quarrel with you. It's these two we want."

From behind one of them called out, "Yeah. The nigger lover is mine."

Chip made a mental note to try to deck him. They all stood there until one of the men said, "Sorry" and walked to the bus, his head down. Another followed, then all the rest except the little veteran and the old woman. The veteran wavered and then said, "Sorry, guys! There's nothing I can do for you and there's no use . . ." His voice trailed off and he went and got on the bus.

Charles turned to the old woman and said, "Ma'am, you can't help, and you might get hurt."

Her eyes flashed and she waved an umbrella in the air and said, "I'd like to see one of these little scalawags mess with me. I'll give him a good thrashing."

"Ma'am," Chip said. "I wish you'd get on the bus. We're going to have our hands full and . . ."

"Now don't you worry about me. I've taken care of myself for a long time."

Chip started to say something but she shook her umbrella in his face and said, "Don't you sass me, young man!"

The teenagers facing them laughed and hooted, but she turned and marched toward them, flailing with her umbrella. "Scat, you little brats! Go home and get your diapers changed."

One of the teenagers grabbed her umbrella and another grabbed her arms. Charles and Chip surged forward. Charles swung a hard right that caught one of the young boys on the temple, while Chip feinted with his right and landed a left in the other one's stomach. The other boys began to close in, screaming and swearing, but there was a sound of tires on gravel and a shout. Chip looked up and saw a brown sedan with the Department of Public Safety emblem on the side. Two troopers were getting out. He had never seen anything more welcome.

"What's going on here? Everybody freeze."

Charles swore under his breath. Both he and Chip froze. The trooper took the situation in and said to Charles and Chip "You two soldiers going out on that bus?" They nodded. "Well," the trooper said. "You better get on it. Here, you little squirts! Clear the way. Go home and go to bed before we run you in and call your fathers."

The boys scattered. The two soldiers looked at each other and grinned. They nodded their thanks to the troopers and got on the bus. Once there, they paused. "I'll sit in the back," Charles said.

Chip said "I guess I'd better sit here."

They shook hands and took their seats. The old woman got on the bus and the driver closed the door.

Chip looked out; the teenagers were gone, and the troopers were standing watching them. The bus slowly pulled out and moved through the deserted streets. Soon they were out of town. It was very dark, but the horizon in the east was showing some light.

THE POEM LADY

VIOLETTE NEWTON

Me, I'm going tell you story you ain't going believe. Since my wife die, I come over from Abbeville every year, check on my cousin, Madeline. She got no husband or any churrin to look after her. You ask why she live up here in Eas' Texas hills? Well, it like this. When Madeline finish high school, she say she want more out of life than she see at home, she want to go to big town and see some new people. She hear ahout that Normal school up at Nacogdoches, and she talk her daddy send her there, study how to teach.

Madeline find that town nice, but it ain't working alive with skyscrapers, and the red dirt the same as in Louisiane. And she find she ain't making good grade in French class she thought would be snap. Teacher say her French all wrong . . . how you like that? And all those other subject, what in world she going use them for later on? She don't know what to do. Four year of hard school look mighty big in Madeline eye. But she can't go home and be call failure. You know what? She hear about job open to run little post office hereabouts, and she take test, get job of postmaster. And give up school. And save face. And pretty soon, she get little cabin up here, two, three mile in country, and it ain't much different from where she come from. But she save face.

Well, Madeline smart enough to run little office in Eas' Texas hills, but she not smart about some other thing. You just wait. I tell you.

Post office got wide gallery and two rocker chair. Late in day when no business going on at window, she come out and sit with me. "It so quiet here," I say, "you think everbody gone live by Dallas." But Madeline say, "They all live here. They minding they business in they own place." And I say, "Ain't nothing much exciting happen here since everbody but you is good Baptis?" And she say, "Oh, we got thing happening all right, but ain't nobody know about it but me."

I see redbird hop up in dogwood tree all white with flower. "Nobody know about it but me," she say again. That perk up my ear, and she know it. She go in, get us each cup fresh drip Seaport coffee, come back, and we drink, rock. I know she dying tell me, but I ain't going ask her for a while. So we drink and rock, she with little smirk on her mouth. She know we playing cat and mouse.

Flock blackbird come down on post office grass, swoop up when car make a pass by. Some man in car wave. "Who," I say, "that?"

"Oh," she say, and toss her head. "A fellow working up where they strip-mining hills."

"Lignite! Them crazy people tearing up and folks here let them do it!"

"For money. Old man Ambrose, he have Big Black now."

"And he drive by in that Cadillac, see his hill all scar up!"

"They plant back everthing. It in contract."

"Can't plant back hundred year old tree!"

"Humph!" she say, rocking harder. "Ain't your husiness no how!"

"How come you know that man?" I ask, suspicious-like. She raise her eyebrow, haughty-like. "He come in to buy stamp, you fool!"

Well, we play cat and mouse little longer, but I know she ain't forgot she trying raise my curiosity, so she stop rocking, lean out and look down highway where a woman come walking.

"What you see?" I ask, but she lean back, say, "Oh, I think, but no, it ain't the Poem Lady." "Poem Lady?" I say, and I raise my eyebrow like Poem Lady ain't bother enough to take my time. "Ain't she got no name?" Madeline answer, "She got name like everbody else, but everbody call her Poem Lady."

"So?"

"She new, since you been here. I want you to meet her."

"Me! You ain't making me up with no Poem Lady, you crazy woman!"

"I ain't making you up with nobody, you crazy old widower! I just want you to see her. She something else!"

"So?"

"She famous."

"Famous?"

Madeline rocked some more, glad she got my curiosity up. She stop rocking and look at me. "So you feel like driving over a ways to Syrup Sopping Supper?"

"What you talking about? And what happen to Poem Lady?"

Madeline smirk a little and say, "Crisp bacon, scramble egg, biggest biscuit you ever see. Club lady do it to make money for something."

"Scramble egg for supper? No crawfish?"

"No, you fool! This Texas!"

I sit back in my rocker, hands on stomach. "Man! It sound like good breakfast at night."

"Is good."

"Is cholesterol. You hear about that up here? Is bad for you."

"Oh, pshaw! That city talk. I don't believe none of that!" But I keep thinking about that syrup sopping supper, so I say, "Let's go. Everbody got to sin sometime." And we drive and drive, Madeline smile and not talk, and we come up to this place, all screen in to keep the bug out, and go in. Several lady all dress in cap and apron, old-timey, wait on table. I tell you, that Syrup Sopping Supper is enough to make you die happy. Them lady keep giving you all that good eating till my skin don't fit me no more. People sit around in blue jean, plaid shirt and cap on head that say "Bud" or "John Deere." And all sopping that ribbon cane syrup with big biscuit. Man! I got to be Texan right off!

Everbody laughing and talking, and when Poem Lady come in, I know it. Laughing and talking stop. That one good looking woman. No blue jean, her. No cowboy boot. Long black hair. And dress she make, deep red cloth Madeline say she weave herself on loom. And barefoot sandal. She nod to Madeline and go get her place at end of table. That one good looking woman! Why she not come sit with somebody?" I ask my cousin, and she whisper, "I think she shy." And Madeline smile at Poem Lady and whisper me, "Next time, I introduce you." Well, it seem funny to me, but I not say any more until we get home and I say, "All right?" and Madeline say get set on sofa for what she got to tell me, but I can't tell it to nobody else. It between her and me. And now between you and me both. She say everbody know Poem Lady poem in big magazine. Poem on cow and bird and plowing round here. Poem on fishing, hunting. She make this place famous for all the thing they do hereabouts. When anybody round here go to Tyler or Nacogdoches, they flip through magazine at store, see if her name in them. If so, buy magazine, bring it back, pass it around.

"So what make that so special?"

"Cause Poem Lady always to herself, kind of mystery. Oh, she talk to people about garden, what they plant, sometime go in for cup tea. Little one like to hear story from her, too. But ain't nobody really know Poem Lady."

"Nobody been at her house?"

"Me, I go one time when she sick and walk down late that day with her letter. She live in log house, loom in the big room. She weave rug for wall, rug for floor and sell them. She get awful lot mail."

"She live by herself?"

"Yeah. It take quiet to write, she say. No T.V."

"Um. You ain't told me nothing yet." And Cousin Madeline pursed up her lip like she got all the time in the world. Barn owl make its cry out in dark outside. "Well," she say, "she come down ever day after mail truck come by, come walking fast by side of road, black hair a flying. And lately I notice she getting lots letters from one man."

"How you know it man?"

"Just two initials and last name. Ever few days when she see that name up in corner of letter, she smile big. But she don't read letter at post office, just put in her big pocket and go rush off."

"She having romance by mail?"

"Seem so, but nobody else know. And it really none of my business."

"That all?"

"No. She have lots poem in little magazine like you don't see at magazine store. And when they come, most time they not seal up."

"And what you doing is against the law!"

"It ain't hurting nobody to look! And what I see is love poem. Love poem like you never read before. Make me shiver! She writing them to this fellow, I know!"

"And you got fun nosing in other people business."

"Ain't hurting nobody. And nobody else know."

"And if they do, Uncle Sam put you in jail!"

"Oh, pshaw! Life around here so pale, I got to have a little romance."

Some romance, I think. Poor Madeline, ain't nobody writ her love poem, even love letter. Is pitiful. I sit here thinking how she read them poem and play like they to her. Madeline have big imagination. I guess that what keep her going. Well, I ain't never had no one write me love poem neither, so I ask, "Hey, what them poem say?" and Madeline hold back a little like she embarrass.

"Well, I guess I can show you. Sometime she go off for week and mail pile up, so I got time to copy poem."

"It ain't right, though. Magazine her property. Is private mail."

"What you going do? Report me?"

"I never said that!"

"It ain't hurting nothing, and it so much fun!"

I could see lonely Madeline lying in her bed nights imagining thing. And I think of that nice young woman who don't know Madeline is onto her. Anyway, Madeline get up, go out of room and come back with some paper in her hand.

"That the poem?" I ask.

"They hard to understand. But real pretty. I ain't never see poem like these. You think it crazy, but they give me the shivers."

"You done said that already!"

She hand the paper to me and say, "I go sit in swing while you try to read."

I think Madeline go out on gallery because what is writ on paper is so personal, she embarrass. I start looking, but it don't take me no time to get the first one. It give me the shivers too. I look at it with big eyes. I ain't never been smart with poem, but I turn page and see more. It hard to believe. I read two, three more and call my cousin.

"So?" she say, coming in the room. "Don't you bet he love them?"

I look at paper and look at her. Man! I hate to tell her.

"Madeline," I say.

"What the matter? Why you look like that?"

I stand up and hand back the poem. "Madeline," I say, "them poem from one lady to other lady. Ain't no man involve. Just one lady writing love poem to other lady."

She give me a look like I never see before. "You crazy!" she cry. "Why you say crazy thing like that! Ain't no lady write no love poem to no lady, you crazy thing! Old age got you in the head! Is man! He got two initial and last name on letter! Ain't no lady do that!"

"Um. Is style now."

"Why you try tease me, you crazy thing! You ought to be ashame, talking like that!" She come at me like she going hit, and I hold out both hand like to keep her off. She not kidding, her face working up a mad. "I ain't never heard talk like that and I better never hear it again." By now her face red, her hand shake.

"You hush your mouth!" I say. "Neighbor hear you!"

"Ain't no neighbor for quarter mile, and you know it!" she shout.

"Neighbor can hear you for quarter mile," I say.

"How come you think you can come here and get me all nervous!" She look down at page again. "You and your big city talk! This peaceful country here! You come spoil it!"

Right now I feel like little old green garden snake that get in the house, get everybody rile up. Me and my big mouth! I know I done take away her pleasure in the Poem Lady and what Madeline been dreaming about. Man! ain't nothing I can do about it. I see Madeline lip tremble, and she give me one hard look, one long, hard look.

Owl out there in dark still make his call. It sure sound lonesome. I don't see how my cousin stand it out here when owl calling. But she fold up the poem, stack them on shelf. I think she going look some more at them another time. I wish it was tomorrow and sun shining, and maybe everthing be all right again. I don't know what to say. Madeline go to door and look out. Moon shining down bright on yard, making grass look all white. Big tree in front look black. Ain't nothing going on out there, no car pass on highway. Some big old moth hit against window screen, and he better watch out, cause that little old barn owl ain't asleep.

Madeline turn and say, "All right! That the end of that. We ain't had no dessert. I got chocolate and vanilla in freezer. Which one you want? Or both?"

I kind of duck my head, look up under my eyebrow. "Is cholesterol," I say.

"City talk!" she snap back. "I don't believe none of that! I'm going give us chocolate."

EGGS

Homer and I were incompatible. Loneliness was probably the main reason why on several occasions we ended up together. For a bookworm like me, a budding poet reading Kerouac's *On the Road*, it was understandable why outside the library a friend was acceptable. Why Homer elected to search me out, to pick me up in his brand-new 1963 Comet, was a mystery. He was nineteen, a high-school graduate, with a comfortable bookkeeping job at the shrimp basin. Virtually independent, with only a permissive mother to contend with, he was often drunk and cruising the streets like a young Bacchus. But unlike the fertile Bacchus with a garland of maenads, he could not attract even the lowliest girls who gathered at the Oasis Drive-In.

I never knew why.

Ironically, I who had no job and no car (and wanted neither to destroy my freedom) was the aggressor when it came to pursuing girls. I lived with my parents, had just completed my junior year of high school, and was anxious for new experiences. Other than through books, how else would I broaden the range of my poetic subject matter? So Ruby and the Romantics sang "Our Day Will Come," and it was summer and I prodded Homer to pick up girls every time we cruised the downtown streets.

"Use the car well, man." How frustrated I was when the night ended and we had miserably failed to entice any girl. At street corners, busy and colorful as carnivals, the stoplights were wasted. Neither one of us offered the giggling red-lipped beauties a ride. Homer's beer, which a remote neighborhood store had illegally sold him and he guzzled from a brown bag as he drove, did nothing to embolden him. All he did was giggle perversely at my disappointment. "Dammit, man! The girls were right outside your damn window and you said nothing! God bless, shit!" My fuming face thrilled him. When he dropped me off at my house, he promised good fortune next time, a greater daring and strategy. I had heard that before.

Many times at the Oasis, with the outside jukebox blaring all over the boulevard, and the pinball machines swallowing coins inside, Homer had likewise failed to attract willing girls of any sort. They greeted him and his pale green Comet; some even jumped into the back seat, smoking and flirting. Their aggression was intimidating.

"So what are we doing? Where are we going?"

But Homer suggested nothing.

"Come on, man," I whispered, leaning over, "let's take them somewhere. We got them. Let's go to the beach."

"Yeah, yeah, okay. In a minute. Just hold your horses."

"Let's go, man. Come on!"

"So what are you drinking?" the girls asked, craning their pale necks over the front seat. His large bottle of beer in its paper-bag cocoon was erect between his thighs. "Can we have some? It looks nice and foamy."

"Hell, no. This is my beer. Get your own."

"Come on, Homer, just one drink each."

"Okay. Give me a dollar for each drink."

The girls looked at each other and kicked the doors open and slammed them shut. They rushed off to greet and leave with other fellows. And I exploded!

"You stupid, stupid ass! We had a chance to finally do something! You sat there like an idiot! We lost it! God bless, shit!"

And Homer giggled and giggled, his cheesy teeth yellower. Perhaps this was to keep from crying. He did question once, during a rare sober moment, why his car and his looks and socializing failed to excite the girls. There were times, especially when he was freshly showered and dressed, oozing charm and sense, that one legitimately wondered why he seemed to repel even the floozies. Nothing worked and he did nothing but expect miracles. On several occasions when he lingered until midnight at the drive-in, I left him and walked the three or four miles home.

What did the Listerine bottle in his glove compartment prove? He showed it with pride, suggesting he spent considerable time eating women. But one never saw his so-called harem, only his curiously swollen red gums; and if he drove to a dark apartment house, he made me wait in the car while he went inside. Like a fool, I sat indefinitely in the bluish dark cursing my dutiful attachment to him. When he finally emerged giggling and smacking his lips, I was to assume he had just concluded a marathon lovemaking session. His reaching for the Listerine, an impressive medium-sized bottle, and gargling vigorously were to confirm his accomplishment. One time he pulled some panties out of his back pocket and waved them tantalizingly before flinging them to the floorboard in abhorrence. They were soiled (or so I imagined) and his disgust, real or feigned, was bewildering. Once he flung them onto my lap like a purple bat, and I jumped with horror. He giggled all the way home and said nothing about his tryst.

One night, long after a traumatic visit to Boys Town, the Mexican whore-village across the Rio Grande, he came honking for me. One of my sisters entered my room.

"Homer's looking for you. Do you want me to tell him you're not here?"

"I know. I know. Don't tell him anything. Just get out of here."

Images returned to haunt me: the ugly painted whores snatching at my crotch on street corners, Homer telling them I was a virgin, and their snatching becoming more aggressive as they offered a free fuck ("*con cachucha o sin cachucha*," whatever that meant); the relentless bacchic noise and music, smoke and smells and liquor; the hours of timorous waiting, locked in the car, while Homer drank and giggled in the bars. He had said we were only going to the plaza. No matter how furious I had been in the car by two or three in the morning, I was inwardly euphoric when his face suddenly appeared like a nugget out of the brown faces and he said,"Let's go." He had not done any hard drinking or screwing, he said. I didn't care. "I'm sorry, Leon. I lost track of time." We drove home in a terrible silence.

I went out to meet him.

"Howya doin'?" he said.

He turned on the car light and extended his arm for a handshake, his greenish eyes radiant. I felt he was repressing his giggles.

"Peace," he said.

Somehow he looked fresh, restored, disciplined. I shook his hand. He refused to let mine go.

"Hey, wait a good minute. Wait. Where are ya goin' so fast? How about a ride somewhere?"

"No. Some other time."

"Come on. Aren't we good friends, good eggs?"

"Not tonight, man. I'm busy."

"Busy? Busy how? You're a loafer. You don't work. Let's see: what are you doing tonight?"

Though I bristled, I managed to appear calm. I was not going to satisfy his need to aggravate me.

"I'm typing some poems, and I have books to read. I can't just run off every time you come here honking, honking."

"Aw come on, those things can wait. Besides, I've got something special lined up. Very special, right up your alley."

"What? I'm tired of your crap, nothing happening. How many times have we failed? Or I have failed. Time is very important, man. It won't stop: how can I? I'm sick of wasting it."

"I feel sorry for you."

He was not giggling. His eyes looked pensive and forlorn.

"You feel sorry for me?"

"Well, I think you're misplaced or something. Don't get me wrong. I like your company. When we're riding around I really like what you say, how you think, but there's always a pressure to make something happen. I—"

"When I leave my room, my books, it is to do something different. I intend to nourish my senses. I don't walk out of my cave to enter another. I'm not your entertainment, and you must be more than a lure."

"You should be in another world, a room alone with your thoughts, your—"

"I was until you came."

"You're a weird sonofabitch, you know that?"

"Well, I'll see you later."

I started walking toward the house.

"Wait, wait! It'll be worth your while. I'll make a deal with you, okay? If nothing happens tonight, you don't have to trust me ever again."

"What is it?"

"What?"

"Your 'it,' your 'something special.'"

"Okay, I met a woman the other night. Very beautiful, very nice. She gives. . . ."

I half listened since this approach to entice me was old. "Come on, man, get to the substance. How is this relevant to me?"

"Well, it so happens that the woman has a beautiful young niece. And I've arranged it for us to meet them tonight. How about that? All we gotta do is be there."

He could tell I was interested.

"The young niece, hmmm, tight little finger-licking pussy, beautiful! She likes it, Leon, come on! She's waiting for you, dying to meet you."

"Okay, okay, but we need to take them to the beach right away."

"You always want to take girls to the beach. There are other places closer, nicer."

"But not as private. Listen: many times we failed because you ignored my suggestions. If you're going to continue ignoring them, not acting on them, then we might as well forget it. Go and have your fun alone."

"All right, fine. We'll go to the beach. I just hope they can get away for that long."

"We need to succeed. The half-hour drive to the beach is part of being with them. Otherwise, I'm not going."

"We'll get there," he giggled. "We'll get there."

"We'd better."

"You're a crazy motherfucker, you know that?"

He waited in the car. I ran into the house to brush my teeth and put on a clean shirt. As usual, he honked occasionally to irritate me and the peaceful neighborhood. His laughter seemed louder than the honking. It was a relief to drive off. He turned on the radio to KRIO, the rock-and-roll station. Generally laconic, he was now almost charming and effusive. His favorite word, "poon-tang," kept popping up in his conversation. I did not believe he would deceive me this time by driving toward the Gateway Bridge and Boys Town. "Don't look for me because you will find me" was a Spanish saying I had heard while growing up. Tonight, Homer would find me if he deviated from our plan.

The Chiffons started singing "He's So Fine" on the radio. I quickly raised the volume. "This is a good song," I said. We laughed and sang along. This mood generally pervaded when we set out on conquests. "If I were a queen," they sang. "I would get you in-between," I sang.

"You're a poet and don't know it," said Homer, laughing.

I laughed and continued singing. Surfing songs came on and we sang together. Homer often played the fool, altering his voice to imitate a stereotypical Mexican Indian or a homosexual. At times he crudely rubbed the crotch of his khaki pants.

"'If I were a queen,'" I sang, "I would get you in-between. I wish they would play it again."

"Why, you dirty fucker! Try getting this in-between."

He grabbed his crotch and, as on other rides, emphasized the shape of his penis. He turned on the light again. He was semihard.

"Try this man-sized wiener," he giggled.

"Is beer your measuring tape?"

"Why don't you come down here and suck me? I could use a good blowjob."

"So could I."

"We're real good eggs," he said, laughing.

I had trusted his direction, his promises, but then he parked in front of one of the city's housing projects. My expectations quickly deflated. Except for some children chasing each other like hyenas across the grass, no young women were around. On the dark lawns of several houses down the street, plump shadows were moving and altering the darkness. I was now nervous and muggy, hating the lowly neighborhood, and Homer was starting to giggle. Nonetheless, he actually looked around and questioned the whereabouts of the aunt and her niece. Frustration and anger were gradually invading me like a fog.

"Let's get the hell out of here," I said. "There's nothing, not a dent. Another night wasted. God bless, shit!"

"Wait a minute. Wait a minute. They'll be here, man. They're beautiful. You won't regret it. He honked and started driving slowly along the curb, on the left side. I hated the lights from the light posts, from the houses and the oncoming cars, from wherever. I wanted to sink into the seat, to evaporate, to jump out and run home. I demanded that he quit the honking, which like an ice-cream truck had already attracted several rascals to the prowling car. Their voices were so daring, so unafraid. Eventually, we reached the shadowy figures and Homer leaned over the steering wheel.

"There they are. I knew they'd be waiting faithfully. I guess I was at the wrong house. Wait till you meet them."

I was horrified! The so-called beautiful aunt, judging by the little I could decipher, was a darkhaired frump in a shabby dress. When Homer prompted me to get out of the car with him, I was nearly quivering. It was not so much the ugliness of the young woman greeting Homer but the eavesdropping housing project as a whole that upset me. Smudgy children were bouncing like wallabies nearby, obviously associated with the aunt. Among them moved a teenaged girl, perhaps thirteen or fourteen, with a baby boy straddled on her hip. Was she the "beautiful" niece, the nubile goddess destined for me? I wanted to climb back into the car.

Homer and the aunt whispered for a while, their heads together, and I stood still as the teenaged girl and the chaotic kids drew closer. Squabby women were emerging from the adjacent houses, from the shrubs and flowers, as if they had never seen a car. Dogs were barking, as if conversing, not at all alarmed.

"What's the holdup?" I urged Homer.

"We're going. We're going. Hold your horses."

Finally the aunt whispered to the plump teenaged girl, her niece, whose mouth hung open and eyes bulged at me. We were ready to go. The girl was taking the baby boy who was probably not much older than a year. She awkwardly climbed into the back seat with me. Immediately, her body odor repelled me: stale sweat, unwashed hair and flesh, perhaps her period. The boy on her lap also smelled. I needed fresh air. Unfortunately, the open window did little to alleviate the smell. Flashes of silvery-bluish light as we drove on the boulevard allowed me glimpses of the girl. She was a ragamuffin. Her coarse black hair was a hurricane, no doubt swarming with lice. Her face was round and puffy, almost distorted, perhaps mongoloid. She never spoke; she exchanged gestures with the watchful aunt. I was in the back seat of a car with a girl: how erotic it sounded if one did not analyze for details.

So I suffered this perversion of a romantic encounter. I could not hold the girl even if I had wanted to. The boy was squirming and she was still cradling him. She seemed miles away, and we were on the winding road to the beach. The headlights paved the way. The cacti and yucca plants appeared like monsters in a haunted house. Homer was generally silent, as if wondering how to handle the unfolding reality; occasionally, he would turn to ask me how I was doing. In what? Did he seriously think I could embrace the girl shielded by smell and kid, or was he measuring my growing fury? Either way, he was frivolous and giggly as he returned to his driving and the aunt who snuggled quietly against him. They appeared so natural together. His arm looked very strong around her narrow shoulders, and his golden wristwatch glinted like a taunting wink.

About halfway to the beach, Homer stopped the car on the side of the road and turned off the lights. The aunt detached herself from him. He turned around and placed his arm on top of the seat, his watch and graduation ring glinting.

"Do you really want to go all the way to the beach? You know, we could stay here or go into one of the roads."

I imagined how embarrassing our sounds would be.

"No, no. We must go to the beach. It's deserted. Here, the police or someone else can interrupt us. Remember what I said, man."

"I know, I know, but it's still too far and I can't wait for some—"

"Let's stay here," said the aunt. "If we go to the beach, it will get too late. We could get in trouble."

"You see, you see," he said.

"Are you going to listen to her? Are we going to the beach or not?"

"Goddamn! Okay, let's go to the fucking beach!"

The beach was empty and very foggy. I was glad. But Homer was afraid of getting stuck in the sand. He refused to proceed beyond the entrance. Though I sympathized with him, I still urged him on and he reluctantly obeyed. The sand was hard instead of dry and soft; the afternoon cars had packed it well. I imagined the glistening families thrashing about in the sunlit foam, rushing to their cars for cold beer and Cokes and delicious baloney sandwiches; standing by open trunks, their bodies dark-purplish, wet and trembling in long towels. Usually, the families left at nightfall. An occasional church group stayed behind to watch the moon rise and allow the youths time to discover themselves in the water and among the dunes. The thought that instead of coming to the beach with my boyhood love I was accompanied by a girl who stank troubled me still.

Homer was driving slowly and carefully in order to avoid possible soft areas. We encountered no car, no person: the shrouded beach was ours to use as we pleased. After a while, I told Homer to stop and turn the car around. "Park it facing the way we came in," I said, "in case we need to make a quick getaway." I suggested, then insisted, we take off our shoes and stroll by the tide. For the first time it struck me that the girl was bare-foot. Throughout the drive she had not spoken a word, and the boy had fallen asleep in her arms.

We stepped out of the car. The sand was cool and humid. We could barely see each other in the dense fog. The breeze and the tide were powerful, insistent. Gulfweed was everywhere. Paradise did not exist, I had always believed: it had to be created. We left the windows slightly open and locked the doors. The baby boy was sleeping peacefully in the back seat. I imagined him waking up, opening a car door, toddling toward the surf and drowning.

The four of us strolled together for a while, now and then feeling rain-drops, until we could not see the car anymore. The aunt started worrying. So Homer and she returned to baby-sit the boy and perhaps make love in the car. I wondered if Homer had a condom. He never seemed to consider infections. Anyway, I had my own concern. I took the girl's hand, which was dark and sticky like a lollipop, and led her onward. Her flesh was smudgy like an overripe banana. I wished she had been wearing a short summer dress instead of loose Bermuda shorts. Nonetheless, the beautiful fog had me intoxicated, and I started talking to the girl.

"Have you ever heard of *Cielo Rojo*? It's a Mexican film."

The girl was looking at her feet.

"It was popular back in the Fifties. I never saw it, except for an adver-tisement in a movie magazine."

She scampered away from the tide, away from the seaweed and me.

"There was a romantic picture, a black-and-white drawing of—" I cut myself off. She was not responding in any form. It had not struck me that perhaps she was a deaf-mute.

I had clipped the drawing out of the magazine because it reminded me of my greatest fantasy: my boyhood love and I embracing, heads tilted for a kiss. It was a sensual image, the actors idealized on a dark beach, paralyzed forever. The man's black pants were rolled-up to the knees; his calves were white and strong. The woman's flimsy white dress clung seductively to her powerful round haunches.

Paralysis: it was my flaw. But tonight needed to be different. The white beach, like a new canvas, was ours to paint in our fashion. I was going to cast Sara Teasdale, whose poems I had been reading lately, into the frothy waves and produce an undine. First, I had to recover the girl. I skipped through the loose white sand after I grabbed her hand and she grunted. I felt her shivering. Without looking at her face, I embraced her and our clothes were cool and damp. The breeze fanned some of her body odor, but her breath was foul. I released her and took her hand. This time she followed me back to the surf.

I rolled up my black trousers and waded in the foamy tide. The girl waded beside me; she stared at my pale calves. She raised her shorts to mid-thigh as we waded deeper. Her hips were square and heavy like Homer's. We jumped and kicked when the seaweed wrapped itself around our knees. It excited me when a strong wave slapped her against me. "Watch out for jellyfish," I said. Suddenly we noticed the water: it was a crackling silvery fire, like diamonds or bits of mercury exploding. I had never seen phosphorescence before; for a minute I thought I was hallucinating. I expected Chimera to rise from the stormy Gulf. "This is beautiful," I kept saying, "beautiful, beautiful." My trousers and the girl's shorts were now quite wet. It was time to get out.

We returned to the powdery sand, farther from the rising tide. Already I was imagining our embrace, our heads tilted for a kiss. We were cold and trembling, uncomfortable with the sand that stuck to our clothes and feet every time we moved. I wanted us to sit down, embrace, then recline kissing. We could even roll on the sand passionately. I had often fantasized this with a sunlit girl in a white swimsuit, bulging between the legs, as though she were hiding a sea bean. But this girl could not understand my words or gestures to sit down. I tried to pull her down by pressing on her shoulders, but she was a board that only tilted laterally. Her knees refused to buckle. It was frustrating: there was nowhere to touch her for pleasure. Her abdomen swelled like a canopy, a shield, over the part I thought of cupping. Finally, still standing, I managed to wrap my arms around her. I was going to attempt a kiss. I cupped her chin, which felt rubbery and oily, and turned her face toward me. Her hair and smell were blowing wildly. Her mouth was open and mine was slightly open, landing slowly on a revolting egg smell, while our bodies twined and lost their balance. My lips were brushing hers when we keeled over and missed landing on a board with two erect nails by inches. I sprang to my feet angrily. The girl was lying flat on her back, her mouth open. Her legs began to spread. I bent over and jerked her up by the arm. She grunted.

"Hey, you two!" shouted the aunt, emerging from the fog like a shadow. "That's enough fun for one night. The baby's been crying. He's hungry. We need to get going."

It embarrassed me that she thought I had enjoyed her niece in some form. I was anxious to get away from them. I sensed they were communicating, gossiping, the aunt suddenly protective. We were hurrying back to the car. They were struggling to keep up with me, jumping over sea wrack.

"Did you do anything to her?" asked the aunt.

"Nothing," I said, still hurrying.

"I just don't want anything to happen to her. She's very innocent, you know."

"Didn't you hear me?"

When we reached the car, the boy was crying, and Homer immediately started the engine. "Let's go! Let's go! It's way past midnight. Just get in, fucking sand and all. It's just my car."

The drive back to town was uncomfortably silent and tense. The car stank of fish. Homer simply drove, after a feeble attempt to lighten the mood, and the aunt watched the road. The girl cradled the boy, now fast asleep after having cried for almost an hour before our return. I thought of ourselves not as young, spent, and satisfied, but as old, guilty, and resigned. We had not made history; we were leaving nothing concrete outside of us. As usual, time had been the elegant victor. Perhaps on another occasion we could transform desire into magical experience. Tonight had been too foggy, chimerical.

Half a block from the housing project, in front of the aunt's house, we spotted the flashing lights of a police car. Naturally, we were jolted. But Homer drove smoothly alongside the curb with more naïveté than courage. I would have dropped the girls off immediately upon seeing the police-car lights. As soon as he stopped, a squawking bunch of people gathered and gesticulated wildly. We got out of the Comet, quivering meekly, and a fat woman with flabby arms out of a greasy housedress was rattling questions at the aunt. Where had we gone? Why? Who were these boys? Why? Didn't she know her niece was underage? Why? The two policemen were ready to pounce on us, and the lights kept flashing urgently. The fat woman, someone's mother, was gasping and her bulging eyes were anxious to believe anything. She seemed depraved and we were depraved and the policemen wanted to know how depraved we were.

The aunt, as if used to escapades, calmly explained we were old friends and had gone for a root beer. I was trembling, angry, disgusted with Homer for not having prevented this humiliation. We were suffering for nothing. The policemen were asking for our names and addresses. No fine memory, not even an illusion could offset the fear of going to jail. Finally the aunt was convincing the bloodthirsty mob of our innocence, and I urged Homer we should get in the car. But even though he too was sensing a relaxation of pressure he was not moving. Suddenly he was giggling, trying to bullshit the police and the preponderant woman. "The girls looked like they needed root beers. I wouldn't deny anyone a root beer, would you?" One of the policemen even shook his head no. Eventually, Homer and I disentangled ourselves and left. Our drive home was no different from those of other ephemeral nights, except for my realization that no beach, person or thing, shrouded by the most fertile imagination, could ever provide the reality I needed.

Pink Walls

Keddy Ann Outlaw

Zeely fell over onto a glass of water while simultaneously dropping blue food coloring into the glass and trying to take a photograph of the exploding drops. My best macro lens attached to her new camera hit the kitchen floor, along with the waterfall of blue water and shattered glass.

"My camera!" Zeely shrieked.

"Your face!" I shouted.

"What?" She put her hand to her cheek. "I'm bleeding!"

"I know. Let me see." The cut was about an inch or so long, streaming blood. I dabbed at it with a wet washcloth.

"Oh, Zeely, I think you need stitches."

"Sharon, can we afford it?"

"Hush, child. Of course we can. They take credit cards now at the Best Care clinic."

"Please don't call me child."

"Mea culpa, mea culpa."

"I feel dizzy. Is my camera broken?"

"I don't think so. Lay down on the sofa. Keep the cloth pressed against that gash."

She had just turned eleven. It was the summer I went to work as an office temp because I wasn't making enough from free-lance photography to pay the mortgage and keep us in food and trinkets. Zeely had taken up babysitting, and in just six weeks saved enough money to buy herself a fancy auto focus Minolta camera and lots of film. But we couldn't afford to run the air conditioning most of the time, grounds for heresy in Houston's summer inferno. We only ran it on special occasions. This was one of them. I ran around closing all the windows so I could turn on the cool air.

"We'll have to air condition the house when Nana's here next week, won't we? Can we afford it?" she asked weakly.

"Stop asking me if we can afford things, Zeely, please. You shouldn't have to worry about that stuff. Nana will only be here for five days. It won't cost that much. Besides, it will be nice to stay cool for a change, won't it?

"Yes." She studied the washcloth. "Boy, look at all the blood. It's sure a bright red. I bet doctors get sick of seeing it. I bet they don't decorate their houses red."

I went in the bathroom to get Zeely a fresh wash cloth. I didn't want her to know how much I worried about money. We didn't have any medical insurance. I could afford stitches if Zeely needed them, but what would I do if either of us ever got run over by a car or something? It was enough to make me never want to leave the house, not that I really had a choice, and besides, look what happened to Zeely right there within the four walls of our home sweet home.

Then I panicked. What if she needed plastic surgery? I pictured her pale, heart-shaped face gouged with an ugly dark scar. I faked a calm countenance and went back into the living room.

When Zeely sat up, her face bled profusely. She cried when she saw herself in the hall mirror.

"Okay, Zeel, we better go to the clinic."

"Should I change my clothes?" she asked, frowning at her Mexican embroidered dress stained with blood and blue dye. She was very fashion-conscious and never left the house without wearing at least one item of neon-colored clothing kids her age had to have that summer.

"Better not. You'll just get bloody again."

We drove a few short blocks to the clinic. The door on the passenger side of the car was broken due to a small wreck I had two months ago. It rattled its clanking rhythm, reminding me to get it fixed before my mother came to visit. Zeely was looking forward to meeting her Nana. They had talked on the telephone several times but never met, as my mother lived in Maine. Zeely had lived with me for the past few years. Her father was an ex-husband of mine, and when he skipped town, I inherited Zeely. She was his daughter by an earlier marriage. I never even heard about Zeely until after I divorced him.

"Sharon, you passed the clinic."

"I know," I bluffed. "But I want to park in the shade." I parked the car under a skimpy crepe myrtle tree and we slid out the door on the driver's side.

We liked the doctor. He was grandfatherly with white hair and soothing ways. "Are you a brave girl? " he asked Zeely just before he inserted a needle full of Xylocaine into her cheek. "Because I need you to be."

She went rigid, tensing her whole body when the doctor put the needle in. She squeezed my hand but her eyes never left the doctor's face. I could see she trusted him. She was a pushover for anyone resembling a grandfather.

"Forgive me, forgive me," Dr. Rhiardi said. "There now, that part is over. Does your face feel numb?"

"I can't feel anything."

"Good."

A nurse came in to assist the doctor with the stitches. I felt mildly nauseated. I couldn't watch while they threaded the surgical wire through her skin. I stared at a medical poster that was almost as disgusting as the stitching procedure. Dead center was a cutaway of the human heart. Surrounding it were pictures of all the bad things that can happen to the heart from eating fatty foods, smoking or having high blood pressure. My own blood pressure tended to be low. I used to smoke, which raised it from its zombielike state. Though it had been years, suddenly I craved a cigarette like it was a sacrament.

"All done. Just five stitches. And you were such a brave girl."

Zeely grinned at him as he dabbed antiseptic on her cheek. He put a small tan bandage over his handiwork and told us there wouldn't be much of a scar. We made an appointment to come back in four days for a checkup, the Monday my mother was flying in to Houston Hobby Airport.

On Saturday we got up early to go food shopping at the Fiesta store, one of our favorite excursions. Waiting for Zeely to finish dressing, I found a twenty dollar bill in my purse I'd forgotten I had; it had been a tip I'd earned photographing a friend's parent's wedding anniversary, not my usual line of photography. Most of my money-making pictures were still life arrangements or photocollages, usually for greeting cards or calendars. The pay was sporadic and slow. That extra twenty dollars meant we could really splurge on groceries.

I walked down the hall toward Zeely's room. Before I quite reached it, I saw her shadow on the light pink wall. It was Zeely in profile, and she was running her hands over her chest, pushing forth little lumps like breasts. Zeely with breasts already? Surely not. She arched, stretching high and they flattened. The pink wall reflected a young girl again. She sighed and pulled off the shirt, which I thought was probably her bright yellow T-shirt that shrunk in the wash.

She hadn't seen me. I scampered away, straight to my room, where I dove into the bookshelf for the only childcare book I owned, *Your Child, from A to Z.* I looked in the index under breasts but found nothing. What age was that supposed to happen? What a dumb, uneducated stepparent I was. Then I found something under puberty—that oily, awkward word that hadn't gotten any better since I was "pubescent." Sure enough, breasts were standard items for girls age ten or eleven, though their growth could commence as early as nine or as late as fourteen. So Zeely was absolutely normal.

I wasn't ready for Zeely to mature. Her childhood wasn't ending already, was it? My own childhood seemed fairly lengthy while I lived it. Yet my three years with Zeely had gone by in a pinch.

"Sharon, let's go! What's taking you so long?" Zeely called from the kitchen. I heard her open the refrigerator and knew she was probably drinking milk straight from the plastic jug, milk that would make her bones sturdy and strong. Of course I wanted Zeely to grow and flourish.

My mind composed a fluid, time-lapse photo into the future. Zeely would expand in all the right directions. She would become tall like her father. Someday, looking into her familiar brown eyes I would see not a child's playful spirit, but the banked fires of womanhood. Eerie. I thought of my own mother. Had she felt sad watching me grow up? I had a sense of foreboding about her upcoming visit. When I was a teenager we did nothing but argue. It would be the first time she visited me on my own turf.

35

At Fiesta, we passed through the strip of outdoor mercados selling toys, artificial flowers, clothing, and electronic goods. Zeely stopped at one of the stalls. "Look, Sharon, aren't they cute?" She picked up a plastic baby doll. A lock of hair tied in a bow sprang comically from its bald head. "You could pose her in one of your photographs."

"Maybe. We'll see how much money I have left when we're done shopping."

"I'll buy one for you. Well, for us." She dug into her skirt pocket and fished out a handful of coins. I watched while she paid for it, glad to see she still liked dolls. She had on a baggy white shirt and her chest no longer looked pubescent. Her hair was mousse-tossed, and despite the ugly bandage on her cheek, she looked like a young lioness.

In the car on the way there, I had debated whether to bring up the subject of buying her a brassiere. But then she might have realized I had seen her examining herself, and I didn't her want to think I was spying, so I dropped the idea. Months ago, we had discussed menstruation, so I wasn't totally truant in the obligations of parenting a pre-teen.

I believed in allowing kids a healthy amount of self-expression. For instance, Zeely's hair looked very rock star-ish and wild, but I didn't fuss at her about it. I didn't want to be the kind of parent my mother was, so conservative about things like hair and dress. She used to fret about my long hair, worn straight and parted down the middle. To her it was a sign of hippiedom. To me, it was a natural and very fashionable style, worn by most girls at my high school.

The sights inside Fiesta were carnivalesque. Papier-mâché piñata donkeys and clowns hung from the ceiling. Great mounds of produce: pineapples, papayas, onions, oversized daikon radishes, other strange root vegetables, and huge bins of dried beans. Mexicans, Koreans, Ethiopians, Vietnamese, Cubans, all the immigrant groups who found their way to Houston, flocked to Fiesta to shop for the strangest things. One aisle was full of Mexican candles in tall glasses. Every candle had a different spell or prayer printed on the glass. White people were a definite minority at Fiesta. Mariachi music blared from the loudspeakers. Crowds stood around the bakery counter, where tortillas rolled off an escalator-style oven, were packaged and handed out still warm to waiting hands.

"Look, Sharon," Zeely whispered. She pointed to an enormous plastic-wrapped package of chicken feet passing by on top of someone's grocery cart. We giggled together like two school girls.

I was impressed to see a young black woman ask the man at the fish counter if she could smell the catfish before she bought it. She sniffed it with approving gusto. There was octopus on ice next to the catfish, covered with little nipple-like bumps. "Is that where they cut the tentacles off, or what?" Zeely asked.

She knelt down to peer through the glass and get a better look at the slimy, light purple mass of octopus flesh. Ever since Zeely became a photographer, she has studied the world more closely in search of all its colors and textures. She had been worried she had no art talent since she couldn't draw or paint. She took modern dance for awhile but it got too expensive. The camera had given her a new creative outlet and I was glad. She pointed to her reflection in overlay with that of the octopus. "Octopus woman!" We came away from the fish counter with a pound of Gulf shrimp we would cook when Nana arrived on Monday.

That night I was exhausted after cleaning the house from one end to another. There were still some finishing touches to be done, to fool my mother into thinking we led a neat and orderly life. Zeely hadn't been much help, had escaped down the block to a friend's house, where the air conditioning was constant, and where such delights as a VCR and cable television could be taken for granted. We had graduated to a remote control color TV only last year. It was out in the living room. It bothered me how easily I took to the remote control. It made me lazy. There was also a small TV in my bedroom, but that night, as I lay there on my bed, moving just six feet down the bed to reach for the knob and turn the TV on seemed like too much trouble. I stared at the ceiling. I had forgotten to turn on the ceiling fan. I wished it too had a remote control. What a decadent person I'd become.

My mother, on the other hand, was a no-frills person. Our house had always exhibited a Shakerlike simplicity I resented as a child. The only place I had been allowed to hang pictures was on a small bulletin board in my room. Clutter of any form was ruled out. The minute I got to college, I plastered the walls of my room with pictures and posters. I foraged for interesting junk everywhere and became known for my strange arrangements of found objects. Before too long, I was hooked on photography, and on a way of life that would always include mess and clutter.

The last time I saw my mother was four years ago at my sister Carol's home in Kansas, a neutral territory for us because we could focus on Carol's two small children and not delve into the details of my messy life—the two divorces, my erratic work habits and lack of plans for the future. Mother and I had always been an unlikely pair, with little connection that I could see or feel. But since I'd taken Zeely into my life, my mother had become friendlier. We even talked on the phone regularly. By nurturing a child, I had passed some crucial test of adulthood. I hoped to continue to further this illusion. I went to bed full of resolutions for improved mother-daughter relations.

Zeely got a fresh bandage from Dr. Rhiardi on Monday and then we headed out to the airport to pick up my mother.

"Do you think Nana would like to go to the Galleria with me?"

"Well, Zeely, you've got to remember she's sixty-eight years old and used to a quiet life. We'll have to see. Her idea of shopping used to be getting the cheapest price on a carton of canning jars, so I don't know."

"Yeah, but the Galleria is one of Houston's best tourist attractions. If she didn't want to go around to the stores, maybe she'd like to watch the ice skaters, like you do sometimes. It might remind her of Maine!"

"Maybe." I wasn't much of a mall shopper myself. When I went to malls with Zeely, I amused myself by going around to card shops and checking out the competition. The rest of the time I tended to slump on a bench somewhere near the mall foliage or a fountain, feeling claustrophobic and overwhelmed by the barrage of merchandise, and peoples' urgent desires for it. I preferred garage sales or thrift shops. However, I did like airports, with their tableaus of human nature and families in reunion.

I was almost hoping my mother's plane would be late so I could sit around the airport and compose myself, get in the mood for my own little family reunion. But the plane was early, of all things, and Zeely spotted Mom even before I did. Zeely had seen photographs of her, but I don't know how she recognized Mom because I almost didn't. Mom had changed. She was shrunken. Her hair was thinner and had changed from gray to pure, pure white. This made her look even more Old Yankee than ever before. As she moved toward us, she shed her hand-knit wool sweater and I saw she had lost weight. She had always been solid and well-padded, in sensible defense against Maine's interminable winters.

"Sharon!" She gave me an uncharacteristic hug and I felt a fragile dove had fluttered against me. "And this must be Zeely. You do look full of zeal!"

They hugged too. "My, what rambunctious hair! Isn't she lovely? But what happened to your face, young lady?"

"I fell on a glass and had to have stitches. Five of them. They come out in a week."

"And how did you happen to fall on a glass?"

"I was taking a photograph with my new camera and I lost my balance."

"Not another photographer!" But she said this in a teasing voice, and soon Zeely was chatting away with her like they were old friends. We got Mom's luggage and made our way to the car.

"Nana, do you like the *I Love Lucy* show?" Zeely asked from the back seat.

"Yes, I've watched that show," I was surprised to hear Mom say. We never had television at my mother's house when I lived there. Carol and I had been the only kids around (except for some Seventh Day Adventists) who had to suffer through life without TV.

"I got the TV at a school auction. Oh, I don't watch it much, but it is company, especially in the winter."

"Nana, wait 'til you see the photograph I took," Zeely said. "You know at the beginning of the show, where there's a big heart and then those ribbony letters write in script that say I Love Lucy?"

"Yes," my mother nodded.

"Well, I took a picture of that, and it turned out great! We blew it up, and Sharon's going to show me how to tint it, probably pink and blue."

How I loved Zeely for her enthusiasm and wholehearted enjoyment of things. She was a great diversion. Without her, what would Mom and I be doing?

My mother tensed in her seat when I swooped down the ramp onto Loop 610. "My, look at all this traffic. How do you know your way around, dear?"

"I help her," Zeely shouted, and I frowned in the rear view mirror, hoping she wasn't about to divulge any stories about my driving habits.

"Yes, you do, Zeely, and maybe you'd like to tell Nana some of the places you two might go this week."

"Oh, I don't need to go anywhere fancy," Mom said. "I just want to visit with you two." Her hands gripped the seat belt. Mom's hands used to look raw and red at the knuckles from all the scrubbing and washing she did. Now her hands looked pale, old, and crumpled as antique kid gloves.

We got home safe and sound. I gave Mom my room. When she lay down for a nap, I felt worried. I'd never known her to take a nap before. I thought about calling my sister in Kansas and asking her about Mom's health, but I really couldn't afford the long distance phone bill.

I was glad to see Mom eat a good amount of shrimp at dinner. Then Zeely did the dishes. I sat with my mother in the living room. "Mom, are you feeling okay? I mean, you look different. You look smaller."

"Yes, I've lost some bone mass. Just a touch of osteoporosis, the doctor tells me. I can't believe it after all those years of drinking fresh cow's milk, but it's a common thing for women my age." She lowered her voice. "I'm taking estrogen now. You've probably seen lots of articles about it in all the womens' magazines."

"Yes. But otherwise, you're healthy and everything?"

"Why sure. If I wasn't, do you think I'd come all the way down here? How you stand this heat, I don't know."

"I stand it better than those old Maine winters."

"Well, that's just one more difference between us then," she laughed. She fanned herself with a magazine and smiled sweetly.

40

Yes, she had mellowed. I'd been afraid she would be looking in corners for dust, or accusing me of abuse because of Zeely's facial wound. But she seemed content just to be with us. We had an easy evening. She and Zeely played cards. We all looked at the photographs I'd taken of Zeely at ages eight, nine, and ten.

The next day I had to go to work. Leaving Mom and Zeely with a Metro map and a pile of bus schedules, I drove away envying them their time together.

When I got home, I heard all about their day spent visiting the museums. They spread out some art postcards and brochures on the table to show me what they'd seen. "This one looks like something you would do, Sharon," Zeely said, pointing to a Rauschenberg collage.

"I remember when you used to be mad for those color-by-number sets," Mom said. "We used to go all over the county at Christmas time to try and find ones you hadn't done."

I'd forgotten about that, but it came back to me—kittens with balls of yarn, Cinderella and other kitschy subjects, all done in that patchy color-by-number style.

"Really?" Zeely asked, eyes wide. "You mean you weren't a natural artist when you were a kid? You used kits?"

"Yes," I laughed. "I still don't draw so well today, you know that. But I'd like to think I'm artistic anyway."

"Oh, Sharon, of course you are! Zeely exclaimed. "I don't know anyone more artistic than you. I'm the one that needs help. You know, I wish *I had* a color-by-number set right now."

"Do they still make them?" Mom asked.

"I don't know," I said. "I remember I got sick of them when I realized you could always still see the little numbers under the colors after you were done."

"Well, it took a long time for you to get sick of them, if I recall correctly," Mom said. "I still have one, you know. It's a lighthouse, and it's hanging in the upstairs hall."

"Really?"

"Your father framed it. Don't you remember? That must have been right before he died."

She was looking at me, but I felt she wasn't seeing me in the here and now. Perhaps she was seeing me as a child, or seeing the part of me that looked like my father. Zeely left the room. She was going to make macaroni and cheese for our dinner.

"Mom, did you ever feel sad watching me grow up? Was it weird to watch me become a woman?"

"I don't know about *weird*, but I think every mother finds it bittersweet to watch her children grow. From the time they take that first step and toddle away, or when they go off to school, it's wonderful but painful, too. Then later, when you came home from college, I would look at you and think—is that my child? Not that we ever had an easy time of it. I'd almost want to shake you and say, Sharon, Sharon—is that you in there?"

"Really? It was that bad?"

"Oh, it was just the times, I guess. All you kids were so wild, rolling around the country like a bunch of tumbleweeds, *discovering yourselves*, and Lord knows what else. But I can see you've settled down now. I'm pleased for you, Sharon—that little girl loves you. I'm sure you know that."

"I do. But she's not so little anymore. Pretty soon she's going to be, well—busting out all over the place. I just hope I can handle living with a teenager."

"You'll survive," Mom said. "I have faith in you."

No hints to get married, no criticism of my temporary job—I couldn't believe it. Gnawing deep down inside me was the fear that Mom was being so nice because she thought she might die soon. But it was time for dinner and then a round of Scrabble, and I pushed those thoughts aside.

What was strange, though, was that every night Mom was under our roof, I had ugly dreams about her. In the dreams we were always arguing. Sometimes it was about lavender versus navy blue coats, a dream based on an actual shopping trip we took to Bangor when I was eight years old. But most of the dreams were absurd arguments about what to pack for a trip back to the time of dinosaurs, or why I hadn't spun hay into gold. I was

42

always glad to wake up and find that a little old lady with white hair, not the virago of my dreams, was making coffee in my kitchen.

Her time with us passed quickly, like one long hen party. The day before she left, Mom and Zeely came home from the Galleria carrying lots of shopping bags.

"Nana went on a spending spree!" Zeely said. "Look what I got." She opened one of the bags and took out a handful of bras and underpants. "Matching sets! It was about time, you know, Sharon. I was going to buy some with my babysitting money before school started anyway."

I was amazed. I looked at my mother. She looked away. Zeely danced all over the house, full of shopper's joy. She put on her new undies under a very baggy outfit. But I could see what a difference it made. Zeely was growing up.

On the last day of Mom's visit, I set up my tripod and switched the camera to its self-timer position. We took lots of pictures. Zeely got out her costume box and we draped ourselves in lace remnants and posed dramatically. We made large butterfly shadows on the walls. We drew on mustaches and beauty marks. We put on cowboy hats and berets. I never in my life saw my mother so playful.

It's spooky now. I have this fear I'll never see my mother again. Please, God, I pray—let her live—and I'm not even religious. Maybe next summer we can afford to go visit her in Maine. I want to have new memories of the person I call mother, to replace those old stereotypes of her I seem to have stored for infinity in the dark place of my dreams. I psych myself up by looking at the photographs we took. I look at them more than once a day. I see three women who look as girlish as the pale pink walls that frame them. What guile they show the camera is softened by the easy camaraderie of affection. May that moment come again.

WAKEFIELD O'CONNOR

PAT CARR

He was a dwarf. There was no viable euphemism after you realized that his total height was four-foot nine and that foreshortened arms, legs, and neck attached to the large handsome head, the ample, heavy-boned hands and feet. His size and his awkward dwarfish gait would have made him recognizable on any street in any Texas town, but of course when we were in school we never had to articulate the word when we talked about him since everyone knew you were referring to Wakefield O'Connor if you mentioned Wake.

He was also the first real politician any of us had ever encountered, and if there was someone new in the halls, you just had to say, "You know, Wake, the president of our class."

He'd mastered all two hundred and four first names in the class, and he didn't hesitate to yell down the row of lockers, "Hey, Melissa" if he wanted you to do something for him. To be as openly, and joyfully, manipulative as he was, anyone would have to be smart, but Wake was actually nudging brilliance. I used to watch him work the crowd at school assemblies, and I always marveled at how he utilized his handicap and his really startling smile to charm. We were attending one of the best vocational high schools in Texas, and it'd be natural to assume that the kids taking shop and automotive repair might resent those of us in college prep Latin and physics, but that simply wasn't true, and everyone beamed at Wake even when they knew perfectly well he was twisting them around his big capable fingers.

Wake, Neely Prescott, and I rode the same school bus to Pasadena High, and since our dads all worked for Standard Oil, we hung around together, studied chemistry together, and got into Rice together.

I had thought Wake's intelligence might have shone a bit brighter in our school than it would at Rice, but he glittered among all the other valedictorians and salutatorians in Dr. Davies' Biology 100 amphitheater as radiantly as he had at home. He was also just as political, and after the first semester, I could see he'd be easily elected president of our college class.

"Wake is phenomenal," I said to Neely.

"Of course he is." And as usual when she was reminded of his existence, she blushed.

I admired Wake, but poor Neely adored him, and I often wanted to shake her, tell her not to stare at him, her mouth ajar and her eyes replete with worship. But I couldn't quite think how to say that or how to warn her she probably wouldn't ever be more than a buddy to him. I kept telling myself that he was different, that someday his sensitivity and the understanding born of his own distinction would be able to appreciate Neely. But I also knew that in our generation it was hard for a post-pubescent male of any size not to desire the platinum-haired starlet types featured in *Playboy*.

And because her face had been smashed against the dashboard in the same car wreck that had killed her mother, Neely stopped being pretty at ten years old despite her luxuriant ash blond curls and her slim model's figure. In fact, having such beautiful flaxen hair and such a gorgeous body undoubtedly only accentuated the shock when she turned around with her crushed lips and mangled nose whose numerous surgical reworkings still hadn't modified the nostrils into a less equine flare.

I was always arranging double dates for her via whichever young man I was going out with at the time, but only once in a while could I convince Wake to ask her to join a group costuming in sea-urchin drapery for an Archi-Arts ball or to be part of a beach party in Galveston when a crowd was going.

Strangely enough, when it came time for the spring dance of our senior year, however, he didn't have a date, and I persuaded him to ask Neely.

She floated into my apartment to tell me.

And a month early, she'd already laid out her scarlet net dress and dyed-to-match shoes on my couch, where she planned to spend the night after the dance.

I was going with Ron, another pre-law student who was quite happy to drive us all in the fish-tailed Chrysler his father was giving him for graduation.

I remember the dance itself was typical Rice, with an overabundance of set-ups for the bottles secreted into the hotel ballroom in summer tuxedo pockets, plenty of daring strapless gowns, and a plethora of one-time-wearable linen pumps that became increasingly grimed by every girl's lubricated escort. But both Ron and Wake stayed relatively sober throughout the dancing, the midnight bar-be-que menu, obviously selected by some Rally Club jokester on the dance committee, and the drive back to my place.

"If you've got an extra chunk of floor, I wouldn't mind talking you out of it for tonight," Wake said to me as we piled from Ron's car. "I need to drive to Austin tomorrow, and I'd as soon take off from here."

"It's all right with me if Neely doesn't mind. The only floor is in the living room."

That of course was merely ritual. I knew Neely'd be ecstatic to sleep on the sofa and have Wake on the carpet beside her.

"Oh, I don't mind," she murmured, and even in starlight, the blush across her shoulders was visible.

They strolled inside to give Ron and me a chance to neck on the steps, but since Ron's single talent other than a photographic memory of historical events was that he could dance, we stood for a only few minutes before we said good-night and he drove off.

The apartment was dark, but I could see the merged shadow of Wake and Neely entwined in each other's arms on the couch, and I tiptoed silently by to shut the bedroom door before I clicked on the light.

Wake had draped his rented tux jacket on a chair, and it beamed white and broad shouldered beside the night table.

I didn't notice what time it was then or later when Wake came into the bedroom and stumbled against the chair.

"Sorry," he whispered. "I was afraid I might have left my wallet in Ron's car."

It was a weaker excuse than I expected from him as I watched him carry the wallet back into the living room and shut the door again, but I thought that since he'd remembered to bring a condom maybe Neely was in the running after all.

When I came out the next morning, however, I knew immediately that she'd had no chance whatsoever.

He was making coffee in the tiny kitchenette.

"If I could have found a skillet, I'd have scrambled us some eggs."

Neely appeared at the archway in my pink bathrobe. She gazed at him, her brown eyes enormous with doubled—perhaps tripled—adoration.

He didn't acknowledge her presence.

"I use a saucepan to scramble eggs," I said shortly. "Neely, you can get the cups."

It was almost impossible not to lunge against each other in the confined space, but Wake managed to avoid even brief contact with her while he broke eggs into the pan and concentrated on folding the whites and yolks together.

By the time we carried plates of egg and toast into the living room, I could tell he wasn't going to look at her or speak to her.

You son-of-a-bitch, I thought. So it's all right for you to screw, but let any female go along, and she's a slut.

But I didn't know how to snarl my anger at him without flaying Neely, and I had to sit and nod and pretend I didn't notice he was ignoring her, pretend I didn't know why.

A week later we graduated, scattered, and I lost all touch with Neely.

Wake and I moved on to law schools, and while I focused on Louisiana's Napoleonic Code, he stayed in Texas. But I occasionally heard about him, and I knew that around the time I ran into Ned, Wake had married someone named Carla Lewis.

Our tenth reunion came and went, then the fifteenth and the twentieth before I read in the memorial section of the alumni magazine that Neely had died somewhere in Africa. I debated about contacting her father if he was still alive, but I didn't, just as I didn't attend our twenty-fifth class reunion. And it wasn't until the thirtieth that I decided to go back to Rice.

Naturally I recognized Wake from across the room. His black hair was a wavy gray, but his blue eyes were the same intense sapphire, and his assured grin flashed the same deep dimple as ever.

"I was hoping you'd be here." He grabbed me into a muscle-bruising hug. "Did you bring a spouse?"

"Ned's a New Yorker. He wouldn't be caught at a Texas college reunion. Did you bring yours?"

"Our daughter-in-law is about ready to deliver, and Carla decided she'd better stay home this time. We've been to these before when you didn't show."

"Is this one significantly altered?"

He laughed. "At the others, we kept thinking we still had things to achieve, but now we realize we aren't going to do anything except keep making money."

A waiter passed with a tray of champagne and Wake lifted off two glasses.

"Did you hear about Neely?" I said.

He nodded. "She was in Kenya, apparently helping the natives build industries not based on elephant ivory."

We sipped the decent but not extraordinary champagne.

"How come we didn't keep up with each other?" he said then. "We're in the same profession."

I looked down at him. "It was probably the senior dance."

"The dance?"

I nodded. "You screwed Neely on my couch."

"I did?"

"You don't even remember?"

He considered. "And you held that against me?"

"Not that. But the next morning you treated her with complete contempt. I guess I always thought you'd escaped that damned macho Texas mentality, that you were different from the others."

He shook his head. "You and Neely were always such innocents, such idealists." His big hand patted mine, and his blue eye creased and twinkled. "I was never different from anyone else. I was just shorter."

Evangeline's Property Line

Ann McVay

Mary lay on her back on the floor in front of the mirror and watched Evangeline get dressed. She had just about figured Evangeline out. There were certain things the two of them had to talk about. Some things Mary knew the words for and some she did not, but you couldn't talk to Evangeline just any old time.

She watched Evangeline measure a line of white polish on the outside of each shoe with the sponge. It was warm in the house, but Mary could still breathe good. The air always got hot and heavy around them if Evangeline was not in a mood to hear her.

"Careful you don't muss yourself in that dress with that shoe polish," she said, testing the air.

Evangeline stepped across her and straddled her, looking down. She held one high-heeled pump an inch above Mary's face before she spoke. "That's the trouble with you, sweet. You get all worked up about stuff, tiny little business, and you squeeze out all the room in your heart what Jesus meant for joy."

Evangeline backed up into the mirror, studying her hemline in the back, touched the white cotton cloth on the edge with the shoe polish sponge. "Goddamn this skirt," she whispered into the mirror.

Mary felt the room get a little warmer, stuffier, the way she always felt when Evangeline shamed her about not feeling joy for Jesus. You'd think at ten years old—Evangeline claimed Mary was probably close to ten—a person could breathe right. But why was it, she thought up to God, that sometimes the fear in her heart and the need for one good breath of air squeezed out room for anything else?

Revelation, Evangeline's cat, thin and straight, with a sharp gray face, guarded two lipsticks on the bureau. "Move," Evangeline told him. She touched him under the chin before she set him on the floor. Mary watched Evangeline's mouth in the mirror, her own mouth becoming a big "O," as Evangeline traced the color on her lips.

"You think I look fat?" Evangeline asked her.

Evangeline's legs were the color of midnight, even darker underneath the white skirt. They were hard and straight from dancing for the glorification of the Lord. Everywhere else, she was round and pretty.

"You are beautiful," Mary told her. She wished she were even a light brown instead of this washed-out white.

"Liar." Evangeline kicked her lightly once, the pointed toe of her shoes finding her rib bones easy, then finished fixing her hair.

Mary ran her fingers across the shoe and then over Evangeline's ankle. She especially needed to talk to Evangeline about the horses, but she knew now was not the time. The foal was coming soon and she wanted to put clothes on it, maybe some kind of bonnet or dress, like she'd done at times with the stray animals that wandered in and out of the yard. But Evangeline had already said no, they couldn't keep it, they couldn't afford another animal. Evangeline was always taking in some kitten or bird or puppy that was too small or too sick to fend for itself.

When Evangeline was ready to go, the panic filled up Mary's throat again. Always, there was that smothering block that started in her chest and moved up into her neck and then her head, affecting her breathing, when she became nervous or when Evangeline left her even for a little while.

Evangeline hugged her and rocked her, standing at the door for a few minutes. "Hey, now. You're gone be just fine. I won't be long and I always come back, don't I? You're my baby, sent to me from Christ the Lord. Just set yourself down and have a little prayer with Him, and I'll be back soon. Me and Jesus, we're gone take care of you."

Mary watched her out the window until she couldn't see her anymore. There was a fluff of dust at the end of the road where Evangeline turned her rusted blue pickup onto the blacktop. The blacktop pulled Evangeline into town, farther away from her, into the arms of friends. Sometimes the friends sent her back home with money.

Evangeline had been excited about the farm when Mary and she had moved from South Plains, Texas. Sometimes Evangeline was excited enough to even work on the land when she came home from the Dairy Queen. Most days, though, she just danced in the sun along the shallow rows, instead of chopping up dirt and planting things.

Five years ago, Evangeline had found Mary on the turn-off of Highway 305. It was a bad time for Mary. She kept shivering even though it wasn't cold. Evangeline had kept talking to her until Mary, herself, could remember how to talk again. Mary understood Evangeline's words long before she could answer her. Even now, many of her own words were trapped in her head, making faint noises, trying to get out.

"God has told me I will grow something here," Evangeline told Mary when they moved to Old Glory after Evangeline got a message from God. "I just don't know what."

The dry and rutty piece of land bucked up against a timber plot without a fence. The shack was like the one they'd had before, only this one had a step outside the door and a leaky tin barn about fifty feet away.

Evangeline's hat hung on one wall. Mary fingered the long, pink ribbons. When they had moved in, Evangeline had placed the hat on one wall and a picture of Jesus in a crown of thorns on the other.

"There you go, it's home now," she had said. But for Mary, it was not the Jesus picture that made her feel safe, it was Evangeline. It was not the red-letter words of the Son of God that offered her salvation, but Evangeline's low voice, full of music, reading those words to her.

Mary squinted out the window, trying to see one last puff of dust from Evangeline's truck. But she could see nothing, not a trace of her. She pulled a chair up to the window so she could keep watch. One of the puppies wandered in, sniffing at her toes, and she put him in her lap.

Sometimes Evangeline still said, "Onliest thing I ever wanted was a baby and a farm." Mary did not answer when she said that, not because she couldn't talk, but because she wasn't sure she still qualified as Evangeline's baby. Or anything else that Evangeline wanted.

In case she didn't, she often crawled up beside her and put her head in Evangeline's lap. Sometimes her thumb slipped into her mouth again. There was nothing so close to home, in as much as she knew about it, as the feeling of the warmth and wetness of her own mouth on her hands as she lay with her eyes closed, breathing slow and even against Evangeline's thigh.

"You like a piece of jigsaw puzzle," Evangeline would tell her, stroking her head. "You the piece what's been missing. Now you know where you fit good. Now you home."

Mary did not know how long she napped at the window, propped against the sill, but her sleep was fitful with broken sounds attached to pictures that she could almost remember. In her dreams, Mary was as dark and graceful as Evangeline, with black hard legs dancing against the sun, and hair like a thick brown mane whipping behind her.

Until her legs began to hurt from the dancing. A dull climbing ache that moved up past her knees and hung heavy at the top of her legs and in her stomach and she had to stop.

She awoke knowing that the Lord was disappointed with her because she had not prayed, because she could not be happy about the dry hard dirt that was part of His Plan for them, and because she did not always want to do what Evangeline wanted her to do, even if He had sent Evangeline to take care of her.

It would be dark soon. Didn't Evangeline know she would be worried? There was only one thing that came close to making her feel safe when Evangeline was gone. She would go to Caramel, even if it meant staying out there with her in the dark. The horse was breathing and warm and never said anything to her about what she did wrong. It was the first thing she and Evangeline had ever wanted together and the only thing Mary could ever remember wanting with anyone else.

She picked her way across the hard ridges of dirt to the barn. The rows of land between the house and the road were straight for awhile, then twisted and dry like someone long ago had tried to make them straight, but the land had won out. The light between day and night on the farm was tan and dirty, making the ridges in the earth harder to see. She didn't want to fall on the bony ledges, but she was breathing faster, gulping air, feeling as if it were all being sucked away from her. She had to get to Caramel.

Mary stepped carefully over a mound of dirt, but her ankle twisted and wrenched her downward. Next to her the ground darkened, and she was relieved. "There you are," she said to Evangeline.

But then she saw Evangeline's face.

If only Evangeline remembered how frightened Mary was about being by herself, then maybe she wouldn't be angry that her dress was soiled, that her knee was skinned.

"You stayed too long," she told Evangeline from the dirt. "I almost couldn't breathe."

"Get up," Evangeline said. "Go down to them trees."

Mary did not like the straight and toneless sound of her voice, flat like one of the slabs of clay on the Texas ground, with none of the music in it that had been there before she left.

"Something I got to show you to stay away from."

"What is it?" Her stomach lurched as it always did when Evangeline had this shadow on her face. "Can't we go see Caramel? Tell me, and I will stay away from it."

Ihateyou Ihateyou, she thought, before she could help it, *when your eyes are like this, this blue-black on brown, the center of them pulled far away from me into small dots of dark.*

"Mind me," said Evangeline. "Honor thy father and mother. Or whoever it is what God give you for one." Her large hands implied a veiny punishment from Jesus if she did not obey. Mary hobbled behind her down to the property line at the trees, her ankle throbbing.

There was no fence on the back acre that led into the woods. Brush and weeds grew thick around the division of property. The trees had created a tangle of black and brown shadows, twisted arms extending a dark invitation.

Evangeline pointed to a growth on the ground. "This here is a thistle bush you ain't supposed to go past," she told her. "There's thorns all through. When you and Caramel go for a walk, don't you go no further than here."

The air around them tightened, pressing against Mary's chest. "Caramel wouldn't go in there." Mary took a few steps back from the tree line. "She wouldn't like it."

Evangeline wasn't listening. She studied the tops of the trees in front of her, raised her arms and swayed with them. Mary relaxed a little. If Evangeline was going to dance, then maybe she was not too mad.

"Tell it to me again. How do we know which part is ours?" Mary asked her. *Talk about the thistle, talk about the line you cannot see between two*

pieces of land, anything to forget about other things, things like men friends
not meeting you in town like they were supposed to.

"There," Evangeline pointed. "Just where I wanted it to be and just
where it's supposed to be." A short ways into the trees, someone from
years ago had marked one of the scrubby trees with a white spray-painted
"X" to show the separation of properties.

"Anyways, when something belongs to you, you kind of know where
it stops and starts," Evangeline said. "It's a feeling kind of thing." She
closed her eyes, and Mary knew she was feeling for the line of division.

"What if the man on the other side thinks the line is in a different
place?" Mary asked while she tried to shut up her evil mind. *Cause-it-*
ain't-marked-what-if-it-ain't-marked-do-you-think-he-might-come-at-you-
with-a-shotgun-jesus-no-oh-please-i-hope.

Evangeline stared at her blankly, and Mary felt the air around them
grow even thinner. "I'm just trying to grow something," she said slowly,
"in a bit of earth that happens to be next to him."

"If you can't grow nothin', then what happens to us?"

"It is a bad thing, doubting the wisdom of the Lord," Evangeline told
her, pupils like hat pins coming into focus on her, and it was then that
Mary knew both God and Evangeline had heard her hateful thoughts.

To prove it, Evangeline tore off a piece of the thistle bush and switched
her ankles three times. "See how these'll tear up your legs?" She lifted
Mary's skirt and slowly raked a thorny twist across her thigh. "So don't
you come down this way. Stay away from the trees. Hear me?"

Evangeline held Mary's hand while Mary cried walking along the row
back to the barn. She had not held her hand in a long time and Mary felt
forgiven. How could she have been so stupid, so faithless as to doubt the
promises of Jesus? The Lord would provide. Hadn't he sent Evangeline to
take care of her? Her legs were stinging, bleeding, but this time she would
not complain. Didn't Jesus suffer even greater pain than thorns and thistles
for her and her sins?

Inside Caramel's stall, Mary was hypnotized, as always, by the sounds
of Evangeline's voice. She spoke in low and musical tones to the horse,

with the same soothing words and sounds that she had used long ago when she found Mary. She had held her and rocked her, easing her to sleep. Evangeline pulled gently on the harness, caressing her neck and face until the horse turned toward her and nuzzled her hand.

"See the withers, how fine and high and hard her legs are now?" Evangeline slapped Caramel's rump affectionately. "She going to be a good mama, now that we fixed her up."

Mary buried her small fingers in the horse's coat. What must it feel like, she wondered, to be a mama horse that is carrying a baby horse deep inside you?

"Cain't believe people treated her that way," Evangeline said. "You got to tend to the things you love or they just shrivel up and die." When they had found Caramel, she had shown Mary how to rub the horse's mouth with a wet sponge, gently kneading it back to life and moisture. "Only thing is, once you start, you can't stop. You going to love her now, you got to always take care of her."

Mary was sure that Evangeline had found her, cast out for dead, in much the same way. She couldn't remember much about it, and she was afraid to ask.

She only knew that before Evangeline there had been a screaming black hole that melted into little gray pieces of rain in her head, numb fragments that made no sense to her at all. Evangeline had fed her bean soup and tried to keep her warm. That was the earliest thing she remembered, sucking soup from a spoon and finally not being so cold.

And that she could breathe. Even if sometimes the tops of her legs hurt all the way up through her chest.

"Caramel is the color of our mixing," Evangeline said. "It is a sign from God, the Father Almighty, that me and you are supposed to be together, take care of each other. It is the color God got when he put all my blackness with your faded white self."

Eyes half-closed, Mary listened, standing next to her, a fistful of Caramel's mane in her fingers. The smell of damp hay, horse and leather filled her nose. Without looking she knew that the leather smell came from the saddle, reins and curries that hung on the wall behind her.

"Will she let me ride her?"

Evangeline took Mary's hand and moved it over Caramel's neck and nose, then held it under the horse's mouth as if the animal would speak, as if words, in answer to her question, would fall into her hand. The horse blew on their fingers, white in black, and lowered her head.

"No. Too tired. Two, three weeks, maybe and she gone have that baby. We got to take care of her."

"How do you know when?"

Evangeline frowned and squinted up at the wooden beams overhead. "I don't remember. Jesus, maybe, give it to me somewhere along the way. He gives me the power of understanding now and again . . . Come on, we got to go pray for this horse." She scooped Revelation out of the corner where he was playing and took Mary by the hand. "And this ground. The Lord can make this dirt green with something, but we got to pray."

After they prayed and ate, Evangeline pulled her close to her in bed. "It was not a wasted trip to town," she told Mary. "Carlton wasn't there, but I put a ad in the paper to get me a farmhand."

Mary snuggled against her.

"'Course, we don't got no phone, so he'll have to come here so's I can check him out."

Mary hoped that Evangeline was not going to teach her anything tonight about what the men would do to her when she was older. But she didn't. Instead, Evangeline threw one leg over hers and rocked it slightly, so that the rhythm took them gently into sleep. This time when she dreamed, she and Evangeline raced together like wild horses. When she danced there was no dull pain in her legs to stop her.

"Good," Evangeline said, when she opened the door to a man who called himself Latham Jones and said he was answering her ad. She straightened the scarf on her plaits. "Yes, well, good, then. We're having a time growing anything around here."

"Don't look like you got a whole lot to work with."

Mary watched while Evangeline soaked up the sight of him from top to bottom, taking in the tight gray and black curls in his beard and the worn spots in the knees of his pants. She looked at him from toe to top, then stopped on his dark face with cold, black eyes. "We're barren as Abraham's Sarah here."

Latham Jones began the next day. In the afternoon, when Evangeline began dancing in the field, he leaned on his hoe and watched.

"It's for the glory of God," Mary told him, proud of her Evangeline.

"Just you and the baby here? You two and the Lord?" Latham asked Evangeline when she danced near the end of his row.

Evangeline frowned. "No," she said and led him to the barn. Mary watched as Evangeline's joy for Jesus opened her hands and lifted her arms high.

"I ain't no baby," Mary almost whispered and was brave enough to mouth the words without sound. She trailed behind Latham, who followed Evangeline and her weaving arms. *What I say to you in my head*, she thought at him, loud as she could without saying anything, *are all the things Evangeline has told me, me, Mary, important things that you wouldn't know about. All about the rules of the house and joy for Jesus and taking care of business when you got to.*

Evangeline pointed to Caramel. "This horse used to be dead, near bouts. We raised her up in prayer to Jesus along with all them other animals and now just look at her." She stroked her softly and thumped her hind quarter.

Mary stepped between Latham and Evangeline. He needed to know that she had seen the way that he had watched Evangeline while she danced in the fields and again when he walked behind her.

But instead she said, "Caramel's going to have a baby. You can't ride her."

"That's okay by me," Latham said. He kept looking at Evangeline. Mary ducked under Evangeline's arms, stomach brushing against Caramel's as she moved to the other side of her.

She buried her face in the horse's side and rubbed her cheeks against the rough softness. Spreading her hands wide and stretching down and around, as far as she could reach, she felt the fullness of the animal and the tight mother's skin.

Evangeline slapped the horse's rump again and this time, Caramel stepped into Mary, trapping her against the leather tools on the wall. A feeling of panic, almost with words, dangerous and bad words and pictures from where she used to be, rose within her. She pushed against the horse.

She couldn't breathe and, at the same time, she breathed in more of the tight small air than she wanted. The smell of the horse enveloped her, swallowed her, as if her nostrils were as big and open as the horse's. The scent of animal and leather, the big brown belly pushing down on her, squeezed out all other thoughts. She could see nothing, only smelled sweat, smelled leather on the walls, smelled sour hay at her feet. Just as it happened in her dreams, her legs began to ache, became numb at the top and in between.

"No, no!"

The horse snorted, whinnied, reacted to her flailing.

Some of the words trapped in her head squeezed out, words used somewhere before. "Let go, let me go!"

It was a moment, an eternity, before she could hear Evangeline's low laugh. "Come on over here, baby." Mary could not be sure which of them she was talking to, but at least she had some breathing room now, enough to slip out and scramble against Evangeline for protection. The air around Evangeline was open and clear, at least when she was in the mood for taking care of her. Near Evangeline Mary breathed clean, straight breaths instead of painful, raggedy gulps.

"You're all right, baby, now close that door and let's leave her be," Evangeline said, and she pecked her on the forehead. Mary clung to her neck and pulled her legs up, wrapped them around Evangeline's waist.

"Girl, you're too big for this," Evangeline told her. But she carried her to the house, hugging her close.

Mary opened her mouth wide to let in as much air as she could so that it could swish in and clean out the noise in her head. She concentrated on the ground and wondered if Latham, trailing behind them, could see that nothing was growing.

Within a week, Mary knew that things had changed. Evangeline was spending less and less time with her and the animals. Revelation weaved in and out of Mary's legs as she fed and watered Caramel. Mary was sure that the cat was as puzzled as she about why Evangeline was not sharing the task with her.

She wanted to talk to Evangeline about Latham almost as much as she dreaded it. Why did Evangeline keep getting closer to Latham, if all she wanted was help with the fields? This was different from how she used to be with the men in town. Mary studied him in quick, secret glances. Without looking much, she knew that he was slope-shouldered and brown and that she didn't want to be near him for more than a few minutes.

There was something about Latham, men in general, that made her uneasy. There was something about how, whenever he stopped hoeing long enough to look over the land, he was taking in more than rows of dirt and trees, as if he were going to be there longer than just to get things growing.

Surely when the foal came, though, things would be different. When the foal came, Evangeline would pay attention to the horses and to her again, to all the small strays that had come across her path. Mary would dress the baby horse in ribbons and a bonnet, and Evangeline would see that it couldn't walk good yet and she would love it . . . wouldn't she? Evangeline couldn't turn a sick or baby animal away. Hadn't she said that that was the Lord's calling for them, the rules of the house, to take care of small and sick and lonely things?

She waited to ask Evangeline again that evening when she came in from work, when she thought the foal was due, just to remind Evangeline that soon things would be the way they were again.

She practiced asking her, even out loud sometimes, but Evangeline was late. And it wasn't until the sun had gone down that Mary finally saw her through the window, dancing near the end of the property at the edge of the trees.

Evangeline was a dancing angel. In the gray space between evening and night, she whirled and twisted and bent herself in shapes that Mary had never seen. There was no music, but Evangeline was alive with some melody of her own that spun her about the orchard and whirled her back to the tree line where she moved her hips in slow circling patterns.

Latham stepped out of the trees, and Mary's knees trembled. The old panic pressed down on her chest and rose in her throat. Latham's face moved in different shapes, too, from what she could see, as he responded to Evangeline. Had he seen this before? She watched him watching her.

From this distance she could not tell which it might be, this woman or this dance, that he had seen before.

"Evangeline, don't," she whispered. Tears stung her skin and she slapped at her cheeks, brushing them away. She had known about the dances in the sun. Those had been hers, theirs, to share. Now she felt hurt, betrayed at not having been allowed the dances at night. It sliced into her, this thought that someone else could be connected to Evangeline in this way.

Evangeline disappeared into the timberline, and Latham followed, past where Mary knew the thistles and the surveyor's mark to be. For more than an hour she waited before Evangeline came in.

Evangeline was still floating, it seemed to her, still moving to music that came from inside and glowing with a magic you could almost touch around each of her limbs, those arms and legs that had danced and wrapped around the man in the trees.

When Evangeline lay down, Mary reached out and opened her palm against Evangeline's breast.

"Don't." Evangeline shrugged her off.

"Evangeline?"

"Shhh."

"Do you still love me?"

The silence stretched until Evangeline kicked one foot out of the end of the covers. "Why you asking such a stupid thing?"

"Because you don't do what we used to do."

Evangeline turned away from her. "You stopped it."

"I know I did." Mary studied the back of Evangeline's head. Evangeline was turning her back on her, finding someone else to touch and hold. Soon Evangeline would leave her and Mary would be cold again. She closed her eyes tight against the heavy slivers of memory that waited like sharp rain in her mind, threatening to fall, to cut through the cloudy webs of her thinking.

"I'm sorry," she whispered.

"Go to sleep." She could feel Evangeline growing angry with her in the dark.

Mary put her thumb in her mouth. The steel splinters in her head were hard and sharp and icy, ready to pierce like spears through the fog in her thoughts. But she would not let them through. She made herself breathe and pray. In and out. Our Father who art in Heaven. Breathe. One and two and three. Christ Jesus. Out and two and three. Jesus saves.

Evangeline was gone to work when Mary woke, so she cleaned the place the very best that she could, mopping, wiping, scrubbing everything. When Evangeline came back, Mary would wash the pickup, taking care to scrape the mud off all the edges. Evangeline would see that she needed Mary, that Mary would be a good girl, a good girl to have around.

She wished Evangeline had not had to go to work today. She wished Latham had never answered the ad and come to work for them.

To get out and away from him, she rinsed out clothes and took them out to hang on the line. Latham sat outside the door, working with a tangled harness, and she had to pass him with Evangeline's white skirt and her own other camisole.

"Soup on the stove," Latham offered to her, not looking at her as she passed.

She did not answer him but ignored the fact that he had come to live with them, had intruded on her world.

Caramel, she decided. The horse was the only other who knew her well and loved her. If she could just go bury her face and her hands in the soft coat, against the tight belly, have the horse nuzzle her neck with her warm breath, that would make her feel better. No one understood her better than Caramel. She left the clothes flipping in the breeze.

She stopped at the door of the barn. She could not see the horse. "Caramel?"

At a sound from the other side of the stall, she moved closer. The stall door was closed. She peered over the edge.

The horse lay on her side. When Mary approached, the horse's legs twitched and she raised her head a few inches. Mary opened the door and was surprised to find the floor wet with stickiness. She squatted down close to the horse and saw the blood, the gaping hole.

The tightness in her chest rose suddenly, and she scrambled back, bracing herself with her hand, slipping into the wet hay.

She backed out of the stall, looking at the bloody hand. Remembrances of blood and pain threatened to loosen in her mind, and she ran screaming to the house, covering her ears so she would not hear the screams.

She pounded into Latham at the door. She opened her eyes and struggled to see, fighting a thick darkness that seemed to swallow her from inside her head.

"No, no, no!" She beat him with all her might, pushing him away from her.

"What the hell you doing?"

The sound of his voice, slow and warm, quieted her a bit, though she still did not trust it.

"Caramel, she's dying." She trembled like the clothes on the line.

He dropped his harness with a clatter and bolted toward the barn. She ran after him, then stopped and squatted into a ball, covered her head with her arms. She ran toward him again and inched in behind him, shaking, stopping before she had to see.

Her back against the wall, she could see neither of them, but she heard Latham moving around on the other side, his boot scraping in the wet stuff, rustling in the moist hay on the floor. He grunted.

"You stop that screaming right now," she heard him say and realized he was talking to her. She bit as hard as she could on both of her hands.

"She dead?" she asked finally.

Latham didn't answer.

"Is Caramel alive or dead?"

"She's alive." He grunted again and there was a sucking wet sound. "But she ain't going to be if we don't help her."

"There's blood and she can't stand up, and she's been hurt."

"Ain't that much blood. She just trying to have this baby, girl, but it's stuck. You got to help me."

Mary slid down the wall, her eyes clenched shut like fists, her fists scraping rough barn board and nails. Nails into Jesus' hands. Who died for you.

"No, I can't, I can't, I can't!"

"Get me my gloves out of the house. And stop that whinin'."

"Oh, Caramel," Mary said, pressing her face into her knees.

"Now!" Latham roared and Mary scrambled up. Her legs were jelly, numb from ankles to knees.

Jesus, father, please forgive me, I'm so sorry, I'm so bad, I am weak and there is blood and there is blood and hurting here, she's hurting bad, we're hurting bad, the legs, the blood and please forgive me.

"Go, girl!" Latham yelled and she made herself hug the wall.

The familiar ache was starting in her thighs. She put her hands between her legs and held tight, trying to ward off the pain that threatened to climb higher. She moved her left leg with her hands, making it bend until it took a step and she had to follow it with another, then another.

The next thing she heard was Latham.

"It's a funny thing," he said to her as he reached and stretched and pulled. Had she come back to help, after all? What had happened to that time? She must have found the gloves and brought them to Latham. "There is one certain place I got to get to. From there it's a song."

She felt herself floating, partly in a dream, partly in a prayer that heaven was holding frozen in a cloud. Latham's face and then his arms were all she would let herself see as she knelt beside him. Sweat dripped down his cheeks, past the whiskers, and onto the veiny muscles in his arms. Jagged veins like jagged lines etched into earth too dry and tired to grow. Those same hard arms that had strained behind the harness now pulled life from life and there was blood and there was pain and there was fear and there was Jesus and—

"It's a song, now, baby, you hold her good now, take care of her."

Take care of her. Take care of her, yes. This was Mary's job, to take care of the animals, take care of Caramel as she always had. Her mistrust of this man could not undo this. These legs, hurting so bad, hers, the horse's, could not undo this.

Even Evangeline not being there, with all the good breathable air, could not undo this.

Somehow in the dreamness of it all, Mary knew to throw herself on the horse's neck, hold her down and talk to her, keeping her face away from the teeth. Latham pulled, and something ripped and screamed, Caramel bucked and knocked the breath out of her. A dark and wonderful thing, slippery, shiny with his mother's gift, unfolded itself out of Caramel.

"We got us a new baby around here," Latham said. "You got yourself a new friend."

And when Mary stopped crying and could look at the foal on purpose without looking away, she knew in her heart that it was true. If Latham, this man who had not touched her, had said it, it must be true. Evangeline must let her keep it. She had made Evangeline stop touching her in the way that men touched her. She would make her keep the new baby. She would watch over it and love it, tie ribbons and flowers around its neck.

Latham would be in the field, growing things. Mary would be the one to play with the pony. It was her job to take care of the animals, to teach it to come to her. She would tell it where to eat and where to run.

And she would teach it to keep away from the timberline where the thistles, sharp and hidden, lay waiting while Evangeline danced in the sun.

An Evening on Mustang Island

H. Palmer Hall

The salt water, clear even in the dark, but speckled with small tar balls, the residue of an oil well blow-out in the Bay of Campeche years earlier, washed over Elizabeth's bare feet. She stood, silent, holding Matt's hand lightly. Looking out at the oil rigs, platforms lit up like small towns in the darkness, she felt the tepid water around her ankles, felt the sand sliding, seeming to slip away under her.

"What are you thinking about, Matt?" she broke the silence, not seeing his face clearly in the moonless night, sensing that his mood had shifted.

"What I always think about the first night we're here." She watched Matt look out into the surf washing the debris onto the shores of Mustang Island. "Dad was fifty years old," she heard him say, "would have been eighty this year, barring heart attacks or cancer."

Elizabeth had heard this same speech, about the shock, about the problem of not knowing, many times. Each time they came to the coast. Her mind drifted as she listened; her fingers drew meaningless lines in the damp sand. "The ship simply vanished," he had told her. "Seven days out from port."

As he talked, Elizabeth grew more uncomfortable. She and the children, now grown, one in college, the other married, had heard the story so often, they could almost speak it with him. She understood, she thought, why he had to tell it so often. Not "Ancient Mariner" stuff, but still some compulsion to keep his father alive. *He should let him die*, she thought.

"It's so strange, Elizabeth."

She blinked her eyes in rhythm with the pulsing of a bright red light glowing just above the horizon.

"All those years, all those ships, and the *Queen* was the only one I had ever actually stepped on. I carried my father's suitcase into his cabin. I remember telling him I thought it was awfully small for someone whose title was First Officer. His cabin was maybe eight feet by six feet, just enough room for the cot, welded to the floor, and a small table. The deck was gray, slippery, and the whole ship smelled of sulphur, like rotten eggs, but more pungent."

Elizabeth smiled, knowing Matt wouldn't see, but knowing, too, that it would lighten her voice. She had heard the story so many times. The first night at the coast, the sound of the surf rolling onto the island, the view of the lights bouncing off the water, always took Matt back to that night in 1963, built up the words in an almost set piece that he released in a low, slowly rhythmic monotone. "Let's sit down, Matt, here in the sand, by the water."

As she sat in the damp sand, Matt lit a cigarette. In the flare of the match, she saw the tension in his face, his jaws working, his eyes staring out at the dark horizon. She waited for the rest of the speech.

She saw him inhale deeply and let the harsh smoke slowly out into the salty air. As he knelt down facing her, facing the sea, she thought about the few changes she could notice since they had bought the beach house ten years earlier. A little more weight, not much; his knees made quiet popping sounds as he knelt in front of her, but the motion was effortless; his hair was thinner. She had not changed much more, she knew. Oh, there was less tone to her muscles and some gray, now, in her hair. Matt had wanted her to put a rinse on it, but she would not. He had backed off quickly when she asked if he found her less attractive now that she was well into middle-age.

She knew he had almost worked the story out. The beat picked up, his voice grew slightly louder. The montonous tone found variety. She tuned him out, not listening to anything but the cadence, nodding from time to time.

"I'm sorry, Elizabeth," he said. "It must bore you. Every time we come to the beach, I blather on about it. But there's something about the place. Dad always wanted a beach house, but we could never afford one."

Elizabeth clasped Matt's hand tighter. Over his shoulders, she could see the dark waters and the moon just beginning to rise behind the rigs.

The red lights blinked with infuriating regularity and she heard a ship sounding its deep horn to signal its intention of moving between the jetties and into the pass leading through the intracoastal canal to Corpus Christi.

She sensed, rather than saw, Matt bury his cigarette in the sand, felt his quick kiss, tasted the salt air and grit of the beach on his lips, watched him stand up and run out into the surf. She breathed faster as she saw his body arch, his legs kick up. He dove into the waves cresting over the first sandbar and swam with deliberate strokes, as if to the metronome that marked the cadence of his father's death story, beyond the second. As she watched, her eyes focused on the slim whiteness of his body moving out in the direction of the shining rigs.

"Matt!" she screamed. "Matt! Come back!" She lost sight of him as rows of dark swells blotted him from view.

Elizabeth waded out into the surf. When she reached the first sand bar, she stood and looked out toward the blinking lights. She was not a good swimmer, had always been afraid of the night waters of the Gulf of Mexico. She hesitated on the shallow sand and then, still unable to see him, waded farther out.

When the water rose above her head, she dog paddled slowly toward the next barrier of sand, toward the second row of white-in-the-moonlight breakers. There the water came only to her waist and she could stand on her own, jumping high as the waves lifted her from her feet.

"Matt," she whispered quietly into the approaching waves, coughing the salt water out of her mouth. "Matt! Where are you?"

A large wave rose above her and the immense force of its undertow pulled her farther out, plunged her down into the water, scraped her arm as it rolled her along the sandy bottom. Under the dark water, she sensed motion. Opening her eyes to the burning salt, she saw a vaguely white shape moving swiftly toward her. Her feet once more on the sand, she backed frantically away, and then felt something pushing her upward, grabbing her and pulling her down. She shrieked, jerked away, turned back towards shore. And then, her heart beating faster, relaxed as Matt's arms and a towering wave lifted her gently toward the sky.

"You son of a bitch," she laughed, then cried. "I thought you had drowned." Holding his head, she felt the wet coarseness of his hair from the salty water, looked into his dark eyes in the moonlight and saw the depth that had always been there, the pain not quite washed away. "Don't ever, ever do anything like that again, Matt. Ever."

"Did it frighten you that much? I thought you were used to the ocean, would know that . . ."

"Of course I was frightened, damn it. You know I hate the ocean at night. But that's not all. All that talk, Matt. Your father and his godforsaken ship. Stop it! Just stop. I thought you'd decided to just keep swimming until you no longer had the strength to return."

"That was a long time ago, Elizabeth," he said, "more than half a lifetime. I'd still like to know what happened. I just needed to swim, to spend energy, to dive as deeply as I could."

His arms pulled her closer and they stood there for several minutes, holding each other, rising and falling with the waves, washed in warm water.

DEVILFISH

PAUL RUFFIN

It was like most days that we fished the wreck or section of pipe or whatever it was lying fifty feet below us that attracted snapper and grouper and kept our freezers full. A diver friend once offered to go down and see exactly what it was in that blue-green deep, but we argued no, it was better to imagine a twisted shrimper or storm-breached snapper boat where more sealife swarmed the decks than the men who once walked them could ever have imagined. A snarl of net or piece of dredging pipe might satisfy the fish—not me and Sam.

It was the mystery of it that hooked a fellow, not knowing what lay in the sand beneath you or what was taking your bait way down there, not knowing its color or shape or size, whether it had two eyes, each on a side, or two on one side, or one eye or none at all. It might weigh in ounces or tons. There was a lot I didn't know about what swam down there and what it swam around.

Sam and I were brought up inland, fishing rivers and creeks and farm ponds, where what jiggled your line was sure to be no heavier than a boy could lift with one arm, no longer than the length of your leg from the knee down. Familiar as family, ordinary shapes, with an eye on each side and the colors right—*predictable*. And no more dangerous than a cottonmouth or a loggerhead—one you just whipped at the end of your pole until his body snapped off from the head, the other you slid up on the bank and bashed with a big rock or stick until he quit moving.

The Gulf was another world for us, when we finally got there, Sam a few years before me when he took a job with a seafood place in Galveston. I came later, after my college work, got a math teaching job at a high school not far from where Sam lived. Sam got married right away and had three kids before he was twenty-five, all gone now and married, with kids. I still batched.

Once we were there on the Coast, where we could look out every day and see that water arching over to the horizon, it drew us like a mistress. It was a rare weekend when we weren't out on Sam's boat, a twenty-two footer, anchored off one of the islands fishing the surf or, better for our freezers and tables, hauling up snapper and grouper from the wreck. But it wasn't just the fishing that kept us out there—it was the sense of mystery, of the unknown. I guess Sam explained it best one day when we were pulling a small shrimp net behind the boat, catching a few pounds of shrimp along with all kinds of fish and trash. He stared at a big pile of seething sealife we had just dumped on the pickboard, then up toward the pale disk of a daymoon off over the sea and shook his head. "It somehow don't seem right to me for us to be looking around up there for little green men or whatever"—he gestured toward the moon—"when most people on this planet ain't got the foggiest notion what we got right here." He raised his raking fork toward the Gulf, stretched out like a silver lid to the horizon, then pointed to the pile on the board and fell silently to separating the confusion of colors and shapes into squid and stingrays, crabs and fish of every type imaginable, lumps of mud, and the handful of shrimp scattered among them.

This was just another snapper-hole day, one of twenty or so we had each year. We popped a couple of good-size snapper no sooner than the boat stabilized its swing on the anchor rope, the way we always did, but the strikes slacked off except for the bait-snatching of triggerfish and spades. No more gunwale-slamming tugs. But these lapses were normal, just part of the cycle of being there, so we drifted out a freeline and slipped our snapper rods in their holders, letting the lines dangle, and leaned back for our first morning beers and cigarettes.

The early breeze had dropped off and the sea was as flat as a sheet of lead. Hot already. Hot and still. And it not even nine o'clock. There was one bitch of a sun coming on. But that's what we had laid in two cases of beer for. We knew it was coming.

Sam shook his head, removed his cap and ran a weathered hand through his hair. He flicked his cigarette butt over the stern. "I wonder if it's any hotter off the East Coast."

"Probably. August's the same everywhere I've ever been. More breezes some places. Still hot as hell." I could see stacks from a refinery. A haze of smoke hovered right above the plant, the burn-off torches holding steady and straight up like dark candles sticking out of the sea. Back in the old days, before he could afford a Loran to feed coordinates into, Sam would run a course out to the general vicinity of the wreck, then jockey the boat until the main stack at the refinery just touched one side of his upheld thumb and the western-most marker of the channel touched the other; then he'd run north and south until the depth-finder indicated the wreck. We trusted his thumb in those days.

Sam belched and leaned and tapped his rod with his beer can. "Guess we ought to reel in and put on fresh bait. My rod's jiggled a few times. Goddamned trigger fish, I bet."

I nodded and threw away my cigarette and reeled in too. The bait was gone, so we both strung on cigar minnows and dropped the heavy lead weights back down until they bumped the bottom, then set the drag and holstered the rods and waited.

The morning wore on, the furnace of the sun building and building until we were drenched with sweat and downing one beer after another. Funny, but you can drink a six-pack in thirty minutes out there in the sun and not feel much more than a mild buzz—the heat sweats it right out of you. We picked up a snapper each an hour or so apart and Sam landed a small grouper, but we had to wait, as we always did, for the feeding hour, which would come whenever the fish were ready, the hell with us and our bait; and when it came we would fill the fish box. It always happened—if we had the time and patience. Sometimes it would be on up in the morning, sometimes early afternoon, sometimes mid-afternoon, but it always came.

There was a time when we got out to the wreck before daylight and caught all we wanted before the sun got fierce, but we got old, or older, and neither one of us liked to get up at two o'clock anymore to make that run in the dark, around logs and crab traps in the river and only God knew what in the Gulf and bay. Then we had to find the wreck in the dark, hell enough in the light of day, and nearly impossible before sunup—but we used to do it, sometimes circling for an hour until we finally saw the depth-finder spike. And if we happened to be looking away or didn't have the light right on it when the needle leapt, it was like not having run over it at all. You couldn't see the boat wake well enough in the dark, even with the light, so that you could just circle back over the same path. We would know by our Loran readings that we were right on top of the damned thing, but you had to be ready with a buoy when the needle spiked or you might as well start over on the circle again. It's just a hell of a lot harder in the dark, even when you know you're just as close to it as you would be in the daylight.

As I say, we got old. So we stopped that early foolishness. We weren't kids anymore and didn't have the patience to flounder around in the dark. Sam says, what's the fun of coming out if you catch all you want before the sun's up and have to go right back home without getting to smoke cigarettes and drink all that beer? So what if you miss that early feeding period—you just wait for the next one.

That's what we were doing, waiting for the next dinner bell, which usually announced itself with both our reels screaming out and the rods groaning and arching almost to the water, the lines singing. And, by God, you can't do more *than* wait. The schedule down there doesn't take you into account at all, not at all, your boat and you no more to the laws that operate beneath that water than a log migrating with the Gulf Stream. If you have your bait down there when the fish feed, they will take it; and *if* they are feeding they will snatch just about anything you drop to them— mackerel strips, squid, croakers, cigar minnows, or a piece of tennis shoe, if it smells bad enough. So you wait.

It happened just as we were finishing our sandwiches and eighth or ninth beer on up around noon, just like the fish decided to join in our lunch hour. The sun, straight overhead, was hammering down, the sea was dead flat, slick as oil, the anchor line slack, no more movement to the boat than we would have had on a slab of stone. Then the reels squawked, simultaneously, as if on cue, and Sam's half-can of beer hit the floor in a gush of foam as he lunged for the rod. On his knees at the gunwale he leaned back against the heavy downward pull as I stood solidly planted against whatever was trying to pull me down. We cranked as we lowered the rods a couple of feet or so, pulled hard, then cranked again, winching the fish up a foot at a time until with one smooth motion I swung mine into the boat, just behind Sam, and he swung his in just behind me. Two fine snapper, at least a dozen pounds each, like twins. Brief fumbling with the hooks and we scooped the fish into the box with the others, baited, and dropped the weights again.

For half an hour we baited, dropped the lines, hooked, boated the fish, baited and dropped and hooked and boated again until our arms ached. There was no time for beer or a cigarette, no time for anything but breath and muscle as the fish tried to pull us down and we tried to pull them up.

"God, I love this," I heard Sam say, time after time. "I need to piss, I've got to piss," he said once, but he went on fishing. Pissing could wait. Beer and cigarettes could wait. This was what we had come for. This was snapper fishing.

Then, quite abruptly, it stopped. No strikes. No jiggling of the line. The rods went dead, the lines tight from their weights alone. Not even nibblers.

"What in hell is happening here?" Sam asked, holstering his rod and upzipping. He peed into the sea. "This ain't right."

"I don't know. Shark maybe?"

When the feeding period ends, it doesn't end abruptly like that. It slacks off gradually. You are dropping the line and catching a fish every time, a process that usually takes three or four minutes, depending on how long you have to fight him; then the big fish begin to fill up and lose interest and the nibblers set in on your bait and you catch a decent fish every second or third drop, then every fourth or fifth, and on and on until finally you conclude that lunchtime is over and you must decide whether to wait for the next feeding or go on home.

"There's something down there," Sam said, leaning on the gunwale and squinting into the water. "A shark or something has run the snapper and everything else off the wreck. Ain't nothing even nibbling." He lit a cigarette. "God-*damn*, that was going good."

I nodded and opened the fish box. "Hell, Sam, we got at least twenty or thirty good fish in here. It's not like it's been a bad trip."

He popped open a beer and tilted it back. "Yeah, but it quit too damned soon. Something ain't right." He leaned and looked back into the water.

I leaned and looked too, my shadow weaving slowly beside the boat like some dark dancer. I expected to see nothing but sea, deep greenish blue sea. But there was more, something black and enormous, darker than my shadow, one of the strangest shapes I've ever seen, more like a wing stretched to filament thinness, but before I could utter a sound Sam's voice came to me, a sharp, distant whisper.

"Christ, look at that!"

I wanted to raise my head and look, but I couldn't tear away from what I was seeing on my side. "What in hell, Sam, what in hell is this over here? Look here." I gestured to him without turning my eyes from the thing below me.

"I don't know what you're seeing, but what I've got here is one of the Goddamned biggest devilfish I've ever seen, and I ain't seeing but a part of him. You see him from that side?" His voice was thin and squeaky, the way it used to get when we were kids together and talked about girls we wanted to take the clothes off of. Kind of goofy, silly, almost shrill.

"I don't know what it is over here, but I'm not seeing but part of it either."

I could feel the boat shift as he left his side and slid up to me, thrusting his head out over the water. "Oh, shit, it's the same fish, man, a giant manta ray, a damned *devilfish*." He turned and looked at me. "That sonofabitch is at least eighteen feet wide. He's sticking out on both sides." I didn't sense any fear in his voice, but his face was a lot paler than it should have been, and he looked a hell of a lot older than fifty.

"What the hell's he doing here, Sam? I've never seen anything out here this big." The enormous ray just hung there, a few feet down, his wings waving gently like a bird drifting in easy wind.

"I've seen'm before, a couple of times this big, but it don't happen often." Sam had fished the Gulf a lot more than me, had worked the shrimp boats and barges, and what he didn't know about it I probably didn't *need* to know. "He's just hiding under the boat, like a damned ling, just like we was a log or something. Resting maybe, or looking for food, the way ling do around the buoys."

I leaned over and reeled in my line. "Get your line in, Sam, or he'll snap it off when he moves out." I brought in the free-line and stowed the two rods. Sam wound his in slowly.

"That explains why the snapper quit," he said, sliding his rod into the cabin. "He's run ever damn fish off that wreck." He handed me a beer, opened one for himself. "They probably won't start up again either. No telling what they thought when he come over. Probably thought it was getting dark already, the way he must have blotted out the sun."

We leaned over and watched his slowly swaying wings. Fish zipped all along his body.

"Them's pilot fish running with him. They got suckers like shoe soles on their heads that let'm attach to him."

"They look like ling," I said.

"Well, they ain't. You can catch the damned things, but they ain't fit to eat."

There were jags of shadow wing stretching out on either side of the boat, like a giant open hand curling up to take us in a fist. Sam sat on one gunwale leaning back and watching the wings weave. I sat on the other.

He coughed and leaned toward me, speaking quietly. "I seen one of these sonsabitches hung up at the dock back there one day, not long after I got down here. Some guy had been fishing way the hell out there and the ray come up under him, and he just quit fishing and rigged up a harpoon he had on board—people don't carry harpoons much anymore—and throwed it right through the body of that bastard. Fought him for hours, but he finally drowned him or bled him to death and brought him back." He shook his head in reverence. "Better'n dragging in a shark anyday. Anybody can bring in a shark. That thing weighed over a ton and a half, stretched over twenty feet from tip to tip. Half tore his boat up. But he had him hanging." He held up his hands and laid one forefinger across the other. "On a cross, like Jesus on the cross, with a spike through his head and at the ends of his wings and one through his tail. Like a big flat, black crucified Jesus. Kids and grownups, the newspaper people, everybody came down to see it. Most people didn't have any idea there was things like that in the Gulf." He leaned and stared at the black wing. "It was like somebody had finally brought in proof of the Devil."

I might have known something was working away in his brain, the way his eyes glassed over when he was talking about seeing that twenty-footer strung up and all the people there. He pitched his half-smoked cigarette into the water and disappeared into the cabin. I could hear him fumbling around beneath one of the seats, where he kept flares and tools and stuff, grunting and swearing, and finally he crawled out and plunked a giant treble hook, big as ice tongs, at my feet.

"Tie this end to that eye." He had reached into the rear locker and yanked out the stern line, a fifty or sixty foot piece of half-inch nylon cord he kept there. He handed me one end and secured the other to one of the cleats on the transom.

I looked at the piece of line in my hand. "Sam, I don't know what you've got in mind, but—"

He spun around and glared at me. "What I've got in mind is hauling in my own devilfish and hanging his ass up beside my boat for people to look at and take pictures of. Now tie that line on."

I just held the massive hook in one hand and the line the other. "Sam."

"Then, Goddamnit, *I'll* tie it. Fuck around all day and he'll be gone." He snatched the line from me and held his hand out for the hook. "Let me have that hook."

I moved the hook away. "Sam, this is crazy."

"Give me the hook." His eyes were blazing.

I handed it to him. In a flurry of fingers he tied the hook on and rose to his feet, the giant treble dangling on a two-foot length of line from his right hand. "Ain't no way I'm going to let this chance go by. It ain't likely to come again. Now stand back."

I stood and touched his shoulder. "Sam, let's don't do this. He's just going to tear up the boat and maybe drown us. If you hook him, something is going to have to give, and I don't think it'll be him."

He turned and glared at me. "I don't expect you to under*stand* this. I just expect you to stand back and let me alone." He hoisted the hook. "This is a stainless salvage hook. You could bring up a Volkswagen with it. It ain't barbed, but if you keep the pressure on, it'll hold *any* Goddamned thing, and I doubt he'll break that line—he'll just drag us until he dies. Did you ever read *The Old Man and the Sea?*"

I stared down at the dark wing on my side of the boat. "Sam, that's not a marlin." Off to the south two big thundercells were building, leaning toward us.

But I might as well have saved my energy for the fight, because Sam stood up on the stern of the boat and held the hook out over the outdrive. "Get the M-1," he whispered. "If I can get him up close enough, I want you to put a round right through his head, between the eyes."

I scrambled into the cabin and hefted the big rifle from a rod rack. Sam always carried the rifle, loaded. I jacked a round into the chamber. "How the hell," I grunted, crawling out onto the deck, "will I be able to see where his eyes are? I don't know where the eyes are on one of those things."

He still stood, watching and waiting, the hook swinging from his right hand. "He's got little fins that look like horns coming out from the head end. Just shoot into the solid part between the horns, back about half a foot, and he won't give us much trouble."

"Right." I eased up beside him, the rifle poised. "But I think you ought to leave him alone."

"I figure," he said, swinging the hook back and forth at the end of the line, "that I can pitch out just in front of him and come up under, snag him right about where his mouth is. I wish we had something with barbs, but the hook'll hold if I drive it in deep and keep the pressure on."

"Sam," I said, stepping back, "the pressure's already on."

Then he flung the big stainless treble out behind the stern, hesitated, and started hauling the line in, an arm-length at a time, until I saw him jerk tight. I was down on my knees, to avoid the hook if he happened to yank it back into the boat, Sam was poised against the sky, thrusting with his legs and back against what he had latched onto below. Out of the corner of my right eye I could see lightning break from the base of one of the storms moving toward us.

The rest is a blur, just bits and pieces, a sort of stop-frame horror movie. The manta could have sounded and snatched Sam from the transom and into the sea—this I know—and probably taken off the transom too, if the cleat held, but he rose, like some magnificent dark angel, rose until I felt him heave the boat by the outdrive, boiling up a great green dome of water, then turning toward us, not twenty feet out, turning and rising until he completely left the sea, the end of one wing blotting out the sun, sailing with his white belly above us. I could see two streaks of red where the hook had torn across just beside his mouth. He landed, half in the boat, half out, springing Sam like a diver over the outdrive, slamming me into the gunnel. The rifle skittered across the deck and into the cabin.

And then he was gone, off toward the southeast. He struck the line of our buoy, yanking the big yellow marker out of sight, but it bobbed up again far off, just a tiny spot in that great stretch of green swells. Sam hoisted himself onto the outdrive, sputtering and yelling for me to shoot, while far out behind the boat I saw the devilfish rise, swelling a vast dome of water, his wings gently arching like a dark hand waving goodbye.

CASTRATING LITTLE MAN

CHARLOTTE RENK

Flo leaned into the turn as if her weight could ease the way or soften the growl of the engine which might betray her presence or intent. She had already turned off the headlights and the engine to allow the car to coast to a stop in the driveway. The rack and pinion going out on her old Pontiac, she wondered how many more turns she could force . . . how many more twists of fate she could absorb before her wheel snapped, stripped from its screwed positions. Would she, like her car, whip helpless and uncontrolled, bumping and scraping curb to curb between gutters?

"The car's worn out, and so am I," she sighed. 167,291+ miles, the transmission just overhauled to the tune of $1235.08, the paint fading into pink continents, peninsulas, oceans splotched all over the once maroon finish, drew attention to its worn barge-sized bulk as downsized magenta, forest, or teal models darted past, honking as she hoisted herself onto the reluctant wheel forcing slow wide turns from the traffic's flow. Growing more distracted and annoyed daily, she blew back at drivers and shook clenched fists and fingers, virtually daring a confrontation. She'd had a near altercation with a tobacco-spitting old man in the Winn Dixie parking lot earlier that day, and she'd scraped the paint on a pick-up at Twin Oaks Nursery. She was in no mood. . . .

Then this . . . this filth going on right under her roof! "Jesus," she thought, as she closed her eyes and pressed her head against the head rest, unwilling to see into the darkened bay window of her bedroom, "don't let them . . . not now, not this." Again, she felt sluggish, slipping, fading, conspicuously brittle and out of place. She sat dreading. She hated what she would do. She relished it too.

Recently, she has hated going home.

Until recently, Russell would be there . . . lounging in his lazyboy, reading the *New York Review of Books*, *The Times*, or any one of hundreds of half-read books pulled from the shelves or stacked against the walls or piled upon the tables. One of his five cats would be curled in his lap as he read. Russell would stroke lightly whichever cat he held as he had stroked Flo—if and when he ever stroked Flo at all. You see, Russell did not like sex. He had not touched Flo in nearly three years, and she had tried everything to excite him—sexy nighties, candlelight, caresses—which he invariably shrank from with embarrassed chuckles, turns, whisking away hands and squeezing his neck and ears into his collar to avoid breath and kisses. Nothing worked, so she gave up.

Beyond the issue of no-sex, Russell was eccentric. Because he was a little man—5'6" at 139 pounds and because the cheap suburban house had 8' ceilings, he had cut the legs off every stick of furniture in the house, cut them down to size, so-to-speak. Granted, the house had low ceilings, but not that low! Flo was a shorter 5'1" at 144 pounds, but she launched a mighty fury at Russell's "small-mindedness." ("leggedness"?)

First, he cut the legs off the buffet and chopped the legs off the china cabinet. He set one on the other to produce the squattiest, most tasteless, legless hutch hugging a floor that Flo had ever seen. Proud at first for cleverly having saved so much room, he defended himself against Flo's outrage by declaring, "Well, legs are useless! On anything really"—he shrugged. An aversion to long-legged women, curved legs on tables or chairs, high heeled shoes, Granddaddy-long-legs, spiders, tarantulas—legs in general. Then, like a skink, he scurried from the dining room, refusing to discuss long or short legs ever again.

Flo stood stunned and gaped at the hutch that he had made.

Russell did not work either. Not at all athletic, the hardest he ever worked, she supposed, was when he lifted her furniture to amputate the legs or lifted a dictionary to check some point, or shifted a stack of books from one place to another to make room for his latest acquisition. Occasionally, he slipped or stumbled across a stack of newspapers and magazines surrounding his chair. Now Russell was not lazy; he just loved reading. He could have been a "professional reader." He underlined, circled, checked, and starred key passages with his ever ready red, blue, and black pens in what appeared to be a code for significance, a significance Russell never shared.

And when Florence Annette Gautreaux's Cajun temper flared, he sat or stood fixed, thin shoulders hunched, pinching forward, bending, stooping to cup across his chest as if to protect his most vulnerable self from the slash of verbal claws and the pierce of worded fangs. His eyes lowered, unwilling to face the wrath of the woman whose flushed rage increased with every second he stayed silent. "I cannot believe you; what did you mean? You ruined every stick of furniture in this house, and every goddamned stick of it was mine except your mother's green love seat, also ruined because of your stinkin' cats' clawin' and pawin', shittin' and sheddin' all over the goddamned place! How the hell am I goin' to ever have anything worth havin'?"

"Don't you care, Russell? I thought you were different from that shit-ass Hampton Bernard, who chased every crotch nestled between two legs . . . and, and . . . and you are different . . . God knows, you are! You are—without a doubt—the weirdest, most bizarre human being I have ever known in my life! Do you know Walter Mitty, Russell? Prufrock? Woody Allen? for crying out loud?" (She did not wait for an answer, for she knew he knew them.) "Good! Well, Russell, *they are positively NORMAL* compared to you!"

Russell said nothing. That's what Russell always said. He had married Flo for her Cajun spunk, her vitality, her independence. Educated right out of the bayous of Pointe Coupee Parish, rescued from an early marriage to a crawfish-sucking, gumbo smacking, coffee slurping, loud-mouthed honky-tonk carousing, woman-slapping bastard of a husband, Hampton "Pappy" Bernard, Flo went on to LSU and became a teacher with single-minded determination. While teaching and studying, she met Russell browsing in Tiger Town's Co-op Discount Books. He was intelligent, shy and gentle. She married him.

But seven years of his cats had made her crazy. Flo lost all traces of her limited, acquired refinement when she reacted to the cats—CC, the Siamese saved from premature death by a medicine dropper; Alegorn Miracle—the Calico that fell from the attic and was pulled safely from a hole drilled in the wall where she surely would have died; Killer Cornflake, who attacked Flo's skirts and scratched bare legs, Ralph Waldo Emerson, and Little Man—Russell's long-haired favorite among the "pride."

The cats had free run of the house. They clawed threads and stuffing from the living room sofa, the love seat, and from the dining room chairs. They pricked and soiled every carpet in the house. Because Russell seldom dumped the litter boxes (and since Flo had absolutely refused to tend cats since she felt that she carried most of the domestic load anyway), every corner and closet became dumping grounds, every curtain contained the yellowed, oily musk of urine stains. The house reeked.

The bitter dust of litter, the foul fume of cat turd sabotaged Flo's joy of cooking—whether stirring rue for gumbo, sautéing sausage, bell peppers, onion, garlic, and celery for the creole or the dirty rice or the jambalaya. Flo lost her appetite for cooking the foods she loved. Russell never had an appetite for spicy foods; he preferred hamburgers—cut the onions, tomatoes, pickles, mayo and mustard. He preferred bland.

Every surface and corner collected hair. Every garment wore hair; Flo felt as if she were about to choke on it every minute; the cats' hair balls hung in to her throat with the same tenacity they held to the carpets. Drapes sagged from having been pulled and climbed. Flo felt degraded by their damage. She felt wicked for hating the cats so. But Russell did not seem to notice nor mind the mess. In fact, he pouted when she scolded them, and fed them her tuna when they needed something special. However, he did stop calling her to notice how cute they were curled in boxes or laying their little heads in his little shoes. He began to scoot them from tables and counters to rescue them from Flo's rolled-magazine, water bottle, and abusive curses.

Flo, whose own parents were hardworking, hard-cleaning country stock from New Roads, La., valued clean houses, physical labor, good food, and good times. Four years earlier when they walked into her house, she felt the hairball rise in her throat. To them and to her, pets belonged outside with the kids. Flo had no children, and her family had not visited again in four years, repelled by cats and Russell's retreat to reading in the bed-room. Flo lost her folks to books and cats.

She felt sick and alone. When she heard cats scratching furniture, the carpet, or themselves, she grew furious. When she heard them licking their bottoms or purring beneath Russell's caress, she threw things, swatted them, yelled more profanities, and ousted them. Alarmed, Russell would lower the foot-lift of his recliner, stumble across slippery clutter, and stand gri-macing against the door to assess both commotion and damage . . . hers, not theirs. Still, he said nothing; he simply glared as one corner of his mouth twitched from its thin disgusted press. At that, Flo hurled whatever she could grasp at the offending cat, missing almost every time.

At night, as she lay wide-eyed beside Russell, who snored oblivous to her, she heard vases and cups knocked from counters . . . her maw maw's milk-glass vase crashed, and her dead baby's picture shattered. Cats treaded everywhere. They stalked her life and her sleep. Twice, she dreamt that she had amputated each cat's legs and presented each to Russell, grinning as she called them "chicken-fried *CATerpillars*." She woke laughing to share her dream with Russell, but he was not amused. Her cruelty appalled him.

Once when she caught Ralph lapping her tuna when she turned to get a TAB from the refrigerator, she fantasized ways to kill him and the others. She became obsessed with the cats and repulsed by the man who insisted without one word that they share their low ceilinged, legless space with them.

Still, Russell slinked about the house with the same quiet persistence and self-sufficiency of his cats. He did not need Flo. He had no need for legs nor love nor her; he tolerated Flo because she was seldom home.

And Flo was seldom home because Russell was always there reading and stroking cats. Russell was perpetually unemployed, "too introverted," he said, "for the public life." He had opened two bookstores in their small town. Both failed. Not enough people to sustain such a venture, even though the Peapicker had catered to the romance and western paperback public. Wal-Mart still sold more books than he did.

And Flo never went home because she was either teaching (both day and night classes at the community college), which she enjoyed, or she was meeting Taylor, whom she also enjoyed. After her stormy short-lived marriage to her curly-haired, brown-eyed Hampton and after her bizarre, dispassionate liaison with her sliver of a Russell, Flo was about to give up on men until she met Taylor.

"Beautiful Taylor. Sensitive, sophisticated, charming, thirty-four, intelligent, passionate," so she thought. He had actually been Flo's student in humanities at the college. He had been to the Louvre; he had been to the Dallas Museum of Art and to the Meyerson! Voluntarily! He did not suffer from Hampton's macho insensitivity or Russell's peculiarity. He was unintimidated by Flo's intelligence and vivacity. In fact, he was stimulated by her scintilating, sometimes crude wit and acquired love for Verdi, Cezanne, Baudelaire, and her capacity for articulating that love in class.

Taylor's charm astounded Flo as they conversed in class, assuming the posture of an exclusive dialogue. Stupidly operatic and melodramatic, the dialogue would go like this:

Taylor: (hand raised) Ms. Barnes, isn't *La Traviata* based on some real conflict Verdi had with his own family's disapproval of his live-in-lover?

Flo: Why yes, Taylor! (obviously surprised and delighted) And also based on Alexander Dumas' *La Dame aux Camelias*, which depicts, in part, Dumas' own conflict with the world over his love of a "fallen woman."

Russell: (teasing) Of course, such scandalous affairs do not exist here, today, do they, Ms. Barnes?

Flo: (stunned, enchanted, staring into his eyes) Not . . . easily . . . not without sacrifice . . . and certainly not accompanied by such glorious music! (They laughed, as other students rolled eyes and exchanged knowing looks about their kind.)

Then talks in her office, both leaning into the dialogue as if every word were crucial, and soon in his bed. He was tender and yet passionate. He "admired" her, he said, "wanted" her. They met at small motels . . . uneasy at first, but adjusting eagerly to the intensity of their encounters within darkened rooms.

Taylor made excuses to stop by her house, prompting knowing smiles from Flo, not only because Russell was always there (though he never answered the door), but also because Russell would slink through the living room, den, or kitchen two or three times each visit as if to check the tempo and intensity of Taylor and Flo's discussions.

As Flo recalled their passion, Taylor's circling her nipples after making love in those dark motel rooms, she wondered what had happened. "Infatuation, after all," she thought. "Her age? Her body?"

Had she forgotten to smile as she fell asleep after making love? She had always been so careful to smile, to keep a careful taut profile so that the skin from her jaws did not sag into jowls. But as she lay sleeping on her side, had he seen her? Had her jaw sagged like a limp pouch pulling the line of her mouth toward the pillow, the other jaw piled like a water balloon folding onto her nose and squeezing her upper lip to a disgusting anal pucker. Had the side that pulled to earth's center drooled? She knew that he must never see her like that. Was it when they stayed at the Waco-Hilton with its wall-to-wall, floor-to-ceiling window opening onto a balcony— the Waldorf of their entire romance? Too much light?

Was it her skin, slack and porous; her belly folding over her pubis, the cellulite saddle riding her hips and thighs? Had he seen these things as she lifted from the side of the bed to go to the bathroom in spite of her sappy over-the-shoulder wink and smile that accompanied her exit.

"God," she thought, "I hate my body, my life." He stopped dropping by her office, her home; he let afternoons and evenings pass without phone calls. So she called him. She sensed something wrong, but would not, could not admit the inevitable.

His infatuation had turned to irritation; revulsion to loathing. When she expressed her need to see him, she began to hear irritation and frustration in his voice, and she felt his need to devastate her, a need she never understood nor, perhaps, ever would.

Determined, she supposed, to make quick end to the affair, he had called her at 2:15 to meet him at Catfish Palace in Palestine. From the tone of his voice, she knew something was a little "fishy," so she punned to lighten the menace. He did not laugh.

"What's wrong?" she whispered over the phone.

"Nothing really, I just need to talk to you."

"Okay, so talk; you've got me on the 'line', baby, heh, heh."

"Not this way; I want to see you, okay?"

"Okay, but I can't meet right now. I've got to be at school in fifteen minutes for a boring curriculum meeting. We could meet after."

"Sure, after the meeting at the cemetery where we used to park."

"I see," she said, "from the Palace to the pits. I'm 'dying' to see you there." Taylor hung up.

The meeting went long. So when Flo drove past the planned rendevouz spot to discover no sign of Taylor, she went on home. Surprised and irritated to find Taylor's car in her driveway, she sighed and went in. When she walked in, Taylor and Russell were seated on the sofa. Little Man was in Russell's lap, and Emerson was sleeping beside Taylor with one paw draped across his thigh. The domesticity of the cat scene provoked Flo so much that she sighed audibly and snipped, "Well, this is rich! Excuse me, I have papers to grade." She went to her bedroom and did not reappear. She left Taylor to Russell.

Two hours and fourteen minutes later, Taylor left. Neither guy spoke as she stomped past the door to the living room twice to run a glass of water. She drank neither.

The vibrant movement of arms and hands beneath her flowing poets' blouses slowed and no longer matched the eloquence of her voice—musical and melancholy, cello grown from a country fiddle. Melodramatically, she sat alone for hours in her darkened office, immersed in Violetta's despair as violins wept and plucked their abandonment. She replayed Act III again and again.

Soon, however, Taylor began to drop by the house again. Russell invariably moved to the sofa in the living room. Their conversations became more animated. They talked of declawing cats and ways to improve the decor of the living room without much expense. Taylor loved French cuisine, a subject that had never interested Russell much, but which Taylor enjoyed along with all things sensual. Flo caught only bits of dialogue as she stood barely breathing before her uplifted glass staring through water, straining to hear: "Little Man loves tuna and affection . . . can't get him out of my lap. Now, Ralph is the talker of the bunch."

"Meow?" Russell meowed.

"Meow," Emerson replied.

"You are such a smart fellow." Turning to Taylor, "We talk all the time."

Taylor chuckled at the gorgeous calico that peeped from beneath the coffee table . . . to which Russell replied, "Distant . . . timid . . . a miracle, really," explaining the miraculous rescue from the black hole in Flo's wall. Taylor whispered, "like some other miracles I know?" They chuckled more.

Flo was dizzy. Her legs went limp. She was sure she had not heard that, but then she thought they might have meant her, but she knew that she was neither distant nor quiet nor miraculous. Suddenly, she called to the living room, "I'm going to make some of my famous chicory Community dark roast coffee. Anybody care to join me in a cup?"

"Sure," said Taylor. "No thanks," said Russell. "I'll set it dripping," said Flo. She loved the fragrance of coffee. She moistened her finger, touched it to the grounds in the canister, lifted her finger to her tongue, and tasted. "Bitter . . . coarse . . . and so black," she thought.

Unwilling for the guys to think her solicitous, she returned to the papers she was grading while the coffee dripped. When she came back to the kitchen to pour coffee for her and Taylor, she selected the sapphire-colored mug, which Taylor had bought for her birthday at the Texarkana Holiday Inn as a souvenir of their love. (Not a camellia exactly, but she was no Violetta either.) Entering the living room prepared to scold whichever cat was clawing the upholstery and preparing her knowing smile to tease Taylor as she handed him the mug, she stopped so abruptly that she sloshed hot brew onto the carpet and burned her hand. But more than fingers burned. Russell was leaning toward Taylor, delivering his coffee, and as Taylor expressed his gratitude, their eyes met, their hands brushed slightly in the exchange, and they smiled.

87

"Oh! I see you've poured Taylor's coffee, Russell! Good! You're unusually gracious this evening. I guess I'll get rid of this cup." Her hand raised, still burning and dripping from the spilled coffee, Flo turned and concentrated on each step to the kitchen. The cup shattered as it hit the sink.

As she exited, Taylor called, "A little cream might be nice."

Flo stopped, stiffened, and asked, "Would you care for anything else in your little cat nip?"

Russell replied, "Are we feeling a mite 'catty' this evening, Flo?" The door to the bedroom slammed.

Although Taylor continued to visit Flo and Russell at their house, he never phoned Flo. Occasionally, he did call to leave messages such as these: "would miss Thursday's class because . . . would reschedule their conference . . . would like to drop by to discuss. . . ." Once as she turned onto Colonial Drive, she thought she saw Taylor's car pulling away.

And so on that evening, she did not want anyone to hear her. She did not want to go in, much less see what she knew was there. She did not want to do what she knew she would do.

Quietly, she reached to her back seat, lifted the paper bag from Winn Dixie. As waves of nausea swelled the pit of her belly, she firmed her resolve. She had nothing left . . . certainly no place, and nobody close who thought she was either good or beautiful. Student-love was good, but it was not enough. And she had no children. So she sat bitter in her darkened car. Carefully, she lifted each can from the sack, clamped and turned the can opener she almost forgot to buy at Winn Dixie earlier. When the first whiff of fish hit, she felt faint. But she proceded to open the cans: one, two, three . . . five cans of Blue Bay chunk light tuna. Afterwards, she tore the lid from the box of Hi-Yield gopher and mole pellets she'd picked up at Twin Oaks, and with her very own fingers, she pinched many pellets-one by one-into each can of flesh. And though the cans spilled oil onto the floor and seat of her tired car, she did not care. She sat still to the sound of Verdi's violins' strumming, pizzicato as the pellets soaked.

Like treasures, Flo placed each can to the bottom of the sack, and clutching the sack in both hands, she eased toward the front door, set the gift on the mat, and unlocked the door. Predictably, the cats came to the door's click to either slither out the door or to assess the intruder. Placing the bag just inside the door's entrance, she watched as the cats closed in and nosed eagerly. Flo pushed the front door closed without a click, stooped down, reached into her bag and meted offerings for each cat—one can for CC, one for Ralph Waldo Emerson who kept his distance at first, one for the calico Miracle, one for Killer Cornflake, and oh yes . . . the fullest one for Little Man.

So when Flo finished setting the cans, she listened. Only the hum of the bedroom fan, the licking and lapping of cat tongues, and an occasional scoot of a can on the floor. And though she'd planned to leave Russell to discover the plight of his beloved cats when he woke, she chose to wait and watch reactions—the cats and the lovers.

She closed the living room door and sat on the sofa. Miracle went first, retreating beneath her favorite chair. Mr. Emerson was silenced next, not without substantial protest by drooling, salivating, convulsions. Little Man followed. "Hell, Little Man," Flo mused, "I'd hoped you'd suffer longer, heave more, finish last." The other two followed, the Killer last.

And when they were done, Flo smiled and sat. "Still not enough," she thought as she scooped Little Man—lukewarm and limp like Russell—and toted him to the sagging drapery. She wrapped the cord round and round his skinny little neck 'til he hung stretched and open for Russell's eyes. Then, she slipped to the kitchen and withdrew a knife from the drawer. Carefully, deliberately, she carved seams around Little Man's protruding, dark testicles, and then dug them out with her knife. "Oh my," she whispered, now where shall I put these bloody little pockets?"

When the guys found Flo about 3:17 A.M. as Taylor planned to ease out the door, they found her asleep, her head leaned against the wide padded wing of the couch. And cradled in her hands, resting in the lap of her full floral skirt, Little Man's balls nestled black and bloody.

"No romantic opera here; no grand finale. Just one of life's absurd little 'cat-astrophes,'" she answered when they asked.

McLife

JERRY BRADLEY

In the crew room Manager Tom clucks us to silence before he loads the video telling us about our famous fries. Even if I last, I won't get fry duty for several more weeks. He talks like we're marines, everyone part of a unit in uniform working together to make things run right. Tom reminds us that pride is important. I try to remember that when I'm picking up loose trash around the dumpster.

The retarded guy who had this job before me never made it to fry duty. I see him every now and then busting up boxes behind Albertson's. Some old guy in a green vest shows him where to stack what. Poor bastard! He probably needs the work, but he just wasn't cut out for fast food. Fast food means fast feet. Or a fast spatula. Speed counts, except in the morning before we're open and I have to mop. In some other store that would be a gnarly chore, but the night boy Rick does a good job, so there aren't too many spots left to work on. I've heard at the Mister Burger the grease gets so bad that they sprinkle flour on the floor to keep from falling on their asses, but here it's not so bad. I just slosh the water back and forth really quick like and read the paper.

I try to catch the sports and comics before Manager Tom comes in and takes it into his office. Once we unlock, paper reading is strictly forbidden. He says it's some sort of franchise rule, but apparently it doesn't apply in his office.

On the screen some dork in a paper hat is demonstrating perfect salting. His motion, three rounded swoops, mimics the company logo. He's probably a manager by now just because he has a talent for shaking. Five grams, five grams every time. And it's shortening, not grease. "Don't let me catch you calling it grease," Tom says.

Janeen is my crew trainer for lunch rush today. I tell her I'm ready for a crack at the fryer, but she says Jeff will be handling the dropping baskets today and Dave the salting and scooping. Jeff is a college student who took the job because it's a no-brainer. It doesn't take away from his studies at the juco. I pick up the gray shaker and make a rhythmic pass like I've seen on the video, showing I can salt as well as he can. Janeen smiles, but she doesn't want me learning on her shift. "Out from behind the counter," she orders.

I take my broom and play like I'm cleaning up. Actually I'm watching Jeff. If he gets promoted to headset or night manager, I want a shot at the baskets. There are six of them, and the fryer unpredictably signals him with beeps and lights. He shakes the shortening from the first basket of fries before dumping them into the steel tray.

In the lobby the first lunch customers begin to line up. The last break-fast burritos and sausage biscuits have been removed and hauled into the back room. I'm not supposed to carry them to the dumpster until after lunch. Manager Tom doesn't want anyone going through his garbage for a free hot meal. "Let them line up out front and pay," he says. And they do. Women in stretch pants with snotty children. Old folks. Working jerks. They all come here.

"When you have a minute," Janeen says, "check the toilet. Some kid missed the mark."

Janeen's okay, but I hate cleaning bathrooms most. Even with a wringer on my bucket, my hands always get wet. Whatever I touch gets sprayed with bleach. I ruined my best jeans because of it. I quit biting my nails too because sometimes I forget to wash up. I think about it every time I filch a fry. We're not supposed to do that, but everybody does. What are they going to do? Manager Tom can't fire us all.

I get a paid twenty-minute break which I always take right after lunch. Dave usually joins me out back. He smokes a cigarette and shakes his ashes against a pipe. Jeff will start cleaning the fryer without him, as he always does. Dave thinks Jeff is a sap and wants to man the dropping baskets, but Jeff was there first. I don't tell him I've got my eye on that job too. We punch "20" on the LED timer on the oven. When our time is up, it goes off with three loud beeps, louder than the ones the fryer and freezer make. If you try to fudge an extra minute, the crew manager will yell "break's over" at you, and everyone will know you've been goofing off. When I come back in with my mop, Janeen is going over the SOC, that's the station observation checklist, with Jeff. Jeff is rubbing his wrist. It probably hurts from a long lunch of lifting heavy baskets of fries.

Most girls learn the drive-thru first or the ice cream machine. They seem better at the ball and curl. I tried it once, but the ball all glopped off to one side taking the curl with it. Guys typically start on the grill. But Janeen is in her second year, so she knows how everything is supposed to go. She could be in a regular restaurant, she's that good. I ask her what she wants me to do next. When she turns toward me, I see a hickey inside her blouse, not really on her neck but visible anyway beneath her collar. She tells me to gather up the trays. I know I'm supposed to, but it makes her feel good for me to ask. The store is quieter now, and I hear Laura announce into her mini-mike, "Pull up to the first window, please." She thinks she's cool, acts like she's on the bridge of the **Enterprise** surveying a drive-thru universe. Dave and I wish there were a Tailhook convention for girls like her. She's pretty, but they shouldn't put girls on the window.

Manager Tom comes in and cashes out the first register. The machines are almost foolproof, which is why he can afford to hire teenagers like us. You just have to punch up the right size burger and drink and be able to count out the change when it tells you to. It's a slick operation, and the only headaches come with special orders. There are no picture for special orders. "Make mine with ketchup only," they whine. Or "I don't want it to have even a hint of onion." I've seen Jeff squeeze onion juice all over the patty of a ready-made burger after he'd peeled the onions off. But Tom never caught him, and now he's running the fryer, so big deal. And I know that Laura says "fuck you very much" under her breath to the hard cases at the drive-thru. Customers are usually too embarrassed to make a stink anyway. I accidentally sloshed a guy's boots while mopping under a stall one day, and he never said a word. He probably deserved it. He was a cowboy anyway.

Manager Tom announces he'll be gone for a while, tells Janeen something about a doctor's appointment with his back. I think he goes home for a nap, but he wants us to think he might be back any minute. I don't sympathize. I've got a plantar wart which makes it difficult to stand all day, but you don't see me running to the doctor. I'm usually wiped out when my shift is over anyway, and I don't sleep well either. But I eat good. Sometimes on my way to the dumpster I'll take some of the spongy burgers left over from lunch and pitch them through the open window of my car. That's what Tom gets for making me park behind the store. And besides, it's not stealing. He can't sell them.

Before he goes, he tells us all to keep smiling. He says happy customers eat more. But when a day sucks big time, like when I have to clean up puke in the parking lot, I don't even try. Or like the time the guy in the warm-up suit grabbed the fat kid Brian who used to work here, and the police had to come. Brian was scared shitless. He thought the guy was going to hit him just because he shorted him a fish sandwich. Afterward they put him on cups and lids for a few days. Then he never came back.

As Manager Tom heads out, he reminds, "If you've got time to gripe, you've got time to wipe," and cuts a look in my direction. I ask Janeen if she wants me to check the ice bins. She sees my suck-up exactly for what it is, but she waits for Tom to get outside before telling me to sweep the lobby again. I dig with my broom beneath the tables, and all kinds of body odor and meaty smells well up from the booths. Sometimes when they're occupied, I offer to sweep under people's feet. A lot of them like that. It makes them feel superior. I don't mind. I'm only getting crumbs and trash off the floor.

As I work my way around the dining room toward the counter, I see Dave jawing with Janeen. Apparently he'd dropped a fry during lunch. Instead of picking it up, he kicked it under the fryer, and she was giving him what for. But if he went by the book, he'd have to go to the back and wash his hands before doing anymore bagging and salting. I see customers drop their fries on the floor all the time, and they pick them up and eat them without washing their hands. And most of the crew hide food and soda pop at various places in the kitchen. But customers can do what they want. Face it, everything goes into your stomach or the trash.

I saw Dave's face redden, then he said something about Janeen's hickey, or maybe about the fellow who gave it to her. He took off his paper fry cap and threw it into fryer #3. Then with us all looking on, he pulled his brown-

and-gold tunic over his head and waved it about before exiting through the kitchen. On his way out he tossed it in the crew commode and flushed. Luckily it just stuck there, and the toilet didn't overflow.

I hate to see Dave go, but I figure I'm one step closer to the deep fryer. I want to say something, but I don't. I just start sweeping faster. Sometimes I sweep or mop left handed just to break the routine, but today I don't. I want Janeen to think I care about my job. I start sweeping my way to the playground where they let the homeless guy sit. Sometimes he orders coffee and asks for the senior citizen discount. He makes me glad I'm not on closing shift. I wouldn't like having to run him off. Besides, they have to check for robbers in the parking lot before they can go home.

On payday my twenty-six point five hours will net me just over a hundred. I spend a lot of it on food, but I don't spend it here. I like pizza, and I don't care if Manager Tom sees me eating it either. Sometimes I fantasize about being the secret shopper and strolling up to every counter in Fort Worth and ordering all I want for free. I could order a cone if I wanted and bitch about the curl, then drop it on the floor for some other schmuck to clean up. But more than likely I wouldn't. I've got too much respect for us working guys.

Payday is always followed by inventory day. That's when I have to help count the cups and ketchup. Manager Tom doesn't want some old biddy complaining because we're out of straws or fun packs. Last time I got a 100 on my SOC in stocking and window cleaning, but if I'm too good I may never get a crack at the fryer. I practice sweeping ones and zeros trying to look busy.

At the counter three giggling girls are taking forever to order, but typically they're not as bad as the pot smokers. On day shift you don't see too many of them, but the ones that do come in are really wasted. You could knock them over with a fried pie, and they'd be glad you hit them. Sometimes they spill their stuff before they get to their car. It's so cool when shit like that happens. If I were cooped up in an office, I'd never get to see that kind of thing.

But people in offices get to give looks to the rest of us. They always look like whatever we're doing is wrong. And they can make us do it again and again. The orientation videos never give pointers either on how to kiss butt with the boss. We're just taught to say thank you and show up on time.

That's about it—that and the salting. Salt sells drinks, and that's where the money is. So when Manager Tom comes back looking sleepy from his visit to the doctor and before Janeen can tell him about Dave and the toilet, I smile at him in a humble-pie way. Two hours from now when I do my final mop, I'll be wondering who'll be at the fryer with Jeff tomorrow. I know who it ought it to be but won't. And when I go home, I'll stuff a fun pack under my shirt and think about how much worse things could be. Then I'll thank my stars I'm not busting boxes.

One Woman's Trail of Tears

Ernestine Sewell Linck

(This story is based loosely on the life of Rebecca McIntosh Hawkins Haggerty, born 1815, died 1886 or '87. She was an extraordinarily successful plantation matriarch, but, in pursuit of success, she became known as the most hated woman in East Texas.)

The doctor paused as he reached for the cheap white china knob of the boarding house bedroom door, upstairs back. He knew what scene awaited him. As the weeks passed since his first call, the emaciated man lying on stained sheets had grown weaker, his cough more persistent, the sputum bloodier. It was consumption. The man could not last much longer.

It was not the odor of sickness and death that made him hesitate. No, it was the old crone, the man's mother, sitting cross-legged in a far corner rocking back and forth.

Every morning by dawn she came down the dusty road from Old Refuge, her plantation, an ancient mule drawing an equally ancient wagon. Every evening at twilight, she left the sick man's room to make her way back those long fourteen miles. She never looked up; she never spoke.

He entered the room.

The man's eyes fastened on him, moved to the figure of the old woman. He struggled to turn his body to avoid the sight of her. The effort caused a spasm of coughing that racked his whole body. The doctor hurried to his side. The old woman continued to rock back and forth, lips moving soundlessly.

The doctor was there the first day she came in: a small, shapeless, bent figure, gray stringy hair falling down her back, wrinkled, sun-baked face, her dress faded, her shoes heavy workingman's. In no way did she resemble the woman he had once known. Rebecca McIntosh Hawkins Haggerty. She had been a beauty. Raven black hair, dark, penetrating eyes, a bearing straight and proud. Dresses of fine silks, hats furbished with ostrich plumes, high-buttoned shoes polished to a high sheen. He knew, as everyone did, that Rebecca was Indian but her ways were white women's ways. She and Peter Hawkins had built a plantation on the labor and league of land Sam Houston had granted them—almost 4000 acres.

The house, just a short walk from Cypress Creek, was big and square, high above ground, dog trot down the center for trapping what cool breezes might be carried their way in the hot, humid country so near Red River. A large veranda wrapped three sides of the structure. The kitchen was out back lest there be fire.

How many times she had called him to the house—and paid him well—to tend the Muscogee children she had brought from Oklahoma to rear. He had always admired her furnishings, shipped upriver from New Orleans, especially the great, square, heavily carved piano.

After the murder of Peter Hawkins, she had managed the plantation as well as any man could have, leaving only to go into Jefferson or New Orleans to deal with the cotton brokers and her bankers. As her wealth increased, so did the respect paid her. It was well known that she owned more slaves than anyone in East Texas. At one count, 264. The doctor shook his head at the vagaries of fate. He pitied her, yet he was, like her dying son, repulsed by her crazy Indian ways.

As twilight drew near one evening shortly after his visit, sheet lightning flashed across the western sky followed by distant thunder. A heavy fog moved up from the bayou, a ghostly protoplasm creeping sinuously through the streets and alleyways. Suddenly there came a keening from the boarding house, so high, so penetrating, so unearthly as to make the black folks seek cover from the "haints" their gran'daddies had warned them of. White folks shuddered and wondered. The doctor strode to the window of his office to look toward the boarding house. Not that he could see anything, the shutters closed. Consumptives had to be protected from the noxious vapors of the night. But he knew. The cry faded into a moan and rose again to shrill keening, the sound carried along with the fog as it enveloped the town. It was the woman's death cry.

She appeared next day at the undertaker's. He hoisted the pine box in which he had laid out the body into her wagon, and she turned the old mule toward her place. A few curious folks stood on the street corners to watch until she was out of sight. Spire Haggerty had been a drunk, a gambler, a disreputable man. Good riddance!

Months later, the doctor, on one of his calls, had stopped by to see the pillaged, deteriorating plantation home. His eyes were drawn to the family cemetery where Peter Hawkins was buried, a marble monument marking the place. Nearby a curious small house made of slats, much like a large square chicken coop, covered the grave of Spire. Must be the Muscogee way, he thought. The body and the house would return to earth together.

A few days later Rebecca appeared again in Jefferson. She was walking—westward. With a few necessaries and some possibles tied in a deer-skin strapped to her back, she had embarked upon her own Trail of Tears. Her mind moved back in time to Alabama along Okmulgee Creek. She recalled running like some wild thing with her childhood friends in the lushness of the forests, of tumbling about in the tall grass where often they could see deer, and of playing along the creeks, sometimes gurgling, sometimes rushing waters for which the White Chiefs had named her people.

Evenings, as the moon and stars smiled down upon them, she loved to sit quietly and listen to the grandfathers tell tales of how the Sun, making its ride across the sky, let fall one drop of blood from which the Muscogee people sprang. And of how these brave First People proved themselves worthy. The Maker of Breath, the Good Spirit of the Upper World, looked down on them benignly. He made the water pure, the hunt successful, and the corn abundant in This World so long as the People preserved the lessons of those stories in sacred rituals.

Rebecca, moving along at a steady pace, reached for the star she had hung around her neck before leaving. A copper star with four points, one point for each direction and for the seasons of the year. Her father had made the bright, shiny star for her, trusting she, his favorite daughter, would guide The People in the ways he had instructed her, the White Man's ways. As she clutched the star, forcing the sharp points to pierce the flesh of her fingers, she felt a hollowness, something missing, a legacy of failure.

Restitution: the Muscogee commandment for living a good, rewarding life. A bad act had to be paid for. A good act—or punishment—could wipe out the bad act. Naughty children were scratched on the leg with a sharp thorn that left an ugly scar. Her thoughts raced ahead to the peach tree limb she used to punish the children in her household. She would not act like an Indian and use a thorn. No, but she had slashed many with her limb. Tight-lipped, she had swung the limb mercilessly if the children—in all there had been sixteen—disobeyed her. And if her limb fell on an innocent child, she shrugged, saying it didn't matter; let the punishment be a lesson to all.

Rebecca thought of her own gentle father and mother. White men frequently came to their house, for her father was leader of a party that wanted to sell the Muscogee land and move west, across the Great Water, where, the white men promised, they would live in peace and plenty. There was dissension that, Rebecca learned later, culminated in the Redstick Rebellion.

It was futile to try to erase the horrendous scenes of the Rebellion. Her life was changed forever. She had gone to visit her grandparents who lived some small distance down the creek. As evening drew near, the old couple and the child strolled toward her house. When they neared the clearing that marked McIntosh land, they saw flames shooting skyward, enveloping the house. Near naked bodies painted with red and black stripes, some of the men still stomping the ground as if continuing the frenzy of the war dance, others running round and round the house brandishing their clubs and shooting off their guns, the night filled with their hideous war cries: it was a frightful scene. Worse, she thought she recognized some of the men; they were fathers and brothers of her friends.

She tried to run forward, but her grandfather caught her and hastily pulled her and her grandmother back into a dense copse of oak where the scrub hid them. He was not fast enough, though, to prevent the child from seeing her mother and father run from the house to escape the flames only to meet the gunfire of their enemies. Death was not enough for the Redsticks. They filled the bodies with lead; they mutilated the bodies with their knives. Her grandfather covered her mouth with his hand to prevent her screams.

When the fury of the Redsticks had abated, they slipped carefully back to their own dwelling where the child finally cried herself to sleep—she was only five years old. Then they began preparations to leave for Oklahoma. They called the old man's African boy and gave him orders to hitch the finest pair of mares to the carriage and make ready the sturdiest wagon for supplies. The old man took a bag of gold coins, secreted it in the wagon floor, loaded his guns, giving one to the boy, in case there were outlaws on the trail, and by dawn they were ready to leave. The old couple feared that the anger of the Redsticks would spill over to include them, for they had supported Rebecca's father's party.

It had been a Trail of Tears of sorts. There were lots of tears shed by Rebecca. Her grandfather was stoic about the move, trusting that the Maker of Breath was directing them to move on to promising new lands. To avoid trouble, he and the boy sought out the old Cherokee trace across Texas that led to a bend in Red River where they would cross into Oklahoma.

Now Rebecca determined that she, too, would leave the well-traveled road to find the Cherokee Trace. Sam Houston and Peter had often talked about taking the trail on their trading trips to the Cherokees. She crossed fields, shying away from farm houses, and by evening she was trudging along, following the deep ruts of the earlier trail. But she did not wish to cross the river at the bend; rather she would follow the river to find the crossing where the Kiamichi poured its waters into the big river, That was the crossing where she and Peter had camped, on their way to Jefferson so many years ago.

Memories of her childhood in Oklahoma crowded into her consciousness. She suffered a lingering illness, despite the herbal concoctions her grandmother gave her. There were nightmares that resolved, as she improved, into bitterness toward the Muscogee. Those same Redsticks who had murdered her parents had arrived shortly after their rebellion, their lands taken by the whites with fewer concessions than her father had bargained for. Ha, they had gained nothing.

As she bloomed into maidenhood, she attracted the young braves, but she scorned them. Let them play their flutes 'til their lips swelled. She would not listen to their love songs. Peter Hawkins was the one she had eyes for. He seemed as determined as she to turn from the Muscogee and follow the white man's way. His father had been a friend to her father. Besides, he and his good friend, Sam Houston, had a lucrative trading business with the Cherokees. Peter was a worthy man. She knew her grandfather would approve of him.

One day Rebecca went to a secluded place along a creek. She disrobed, stepped into the sparkling water, gingerly, and swam about, feeling the waves of cool water wash over her body, feeling the resistance of the energy of her body as it met the rushing waters. She turned over and over, rolling about sensuously in the water. At last she stood up, moved her arms along her sides and down her thighs to wipe away the drops of water clinging to her flesh. She shook her long hair, and looked down at her body, at the shapely breasts, her narrow waist, hips broadening slightly. She knew she was beautiful. Her reflection in the water told her so.

A slight movement drew her eyes to the bluff above the creek. There sat Peter Hawkins. Rebecca stood up straight and proud, continuing to feel her body as she brushed away the glistening drops of water. She moved up on the bank, a green sward of lush grass. A redbird twittered at her from a branch of a giant cottonwood tree nearby, a sign of good fortune. As if she had willed his actions, Peter rose slowly and came toward her. She stretched out her arms to meet him. Peter took her in his own strong arms and enfolded her to his breast. She raised her lips eagerly to his, and the kiss was long and sweet. He pushed her away; with his own hands, he felt her body and wiped away what drops of water lingered. Then, without a word between them, he turned, made his way up the bluff and disappeared. Rebecca hurriedly dressed herself, content that he would soon be talking with her grandfather. She had not known such happiness since before that horrendous night in Alabama.

It was several days before Peter returned to speak with her grandfather about marriage. He brought with him a fine pair of horses for the old carriage, a pile of deerskins and bright cloth for Grandmother, and for her, beads. No house was prepared for the happy pair. No fine shirts or beaded moccasins or fine blankets were made for them. Peter simply led her from the house, after making their farewells, helped her into his carriage, and together they started to Texas. When they stopped to camp along the trail, Rebecca gave herself to Peter with inexhaustible passion. She trusted him to make all her dreams come true. But their love was more than a commitment to the white man's way. Their bodies seemed to melt into each other and they clung to one another, spent, the consummations a sacred acknowledgment of the power within themselves to create their own perfect world.

When they reached the land Sam Houston had granted them along Cypress Creek, they walked hand in hand, hardly daring to believe this land was theirs to make into their own place. They chose a location for the house and dreamed of fields of cotton. Within a few years, Peter and Rebecca had a thriving plantation. Houston came to visit often. He liked what he saw. Africans singing contentedly as they worked. Cotton hip-high. The house magnificent. And what a spread of food she commanded from her kitchen. All the things Sam liked. Chicken, pork, sweet potatoes, rice pudding, his favorite, cornbread and coffee. Often Peter left with Sam, on a trading expedition to the Cherokees, to be gone sometimes several weeks at a time. During his absences, Rebecca managed the plantation, riding out daily in her carriage to the fields, to watch the slaves at work and confer with the overseer about the crops. She learned how to keep accounts and deal with the cotton buyers in Jefferson. Peter bragged about her competence. He liked to call her the Bright Star of Old Refuge, and she would playfully frown and remind him with a pout on her face that her name was Rebecca, that Bright Star may be her Muscogee birth name, but if he wanted her favors, he would do well to forget it!

Shots and a cry in the night changed Rebecca's world. She was aware that the white settlers along the Red were angry with Sam Houston for granting lands to Indians. It was no secret. But Sam had been so confident of his plans that she did not know how dangerous the situation had become. Several days after Sam's last visit, Hawkins took her into his arms, explaining, "Today I will go into Jefferson for supplies." He pulled out a long list he and the overseer had compiled the evening before. "And what can I bring from town to please my beautiful wife?" He brushed the tips of her fingers, which he held in his hands, with his lips.

Rebecca smiled, wondering what he might bring this time that she did not have. What more could she possibly want?

"Bring yourself back to me; you are all I want—or need," she said, moving closer within his embrace and lifting her face to him for a kiss that told of their mutual love. "Only yourself," she repeated. "I'll be waiting."

Her world had been complete. But no longer. Ambushed, Peter Hawkins had been shot as he turned the buggy into the lane leading to her, once in the back of his head; a second shot found his heart. And her heart.

Peter was found lying at the side of the road where he had been thrown when the horses bolted. They stood off the road under the pines, frightened by the smell of blood. When Rebecca arrived at the scene, the hatred she had harbored for her own people since she was a child of five rose in her throat, black bile nauseating her. She clenched her teeth, swallowed, and in that moment, the hatred targeted the white people who wanted to drive "injuns" out.

The murderer or murderers were not robbers. The supplies were untouched. On the floor of the buggy she found Peter's last gift to her—a silver looking glass.

Rebecca mourned for Peter—and she brooded. She was convinced the bankers and brokers had plotted to get the Hawkins land. They believed she would leave for Oklahoma if Peter were dead. How wrong they were! She resolved to stay, work the plantation, and find some way to avenge the death of her beloved.

Though she had borne no sons or daughters to Hawkins, she would create her own dynasty. Relatives in Oklahoma had children. She would bring them to Jefferson, educate them like white people, teach them the lesson she had learned: "White people will betray you. You must not trust them. Take the white man's road. I will help you become rich and powerful. Then you will fulfill your obligation to me. Outwit the white man, deprive him of his power, bring him to his knees, destroy him!" She liked what she saw in the mirror those days: a strong, determined woman, with taut, severe lines where smiles used to appear.

Her plan had failed. Most of the children left Refuge Plantation to return to Oklahoma where they drank the white man's whiskey, misfits all. Some few had remained in Texas, far from her. Two of the girls, she heard, had gone to New Orleans, where they were known on the streets along the docks.

Peter had taken on Spire Haggerty as overseer shortly before his death. No one knew where Haggerty came from.

He was a man with the go-yonders, but when he reached the Hawkins place, he appeared to have come to the end of his road. His treatment of the slaves was not what they had experienced while Peter lived. There was a cruel streak in him that he made no attempt to conceal when he was in control. For the slightest infraction, real or imagined, he would have the Negro stripped, male or female, and whipped, forcing the rest of the slaves to watch the writhing, crying punished one. Rebecca would stand in the shadows of the porch and watch too, enjoying the mastery of the man. Why should she not bring him into her house?

There had been no courtship. This was no love marriage that she arranged and to which he acquiesced. After all, he would be master of the plantation. What more could he want? But Rebecca had given much thought to this arrangement. As Rebecca Haggerty, the brokers and bankers who, she was sure, had been responsible for her husband's death, would hesitate to take further steps to drive her from Refuge Plantation. And, more, he might father a son for her, a son she could trust to carry on her plan for revenge.

In time there was a son, named Spire, her one concession to the father. He received the same treatment from Rebecca as did the other children in the house. She wielded her switch with the same determination as Haggerty did his whip.

Though Haggerty insisted it was his right as master of the plantation to care for financial ends, Rebecca dismissed his arguments with scorn. The plantation continued to thrive; her wealth seemed boundless for a time under their uneasy agreement. Over the years, however, Haggerty began to drink—heavily. He became even harsher with the slaves. The outbuildings began to show decay. Whole sections of good cotton land lay fallow. Some of the slaves had sickened; others ran away.

There came a day when the boy stood in the doorway of his father's bedroom and watched as Rebecca slashed his father's bare buttocks with a heavy limb of the peach tree. Rebecca was drawing blood. The boy cried aloud and she turned one quick moment. The fury he saw in her eyes drove him away from the scene. He hid in the barn with the horses. A short time later he saw his father, carrying his clothes and struggling to get himself into them to be decent, jump on an unsaddled horse and beat the horse with his quirt savagely as he galloped off, never to return. Without a goodbye to the boy. Not that he had paid much attention to him before. A few days later—he was almost ten now—he bundled up his clothes and walked into Jefferson There he found himself a job in a saloon. Not many years passed before he acquired his father's whiskey habit.

She had never seen him again until he took sick. When he needed money, he sent messengers. Fearful to approach too closely, they would call, "Ol' Injun woman, Spire wants gold." She never failed him—until after The War. The gold ran out and the Confederate paper was worthless. But the messengers kept coming. Piece by piece, Spire took from her the white men's things Peter had been so proud to give her.

Rebecca no longer cared. Perhaps someday Spire would come home or send for her. He never did. She happened to find out from a passerby that he was dying and she had imposed herself on his space, knowing he hated her.

Why had she failed so miserably? She knew the answer. She had not kept the Good Spirits of the Upper World in harmony with the Bad Spirits of the Under World. Harmony in This World necessitated respect for human life and nonhuman life alike. And what had she done? She and Peter had cleared the 4000 acres of pine and oak and all vegetation without regard for the spirits that lived in all things. How long had it been since she had listened to the talking of the trees and the waters? As they built their own Refuge, they had deprived the birds, the deer, foxes, some bear, and the little animals of their native refuge. They had killed the deer without proper rituals, never asking forgiveness of the animal spirit for supplying meat for their table. And they had enslaved Africans to cultivate the land for gain. The Muscogee way was to use the land only for what they needed to survive.

Rebecca's anguish over her misspent life contributed to her exhaustion, though the Trace was not difficult to follow. She found herself stopping more often to rest, to chew a bit of jerky and parched corn from her pack, or snare a rabbit, pick some of the young leaves of poke to boil, dig some onions, or chop out a root of sassafras for tea. Whatever would lend her strength. After one such stop, she looked about for buzzard feathers. That was easy. Some buzzards were even now circling the place she had last killed a rabbit. She picked up some feathers, trusting they would bring her closer to the Powers of the Sacred Realm. Reaching into her pack for a strip of deer hide to tie the feathers to the stick she used for a cane, she felt the mirror, the only item she had kept of that former life. She looked into it. What magic was working here? How could it be? There were two faces reflected. Bright Star, the beautiful Muscogee maiden. She was given the name by an old uncle, who took the baby from her mother's arms, lifted it skyward and asked for the blessings of the Maker of Breath. Rebecca watched as Bright Star's face slowly changed, love and tenderness lost in ugly lines criss-crossing her face, features sharp and angular, eyes color-less and passionless. Wisps of gray hair played around the face, not soften-ing its features. Dismayed, she flung the thing away, but the sun's rays caused a blinding flash, a flame that burned into her soul the image of what she had become.

The sun had risen maybe fourteen times before she reached the Kiamichi crossing. As soon as she stepped on Choctaw ground, a flicker of movement caught her eye. Ah! The vicious Choctaw Little People were watching. Peter had told her she must be wary of them. Her first night was a misery. The Little People threw pebbles at her, disturbing the rest she so sorely needed. One morning a sizable boulder blocked her path. She thought she could move it, but, strangely, all her efforts failed. She attempted to go round it but found herself in dense undergrowth and lost her way. She wandered about, limbs from low-branching trees slashing her face; thorny brush scratching her arms. Exhausted, she found a spot to sleep. But she was restless. She dreamed of trying to move the rock. Suddenly she woke, startled, her hand reaching for her heart. The meaning became clear. The bitterness she harbored, first for her own people and later for the white men had hardened her heart. It was like granite. Unmovable.

A single tear rolled down her cheek. "Humph!" she thought, "I am really on a Trail of Tears." Scornful of her weakness, she took up the jour-ney again. But she was weaker, her food supply almost gone. She would have to feed on elderberries, wild grapes, and sumac berries for tea. Would she have the strength to reach the Canadian River, the dividing line be-tween the Choctaw and Muscogee nations?

The heavy workman's shoes had worn through. She stopped, emptied the deerskin pack, keeping only a little copper pot. She cut the skin into pieces, used the thongs to tie them on her feet, and stood up. How good they felt! She wanted to dance, as Bright Star once had, toe, heel; toe, heel. Yes, she could still feel the drumbeat of the earth's heart. The beginning of a smile appeared on the stern old face.

She was stopping more often to rest now. Once, finding a spring, she started a fire for making tea, chewed on some coarse wild spinach, sucked the nectar of nearby honeysuckle, and snared a rabbit. As she took the struggling animal to kill, she heard herself repeat:

"Forgive me for taking your life that I may live. I must have meat." Again she felt the smile on her face. It was good to recall Muscogee ways, to be Bright Star again.

She lay back on a soft bed of leaves. Above, an eagle soared. Her smile disappeared. Was this the primordial eagle of the elders' stories that threatened the First Men? Would it swoop down to take her in its talons and kill her? Nothing prepared her for the terror she felt. The eagle dropped lower and lower, then suddenly soared off into the blue. Bright Star closed her eyes and thanked the Maker of Breath.

Next day she came upon a large forbidding water moccasin stretched across her way. Had the Little People put him there to kill her with his poison fangs? She recalled terrifying stories of Tie-Snake from the Lower World. Had Tie-Snake changed his colors and come to steal her soul? In a quavering voice, she addressed the snake: "Mr. Moccasin, if you are indeed Tie-Snake, I beseech you to recall I lost my soul once when I left my people for the white man's road. Let me return to my people that they may learn I was wrong." The snake slithered into the brush.

Shortly after her encounter with Tie-Snake, she sat before her fire, eating a piece of rabbit from her last kill. An eerie cry, almost human, broke the silence. Again she was stricken with mortal fear. She saw eyes shining as a panther drew near. It held her gaze for what seemed an eternity, then turned, and was lost in the wilds. Bright Star, her heart still pounding, wondered: had she passed the tests just as the First Muscogee had? First, encountering strange people, then an eagle, a snake, and a deadly cat? She lifted her arms to the Maker of Breath and prayed that the law of restitution had been satisfied, that she had proved herself worthy.

She was sure she was near the Canadian and her own people. It must be time for the "busk," the harvest ritual of gratitude for corn. She must be ready. She must fast. That was easy. She had had so little food lately. Then she must find the yaupon tree to make a drink of the berries. A dark, black bitter drink. The Muscogee called it "white drink," because it was purifying. Bright Star's spirits rose in anticipation.

The Canadian was not high at this time of year. She did not have to go far to find a fording place. But she was feeling weak. She must not hurry.

Yet her heart cried, "Go, go." Bright Star stepped into the water. She was about to step out onto Muscogee land when her foot slipped on a slick rock. She tumbled backward, striking her head on a rock under water. Bright Star lay there unconscious. The water moved slowly over the inert body. When she woke, she was looking upward into the early evening sky. One bright star hung low in the sky. Was the Maker of Breath calling her spirit? The waters gently moved against her body, turning her so that she caught a reflection of herself, as in a mirror. Her face no longer told of anger and hate.

She was aware of a slight movement on the Muscogee shoreline. It was the Muscogee Little People. Oh, they were mischievous but they were helpful too. She knew they would lead her people to find her. Perhaps the Old Ones would tell her story. The waters gently pushed the body over. Bright Star lay face down. The rippling waters, fretting and curling around her, made lulling, murmuring sounds.

Bright Star slept.

THE PROMISE

MARK BUSBY

As he looked through the colored glass down on the world outside the hospital, all looked like a fantasy. Pressing his nose to the window, Tommy Swindell could hear calliopes whirling round and round with clowns hanging from bobbing horses on a merry-go-round. This quiet room's cut-glass, colored window and short bench, just his size, excited his imagination.

He didn't like the hospital, but someone his mother knew was sick, so for the third time in two weeks he dutifully followed her. He discovered the chapel the second day, breaking the waiting room monotony where adults constantly watched something about politics. Ike or anybody else, he didn't care. His father was going to vote for Stevenson, even though he made fun of Stevenson's bald head, calling him an "egg head." All three channels carried the Republican convention, so it didn't matter that visiting hours came when Western Movie Theater was usually on. He thought for a moment about the still picture that introduced Western Movie Theater—a man on horseback looking at a bullet fired toward him from the distance. Every day the show began with the same image, and every day Tommy wondered about the lone man on horseback. Who was he? What happened to him? And so Tommy would begin a story in his head about the cowboy. Not today though.

At first he thought the chapel his special place. Down the hall across from the waiting room, he first noticed the sun streaming through the window and stepped inside. Sitting on the little bench, he could look out the window through several colors. Red, his favorite, made the Dairy Queen across the street vibrant and alive, even without any cars parked out front. Green produced islands like the picture on his mother's lp cover of *South Pacific*. Blue was cool and icy, slowing the Studebaker on Clay Street, but yellow speeded it up and made everything anxious. The driver's face through yellow stared back at him with eyes of dread.

At first he thought the little bench built for him, but he learned it was for people to kneel. Catholics kneeled, his mother said, and prayed. To the Pope, he thought, and kneeled, imagining the Pope. The Pope wore a special hat, he thought, but the only picture in his mind was a dark man wearing a war bonnet with magnificent eagle feathers and strings of teeth.

His family was Church of Christ, or at least his mother was. His father never went to church with his mother.

"Jim, wouldn't you like to go with us today? The boys would be delighted to see you there, and I'm sure you could keep them from misbehaving in church better than I can."

He would tell her forcefully that he was not interested in going to church and would turn to Tommy and Larry, telling them to straighten up and behave at church or he would take his belt to them. But Tommy knew how his father felt; church bored him too. His friends' churches seemed more interesting than his mother's. Most friends were Tabernacle Baptists with a piano and a big BYA, or Baptist Youth Association. They went bowling and to rodeos in a blue and white bus, his father sneering "Grab-a-nickel" Baptists whenever he saw their bus. Most of the kids his mother called "better off" went to the Tabernacle. Their fathers were younger than his, and they wore suits to work.

His mother's church, the Church of Christ, never associated with other churches. His friends would invite him to come to church, but his mother would say, "Tommy, you can ask them to church with you, but we do not attend those denominational churches. They do not preach the truth." Methodists and Presbyterians and Baptists could go visit one another, but not Church of Christ. He felt isolated but never invited friends to his church. Nothing ever happened there. They didn't even have a choir. No organ, no piano, certainly no electric guitar like the Assembly of God across the street, "Holy Rollers," his mother said disdainfully. "They do not have the truth," she would say.

Sometimes on Sunday night, waiting for his mother to finish in the nursery where she worked, he would stand by the blue neon "Avenue Church of Christ" sign and crunch crickets, imagining he was fighting giant black-winged demons like the flying creatures in *The Wizard of Oz*. Crickets in fall lined the sidewalk, and he would skip along them feeling and hearing their breaking bodies.

After that, he would listen to the guitar sounds waft across the Avenue from the Assembly of God. The wailing guitars would beckon, and he would imagine people rolling on the floor. It was much more interesting than his church. Inside his church, he would sit in the back and carve his initials in the pew, passing hours with his pocket knife. With each stroke he would think of knife fights, charging into a hoard of A-rab, Japanese, or Nazi enemies.

Although the hospital chapel gave him a place to escape, he found his mind wandering to thoughts of church as he looked at the open Bible lying on a small table in front of the kneeling bench. Just now, though, he heard sounds in the hall, as nurses wheeled someone along. His mother and her friend Mandy were walking beside the gurney, and he tried to shrink into the chapel. As they approached the door, he heard the man being pushed ask to stop at the chapel door, where Tommy sat on his bench. The man rolled over and looked in at the cross on the wall, when he noticed Tommy.

"Hello, son. What's your name?"

The nurse stepped up, "Now, Mr. Wallace, it's time for you in the operating room. Doctor's waiting."

"Just give me a minute with the little man. C'mon over here son."

Tommy walked over, looked up, and noticed he was looking right up the man's hairy nostrils. He thought briefly of escaping into a dark cave filled with spiders, but the man's voice brought him back.

"Son, what's your name?"

"Tommy Swindell. I'm nine years old."

"That's fine, Tommy. What I want to know is what do you want to be when you grow up?"

Often asked this question, Tommy had a pat answer.

"Doctor, lawyer, and Indian chief," he said quickly. Then he looked toward his mother and added: "And preacher."

The man on the cart responded with a muted snort, a laugh cut short. "Well you can't be all of those son. But that doesn't really matter now. I just want to ask you something. Let me have your hand."

Tommy reached out and the man huge hand covered his. He noticed the thick, dark and wiry hair on the man's fingers. It looks like a gorilla's hand, he thought, and had a fleeting image of a gorilla grabbing a vine to swing from tree to tree. He saw himself as Tarzan's companion, Boy, swinging limb to limb with Cheetah, but the man again intruded into his imagination.

"Tommy, there's just one thing I want you to do for me, will you?"

"Yes sir, I sure will."

"Well, this is it, my boy. If I don't make it through this, I want you to promise you'll have a good life for me. Will you promise me that?"

Tommy looked at him blankly. Mr. Wallace pulled him closer by pulling on his hand.

"If you don't make it through?"

"Yes, son, you know, I'm going under the knife, and it's dangerous. So, if I die, will you promise me to have a good life?"

"I guess so," Tommy answered, trying to imagine the man going under the knife. He saw a large scimitar, the kind Sinbad the Sailor carries, hanging down over Mr. Wallace's stomach.

"Thanks, son. That's all I needed. Let's go, nurse."

Tommy watched as the man was wheeled down the hall. His mother stood beside him, putting her hand on his head and tousling his hair.

"We need to say a little prayer for Mr. Wallace, Tommy. He's about to have a serious operation, so we should ask God to watch over him. Let's step inside the chapel."

As he stepped back inside the chapel, it felt different, not a magical, special space for him to play, a place for imaginary games. Now it felt like church—oppressive and threatening. He knelt down on the little bench, but his mother chastised him.

"No, no, Tommy. You know better than that. We don't do that. Only the Catholics, Holy Rollers, and Pharisees make a spectacle of themselves. We believe that we speak to God quietly. Now stand up and bow your head like a man."

She bent over and spoke reverentially, "Dear God, we come in this moment of humility to ask you to look down on our friend Mr. John Wallace in his hour of need."

Tommy listened, thinking about God. God was wearing a dark gray suit, sitting at a big desk with a small tv screen with his mother's face in close up in front of Him. God's tv was in color! God was bald, and He looked like both Eisenhower and Stevenson, Tommy thought. There seemed to be hundreds of tv sets in front of God, but the only voice He could hear was Tommy's mother's.

"We know that you are all-powerful and that if you decide to take Mr. Wallace into the bosom of heaven that you do for reasons that we cannot comprehend. But, dear God, Mr. Wallace is a good man, a young man, and if in your wisdom you can see your way to spare him, we supplicate you to consider it. In Jesus Christ's dear and holy name, we pray. Amen."

"Amen." Suddenly, Tommy saw his face in color on God's tv set saying "Amen." He looked up and winked.

"Do you have something in your eye, Tommy?"

"No, m'am."

"Now, Tommy, I'm going back into the waiting room. Do you want to come watch the tv there?"

"No, m'am. There's nothing but that political junk on. I'll stay out here and play. Mommy, when are we going home?"

"Well, Tommy, the operation will take about two hours, and I promised Mandy to be with her. Stay here and play. I'll be with Mandy in the waiting room. Play quietly and don't make any noise."

He looked carefully at the little room, at the wall plaque: "In loving memory of Mrs. Vivian Smoltz, this room is generously furnished by the ladies of the Tabernacle Baptist Church." He tried to think of what Mrs. Smoltz might look like, but all he could see was a huge stomach with a knife hanging over it, and he didn't want to think of it. On the other wall was another plaque: "The Lord is my shepherd. Psalms 23." He imagined little lambs playing in the field and remembered one of his mother's books with a fluffy white lamb with black feet on the page across from "Mary Had a Little Lamb." Suddenly, in his imagination a gigantic sword from above plunged into the side of the lamb, and bright blood pulsed.

He shrieked and then realized he was making noise when his mother stepped into the room, although he was sure only a few minutes had passed. He thought she was going to be mad at him for making noise. But she just sat quietly on the bench.

113

"I'm sorry I was making noise, Mommy."

She sat quietly with her head down and eyes closed and didn't answer.

"Can we go soon?"

She sighed, "Yes, Tommy. I'll take you home and then meet the ladies of the church at Mandy's."

He sat quietly beside her trying to create a story in his mind so he wouldn't have to think about Mr. Wallace. But his mind was blank, and he could imagine nothing, nothing at all.

PATTERNS OF ILLUSION

JAMES HOGGARD

"There's just something about her," Aran said, "that bothers me."

"Why?" Mary asked. "She's attractive enough. Is that it?"

"No, it's something else," he told her. "The look about her: big doe eyes but they somehow seem vacant—or mean even. I can't figure it out."

"You don't even know her," Mary said. "At least I don't think you do," she added, looking at him askance. Quickly, though, she turned her attention away. She asked the two children, her stepchildren, if they'd like another lemonade or Seven-Up.

Aran watched them shake their heads that they were doing all right. They had just gotten into San Miguel an hour before, put their bags in the apartment the Instituto had assigned them, and come immediately across campus to the hotel for lunch.

Suddenly Aran's daughter Gaddi was laughing. She was nodding toward a little boy running naked around the pool outside. Periodically he'd stop and stomp the shadows of giants' hands that the banana leaves cast on the cement. Aran glanced back at his own children. Although he and Mary would be here for close to two months, the children would leave after two weeks to go back home to their mother. Squeezing Mary's knee, he once more heard his son Damon announce to the table what he had said three times already: that though he was just ten he was going to get to take Spanish in a college.

"You'll probably flunk, too," Gaddi said. "Go ahead, Daddy. Ask me some words," she said to draw attention away from her brother. "I'm taking sculpture," she told everyone. "I'm going to make monuments to make the highways pretty."

"No, you're not," Damon said.

"I am, too. Ask Mary."

"Is she?"

"Let's all settle down," Mary told them, looking worn from two days of driving with them. "We'll get all our schedules straight tomorrow."

"See?" Gaddi said. "I'm taking sculpture and Damon's flunking Spanish. He's dumb," she said, "real dumb."

"Shut up," Damon told her.

"No way," she answered. "And your food looks like something we ran over on the highway."

"Gaddi," Aran said, "now hush."

"It does," she said. "Look at it. Something ran over it and squeezed all its guts out."

"Settle down," Mary told her, but Gaddi was already reaching across the table for Damon's plate, and demanding:

"Let me have some!"

Squeezing her leg to hush her, Aran was struck once more by the presence of the woman who had aggravated him last year when they were here, and now she was sitting with a couple several tables over. He felt foolish. He had no idea what the source of his anger was—or was it even anger? He didn't even know the woman's name; he had only seen her several times last summer. She was tall, statuesque, her clothes were elegant and her cheekbones high, her skin was smooth and olively tanned, and the silver of her hair was as striking as the large pieces of jewelry she wore. She looked like the spirit of a place, but which one? Maybe that wasn't it. Maybe the trouble was he couldn't attach her to any place, or to anyone; but if that were true, he noticed, she gave off no look of misery because of it.

During the last year when anyone had asked him what San Miguel was like, Aran had always answered, "Shangri-La," and each time he had used the cliché he had felt as if a membranous element were peeling inside him. The sensation was with him again. This year's apartment was much plainer than the one they had been given last year, with its thirty-five-foot high living room ceiling domed in exposed brick; bathroom fixtures, upstairs and down, golden; two patios overlooking a tropical garden, and the leaves of the aloe vera bordering it as large as broadsword blades. Even the roof had been brilliant with a spread of bougainvillea. Although homely in its appointments, this year's apartment was large—two bedrooms joined by a patio and living room; there were terra cotta tile floors throughout, and a plague of huge termites swarmed on the vigas. "It's the season," the school's vice president insouciantly told him.

He glanced again at the woman. He couldn't get rid of the botherment she brought him.

He and Mary had first noticed her last year at an afternoon program given by a painter who had quickly managed with his palette knife to turn a promising sketch of the parochia into mid-level motel schlock. Aran had noticed the woman narrowing her eyes at the lecturer. Her attitude of earnestness at such sober drivel had made him want to stick his foot out and trip her when she moved closer to the canvas or backed away from it as she purred about the "delicately eclectic" things the painter was doing with light. All about her seemed studied. She fit her white jeans well; the two top buttons of her blouse were stylishly unclasped; and her silver necklace, its pendant a large crescent, dipped at her cleavage, not so much, it seemed, to emphasize the swelling of her breasts as to say: *This is the casualness affected by those of us who are wealthy with taste.*

"Her features are perfect," Mary had said.

Glancing at them, the woman tossed her head to indicate how interesting all this was, whatever this was. Aran's stomach, that afternoon and for days later, felt full of ants and frogs, and each time he saw her he found himself doing battle with himself. He was confident, however, that the stomach disorder had nothing, or little, to do with the woman. It had a lot to do with noxious bacteria: *Amino acid ergo sum.* Psychology, after all, his anger said, was often little more than clever fiction.

"Don't worry about her," Mary said. "She's not important."

But to him she was. She herself was what she called eclectic, and the term was nothing more than a euphemism for mishmash.

"Perhaps you find her attractive," he imagined Mary saying, but he knew that that was not the problem. The force of her presence called to mind something else, some factor that made him feel diminished; and unreasonable though it was, he found himself spewing at her in his daydreams. He fantasized himself striking her. He also felt the same about the wise-cracking painter with the ruinous palette knife, so maybe, he thought for awhile, it's only the corruption in my belly making me feel this way. Then she had come to his reading.

Sitting on the front row, she had seemed to be the fulfillment of the surfaces being developed by others there before him. The glitter, being cultivated by them, was already fully developed in her; and the grandness of her presence said she knew it, but the lines flaring from the corners of her eyes indicated that something within her was hungry, desperate even for a kind of certification that only the makers could provide. Still, like many others he had seen here, she was too genteel to look greedy. Hell, he thought, maybe she's just more interested in her illusions than mine, and that's always, he laughed to himself, ample enough reason to kill someone.

Flipping pages, he had found his next poem, one about the nausea that came when he missed his children. Then his fingers and voice found another, this one full of outrage at their mother for taking them from him; but when he came to the ending, he found himself surprised. He had closed with something other than an outburst of bitterness, with something other than a cry against injustice. The poem ended with a reference to his own loss of redemption. Instantly the woman got up and left. He thought he had somehow stung her, and himself with her, until he noticed that her eyes looked as blank as marbles.

The malachite setting was round and far too large for the man's finger, but the man was desperate, Aran and Mary discovered early in the evening. After his wife had died, the man had taken early retirement, for the second time, he said, from his job as managing editor of a Chicago newspaper. He was going to travel until, as he said, "I drop, and I might do a novel on the way—get serious scribbling myself," he told Mary then quickly asked, as he patted her leg, "You really happy with your husband?"

"More than happy," Mary told him, and Aran stayed silent.

Caressing now the mouth of his glass with his lips, the man said, "You're pretty. I'd like to kiss you. May I? A kiss because you're pretty?"

Giving the man little reaction, Mary leaned against Aran. Looking from one to the other, the man affected a courtly air and asked Aran, "Do I have your permission? There's nothing to fear."

"I realize that," Aran said.

"Then may I?"

"What's the point?"

"She's so pretty."

"How about another drink?" Aran asked. "A bit of sublimation might be good for you."

"I don't think," the man told Mary, "he's letting you get very far."

"I hope not," she said.

"You might come to resent that," he told her. "Most women do."

"Maybe so."

"Then a friendly kiss? It won't hurt anything."

"I don't think," Aran said, "the issue we're dealing with is her pain."

"Certainly not. Maybe yours, though. After all, we men do have a weakness: being smart enough to know we know far less than we need to know. So how about it if I give her—probably—just one kiss?"

"No," Aran said.

"Very well," the man said and turned away, his eyes as superciliously self-possessed as the woman who bothered Aran.

The party soon moved from the house where they were having cocktails to a restaurant off the *jardin*. The man leaned over to speak to the hostess who, though she nodded distractedly, pointed to the table and told Mary that the seating arrangement called for her to sit here, next to the man. Aran's place would be at the far end of the table.

Mary caught his arm as Aran turned away to leave. She reached up and kissed him. "After awhile," she said, "come ask me to dance."

"Sure," Aran said, trying not to sound pissed.

The meal began with Aztec soup. The entrée was broiled chicken. The wine, red and white both, came in carafes—to hide the screw-top bottles, Aran mused. The vegetable was broccoli smothered in a white cheese of the region and steamed onion. From around the table, and beamed down upon it by waiters and others slipping by, came the animated singing of flirting, eyes dancing at necklines and laps, hands spasming to pat wrists as if something serious had just been emphasized. Then sudden gestures of sobriety fell when it came time to whisper while waving at someone else across the room or down the table where a new pair of bobbing eyebrows munched the atmosphere. Alien to the gaming, Aran finally caught Mary's eye. Rising, he said he was coming to get her, and moments later, when he asked her to dance, the man from Chicago who wanted to kiss her and who had said he was dizzy for her stood up and told Aran that he had just been planning to ask her himself:

"You wouldn't mind, would you?"

"Not at all," Aran said. "Say what you want. It's just that she and I are having this dance."

"Certainly," the man said. "I just need to be faster."

"A lot faster," Aran said. "Next time, though, I'll let you lead."

Smiling, the man nodded to acknowledge his rival's temporary victory, then Mary kissed him on the forehead.

Putting his arms around both of them, the man said, "After you finish, come on back here and get me. Ask me down to your end of the table," he told Aran. "The people here are worse than the wine."

When they came back to the table after two dances, the hostess was inviting the group next door for a drink at the opening of a disco-bar. Feeling absurdly responsible, Aran tried to find their new friend, but the man was gone.

"We don't like our room," Gaddi said, their first night in the apartment. "The dressers are built like coffins."

"Yeah," Damon said, "why don't you give us your room? Our room smells creepy."

"Something's going to bite us when we're asleep," Gaddi said. "I'm not going in there, not unless you're in there with us."

"Look," Aran said, trying to be patient, "we've opened the windows. It'll air out. It's just been closed up for awhile. And besides, you've even got your own patio. We don't."

"Sure," Gaddi said, "where something can climb up the wall and get us. You won't be able to hear it either."

"They don't care," Damon said. "They probably hope a thing'll get us."

"That's ridiculous," Mary said.

"Then give us your room," Damon told her.

"Right," Gaddi said. "Girls with girls and boys with boys."

"I've already told you," Aran said, "you've got your own room. If anybody comes in, they have to come through our part first. Nothing's going to get you. Besides, the door has two locks on it, and we'll always lock the screen."

"That won't do any good," Damon said. "The locks are made in Mexico. They don't work right."

Although frustrated, Aran couldn't keep from laughing as he told them it was late, way past time for them to be in bed, "And I'm taking you in there now—both of you."

"If we have to go to bed," Damon said, "you and Mary do, too."

"Fine," Aran said, rounding them up in his arms and pushing them toward the door, pinching their bottoms and woollying their hair to distract them.

"I'm not going first," Gaddi squealed. "Something'll kill us!"

"Right," Aran said, leading them across the patio, "maybe me." Opening the door to their room and caught up in the mayhem of his children, he howled like a ghost to tease them, but instantly knew he had made a mistake. They were crazy with anarchy again.

After finally getting them dressed for bed, he gave them massages, but they stiffened under his hands. Damon insisted he was sitting up all night: "I'm working on my stamps," and Gaddi told her father he'd probably never see her again because something would kill her during the night and stuff her in the dresser. She screamed.

"At least I'll know where you are," Aran said, bending down to kiss her, but she bit his nose and, throwing her arms around him, told him she wasn't ever letting him go, he was going to sleep with her forever.

"We're gonna smooch, too," she giggled. Laughing, he pinched her foot under the cover. "I want my hiney scratched," she told him. "There's a flower in it."

"Night, little booger," he told her, then kissing her again told her he loved her.

"What about me?" Damon asked.

"I've already kissed you good night."

"You didn't say you loved me."

"I did, too."

"You didn't mean it very much."

"Sure I did."

"Prove it."

"Sweet dreams," he told them. "I'll see you in the morning."

"We'll probably be dead," Gaddi said, then Damon told his father:

"Make Gaddi quit. All she does is cut the cheese all night. I'm tired of her farting."

"I'm never gonna stop," Gaddi said, "it feels so good." Damon started laughing but quit when Gaddi said, "Every time he wets the bed, it sounds like rain, and I get cold."

He tried talking them into taking siestas, but they had no interest in such, and when he explained that siestas were an old Mexican custom, Damon said, "So what? We're American."

In spite of their protests, the children would often fall asleep at night in restaurants, with Gaddi even dropping off before they got served. Both Aran and Mary repeatedly told them why they were so tired: "The rhythm here's different from what you're used to, and the altitude's high. So tomorrow we'll all take a siesta."

"Not me," Damon said.

Curled up in Mary's lap, Gaddi jerked, but her eyes stayed closed.

Walking home, they crossed the crowded *jardin*, and Gaddi, who had become lively again, skipped, like the cool gusting breeze, around the people who were standing and talking, walking in couples, sitting on benches. A block and a half later, though, she said she was tired and wanted her father to carry her home.

"Would you like a ride, too," he asked Mary who jammed her thumb up under his arm then puckered her lips for him to lean over and kiss her.

"Maybe later," she said.

"What're you talking about?" Damon asked.

"Making love," Gaddi sang. "They're gonna smooch and I'm gonna watch. Now carry me," she demanded.

"I'll carry her," Damon said. "Piggyback. I do it all the time."

"She's too heavy," Aran said, squeezing the back of his son's neck.

"I'm warning you," Gaddi said, pulling her brother's arm from around her father's waist. With hip-flicks she pushed herself between them. "Carry me!" she ordered, and grabbing her father's arm, told Damon, "Get lost. Me and Daddy are tired."

"My God, she's brilliant!" the big-girthed, red-bearded painter said at the reception after his talk. "I've got her in two classes and she does twice the work of anyone in there."

It took Aran, who had just come into the gathering at the snack table, awhile to realize that the woman being praised was the one who had been irritating him. Glancing across the room, he saw her; she was talking with Mary. Ignoring the conversation he was standing now in the middle of, he watched the two women. Instantly turning toward him, the woman waved as if, of course, she knew him. A big hand clapped him on the back.

"Keep looking," the painter said. "She's worth it. Gave me sixteen yards of Belgian canvas this week. Said she didn't think her painting was good enough to justify flying it home."

Aran laughed hollowly, then sipping his beer, noticed the large wooden tribal mask on the wall, its red and white teeth painted bone. Glancing away, he saw the calm image of Mary, alone now, then heard another woman saying his name. Turning to meet her, he saw the smartly dressed woman who had been bothering him. She was coming directly toward him.

Announcing her name, she extended her hand and said, "I've been talking to Mary. I was at your reading last year."

"I remember," he said.

"Got to go now," she said, "another engagement—but maybe sometime while you're here, we can all get together."

"Sure."

"Take care," she said rapidly, "loved seeing you again," and Aran, noticing how rapidly his attitude toward her had changed, began wondering if he were so impressionable he was characterless.

The spread of crackers and cheeses, raw vegetables, tostados and chips was now meager. Shapes of buzzing people floated around him. The children, he imagined, were sleeping in peace—or having nightmares; they often did, especially Damon. Aran felt adrift. Missing his children confused him.

"Are you all right?" Mary asked.

"Sure," he replied, bewildered to realize that sometime before he had sunk himself into a rawhide-backed chair.

Mary was sitting beside him, whispering. Others in the room were talking. As Mary touched his thigh, Aran heard a man saying, "An inclination to hallucinate, you know, might be at the source."

"I don't know," the painter said, stroking his beard upward until it rose from his chin with the roundness, stiffness and size of an earthenware plate. "What do you think?" he asked Aran.

"I don't know." He didn't even know what the conversation was about. He was thinking of his children, of the blocks of time spreading without them, of the nausea that came when he missed them, of the fact that their time here together was ending. He wouldn't see them again 'til Christmas, and maybe not even then.

"Indeed!" Leonard cried, his face radiant, and Aran realized he had missed another part of the conversation. The man thumbed his glasses back up the bridge of his nose and began telling about his boyhood hero: "I was just eleven. We were living in Framingham and he was the champion pole-vaulter at Harvard. Hell!" he said, laughing, "he probably couldn't even go fourteen feet, but I thought he was God."

"No!" the hostess shrieked, "no!" she cried, her white caftan billowing. "Don't start it! Not again!"

Ignoring her in his enthusiasm, Leonard said, "My real hero, though, was a guy in my own prep school. I was fourteen and he was around sixteen, but something like six-four," he said, "and he walked with a slump," Leonard added, rounding his shoulders and strolling around the room as he told them, "He was the most heroic figure I'd ever seen—played end—and for two years I walked in a slump myself—just like him. It made me feel tall."

"Magnificent!" the painter roared as Leonard pantomimed jostlng a pole to show them how he had tried to combine the football star's slump with the pole-vaulter's lope.

"That ended up disaster," Leonard said.

"Good way to get a rupture, too," the painter said.

"That's why I switched to doing dashes."

"He set a record, too," his wife said.

"How long did it last?" Mary asked, her palms pressed together in friendly mimicry of rapture.

"It's still standing," Leonard's wife said, squeezing him high on the back of his leg. As he glanced down at her, his glasses fell off on the rug.

Retrieving them then sticking one of the earpieces in his mouth, he said, "Listen, dear, the boys who run the dash in my time now can't even make the team."

"Lord!" the agitated hostess raved. "This is disgusting—worse than last week when you spent half the evening describing Notre Dame playing NYU."

"SMU," Leonard corrected her.

"The first time?" Aran asked, and when they told him yes, he said, "I was there. We were living in Dallas. It was a cloudy, misty day."

"Dammit!" the hostess said, "you stay out of this."

"Kyle Rote," he said reflectively.

"Who the hell's Kyle Rote?"

"Three touchdowns," the painter said, with Aran adding: "And Doak Walker on the sidelines, tackled out of bounds against a wheelchair during the Rice game, and tears coming down his cheeks during the coin-flip because all his life, he told the papers, his big dream had been to play Notre Dame."

"Who the hell's Doak Walker?" the hostess asked.

"Maybe the best football player ever," the painter said, winking at Aran to celebrate their new friendship.

"I was a freshman that year," the host said, speaking for the first time. "I was there. Remember Johnny Champion?" he asked, smiling as he wiped the back of his tonsure down. "Little stocky guy—five-six and having to block Leon Hart at six-six—diving between his ankles to trip him."

The hostess, with whom he'd been living for six months now, slapped air at him.

"Settle down," he told her, then turning to the others, he said, "And for all the first half, little David gave Goliath the fits."

"No!" the hostess cried. "Hush! You talked about this same thing last week."

"I know," Leonard said, spreading his fingers over the ends of the arm-rests on his chair, "but we left a good part of it out."

Sitting on the floor, the hostess wrapped her arms around her knees and pouted. She looked to the other women for aid, but they offered none; and when Aran said Notre Dame had been a forty-five point favorite, she butted in, saying, "You're making this up. You weren't even born then."

"The greatest thing, though," Aran told them, "was the Sunday head-line in *The Dallas Morning News*: Ponies Stomp Irish: 20–27!"

"That doesn't," the hostess said archly, "even make sense. They lost."

"Not if you were there," the host said. "It was wonderful—back even before I met my first wife."

"You leave her out of this," the hostess told him.

"Listen," Leonard said, attempting to include the hostess in their play, "didn't you have heroes?"

Peremptorily she announced, "I don't believe in heroes. I didn't back then and I certainly don't now."

"I mean when you were a kid."

"Never!" she swore.

"I don't believe it," he said.

"Maybe one," she relented, "when I was twelve, maybe ten: Katherine Mansfield."

"Hell!" the host said, "when I was five I was partial to Marcel Proust myself."

The guests laughed, but the hostess found nothing funny in the un-called for effort at lightness.

After he came back from market the next day with the children, he and Mary decided it was time for a nap, for all of them. They had stayed out late and gotten up early. Defiantly Damon told them he was going to play.

"Sure," Aran said, "no problem."

"I don't ever need naps," Damon insisted, determined to get the fight he obviously thought he was due.

"You're probably right," Aran said. "A lot of us, though, aren't quite so strong."

"I mean I'm going outside," Damon told him. "That's where I'm going to play."

"Sounds good to me," his father told him, and Damon and his sister hurried out the door.

Several hours later, shortly after Aran and Mary had risen for coffee, Damon came running into the apartment chattering about what he and his sister and one of their friends had just seen: a man and a woman up on the roof of the art building, photographers below them taking pictures of them. Aran glanced out the window; patches of rainclouds looked like bruises on a clear blue sky.

"And they were naked!" Damon said, "naked! You could even see their hineys—and front things, too," he added, "hers and his, too."

"Where's Gaddi?" Mary asked.

"She and her friend," Damon said, trying to stop panting, "they're still out there looking."

In memory Aran could hear his daughter's throaty laughter. "Look!" he remembered her squealing one morning during a summer visit two years ago when she and Damon were helping him fix breakfast. On an impulse she had yanked up his bathrobe, and with it his nightshirt. "Ay!" she had shrieked, trying to defy her surprise, "his thing's got a ring around it!"

Now, though, he was thinking about the woman he had met on his way back from market: the woman who'd been talking to Mary last night and had then come over to introduce herself to him. But she hadn't even really stopped; she'd sashayed away almost the moment she'd announced herself to him.

Awhile ago, passing on the sidewalk, they'd met again. The imagery of her still vivid, her blouse was turquoise, her well-fitting pants the color of bone. Bracelets torqued her wrists and an opal moon-crescent rocked at the nadir of her lavalier. Her hair as silver as a polished ceremonial shield, she had asked him why he had the bunch of orange flowers.

127

"For squash blossom soup," he had answered.

"You mean you just use the flowers, and not the zucchini itself?"

"Sure," he'd said, "along with a leek and some other items. I'll give you the recipe."

"I'd love it," she'd said, reaching out to touch his arm, then flipping the gesture into a wave, she'd said she had to rush on; and she did, though a ghostly remnant of her remained oddly antic with him. A trick of memory making him repeatedly watch her rush off, she'd suddenly be before him again. Always, though, she'd hurry away.

Burning his eyes, the onion he was dicing was making his nostrils weep. Imagining he and the woman were again on the street, he tried sniffing his head clear. Were the two of them going in the same direction? And if they were, had she noticed? Backhanding the onion bits into the hot oiled skillet to sauté them just enough to mellow their tart fragrance, he found himself wishing he'd been on the roof with his children when they'd seen the naked people. He enjoyed the bursts of anarchy they brought him, but soon they'd be leaving, disappearing from him; and they and the portions of the world they'd all passed through would turn into little bursts of memory, shapes that were vivid but dimensionless.

Summer's Child

Joy E. McLemore

It wasn't easy being a girl, and four older brothers didn't make it any easier. All her life Sister had been hearing about how the Millers had given up on having a girl until she came along, so she couldn't figure out why Mama wouldn't even let her have a bathroom of her own now. Sister recalled her third birthday, her first memory. There she was with a huge Madame Alexander doll almost exactly her size. Everybody watched her opening that package and finding the creature inside. As soon as it made a "wa-ah" noise, she threw it right down and never picked it up again. Mama perched it in the baby rocker at the corner of Sister's bedroom where it was still waiting.

Then when Sister was about five, Mama had wondered why she was running around with her hand clamped tightly over her belly button all the time. "My seeds!" Sister had wailed. One of the brothers, it turned out, had told Sister that the seeds to grow babies some day were deep inside, and they'd fall right out if she weren't careful. She checked her navel and found lint. Seeds. Sister didn't know the difference. The whole family had teased her a good deal, and Sister laughed along with them most of the time, although she didn't think it was funny at all. Somewhere around eight or nine she decided she'd never have any babies anyway, not if they had to come out the way Mama said, so she didn't care if all the seeds fell out.

Now, being thirteen was the worst of all. Mama and Sister had had a woman-to-woman talk, and sure enough, this fall after school had started, Sister "started" too. "You can't walk like that for twenty percent of your life, Sister," Mama said. Sister was aghast. This nuisance was going to occur with some regularity. Mama had forgotten to explain that part. "Besides, it's better than being a boy." Sister considered that alternative as she made herself a peanut butter and grape jelly sandwich. The mixture turned a horrible gray when Sister mixed the two ingredients with a fork, so she added jelly for a marbled effect.

"Could you start getting peach preserves again, Mama?" No, she wouldn't want to be a boy, that's for sure. A book she was reading said those things boys had got stiff when they didn't want them to. Maybe she'd get the hang of being a girl eventually. Mama managed well enough when she wasn't yelling or reading. But what Sister really wanted was to be five years old again, catching lightning bugs just after dark until Mama called her in to take her bath.

This particular April day, just in time for the annual diocese picnic, it had happened again. Sister decided to sit with Mrs. Hammer, her algebra teacher, on the grass beside the vollyball game, so that nothing would leak out if she went running and jumping around that net. Mrs. Hammer was good company anyway, no matter that she'd had a cake with seventy candles last year. She'd taught four Millers already, even Daddy. And Daddy had been a Rhodes scholar, whatever that meant. It had impressed Mama sufficiently that she had married him. Sister liked Mrs. Hammer and visited with her whenever she got the chance. Besides, she was glad to avoid the volleyball game on account of being a first-class klutz. Mama had said that was all right, so was she, and it didn't matter on account of they were both pretty. Sister didn't feel pretty.

"Nobody your age feels exactly right with the world, Mary Margaret," Mrs. Hammer said.

"But *nothing's* right these days." Sister had decided long ago she could trust Mrs. Hammer, if anybody. "All the family's on my case, nobody here at school likes me—"

"Nonsense, Mary Margaret."

"I'll probably get two C's this quarter too."

"Not in algebra."

They watched the volleyball game. Once the ball came out of bounds to Sister, and when she tried to throw it back, it went only a short distance in the wrong direction. So she kicked it hard.

"Hey, we need a football team at St. Stephen's!" somebody yelled.

"You're almost as pretty as your mother," said Mrs. Hammer, as they got in line for their paper plates.

130

Sisters arms and legs felt too long, and her brown, naturally curly hair frizzed most of the time because of the dreadful Texas humidity. She pulled it back into doggie ears usually and was wearing her glasses more and more, which covered up her cornflower blue eyes. All the girls in St. Stephen's eighth grade were getting boring because they spent half their lives trying to be gorgeous and the other half talking about boys.

The next day after the volleyball game the Millers were late to school, as usual. St. Stephen's first bell wouldn't ring for about twenty minutes, but for some reason Mama decided to drop Sister off first for a change. Usually all the brothers got deposited at the junior college or big high school first—at the field house, chemistry lab, or parking lot where the cheerleaders convened. The boys said they were going to fix their engine in the van this summer and solve all the transportation problems, but Sister didn't mind the morning confusion. She'd been last so long that she was quite amazed when anything in the way of luck came her way.

The brothers could be late for a change. Sister would be on time for safety patrol for the first time in eleven weeks. She'd counted. She enjoyed dressing up in the yellow suit and lugging around markers, whistles, flags. Noticing somebody had changed the Easter sign, "Hallelujah, Christ is Risen" to "Barbeque—11:00–2:00 Sunday," she stared at the sign again. That "barbeque" always bothered Sister. The last syllable looked to her like "kwee." That's the way they do things in Texas, Mama had said, but having Daddy teaching languages had driven Sister mad most of her life. And Mama had said Sister was going to wind up just like him if she weren't careful, worrying about things like phonics and spelling.

No way Sister'd wind up like that. She'd show them all. She'd go to Texas A&M and major in veterinary medicine, that's what she'd do. That would get even with everybody. Mama had spent five years at the University of Texas and had absolutely nothing to show for it but a stupid education degree she never used.

It would give Sister tremendous satisfaction to be an Aggie, especially when Daddy came apart during football season. It was all his fault Sister had had to take tennis lessons, and he'd talked Mama into that icky ballroom dancing too. And the person Sister'd wound up dancing with most was the boy down the street who had pimples not only on his face, but his arms, too, the squeezy kind. Mama wasn't all bad though. Everybody had

131

missed her carrot cake yesterday at the picnic when she and Daddy had sneaked off to Shreveport to eat gumbo. And she had also delivered Sister to school first this morning.

Mrs. Hammer saw her first.

"Morning, Mary Margaret. You're on time for patrol."

"Yes'm." Sister mumbled and grunted a minute, not really wanting to visit this morning because she'd dug fishing worms yesterday after the picnic, worked on the treehouse, and planted some horrible bulbs Daddy had dragged in from a neighbor's garden. No time for algebra homework. She had read recently those bulbs were poisonous and remembered the time one of her brothers had planted a light bulb and thought it would grow into a fine gas patio lamp like the Mannings had next door. This morning her fingernails were dirty, and she didn't have on regulation knee socks with her plaid jumper uniform. Nice as Mrs. Hammer was, she was big on rules.

"Did your mom and dad have fun at the races?" asked Mrs. Hammer. "I hope you said we missed them at the picnic yesterday." How did Mrs. Hammer know they loved horse racing as much as eating out in Shreveport? Sister didn't account for her parents. "I enjoyed my visit with you though. Can't believe you're leaving us soon." Sister thought about the big high school. Mama said it was full of alcohol, drugs, and fresh boys. She'd been fighting with two male Millers this weekend because when Sister arrived next year, they were planning to punch out any guy who looked at Sister funny.

"Oh, they got back late last night." Sister looked at her half-chewed fingernails. "Sometimes they just have to escape all of us."

"Parents do that." Mrs. Hammer smiled. "Listen, Mary Margaret, I need to speak to you after school. It won't take too long."

"Yes'm, but I'm on patrol, and—"

"I'll get you out of patrol. It's important, Dear."

"Do you know how long it will take?" Sister asked in a small voice.

"Not long. See you at 3:30."

On the way to the girls' rest room Sister thought about how it wasn't fair her brothers planning her social life next year. They planned to scrutinize, interview, and threaten any boys who looked at Sister wrong because she was "such a baby." It didn't make any sense at all. They looked at girls plenty funny, and Sister had found a package out in the garage apartment which read "to be used for prevention of disease." She had read about those things and decided the package belonged to Billy Bob, her oldest brother, 'cause one day she'd come home quickly when Mama and Daddy were in Dallas and Sister was supposed to be down the street at her grandmother's, and Billy Bob had about died. He had been lying right on the couch next to Suzy Martin, a girl from the next block who went to First Baptist training union every Sunday night. Sister enjoyed listening to crickets or remodeling the tree house on those evenings and rejoiced that she could manage the whole religious business in the hour's worth of mass on the weekends. Well, and there was mass at school twice a week, but none of the sophisticated eighth graders paid any attention to Father O'Brien. In fact, they generally passed notes through all his rituals, and only rarely did Sister catch Mrs. Hammer's evil eye and feel guilty.

Digging worms, which Sister also found time to do on weekends, wasn't a bad business either. She'd decided not to babysit any more after her little cousin had dirtied his britches the afternoon they left him with Sister, and the pay wasn't so good. But sometimes she sold her worms around the neighborhood and had made a pile of money. Right now she had forty-three dollars squirreled away in a Maryland Club coffee can, third drawer down, right behind the locust shells and rock collection in her jewelry box.

She stayed in the little cubicle in the bathroom 'til everybody else left, adding a little tissue to her 32A bosom. Oh, well, at least it wasn't double-A any more. She didn't want to talk to anybody. Something must be the matter with her. Daddy said she daydreamed all the time, too, but then, so did he when he wasn't reading. Sister went back to her locker, but by then had forgotten what she wanted to get there. Only five minutes remained for patrol duty, so she decided to skip it. And she'd miss it again this afternoon because of the mysterious conference with Mrs. Hammer. They'd probably throw her off patrol.

The day grew progressively worse. Sister had forgotten her homework in American history, and during lunch everybody seemed to have something going on which didn't include her. She sat down close to Sherry and Terry Spencer, who had asked her to spend the night at their house a couple of times this year, but she didn't much like spending nights anywhere but her own little room—"the swamp," Mama called it.

"Hi, Mary Margaret," sang Sherry. "I don't mean to be rude, but we're discussing something." The girls stared at Sister. "It's sort of private."

Sister just shrugged. She knew the cue, as well as just exactly how to get into the conversation if she wanted to. All the girls were always talking about John Buskirk, the smartest and cutest boy in St. Stephen's eighth grade. Sister was easily bored lately though, and Big Bad John, as she called him, had disenchanted her last August at her birthday party by ducking her in her grandmother's swimming pool.

Sister decided to disappear into a corner to eat her turkey sandwich by herself so she could really concentrate on worrying about what Mrs. Hammer was planning to say to her at three-thirty. She ambled past some slimy looking okra and decided it was a good thing Mama had packed her a lunch.

Her braces got in the way of eating the apple, so she switched to Fritos instead, ignoring the carrot and celery sticks. Everybody in the Miller family, except Sister of course, was a health nut. She was sick of it. Sister hated anything resembling a sport, partly because, she thought, sports had made her daddy and brothers half crazy. Every Saturday morning Daddy would fix waffles, then send brothers off in all directions with tennis rackets, baseball bats, golf clubs—just anything to keep them out of their mysterious woodsy backyard next to the creek. Sister bet nobody else on the block knew that maples, three kinds of pines, two gums, one hickory, a pecan, and an English walnut were growing right back there on Miller property. They were all happy enough to gobble the cobbler when Sister picked buckets of dewberries, of course.

And surely nobody else had ever seen the mama raccoon spiraling up the oak tree next to the deck with her four babies. Sister had thought about showing Mama late some night how to get the coons out. Maybe Mama would understand. Sister had decided the backyard rightfully belonged to the girls. The boys could have the front as long as Daddy made them mow it. The backyard had so much ivy and such a carpet of pine needles that it didn't need any mowing. She and Mama could manage the geraniums, caladiums, and other exotic plants on the deck.

Sometimes Mama fixed lemonade and lay in the hammock with volumes of short stories while Sister worked on the treehouse, and Mama didn't give a hoot what anybody did with his tennis racket either.

Come to think of it, this conference today probably had to do with Sister's non-interest in sports. She had been making excuses for not playing the athletic event of the day for several weeks now. "A girl can't use some excuses every week and a half, Mary Margaret," the phys ed coach had stated sternly. But Sister really had sprained her ankle the first day of basketball, and she'd gotten hit in the nose with a softball on the second day of that sport after striking out twice in a row on the first day. And now they wanted her to play volleyball which, thought Sister, was the absolutely dumbest game anybody'd dreamed up yet, and her brothers said St. Stephen's had the seasons all mixed up anyway. Even Daddy, who wanted Sister to be a "lady," whatever that meant, went around muttering things about *sane corpore in sane mentis*. Daddy had read her some good stuff over her thirteen years though, things from the Tolkien trilogy even. Today, thinking about the after-school summit meeting, Sister decided to make an effort on the soccer field.

She tossed her paper bag full of trash into the garbage and went outside. P.E. was fifth period, right after lunch, so Sister donned a big green jersey over her uniform and lay her skirt on the sidewalk just as the coach yelled, "Forward, Miller!" She pulled her shorts decently into position and entered the battlefield.

Fortunately most of the action was happening on the other end, near the trees. Sister was studying cloud formations for a couple of minutes when suddenly the right wing, John Buskirk, broke loose and worked the ball down the sideline opposite Sister. She discovered herself paying full attention and moving faster on her long legs than she usually did. She was almost centerfield exactly opposite John when he caught her eye and hollered, "Center, Mary!" then passed the ball to her. She trapped it with her left foot and started sprinting. Sister had the whole half of the field to herself except for the opposing center fullback. Just as she was wondering what to do about him, he slipped on a patch of mud. Before he could recover, Sister scooted the ball around to the left, faked a right to the goalie coming after her, and kicked the ball dead center. One point. It wasn't so hard really, just like kicking beer cans down the street.

"Din' know you had it in you, Miller," said Coach.

"Nice work," said John, giving her a high-five.

The good mood after shooting the goal might have lasted if she hadn't been so concerned about the 3:30 appointment. It felt like five o'clock by the time religion class rolled around. Sister's stomach had felt funny ever since lunch, and she'd been to the girls' restroom three times since she'd gotten to school. Maybe the soccer game after lunch had wrecked her non-athletic body. She had played exactly five minutes—she'd timed it—before stopping to rest. That big old ball had stayed close to the ground most of the time and, therefore, appeared slightly less lethal than all those sneaky little projectiles in the other games. She might play again. Maybe. If John did.

"Good shot, Mary Margaret!" said Sherry Spencer on the way to religion class. "I didn't even know you liked soccer."

"Neither did I," answered Sister.

Everybody in St. Stephen's eighth grade agreed that Miss Rhinehart, the religion teacher, worked hard at being an old bag. Sister wondered why she hadn't gone on to the convent and been a real nun since she was an old maid anyway. Sitting there arranging her incomplete catechism, Sister wondered if Rhinehart were a virgin and decided she probably wasn't, according to Mama at least, who had suggested that most girls, married or not, did not remain virgins long past the age of twenty. And even though Mama was pretty vague on lots of subjects—and absent-minded at times, especially if two or three brothers were talking to her—Sister could count on her to tell the truth. Sister had decided to remain a virgin forever after hearing what Mama had to say about the alternatives. John Buskirk surely would too.

Sister didn't listen to the first ten or so minutes of religion class because they'd covered all that Holy Mary junk thoroughly several weeks ago, and she was pretty certain God went fishing as often as possible and was embarrassed by most matters related to humankind. Now Sister and her classmates were sitting there in a big circle listening to the droning Rhinehart question them, one by one, concerning what each would do if somebody offered him a million dollars to give up The Church. Sister considered that First Presbyterian downtown had some awfully pretty dogwoods, white and pink mixed together against the old brick and blue sky. Furthermore, Trinity Episcopal had wood shingles on top, stucco walls, and those wonderful roll-out windows like her aunt's house in New Orleans. And Uncle Bob had built the Alpine Christian Church, with its nice chapel-like setting in a pine thicket. It seemed to Sister that God would be just as likely to visit any of those places as the modern domed structure her diocese had worshipped. Besides, Sister resented the way her church was so cocksure about everything. She spent most of her life just sitting and thinking and getting more confused.

"Definite" people, as she thought of them, made her nervous. "Beware of anybody with pat answers," said Daddy. So why was he Catholic? And why was he so bossy?

Her mind wandered back to the circle, where three people had answered Rhinehart's question while Sister daydreamed. Everybody with any sense after eight years at St. Stephen's by now knew how to answer a stupid question like "Could you give up the Church?" Only John Buskirk had squirmed at all before answering. Sister pondered her new respect for him as one of the Spencer twins paraphrased what all the rest of the class had been saying: "My soul is worth more than money; I would never give up the Church."

Sometimes Sister thought all that religiosity sounded fine and noble, like during funerals and weddings, and had worried for two or three years now that her spiritual self had slipped out of focus. She'd decided to worry about all this Church business after she got the growing-up-girl stuff out of the way. Religion was just too heavy for now, although she was willing to go through the rituals and mind the Golden Rule, most of the time. Besides, Daddy would lock her in the cellar permanently if she failed to attend. Well, he'd never actually locked her in the cellar, but every now and then he threatened.

Nobody at the Miller house was very scared of Daddy or God. God visited Sister daily, mostly away from St. Stephen's—a robin here, a raccoon there if she sneaked out on the deck after everybody else was asleep. She didn't like armadillos much, though, and always avoided Copperhead Creek, as Mama called it, during July and August when the snakes were shedding their skin. Sister didn't blame the snakes for being irritated by that process—sort of like trimming her nails, getting a haircut, shedding blood. She wondered why God had made water moccasins though, which thrived at Cherokee Lake. They were the meanest breed in eastern Texas. She'd heard horror stories of their dropping out of cypress trees into fishing boats. She also wondered if she were in bad enough trouble that the monsignor would be at the three-thirty meeting.

"Mary Margaret, what would you do?" came the query of Miss Rhinehart, interrupting Sister's reverie.

"About what?" said Sister, all wide-eyed and fidgety.

"If somebody offered you a million dollars to give up the Church," responded Rhinehart in the voice she used when nobody'd figured out any of the answers to the homework questions. John Buskirk stared at Sister and smiled a challenge. She gulped. Between this question, all those brothers beating up any boyfriends she might ever acquire, girl stuff, and the conference this afternoon—Sister could see no future at all.

"What would you do, Mary Margaret?" Rhinehart persisted.

"Well, I—I mean, it's a tough question." She thought of the Presbyterian Church downtown. Her cousins went there. They didn't seem to think the booger-man was going to get everybody outside their church. "Could I—let me think about it and tell you first thing tomorrow," Sister stammered, just as the bell rang. John laughed out loud as he grabbed his books. Rhinehart threw up her hands and looked skyward.

Algebra class passed all too quickly today, and Sister kept watching her watch. There must be demons living right inside her head. Something was distorting time and changing the hands on her watch. Days had passed between breakfast and religion class, and now algebra was going by like a fast videotape. Mrs. Hammer had left the class with an aide, who didn't understand polynomials as well as Sister did. Maybe Mrs. Hammer and Monsignor were devising elaborate torture schemes for the three-thirty meeting. She thought of the rack in the Poe story. And all of a sudden it was three-thirty, and there she stood, with jello knees and clicking braces, right in the headmistress's dreaded office. The monsignor was there, and he didn't look up from his desk while they waited for Mrs. Hammer. Sister looked at the ceiling. It looked just like it always had, white squares full of black dots. Automatically she started to count them. Let's see, twelve on the long side multiplied by—

Mrs. Hammer came in and sat at her desk. Why did she look so serious? Then she pulled out some papers, nodded to the monsignor, and smiled at Sister.

"Congratulations, Mary Margaret," he smiled. She'd never seen this smile. Congratulations? For hating sports? For having food fights in the cafeteria? For skipping student council meetings perhaps? Maybe he'd heard about the soccer goal she'd accidentally kicked after lunch and was trying to soften the blow before the ax fell. Obviously Miss Rhinehart hadn't gotten to him yet.

"Congratulations, Father?" Sister's voiced squeaked.

He nodded. "You've done an outstanding job as secretary of the National Junior Honor Society this year, and your classmates have elected you the most outstanding girl in the graduating class at St. Stephen's School." Sister's mouth had fallen open, and Mrs. Hammer was clearly enjoying her favorite pupil's reaction. The monsignor continued, "We're all very proud of you."

"Yes, Mary Margaret, particularly because we knew you'd be so surprised," added Mrs. Hammer. "Humility becomes you."

"Does this mean I get to go to Bluebonnet State?" Sister asked. For years she'd dreamed of that impossible honor.

"Yes, along with John Buskirk, who will represent the boys," Mrs. Hammer smiled, "that is, if you submit an essay explaining why you think you're entitled to go."

Sister stared at the monsignor, then her teacher, in disbelief. She felt the blood rushing to her cheeks and feared that if she opened her mouth, those mysterious tears might come, as they had so often in this past crazy year. Besides, things like this happened to the Spencer twins, not to her, Mary Margaret Miller, standing here shaking in the main office.

"No mistake, Dear. Congratulations." And she hugged Sister, who wondered how an old lady could have such pretty wrinkles out of the corners of her eyes.

"What took you so long?" asked Mama, as Sister ran out to the old Chevy wagon. "What's the big rush now?" Sister had acquired no fame for rushing.

"You won't believe it, Mama," said Sister, as she began to recount the events of the day. Sipping on her can of sugar-free Dr. Pepper, Mama seemed only mildly impressed. However, she did take the long way home while Sister told her every blessed detail, even about the soccer game and John Buskirk. "Do you think I could possibly have that essay written by next Monday?"

"Calm down, Sister. You can do it if you think you can." Mama sounded just like Grandma with tired old expressions like that. "And it won't take you any longer than digging worms or pounding on your treehouse if you'll just quit piddling around all the time." Mama didn't sound mad, but she nagged Sister every day about something.

Sister felt defensive. "I don't 'piddle around all the time'!"

"I don't see how you can find anything to wear in your room, and I'm not cleaning it up again."

"I didn't ask you to!" Sister yelled. "It's my room!"

"It's just possible you'd *feel* better, not so overwhelmed and all, if you'd get in there and sort things out."

"You think you're always right."

"I often am right, Dear. Experience." Mama smiled her smile that would freeze a tiger at twenty feet. Sister decided Mama really wasn't mad and wondered why her own face felt flushed. Mama stopped and looked at Sister just before she got out of the car. "By the way, congratulations about today, Sister." She handed Sister one of the two grocery sacks to carry. "I am so proud of you."

Sister went into her room, put some fresh water in the cats' bowl, changed the hamster's cedar chips, dumped the litter box down the toilet, gave the parrot some sunflower seeds, and decided to worry about the clothes on her floor later. The parrot said "Go to Hell," just like the boys had taught him. She threw her uniform on the floor and quickly dressed in her dirty sneakers, cut-offs, and one of the boys' big old t-shirts.

On the way through the vacant lot between the Millers' house and the Mannings', Sister grabbed a can of night crawlers freshly dug the evening before. She never charged Mr. Manning for his fishing worms because he always loaned Sister all his wonderful tools Daddy didn't have in the garage, and Mr. and Mrs. Manning had helped her build one classy bird feeder last summer. Mr. Manning had been working just half-time since having a lobe of his lung removed, and he still missed his Lucky Strikes. Almost always Sister could count on him to go fishing with her. They'd just walk over to Cherokee Lake if Mrs. Manning didn't have a faucet or something for him to fix.

Mrs. Manning let Sister in through the kitchen door, where the smell of fresh baked bread caused her mouth to water. Sister ate half a loaf with butter and a glass of milk while Mr. Manning found the best poles in the garage. Then the two headed for the lake.

"Thanks for the bread, Mrs. M!" Sister yelled as they went out the door. Then she went back. "And if Mama calls, I'll be home before supper." She paused. "And I haven't forgotten that I have to sweep the dirt off the deck," Sister said as the pair headed toward the woods.

"Got it," Mrs. M. replied. "Catch a big 'un!"

Sister had always liked Mr. Manning because he didn't talk every minute like most people. He could just pack his tackle, walk through the thicket, and not have to mouth off. He was checking a little sapling near the place where a guy from the next block—also in eighth grade, but in public school—had suggested they lie down and rest a minute on his beach towel last summer. It had seemed an awfully strange suggestion to Sister, and she had right away discovered some poison ivy on the tree under which he'd been arranging his towel. She didn't go with people her age to the lake any more.

"English walnut, I think," said Mr. Manning, still examining the new growth.

"I like the little baby hickories best," said Sister, "and they turn gorgeous golden in November."

They arrived at the muddy lake surrounded by pine trees and wildflowers of many descriptions. Sister decided the cornflower, Indian paintbrush, and those white-blossomed weeds would look nice and patriotic for a bouquet. Maybe she'd take a bouquet home to Mama. Sister was trying to decide if she would add black-eyed susans when Mr. Manning interrupted her planning.

"Let's fish over there." He was already headed toward the sandy beach still in the sunlight. Sister followed. "Id'n that where we caught those perch last summer?"

"Yeah, but they have more bones than bass," said Sister, already thinking she really wanted to go squish mud between her toes over by the old oak tree fallen into the deep water. She walked over there and surveyed all the exposed roots while Mr. Manning threw his line in the water. No, she couldn't squish mud between her toes any more while anybody was watching, so she climbed out the old tree, straddled a limb, and threw her line into the water. Something nibbled at her bait almost immediately and got away with a crawler. Mr. Manning looked at her and stuck his thumb in the air. Sister stuck another worm on the hook. "Sorry, little fella," she mumbled as she impaled him. She sat quietly for a few minutes before hauling in a decent-sized catfish. "Supper!" she exclaimed.

Mr. Manning ambled over. "You're doin' better'n I am."

"Do you have any gloves in your tackle box?" asked Sister. "These things can be nasty." Taking the fish off the hook was the part Sister didn't like, especially with catfish. Without a word, Mr. Manning rescued the fish and threw him in the net and hung it down in the water, just like he always did.

"You're not having any luck, Mr. M." He was fooling around with something in his tackle box. "We can quit any time." Mama wouldn't let her walk through the woods alone.

"Okey-dokey," said her friend, feeling his pocket for cigarettes that weren't there. "I reckin y'all want me to throw your fish back too."

142

"Well, there's only one," she apologized, as Mr. Manning reached into the water for the net. Sister loosened up a little. "Do you think I could throw him back to the deep water?"

"Betcha could." Mr Manning's bloodshot eyes twinkled. "Just don't let him gitcha."

Sister grabbed the fish firmly behind his whiskers and in front of his fins the way Daddy had taught her once on Galveston beach. She threw the fish about ten yards and was pretty proud of herself.

"We'll git you on the baseball team in high school next year," he said, as they started down the path homeward. The leaves and pine needles crunched under their feet.

When they came to the fork in the path, Mr. Manning asked Sister if she wanted to take home a fresh loaf of sourdough for dinner.

"It's getting late," said Sister. "I'd better not." She also wanted to be alone. "Mama's fixin' chicken, and she gets pretty upset if we're not all there at supper."

His smile said he understood. "Well—well, come over any time you feel like it, Mary." He snapped a twig and stuck the end in his mouth. "The Mrs. and I have always thought you're the best of the litter." He waited a few seconds. "Not afraid to walk through the rest of the woods by yourself, are you?"

"Hmmphf!" Sister scowled. "I'll be home before you are!" She trotted down tne path as he stood there and then she yelled back, "Thanks for going with me!"

She slowed down quickly. Why was she so tired after such a little soccer today? She sat on one of her favorite rocks within sight of home, and soaked up the twilight sounds and sights. This was her favorite time of day, the sun playing with shadows and all the squirrels running through their evening rituals. One squirrel stopped three feet away and stared at her. Sister didn't really believe this business about squirrels giving people bubonic plague—maybe in New Mexico, but not right here in her woods. She tried to convince the little animal to come to her, but he wouldn't. Raccoons liked her better, especially when she sneaked dog food to them.

Sister didn't like Mr. Manning's "litter" comment, but Mama had said Methodists always felt jealous of Catholics. He didn't mean any harm. She'd show him though. She'd show everybody, just as soon as she figured out what it was she wanted to show them. For starters, she was going to adopt exactly two children. Maybe she wouldn't even get married ever. Well, it would be interesting to see how John Buskirk turned out.

Mama might be mad again, she thought, as she jumped off the big rock. And what about all this Bluebonnet State business? Maybe she'd try to write this essay and it just wouldn't work. She hurried through the vacant lot, dodging the poison ivy and snakey-looking vines reaching out from the trees. Nobody noticed her sneaking through the downstairs bathroom she always left unlocked. She locked the door into the hall, washed her hands, and checked herself out in the full-length mirror of the bathroom. Too much showed. Sister could no longer hide the fact, even with loose shirts and uniforms, her body had changed. Why had she ever wanted to be thirteen? Sister could not abide half the people in her class for more than five minutes. Life had not been easy lately.

She turned sideways to check herself from that angle. One of Mama's brassieres was hanging on the hook behind the door, so she tried it on. Not bad, especially the lace part, and a little tissue could keep it from poking in on the ends. She put her sweatshirt back on. A definite improvement. Squinting into the mirror, Sister wondered how long she'd make it without contact lenses. Texas females who could afford it generally refused to wear glasses no matter what they failed to see. Her auburn hair flashed interesting lights, and John Buskirk had stared at her out in the sunshine on the soccer field. Being a girl was bound to have some good points somewhere.

Suddenly she was seized by an urge to experiment with Mama's makeup. Sister smeared a little rouge on her high cheekbones but rubbed it right off. Then she tried some pewter-colored eye shadow and then a little green. Not bad. She scrunched her body up closer to the mirror so she wouldn't have to squint. Then she reached up under her shirt and took off Mama's brassiere and washed her face. The fried chicken from the kitchen smelled terrific.

"Mary Margaret, you come out of there right now," hollered Mama, and she only used Sister's Christian name when there was about to be trouble.

"I'm not hungry," growled Sister, because it had just occurred to her that she needed to get an inch or two taller if she were going to get any wider.

"Suit yourself, young lady," Mama said as she stomped down the hall.

Walking into her room, Sister stared at the parrot, took out the noisy hamster's wheel, and lay on the bed beside the calico cat curled on the ruffled sham. She pulled a book from the shelf, then decided not to read. The boys were making noises upstairs, and Mama was hollering at them to come to dinner before she threw it all out.

Sister picked up the phone, looked at Mrs. Hammer's number on the front of the St. Stephen's manual, and dialed.

"Hammer's residence," the familiar voice said.

"It's me, Mary Margaret." Long pause. "I'm not sure why I called. I guess I'm scared."

The voice at the end of the line seemed to be in the same room. "*You* scared? Of what?"

"It's just that—" she searched for the right words.

"Nobody ever said growing up is easy, Mary Margaret." The schoolteacher voice softened. "I'm scared too. Everybody in his right mind is."

Big silence.

"Could I, I mean would you tell me more about the essay?" she stammered strangely.

"If anybody's going to be all right, Dear, you are."

"But how can I *know* that?"

"You can't." Mrs. Hammer waited. "That's the toughest part."

"I didn't mean to bother you at home, Mrs. Hammer."

"It's all right, Mary Margaret. But dinner *is* on the table." She laughed. "And I loathe telephones."

"I'm sorry."

"Do you want me to call you back? No, I have an idea. What if I buy you some ice cream after school tomorrow? You are graduating, after all."

"With marshmallows and hot fudge topping?"

They both laughed. "Be in my office at three-thirty."

"Bye. And thanks, Mrs. Hammer."

Sister lay on her bed and stared at the ceiling. All those strange people she lived with were making a racket in the dining room, and occasionally she heard her name mentioned. She lay there until it grew dark outside, then went to the kitchen around 9:00 where she knew Mama had left a plate for her in the oven. It was there all right, with peach cobbler for dessert.

Weasel Loves

Michael Verde

Coach Ford found the P—the P for Park; he was sucking in a yawn, checking his lips in his Mustang's rearview mirror. The peppermint he was counting on was fresh. It was gray out, his lawn dewy.

He killed the engine. In the driveway there were toys to dodge. He focused, making his every step soft, like an Indian's, an unsteady and not entirely sober Indian entertaining a sleepy hope that his teepee was not locked. It was. Dead-bolted.

He knocked.

Then rang. "Come on, Judy, open up." The neighbor's basset hound, Festus, began to wail.

"Judy, come on, crap," Coach Ford persisted. "I've got to shower and get back to the fieldhouse. Festus, shut the f—" There was movement in the peep-hole. His voice went whiney. "Don't do me this way, Sweet Thing. We're talking district championship here. You know Holbrook and his films—over and over again. I should have called."

"Two bits, four bits, six bits, you sorry no good cradle-robbing *bastard*!" shrieked the voice from the door's other side. It sounded like Sweet Thing meant it.

Woody hated this. But what could he do? Turco had him by his armpits and was hauling him like a human football the length of the bus. This was everyday. At the last row of springy green seats, the Turk, as the hulking baby-faced lineman was known even beyond the county, dropped him, leg braces and all, before a pair of rather large girls—twins: Rita and Lita.

"Who you want *this* morning, Ron Juan?" Turco directed, as if he were instructing Woody to call it in the air. "The healthy Miss Rita or the even healthier Miss Lita? Both girls carry a lot of weight in this county, so I really don't see how you could go wrong."

Woody's hesitation brought an open palm to the back of his neck. When he could see again, two chubby faces, inches away, were staring into his own. He smelled baby powder.

"Come on, Pinocchio, pick and lick," by which Turco meant, Woody well knew by now, kiss. He picked, quickly.

"Hey hey, folks," whooped the Turk into oohing and ahhing applause, "that's three days in a row for the lovely Miss Lita."

His leather and metal bound legs sprawled out in the sticky aisle, Woody, a one man pile up, went to wipe his lips—

Stopped.

Lita—he swore all day this was true—smiled.

Weasel looked at his watch. Then the phone. Then his watch. His room was a joke, a sty. He looked back at the phone, then caught himself. He made a muscle, looked at it instead. The phone did not ring. Then, as a last resort, he called on magic: He whistled Dixie.

The phone did not ring again.

"Dammit to hell, Wendy," cried Weasel, burying his face into trembling fingers.

When he looked up, he was staring at himself in a photo, a newspaper photo tacked cock-eyed on his wall. The article accompanying the photo had put his name above all other names in Angel Falls. *This Weasel Flies*, read the headline. Weasel, as of two weeks ago, was the all-time leading rusher in Golden Panther history. "Ten more minutes," Weasel swore to his tiny self in the photo, his rejoicing thumb-smudged double who had only one thing to add, and wouldn't quit adding it:

"Num-ber One! Num-ber One! Num-ber One! . . . "

"I'm telling you," Weasel insisted, shaking visibly now from head to toe, "if she ain't called in ten minutes—*this* Weasel flies."

That was his vow. Four minutes later, he broke it.

That's not what I mean, no. All I mean is that for awhile, Wendy, things will be, you know . . . subdued.

Subdued? It means, well—

Coach Ford was hunkered over the telephone in the Coaches' Office. He was holding a pink comb, Coach Potter's, up to the fluorescent light, mindlessly raking through its teeth with a thumbnail. He was wet, and except for a thin white towel with "Varsity" magic-markered on it, naked. His hair was dark, receding, parted in the middle, and plastered to the rear three-quarters of his head. Among other inconveniences, he had a hangover.

And if by chance my wife calls—I don't think she will, but if Judy does— just act like you think she's crazy. She thinks she's crazy anyway. Hell, she is crazy. But don't get into some long drawn out discussion with her. Don't let her pull her Perry Mason routine on you.

Perry Mason? He was a real famous lawyer, used to come on TV. Yeah, kind of like Matlock.

Shouldering the receiver to his ear, Coach Ford clicked open his locker and poked around for something to soothe his head. He found the Bayer behind his history book, but the plastic bottle was empty. As he blew away the Bayer dust, his eye fell on a transparent cube, a photo display, sitting atop his playbook. There were only two snapshots in the cube: one of Judy in his coaching cap and a long T-shirt, hip cocked, a whistle in her mouth, giving the signal for a personal foul; and another, of himself in cut-offs at the end of a pier, a fish in one hand and a Jim Beam, White Label, in the other. He was blistered mercilessly and laughing to high heaven.

Of course I still love you, Wendy. You know I—who's that in the background? You are in the cosmetology room, aren't you? Look, Two Bits, all I'm saying is we need—

Coach Ford removed the picture of himself from the cube and turned it over. Taped to its back was another picture, a much smaller one, the kind of black-and-white head shot that went into high school annuals. It was of a girl, a beautiful girl. The picture, if the yellowing borders and the girl's black bouffant were any indication, was not taken yesterday.

Come on, Sandy. It's just a little holding pattern we're in. Sandy? No no, I called you Candy. You know—as in candy cane. Jeez, Baby Cakes, why the fangs? Now listen, I'll see you in class in just a sec. Hey, by the way, you seen Weasel around this morning?

Weasel gunned his pick-up around. Even in reverse the fourwheel monstrosity rumbled like a Harley. The tires, huge black knobby things which made the body, in comparison, look like a Hot Wheels, spat caliche on his mama's fake deer. The sticker in the back window said it all—NO FEAR.

From pot-hole to pot-hole Weasel whipsawed his truck down the dirt road which connected his mama's trailer to 273, the farm road into town. When he hit the asphalted 273, he dug his Copenhagen out of the seat's crevice and really worked the pedal. A half a mile down the road he clipped by the sheriff doing 90, easy. The sheriff, one of Weasel's biggest fans, gave the sign: the panther claw.

At the caution lights, Weasel hung a squealing right. A block farther, past the high school, he came up on a pack of shirtless boys fakejogging in raggedy P.E. shorts. One boy, tottering far behind the others, frantically waved Weasel down.

"Coach Ford's been looking everywhere for you," the pale kid in metal braces panted into Weasel's cab.

Weasel killed the radio. "I don't give a rat's ass, Woody. You seen Wendy this morning?"

"Seen her first period. Weasel, if you miss more than half a day you can't play tonight. And if you don't play—dog, what are they gonna do, put me in?"

"I don't give a flip what they do. I'm hurtin', man."

"You sick?"

"Sick? Hell, nigger, I'm dead."

"What's wrong?"

"Wendy, she don't—she don't love me no more." Weasel's forehead fell sharply against his steering wheel; his biceps twitched.

"Come on, Weasel," said Woody, patting Weasel's spastic arm consolingly, "Wendy loves you. You know that. Heck, who don't love you?"

"Son, I'm telling you, something's changed. I don't mean nothing to her no more. I'm history, man."

"Weasel, come on now, that girl ain't never gonna leave you. Ya'll were matches made in heaven. 'Sides, who's she gonna leave you for—God?"

Coach Ford stepped into his room sucking on a fresh mint. He glanced around and called the roll—nearly. He called everyone's name but Buck Lejeune's, Weasel. That desk was empty. On the absentee slip he wrote *All Present* and handed the slip to the pimply office-helper.

"Today," he said, addressing the class, "we're gonna step back from the Emancipation Proclamation and look at the big picture. What is history?" He gave a quick hitch to his black polyesters.

The faces up and down the five rows of desks were blank. Except for one, a girl's, a girl in a black and gold cheerleader outfit sitting in the front of her aisle. Her face was an arrow; and she was aiming herself right between Coach Ford's eyes.

Breaking from the girl's deadly glare, Coach Ford stepped over to the chalkboard. On it he wrote, in big letters: HISTORY.

"What is it—History? Ever asked yourself that question, people?" He moved from the board to his portable lectern, leaned on it. "Change."

"Change," he repeated, energized by the sharp sweetness of his minty breath. "History is change. Hence, we, as students of history, must ourselves become open to, receptive of—heck, even thankful for change. That's right," he agreed vigorously with himself. "We must, each and every one of us, myself included, accept change, accept it maturely, like adults, and not—listen to me now, folks—and not, when things don't go exactly our way, cause a big scene—yes, Wendy?"

The cheerleader's eyes were water, her jutting chin a quaking dam. "Can we, can we"—suddenly the dam broke, and wailing, she threw herself across her desk.

"Where we goin'?" an excited Woody asked, searching for his seat belt.

"Where the lonely go," he hollered, nailing the accelerator and sending the joggers ahead leaping for the ditch. "Mudding."

At the old Texaco oil field, Weasel whipped the four-wheel Goliath across the cattle guard. "I told her, 'Fine, Wendy, but think it over and let me know either way by in the morning.'" He was onehanding the wheel, spying out mud holes across the ragged pasture like a hawk would mice.

"What'd she say?" asked Woody.

"Hell," said Weasel, "she didn't even call. Didn't even call my ass this morning. Is that cold, man, or what?"

"That's cold, man. Cold as a . . . as a . . ." Woody never excelled in English.

"Hell it ain't cold. It's freezing."

"Damn straight," agreed Woody, "that's freezing—freezing as a . . . as a . . . as a cube of ice in the freezer."

"Woody, tell me the truth."

"About what?"

"About my face—think it's too thin? Do I really look like a Weasel? Tell the truth."

"Naw, you don't look like—Yow!" bellowed Woody as his head struck the roof of the cab and a fat pancake of oil and mud slapped the glass.

"*Fuckin' A!*" yelped Weasel.

When Woody could talk again, he asked, timidly: "Weasel, would you ever go with a girl that was kind of—well, kind of a little on the healthy side?"

"What's that?" hollered Weasel over the screaming engine, his misery, for the moment, quenched.

"Would you ever go with a kind of a big girl?"

"Plug a fat chick?"

"Well—"

"Look, man, there's only one girl I want to go with as long as I live— Oh, God!" He slammed on the breaks and grabbed up a fist full of his own hair. "She didn't even call."

The coaches' office was nippy and smelled of feet. A butane heater hissed beside an iron desk.

"Well?" implored Coach Holbrook the second Coach Ford stepped through the door. "Was he in class?"

Coach Ford plopped down in a backless swivel chair and spun himself slowly, despairingly, around. "Nope."

"Try calling his house then," Holbrook, the head coach, instructed him. "The little fucker's gotta be somewhere."

Ford dug out the Student Directory and a pack of Red Man chewing tobacco from the desk in front of him. The tobacco was old, real old, but it was tobacco. He found Weasel's number, dialed it. At least a dozen times it rang as his shoetip tapped under the desk for the resident Folger's can; there would be a paper towel, stiff and bespattered, still in it. "No answer," he finally announced. "Where's the damn spit can?"

Holbrook was staring at O's and X's on a beat up chalkboard; he gestured helplessly to the ceiling. "Where's my damn running back?"

From the bathroom the line coach hollered—"We'll have to go with Harris at tailback!"

Holbrook grunted. "He ain't got the balls."

A toilet flushed. Coach Potter came out of the john.

"Shit Coach," complained Ford, fanning his cap, "burn a match or something—lord!"

"I'll tell you," muttered Potter, diddling with his fly and not paying Ford any mind, "that Harris kid really showed me something in the Old River game."

The phone rang. Hearts leapt. Coach Potter almost knocked Ford down grabbing for the receiver. "Yello. Who? What's that?" Squinting, the chubby line coach looked like a sharpei. "I sure will," he said. He hung up, chuckling. "Coach." He nodded to Ford.

"Yeah?"

"That was your old lady. She wanted me to tell you that sixteen might be sweet, but it ain't legal."

Neither Holbrook nor Potter knew whether to laugh or cry. They howled.

Weasel was three rungs up the ladder, barefoot, a thin slice of sandpaper angled out of his back pocket. His truck, what was still visible of it beneath the mud, was parked at the base of a water tower.

"What are you doing?" Woody kept asking. He was standing outside of the truck, calf deep in mud, holding himself up with the help of the passenger door.

"Got a little business to tend to," Weasel finally allowed.

"What kind of business?"

Weasel kept climbing. "She's yours, Woody."

"Who? Who's mine?" Woody was lost.

"The truck," called Weasel. "Treat her right. Quaker State. Nothing but. And you can have them boots too."

Woody considered the abandoned black Ropers on the pickup's hood. "I can't wear regular shoes, Weasel."

"Then give 'em to Coach Ford," Weasel hollered down. "About the only daddy I ever knew."

Coach Ford was starting to feel it. He stood up. "Anybody else for coffee?"

"You're a man after my own heart," said Coach Potter.

"Black?" Ford yawned.

"Like my women," Potter grinned.

"Shit, Coach," snapped Holbrook, "Rome's burning and you're making nigger jokes. Hey, Ford?"

Ford halted at the door. "Yeah?"

"*Just* coffee. You hear me? I need you tonight."

The nearest coffee was in the teachers' lounge. Up and down the Senior Hall, inspirational messages were painted in black and gold across long runs of meat-wrapping paper. *Claw the Bumble Bees. Bi-District Bound. Thanks for the Honey—Here's your Wings.* Mrs. Lumpke, FCA sponsor, remedial math teacher, and no spring chicken, spied Coach Ford coming down the hall and leaned out of her classroom to give him the claw, adding with relish, and three rolls of belly, her trademark growl.

Coach Ford double-clawed back, extending his paws in the direction of her Guinness-size breasts. He winked dirtily.

"Oh, Carl," Mrs. Lumpke chided.

The coffee was nasty. Coach Ford started a fresh batch, then collapsed in the room's sole comfortable seat, an old orange plaid springless couch that fat teachers like Mrs. Lumpke avoided for obvious reasons. What he needed, really needed, was in his car, under the seat, in a water bottle. But he was too tired, the couch too deep. He was out like a light. He awoke by a river in the valley of two green hills. His head was in a young woman's lap. She had been watching him sleep, shielding his face from the sun with her long black hair. She was smiling and gently stroking his forehead. He tried to speak, he had so much to say, so much to catch up on, but the words were hard, his mouth not obliging. She understood. She was wearing his letter jacket with all his patches. And his ring. She had not changed. He wondered if he had, and sat up to find out. He looked in the river.

"Carl?"

Coach Ford started.

"You're not sick are you, Carl?" It was Mrs. Lumpke.

"Oh no, I'm fine," he grinned it off. "Coffee ready?"

"I don't know, but that little crippled boy, Woody Martin, is out in the hall. He says he needs to talk to you. He looks a mess. It's life or death, he says. He doesn't have a hall pass. What should I tell him?"

Gasping, Woody managed: "W-Weasel's on the water tower, Coach. I drove his truck." The boy was all mud and eyes.

"Do the other coaches know?" asked Ford.

"No, I just got to school and I seen you going in the lounge." Any less air or any more nerves and the poor kid would have been out. "He's gonna jump."

"Jump? My God, son, what for?"

"He says Wendy's gone sour on him. He told me life ain't worth living. I drove it all by myself, Coach Ford."

"You talking about the tower in the old Texaco field?" asked Ford, on the move.

"Y-Yes sir."

Inside the fieldhouse, Ford hopped a bench and side-stepped a 45-pound free-weight. "Found him!" he yelled.

The coaches' office flew open and two capped heads appeared.

"He's on the water tower. Says he's gonna jump. Throw me my keys!"

A cap disappeared. Coach Holbrook said, "He's where?" and as Coach Ford explained all he knew, the head coach went visibly pale. "He's going to kill himself before the district championship? What kind of commitment is that? Good God, I'm snake bit."

Coach Potter tossed Coach Ford his keys. "And take this," he added. He was holding in his pudgy hand a little green Bible, pocketsize, the New Testament with Psalms. He had been using it to keep his desk from rocking.

Ford caught it.

"Never know," observed Potter.

"10-4," said Ford. "Thank you, Jesus."

Like a box of rocks Coach Ford's Mustang rattled over the oil field cattleguard. At the rear of the weedy cemetery of corrugated toolsheds and rusty pumps and derricks, he found Weasel a good two hundred feet up in the sky where Woody said he would be. The boy was scrubbing away, it appeared, at the water tank's bulbous belly.

Coach Ford pulled up beside a pair of colossal ruts; his nerves were on edge. Time out. He needed one, bad. He reached under the seat for his water bottle. What a day. What a last twenty-three years. He rested the plastic straw attached to the clear bottle on his tongue. It was not water in the water bottle. The first suck deserved another. And another. A gurgle, then air, and that was it. Time back in.

With something less than enthusiasm, he got out of his car and snaked his way around the puddles to the tank's iron ladder, investing what athletic ability he had left in keeping his new Nikes new. At the base of the tank he looked up and saw a track of thin stitches running up the fat leg of a mighty tall woman. The iron stitches ended at the dirty pads of two white socks, way the hell up there.

Coach Ford yelled: "Me and you, big man. Come on down."

Weasel did not reply. He seemed intent on eliminating one of many messages decorating the tower. Ford could make out several: *I love Kelly: Srs. '85: Fuck You.*

"Weasel, buddy," Coach Ford tried again, this time clapping sharply, "Huddle up."

Weasel didn't so much as flinch. The message he seemed intent on wiping out now read: WEASEL LOVES WEN. Ford could guess what the two other letters had been.

Annoyed, he hollered: "Weasel, son, what in the hell are you doing?"

This time Weasel replied. "Ain't doing nothin', Coach. I'm undoin'."

"Undoing? Undoing what?"

"A lie!" Weasel yelled down, steady scrubbing.

"Then are you coming down?" hollered Coach Ford.

"Oh yeah. I'm comin' down all right."

That didn't sound too good to Ford. He tried the ladder; it shook from side to side—more like a vine than something a man, particularly a man so well watered, should climb.

"Weasel?"

Coach Ford had his hand out. The N had gone the way of the D and the Y. WEASEL LOVES WE read the tank. The sandpaper in Weasel's hand was a tissue.

Having secured, with assistance, a seat on the metal grate, Coach Ford braved a peek between his legs. "Mutha Fudger, Weasel," he panted, "we're in heaven."

"Naw, Coach," replied the boy, resuming his work. "We're in hell."

The noon sun had begun to bake the tank. A dead something or another not far away had attracted buzzards. On the far side of a distant line of dead and dying pines, the unfortunate sounds of the marching band, warming up, could be heard.

Coach Ford looked on as Weasel, with virtually nothing but the skin of his hand, scrubbed away at the E. Blood was involved.

"You're lovesick ain't you, son?"

Weasel offered no response, pressed on with his undoing.

"There ain't no worse pain. No worse pain on God's green earth than the one you're feeling now."

Weasel quit scrubbing. Coach Ford had his ear. He could work with that.

"But you know, son, I've always said—what doesn't destroy me makes me stronger. Hard to believe, I know. Hard to believe that right this very second, right now, even as I speak and as you feel the blades cutting away at your soul, that a champion, a *real* champion, is being born. That's right. What you're feeling—them are birth pangs, son. Sure are. And I'll tell you this: the Weasel that came up this tower ain't gonna be the same Weasel that goes down it. The Weasel that's gonna be going down is gonna know something that the Weasel that came up never dreamed of. Know what that something will be?"

The boy's head shook No. Tears weren't far from his eyes.

"He's gonna know what he's made of. Know what you're made of, Weasel?"

He bit his bottom lip.

"You're made of gold, son."

A tear appeared on the boy's cheek.

"The gold of a district champion. The gold of a good man who knows what it takes to win. The gold," said Ford, his voice mounting to a triumphant conclusion, "of a *golden* Golden Panther."

Weasel looked up, his face red, eyes bleary. He dipped his cheek into his shoulder, wiped away an errant tear. "Coach." He took a deep breath.

"Yeah?" smiled Coach Ford encouragingly.

"Save that crap for somebody who cares, would you? This ain't fourth and long here. This is my life." And he wept, like a baby.

Woody had angled himself in the hall strategically. Miss Tompkins at the chalkboard on the other side of the closed door couldn't see him, but Wendy, if she would just look up, could.

The metal on his leg proved handy. He tapped it against the door, but unfortunately the kick was a bit hard. Other heads, not Wendy's, turned; then there were footsteps. He hobbled to the wall on the hinge side of the door and closed his eyes. As the opening door swung his way, it caught, miraculously, against the unshut locker on Woody's other side, pinning Woody between it and the cold tile of the hall wall. Miss Tompkin's straw hair would have been in his mouth if the little rectangular window in the door had not been between him and her. This was a risky game Woody was playing. He loved it. At last, he was on the team.

After a lengthy gander didn't turn up anything, Miss Tompkins retreated. Woody pivoted back to his spot. Wendy's head had not moved, and it did not appear to Woody that it was going to any time soon. But the clock was ticking, the team down. "Okay son," Woody said to Woody, "let's see what you got. It's all or nothing. Air it out."

Woody took a deep breath, knocked, stepped in the room. "Excuse me, Miss Tompkins, may I have a word with Wendy Rayburn?"

Miss Tompkins, obviously irritated by now two interruptions, just glared. Then snapped: "You certainly may not have a word with Wendy Rayburn. Where are you supposed to be this period, young man? Does it look like we're having recess in here?"

Here it was, everything the team had worked for, talked about, dreamed on—the district championship. And coming down to one play. With a textbook joke, Woody replied spiritedly: "Miss Tompkins, I'm sorry, ma'am, but there has been a death in our immediate family and I must speak with my cousin right away,"

Miss Tompkins fumbled for a reply. Woody smelled goal line, lowered his head. "There's really nothing recessy about a heart attack, Miss Tompkins, and I'm sorry if you think there is."

But Miss Tompkins hadn't won the VFW Teacher of the Year Award 17 years for nothing: she knew when her donkey was being dusted.

"On your mother's or father's side?"

"Ma'am?" said Woody.

"On your mother's or father's side? And is the relation, pray tell, first, second, third—or is it, young man, entirely mythological? Do be specific with your genealogy."

"Well . . ." stuttered Woody. And this is how it always went for him. There a cripple, here a cripple.

"As I suspected," soliloquized Miss Tompkins moving briskly to her desk and removing from its middle drawer a red pen and yellow pad. "Take this to Mr. Sharp," she said scrawling, "and bring me back a like slip in kind."

Woody limped forward before the class, the season and the championship shot. Then, he almost soiled himself as a fog horn-like scream shattered the room. Lita, who Woody had not even noticed was in the class, was out of her desk and pounding toward the window. "The cafeteria!" she screamed, "it's burning. It's burning. People are on fire!"

Miss Tompkins clutched her hair and scampered to the window.

Lita stepped aside for Miss Tompkins, then fell in behind her, gently pinning the brittle woman snugly against a shelf of dictionaries. From behind her well-padded back, Lita waved Woody and Wendy out of the room. An angel block.

In the hall, Woody set Wendy straight on Weasel's whereabouts and his proclaimed intentions. She took it hard. "Come with me, Woody," she implored.

"Woody Martin! Wendy Rayburn!" a teacher's voice lit up the hallway. "What in heaven's name is the matter?" Mrs. Lumpke was on the move. "Was that a gunshot I heard?"

"I'm getting my car, Woody," said Wendy hysterically, "meet me on the street."

To leave the building Wendy and Woody had to pass the office. As they did, the principal's door opened. A woman stepped out, all but colliding with Wendy. "Excuse me," said the woman, who looked to Woody as if she had been, and maybe still was, crying. The woman, only now glancing up in earnest, seemed stunned when her eyes lit upon Wendy. "Sandy?" She covered her mouth. She stepped back, dropped her stare to the gold-stitched name which was fancily spiraled across Wendy's formidable chest. "My God, you even look like she did." The woman, more shaken than before, turned and fled the building.

Weasel was done. You'd have thought he had just removed his fingers from a grinder. WEASEL LOVES. That's all the paint said.

Coach Ford had not moved from his seat on the tower's perforated metal skirt. He was looking up at Weasel who, exhausted and dispirited, was leaning his head against the tank's fire-hot belly. He wanted to say something, make the boy's hurt go away, but for the first time in God only knew how long, Coach Ford was digging for a song and coming up with sand. Now and again he would glance up and offer an expression of sympathy. That was all he had to offer. Resurrecting the dead was not, damn it, a play in his book.

"Coach?"

It was the first thing said in some time. Coach Ford had been trying to spy out what all the buzzards were circling. He didn't know what Weasel had been doing, but the undoing, as far as he could hear, was finished.

"You've been drinking, ain't you?"

"No, why you say that?"

"It's gotten worse, Coach. I mean the whole team knows. Willy Taylor said his daddy sees you at the Pine Tree Lodge in Stonebriar twice a week."

"Old man Taylor is full of—"

"Coach, tell me—"

"Weasel, I like to shoot pool. That's—"

"Not about that. About my name. Why'd you give me that name, Weasel? Tell me the truth. It's my face ain't it?"

"No," laughed Ford, relieved to change the subject, "because you play like a weasel. Ever seen a weasel?"

"Don't think so."

"You'd know if you did. Little brown ribbon looking things. Fearless. Absolutely fearless. They'd tree a pit bull."

Flattered, Weasel almost smiled. "You ever seen one?"

"Oh yeah. Seen one in old man Coon's hand. Bit the old man in the palm and wouldn't let go. Me and a girl named Sandy were on the swing and here they come around the barn. Hard to say who had who. 'Sandy,' he hollered—the old bastard was too proud to talk to me or even to let on he was hurting—'quit your slobberin' and bring me that goddamn bucket of water.'

161

"I jumped up, ran the bucket over—and man, that weasel was sunk into that old fart like a steel trap. Talk about putting your game face on. Son. That skinny little sucker came to play. No, it's a fine thing to be called a weasel."

After a rather healthy pause, Coach Ford remarked, half to himself, half to Weasel: "That's what she called me too."

"Who, Coach?"

"Sandy. Sandy Coon. My very first girlfriend. The one on the swing. Said I was the only boy her daddy couldn't scare off. Said me and that weasel had the same kind of head. Hard."

"Did you love her?"

Coach Ford hesitated, then nodded. "That's a fair thing to say."

"What happened?" asked Weasel, noticeably interested.

Coach Ford tapped his knuckles to his head. "Like she said—hard."

"Miss her?"

"Who Sandy?"

"Yeah. Sandy Coon. The girl on the swing?"

"Aw hell, son, that's"—Coach Ford pulled off his cap and wiped his bald forehead on the sleeve of his shirt—"history."

"Whatever come of ya'll?"

Coach Ford eased himself into a slant of shade. "You ain't hot?"

"I'm all right," said Weasel. "Whatever happened to you and Sandy?"

"Son, that was a long time ago. Whatd'ya say we run up to the Gook Store and get us something cold to wet our lips? A Mountain Dew or something?"

What little relief Weasel seemed to be experiencing disappeared at once. He hadn't forgotten why he came. "You down one of those somethings for the both of us," he said. Then he stepped out to the one cable of rail that circled the tower's platform and turned his attention to the ground.

"Whatcha looking at, Champ?" Coach Ford asked, as coolly as he was able.

Weasel said: "What about the weasel? What happened to him?"

"Well . . ." Coach Ford was moving ever so calmly in Weasel's direction.

"That water wake him up? What'd that weasel do, Coach?"

"Let me ask you," said Coach Ford, almost within arm's reach now of Weasel, "what would you do? Say you're a weasel"—not wanting to spook the boy, Coach Ford was cutting the last yard between them by the inch—"and you got your teeth deep into a hand, and then that hand dips you into water—what would you do?"

"Depends," muttered Weasel, his eyes as fixed on the ground as ever.

"On what?" asked Coach Ford.

"On how much I hated the water," mumbled Weasel.

"Or loved the hand," Coach Ford replied, not intending to.

"Or," returned Weasel, "*hated* the hand."

"Or," said Coach Ford, "loved the water."

Weasel turned suddenly, faced his coach. "What would you do if you were that weasel?"

This time it was Ford who looked away—not down but out, out there, beyond the buzzards, somewhere. He didn't answer right away. "I suppose," he said when at last he did respond, "that I'd do just what that weasel did."

Weasel's hand dropped from the rail. He and Coach Ford were face to face. "What'd that weasel do, Coach?"

Coach Ford took Weasel gently by the shoulder. He could smell his own breath. "Drown," he said.

Ford and Weasel made it to the ground about the time Wendy and Woody pulled up. Had the embrace that followed been any more feverish, Weasel's t-shirt and Wendy's cheerleader top might have burned away between them. Somewhere a dog was fussing at something, but otherwise the only sounds in the oil patch, save the hugging and cooing, came from the rustling limbs of a nearby chinaberry tree.

Wendy took Weasel's face into her hands. She looked deeply into his eyes, then nuzzled against his bristly chin like a baby cat. "My Weasel," she said. Then she said it again. There were tears, in her eyes, on her cheeks, in her mouth. "My Weasel. My Weasel. My Weasel."

Coach Ford was losing his hair, not his memory. The tiniest thing, a word, a gesture, the scent of the wind—that was all it took.

They were standing by the little hump of dirt, far back in her daddy's pasture. He had the shovel, Sandy had him. The funeral was over, the weasel history. He said, "I ain't never seen nothing that brave." And she said, "My daddy really don't hate you as much as you think." And he said, "That's the kind of ball I'm gonna play." And she said, "He even said I might can go with Mama on the bus to see one of your games some time." And he said, "Carl Ford's gonna teach that state a trick." And she said, "They say Texas girls'll come on to a guy pretty as you please." And he said, "Better not come on to me." And she said, "My Weasel. My Weasel. My Weasel." And he said, "Bravest thing I ever seen." And she said, "Carl, you ain't never gonna forget about me, are you?" And he said, "Never."

POLLY SUNSHINE

JILL PATTERSON

Nadine Trellis had a soft spot for hitchhikers. She admired their nerve, the way they risked their lives, standing on the side of the road, their thumb out, because they knew about the lure of the open highway. Nadine understood that attraction. Many times she herself felt the urge to drive off, leaving everything behind, speeding a little, watching the pine trees rush by, listening to KKRR. She was a grown woman despite the town gossip, and she refused to be Troop's Polly Sunshine any longer—had never, in fact, liked that reputation. Why, the whole town constantly reminded her she was even dependent on others to drive her where she needed to go because she'd never owned a car. Never mind this dependence made her a hitchhiker of a sort. No one noticed that.

But, to be honest, no matter how much she regretted her past, hitchhiking just wasn't her cup of tea: she could never bring herself to take a ride from a total stranger. So finally she paid her boss $400 for his old green Subaru and made a solemn promise to work on her image in other ways. She began by closing the five-and-dime early, walking out the door around 4:45, jingling her new car keys and singing little tunes to herself. Then, just one week after buying that green Subaru, she got her own place, the little yellow house on Cherry Street, and started watching late movies on T.V. She even moved the set into the bedroom (although her boyfriend—her ex-boyfriend—Ronnie told her that was a stupid place to put it) and turned out all the lights (although her mother warned her she could get radiation from watching T.V. in the dark). That black and white screen flickered against her bedroom walls 'til the sun came up. Of course, Nadine fell asleep shortly after midnight every evening. But it was, after all, the point of the matter.

And that's exactly what she told Ronnie when she drove out to his house to say good-bye to him—forever. He could laugh all he wanted. She liked late movies, she could put her T.V. set anywhere she wanted, and she didn't care if he thought her new Subaru was a trash heap: she did not ever want to see him again. Afterwards, she got in her Subaru and drove all the way to Fort Worth and spent Friday night in a Motel 6 just to let everyone in her family and Ronnie know she was a woman now. She never told anyone she checked under the bed and in the shower five times for strange men before she could finally go to sleep. She'd gotten over her fear of strange men by the time she got back to Troop.

It was in Fort Worth that Nadine met her first hitchhiker. He walked right up to her, after she'd checked out of her motel room, when she was walking out the double glass doors at straight up noon. He was wearing a three-piece suit, but his hair was a little flyaway.

"Where am I?" he asked her.

"Motel 6?" She said it like a question because she figured he could read that big sign in front for himself.

He shook his head. "What city?"

She still wasn't sure what answer he was hunting. "Fort Worth?"

"Texas?" His eyes opened wide.

That made Nadine a little leery, almost angry. "Murder, yes, Texas. Where else would Fort Worth be?"

"Listen, lady." He ignored her frustration. "Could you give me a lift? I need a lift."

Nadine looked at him. She thought about that open road and her reputation and decided it was time to take drastic measures. "Sure," she said. "No problem."

"Thank you." He exaggerated those words, even grabbed her arm and shook it a little. "I thank you. I got to get to AA. Last thing I remember I was playing cards up in Arkansas. And drinking." He pressed his thumb and fingers to his forehead. "God knows I was drinking. Hard."

Nadine went back inside and asked for directions to the nearest AA. The desk clerk told her she shouldn't be giving rides to strangers, but she didn't listen to him none. She remembered her vow to change her image and thought this was an excellent opportunity. It didn't matter Nadine's first hitchhiker slept in the car all the way to AA or that, when he got out of the car, he gave her a five dollar bill and said, "God bless." Her hands shook nonetheless.

And when Ronnie lectured Nadine about hitchhikers the following Sunday morning at church, she told him that five dollars just went to show you God was on her side and she had done the right thing. She thought of that excuse long before church started because she knew Ronnie would give her a going-over. She only told Ronnie in the first place because she wanted him to know just how much she'd changed. She wasn't afraid of hitchhikers. She could be a dark and desirable woman if she wanted.

But she didn't tell him how her hands shook, and she couldn't explain that feeling she got after she left her first hitchhiker and headed back to Troop, speeding a little, listening to the radio, trying to sing past that lump in her throat before the tears came. That hitchhiker had been a perfect gentleman. There'd been no reason to be afraid.

True enough, Nadine herself would have never hitched a ride with a stranger. That wasn't her cup of tea. And, honestly, she would have never even had the courage to pick up one if it hadn't been for *The Long Hot Summer*, the remake with Don Johnson. It was the feature film on cable T.V. that Friday night in her single room at the Motel 6, and it was a good movie for her to watch right when she was making all those changes in her life. She needed a little fire, and she'd always wanted Ronnie to sing her name like in the movie when Ben Quick sang Noel's name from her balcony while she lay in her big four-poster bed. "Nadine. Oh Na-dine." Just like that, with two pitches on the last syllable. Ronnie only called her Polly Sunshine and she hated that name. She could be a dark and desirable woman.

Of course, she hadn't had a single date since she'd said good-bye to Ronnie four weeks ago. But he still drove by her house every Friday night to see if she was there, and she'd learned to park her car down the street and keep all the lights turned off so he'd think she was out. Furthermore, she told herself every morning when she stepped out her front door to face

167

a new day at the five-and-dime that today might be the very day when her Mr. Right would walk into the store and ask for a pack of Camel cigarettes or a quart of Quaker State Motor Oil. And that's why she decided never to drive past another hitchhiker again. She never knew but one of those men might be her Ben Quick, and she would hate to keep driving on by, leaving him stranded in the middle of nowhere.

She hadn't deserted one hitchhiker since that alcoholic in Fort Worth, and it'd been four whole weeks. But when she saw that high school kid with his fishing pole right outside of Troop on Monday morning, she was tempted to drive past him. She was tired and in a hurry, on her way to see her mother in the Jackson Hospital. Then that nagging little spot on her right eyelid started twitching, and that was her conscience reminding her about her promises. So she did pull over, but by then she'd already gone too far and had to back up a little. The dust swirled around her car, driving so much on the shoulder, stirring it up like she did.

The boy she stopped for had a bandanna wrapped around his head like a gypsy and dark brown hair that hung out of it past his shoulders. Nadine knew the boys who lived on the Troop Loop often wore their hair like that, and she thought she recognized this one. The Loop wasn't a very encouraging neighborhood for a boy who looked so awfully young. She could tell by the way he dropped his cigarette and then snubbed it out with his boot he was used to a lot of things. He opened the front door of Nadine's car on the passenger side and kind of stooped over to look in. He didn't say a word. And that was odd because Nadine had learned that hitchhikers in Troop normally told her where they were going after they were already in the car, when it was too late to tell them she wasn't going that far. But this boy just stood there, holding his fishing pole, peering in at Nadine.

"Where you going?" she finally offered. She really wasn't in any mood for hitchhikers.

"I'm rolling class," he answered, confessing straight up.

"I could tell that. Being Monday morning and all." Nadine smiled. From the shape of his lips, Nadine thought he must be a good kisser. She liked his hands, too. She was a hand and lip woman, and she decided maybe she ought to be a little more friendly. "Where you going?" she repeated.

"Just a ways or so. About fifteen miles. There's a fish pond." He nodded his head up the road and tugged on the bandanna knot at the back of his head. "About fifteen miles. Good catfish."

"Get in. Heading toward Jackson myself."

He opened the back door, slipped his pole gently inside, closed the door, and sat down in the front. He slumped in the seat, almost sitting on his lower back instead of his rear, and placed one hand on his knee and the other halfway into a front pocket. His jeans had holes in the knees, and he looked like a rock singer Nadine had seen on the cover of a magazine at the five-and-dime. He told her his name was Jim, and then she remembered he had been a freshman her senior year at Troop High. Nadine quickly added it up. She was twenty now, so he must be seventeen.

"I remember you." Nadine smiled and nibbled the skin around her right thumb nail.

"Yeah. I remember you, too. You dated that Ronnie guy." He looked out the window when he said that, like it didn't matter much to him whom she dated. Nadine thought maybe she should tell him she didn't go with Ronnie any more, but she wasn't sure how that would sound.

Ronnie's lips were too thin, and his hands were pudgy. Not that it mattered. He didn't believe he should kiss Nadine in certain ways. She was his Polly Sunshine, and a man ought to keep Polly Sunshines 'til they were ready to marry. It wasn't proper to act otherwise. Her mother had agreed. A man would go as far as you let him, she had told Nadine, and a good woman always said *Stop!* Otherwise, an angel from the Lord might dive straight from heaven and snatch her bald-headed. That's what her mother had told her when she turned thirteen.

As a result, Nadine was known at Troop High as the kind of girl a guy wanted to marry—not date. A clean woman. Nadine guessed any day her front porch would be crowded with all those boys who'd never asked her out but now wanted to get married. Murder, she thought. She could be a dark and desirable woman. She wanted a real kiss. She wanted to feel it in her thighs like she'd heard about in a rated R movie once.

"I'm not going with Ronnie. Now," she said, but it sounded as dumb as she thought it would.

"That's too bad." She could tell he was looking at her, so she bit her bottom lip just a little. He pulled his bandanna off and tied it around his wrist. "Mind if I smoke?" he asked.

She shook her head. He pulled out a pack of Camel cigarettes.

"You smoke?"

"Sometimes," she lied. "But not right now."

He smiled and looked out the window. Nadine thought she should say something, like maybe he should stop by the five and dime sometime. "I'm going to the hospital," she said instead.

He nodded. "That's too bad."

"I'm going to see my mother at Jackson Hospital," she added. "She has kidney stones."

"That's too bad," he said again. "You can let me out right there. By that first fence post."

"Sure." She didn't know what else to say, but right before he shut the back door, she said, "Have fun." He closed the door before she could finish the sentence though, and he opened it back up.

"What?" he asked.

"Nothing. Just have fun. That's all."

"Shouldn't pick up hitchhikers. It's not safe." He closed the door.

Nadine didn't cry this time. Her right leg bounced up and down a little, nervous, pressing on the gas, but she didn't cry. She wasn't afraid. Maybe she'd see Jim again.

Her mother told her there was plenty to be afraid of if she was picking up hitchhikers, and she probably ought to refrain from doing so. People might start to think she'd become a floozy.

"Nadine Trellis," she said, "You'd better watch yourself. You're going to go too far. I swear. I didn't raise no daughter of mine just so she could go straight to hell in a hand basket."

When Nadine finally arrived at the hospital, she'd found her mother sitting in a stiff white bed watching *The Guiding Light* on T.V. The sun was shining through the window, putting a glare on the screen, so Nadine could barely see the picture. She turned and looked out the window instead, pretending if she looked hard enough, she might see Jim, 30 miles away, fishing.

It had obviously been a mistake to tell her mother about *The Long Hot Summer*, Ben Quick, and Jim. Her mother liked Ronnie, mostly because he objected to Nadine's new image as much as she did. In fact, her mother sounded just like Ronnie had when Nadine told him she was going to rent her little yellow house. He laughed at first and said he didn't see how she was going to sleep in a house all by herself when she couldn't even go to the bathroom alone at the picture shows. Nadine didn't answer, and then Ronnie got mad.

"What the hell you want a place of your own for? Nadine. Miss Polly Sunshine." He nodded his head from shoulder to shoulder and did a little dance with his behind, making fun of her. "Ooo-ee. Don't Miss Polly think she's getting maturelike."

That was the afternoon Ronnie was sighting in his new rifle, and he had stood five tin cans and one glass bottle on a wooden cattle guard despite the fact Nadine hated guns and asked Ronnie to take her home if he was going to shoot his off.

"I'll take you home when I'm damn good and ready. Miss Polly Sunshine."

Nadine wanted to tell her mother what Ronnie had said, that he said *hell* and *damn* almost in the same breath. Why, he could have aimed that rifle at her. After all, he'd stood behind her the whole time, and she could just imagine that barrel pointed at her back. She'd drawn her hands up to her chest and tightened her fingers around one another. Her legs shook under her weight. She anticipated that shot.

When she finally turned around, Ronnie was standing beside his truck, the door open. "What you waiting for?" he asked. "I thought Miss Polly wanted to go home? If you afraid of a little ole rifle, you better reconsider that yellow house. Might be biting off more than you can swallow. You better watch yourself, girl. Miss Polly."

And that's exactly what her mother was saying when Nadine spotted her next hitchhiker through the hospital window. That little man with the neck brace was still sitting beneath the tree by the main entrance of the hospital. Just like he was when she'd got there an hour ago.

"You better watch yourself, Nadine," her mother said.

171

"Mister." Nadine tapped the little man on the shoulder, and he had to shift his whole upper body to look at her because of that neck brace. "You need a ride, Mister?"

"Crawford. My name's Crawford. And I called a cab." He drew up his top lip after he finished that last sentence, like he was showing Nadine his fangs.

"You been sitting here over an hour, Mister. Are you sure? Maybe that cab's not coming."

"Crawford. My name's Crawford." He shifted again and stared back out at the main road. Nadine knew by the way she could hear him inhale that he'd been a heavy smoker for years. "Think my cab's not coming, do you?" He nodded and breathed. "I see."

"You got any family? Crawford?"

"Mary Gail. My wife, Mary Gail." He smiled. "Maybe you could take me home. Mary Gail will be so surprised. I'm let out earlier than expected."

"No problem. That's my green Subaru parked right over there." She pointed. "Where you going?"

"I'll show you." He picked up the little bag sitting beside him on the bench. It looked like a lady's clutch purse.

Nadine unlocked the passenger door for Crawford, but he tapped his long fingernails lightly on the window of the back door. "You want to sit in the back?" she asked, a little surprised. He nodded and winked at her.

She drove about ten minutes out of Jackson, toward Troop, and was starting to wonder exactly where Crawford wanted to go when he finally told her to turn down a thin dirt road just before Whitehorse. He leaned forward over the front seat, lay his arm on her shoulder, and pointed one of his skinny fingers toward the road he meant her to take. Nadine wondered how long it had been since he trimmed his nails or, at least, cleaned the dirt from underneath them, and when Crawford pulled his arm back, he ran those dirty nails through her hair.

Her shoulders felt a little tense, and she tried to shake out the muscles, rolled her head from side to side. She looked in the rearview mirror and noticed Crawford was mimicking her, rolling his head from side to side too, only in exaggerated movements as if he were slinging his head rather than trying to relax himself. Nadine turned on the radio. "You like music, mister?" she asked.

"KKRR. Double-K, Double-R for the best Rock and Roll in East Texas," Crawford recited proudly. Peering out the window, he studied the thick forest of pine trees. He rolled his head in big, complete circles now and mumbled over and over, "KKRR. Double-K, Double R."

Nadine stared straight ahead, gripped the wheel tighter, and tried to control her anxiety. She could feel the muscles in her thighs weaken and start to shiver a little. There was nothing in sight except the tall pines and the thick fog of dust her car stirred up. Then Crawford giggled, mechanically, like someone pulled his string and laughter was the forced response, like he was simply a talking doll.

Nadine smiled. "What you laughing at, Crawford?"

He giggled again. Then he raised his shoulders and clapped his hands together. "They don't know I'm gone," he squealed.

"What do you mean?" Nadine continued to stare straight ahead, afraid if she turned around she'd find out why Crawford was partial to the back seat.

"I mean exactly what I say. They don't know." He breathed between each word: they—don't—know. She heard the scratchy smoke in his voice. "From the hospital. They don't know I'm gone."

Nadine's hands trembled. It wasn't safe to pick up hitchhikers.

"I's going to surprise Mary Gail. Thinks she can keep me in that stinking hospital. I tell you. I's going to catch her. Her and that young cowboy fella of hers. I'll shoot them both deader than a damn doornail—" He giggled again and then repeated himself, this time singing, proudlike, giving two syllables to the last word. "They don't know I'm gone."

Nadine made herself look in the rearview mirror now. Crawford opened his small bag and dug frantically in the bottom. Not lifting his head but simply raising his eyes, he glared up at her. His eyebrows jerked down with anger. "Watch the road," he hissed. "And pull over under that mimosa tree. I'm going to surprise them. For certain."

Nadine pulled under the tree and put the car in park. The motor moaned quietly, and Nadine closed her eyes. She could hear Ronnie. *Nadine. Polly Sunshine. Desirable women better watch themselves.* The nerves fluttered all the way down into her thighs as Crawford continued to rustle through his bag. Then he stopped and giggled again. "This is for you." He breathed right into Nadine's ear, his lips brushing her ear lobe. "Take this, missy." She drew her hands to her chest, prepared herself, then cocked her head slightly toward Crawford, wanting and not wanting to see what he offered.

"For your trouble," Crawford said, and he dropped the one dollar bill in her lap because her hands were still wrapped in tight little fists. He opened the door and walked off down the road, turning once to raise his hand to his shoulder and wave it just slightly.

Nadine laughed out loud. She laid her head on the steering wheel and laughed out loud. She could hardly wait to tell Ronnie about Crawford. It was only Monday though, and unless she stopped by his place, she'd have to wait six more days until Sunday to tell him. She wasn't afraid of hitch-hikers—not alcoholics, not Jim, and not Crawford. She could be a dark and desirable woman. She could seduce young cowboys like Mary Gail, and someday soon, men would sing her name. "Nadine. Oh, Na-dine," she sang softly.

But Nadine couldn't explain why she laughed so hard she started crying, why her body shook with every sob as she lay her head on that steering wheel, still parked on that thin dirt road. And when she picked up Jim again on the way back in to Troop, she didn't say much. She didn't want him to hear the hiccups left over from her crying.

CHIPPING AWAY AT BASEBALL

JERRY CRAVEN

Jeremy Ryan tossed the whiffle ball. Just as he started to swing the bat, he saw his mother steer the blue Buick into the driveway. He missed the ball. "Ryan misses," he announced. "José Guzman is throwing heat that anyone can miss. But this time it might be that Ryan was distracted by the blue cup of ice tossed by a fan onto the field." Jeremy bent to get the whiffle ball. He gestured toward the Buick with his middle finger. "Ryan points at the blue cup. He's saying something to the umpire. I believe he's complaining about the unfairness of the distraction."

Jeremy kept up the running commentary while his mother got out of the car. He knew she would spend about five minutes fussing at him over nothing before going into the house and putting Vivaldi on so loud it would run Dad out of the house. She would sing along with it. Loud. "Dee tweet dee dee dee da dee dee." She called it singing, anyway. He tossed the ball again.

"Jeremy Taylor Ryan, you hush that up." Sabrina stood beside the Buick, arms akimbo.

Jeremy let the ball hit the ground without swinging at it. "Ball two. The fans jeer. The loudest boos seem to be coming from the general area from which a fan threw the cup of ice. Will Ryan pull it out for the Rangers? It seems unlikely. The Cubs are up by one. Top of the fifth in the seventh game of the World Series. A runner on third, and Nolan Ryan at bat with one away. This is Harry Caray calling the action, live, for sports fans across America."

"You're obsessed with baseball, Jeremy. You hear me? Obsessed. You know I can't stand a member of my family to be obsessed with anything. It isn't healthy, not for a ten-year-old. Not for anybody. Hush up or I'll take that ball and bat and put it where I put those stupid cards." She took a bag of groceries from the car.

Jeremy picked up the ball and threw it into the air. "A curve ball. It breaks fast but not enough to catch the corner of the plate. Ball three. Ryan steps back, knocks the bat on his shoe, picks up dirt and rubs it on his hands. The count is three and one."

"That's a nasty habit, Jeremy, rubbing dirt on your hands like that. You'll get ringworm from the dirt, do you hear me? Ringworm. Jeremy, would you hush and listen to me? I'm cooking some spaghetti tonight. You know what that means for your stupid whiffle ball, don't you?"

Jeremy knew. He tossed the ball and swung, tipping it off to his left. "Ryan swings and fouls toward third base. The ball bounces into the stands. A woman grabs it and stuffs it into a bag of groceries. The count is three and two." As he retrieved the ball, he kept talking in his best radio voice. He glanced toward the house and saw Mom standing on the porch, one hand on the doorknob, glaring at him. She fixed her eyes on him like an owl he had seen on *Nature* watching a mouse it planned to have for dinner.

Jeremy remembered how Dad used to play catch with him in the back yard, used to talk baseball with him. "Ryan is the greatest name in baseball," Dad said once. "And that's your name and my name. Ryan." Dad even took him to Dallas once to watch Nolan Ryan pitch, and Dad had joked about the greatest name in baseball being a distant cousin of theirs, though Jeremy knew better. Used to be, back when Dad played catch, he would buy Jeremy baseball cards.

An image of his baseball cards came to him, cards he had collected and traded for and memorized, cards he treasured. They lay in the bottom of the Dumpster, awash in spaghetti sauce. Roaches nibbled at the edges of them, and someone had raked older garbage across the cards, along with some crawly things. Maggots, maybe. As soon as he thought the word *maggots*, Jeremy gagged and slammed the lid to the Dumpster.

Mom had turned down the volume of the stereo when he came in from school so she could tell him that she had thrown his baseball card collection into the trash. Jeremy didn't believe her, not until he checked in his room and found them gone. He headed out back for the Dumpster. On the way he stopped in the doorway to the kitchen to announce, "I'll get them back." His mother said nothing. She stood with her arms crossed, looking over her nose at him, smug and righteous. He thought he saw a look of triumph on her face. Mom the camel, he thought—her lips, clamped and puckery, looked like they weighed two pounds. They struck Jeremy as twitchy, rubbery lips, ready to draw back and spit in his eye. He had seen a movie in which a camel had spat on a shepherd boy. The boy's offense? Playing too near the mouth of the camel.

When he got to the Dumpster and saw the way his mother had ruined the cards, he understood the look of triumph. She must have been watching, he decided, because *The Four Seasons* got loud again just as he closed the Dumpster lid, and he heard her singing along.

Back in the house, he tried not to look at Mom. "I did it for your own good," she told him, yelling above the music. "Because you were becoming obsessed with those stupid cards. Obsessed. And no kid of mine is going to become obsessed with anything. You hear me, Jeremy? Do you hear me?" He had pretended that he did not.

Jeremy's shoulders sagged at the memory of the ruined baseball cards. He tossed the ball again. "Ryan swings and fouls. That's foul number thirteen for his turn at bat. Ryan might not get many hits, but he knows how to foul . . ."

Taylor dreamed of George's Pub, where he liked to go when Sabrina made the house black with sound. George drew cold beer in a mug carved from yellow ice while Taylor dropped quarters into the juke box. He slid into a booth, yellow mug in hand, and waited for the music of Buck Owens to wash over him.

But something was wrong. The music. It was a tangle of yellow slimy things that made no sense. George perched like a turkey buzzard on the bar, his beak snapping, biting chunks out of the head of a drunk who looked like Jeremy.

"If you don't stop, I'll tell dad," the drunkard who was Jeremy told the buzzard, "and he will run away from us both."

As Taylor watched, George flapped vulture wings and flew to Taylor's booth to eye him with eyes that looked like Sabrina's. It stood, wings akimbo, screeching, screeching.

"Taylor Joseph Ryan!" the bird yelled.

Taylor bolted upright on the couch. The vision of George-buzzard vanished into a weird yellow mist of cacophonous noise. Sabrina stood not three feet away, hands on her hips, glaring. On television, a man in a cowboy hat sang about being on the back side of thirty and back on his own. The words bounced against the violins of Vivaldi's "Summer" in a terrible way.

Taylor realized what Sabrina had done. She returned home and found him asleep with country music playing on the TV. Instead of turning off the TV, she had turned on Vivaldi, and it was the clash of baroque and country that made the noise of the yellow mist.

"That moron cowboy is ruining my music!" Sabrina jerked a thumb toward the television. Taylor stared at the thumb. A claw. That's what it looked like. A bloody claw, maybe from a hyena. The hyena babbled something at Taylor. He drew his shoulders up to ease a pain in his neck, trying to recover from the vision of George as a vulture biting Jeremy.

Was she singing? Oh, yeah: that was it. Singing. Sabrina's rendition of Vivaldi—though how she got those sounds from *The Four Seasons* was beyond him. "Dee tweet dee dee dee da dee dee." She had said something else, though. What was it?

He raised his brows, held a palm up, and asked her to repeat what she had said. The yellow mist from the blurring of Vivaldi with the cowboy's song hammered at Taylor.

Sabrina added to the noise, Taylor realized. She's trying to drown me out. She doesn't want to hear me.

Her nastiness hit him like a physical blow, and Taylor felt something he seldom allowed himself to feel. Anger. Red, ropy with fibers.

He held it in a delicious way, close to his chest, knowing he could reduce it to a thread or release it to explode across the room. Sabrina had never seen the explosion of his anger. Taylor had always contained it, kept it small and pink and inside—but this time. This time.

He let the red fibers play across his chest, holding, holding. What was she saying? Her voice came to him through the noise of the yellow fog. What was she saying?

". . . can't stand it for a member of my family to be obsessed with anything, especially with something so stupid as . . ."

Taylor released the red. It laced through him, lifting him from the couch in a slow, measured way. He felt his eyes narrow to slits, felt the red lift him over Sabrina like a mountain lion standing over a fox sparrow. She fell silent.

The red fibers, moving him like a puppet, took him to the hall closet. He watched, almost amazed, as his hands took out the bowling bag, took out the ball. Back beside Sabrina, he looked at her in the yellow noise, the violins of Vivaldi and the guitars and drums from the TV; she stepped back in fast, sparrowlike jerks. His arm lifted the ball.

Taylor could feel the red move the arm higher, higher. Sabrina fluttered back again. Taylor almost laughed. "You will never have to be bothered by country music on TV again," he heard his voice say.

Sabrina fluttered, stumbling, her arms flapping. She fell. Taylor watched the red that controlled his arm lift the ball higher, then smash it into the screen of the television in an explosion of glass, cleansing glass that showered the room, washing out the yellow mist, leaving only violins playing Vivaldi, violins he had loved like fresh-shined copper before Sabrina ruined them with volume and repetition that hung the air with the black of tarnished copper. He could taste it, dark and metallic, even as the red lifted him in a leap to the top of what remained of the television.

After a few satisfying jumps on top of the TV, then flinging it to the floor, face down, Taylor allowed the red to recede to pink threads. He gathered them enough for stepping across Sabrina to turn down the black copper of the violins so he could tell her she had won.

What did that mean—that she had won? Taylor wasn't sure, but the telling of it felt like victory, not defeat.

He walked to the door, holding only enough pink threads to allow him a song of victory, a mockery of "Summer" and of Sabrina:

Dee tweet dee dee dee da dee dee
Da dee dee da dee dee.

On the front porch, he looked at Jeremy tossing a whiffle ball. The dream image of George the vulture flickered in front of him. He tried to push it aside. "Run away from us both, run away from us both," the voice of the drunkard said. Taylor winced.

Jeremy picked up the whiffle ball. "That's foul number twenty-five. Nolan Ryan might set a new ballpark record for fouls here at Wrigley Field."

When he had heard the scream of Vivaldi start up, he knew Dad would soon come out, get into the Buick, and drive off. Resentment fluttered around him like the yellow-black leaves, diseased in mid-summer, drifting from the locust tree in his back yard, the back yard where he and Dad no longer played catch, the yard he walked through to the Dumpster to find maggots crawling through the spaghetti sauce on his baseball cards. He felt resentment of Mom's chipping away at baseball. Trashing his cards. Using Vivaldi to keep Dad away, to keep him from playing baseball or talking baseball. Resentment of Dad for abandoning him. He saw his anger as a storm of diseased locust leaves dancing about him to the beat of *The Four Seasons.* "I hate Vivaldi," he muttered. Hate him, hate him.

But at least, Jeremy told himself, he had a piece of baseball left, a game of solitaire with a whiffle ball. And I'm Harry Caray, the number one sportscaster in the world. "José Guzman delivers the pitch." Jeremy tossed the ball and hit it straight into the hedge near the sidewalk. "Ryan connects. You can hear the crack of the bat all over the stadium. The crowd goes wild. Ryan races for first."

Jeremy dropped the bat and ran to the hedge. He glanced back at his dad standing on the porch, watching. Watching me? This is something new. It felt good.

"Wayne Wilson tries to catch the ball, but it hits the center field fence and vanishes into the vines. This is Wrigley Field, ladies and gentlemen. Vines grow all over the outfield fence. This will be a ground rule double." The whiffle ball, he knew, had to be in there somewhere. He pushed into the hedge, saw the ball, and reached for it without seeing the nest of paper wasps until it was too late.

"Yikes!" Jeremy leaped back. Wasps flew right into him, stinging through his tee shirt. "Yikes! Angry fans pour onto the field." He jerked back from the hedge. "The umpire didn't call a ground rule double, and Nolan Ryan runs past second." Jeremy whirled around, yelling with each sting. He ran toward his father, making his voice take on the urgency of a great sportscaster. "They blame Ryan. The fans blame Ryan for the miscall. They pile all over him. Yikes! Ryan has to roll on the ground to get the frenzied fans off him."

Jeremy threw himself to the ground and rolled to squash the wasps. "He slides into home plate, in the nick of time, and the Rangers take the lead!"

Wasps kept diving in, but something was knocking them out of the air. Jeremy stopped rolling and saw his father slicing the air with a towel. No. A shirt, he realized with a start. Dad took off his shirt to knock the wasps off me. Me.

"Even the umpire is in on the act, swatting crazy fans away from Ryan like so many flies. Ladies and gentlemen, never in the history of baseball has there been anything like this." Jeremy stood up and turned around so his father could get at any wasps that might be crawling on him. In the middle of a swing, Taylor hopped back and yelled.

Wasps are going after Dad! "The bullpen!" Jeremy pointed at the Buick.

Taylor picked up his son and ran toward the car. Jeremy clung to him, talking in his best radio voice. "The manager is on the field. He kicks away the mad fans and now has Nolan by the foot. He jerks him from the frenzied people and picks him up. He's running for the bullpen . . . "

Inside the car, Taylor squashed two wasps with the heel of his hand. "Jeremy, are you all right?"

"Those things hurt."

"Yeah. They got me, too. You all right?"

"Sure." Jeremy was aware that he was on the edge of tears. "Why wouldn't I be all right? The Texas Rangers just took the lead in the World Series." He heard himself laughing in a way that scared him. Taylor lifted Jeremy's shirt and looked at the swollen places.

Wasps bumped on the windshield, then drifted back toward the front hedge. Taylor rolled his window down. "It's hot in here. If the wasps come back. I'll roll it back up." He fumbled for his keys. "I'm getting you to a clinic to have those stings checked out. Then. Then."

"Then?" Jeremy prompted.

"Then how about going to the park to warm up a couple of pitchers. Major league stuff, with two Ryans on the team. We will be a winning combination for sure. You can be the color commentator."

"Play catch at the park? Cool." Jeremy rolled down his window. "Listen, Dad."

"To what?" Taylor struggled to get his shirt back on.

"Vivaldi with static. Mom cranked the CD until it blew the speakers."

"Yeah? It sounds like black noise but without the taste of copper." Taylor laughed and started the car.

As Dad pulled cut of the driveway, Jeremy looked for the wasps around the hedge. But he didn't see any. While they drove off, he listened to the Vivaldi static becoming smaller and smaller behind them.

An Adventure Is Made for Having

Jan Epton Seale

From the time the boy had told her the plan, the girl daydreamed about the last day of her visit. The other four days she and the boy had played Monopoly and Slap Jack, teased the dog, and spied on their older sisters as the girls were doing dumb things like mooning over pictures of James Dean or bleaching the front of their hair with lemon juice. This morning, while it was still dark, the boy had come into the guest room and jiggled her foot to waken her. She had already penciled the stuff into her diary: *Gainesville, Texas / June 25, 1950*—so she could start right in recording the adventure after it happened.

He called the thing they were going to do "bagging frogs" and promised her it would be fun. His mother would fry the frog legs, and eating their catch for lunch would be the high point of the visit. In the late afternoon, the boy's mother was to drive the girl and her sister to Dallas where their parents would meet them for the rest of the trip home.

Of course, the boy wasn't about to let the girl touch his BB gun. She knew that. It would be her job to stand a little way out in the water while he shot at the surfacing frog, keep her eye trained on exactly where the widening ripple started, wade out to that point, and bring back the dead frog. In other words, she would be his hunting dog.

Anyway, it *was* his gun and it *was* his dad's cattle tank, and the girl and her older sister *were* the visitors. That was one reason to keep the diary, to remember all the places they had lived. They sometimes got to go back to re-visit like this. Their father was in the military. He had brought them for only a little while to Camp Howze, but it was long enough for the girl's sister to make a friend at school.

The boy had promised that she would like the frog legs, that they tasted exactly like chicken, the way his mother fixed them—maybe better. All in all, it would be something to write about that first day back at school when the teacher assigned the theme about summer to be written while the textbooks were being issued. She would not title it "My Summer Vacation." Hers would be "My Summer Hunting Wild Game."

"But what about the cow stuff?" she asked, following the beam of his flashlight as they walked through the dry summer grass.

His uncombed hair stirred in the dawn breeze. "There's not any out in the water and you ought to be smart enough to step around what's at the water's edge."

They crossed over a little knoll and descended to the tank. There was a faint wafting of cool air off the water but that didn't mean a thing. By eleven o'clock it would be a hundred degrees. This was Texas in the last week of June.

She bent to roll up her blue jeans, carefully folding them over and over so they would fit above her knees. "What do you mean, 'There's not any out in the water'?"

She had seen the cow plops all around the edge of the pond and it didn't make sense. cows were smart enough to cut it out when they waded in to cool themselves in the parched summer afternoons.

"I told you, there's not any out where you're going," he said, fiddling importantly with his rifle.

"How do you know?" she persisted.

He looked at her. Maybe he was sick of her. Still, he had been pretty nice to her all week even though he hadn't known until the last minute that she was coming. Their teenage sisters had planned the visit and at the last minute, the younger girl was sent along to be the boy's companion so he wouldn't spend the whole week pestering the older girls.

The girl was eleven and the boy was barely ten but that was okay. She would forget that he was younger, if he was the means to an adventure. Nancy Drew had adventures. Clara Barton did. It was time she was having one but it seemed a little hard to find one. So she had said to herself, Put up with this stinking boy long enough to have an adventure.

The boy sighed, sounding grieved but patient. "Cows have got more sense than to poop where they're fixing to drink and if you don't hurry, it's gonna' be too late." After the sun rose and the day swooned hot, frogs were not as active. In the pre-dawn lull they cruised the pond, snapping at insects.

The girl stepped gingerly into the water that barely moved at the shoreline. Her toes disappeared in green ooze. She bit her lip and took another step, balancing with outstretched arms.

"What if the cattle come?" she asked.

"Shhhhhhhh! You'll scare the frogs." His voice was louder than hers.

"I don't care—you answer me!" She had some rights.

"They won't," he said.

"Yes, but what if they happen—"

"I'll take care of you, sissy," he said.

They settled in to wait for the dome of a frog's head to break the stillness. The dark water circled her white legs higher and higher as her feet sank in the mire. He cocked his rifle and studied the surface of the pond.

In a moment they were rewarded. A beginning ripple revealed two eyes about twenty feet beyond the girl. The boy fired, cocked the gun, fired again. There was a flurry, a plash, and the ripple deepened and hurried out in all directions.

"I got it!" he called. "I know I did. Go pick it up now."

She extricated one foot, then the other, and moved out. Each step was soft, with no promise of a firm bottom. Each foot twisted a quarter-turn before she could straighten it. She discovered her arms flailing the air to keep her balance and quickly put her hands on her hips. Maybe the boy hadn't noticed.

She concentrated on the exact center of the widening ripples. It was hard to keep looking there and watch her step too.

"Hurry up!" he called. "Get on over there. I've done it a billion times."

"Shut up!" she answered. "I'm going as fast as I can."

Arriving at the site, she gingerly reached down and began to grope, half fearing she would touch the frog. The slime filled her fingernails. Soon she felt a kick, and, closing her eyes, she grabbed. A large grayish bullfrog with a hole in its side mustered a few kicks as she raised it dripping from the water. She felt dizzy and desperate. "Can't you come get him?" she called. She had done her part.

The boy was reloading, though he still had plenty of BB's in the gun. "Hell, no. I've got my boots on. Bring it on in." He continued busily with his gun. "For crying out loud."

She waded toward the shore. The frog gave one last furious twist. She tightened her grip, feeling it splutter against her face. Then it went slack.

The boy held open his game pouch. "Drop it in there." She did and leaned down to rinse her hands in the muddy swirl.

Now the boy shot repeatedly, shooting at anything, it seemed to the girl. She could have sworn he shot at dragonflies touching down on the pond. She waded out dutifully each time and groped for the frog. When she failed to find it, he told her she hadn't been fast enough. Once he said, "Hurry up and get the damned thing. Don't be a slow poke."

"Come out here and get it yourself, smarty-pants," she said.

"That's your job," he said, and spat boldly.

She was glad to be going home. He had gone braggy and ugly all of a sudden.

They had four frogs when the sun gilded the knoll and they heard the yard bell. It was strange, because his mother had not called them for breakfast all week. They got their own cereal and milk whenever they wandered into the kitchen.

"What does *she* want?" the boy asked.

"Yeah," the girl joined, trying not to sound too disrespectful.

Despite her care, the cuffs of the girl's jeans were crusted with mud and her blouse sleeves were wet. Her toenails were little islands of silt and each fingernail harbored a half-moon of mud. She brushed back a strand of hair, at the same time streaking her face.

She had done it. She had had an adventure. She had rolled up her pants legs and gone straight into the tank and retrieved frogs. She had waded out past the cow manure, and with the prospects that dangerous cows and bulls might come.

"From the depths"—that's how she would put it when she wrote about it in the essay. "Battling unknown dangers." She would use "suddenly" several times. She would write "very dirty" to describe the edge of the tank and underline it—hoping the teacher would understand and nod approvingly at the way she had avoided saying "cow poop."

Of course, the end of the adventure was yet to come, eating the frog legs. She would be sure to tell about this in her essay. She would not tell her parents about any of the adventure, because her mother would say it was a wonder she had not drowned or been gored by a bull, and her father would say whoever heard of a girl doing such things.

186

And when she came back the next summer, she would ask the boy to let her shoot the gun.

They started toward the house—he, limping in fake heroism with the weight of the frog bag; she, picking at the caked mud on her forearms.

The boy's mother was at the back door. "You children need to hose off before you come in the house," she said. The mother was pretty, kind of la-di-da and fancy.

"We got four frogs," the girl said.

"That's nice," the mother said.

"Remember you said you'd cook the legs for lunch?" The boy was wiping his boots furiously on the backyard grass. "Oh Buddy," his mother said, "I don't think so now. There's been a change in plans. We're going to take the girls to Dallas right away."

The children's shoulders slumped. "Awwwww."

"Something's come up," the mother went on. "We've just heard President Truman on the radio. There's a bad disturbance in Korea. The girls' parents called. Their dad may have to go on active duty. They're coming right away to Dallas to meet us."

"Active duty?" the boy said. "Gosh." The girl dribbled the cold water from the hose over her greenish legs. Gradually they turned white again. She rinsed her arms and slung them dry.

She would go in the house now. She would take off these things and put them in a plastic bag the boy's mother would provide. She would put on her clean blouse and skirt and they would go to Dallas, she and the boy being careful not to touch as they sat in the back seat with one of the sisters. And the frogs would lie, dead and stinking, in the corner of the yard all day, or until the dogs found them.

She walked slowly toward the back door in the early morning light. The title of her essay would be "War Ended My Summer Adventure." It reminded her of the "Heidi" film at school that had made her cry. She could still tell everything that had happened so far in the adventure. The thing was, she would never know how many more frogs they might have bagged before the sun got hot, and, if the frog legs really tasted like chicken.

Even though it was getting warm, she shivered in her damp clothes. She wondered if there might be other events, things she didn't know about right now, things to spoil the adventures she just knew were out there waiting for her.

KYLA GENE'S WEDDING

RHONDA AUSTIN

"Listen to this, Kyla Gene. This magazine says that an unmarried female over forty has just about as much chance of getting married as she does of getting struck by lightning. What do you say to that?"

"I say you read too much crap, and the garbage needs taking out. Put that magazine in there while you're at it. That's where it belongs."

"Touchy, touchy. I didn't mean nothing by it, just telling you what it said, that's all. Don't take it so personal."

"I ain't taking it no way at all," said Kyla. "I'm just tired of everybody sticking their big, fat noses in my personal life. If I wanted to be married, I would be. I tried it once and it didn't take. Unlike *some* people I could name, I learn from *my* mistakes."

"Kyla Gene Woolsey, this is me you're talking to, your sister, remember? I was there when you and Rod ran off together when you was both sixteen. That so-called marriage lasted all of three days 'til Ma and Pa drug you both back by the scruff of your necks and had it annulled. I fail to see how you can call that a marriage. If it's annulled, that means it wasn't no real marriage in the first place."

"Well, I guess you'd know all right, Cora Nell. You've been married to half the men in the county. How many times is it now, five, six? I guess that makes you an expert on marriage all right. Get on out of here before you get me really mad at you."

Cora Nell knew she had struck a nerve, and even though she hadn't really set out to upset Kyla, she had to admit that she took a certain perverse pleasure in getting her stirred up. After all, Kyla needed a little stirring up now and then. Something, better yet someone, needed to get her female juices flowing. Even though both women were only in their early forties, Cora Nell thought Kyla looked and acted a good ten years older. She was convinced that was because Kyla had no man in her life. She didn't really know why either. Kyla wasn't ugly or anything. In fact, when they were younger and went out partying together, Kyla was the one who got the most attention from men. Since then though, she'd let her figure go and cut her hair real short. Seemed like all she ever wore any more were jeans and those ratty old houseshoes from Wal-Mart. Jimmy, Cora Nell's husband, said that women who wore their hair real short and wore pants all the time looked butch. She'd get mad at him for saying that because she knew it wasn't true about Kyla, but she had to admit that sometimes she was even a little bit embarrassed about the way her sister looked when they went out together. She felt guilty about it, but a person can't help how they feel in their heart of hearts.

Besides, it wasn't Kyla's fault. She knew Kyla couldn't help the way she was. There was only the two girls in the family and their dad always treated them like boys while they were growing up, especially Kyla. He even named her after himself, kind of. He just changed his name, Kyle, into Kyla by putting an A on the end instead of an E. He even spelled her middle name like his middle name, G-e-n-e, like a boy's, instead of J-e-a-n, like a girl's name. Cora Nell supposed she'd just have to work harder at finding the perfect man for Kyla. Heaven knows she was never gonna find him by herself.

Cora Nell and Jimmy lived across the street from Kyla, so she walked on home after carrying out the trash. In her yard, she picked up a beer can that had spilled out of Jimmy's truck when he wheeled into the driveway. She wished he'd clean his truck more often, but she knew he worked hard and was tired when he got home. She decided she'd run it through the carwash for him on Sunday while he was watching the game. That would make him happy.

When she opened the kitchen door, Jimmy was sitting at the table in his undershirt and work pants, drinking a beer. She wanted to ask him if there were any new guys at the plant that he could fix up with her sister, but she thought better of it. That was what their last big fight had been about and he'd made her promise not to bring it up again. She hadn't either, hadn't even thought about it 'til she read that magazine article.

Two weeks later, Cora Nell got the shock of her life when she walked into the Denny's Restaurant where both she and Kyla worked as waitresses and Kyla announced to everyone there that she was getting married.

"You're what?" asked a stunned Cora Nell. She dropped her cigarette and it landed somewhere in the folds of her uniform. She was dancing around trying to find it before it burned her when she smelled burning nylon. She fished the cigarette out of her pocket where it had landed and ground it out in a nearby ashtray. Looking around to see where Kyla had gotten off to, she spotted her over at one of the booths, calmly taking a breakfast order. When Kyla came up to the window to turn in her order, Cora Nell asked her again, "What did you say?"

"You heard me. I said I'm getting married."

"Oh yeah, who to? The paper boy? He's about the only male I ever see you talking to, except Jimmy when we're playing cards."

"You'll know when I'm ready to tell you. You don't know everything there is to know about me, even though you think you do."

Cora Nell couldn't help herself. In her most sarcastic tone she asked, "So when is this wedding taking place? Am I invited or will you be jetting off to the south of France?" Cora Nell was using her best imitation of a snobby voice, but mostly it sounded like she had a head cold.

"Oh, you'll be invited all right. In fact, you played a very important part in my decision to do this."

"Huh?" Cora Nell stood there with her mouth open, sugar streaming from the jar she held, now dangling limply at her side. The hostess was giving her one of those get-back-to-work looks.

Just then a charter bus pulled up in the parking lot and the place filled up with tourists. Both women were so busy they barely got to speak to each other again all morning. Cora Nell was dying for more details, but about ten minutes before their shift was over, Kyla turned her last two tables over to one of the other waitresses and hurried out the door. Cora Nell wanted to catch up to her, but a baby at one of her tables squirted ketchup on the man in the booth behind him and she had to go take care of that mess. Both the man and the baby were hollering.

"What the hell are you looking for, flying saucers?" asked Jimmy that night while Cora Nell was washing dishes. She'd been staring out the window all evening long, watching for Kyla's car to pull up in the driveway across the street. She didn't say anything to Jimmy because she wasn't sure that Kyla wasn't just making the whole thing up and she didn't want to look foolish if that turned out to be the case. That wasn't out of the question, either. Sometimes Jimmy and Kyla got together and played really mean tricks on her. They always got a big laugh out of it when she fell for their pranks and this very well might be one of those pranks. If so, she wasn't going to give them the satisfaction of falling for it.

"I'm just looking at the sky, Jimmy. Looks like it might hail. Maybe I ought to go cover up Kyla's tomato plants. I don't think she's home."

"You're crazy, woman. Those aren't hail clouds. Come on over here and sit down. *Roseanne*'s about to start." *Roseanne* was Jimmy's favorite TV show.

The next morning, Kyla's car still wasn't home and Cora Nell could hardly wait to get to work to find out where she spent the night. Relieved to see Kyla's little blue car in its usual spot in the parking lot at work, she hurried inside to ask her.

"Who do you think you are, my mother?" Kyla asked her. "I'm a grown, engaged woman. You shouldn't be at all surprised if I start staying away from home a few nights now and then. After all, I'm free, white, and over twenty-one."

"Yeah, way over twenty-one," said Cora Nell under her breath. "So, did you stay with your fiancé?"

"That's for me to know and you to wonder. Look, table two's waving for you. Get to work, girl."

Cora Nell couldn't figure out whether or not Kyla was teasing her. If she was, she sure was going to a lot of trouble to pull it off, staying away from home all night just to make her curious. On break, she tried again to get more details. "So, have you set a wedding date? Do I know him? What's his name?"

"Yes, no, and none of your business."

Cora Nell could tell that Kyla was enjoying keeping her in suspense. She began to think maybe it was true after all. Kyla sure *looked* different, and she seemed happier. A man in her life would account for that, she thought.

The next day when Kyla came to work, her nails were painted and her hair had been colored. No longer gray, it was now a soft brown, like it used to be. Once again, Cora Nell pressed her for details and once again, she got nothing.

"Cora Nell, I'm going out of town for the weekend. Do you think you can water my tomato plants and feed my cat?" asked Kyla after work on Friday.

"Only if you tell me where you're going," Cora Nell answered.

"Well, if you don't want to do it, I'll ask somebody else. It's not like I'm asking for the moon." Kyla was using her little pouty voice and acting like her feelings were hurt.

"Geez, Kyla. You know I will. I was just kidding you."

"Thanks, I knew I could count on you. I'll be back on Monday and then I'll have some news for you."

Cora Nell couldn't get any sleep all weekend. She thought about trying to follow her sister to see where she was going, but she couldn't afford to miss work. By Monday, her curiosity had almost consumed her. She had chewed her fingernails practically up to the first knuckle. When she saw Kyla in the driveway Monday morning, it was all she could do to keep from pouncing her down on the grass and tickling her 'til she talked. That always worked when they were kids. Instead, she sprinted across the street, causing the garbage truck to swerve to miss her, and casually asked Kyla for a ride to work. "My car battery's dead. Can I ride with you?"

"Sure, but you'll have to find your own way home. I have somewhere to go after work. By the way, thanks for looking after things for me while I was gone."

"No problem. Did you have a good weekend?"

"The best. Do you notice anything different about me?"

Cora Nell looked her over, her eyes coming to rest on Kyla's left hand which was balanced on the steering and sporting a *huge* diamond cluster ring. She grabbed her sister's hand and gasped, "It's beautiful. Where did you get it?"

"Where do you think, goofy?"

"Kyla, it must be a full carat, but it doesn't really look like an engagement ring. What does this guy do that he can afford a ring like that? When am I going to meet him?"

"Well, I guess it's time to put you out of your misery. The wedding is two weeks from Saturday. You'll meet him then. Unfortunately, he won't be able to get here before that. I would just love it if you'd be my matron of honor."

"Of course I will," said Cora Nell, her voice cracking with emotion. "It'll be just like we always used to talk about when we were kids. I'll give you a shower and help you pick out your dress. You know how much I love weddings."

"I should say so. You've had enough of your own." Cora Nell knew Kyla was teasing this time and they both laughed about it. For the next two weeks, the sisters planned Kyla's wedding. Cora Nell wanted to give her a shower at the VFW and invite all their friends. Jimmy was a member there, and, as a veteran's wife, she was allowed to use the party hall. Kyla wouldn't hear of it, though. She kept saying she didn't want a traditional wedding because it wouldn't be a traditional marriage. The two women shopped for days for Kyla's wedding dress and Cora Nell's matron of honor dress. They spent one whole afternoon buying clothes for the honeymoon. Kyla said they were going somewhere tropical on the honeymoon, so they bought shorts and beach towels and suntan lotion. Cora Nell teased Kyla unmercifully when they shopped for lingerie.

"He said I could pick the place, so I picked Hawaii," Kyla told the lady at the travel agency. "I've always wanted to go there." Cora Nell watched as Kyla bought the deluxe package at the Maui Hilton. She tried peeking over Kyla's shoulder to see the name on the credit card she was paying with but all she could see was that it was an American Express Gold card. Finally, Kyla relented. "His name is Marcus Perez and he's from Colombia."

"Colombia? This is so unbelievable, Kyla. A foreigner. Wherever did you meet him? I'm so excited I can't stand it. Why are you being so mysterious? Is he a spy or something?"

"Well, there are some things I can't tell you just yet, but one thing's for sure. We won't have a marriage like any of yours. There won't be any nights sitting home watching TV and there sure won't be any knock-down-drag-out fights like you and Jimmy have."

"Oh, Kyla. Every bride thinks that. There's not a marriage in the world that doesn't have boring times and problems. Take it from me, no marriage is perfect."

"Mine will be. You'll see. I'll get everything I want from it."

Cora Nell was beginning to worry about her sister. "Well, I hope you do, honey, but I think you ought to be a little more realistic."

"I wish you'd make up your mind. For years now, you've tried to tell me that marriage is the only proper state for a woman. A few weeks ago, you couldn't wait to fix me up with somebody, anybody. Now, you're trying to convince me marriage is not so hot."

"No, that's not what I mean. Hell, I don't even know what I mean. I just want you to be happy is all."

"I will be. You'll see."

"I hope so, Honey. I surely hope so."

Finally, the big day came. Everything was ready. Cora Nell had planned Kyla's wedding down to the last rose petal glued onto the archway she had rented and set in front of the county judge's door. In spite of all her begging, that's where Kyla insisted the wedding was going to take place. Cora Nell wanted to invite a lot of people, but Kyla made her keep it small, only inviting her and Jimmy as witnesses. "Marcus doesn't want a big wedding and this is his wedding, too, so I'm respecting his wishes," she said.

"But, what about . . ."

"No buts, Cora Nell. This is my wedding and I'm doing it my way."

Fifteen minutes before the ceremony was supposed to start, Cora Nell was pacing the floor. The bride, on the other hand, seemed perfectly calm. "Relax," she told her sister. "Everything is going just as I planned." At exactly 3:00, the judge walked in, followed by a very distinguished looking man of about fifty, dressed in an Armani suit. Right behind him was a much younger man in casual clothes, carrying a small suitcase. The older, handsome man smiled warmly at Kyla and she smiled back.

"Is that him?" Cora Nell nudged her. "He's so handsome, and look at that suit. Wow, I can't believe this is happening. Are you ready?"

"Let's do it," said Kyla. "Oh, by the way, Marcus asked the judge to perform the ceremony in Spanish. He doesn't speak any English."

The two men and the two women assembled at the judge's desk and the judge began to perform the ceremony. Although Cora Nell didn't understand a word of it, she was so caught up in her own excitement that she didn't notice much of anything until she heard the younger man say, "Si."

"Si, why is *he* saying that? Kyla, do something," she interrupted. "You're going to marry the wrong man." By now, the judge was looking at Kyla, who was glaring at Cora Nell, who was sputtering uncontrollably. Jimmy was sitting in a chair at the back of the room, smirking and shaking his head. Feeling suddenly paralyzed, Cora Nell sat down in the floor, right there in front of the judge.

"Is everything all right, Miss Woolsey?" the judge asked Kyla. "Would you like to take a break to look after your sister before we continue?"

"No, Judge. Everything's fine. I would like to get married now." In a few minutes, Cora Nell heard her sister say, "I do."

After the ceremony was over, the young man and Kyla walked over to the judge's desk and signed some papers. The judge congratulated them, then left the room. Cora Nell continued to sit in a heap on the floor, her legs too weak to hold her.

"Jimmy, I think you better take her home now," said Kyla. "We're off to the airport. Tell her I'll be in touch."

"You and your crazy sister kill me, Cora Nell," Jimmy said on the way home. "You two are just like the sisters on *Roseanne*, always trying to put something over on each other. I think she really outdid herself this time, though. You'll never be able to top this one." Every few minutes, he'd bust out laughing. Cora Nell, still in a fog, couldn't figure out what was so funny. Finally, she found her voice.

"You shut up, Jimmy Dale. This is not funny. Kyla Gene's married some foreigner half her age and to top it off, he don't even speak English."

"Listen to yourself, Cora Nell. Why do you think she didn't tell you all about it? She knew you'd get all bent out of shape over nothing, just like you did."

"NOTHING! How can you call this nothing? My only sister just married a gigolo."

Jimmy wheeled the pickup into a Sonic. "Man, Kyla's gonna really hate missing this. She wanted me to keep it a secret 'til she got back from the honeymoon so we could tell you together. We didn't think you'd take it *this* hard. After all, there's nothing you like more than planning weddings and you've been trying to marry Kyla off for years. As it is, you got to help plan her wedding and you had a ball doing it, didn't you?"

"You better spill your guts right now, Jimmy Dale. I swear you won't live 'til sundown if you don't."

"Okay, okay. Let me order first. You want a milk shake?"

"No! I don't want a milkshake."

"You're gonna get a good laugh out of this." He leaned out the window and ordered a chocolate shake and a large order of fries. "Remember the old guy, the one in the fancy suit? You thought that was the guy, didn't you? Kyla said you'd think he was the one. Well, that guy's a lawyer. He and Kyla met a couple of months ago at Denny's. He was sitting at one of her tables and they just struck up a conversation. Turns out the kid is here on a student visa that's about to expire. The only way he can stay in the U.S. and get a Green Card is to marry an American citizen. Who knows how Kyla got involved, but nothing surprises me any more about your crazy sister. I guess she didn't have anything else to do this summer, so she decided to get married. Hell, maybe she did it just to make you happy. The kid's old man paid for everything, even the ring and her vacation. The kid's off in San Antonio and Kyla's on an all-expense-paid vacation in Hawaii. Hell, I'd have married him myself for a free trip to Hawaii," said Jimmy.

For the next few days, Cora Nell went back and forth between feeling shocked and feeling furious. She couldn't wait for Kyla to get back so she could tell her what she thought, as soon as she figured out exactly what that was. On the third day after the wedding, a postcard arrived from Hawaii. It read:

Dear Cora Nell,

Having a wonderful time. Wish you were here. I hope you're feeling better. You didn't look too good the last time I saw you. I'm sure Jimmy has filled you in by now. Maybe you can forgive me by the time I get home. My love to you and Jimmy, and please don't forget to feed my cat.

Your loving sister,
Kyla

P.S. You can have the ring when I get back. It doesn't really go with my jeans.

Black and White

Greg Garrett

When Lynette wasn't home at five like they'd agreed, Cal walked back out to his car and squeezed in behind the wheel. He would wait; he had taken off from the store early to pick up his son Walter and he wasn't going to leave without him. Cal sat in the shade of the pecan trees that lined the long driveway, radio tuned to a country station out of Fort Worth, his arm stretched across the wheel, his fingers just brushing the dashboard along with the music. First he thrummed the dash lightly, rhythmically, with the tips of his fingers, then with his full fingers, then with the palm of his hand. By the time the sun had set, he caught himself pounding the dashboard with his fist, completely oblivious to the music. He had to admit it: she had lied to him again. She wasn't going to meet him. He walked up to the house, wrapped his fist in a sweatshirt, and put it through the beautiful etched glass window in the front door of her new husband's house. The glass clattered musically to the terracotta floor inside as Cal extended his arm through the window and twisted the deadbolt. He went into the living room, surveyed the scene to figure out how he could do the most damage, then hoisted the twenty-seven-inch Mitsubishi stereo television set off the entertainment center, and walked out with it.

He was halfway home before what he had done really struck him; it was like those times when Lynette was still his wife and he used to get so mad at her that he honestly didn't seem to be able to do much more than watch from a distance, a feeling like swimming underwater, as his body slammed doors, put its fists through walls. That was how he had felt as he lugged the television out to the car, balanced it on his knee as he opened the rear right door, wedged it into the back seat. Sometimes things just happened.

Now he pulled over onto the side of the road and sat, taking deep breaths like the marriage counselor had told him to, counting the passing seconds. When he felt like he was in complete control of his actions, he knew that what he'd done was stupid, that it could get him in big trouble, and he knew that there was only one thing he could do.

He drove the backroads where he and Lynette had once courted until he located an old timber trestle bridge on a lane overgrown by trees. Cottonwood fluff drifted down onto the windshield and the bitter smell of tar or creosote drifted up from the bridge timbers as he parked the car, tugged the TV out of the back seat, raised it as high as he could, and heaved it over into the gully below. It landed in the shallow creek with a satisfying noise, a sort of simultaneous crunch, crack, and splash that startled a group of white-faced calves watching from the fence. They galloped away, heels high, and Cal drove home to wait for her call.

He knew it would come, and what form it was likely to take. This would be another in her long line of reasons why he couldn't see Walter. It wasn't fair for her to keep his own son away from him, wasn't right. He hadn't been a bad father, hadn't really been a bad husband, certainly not any worse than lots of others. No, it wasn't right for her to keep Walter from him, but he had to complain to the judge every time she missed a meeting and it cost money to send even his polyester-pants lawyer to court and then her lawyer always showed up and made some perfectly reasonable excuse and nothing ever happened. Nothing ever happened to people with money.

Thing was, until they had started trying to keep him away from Walter, he had been perfectly willing to stay away. Walter was an odd kid, thick glasses and slanting shoulders, more interested in reading about baseball than playing it, and ever since Walter and his mom had moved in with Dr. Donald Wise, they were cramming his head so full of culture that he could hardly talk to the boy. They took him to plays, they took him to the opera, every other week it seemed they were off to Dallas. When Walter came over one weekend talking about Rossini and Puccini, Cal, who hadn't been across the broad aisle from Electronics to Toys lately, first thought that they must have slipped in some new Ninja Turtles while he wasn't looking.

When he opened his front door and the phone rang, he stepped over and picked it up immediately. No sense putting it off. "Yeh-lo," he said.

"I know you did it," Lynette said. "You set off the goddamn alarm when you broke in. The police were here, all over the place. I'm sure they'll find fingerprints."

The only thing they might get would be a smudged print on the door knob; he hadn't touched anything else bare-handed except the television, and they weren't likely to even find it, let alone pull prints off it. "I waited for you for hours," he finally said; this was how it always worked: they had two completely different conversations going at once. He wondered how they'd ever communicated, if they ever had. "Then I came home. Where were you? Did you expect me to sit in front of your house all night?"

"They're going to lock you up for this," she said. "You're never going to see Walt again if I can help it. This week it's the television. Who knows what you might do next?"

"I'm going to drag you back into court," Cal said. "One of these days the judge is going to get tired of it and throw your scrawny butt in jail."

She sighed, as close as she would get to acknowledgment. "The police should be pulling up to your house about now. Don't even try to deny it. They'll search. They'll find it. You might as well just admit it and turn yourself in. Save us all the humiliation of a trial. Think of your son for once."

And, in fact, there were flashing lights outside his front window and he had to excuse himself. "Some people are here," he said. "I gotta go."

The police came in, sat on his couch, asked him some questions. He served them coffee, and when they were done asking, he agreed to let them look around. "Whatever she's talking about," he said, "it sure as hell isn't here."

It didn't take long for them to see he was telling the truth. The house was small, and mostly empty now that Lynette and Walter were gone. He had a recliner and couch in the living room facing the small color TV he had saved up for three months to buy with his employee discount. He and Walter ate off TV trays stacked against the living room wall. His bedroom had one dresser with an ancient black and white set on top and a bed, and Walter's room had only a bunk bed they'd found at a yard sale and a battered crate that held some toys and books.

"Sorry to have bothered you," the younger cop said. He looked familiar, and Cal thought that maybe he had seen him at the store, although at that age all cops looked the same, smooth-faced, earnest, play-tough. "We may have to come back and ask some more questions."

"If you do, you do," Cal said. "She can be"—he fumbled for the word—"persistent. I remember." He did; more than that, he recalled how in the old days she could slice him to ribbons with that tongue, reduce him to sullen smoldering silence without even raising her voice. He couldn't answer her; anything he said, she would shape into something new, sharp-edged, damaging. *Persistence.* Those were the times when he drifted into that absence, that distance, broke things, threw things, kicked down doors when she got too scared to insult him anymore and tried instead to put something solid in between them. Afterward they would always apologize to each other, make up. He never hurt her, never hit her; he had been taught that no man ever struck a woman. He just had a little trouble managing his temper, that's all.

Then suddenly eight months ago she must have decided he was a potential childbeater and every other dirty thing she later called him in court, because she moved out and started seeing Dr. Donald Wise during *and* after work. Cal figured Lynette and Dr. Wise must have been previewing the marriage act on the receptionist's desk, maybe in the dentist's chair, and more than once, his sense of outrage stuffed him into the car, steered him in the direction of the Wise's high-rent neighborhood to demand satisfaction, but somehow it could never push him all the way up to that front door, and for that, Cal felt weak and powerless, warm in the face, even though he knew he could give Dr. Wise a three-punch head start and still kick his ass.

"Your stepdad is a pantywaist," he sometimes told Walter when the boy talked about going to museums or to Santa Fe, just to get Walter to look down, scuff his feet on the ground, stop talking. "He's just the kind of man your mother ought to be married to. She can run all over him."

"Why do you and Mom hate each other so much?" Walter would ask. At some point children learn not to ask what they really want to know, not to show that they see straight to the heart of things, but at eight, Walter had a ways to go.

"Things just happen," Cal said. It was hard to explain. Mostly he was mad at her for leaving after he'd given her every advantage, sacrificed for her the way he did. It wasn't right for her to think she was better than him. He could have been somebody too if he'd had the chance at two years of college like he gave Lynette. He wouldn't have become a dental technician, of course, but he could have made something of himself instead of finding himself stuck at Wal-Mart for the rest of his life. "Some people get the breaks, and some people don't," he sighed, ruffling Walter's hair. Walter immediately smoothed it back into place.

The police didn't come back, although that didn't mean Lynette had given up. For a week and a half she left smoldering messages at the store—the secretary who took them looked at Cal wide-eyed with new curiosity—and made scalding calls to him at home. Then on Wednesday night her voice was dripping with defeat. "The lawyer says I better let you see him this weekend," she said. "But that doesn't mean I have to see you. Pick him up at school. Drop him off at church on Sunday night. Stay away from my house."

"Okay," he said.

"I mean it," she said.

"Okay."

Cal rearranged his schedule so one of the high school kids could come in Friday evening to run Electronics and cautioned him about the volume and the venom of the music he'd been playing in his absence. The last time he'd left Ronnie in charge, Cal had come in early the next morning, flipped on the power, and been assaulted by a hard rock chorus at maximum volume: "Why do we dream in black and white?" Who knew? Who cared? Certainly not Cal. Not even a full day of Travis Tritt and Reba McIntyre had restored his equilibrium.

On Friday afternoon, Cal parked outside the school and slid down low in the driver's seat; the other cars, bright new Hondas and Dodge minivans and Volvo station wagons, were all driven by brisk perky mothers who always looked suspiciously at him, the outsider, a potential murderer or child molester, as they eased to a stop, shut off their engines.

The bell rang, a stream of screaming children passed, and then Walter pulled open the creaking passenger door and slammed it shut behind him.

Those were the only sounds for some time, until, as they drove past the car wash, Walter asked, "Why did you steal our TV?"

"Who says I took your TV?"

"Mom did. She said if I see it to call and tell her and she'll send the police over. Would they arrest you?"

"Probably," he said.

Walter nodded and twisted his lips to one side of his face, then the other as he considered. "I wish you hadn't done it. We haven't gotten a new one. Every time I ask why we can't watch something Mom says it's your fault."

"I'm sorry about your TV set," Cal said. "But that's not saying I did it."

When they pulled up in the driveway, Walter made a beeline for the living room, dropped his bag on the floor, and flipped on Cal's television with the remote control. First there was velvet blackness, then a pinpoint of light that expanded to fill the screen.

Walter sat down on the couch and flipped through the channels until he found a nature documentary, something about sharks and feeding frenzies.

"Cool," he said.

"You like this stuff?" Cal had been hoping for the Bulls and the Lakers. "This is just fish eating each other." That reminded him of dinner—the kid had to eat—and he got up to check the freezer; he thought he had some fishsticks and french fries left over from last time.

"Well, it'd be better on a big set," Walter called from the living room. "Our TV, the one you stole, was a lot nicer than this one."

The food was rock-solid and covered with tiny sparkling crystals of ice, but it was nothing forty minutes at 350 degrees wouldn't cure. He stuck everything on a cookie sheet and went back in to sit with Walter.

"You miss your TV?" he asked.

"Sure," Walter said. "Wouldn't you?"

After Lynette had left but before he'd gotten this set, Cal had spent his evenings in bed with the tiny black and white perched on his chest, continually fiddling with the antenna so the people wouldn't look like they were wearing gorilla suits. "Oh yeah," he said. "I see your point."

"So I think whoever stole our TV set ought to get us a new one."

202

"I thought about buying you a new TV," Cal admitted. "But I don't think your mom would take it. Do you?"

Since a commercial about veteran's life insurance was on, Walter turned to look at him thoughtfully. "No," he said at last, after the shark program came back on. "I think she'd like for you to offer it so she could turn you down. That would make you mad."

Cal smiled ruefully. "I guess you know us pretty well."

Walter didn't answer him; onscreen they were cutting open a great white shark to show the stomach contents—a dolphin skull, a couple of seals, a tarpon or sailfish—and he was engrossed. "They have triangular teeth," Walter said without looking away. "With serrated edges. Like a steak knife. And they grow forward in rows, so they always have sharp teeth at the front. They can chew the crud out of anything."

"I'll go check on dinner," Cal said.

"I think it would be neat to be a shark," Walter said as Cal got up.

"But not that shark," Cal said.

"No. Not that shark. But one just like him."

"Me too," Cal said—he could almost imagine splintering Lynette's front door with his powerful jaws, gnawing off Dr. Wise's legs—but Walter was engrossed in the show and didn't acknowledge him.

After dinner, the two of them took their dishes into the kitchen and while Cal washed and Walter dried they planned their weekend.

"TV," Walter said. "Lots of it."

"I vote for some time in the park, if the weather's good. Maybe take in a baseball game."

"I don't have a TV at home," Walter reminded him. "I'm deprived. I don't have anything to talk about at school."

"I'm sorry about your TV," Cal sighed. "You sure that's what you want to do?"

"Yup," Walter said. He nudged his glasses back up the bridge of his nose and went back into the living room. There was a sudden shrieking burst of sound—"Sorry," Walter called—and then Cal heard a snatch of MTV before Walter settled in with *MacGyver*.

"We'll need some more groceries," Cal said, surveying his empty refrigerator, probably starting with breakfast. He left as MacGyver was concocting some sort of explosive device out of soaps and other household items, and drove slowly, window rolled down, to the store, savoring what might be his only taste of the outdoors all weekend. The night was just slightly cool, and in the far west he could still see glimmers of orange and red and purple in the high strands of clouds catching the final sunset.

Saturday was warm and sunny, with hardly a gust of wind, and while Walter sat glued to the television, Cal sat gazing out the front window. Two joggers bobbed past, then that cute black girl up the street with her sniffing Labrador, and then some guy wearing neon biking shorts and a white plastic helmet pedaled leisurely by.

"It's gorgeous out there," Cal said. He opened the window, felt the slight sweet breeze as it swelled the curtains. He looked back at Walter. A documentary on sight in the animal kingdom. Dogs lack the fundamental receptors for full color vision, and their visual acuity is instead attuned to movement. Cal looked back out at the world, green and blue, tried to imagine it without color.

"I'm going to wash the car," he said, finally. "Call me when you get hungry for supper." He gathered soap, his rags, a pail, and a brush to scrub the whitewalls, and he went out to give his ramshackle Dodge a bath.

That night, after a dinner-long plea, Cal relented and let Walter watch a Steven Seagal movie on HBO. "Don't tell your mom," he said.

"I don't tell her anything we do over here," Walter assured him.

"That's probably a good idea."

Cal himself dozed until the grand finale, when Seagal strolled through a roomful of bad guys breaking arms, legs, vertebrae. It sounded almost exactly the same as Lynette's television landing.

"He's pretty strong," Walter murmured.

"Oh, I'll bet I could take him," Cal said.

Walter looked over and smiled. "You could not."

"Well, I'd have to get back into shape. But there's just no telling what your old dad is capable of when he gets worked up."

Walter got up reluctantly as the closing credits ran. "I had a great day," he said, giving Cal his sort-of hug, a drawing close and pat on the back.

Cal noticed that Walter's eyes were rimmed with red. "Now I want you to go right to sleep. And don't feel like you have to get up early, okay? Don't be in such a hurry to get to the TV."

"Ah, Dad," Walter said as he retreated down the hall to his room. Cal flipped the set off with the remote control, the vibrant light and color shrank to a white pinpoint, and then, with a static crackle, the screen went black. Cal sat looking at the screen for a very long time, long after he would normally have tuned in *Sportscenter,* and at last he got up, turned out the lights, and went to bed.

"No television this morning," Cal said at breakfast as he spread margarine on his toast. Walter took his toast straight, with just a dab of grape jelly, and now he set his piece of toast down, rested both elbows on the TV tray, and looked across at Cal, his blue eyes magnified slightly by his glasses.

"Why not?" he asked.

"You've spent enough time with it. It's time we did some things together. It's hard enough to get your mother to let me keep you, and I'm not going to spend our last day together watching you watch TV."

"It's not fair. Who knows when I'll get to watch anything again?"

"Life's not fair. Ask your mother. She's an expert on that. I said no television and I mean it." He crunched off a piece of toast and chewed slowly.

"So what are we going to do?"

"I haven't decided yet," Cal said. "Help me out."

"The Art Center?"

"Cameron Park?"

Walter did his side-to-side lip thing. "Okay. How about the Art Center, *then* the park?"

Cal held out his hand and they shook. "Deal." He noticed that Walter's fingers were thick and stubby like his own—Lynette had long graceful fingers—and on impulse, he leaned over and kissed Walter on top of the head.

"What was that for?" Walter asked.

"Just because," Cal said. "Come help me with the dishes."

At the museum, Cal walked with arms folded from painting to painting. It was another sunny day outside, and he'd loaded up their baseball stuff in the trunk. "Come on," he told Walter, who had settled in front of a canvas that looked like so many random squiggles, his head tilted slightly to one side.

"Just a second," Walter said. "This is a good one. See all the color?"

Cal turned back to the painting for a moment. "Sure," he said. "Let's go."

Walter looked up at his father. Cal was gazing at the glass doors leading back outside. A group of teenage girls entered, clutching notebooks, and fanned out. Two of them headed in their direction, and Walter stepped back so one of them could read the tiny card next to the painting that gave the painter and title.

"Let's write about this one," she said to the other. "Look at the colors."

Cal put his hand on Walter's shoulder and turned him toward the exit. "Let's go," he said. "We don't have much time."

"Good," Walter said, softly, but not so softly that Cal couldn't hear. A wave of heat rose from his chest to his forehead, and he had a momentary impulse to break something, one of these statues that Walter liked so much, maybe. A boy shouldn't talk like that to his father.

He felt better when they got to the park, though, and stood about thirty feet apart beneath a green canopy of tall trees, the grass lapping at their ankles. "Now this is living," Cal said, and he tossed the ball up almost into the oak branches and caught it. "Here."

Walter stood uncertainly, glove hand extended, glove turned basket up. His glasses were momentarily opaque—the angle of the sun or something—so Cal couldn't tell for sure if he was watching.

Maybe he wasn't. The ball arced lazily through the air and thumped him in the chest. Walter drew himself inward like a turtle retracting head and limbs.

Cal shook his head, looked heavenward for guidance, and finding none, walked over to the boy.

"Are you okay?" he asked, crouching beside him.

He was pleased to see that Walter wasn't bawling, although he did sniff once or twice before he got out, "Yes."

"C'mon. Hop up and we'll try it again." He patted him on the shoulder and stood up.

"I don't want to," Walter said. He took off his glove and gave it to his father. "Can I go swing?"

"Swing?" Again Cal could feel something big and hurtful trying to escape, and he pulled his lips tight and just nodded. Walter scampered over to the swings, then the slide, while Cal sat silent on an aluminum bench beneath the trees.

That afternoon, Walter was packing up for home. He had showered and dressed for the evening church service, and sat fidgeting in front of the blank television set while Cal fixed a cowlick. Cal still had on the blue drawstring sweatpants and Cubs jersey he had worn to the park.

"I think it's a gyp that I have to go to church and you get to come home and watch TV. I don't get to. It isn't fair."

"Maybe so," Cal said, trying to hold Walter's head still. "Tell your mom to bring you over anytime and you can watch it all you want."

"I don't think so," Walter said.

"So what would you like me to do? Promise that I won't watch mine until you get a new one?"

"Maybe," Walter said. As soon as Cal turned his back he ruffled his hair back into place. "That would be fair."

Cal sighed. "I was pretty mad at your mom. You can understand that, can't you?"

Walter nodded. "But you can't do bad things just because you get mad, can you?"

"No," Cal said. "You can't. I wish it hadn't happened. I wish I could make it up to you."

"Right," Walter said gloomily. "But that doesn't get me a TV." He collected his bag and walked hang-dog out to the car.

Cal watched as Walter slid into the front and slammed the door shut. Everything he did next seemed natural and appropriate: he didn't answer Walter's questions when they finally got underway, just drove to where they needed to go.

When he pulled onto the wooden trestle bridge, Walter rolled his eyes. "Where in the world are we?" he asked.

"Hop out," Cal said, and he directed Walter's attention down to a huge snag where, perched in the branches of a washed-out Texas liveoak, hung the remains of Dr. Wise's shattered television.

"Okay," Walter shrugged.

"Now watch this," Cal said, smiling, and he pulled his nineteen-inch television from the back seat and carried it over to the brink. Walter looked on with some interest as Cal did a clean and jerk, poising the television precariously over his head for a moment before heaving it downward with all the strength and frustration and indignation of his thirty-seven years.

Like before, the television hit with a simultaneous crunch, crack, and splash that sent water coursing high in the air before falling gracefully back to earth. The white-faced calves leaned in a little closer to watch, peering through the strands of barbed wire.

"Cool," Walter breathed, turning up to give his father a tentative smile before looking back down as the color television bobbed once, twice, the cabinet filled with water, and it settled gently onto the creek bed.

They stood there in silence, looking on, Walter, Cal, the white-faced cattle. The last ripples spread to the shore or were carried downstream. In the distance they could hear a dog barking rhythmically.

"Sharks got it," Walter said at last. "Got both of them."

"They can chomp up just about anything," Cal agreed, unclenching his fists and lowering them to his side.

He held the door open and Walter scampered up into the seat. "You gotta watch out for those things," Walter said as the door closed. Cal nodded to himself, took a deep breath, and got in the car to take his son back to his mother.

RETROSPECTIVE

D. R. MEREDITH

Her granddaughter Elizabeth came to fetch her. . . . .

It was early June and Mattie's day to weed the graves in the family cemetery on the bluff above the Canadian River. Not that there were many weeds nor much grass either—the drought had seen to that—but Mattie still came to sit a spell with old friends from past times. Visiting the dead was sometimes a refuge from the living, most of whom, like Elizabeth, were much too young to be good company. Loneliness often accompanied too long a life, and Mattie had lately been feeling the burden. So few remained who remembered her beginnings in this windswept land of the Texas Panhandle, fewer still who wished her well. Hard women were respected but seldom admired, and Mattie Jo Hunter knew herself to be a hard woman. She was what the land and the times demanded, behaved according to those demands, and apologized to no one.

As for her sins—she could not take back what she had done, and times like these, sitting quietly with the bones of those who knew her best, she admitted that under the same circumstances, she would likely behave the same way again, given her nature and the nature of sin. A woman more than a man had to earn the right to sin, and once Mattie used up all the sin she had earned and then some, she never flinched when the time came for the reckoning. Neither had Jesse.

She did not flinch this time either when Elizabeth bid her come back to the house, for Jesse waited and they must hurry. Mattie had expected this final reckoning, felt the bond joining the two of them grow strong again as it had been in their youth and all the days that followed until she had denied their past for the future's sake. Now was the time, and the locked doors in her past were about to swing open. . . . .

Her granddaughter Elizabeth came to fetch her.

"How bad is he?" asked Mattie.

Doc Tobin rubbed the end of his stethoscope. She remembered his doing that same thing back in '18 when Rachel died from the Spanish influenza, and in '20 when Leon turned his face to the wall lest he be tempted to forgive his mother, and let the cancer in his belly take him. And again in '25 when Joe finally died. But she was expecting that death. Joe came home from the war with his lungs all burned from mustard gas. Sometimes she'd still wake up thinking she could hear him out on the porch coughing his life away.

But she never expected to see Leon again, hadn't seen him for nearly thirty years until he came home to die. But not to forgive. He never forgave her. Never forgave Jesse either. He left her six-year-old Elizabeth to raise, but the little girl had nothing to do with forgiveness.

All her sons and daughters but one were buried on that hill overlooking the Canadian River. And with each death Doc Tobin had rubbed the end of his stethoscope like it was some kind of talisman, and if he rubbed hard enough, he wouldn't have to tell her another child had died. His talisman hadn't worked all those other times, and she doubted it would work this time either.

"Jesse's pretty bad, Mattie," he finally said. He rubbed his stethoscope and Mattie noticed the age spots on the backs of his hands. He's an old man, she thought suddenly. Almost as old as Jesse and me.

"God damn it, Mattie!" he burst out, his voice sounding almost as strong as it was thirty-odd years ago when he helped her birth her last child, the one she shouldn't have had. "What was Jesse thinking about? Riding a half-broke horse like that. How old is he anyway?"

"I don't know; he never would tell me. Past eighty, I think. But he's a strong man," she said, reaching out to grasp his sleeve. "Can't you try some of those new medicines I hear about? Isn't there supposed to be a miracle drug? It's 1937, Doc. Haven't you learned how to save one of mine yet?"

"I'm sorry, Mattie."

She released him. It wasn't right to rub a man's face in failures he couldn't help. And Doc had always been good to her and Jesse, better than they had a right to expect. "If he stays down, gives himself a chance to heal, he's got some more good years left, Doc. He's too ornery to die."

210

Doc shook his head and patted Mattie's shoulder. His hand was as gnarled and swollen as her own. "He's all broke up inside. I don't know how he's lived this long except he waited to see you. Go sit with him, Mattie. Help him slip away happy."

"You'll keep everybody away?" she asked, conscious of the pairs of eyes staring at her. Particularly one pair, large and blue and bitter with hatred. She squared her shoulders. No sense in getting upset. The owner of that pair of eyes had hated her for sixty years. Jesse's dying wasn't going to change that. Sometimes Mattie wondered if hate didn't last longer than love.

His red-veined eyes looked grim. "If I have to hold them off at gun point." He took her arm. "He's upstairs waiting."

He escorted her up the wide oak staircase, the one she'd watched the cowboys build back in '80. Lord, but they had been angry. Carpentry wasn't cowboy work; it was unmanly. Several times she had thought she would have to keep them at it at gun point. But Jesse had always laughed and picked up a hammer to drive a few nails himself.

She stopped and clutched the bannister, her mouth suddenly painfully dry. "I always thought I was a strong woman, Doc. I had to be, a lone woman out here miles from anybody with children and a ranch to worry about. But I wasn't so strong as I thought. Jesse was always there to back me up, and I never admitted it out loud before. Lord, but who will back me now?"

Doc Tobin urged her up the stairs. "Jesse never gave you backbone, Mattie. You always had it. For God's sake, woman, he's just dying. He's not wiping out your memories. If you need him, he'll be there."

She nodded and took the last few steps up to the door at the top of the stairs. She smoothed back her hair, feeling its thick texture. It was silver now; nothing left of the molten gold color Jesse had always admired. Time stole so many things, and returned so few other than regret and wisdom. Regret never changed what had gone before, and wisdom always came to late to be of any benefit.

She glanced over her shoulder to the bottom of the stairs, met the bitter blue eyes, and shivered. "Remember, Doc, keep everybody out."

Doc Tobin opened the bedroom door and gently pushed her inside. "This is your time, Mattie."

She heard the door click behind her, heard the clock on the dresser ticking, heard a horse neigh down by the barn, concentrated on those sounds rather than the liquid noise of Jesse breathing.

His head turned on the pillow and he opened his eyes. "Mattie?" he asked, his voice raspy, weak. So unlike her memory of the last time they spoke seventeen years ago—when Leon died and left Elizabeth in her care.

"It's me, Jesse," she answered, coming closer, seeing the dark smudges under his eyes. At least his eyes were as she remembered: so light a gray as to look silver.

"Had the boys carry me here. Wasn't sure you would come otherwise."

"I would have come, Jesse."

"Didn't know if you would break your word to Leon."

Mattie drew a breath. "My son is a long time dead and Elizabeth is a woman grown."

"Sit by me," he whispered, lifting his hand to reach for her. "On the bed, Mattie," he continued when she hesitated. "Won't nobody care."

"You said that before. Remember? When you were laid up with a broken leg back in '78?" She sat down and took his hand. "You laughed at me when I said it wasn't proper for a young married woman to be sitting on the same bed with an unmarried man." she sighed. "Times have changed some. Used to be a woman worried about so many things. It was important to be a good woman."

He drew a shallow breath and she heard the air gurgle like water through a busted pipe. You were a good woman, Mattie."

She laughed and was pleased the laughter didn't have a bitter sound. Folks didn't call her that Hunter woman because they believed her virtuous, but Jesse knew that better than anyone. "Most folks didn't think so. Remember what they said when I wore pants and rode off astride my old mare. I don't know what shocked folks the most: my wearing pants, or not riding sidesaddle."

"You scared the hell out of me, riding off like that across the damn prairie all by yourself."

She believed him because she could see the remembered fear in his eyes. "I knew you would follow me. I knew it was time."

"I finally caught up with you under that old cottonwood tree."

"The one out in the front yard," she said, remembering how he had yelled at her, remembering too what happened when he stopped yelling. She felt warm and breathless, not with desire, but with its memory. For a heartbeat she wished she and Jesse were young again, could feel hard, firm flesh against flesh instead of the memory of it. The moment passed as it always did. A woman couldn't go back over her own tracks.

"You were pretty, Mattie, sitting there on a blanket under that tree, sipping cold water from the spring you found." Again the sound of air rushing through fluid-filled lungs. "And determined. you always were as stubborn as an army mule. You stuck that chin of yours up in my face and announced this was where you were building a house. Said you were tired of living on dirt floors in a sheepherder's old placita."

She said more than that and saw those memories in his eyes, too. "I was tired of the bugs and spiders falling between those cottonwood rafters from that sod roof. I used to hang a sheet over Leon's crib. And I knew you men weren't going to find a better place. Men would live in a cave and never wash from year to year if it weren't for women."

He choked on his laughter and she wiped the bloody foam off his lips. "Stubborn little Mattie," he continued, his voice weaker, the silences between sentences longer. "You got your house. Freighted the lumber in by wagon from Dodge City to Tascosa, and you would send the cowboys over to pick it up."

"I made them draw straws to see who was making the trip," she said, remembering faces of men years dead. "They all wanted to go so they could get drunk down in the Hogtown district."

"It was a place a man could let off steam. I used to go down there myself when we first came to the Panhandle."

She could still feel the anger she felt then, and resentment that she had no right to her anger. "I never asked you to stop."

"I never went back after I caught you under the cottonwood tree," he said, squeezing her hand with fingers already cold.

She looked away so he couldn't see the tears. "It was a long time ago, Jesse. Just like Hogtown and Tascosa. Nothing left either place but a few crumbling mud walls that didn't wash away when the Canadian flooded, and they're going to tear those down to build a boys' home." She laughed and heard the bitterness this time. "The town where more 'boys' got in trouble than anywhere I know of, and it's going to be a home for troubled boys. Maybe that's good. Maybe it will cancel out all the grief Tascosa caused."

"Tascosa didn't make Leon run off, Mattie."

She raised her eyes to look at him. "There was ugly talk about me in Tascosa."

"Always was, Mattie. Leon never believed it before."

"Sons expect their mothers to be without sin."

Jessie closed his eyes and Mattie caught her breath for fear he slipped away thinking she blamed him. "Jessie?"

He opened his eyes. "They never tore down the old courthouse."

She let out her breath in a sigh. "No, it's still there. The boys are living in it until Mr. Farley can build something more suitable. Then it will be a museum, but I doubt I'll ever go visit it. I don't need exhibits of bits and pieces to remind me of what Elizabeth calls the old days. I have memories enough of my own."

He smiled. "Remember when we used to go dancing in the old courtroom up on the second floor?"

She remembered. Everyone went, even the babies. The mothers would bring blankets and put the little ones to bed off in the corners. Once the musicians started playing and couples began whirling around the floor, Mattie could forget this was the room where Jessie was tried for murder and sentenced to prison, where she was figuratively stripped naked for all who attended the trial to gawk at. She reckoned a dying man would rather remember the good times.

"Remember when we caught Rachel and the young Williams boy kissing out in the old buggy?" she asked, rushing on before more bad memories crowded out the good ones.

He chuckled and his breath wheezed in and out. "You blessed them out and sent them back to the dance." His voice softened. "And we took their place in the buggy."

"We were too old for that kind of foolishness," she said, feeling again the awkwardness of the position, the fear of being seen, the joy of not caring.

"I was never too old with you, Mattie. But here just lately I don't think I'd be much use."

214

He sounded embarrassed, Mattie thought, as if a man in his eighties ought to be ashamed of not being able to make love. "Is that why you tried to ride that horse? To prove you're still a man?"

He closed his eyes and his breath caught in his throat. She clutched his hand tighter, trying to keep him just a little longer. After a few seconds, his breathing started again, and he opened his eyes. "Maybe I just wanted to choose my own time and my own place. Not live until I'm helpless and one of the grandkids has to help me to the breakfast table every morning. Or I lose my sight and stumble around the house like a useless old coot, and can't find my way to you."

"But you're leaving me, Jesse! It doesn't matter that we haven't lived together since Elizabeth came; I knew you were close. All my children gone, and now you, too." She swallowed, her throat so tight it hurt. "Grandchildren aren't the same. They don't remember our times. To them I'm just a crazy old woman who tells stories and never the ones they want to hear."

"I left when you asked me to, Mattie."

She didn't need reminding. Of all the doors in her past, she dreaded opening this one the most. "There was not a one of our children who did not bear us a grudge, Jessie. I did not want another generation growing up to despise us. I could have the past and you, or I could have the future and Elizabeth. Of my own free will I promised Leon to deny you. I've kept my word until now."

He was quiet, his eyes closed, his chest barely rising and falling. His face looked gray, his cheeks more sunken than even an hour ago. Perhaps an hour more, maybe less, and another door in her life would close. She was a house full of closed doors.

He opened his eyes and she knew he was standing in front of another one of those closed doors, begging her to open it. "Do you ever blame me for the baby, Mattie?" he asked.

He'd never asked her before. It was one of those times they had shared, but never talked about. She started to lie, but the time for lies was when it happened; not now. "I was forty-three years old, too old to be having babies. And the birthing was hard."

"I know, Mattie. I stayed with you."

His voice was soothing just as it was that afternoon more than thirty years ago, soothing and calm when she was neither. The bedroom had been hot and her hair was plastered against her head with sweat. The wind had stopped blowing that morning, and the lace curtains hung motionless at the windows. She remembered his holding her hands while she cursed him with every contraction that ripped through her belly.

"I hated you then, but it didn't last. And it wasn't a real hate, Jesse, just the kind every woman has in childbed when she realizes nobody can help her, especially the man that put her there. Birthing is lonely work, and I guess womankind's never gotten over being mad about the way the Lord arranged things, so we take it out on our menfolks. My blame wasn't the hateful kind, just normal."

"I never knew that."

"I never told you. Wasn't any point in talking about it." She rubbed his cold hand, knowing how useless it was, but needing to do it. "Did you blame me, Jesse, about the baby dying?"

His eyes were liquid silver with tears. "He was the only child of mine I ever saw born, Mattie. He looked like you. Had lots of that golden hair."

She wiped her eyes on the bedsheet. "I never saw him. I fainted after he was born, and when I woke up, he was already buried."

"Doc Tobin and I washed him, and I dressed him in that little christening gown you made. I never blamed you, Mattie. He wasn't meant to live. There was something wrong with his lungs and he couldn't breath right. I figured it was God's judgment on us, but Doc Tobin explained we were too old to be making babies."

"We did a lot of wrong things in our lives, Jesse, but I don't think God punishes people by killing their babies. It wasn't our time or his, that's all."

"Is it our time now, Mattie?" His voice was weak, weaker than a few minutes ago, she thought. "Because I'm going to say the words, and I want you to say them, too. We never have before, not in the more than sixty years we've shared. I'll say them first, then you, because I want to take your words with me. He took a breath, and she knew it was his last one. "I love you, Mattie."

She hesitated, and he looked at her one last time. "I love you, Jesse," she said, and watched his silver eyes tarnish into dull gray as he died.

216

But she wasn't dead, and there was one more task she had to do before she closed this door. She closed Jesse's eyes and pulled the sheet over his face, so long beloved and so often denied, then stepped out of the bedroom. While he lived, Jesse had been hers; dead, the husk of his body belonged to another. She straightened her shoulders and walked down the stairs to meet the woman she had hated and wronged for sixty years.

She looked into Caroline's hostile eyes. "Your husband is dead."

SLIM

CAROL CULLAR

Shamrock, Texas
August 1937

The rolling prairie stretched from the Rockies to the Ozarks across a thousand miles of gently rolling hills cut by dry river beds and small farms plowed higgledy-piggledy and sown with acres of wheat—millions of acres of wheat planted to answer the government's cry during World War I. Slow to convert, some of the farmers were switching to cotton and corn, but too few had gone to modern agricultural methods. Spirits reeled from the War, the Influenza of 1918–19, the Crash. When the market collapsed, they lost money, then equipment, their farms, and heart. As if unsatisfied with the havoc wreaked, Nature unleashed The Drought and aimed it like some great magnifying lens focused incessantly on the western farmland of Oklahoma. Fickle rains fell, only to be sucked away by the burning air. Elsewhere, entire sections flash-flooded away for want of contour plowing. The atmosphere became a destructive engine powering itself on heated updrafts, pulling erosive ground-winds into its maw, along with the topsoil, then the subsoil, and the hopes of all those tied to the land. Thousands quit when the dust storms began to rage; some went insane as the dust-laden, ionized wind scoured every crevice and left nowhere to hide, nowhere to run except away—to California, to South Texas, to sanity—away from the burning eye of the sun. But some stayed.

Bessie Mae stepped to the screen door with the battered tin dipper in her hand and with a deft flick of the wrist splashed what was left of her drink over the top portion of the flour sack stitched there. The cascading droplets wet the thin fabric, and a breeze blew the cooler air over her. She closed her eyes and breathed.

"Hey!" The startled voice was deep and unfamiliar and came from the glaring haze on the other side of the screen.

"Oh! I'm so sorry! Let me get a towel!" Bessie pushed the screen past its buffer catch and opened it wide. A hobo stood on the stoop, his cap in hand; he mopped his forehead with a red bandanna.

"You didn't get me very wet!" After his first quick glance upward, he fixed his gaze respectfully on the yellow tom that came to swish about her ankles.

Bessie searched the high-buttoned front of his faded work shirt and saw only a few droplets. Clasping the latch in her hand, she looked higher at the averted head, flushed with heat. When she realized he intended to say nothing, she asked: "Can I help you, Mister?"

"Just gettin' ready to knock . . ." the stranger darted a quick look at her face, his hands betrayed a sudden nervousness. "Could . . . could. Do you reckon I could have a drink?" He finished in a rush and looked up again.

"Oh! Of course, just a moment." Bessie let the screen door close and stepped to the stone lip of the cistern where the water bucket stood. Taking the hobo dipper from its nail on the closet wall, she scooped it brim full and carried it back to the door.

The drifter had replaced his cap and tied his bandanna about his neck. His bony wrists dangled from the too-short sleeves and frayed cuffs of his shirt. Bess continued to watch him as he gulped from the tilted dipper, his head thrown back, adam's apple bobbing. He lifted his cap and poured the last drips on his head, then swiped across his forehead with his sleeve before resettling the battered tweed. He returned the dipper with great deference.

"Thank you, ma'am . . . mind if I sit in the shade over there and have my lunch?"

"That would be fine, Mister." Bessie looked him up and down. "Where's your lunch?"

He blushed. "Ah . . . here. I got me some crackers." He patted his breast pocket.

"Hump! Wait right there." She disappeared. In a moment she was back with a glossy red tomato and a large green onion. "These go well with crackers."

"Thank you, ma'am!" He bobbed his head and touched his cap. His faded blue eyes shown. "Yes, sir-e-e, thank you!" He turned and strode away, loose in his gait.

Bessie let the screen door close with a snap, hooking it behind her to keep the baby from wandering out. In the kitchen she stirred the black-eyed peas on the back burner, checked the cornbread in the oven, then set Jabe's place at the head of the table after giving the worn yellow oil-cloth a final swipe. The hobo was just in sight out the east window, seated, resting his back against the black locust at the margin of the road.

"Shoo, Tom!" She toed the persistent mouser-turned-bum out of her path and peeked around the corner of the dining room door to check on Baby Lester. She always thought of him as Baby Lester and was assured to see that he still sat in the middle of the turkey carpet with his nesting cups scattered about. He was chewing one and banging another against the rug.

"Bessie! Bessie, you got the screen locked!" Jabe was back from the gin! She clapped her hands for the baby and scooped him up to hurry to the back porch.

She smoothed the sides of her simple bun and wiped her nose and forehead with the back of her left hand to erase any stray flour. Jabe was prone to tease if he caught her with flour on her nose. An unconscious smile lit her coffee-brown eyes as she undid the latch and stood to one side.

"Here! He's too heavy for you! Come to papa, Lester! Has he been all right today?" Jabe lifted the slack form of the three year old into the crook of his arm and hooked the other about Bess' petite shoulder. His blunt fingers plucked at her left earlobe.

"Oh, yes, he's fine. Very happy today. Your lunch is ready to put on the table." She tightened her apron and hastened toward the kitchen.

Jabe set the baby down and splashed a dipper full of water into the granite wash basin. Lester toddled on unsteady legs, clinging to his father's tan work pants as Jabe scooped a fragment of lye soap out of the dish and began to scrub. When he had finished he sloshed the dirty water about in the pan, then lifted the lid of the slop crock by the door, reminding himself to take it out to the pigs when he had finished his meal. He smoothed his thinning hair in the tiny mirror, then hoisted the baby back onto his hip for the few steps to the kitchen. Ten steps more than Baby Lester could have made on his own, more than he might ever take. Jabe settled him into the high chair and put the tray down. Lester began to pat the smooth wooden tray.

"What chores did you give the hobo fixin' the gate to the chicken pen?" He seated himself at the head of the table and reached for the brimming goblet of buttermilk at the head of his place.

Bessie Mae straightened from the oven, her face reddened by the heat. "Oh! I didn't! He came askin' for water, then went to set under the black locust just a few minutes ago!"

"Well, he's found himself a job without having to be told. Did you give him any food?" Jabe tucked into the black-eyed peas as she shoveled a huge slab of hot cornbread onto the side of his plate.

Jabe looked up at her flushed features and ran his free hand up the pale cotton print of her skirt, cupping her thigh.

"Jabe! The baby!" Bessie jumped from his caress, but smiled at his boldness. She busied herself at the sink and spoke over her shoulder. "I gave him a tomato and an onion. He said he had some crackers, but I doubt it." Jabe's chair squeaked back as he left the table.

"Mister! Ho! Could you come over here?" Jabe waited until the stranger hung the hammer back on the wall of the garage and made his way to the stoop. "Come on in here and wash up. We was just settin' down to eat."

"Well, sir, I ate just a bit ago, but don't mind if I do!" He followed Jabe up the steps, went to the wash basin and scrubbed his hands, but wiped their wetness on his pants rather than dirty the pretty towel on the nail. He stepped to the kitchen door. "Ma'am, thank you kindly for the tomato and onion. They was right tasty."

Jabe pulled out the white wooden chair across the corner from his own place, "Here, set."

Bessie filled a plate at the stove, topping it with a slab of cornbread and set it before the gaunt-faced man. "For this bread we take, for our way we make, thank You. Amen!" The stranger ducked his head and began to shovel the peas in with an economy of motion that spoke volumes of the days it had been since his last meal.

"Amen! Amen!" Lester chimed in from his place on the other side of the table, banging his tray with more fervor. "Peas! Peas!" he chanted as his mother placed a saucer of cooled black-eyes before him, then went to fill her own plate.

"You were fixin' the chicken fence when I came up . . . ."

"Yes, sir. Gate was saggin'." He spoke around a mouth full of cornbread.

Lester chose this moment to begin whacking the tray of his high chair again. "Nilk . . . nilk!"

Bessie moved to the blue Indianhead pitcher on the far end of the table, lifted the cup towel from its top and poured a small mug of buttermilk, placing it on Baby Lester's tray.

"That's a fine boy, there." The stranger spoke as he neatly polished the last of the pea juice from his plate. He smiled at the child, who chose for once to return the favor.

Jabe continued to eat, his head down toward his food. He spoke finally without raising his head. "He's slow, Mister, real slow."

"Yes, sir, I ken tell . . . ."

But Jabe went on, as if the hobo hadn't spoken.

"A mite slow to walk, he was, and last spring he followed Nettie, she's our middle girl, out to the clothes line. He was playin' in the dirt, botherin' nary a soul, and when she went back with the second basket to hang up, there he was . . . covered with red ants! She brushed them off and ran screamin' for her mother, but when they got his diaper off and got 'em all off him, he was bad stung. Bad stung. Like he never had a chance. Nearly lost him, we did. Had a terrible fever for days! Since then he seems slower. Won't walk, or nothin'." Jabe's midnight blue eyes turned to the stranger, daring him to condemn.

The hobo's adam's apple convulsed. "I seen he was slow . . . like me, I reckon. 'Like to like' my grannie used to say. . . . They gave up on me. Sent me away when my momma didn't want me. Been on a farm ever since. Them folks was nice, patient with me, you know?" He forced himself to continue, afraid that the father beside him was going to give up on this child. "Slow folks just take some extra patience. This is a fine boy here." He blushed at his temerity and stammered, "Well . . . I'll get back out there and have that gate hung proper in a jiffy! Much obliged, Ma'am, for that fine meal!

Jabe's eyes glanced over Bessie Mae's tear-filled ones. He nodded his thanks for the meal and followed the hobo out the door.

"The farm you left burn out?"

"Well, yes and no. The Tollivers was real old and when this drought hit, it seemed to dry them up along with the wheat. They both died within two months of one another, and their own son sent me on my way. . . . Didn't want no dummie around, he said. . . . Reckon I'll walk out to Californy and get me a job pickin' cotton." He set his cap, hitched his pants and wiped his hands down the seat of them. "I was just about to finish hangin' that gate when you called me in to eat; reckon I'll get back to that, if it's all right with you?" He looked around at Jabe on the step behind him.

"What's your name, Mister?" Jabe's hand was extended.

"Slim . . . just Slim." The hobo shook Jabe's hand and met his smiling eyes before glancing quickly away.

"You got family in California?" Jabe searched the face bent before him.

"No family . . . nowhere. On my own." He kicked a dusty clod toward the ragged pale petunias beside the stoop, the ones that got the water that was too dirty for the hogs.

"I could use a hand around the place here; there's a cot in the garage over there, if you've a mind to stay. This here drought can't last forever, and we're gonna have a mite of cotton make it through the summer. . . . 'Less you particularly wanted to go to California?"

Slim looked up, his face wreathed in joy, "No, sir-e-e! I've a mind to stay!"

And stay he did. For twenty years he shelled peas, hoed cotton, and ate watermelon on the back porch with the family until late one November night in 1956, when a semi, bowling out of Oklahoma City on its way to California, knocked him like a stray pin off the highway on his way back from the domino parlor. In his meager effects Jabe found the address of a prominent physician in Monroe, Louisiana, but when he telegraphed them of the death of their brother, there was no response, so Jabe and Bessie buried him in the family plot on a barren, windy hill south by southwest of Shamrock.

ALL IN A DAY'S WORK
FOR THREE COWBOYS

LAWRENCE CLAYTON

They left the house before dawn, three cowboys out for a day's work. Tim drove the pickup truck pulling the trailer with the three horses. Bob and the father—everyone called him Dad—were in the three-quarter ton truck pulling the long gooseneck trailer that they would haul the cattle in. Not long after sunup they pulled through the gate of the pasture ten miles from the home place. They parked near the pens and unloaded the horses. "Should we hide the trailer so the cattle won't see it?" Tim asked.

"Let 'em see it," Bob growled. "We'll get 'em anyway." Dad agreed with Bob, as he usually did. They were that much alike. Bob had stayed at the ranch after his graduation from high school. Tim, two years younger than Bob, had gone on to college, to play football, mostly. And he had made Little All-American at linebacker. He taught and coached for awhile in high school until what he called "a screwball school board and a crazy superintendent" convinced him to return to ranch life. His wife liked it all right living out on the ranch. At least she complained little but went to town as often as she could. After the mother died she was the only woman there, since Bob had never married. But Bob had his share of girlfriends and late night escapades.

The trio swung into their saddles and headed for the mesquite brush. Bob's horse tried to pitch a little in the faint morning coolness, but Bob spurred the mare and jerked the reins to settle her into a trot. He even liked wild horses. They spent most of the August morning chasing cattle through the mesquites and finally got the herd to the corral. In the course of the morning, Bob had roped three calves and bulldogged one old cow. Tim had not seen much need for any of it. "Damn," he shouted, "I haven't much had this much fun in a long time. Maybe I ought to give up this slow ranch life and go on the rodeo circuit. I'll bet I could make a bunch of money. And I hear those girls flock to those rodeo heroes."

Tim laughed to himself. "Those girls have a lot to pick from because of the ups and downs of the fortunes of the heroes," he shouted back. "And I can't tell you have any shortage of that kind of activity anyway."

"The grass is always greener in the other pasture," Bob taunted.

Tim knew Bob had missed the proverb. "It only looks that way," he muttered.

The heat was dizzying by late morning, and the hornflies viciously attacked the cattle, which were bawling and circling in the dusty corral. On his lathered mare, Bob chased the last yearling into the pen, and Tim slammed the gate. "Got 'em all." Tim said with a grin, but his father scowled.

"You damn near ran some of 'em to death doin' it, though, an' in this heat," he said. "That last one lost ten pounds before he finally got in the pen to get away from you two, and you call yourselves cowboys."

Bob grinned at Tim, even though both were familiar with the old man's rough ways. They were a little wild but they worked at it, just to keep up their image, even if for their own eyes. Bob was especially diligent about it.

"I remember hearing one time Dad chased one old steer 'til it died. Ruined a good horse doin' it, too. Guess age is gettin' to him," Bob said.

"Yes, old age and hard knocks."

They cut out the cattle they wanted to sell: four older cows and eight yearlings. Dad wanted to test the market before he sold the rest of the calf crop. They turned out the rest of the animals, which made a beeline for the tank and a drink of water. Tim backed the gooseneck trailer to the chute with Bob waving him directions. Finally a jolt and a loud bump announced that he was back far enough. "Bob," Dad called. "Try to keep him from hitting the damn fences. You boys are goin' to tear up everything I got."

Bob grinned, his good-natured humor coming out even in the face of the almost constant tongue lashing of his father. "Dad," he called. "Damn if you don't get grouchier as you get older."

"I'm not old, you young outlaws. I can still handle cattle as well as both of you put together. And I can still handle either one of you, too." He grinned as he said it.

Tim walked back to the crowding pen and pushed the four cows on toward the chute. "Let's get them in the front section and close the gate on 'em."

One old cow had a long set of sharp curved horns, those kind that turned up but slanted toward the front. She was mad and didn't care who knew it. Finally all four were going up the chute and hit the back of the trailer in a line. Two went in, but the third wanted to wait. The old horned cow was last. Tim followed up, but Bob jumped in behind the last cow, shouting and twisting her tail to crowd four cows into space that three pretty well filled up. The old horned cow was switching her tail rapidly and her bowels were loose. The green spattered on Bob's left pants leg and his boot. He was outraged, and his language showed it. "You old bitch, I'll show you." He jabbed her with a stick, and she made a supreme effort to find room in the trailer to escape her attacker. Dad had jumped up on the side of the trailer to try to make the others give the newcomer some room. He shouted at her and encouraged Bob. That last part was a big mistake. The old cow got her head down and the horn ran through the pipe sides of the trailer. Bob poked her again, and as a result, one keen horn ran through Dad's faded denim jeans just above the boot top and slid into the muscle of his calf as slick as a surgeon sinking a scalpel. Dad jumped back, pulling the horn out but leaving the tip red and his pants leg sporting a growing red spot. Blood began to collect in his boot. "Damn," he yelled. "Bob, slow down. You're going to kill her and me too."

Bob, who had not seen the goring, couldn't figure out the sudden change in attitude. "You sure do change your mind quick," he muttered.

After some personal first aid, Dad resumed his role as straw boss and the loading continued. He limped some but tried not to show it. Eight yearling calves bad been cut out, and Tim had them started up the chute to fill the back of the trailer. Two didn't want to make the trip and started trying to turn around.

Bob got into the act by kicking the animals from his perch on top of the chute fence. "Get on in there!" he screamed and kicked with his green spattered boot. He slipped but caught himself before he got all the way down; and one of calves kicked him, catching his manure-smeared leg and giving it a resounding thwack.

226

Dad, in pain himself, giggled. "Hurts, don't it." he taunted.

"Didn't hurt much," Bob grimaced. "I'll get the little bastard for that," and he kicked one of the following calves, almost causing the three remaining ones to back down the chute.

The loading continued, with Tim pushing the last one in. As it entered, Dad got excited and jumped on the back of the trailer to help, or boss, being careful to hold his game leg out to keep from hitting it on the fence. Bob, not really watching what he was doing, slammed the tailgate hard on the door jamb of the trailer. The metal bar cut the end off of Dad's middle finger on his left hand as if a knife or sharp saw had been used. Blood spurted and curses followed. "You cut my finger off," Dad moaned.

Bob, seeing the plight of his father, spotted the end of the first joint of the finger lying on the board serving as the end of the chute. "Sure did," Bob said, and he kicked the piece through a crack. "Damn sure did."

Dad howled at him. "That's my finger. Don't throw it away."

"It won't do you no good now," Bob said, rather matter-of-factly.

Dad was wrapping the stub in a handkerchief and trying to staunch the flow of blood. Tim, taken aback by the incident, went to his father's aid, but the old man refused. "You boys are just wild and can't help it, I guess. But I didn't think you would try to cut my hand off."

With all of the stock loaded, Tim jumped the horses into the trailer of the other truck while Bob jumped behind the wheel of his truck, glared at Did until he got in, and then they headed out. Tim knew they would wait for him at the gates so that Bob would not have to get cut to open them. Dad probably wouldn't try. Tim drove off chasing the dust of Bob's truck and trailer. It worked out as he thought on the gates. When they were going through the last one before pulling onto the highway, Bob leaned out and said "Why don't you leave the horses and that trailer here and go on with us. Leave it in the shade, and it won't hurt the horses." Dad seemed to be holding up pretty well.

To Tim, the miles seemed endless. About ten miles down the road, a thought struck Dad. "Let's stop at Rosie's Place. I could use a beer," he said.

Despite Tim's protest, Bob wheeled in as they approached the shabby low building just off Highway 36. At night it looked all right, with the neon lights flashing. But in the harsh light of daytime, the reality was not a pretty sight. Inside, however, it was dark and cool. "What happened to your finger, Dad?" the waitress asked. "Got it somewhere you shouldn't had it, I guess. I warned you about foolin' around with that kind of women."

"Damn it, bring us some beer," Dad growled, and the girl—Candy, they called her—giggled on her way to the cooler for the bottles of Lone Star.

Tim was still trying to make his point, "We can't stop here. We need to get Dad to the hospital before he bleeds to death."

Dad glared at him. "I need a beer or two. Sit down and relax. I won't die." Tim relaxed a little and waved to Candy to serve him a beer too, which she did.

"I told the old coot to stop fooling around with those young girls. I told him he'd lose a finger or somethin'. He finally got what he deserved, didn't he?" She directed her remarks to Bob, who seemed grateful. Dad guzzled his first beer and beckoned to Candy for another one. Tim shook his head for no. It was hot outside, and the cold of the beer caused beads of moisture to form on the bottles. Bob took to peeling off the paper labels from the longnecks. He played two songs on the juke box—"All I need Is 'Round the Clock Lovin'" and "Good-Hearted Woman." He watched Candy, who seemed not to mind. The gathering had all the trappings of a party.

Tim was getting nervous again. After what seemed an eternity to him—at least it was three beers later and without lunch—Dad was finally ready to go. "Pay the girl," he said to Tim.

"Come back, Dad, when you feel better, and I'll console you," Candy called as they walked out into the bright sunlight. "That goes for you too, Bob." Tim felt left out but did not worry about it. He even felt grateful.

Tim, who had only one beer to the three each for Bob and Dad, beat Bob to the driver's seat since Bob had turned back to say something to Candy. Dad limped along. Tim drove as fast as he dared to the hospital. When they reached the emergency room entrance, Tim couldn't find a place to park the truck and trailer and had to let Dad and Bob out. The cattle were bawling and people were staring. Dad, who was in some pain by now, said, "Go on to the auction barn with these. The sale is still on. I don't want them to have to stand over 'til tomorrow. Come back and get me later."

Tim drove off as Bob helped Dad in the emergency entrance. Inside, the coolness felt good as Dad eased into a chair and Bob walked up to the admissions window. Dad couldn't hear what was said at first but he saw Bob getting mad. He knew it because Bob's face got red and he slapped his hat on his leg, the left one. "All we need is a doctor to sew up his leg and his finger. Can't any ole doc do that? It was an accident. I didn't stab him; a cow did. No, we don't have a regular 'physician.' We ain't often sick. What kind of hospital is this, anyway?" Bob was really getting work up. Finally, the young clerk blushed, rose suddenly, and left. Dad could not be sure but what Bob reached for her through the pay slot in the bottom of the glass. When an older, burly nurse walked up, she told Bob a doctor would be right out. And he was. A young intern walked up to Bob and then followed the glance to Dad, who was a little pale by now.

"You sure you're a doctor?" Bob quizzed. "You look too young to be a real doctor."

The intern ignored the question. An orderly helped Bob get Dad into a wheelchair, and the doctor followed them into the treatment room. They got Dad on the table, and then the doctor cut Dad's pants and boot top. That stirred him up some, but even Bob agreed it was the only way. They finally got the boot off the swelling leg and ankle. After the deadening took effect, the intern cleaned the wound and stitched it. Then he turned his attention to the bloody stump of the finger. "Just the fleshy part and most of the nail are gone," he said. "I think we ought to give it a chance to grow back. If it doesn't, we'll have to amputate it back to the first joint." Dad paled and readily agreed to try it that way. The young doctor cleaned and bandaged the wound. After a tetanus shot, which Dad protested he didn't need, the doctor talked to both of them, though it is doubtful Dad heard much. He was pretty ill by this time. "Keep him off that leg for at least a week. Elevate the hand and arm to help alleviate the throbbing. These pills are for pain; these will keep infection from developing. Change the bandage every day on both wounds." The doctor seemed glad it was over.

Tim came in then, sweating, his hat on the back of his head, and was sent back for the truck he had just parked three blocks away in the Safeway parking lot, the only place that would accommodate the trailer. Bob wrote a check for the bill. The young clerk looked at it suspiciously. "It's good," Bob protested and stalked away. When Tim pulled through the entrance tunnel, the smell of fresh cow manure swept through the open door into the waiting room. Two orderlies helped Dad into the cab, despite a very weak protest on his part. As the truck pulled away, Tim breathed a sigh of relief. Dad was pretty groggy from the medicine and the beer on an empty stomach. Bob laughed, "Ain't it been a hell of a day. I love it."

"Yes," Dad said. "Hey, why don't we stop off at Rosie's on the way home. I could use a beer."

Bob said, "Yeah, maybe Candy is about to get off work." When they passed Rosie's, Dad was asleep, and Tim was glad. Bob got mad because they didn't stop.

HORSE ON THE HIGHWAY

ALBERT HALEY

At noon the Dallas-Ft. Worth airport was a busy sprawl. Dark skinned people pushed mops over concourse tiles. An electric cart beeped as it carried a load of geriatric men wearing ten-gallon hats and string ties. Though Brice Stockwell hadn't been Texas way in a good while, here on the ground it was all familiar. He knew his way around. The advantages of being a hometown boy.

He continued his steady walk toward baggage claim, swinging his hardcase as he went. He passed lighted signs designed to boost the local sports franchises: Go Cowboys, Rangers, and Mavericks. Brice smiled at the pushy, clenched fist sentiment. How might one translate it for the non-native? Our team is headed for number one or ol' coach is out the door. That was civic pride, Big D style.

In the claim area he continued his hopeful search for a familiar face. So far the Stockwell family had not turned out exactly en masse. Brice accepted this and killed the bag-waiting time by cavesdropping on his fellow business travelers. They were tall, big-shouldered guys, possibly oil men like himself, and they were sharing the weather report. Temperatures across the state were in the mid-70s, only a week 'til Thanksgiving, definitely a hardcore case of Indian summer, can't beat it with a stick. It made Brice think of back home: Chicago, snowbanks, fifteen icy degrees. A few hours ago he had said good-bye to Judy with more of the white stuff drifting down. The Yellow Cab idled behind him in the driveway, its wipers flicking, as he warned Judy not to try to shovel out by herself.

"Pay the kid next door," he said. "You're too far along."

Judy laughed. "Brice, you make it sound like it's going to happen tomorrow. I wish."

"Well, I'll be calling every night."

"Good. You'll keep me posted on how it goes with your brother and all. Now how about a kiss before the man drives off without you?"

Aboard the plane Brice had closed his laptop and napped intermittently. He kept waking to find himself thinking about Judy's good-bye. In a way, her kiss was her last word and that word was "Randall." Ever since he'd penciled this trip into his planner she'd been campaigning for Brice to find a way to let the bulk of his business hang fire and use the time in Texas to concentrate on his poor, screwed up brother. Extend the trip if he had to. Work on family ties. But how could he? Here came his pieces on the rubber belt—a burgundy garment bag, a taped-up box containing frozen steaks for his dad who thought Chicago was the center of the beef universe. Still no sign of anyone from his family, especially Randall. Brice checked out a baggage cart and headed for the car rental area.

Five minutes later he was about to ink the contract when someone began to speak into his left ear. Brice turned from the counter, using peripheral vision to make sure the laptop was still at his feet.

The man wore a chalk-stripe suit with a pink tie. Brice looked from the queasy tie to the man's feet. The oxblood loafers had tassels on them. It was the craziest thing. Brice was pretty sure he recognized his little brother's feet, but that was all.

Randall took off his sunglasses and slammed his hands on the counter.

"Can't bull-leave it! You know what you did back there? Walked right past me. Like I was nigh invisible. Didn't you know I'd be at the gate? Sure you did. Know what I did then? Followed you to see if you'd ever look around and notice me."

"I can't believe it either," Brice said, trying to recover. He was glad that Randall seemed to be laughing. How had he messed up like this? It was so obvious now. The wide open face could only be Randy; it was just that he looked—

"Staring right past me, I tell you!" Randall bawled. "Hell, I can't blame you, bro. It's been a few years."

"You're looking real good," Brice said.

"No way. I should be dead. But that's another story. Tell this good lookin' gal there's no sale." Randall winked at the car rental agent. "Don't worry, ma'am. This here's my big brother. He's confused about what he wants. It's unusual for Mr. Brice Stockwell, but it's true."

"You're brothers?" She smiled.

"Hell, think it's our fault?" Randall laughed some more. He picked up Brice's computer and they were on their way.

In the parking garage Randall stopped at a news box where he bought a *Morning News.* "Look here, Brice. It's about you guys. This must be some pow-wow you oil boys are having."

"Just a regular regional meeting." Brice didn't want to look at the business page headline. He still felt dazed and embarrassed about his failure to identify. What exactly was it about Randall? That he'd lost more hair? The deepening lines in the forehead and around the eyes like someone had been working on him with hammer and chisel? Or was it the fact that somehow he seemed shorter than ever, a squat post that had been pounded deeper into the ground? Brice couldn't put a finger on it. It was more than physical. How could it be explained to Judy? *I didn't know my own brother.*

Randall was riffling pages, trying to find the continuation of the article. "You call this just a meeting, Brice? With environmental pressures, escalatin' taxes, and declining wellhead production? You can't PR me, boy. It's all here." Randall punched the newspaper with his fist.

Brice glanced at it. "The media ought to find something else to write about."

"Spoken like a company man!" Randall laughed. "But get with it. Like Dad always says, in Dallas if an oil man pees in a closet, sure enough someone's going to write about it. Velocity, range, and how's the aim. It affects all those mansions on the hill."

They started walking again, Randall not remembering exactly where he'd parked. He remained nonplused, however, a happy guy, arms swinging loosely, intent on playing the personal spotlight onto big brother. What about Judy's sonogram? Why had they asked not to know the child's sex? Hell, they weren't going for that natural childbirth crap, were they? No woman, even the bitchiest one on earth, deserved that kind of pain. And what about Dad?

"Dad? You mean how's he feel about becoming a grandfather?" Brice asked.

"That's right. What's the old man say?"

Brice bit his lip in a spot where it itched. "I thought he might come out to meet me." He had been waiting to say that.

"Don't worry, bro. You'll see plenty of him. He told me I had to bring you straight to the house. He's got a room fixed up for you. No way his son is staying in one of those damn sterilized hotels, quote, unquote."

"But I've got to be downtown for my meetings."

"You work it out with Dad. I just follow orders. You ought to know by now."

They came upon Randall's old Cadillac and they got in. When they pulled up to the exit booth, Randall buzzed the window down. "Keep the change, honey. That's right. Raise that gate. I've got an oil man from Chicago ridin' shotgun. That makes us the last of the high rollers."

Randall stomped on the gas. The Cadillac hesitated, making a dull roar far away beneath the hood before slowly gaining speed. Randall glanced at Brice.

"Wastes gas starting up like that, Carol says. Good, I tell her. I'm helping support them poor ol' oil companies."

They cruised beneath the burning sun, and the light pounded Brice into an overloaded amazement. He'd forgotten so much. The way people drove down here. Long, air-conditioned cars moving fast, tailgating all the way. The triangular highway signs that suggested everyone "Drive Friendly."

Randall laughed. "Look at you, Brice. They transfer you north and you become a dude. A damn Yankee."

"That's about it."

"So you guys have a load of early snow in Chi-town this year?"

"Yeah. Almost didn't get out of O'Hare." Brice thought briefly of Judy. "How's your family, Randy? Sorry I haven't asked. The flying throws me off."

"That's all right. Nothing to ask about. We're hanging in there. If we hadn't moved out to the ranch, however." Randall took his hands off the wheel. "Look at that. Needs a front-end alignment."

"How's the insurance agent thing going?"

"I'm not an insurance agent. I'm a financial planner."

Brice had been noting one of the numerous billboards staked out along the freeway. VASECTOMY REVERSAL, MICROSURGERY. He turned back to Randall. "Sorry. Guess I got the story wrong from Dad. So what is it you do now?"

"I sell insurance!" Randall laughed. "Let me show you." He reached over to open the glove box. "Aw, forget it. The brochure's not in there, but hell, you understand. Financial planner is a marketing tool. That way it sounds like we're guys in suits in the business of making people rich. Steering them toward able investments and crap. What we're really doing is selling thick-as-mud universal life policies to cover their sweet asses when they croak."

"How big's your ranch?"

"Dinky. Forty acres. Pretty rundown. I had to rewire the whole house after the first time Joey plugged in his guitar amp. Got the place for a good price, though. Country property has been beat up by the drought. That's why I had to bail out of real estate."

"Has moving out there cut down on the stress?"

"That's one way to look at it. Now when life turns up black roses, I can go into the field. I walk along and count fence posts. Nice substitute for drinking. Some people are on the wagon. I'm sittin' on the fence."

"I'm proud of you for doing that." Brice was thinking of Randall at Mother's funeral four years ago. It was the last time he and Judy had seen him. Randall had been wearing a blue blazer that was too small for him and he was barely on his feet. He was supposed to be a pall bearer and help move the light casket down the steps of the First Presbyterian Church, but the minister had wisely called for a discreet, last-minute substitution.

"You really didn't recognize me back there, Brice?" Randall suddenly asked.

"No." Brice wondered again how he could effectively explain the slip-up to Judy who expected reunions to be all hugs and kisses. The trouble with Judy was she didn't understand the rich history of Randall and his place in the Stockwell family. Randall was simply Randall. Like the time Randy was at A&M for his one and only semester and Brice got a call to come over to the freshman dorm because his brother had been fooling around, shooting off bottle rockets from out his window and had accidentally set the curtains on fire. Or further back, the day Randall lied to Mother and said he was going to a friend's to do his homework. But he didn't return for supper and soon as Brice was through eating (Dad wasn't home from the office) Mother sent him on a search and rescue. Brice pedaled around the subdivision until he spotted Randy's bike lying on its side at the end of an undeveloped cul-de-sac. Brice raised his knees high and slashed through weeds until he found Randy in a clearing hidden from the street. Randy was staring at a set of sterling silver serving pieces—cold meat fork, gravy ladle, cake slicer—all filched from the bottom drawer of the Stockwell china hutch. He'd been using the utensils to dig holes in the hard clay.

"I can tell time by the sun, Brice. I thought it was only four o'clock. Guess I ain't got it right this time, huh?"

"Come on home. I'll tell her you were working with Billy on a report on the products of Brazil. You guys lost track of time."

"Brazil?"

"Sure." Brice took the silver so he could clean up the pieces and put them away when Mother wasn't looking.

"Hey, Brice," Randall said now. "You watch what the Cowboys did last week to your Bears? We mounted you and rode. Texas is still number one."

Brice looked over at his brother who had his hands clamped to the wheel of the not-so-shiny Caddie. The truth was Randall wasn't likely to change. Thirty years later he remained an amiable foul-up. You couldn't help feeling for him. At the same time he exhausted a brother's creativity. So what did you do? You cut him lots of slack. You let him be. Brice wished he could make Judy understand.

Their father's house was a freshly painted English Tudor job with plastic looking grass in front of the first story's brick facade. Inside were five bedrooms, standard for this upscale neighborhood. A pewter Lincoln occupied less than a quarter of the circular drive.

"He'll be by the pool," Randall said. "These days he spends the afternoon there."

They opened the gate to the backyard, and Mr. Stockwell, shoulders deep in bubbles, looked up from the whirlpool. "Brice!" He did a sort of wiggle in the water, then decided to stay in. Brice was bending at the knees so he could reach down to take his father's hand. But there was no handshake.

"Excuse the wetness, son. This is good therapy, so I ought to give it a minute longer."

"Dad, it must be a hundred and ten in that stew pot," Randall said.

"Yes, Randall? You have further comment?"

"Yessir. It can't be good for your damn old heart."

"Listen to him, Brice. He sounds like my doc. What do those white coats know? These water jets are the best thing. Gets the circulation going. Hand me that towel, please."

Mr. Stockwell lifted himself out of the water and started drying. Standing next to Brice, he was nearly as tall. "Good thing you came to town, Brice. Randall never comes out to visit me."

Randall stripped his pink tie loose and stuck it in his coat pocket. The tip hung out. He sat himself in one of the basket-weave pool chairs.

"You two go ahead and get caught up," he said. "I'll be right here."

"So," Mr. Stockwell grinned, "how's that future grandchild coming along, Brice?"

Brice told him about the good sonogram and at the same time corrected his father's misimpression that Judy was eight rather than six months pregnant. Somehow the old man had mixed that up. Brice was about to get to the box of frozen steaks they had out in the car when his father interrupted.

"Now tell me about this meeting, Brice. How come the company's not holding it in Chicago this year? And are you going to deal with the domestic rig count? Damn pathetic is what it is. What about Alaska? Think we'll get the feds off our back so we can get to something producible in Norton Sound?"

Brice knew that even in retirement his father remained a bit obsessed with what he called "the company." Whenever they talked on the phone,

Dad wanted updates about what his old cronies were doing. Usually Brice didn't know. Brice's things were petroleum PR and HR. His father had been in charge of domestic exploration. It was apples and oranges really, but it didn't matter to Mr. Stockwell. By god, it was fine. His oldest son worked for the company. His son Brice could tell you anything you wanted to know about the oil industry.

Brice looked over at Randall. Randall had reapplied his sunglasses. He was beating a rhythm on the arms of the chair as if he were listening to a low decibel radio station.

"Come on, Brice," Mr. Stockwell encouraged. "You can tell your old man the poop. I'm not a spy for the damn Sierra Club."

"I really need go to the bathroom, Dad. Long flight and all." Brice went into the house through the French doors. He had never actually lived in this house. The parents had bought it after he was out of college when his father got the final promotion, taking him into six figures. The last time Brice had been inside was during the time of the funeral.

He got lost trying to find a particular bathroom he recalled being off the kitchen. Instead he blundered upon the master bedroom. His father had left the room the same as when Mother was alive. The ornately framed family photos were lined up on the bureau. Lace throw pillows tilted back against the headboard of the bed. Brice picked up a picture. It showed Brice and Randy. Brice was preparing to boot a football from one end of a vacant lot to the other. Randy was closing his eyes and holding the ball with his fingertip as Brice backed up for a good run at it.

Cute kids. Long ago and forgotten. That was the problem, the plain reason why Judy's expectations were unreal. What could be shoe horned in between meetings? Certainly nothing substantial enough to untangle all the distance that had grown between him and Randall. It wasn't his fault either. What could you expect when you lived in different states, had different careers and, for all practical purposes, incompatible lifestyles? A lot of things once held as a common bond were simply gone. Like that football that had sailed end over end into the autumn sky. The best he could do would be show Randall that he cared.

The old man and Randall were splitting a six-pack in the shade. Brice stopped at the pool's edge. For a second his mouth must have hung open.

"You're drinking?"

"Always in moderation," Mr. Stockwell said.

"Have one, Brice," Randall grinned. "I bet you've never gotten a buzz on with Dad. It's fun, isn't it, Dad? Besides we know how to pace ourselves."

Mr. Stockwell looked sternly at Brice. "Let's not be damned Baptists here, son. Now listen to this idea I just got. Why don't we all poke around the hardware store. For old times sake."

"Are you serious?" Brice asked.

"Of course, he's serious," Randall said.

"Good. It's set," Mr. Stockwell declared. "You just give me a minute to change into appropriate attire."

Fifteen minutes later they were there. Inside the superstore the old man assessed the merits of new generation power mowers and picked through nail trays. He put his fingers on pointed metal and palmed round rubber gaskets. From the time Brice and Randall were little kids, their father was always saying that if he finished going through the load of paperwork in his briefcase, he would do some fix-up around the house. He never did and Brice still saw no purpose to the boring weekend habit, the aisle by aisle examination of thirty-five cent price stickers and all the rest.

Randall must have felt the same. He wandered off and started talking to the in-store demonstrator. The young woman had a compact microwave oven on a cart, and beside that, a bowl of something and an open bag of tortilla chips. She laughed when Randall took off his sunglasses and said a few words.

"Com'mere, Brice. You gotta try this."

Brice tasted the woman's chili dip. It was warm and spicy but bland enough in the sum of its parts to satisfy many people. Mr. Stockwell came over and smiled at the woman.

"You watch out for these boys," he said.

"No, you watch out for this old man," Randall said. "He's been shopping for nuts and bolts for thirty years just on the off chance he'd run into someone as young and good looking as you at the hardware store."

"Not true, Miss. I was a married man until a few years ago."

"There you go," Randall said. "Now he's making up for lost time."

The girl smiled. "You don't have to buy the microwave to get the recipe. Want it on a card? It's an easy five-minute one."

After that Mr. Stockwell decided they ought to go to the grocery store and buy the ingredients for their own chips and chili dip. He and the boys would pick up some more beer, too. Then they'd go home and snack through the afternoon.

Randall volunteered to do the mixing and cooking. Brice and his father stayed by the pool and pulled up their chairs so they sat in the shade beneath the oak tree. In a minute Randall came out with the chips and dip and fresh beer on a round party tray.

"Eat hearty, Dad. And don't go saying I never did anything for you."

Mr. Stockwell picked up a beer. He looked at Randall and the tray he offered.

"What's that, Randall?"

"I said don't tell me I never did nothin' for you."

"That's what I thought." Mr. Stockwell got out of his chair which creaked.

"Go ahead, Dad." Randall jammed the tray against Mr. Stockwell's stomach. "Help yourself, dammit. You bought it."

Mr. Stockwell looked steely. He pushed the tray away and went into the house.

"What was that?" Brice asked. "I thought he wanted to eat this junk."

Randall looked toward the French doors. He set down the tray and took a drink of beer. He stood still, gazing contemplatively at the blue, unrippled swimming pool. He smiled in a way that alarmed Brice.

"The old bastard hates my guts," Randall said as unexcitedly as Brice had ever heard him say anything.

"What? That's bullshit, Randy."

"Give me a break, bro."

"He's an old man, Randy. He probably had to take a leak."

"You really don't get it, do you? You've moved on. That's what I envy. To be able to always stay a step ahead of the crap down here."

Brice shifted uneasily in the chair. The basket weave dug into his behind. "What do you mean, Randy? Do you mean Mother's passing?"

"Passing," Randall laughed. "You know, you sound like him?" He waved his hand. "Sorry. I don't mean I don't care. But from his point of view he's probably happier than ever. He always had more time for the office than for her."

"You're being too hard on him," Brice said.

"Am I?" Randall stepped forward and selected a chip from the bowl on the tray. He inspected it. "Nice thing about eating outdoors in Texas is the chili dip doesn't cool off. If wind's out of the south, though, chips can get kind of soggy."

"Tell me what happened," Brice said.

Randall dipped the chip into the bowl. He held the chili coated end up to the sun. He popped the chip into his mouth and sighed. He put on his sunglasses. "What makes you think anything happened?"

Brice looked toward the house. "Something did."

"When?"

"Since I was last here."

Randall sighed again. In a minute he moved close to Brice.

"I was bombed," he said. "Nothing new. Carol and I had gotten into another knockdown dragout." Randall wiped the sweat off his brow and smiled vaguely.

"You ever hear about our fights? Nah? Well, I mean to tell you, they're nuclear meltdowns. Then when they're over Carol sulks. I go out to the corral and find a horse to ride to a lather. For some reason that gets me to thinking about my needs. I come back to the house and more or less rape her. Rip, claw, sprint for the finish line. First time I did it to her, I figured I'd go to jail. She'd already said she hated me and wanted nothing to do with me. But when it was over she looked up with this kind of doped expression and said, 'You still got some passion in you, boy.' Ain't life

241

weird? I don't think we love each other, though." He shifted in his chair and took another drink of beer.

"So on this day a couple of months ago we were in the bedroom. Raging lust, you might say. I'd barely got Carol's top off and there was the doorbell ringing. I got off my knees and went to the door and it was Dad. He's smiling and being insidiously nice. 'I've come to get Misty,' he says."

"Misty?"

"His horse," Randall said. "You don't know about that?"

Brice didn't.

"Guess he was being Mr. Humble Pie with you again. Remember hearing about Dad's retirement party last year? Lavish was the word. Too bad Mom couldn't have lived to see. It might have made her feel better about giving up most of her life to the man and his job. You sure as hell should have been there, too, Brice. The son who followed in his footsteps."

"I was out of the country," Brice reminded Randall. "That Siberian deal."

"Right, right," Randall agreed. "Anyway I went to this whoop-te-doo downtown at the Petroleum Club and I mean the company gave the old man one hell of a party. The CEO flew in from Chicago and made a speech. They had Dad's name carved into a six-foot block of ice. There were piles of babyback ribs and Gulf shrimp and all the invites were engraved. Then the climax. At the end of Mr. Bigshot's speech he hands Dad a silver-studded bridle. You know how clever Dad is in public. 'This means you're turning me out to pasture,' he quips. Round of applause. Pasture, sure. They gave the old man two hundred grand in severance and a thoroughbred sorrel."

Brice whistled. "Are you serious? Sounds like a nice animal."

"You could say that," Randall agreed. "So Dad says to me after this major interruption in my sex life, 'Gotta have Misty.' I'd been keeping the horse for him until he worked out a neater arrangement. Now he's telling me that we have to take Misty in the trailer up to a friend's place at Denton. The friend lives close enough to Dad that Misty will be more conveniently located for riding and slavish worship. It was fine with me. 'The hell with doing him any more favors,' I said to myself. He could have his horse. I was wasted on tequila and beer anyway."

"Go on," Brice said.

"All right. We herd the horse into the trailer he brought along. I get everything set up back there. Dad slips behind the wheel of the pickup, of course, since I'm DWI all the way. We're going north I-35 at about seven at night. Traffic kind of heavy. I had just changed the radio station when it happened." Randall paused. He looked around. "You got another beer there?" He studied the sky. "Damn. How do you do it, Brice? You always bring fine weather."

"Randy—"

"Okay. Yeah, the radio. I'd found one of those dumb, pop-slanted country stations. Not exactly Bob Wills and the Texas Playboys. 'Big Ball in Cow Town,' now that's a real song. I was starting to say that to him when the trailer began to wobble. Suddenly Dad's fighting the steering wheel. I swear the thing looked like it was going to come off in his hands. In a situation like that you don't just pull over to the side, not on a zooming freeway. We were a half mile down the road before he got it under control and we could stop. 'Put on your flashers,' I tell him. We get out. Back at the back is where I see how it is, bro. Except for the hay, that there trailer is pretty much empty."

"Hold on, Randy."

Randall stuck up his hand so he could continue. "We start walking down the side of the freeway, Dad and me, shoulder to shoulder. No talk. The whole time I'm hoping those oncoming headlights will slow down. Up ahead we see lights that aren't moving. 'What's that?' I ask. I'd figured it out, but I hadn't, know what I mean? Besides, I had to say something. He doesn't answer. By the time we get to the lights the first wrecker is pulling up."

Randall took a sip of beer, but now the can was empty. He reached forward for another.

"Oo-wee, people were hot. I say, 'Anyone seen a horse?' and this one guy likes to massacre me. 'I slammed on my brakes you so and so,' he's screaming. 'My arm hit the dash and my car's totaled.' I took a look. At what was left of it. Seemed like there had been some kind of chain reaction. Lot of cars in bad shape. Dad, though, he was Mr. Incommunicado. Shocked? I dunno. Then Misty showed."

"You mean she was okay?"

"Okay? Sure." Randall stretched out his arms, exposing his cuffs. "One of the guys who had pulled over to the side had her by the bridle. Misty was more than a little upset and the guy couldn't control her too good. But this old boy knew what to do. When we looked again, he'd swung himself up and was riding her bareback down the side of the highway. He had her at a suitable walk, but it was the strangest looking thing. Maybe it was the way the red and yellow car lights lit the two of them. Horse and man. They had that tinted look. You know, like they'd walked out of a club at two a.m.? Or it was how he was sitting up straight and wearing a suit. A navy blue suit. Here come this horse and navy blue suited dude. He stops her right in front of us, professional-like. He's towering over me. 'This your animal?' he says.

'Her name is Misty.' That was Dad, ending his seven years of silence trick. 'Now get off her please.' The guy gets off all right. He starts toward me, calling me a drunk. But I was plenty sober by then so the guy must have only been smelling that I had been lit. He has hold of me by the collar. Dad doesn't do a thing. He's trying to stroke down Misty and check her forelegs. Must have figured she took a hell of a leap from the trailer to the pavement. The horse gets all shook up again. She snorts as the dude in the suit hauls off and pops me on the jaw. I see Misty toss her head and break away. Then someone pounds their horn and we hear the brakes and the tire skid and—"

"My god," Brice said.

"I had to grab the old man to keep him from running out into the middle of the four-lane. He knew what the deal was. Even after the cops finally got there and set up the flares, we could see she was still alive. Brice, you should have seen her, though, lying down on her side. Guts spilling out from the belly down. When no one was watching, I went close to her, damn it."

"I don't want to hear anymore."

"But you got to know the way the teeth looked, Brice. Right when she opened her mouth and made that noise. It was incredible. I can't stop seeing it. And hearing." Randall pivoted his body so that he was facing away from Brice. The tie hung halfway from his pocket and he noticed it. He yanked the tie out and threw it to the ground.

"See, here's the deal. The old man worked for that company forty-three years. Along the way he passed the torch to his oldest son. Got you a primo job in the industry, Brice, am I right? So we're not talking about a simple career. It was more like a fiefdom. To say the horse was a big deal to him, doesn't say it. And I killed it."

"But it was an accident. He knows that. Besides, you're his—"

"Wait a minute. You're not hearing me. I really killed the horse, Brice. I killed Misty. Do you know how to manage that? Spur of the moment completely kill something that big? Or should I be polite and use a euphemism? Destroyed. Okay, let's say I destroyed her. I, Randall Stockwell Jr., destroyed Misty."

"I think you should stop drinking, Randy."

"Should. Now there's a word."

"Randy, it's over. If he won't get off your case about it, I'll talk to him."

"Do me a favor." Randall got up from his chair and walked to the edge of the pool. "No more favors. Don't beat up the bully that beat me up. Don't tutor me in math. Don't turn me on to your favorite bands. Don't find me a girl friend of your girl friend. Hell. Do you know why I married Carol? She reminded me of Judy."

"Randall. Don't stand so close to the edge."

"Hey, I'm not drunk. Believe me, I know drunk. I'm just jawboning. For your northern information, we do a lot of that down here. So want to know how to kill one?"

"What are you talking about now?"

"Finishing off a horse, bro. You're still the churchgoing one in the family. Y'all appreciate this."

"I don't think—"

"Listen, Brice. Here's how you do it. You use an actual form of prayer. Okay? It does them in every time. You get down on your knees. That's the invocation part. On your knees in the night. You put on the black hood and if you ain't got that, slap on an ol' cowboy hat. Crumple the rim for effect. Then you start in with the words."

"Come on, Randy."

"You say you lousy piece of garbage. I don't need you. I've got another right where you came from. And you never could run that fast. You don't look that good either. You're not nearly as big and well formed as the other one I've got. Think I take you seriously? No way. That's when the miracle happens, Brice. The horse lays its head down. Its eyes stay open. It stops breathing. It oozes blood."

"What did he say to you, Randy?"

"He said, 'You've cost me a horse. You didn't latch the gate properly.' Properly. I remember that. His kind of word. Properly. He went back to the trailer and checked to see it wasn't damaged. That was what he was worried about. Not the seven-car pileup, not the guy still holding onto his arm and cussing a streak at us. Not the couple of little kids crying to their mommies. Or the guy who had ridden the horse who was giving the cops a statement and urging them to take me in. The old man was bawling his eyes out about the horse I killed."

Randall walked over to the bowl of chips. Brice stood up. He wanted to put his arm around his brother. Randall was a few feet away, his coat back soaked through with sweat. Brice reached out, but instead of touching Randall the arm continued on and with perfect quarterback form it launched his beer can toward the pool.

Randall turned his head toward the splashing sound. "Well, I'll be. Messin' with Dad's pool? You know better than to do that, bro."

"Think I care?" Brice was looking toward the house. He was thinking of their father inside. What was he doing? Reading a magazine? Watching TV? Whatever it was, it would be a device to stall until Randall went home. Then the old man would step in to personally escort Brice to a well-reviewed restaurant. What will it be, Brice? The menu's extensive. Anything you want, nothing's too fine for my boy.

"Lookit!" Randall said.

A breeze had come up, causing the leaves of the oak tree to stir and rustle overhead. Driven by the wind, the shiny silver tube drifted toward the shallow end of the pool. The beer can took on some water and sank lower. For a second it looked like it might go to the bottom, but it didn't. There was just enough time for the can to make it to the end where it banged into the curved mosaic side of the pool. It stayed there until Randall walked around. Like a good son, he bent down and retrieved it.

GIVE PEACE A CHANCE

CHUCK TAYLOR

The way I met Flora was I stopped for beer and gas at an Exxon truck stop on I-20 near Terrell, and there, in the john, scribbled on the back of the scratched, metal stall door, was the invitation—"If you want good tight pussy, call . . ."

I always met chicks in strange ways. Once, ten years back, out partying in New Orleans during Mardi Gras, I picked up the phone near the old Jax brewery, and this woman says, "Hello, is that you David?" And when I said I wasn't David she said, "Well, who are you?"

So nearly every time I came through Dallas I'd swing by to party with my pal Flora. When I first knew her she was working as a waitress in this little Italian restaurant in Lakewood. After the place closed, she went back to being a hooker, flashing her long beautiful legs, in a rather shy way, on Gaston close to downtown. About a year later she went on welfare from having her daughter Boots. Of course Flora had no idea who the father was. She used to tease me a lot, claiming that Boots very clearly had my nose and mouth.

I always carried a small bag hidden under the seat in my truck, and that usually guaranteed Flora and I had a good time. She was an easygoing blonde. She liked to dance to Reggae music at this combination pool hall and club over on lower Greenville. She didn't mind if I first stopped off for a few beers in this tittie bar where I had a few friends. This time when I dropped by for a visit—on a warm October day around four in the afternoon—I was worn out and a little disgusted—on my way back from taking a load of disposable diapers to Shreveport. There'd be little profit on this run. I was carrying back nothing but empty space in the trailer. I am an independent trucker. I own my own rig, and I take orders from nobody. For that freedom, you win some, you lose some.

Almost as soon as I got my head in her little apartment on Swiss, Flora was up and all over me, giving me hugs and kisses, pulling me down on her sofa in the living room and playing with my hair.

"Decker, Decker, I am so glad to see you. Where have you been? You don't happen to have any coke, do you, old buddy, old pal?"

I looked up into Flora's big brown eyes, a little dumbfounded. "You know I don't carry that kind of shit when I'm working," I chuckled. "It's too damn risky with all these checkpoints on the roads and drug tests they got now."

"Well, I can get us some if you'll drive us."

I was tired, but Flora gave me one of her big smiles and cuddled up close, implying she would make it worth my while. We walked down the stairs out to the Kenworth where I had eased her in nice alongside the apartment building. I pushed Flora up, handed her Boots, fired the engine up, and we were on our way. Flora pointed the way past downtown Reunion Center onto Interstate 35 heading south.

Just when Dallas was about gone, and we started seeing farms all around, Flora pointed to a turnoff onto a deserted county highway. There wasn't a single store or gas station at the intersection. We drove west a couple of miles through this flat, black-earth territory, and then we turned south onto a gravel road. After ten minutes we hung another right onto a small dirt road. After about fifteen minutes I pulled the rig into this small farmyard, hoping she wouldn't sink too deep in the soil. The ground was a little damp.

To the right was a regular old wooden farm house with some nice looking tall pecans around it. To the left was a rusting yellow metal building, a kind of implement storage area.

Two big black dogs—mongrels that looked mostly Doberman—came out snarling and barking, circling and leaping at the rig. I blew the horn a few times, but the dogs just jumped back a couple of feet and came on again. After a while this big guy, looking like he was right off the old *Hee Haw* TV show, opened the door of the metal building. He whistled and cussed. The dogs quickly slinked off, their heads and tails down. Flora rolled down the window and stuck out an arm to wave.

"Flora, that you?" the big guy shouted, shading his eyes. He must have stood six three and weighed two hundred and fifty, in a neat mixture of fat and muscle. He had a long graying ZZ Top-type beard and wore blue coveralls.

"I didn't know who in the hell it was. No one shows up here in a Kenworth. Come on in. Who's your friend?"

"This is Decker." Flora said, waving and climbing down the side of the rig, her daughter dangling from one arm.

"Glad ta know ya. I'm Pete." He grabbed my hand and it disappeared into his. "Known Flora long? How's your kid, Flora? I forget. A boy or a girl?"

We went through a door in a metal outbuilding and inside found ourselves in a small apartment. The floor was unpainted cement; the walls were constructed out of that wood chip plywood that fills the air with a faint odor of rotting meat from a butcher shop. The plywood was covered with centerfolds from skin magazines like *Dude* and *Hustler.*

"Nice place you got here," I commented, nodding toward the centerfolds.

"I like it," Pete laughed, "but my ol' man sure doesn't." Pete gestured in the direction of the frame house. "My old man—that's why I live out here with the tractors and plows."

"Yeah," I said. "I guess paradise would be to have one of these lovely ladies each night of your life. This is almost as good as having it."

Pete laughed again, pointing to folding chairs and a card table by the window. Once we were all seated, Pete pulled the lid off a red coffee can and produced a small plastic bag full of marijuana. While Flora made a place for Boots on a dishcloth there on the cement floor, Pete rolled a joint.

Pete's country apartment was a perfect setup for a dealer. Close to a big city for clients, but totally out in the middle of nowhere, it was unlikely the law would ever catch on. We all talked for awhile about the drought last summer, and then about the government taking away everyone's freedoms. The more we talked, the more Flora seemed to grow tense. Still, she managed to make us laugh with a waitress story—this one about reloading uneaten food onto the plates of new orders at the Italian restaurant she'd worked at.

Boots, the baby, was happy examining dust balls on the floor, laughing and popping them in her mouth. After awhile, Flora seemed to grow exasperated by the small talk. I could see it in her eyes. "Pete," she drawled, "this is great stuff. But we didn't come for weed. We wanted some, you know, other stuff."

"What stuff?"

"You know."

"What about your friend?"

"He's cool. You know me. How long I've been coming here? Two, three years?"

"Yeah, Flora, the thing is, I know you. You never *had* any money and you don't got no money now." Pete shrugged his large rambling shoulders. He laughed good naturedly, winked at me, and began rolling another joint. "You can smoke all the grass you want, but you don't get the other stuff for free."

Pete reached in the coffee can again and this time dug out a large pile of snapshots. "Take a look at these," he said, handing the pictures over to me with a big smile.

"Well, we are going to pay," Flora interjected, somewhat loudly. "Decker's got money, don't ya?"

I ignored Flora's remark and looked at the photographs. They were shots of two different women. One was a redhead in her early forties. The other was a bleached blond who must have been fifty. Both of them were smiling, a little shyly, at an unseen camera. Both had hiked up their blouses and unsnapped their brassieres, posing like the amateur photos you saw printed in *Easy Rider*, the biker magazine.

"Pretty good, huh?" Pete said. "I took 'em myself." He reached over to the windowsill, behind the curtain, and pulled out a small camera with a built-in flash. "No offense now," he said with southern politeness, "but, Flora, I don't know your friend. I only deal with people I know."

"So, Pete, hold your horses. There's got to be a first time for everyone, right?"

"That was in the old days—before things got weird." Pete rolled his eyes in mock seriousness.

"OK." Flora paused, and then leaned over to whisper in my ear. "Let's you and I have a pow-wow."

I smiled at Pete, set his pictures on the table, and we all got up. I picked Boots up off the floor. Pete went out the door first and chained up the dogs under the pecans.

"So what do you think?" Flora asked when we were standing back over in the shade of the rig.

"What do I think what?" I said. "I told you I keep no coke in my truck. I thought we were going to snort a free line or two and be on our way."

"So did I. Maybe he's hard up these days." Flora bit her lip. "We can give him fifty."

"What do you mean, we? The guy is paranoid. He thinks I may be a narc or an agent. He won't take my money. He's so paranoid he'll think it's marked."

"That's not true and you know it." Flora swept her blonde hair out of her eyes.

"Maybe it is. Maybe it isn't. He could step out that door any minute and blow us both away with a shotgun. Why don't you go ahead and ask him if he's paranoid?"

"All right. OK." Flora looked up at me and then at the yellow metal building. "Just keep your little girl for me a minute, will ya?"

"My little girl. Hell. I don't make enough to take care of my own kids."

Flora went inside. I climbed back in the Kenworth with Boots to listen to some country music cassettes and to get warmed up. The sun was nearing the horizon and the wind coming up had a bite to it. How in the world did I get myself into such situations?

Fifteen minutes passed. I opened the glove compartment and let Boots go through the maps and insurance papers. I gave her my keys and let her play with some of the dashboard knobs. Then it got to be a half hour. I was growing irritated. My boys are ten and eleven. I ain't used to fooling around with babies.

When forty-five minutes had passed, I decided I couldn't wait longer. Sitting in a truck in a farm yard with a two-year-old baby. I had to laugh and shake my head. It made no sense.

I climbed down from the rig, holding Boots close to keep her warm, and went up to the door of the metal building to knock. The wind in the yard was blowing the pecan leaves in circles like dust devils. My rig cast a long shadow.

What about the people in the farmhouse? What did they think of a stranger's large truck parked in their yard? The windows were curtained and still. No one seemed to be peeking out. Maybe they're hiding inside out of fear; perhaps they've already called the cops.

When no one answered the door I gave a shove and went inside to get out of the chill and wind. There was small sink near the card table where we had sat earlier. I carried Boots over there. I found an old paper cup, had a swallow of water, and then fed the rest to the baby.

It did not take a lot of guessing to figure what was going on. Flora and Pete, they had settled on their own terms for the coke. They were in some back room. It was all right with me. I wasn't the jealous kind.

I looked around the room for a phone. I thought I might as well call home and let my wife know I'd be putting in a little late, but the phone must have been in the back room. I opened the refrigerator. There was a Domino's pizza box in the back with a few slices inside. It made me laugh to think of some pimpled young Domino's teenager trying to find this place. I found some bread, broke it in small pieces, and gave it to the baby.

Could Flora be dead, I asked myself? People overdose on the cocaine all the time. A sixteen-year-old girl who lived next door to me in Abilene— a really beautiful child—had a heart attack and ended up in intensive care the very first time she tried the stuff. Her boyfriend had gotten her some for her birthday. Another woman friend of mine in Shreveport had been recently murdered in her apartment. I used to take her out to dinner. The police couldn't figure a motive, the paper said, but I knew. She was a coke and speed freak. The woman lived on welfare in public housing with her eight-year-old boy and she never had any money. Hell, by the time I met her, she was down to two beds and a kitchen table.

Maybe Pete and Flora slipped out a back door and took off in a car. Another ten minutes passed as I ate stale pizza and looked again at the pictures of the two women holding up their blouses. Pete's apartment was quiet as a morgue. I pulled the curtain back and peered out the window. A few stars hung faintly in the sky. In a little while it would be completely dark. If I could have heard some music playing in the back room—or some bodies thumping—I would have been relieved.

I thought of going down the hall into the back, to try to talk to Flora and Pete—but I held back. The big guy might not appreciate being inter-rupted, so instead I went outside and walked around the side of the metal building to relieve myself.

Behind the metal building was a small field of dried grass with a barb wire fence around it. Parked in the middle of the field was a rusting green VW bus—the old kind, maybe a 1966 model. The moon was now up, three-quarters full, so I could see that all four tires were missing on the bus. The bare metal wheel rims were sunk deep into the earth. On the side of the bus facing where I stood, looming larger than the moon, was a large, faded peace symbol, white painted on green. The symbol had been done free-hand, so the circle was a bit lopsided. I squinted to make out the slogan under the circle: "Give Peace a Chance."

Who, I wondered, did the bus belong to? It was hard to imagine Pete as a hippie.

Flora once told me she had been a hippie—but I didn't believe her. Nowadays everybody wants to say there were a hippie. Lots of guys grew our hair long back in those days, but hippies were nothing but college students thinking they could change the world while living on daddy's money and partying. I did a few years in Austin, and remember smoking grass in the basement of the student union, lounging around, never going to class. It sure seemed like paradise, but it had nothing to do with real life—or with real people who have to sweat to earn a living.

"Enough of this shit," I said to myself, zipping up my pants and walking back around front. I hesitated for a moment at the metal door to Pete's place, then turned and walked up to my rig. I climbed inside and turned on the engine.

Boots, she would be all right by herself. I'd fed her and she'd fall asleep after crawling around on the floor and eating more dust balls. Flora was going to be all right too. My guess is she was not only happily fucked, but also happily fucked up on cocaine. Flora would surface sooner or later—and nothing would be said the next time I stopped in Dallas.

After a few minutes letting the engine warm up, I flicked on the lights, put her in reverse, and slowly worked the truck out the yard back onto the dirt road. The wheels spun a little, but she was all right.

Three hours or so to go and I'd be back home with the family in Abilene. I kept my head down in case Flora came dashing out the door with the kid in her arms.

WHEN LUCK RAN OUT

It was the last night of the year, and the last two hours, and cold and dark and quiet on the block, when the door blew open and the friends came in as they have for the past ten thousand years, wanting to play poker with the Baby and me. There was Greg the old Sailor with tattoos all over his body, and Larry the War Vet with his ivanhoe hair, and Young-John still dark and bright from mountain climbing and solitary star gazing, and Steve his friend with the bird eye, and Hedwig the beautiful red-haired queen of planetary exile (what a jazz that woman has, what a smile). I sat Baby down with his special 51-card deck.

"Cut the cards," someone said.

Then you should've seen all the people getting into their pockets and secret stash places, all the coin rolling out.

When we first began, I didn't feel good. I was still blue from before they had come in from remembering my last trip to the edge of the world—Bakersfield via the LA Express—and the misery I had seen: the brother in prison, the woman bereft of her children and too drunk to stand up in front of a judge, her paralyzed lover (my brother's rival) in his wheelchair shot in the back, all of that story playing on the walls of the universe with so much more worry, sorrow. And then I hadn't seen E. Z. since I'd been back in Austin and so I'd been alone with my thoughts. So the poker game seemed difficult, and I lost all my pennies steadily, mostly to Larry the War Vet. But I drank hot rum toddies and when Midnight came, I felt a little better, although I didn't want to kiss anyone. When everyone went outside to shoot off the fireworks I had given them, Larry was strutting, thinking he had won everything because his pockets were loaded down with my coin rolls, but what can I say? I was dazzled (again) by his blondness and happy still that a War hadn't claimed him, so if there had to be a Winner I was glad it was this one who would hurry to spend it on his Girl Friend waiting in bed for him at home. And then the red-haired Queen had taken her share, the Sailor hadn't wanted to play for real money but did anyway and lost it, John the still Young had won just enough to want to keep on playing 'til daybreak but no one else did, Steve had got drunk. The Baby hadn't said anything all night, concentrating on his private card hand, but when the fireworks began to go off he began to cry, and I carried him to the back bedroom while his crying was continuing. Then in the midst of the din, the popping of the Black Cats deepened to an unfamiliar thud and rattatat which I realized was the sound of many guns, and the Baby cried harder. When I looked out the window red fireballs were exploding over the roof of the orphanage next door. Then the house began to shake from the inside with footsteps and shouting and slamming, and something about the sound of the unfamiliar male voices in the hallway closing in on my bedroom told me to run. So I bundled up the Baby and ran out the back door, down the back stairs, down the back alley. Sirens were wailing and what sounded like a hundred thousand voices carried in a night wind inconsolable with loss, accompanying the long cry of the Baby. Behind us headlights appeared and above them a bank of blue and red flashers hot on my back, and I began running. I came to the street at the end of the alley already cratered with the marks of minor explosions, black holes careening in the headlights behind me. But just then a bus appeared at the corner—its doors opened and I loaded us into it and put my last two coins in the box. "What bus is this?" I asked the driver.

"Desolation Boulevard," he said, "via Capitol and Congress."

"Well here's where we get off," I told the Baby. We were already at the capitol building, its dome serenely illuminated against the black night. When I stepped off, a Man and a Woman stepped out of the shadow of the covered bus bench, and the Woman cried out, "That's my Baby!"

And the Baby held out his arms to her, and she took him from me as they embraced, and the three of them walked away and left me alone.

The sound of the explosions had become more distant. The dawnlight was increasing, so that I could make out the dark shapes of the Peace Dogs strung along the capitol steps, awkward and gaunt, pacing nervously through their Night Watch. "Come watch with us," one of them called.

So I took a place in the string and began to watch.

I watched for days and nights. When I slept, I slept on the stone steps and under the stone eaves fashioned from a million billion handstrokes of soul brother prison slaves, smooth and hard as their muscles must have been. Above my head the pigeons. I woke while the sky continued to bleed hard red rain somewhere in the neighborhood of the Other Side of the World, and the news commentators continued their uneducated rap as a Blind War continued amid comedy and intermittent music. But when so many days had gone by, the Peace Dogs began to quarrel among themselves about food—what kind, and how it should be distributed. Soon their snarling was taking up at each dawn with breakfast just as the far-off war racket was slacking off. When a Peace Bus arrived with reinforcements of Mothers and Babies, the Peace Dogs chased its wheels and ran it off the capitol grounds. Then they divided themselves into two groups for each side of the capitol steps: one side for the Homeless, one side for the More Homeless, and spent too much of their daylight time hiding the boxes of food from each other and snapping at the legs of the incoming and outgoing lobbyists and tourists and legislators. Then one would take me aside in the evenings to complain about another; then another the other one; then the other one would take me aside; when I saw there would be no peace with the Peace Dogs as long as they vied for my ear, I took off.

I heard that the War ended fast. I heard that the Enemy had been buried, what with all the coins given our War Buddies. But the year had turned bitter cold and the spring came down with a hard edge to the grass blades, and the trees continued to bleed shadows down the street gutters. I stopped once at the multiple doors of the Landlord Apartments to see about renting a room, and again at Owner Estates and Manor Villas, but the Managers didn't recognize me in my dilapidated state, even though I had rented from them several times before.

So I continued to wander the streets, bearing east, following the indecipherable language sprayed along the sidewalks and walls. I crossed the broad stream of traffic and wandered through a neighborhood of uprooted houses and shattered men bent under loads of black plastic bags, and bodies of men sprawled across the sidewalks out-sleeping their lives. Squad cars whistled by me and Squad Men ducked in and out of the yards with their guns drawn, and helicopters bobbed like dragonflies through the metallic blue summer air. I continued walking. Ahead of me I thought I

256

could see the pavement finally dissolve into some green pastures just on the other side of a wrought iron fence, but when I got closer I saw that the grass was completely occupied with the tombstones of soldiers on the lower slopes and sepulchers of generals and statesmen on the hill crests, with black butterflies fluttering among them like domino dots. I hung my arms between the sharp spikes of the fence and watched the live oak shadows rove across the stone face of Stephen F. Austin's tomb. A white statue of Him rose from it with an arm outstretched and a finger pointed toward some invisible goal, one more neighborhood perhaps to develop on the cemetery's other side. The shadows of the domino stones toppled on top of each other as the sun set. At least they were quiet. I don't know how long I hung there.

"Hello down there!" I heard someone call.

When I turned around, I saw a narrow three-storied yellow house across the street from me, and on the third floor balcony two people waving, and sitting with them on the railing was the Baby.

"Come up here and be with us!"

I turned from the fence and crossed the street to them. As I got closer to the house, I began to hear drums. Then as I climbed the steps to them, keyboards began running and voices began to sing.

It was the Last Refuge of the Musicians, the Man and Woman told me that night as we sipped coffee together amid the broken furniture piled around their upstairs room. The Baby had acquired a drum for himself and two good drumsticks and beat them with an amazing steadiness as the music continued to come from the floors below.

After coffee, they took me downstairs to show me where I could stay. We waded through a roomful of garbage and into a roomful of drums and keyboards and sound monitors and cymbals, and there were two drummers facing off at each other, each with a mountain of drums, and a keyboard player prancing nude in back of three layers of keys upon which he was laying multidimensional fingers. The door to my room was half blocked by the snake coils of electric cords, but the Man rearranged them carefully to make a path for us, and to open the door, and so we opened it and went into the room, and it was very beautiful. It was octagonal like a poker chip holder, with long windows on a three-faceted wall looking to the south.

And of all the rooms we had passed through to get to this one, it had the least garbage in it.

"The Musicians have been wanting for you to stay here with us," the Man confided to me as we leaned against an executive desk that had been placed in the middle of the room for my use. He pulled out from beneath it a black box and unsnapped it—"your accordion," he said. The red and silver inlay of the instrument gleamed up brightly after such a long stay in the silent dark case. Then he handed me a long joint of sensimilla to light up, which I did.

He himself was a Music Man and the Woman with him was a Dancer. He played the Dance—made the records spin and the smoke billow and the red lights smolder and the laser beams splay off the dancing women at the Hard Tit Club.

"It's only a month-to-month lease that we have on the place, and no kitchen facilities at all in the house," he continued as we passed the smoke and watched a Squad Man on the street just in front of the windows jump out of his car with his Squad Gun pulled out of its holster and the Gun pointed then at a middle-aged couple being pulled from their car by other Squad members.

"And the only bathing facilities," he said, "are on the third floor at my place. But it's only a hundred dollars a month that each of us has to pay to make the rent to the last bank that foreclosed on it."

"I saw you," yelled a Squad Man at the couple who were being thrown down on the hood of their car. "Take the packet of white stuff from that woman's pocketbook and hand it out of the window and SELL IT TO ME!"

"And the Musicians have put up a few wall signs to discourage real estate visitors and the garbage rattling anytime someone opens the back door and the cymbals at the front make for a pretty good alarm system. Then the problems with the back parking lot," he said, "the break-ins to the Musician Van, and then to the Club Mobile, and the smoking of vagrant chemicals, have been cut down in part. You know we took your advice. . ." He put out the end of the joint on the top of the desk and left it for later for me if I wanted it.

"And what was that?"

"About the hex signs?"

258

"Oh," I said, "the pentagrams."

"Yeah, sprayed on the batteries and tailgates and such, and they seem to be working. And we brought the gypsy truck you left at the last house and parked it out back there with the rest of the vehicles. We thought you might want some wheels again some day."

I smiled at him and he smiled at me, and we hugged each other, because he was my Son and I loved him.

The drummers and keyboardist continued unabated and the Squad cars had come to be accompanied by the thunder of the wings of their black helicopter surveillance Squad buddies as we picked our way out the room, back through the cord snakes and down a hall marked in red Anal Death Fuck, windows barred with broken glass, walls marked with poetry and threats of bribery and death in crayon and adolescent lettering.

"But how could I ever get any sleep here?" I asked him. We stepped out the back door past the mound of unrecyclable paper and cans of unredeemable value, and a dark man stepped out of the dark shadows of the wild bushes that surrounded the lot and embraced me. And I embraced him back. Because it was E. Z. himself with his dice in his pocket and his dime in his ear and his clover in his right shoe and a fine strand of my own pubic hair in his wallet, and he said, "Maybe your gypsy wagon doesn't run, but it sure can sleep us back here." So E. Z. and I began to sleep there.

I heard that a hundred thousand men in one day were buried alive in sand. I heard that a hundred thousand babies a day were carried off in dumpsters. I heard that the men had begun to hate their women and the women had begun to hate their men so much that they had begun to debate matters of oral unedifications and broken promises of sexual dimensions on day-time television. But the moon and the musicians continued to rock the household well into the fall. On sunny afternoons I carried my accordion across the street and crooned old battlesongs to the buried generals and statesmen—in return they whispered military secrets to me about how to hold ground and never let down your defenses. At night I slept with E. Z. in the wagon on the back lot as the pentecostal singers from across the alley blended their music with that of the pentagrammic rockers in the house, the sirens and the distant grieving. The different strands of music braided so prettily that many a night the corpses would dance out of the cemetery, and we would all dance together, run the keys, snooze, dream, trade ghost tales—Big Foot and Frankie, Yeller Dog and even the Founding Father occasionally making a joke—as the trees around the lot turned to white skeleton hands and the night air became cold again.

And in the house I took over my room and sat at my desk and wondered if after all it might be possible to make some kind of plan for the future, some kind of game where there would be no Winners and no Losers, no upper and no under, no one going away from the table with all of the wherewithal—it was a tricky question. Outside the windows men walked the sidewalks with their suppers in slender brown bags and only occasionally a woman, usually somehow distraught, without a purse.

The longer I stayed at the house with the Musicians, the more I wanted to stay there and continue thinking. The tombstones I had begun to find charming and the Squad scenes quite entertaining and the garbage and pentagram graffiti protective and cozy, and then, too, being with E. Z. made it better—helping the coins roll out of his pockets at night, finding them in the morning scattered across the floor and in the bed covers and on the sidewalks, and sometimes even a dollar bill or a twenty dollar bill in a gutter as we took our evening walks around the cemetery grounds. It was more than enough to pay the modest rent. But the bank had hired a real estate agent to sell the house, as well as the rest of the foreclosed ghost shops and rat houses and infested garages and bushwild lots that comprised the neighborhood since the Squad men had been able to arrest the last of the men, women, and children in just those few weeks I had begun to stay there. I witnessed the last family on the block in the white house across the street get herded out in handcuffs and put in variously marked Squad cars—a man and a woman and three children. So this real estate agent began traipsing prospective buyers through the garbage and snake cords and showing each one of them every room of all three floors. But no one was browsing such a house in such an abandoned block in what could be called anything at all like an uproar of enthusiasm, and so this real estate agent was getting unhappier.

One day he came followed by a man whose eyes were shaded by his black gimme cap. I was sitting at my executive desk gazing at a patch of wily sunflowers which had begun to twist from the weedy lot that edged our drive into the sidewalk with some of its stalks even bent all the way into the street. It was completely blocking the way for walkers but giving out a peculiar yellow heat and leafy insight to an otherwise monochromatically gray day pierced only by a hundred thousand screams from men and women in various stages of physical torture seeding the breeze coming into my room from the open window. At least the real estate agent had the courtesy to knock at my door first.

I said, "Come in," and the two of them did, and the real estate agent asked me, "How many people are staying in this house, do you know?"

I said, "No, I don't," although I knew that since E. Z. and I had come there had been a Full House—Black Alice and her Lover Dawn had moved onto the second floor, then the three musicians, and then the third floor bunch. . .

"Well you might not know this," he said, "but there is only permission on your lease for Four of a certain Kind, the three Ones upstairs and the fourth One being the keyboard player—YOU, in fact," he said, "are not on that lease."

"But no hard feelings," I said.

"No, no hard feelings. . ."

"I only work here," I said, "because the Musicians were kind enough to give me space . . ." No need to tell him, I decided, about the gypsy wagon and E. Z. on the back lot.

"I am thinking," the man with the shaded eyes said, "of fixing this house up for myself and my family."

Oh a family, I thought to myself, and my self brightened despite itself at the thought of babies and ghosts of old holidays past, maybe even bringing some kind of future to this sad neighborhood. And I said, "this would make a very nice family house."

I guess because I had been somewhat touched by his homely vision, I did not mention that my own family, of course, and the musicians who had so graciously hosted me would have to unfortunately be turned out to make way for such a new family plan.

They wandered out of the room. I heard them trip through the cymbals and bang through the accumulated juice jars piled at the back door.

Minutes later they reappeared in the view out my left-most window, and stood by the shaggy sunflowers. They were talking intensely to each other and frowning up from time to time at the outside house walls which were peeling yellow under their gaze. On a whim, charmed I guess by the

Family Man's plan, I pulled out my accordion from under the executive desk and began to play an old tune about love on the edge of a battlefield, and to send the two men a glimpse of the house's music without its defenses, so that large yellow flakes began to swirl off the house like yellow rain, and I saw for an instant the gleam of an eye underneath the gimme cap, and a shiver ran through me like nothing I had ever felt, from even the most stony of the generals and stockbrokers laid out in the cemetery, some little screamy glint of gimme cap greed. But I closed my eyes and kept playing, and when the tune was over and the last note had told the sad love-crossed ending, the two of them were gone.

The next day the real estate agent came back and gave notice to all of us—thirty days to be out—five days before Christmas. So it was the Last Days. And the Musicians began to play in earnest. The drummers took up their stations and armed themselves with a hundred drumsticks apiece. The keyboardist monitored his many dials and tested his most lyrically obnoxious harmonics through his various microphones. The Music Man came down from third with his Happy Stash and the Dancer, who writhed around in the midst of mike cords at the keyboardist's bare feet, and the Baby was given a snare drum of his own, and the two Queens came down from second. Music started in the afternoon, pulsed and pounded on into the evening, and E. Z. and I lay down in the wagon that night and went to sleep listening, and by about midnight the drumming had turned into thunder. Then the rains began.

We all moved out the furniture and musical instruments and books and all our other valuable stuff in small loads into borrowed pick-up trucks with open beds through wind and mud and rain which was continuing without let-up into flooding. One drummer had a running car and he made load after load in it, but one of the Queens used a taxicab to move her valuables, and the keyboardist threw stuff into one of the broken down vans on the back lot and then called a wrecker. We put our money for the move together, and Music Man and the keyboardist split the pot. Music Man got a house with a yard for the Baby and the Dancer, and the Musicians were trying for Housing in the Suburbs, trying not to think about how they were going to pay the gawdawful rents in the months to come. It seemed like E. Z. and I were going to wind up parked by some curb in the wagon. And the wagon and the weather were cold for that, and the constant drumming now, too, of the rain on the aluminum wagon roof coming straight down on my head drowning all my dreams out, and too wetly cold for all parts of me to stay warm through the nights, even with E. Z.'s big warm body steaming up as much excess heat as possible. And I thought, well, maybe the real estate agent and the new Owner would wait just a little bit, maybe 'til just after Christmas came and went, because after all, the new Owner Family would probably want to spend Christmas together in their old house, wherever it was, rather than move through the holiday which is the pits, and no doubt the new Owner would want to wait anyway at least until the first of the year to try and fix the house up to a family's regular living standard, i.e., a paint job, exterminator, and kitchen.

But it was the last day of the thirty-day notice and the last pieces of furniture in the Music Man's third floor living room, having to carry the stuff down the back flights of wooden steps, and the rain was coming down to beat all historical records, and it was mixed with the ash of a hundred volcanoes, the rock now weeping through the clouds of lava water, and on the back parking lot the new Owner sat in his black pick-up truck, and parallel with his truck was the black Chrysler of the real estate agent, occasionally flicking their wipers across their windshields so as to get a clearer image of the moving out we were carrying on. Cemetery ghosts hung like black tatters off the iron fence mourning our passing out of their neighborhood. I was wielding the heavy end of Music Man's worn bedstead which was writhing and sighing its history of dancers and bar maids and singers as we tried to push it down the soggy stairs, when I felt a tap on my shoulder, and when I looked around there was the Owner glinting at me from under his gimme cap.

"Uh Sister," he said, "I need to talk to you for a minute. I just wanted to say—"

With me stopped and turned around, the Music Man was nevertheless trying to push his end of the steaming wet bed down, so that I staggered just a little bit, and the Owner said "—oh go ahead and finish making this load."

So the Music Man and I wheeled and dealed the mattress into the pick-up bed and covered it like you would a corpse with black plastic. The Owner was waiting for me in the stairwell.

"You can stay here, Sister, if you want to—after the others are gone. What I said, see, about this house being for my family was just a joke, see, to get everyone out fast—actually I want to turn this house into offices. I want to dice it up into spaces. I want to stock it with briefcases and master plan guys and spies for the universal business systems. But I can't do this right away because I sunk all my capital into just buying the place. So it's going to take me some months—and in the meantime you could stay here if you want to after the others are gone. . ."

I must have been looking at him odd-eyed as he said this (what a joker this glinting guy was!) because he attempted to assure me along the lines of what he thought was my most resistance. . .

"—for whatever you were paying the Musicians. . ."

I said, "a hundred dollars . . ."

He looked at me solemnly from under his bill. The rocky rain was filling up the stairwell. It was well around our ankles and the upper roof had become a chute of gravel water which we stood under like a waterfall throughout the discussion. His pitch was cut short by Music Man's call for assistance on the removal of his couch that had made into a bed for both babysitters and multiple sex partners so many times that now it wouldn't fold up anymore and was snagged between the banisters.

"I'll think about it," I told the cap-shaded face. He flowed down the stairs and back into his truck where his black silhouette continued to loom at us as we slid the pick-up out of the driveway on its last load.

Myself alone in three stories of yellow house? Protected only by the cemetery ghosts from the Desperate and Needy and preying Squad cars? But then—wouldn't he need some sort of security for the house anyway? So maybe, just maybe, if I forgot the way he had treated the rest of my hosts and my family and how he had lied—joked really—he would Let E. Z. stay with me in the third floor apartment . . .

When the last load was made he was waiting for my answer in the front room, which still had my executive desk in it and my card on the door.

"So maybe E. Z. my boyfriend could live on the third floor and be my security," I said.

Which wasn't what he wanted me to say, I could see immediately from the way his eyes swam back under the cap and he stuttered, "Oh no well you see I am going to live on the third floor—well, because I'm divorced actually and the kids are with my wife so I'm living alone. . ."

He left shortly after our conversation turned negative. I called a wrecker for the wagon and gave them the address on Nowhere Road where the Music Man was. Then I went out to the lot and called into one of the wagon's windows to E. Z.—"Honey, that deal about the upstairs apartment didn't work after all."

But he didn't answer me, and when I opened the back door to see about him, the wagon was flooded and he was gone.

I cannot name for you all the streets I walked those last few days of the yammering year of the rock-ice heart, as I had begun to call it. But I walked through Christmas. On the last day of the year the sun came out in the afternoon and I found myself walking through a neighborhood south of the River, and at the intersection of East Mary and South Fourth, Mary herself came up and joined me and we began walking together.

"Honey you know it's always been hard to get a room," she assured me. She agreed how difficult it was sometimes to go on living—to live with the miracle of your own life—particularly when you see certain Ones humiliated, or stabbed, or gunned down in all sorts of styles before your own eyes. And how *do* you bear up to such action on your own family members? Especially when you're related to both sides of an argument?

She put an arm around me. "Want to come over for a cup of coffee?" We walked past the three-storied Living Christchild Church edged in neon and the Jesus Clapboard Hovel of the Far-Out Worshipers and turned left at the Christus-Mark-up Store into a small grotto off an alley.

"I still can't get over," she said apologetically, "what it's all come to."

She ducked through the small door and I followed her.

"Joe?" she called in the hallway. She opened a side door a small crack and talked into a dark room. "I brought someone home with me."

I heard a man's voice, some indistinguishable words. "Okay, honey," she said.

"Just stick your head in," she told me, "and say hello to him."

"Hello Dad," I said.

The room inside was so dark that I couldn't see him, but I heard his indistinguishable words again. She shut the door. "He's been sick since his last operation on that old War Wound, but I think he's beginning to adjust now to the new body parts. He's too weak to get up and see you now, but you know he's glad you're home."

I followed her to the kitchen. "Your friends were around earlier looking for you," she said, "—Larry and Greg and John and all, wanting to see what you were up to for this evening."

I sat down at the table and studied my hands. "Oh, I'm not all that interested in the Game this year," I said.

She put on the pot and brought out the family albums. We were still looking at them when little fog feet tiptoed into the back of the grotto, and I heard the river and the mist talking to each other outside rolling down the alley, a voice surprisingly distinct calling at midnight from the room down the hall, "Mary, could you bring me a glass of water?"

She got up and said, "I'll be there in just a minute, Joe."

SECOND SADDLE

JAN REID

The horse was a two-year-old dark palomino, a good fifteen hands tall. Bose had picked him out first thing in the picket corral, his neck slung way up over the others in the milling and the dust. His eyes were wild but interested in all these creatures yelling, whistling, assaulting them with coils of rope. There weren't many broncs of such promise in western Texas, and the peelers wasted no time moving these through. They just concentrated on getting Garland Shelton's herd broke second saddle—ridden twice, terms of the contract—and driven hard to the army buyers at Fort Griffin. Otherwise, they'd next be seen at a high lope in south Kansas.

Despite handsome prices, raising horses had been a losing proposition in the Palo Pinto country ever since the distant war that made Bose a free man at the age of seventeen. For a decade Shelton, Oliver Loving, and a few other ranchers had been buying them for ten dollars a head down in Mexico and herding them six hundred miles north to the Cross Timbers, of a mind to get rich. But then the war broke out, Texas seceded, and the federals obliged local wishes by closing down the line of forts that had kept the hostiles at some neighborly distance. The Civil War in Parker County turned out to be a Comanche and Kiowa war. And after the bigger show was over, the federals took their sweet time moving troops back to the rebel frontier. Killings and kidnappings were frequent, but the horse and mule theft was constant. Every new stable west of Fort Worth was built of post-oak tree trunks and locked and chained at night. People who didn't have stables would lock one end of a chain around a horse or mule's neck and lock the other end to a tree. This was answered by maniacs who cut their throats and chopped their heads off. The farmers just gave up. Learned to plow with oxen.

Knowing better than to ask the price of the palomino, Bose decided to deliver him broken fit for a colonel. Unlike the other bronc peelers, all of whom were white boys in their teens and early twenties, Bose had reason to value the efforts and institution of the United States Army. And he didn't mind showing off a little. Bose kept up his quota of the lesser stock, of which there were a hundred and forty head; the round corral behind the Sheltons' ranch house was a dawn-to-dusk frenzy of horse abuse. Two boys would grab and twist the ears of a roped horse and ear him down motionless, jaws clenched and groaning, until a bronc rig could be cinched on him, and a rider climbed aboard. The rodeo commenced from there, and constituted the first ride of the contracted pair. But Bose took his time with the palomino. The horse spent the better part of two days flopping on his side, roped by the forelegs, and lying with his wind knocked out. Then, with the rope around one fetlock, decided it was less wear and tear on him to stand still while the human crooned to him and touched his nose and rubbed him all over with a rough gunny sack. Then, with the rope tied to a hind foot and hitched in a loop around his neck, suffered it as the man pulled on and twisted and put scissors and comb to his cream-colored tail. Until finally the horse was halter-broke and unafraid of the light tarp popped close to his ear in likeness of a windblown slicker. Bose was so patient and steady that by the time he stood up in the stirrup, swung his leg across the cantle, and took a seat, the palomino just trembled. He never even jumped.

Bose didn't use the rough saddle-tree bronc rig they put on the others. He broke this one to the nicely tooled Fort Worth saddle Doctor Ikard had given him, along with a peso-studded bridle and a set of saddlebags that contained his freedom papers. A lot of slaveowners chose to do it that way, once it became clear that the war was lost. It was a point of pride with them; also they desired to get their affairs in legal order, in anticipation of the forthcoming duresses. Milt Ikard, the doctor's son who had grown up with Bose and believed he would one day inherit him, sulked over his papa's act for nearly two months. Almost ruined their friendship, Bose thought, with a bitter little smile. But Milt got over it, and this morning he was among the youths who peered through the pickets and sat on the crossties with the dew still thick on the grass and the sun just up over the trees. Holstered sidearms and a few shotguns were arrayed with their meal bags and canteens along the fence, in case need of them arose. There was a good deal of jeering and drawn-out coffee drinking. They were all beat up and bone-sore.

The palomino stood reasonably still as Bose laid the pad snug against his withers and saddled him the second time. He stepped around more when Bose put the hackamore bridle on him; the heavy strap leather reins were borrowed from a plowman's harness. "What are you going to do with those reins, Bose?" Elbert Doss called as he got on. "Ride skids behind him, comes a blizzard? Tie him way up in a tree and let him tread water, case it floods?"

Elbert was a slender youth with a shock of auburn hair, long-lashed green eyes, and a dimpled chin—in great demand at dances, his mama's pride and joy. His dad was the Parker County judge, and Elbert aimed to become a lawyer and a politician in his own right, if that were still allowed in the rejoined country. There was talk of him moving back East and going to a college, so the war's bitter reckonings wouldn't set him back so much. In the meantime he peeled broncs.

Bose guided the horse away from the boys in a leftward circle, then in answer to Elbert whirled the reins like a lariat, close upon the horse's ears and far out in front of his eyes. The palomino shied a little, but not too much. Bose turned him in a circle, back the other way, then stopped him. He slipped his boots out of the stirrups, drew up his knees, hooked a heel on one of the riggings, knelt with the other leg, and slowly stood up. 'Whoa, now, easy. That's right," he said, playing out the reins and taking light backward steps until finally he stood on the horse's croup.

The palomino cast back curious glances and swished his tail but didn't seem to mind. Bose clicked his tongue and the horse took three steps forward. The others turned up the jeering, trying to spook him, but he stood quiet and just turned his ears back and forth. Bose took two light steps forward and balanced again on the saddle.

"Almost finished horse," he boasted. "Can you do this, Elbert?"

"I can't think of any reason why I would," he answered.

"He wants to join the circus," Milt Ikard said.

Behind the ranch house clearing was a brushy cliff, about a hundred feet high, that leveled off in pasture toward the west. A couple of buzzards lazed out over the valley below. Under some elm trees on the edge of the cliff, half a dozen young Comanches admired the size of the herd, if not its overall quality, and watched the trickster's exhibition on the honey-colored horse. They couldn't do anything about the horses: the sun was too far up, and a few hundred yards away, the other raiders were resting and watering another rancher's herd, about forty head, that they had run off during the night. But Quanah said, "I want the *tu-tah-voa*." The nigger. Or dirty white ass, in their way of saying.

Quanah led the raiding party, and as long as he had the confidence of the others, he could do anything he chose. Cold Hawk voiced his concerns politely. "I count nine of them, and we need to get those horses across some rivers."

"You couldn't hit him anyway," said Toes Grown Together. "It's too far off." Quanah looked at his friend and grinned.

"Two mares and a mule?" he said.

"Done," Toes accepted the wager.

Cold Hawk's misgivings simmered in his eyes.

Quanah stepped quickly to the horses and came back with his .44 Henry repeater. He wore moccasins, deerhide leggings, a breechclout, a red bandanna around his throat, and a ragged and patched U.S. army tunic with master sergeant stripes. It was hot and scratchy, but he wore it always in raids against the whites. The blue army coat was Quanah's signature in those years, mark of *tuibuitsi*, swaggering youth. He had cut it off a bald-headed soldier that six of them caught off by himself loading watermelons in a wagon near Fort Sill. They filled him up with arrows, and one of them sheared off a thin piece of scalp, but due to the arrows, stealing the coat was complicated—accounting for its very tattered condition. They broke melons over the dead sergeant and left him half-buried in the flies and slop.

"Wind coming up," Toes ragged Quanah.

He lay down prone and, using a rock, first squared the sight on the nigger's shoulders, raised it a couple of inches higher for the distance, and waited for the horse to turn him around broad again.

"Which mares?" he said.

Bose felt the whispering shock of the first shot well before its crack echoed through the valley. It passed under his chin, two inches from his throat. The second one came in low, bucked by a shoulder annoyed by the miss and rushing to get another bullet off. Bose thought certain he was hit because his feet were thrown out from under him and when he landed on his hip, there was a sharp jag of pain and his right leg went numb. For an instant the others froze in crouches and perched on the fence like crows; then they began to clamber and jump, in the odd way of humans trying to will themselves smaller. Then, collecting their wits, they picked up speed and dove for cover.

From the dirt where he was sprawled, across the corral Bose watched the bolting horse stagger hard and pull up limping. He'd stepped on the long reins and hurt himself. The saddle was askew. Bose rolled toward the fence and lay there until he thought there wouldn't be any more fire, then got to his feet and with much swearing and a limp of his own backed the palomino against the fence. He read one feint wrong, the next one right, and with a lunge caught one of the reins. Bose talked him down to where he just shuddered, but the eyes were wide and yellow and their expressions were way back in his skull—all the trust Bose had built up was gone.

"You all right?" called Sam Newberry.

"Yeah, but look at my saddle," said Bose.

The bullet had hit just below the horn, ruining good leather and splintering the fork. "Somebody come hold him," he said.

"What are you doing?" said Will Gray.

"He's hurt, and I gotta get the saddle off him."

"Fuck that horse!"

In time they calmed down and milled in an angry circle, ramming bullets in pistols and strapping on holsters. "Indian sonsabitches," fumed Milt Ikard.

"Not necessarily," said Elbert Doss, the would-be lawyer. "Let's don't stir up any unreasoned massacres. Mighta been stray shots. Or somebody hunting."

"Stray shots!" said Bose. "Five feet and ten seconds apart? Hunting me!"

"Maybe a jilted girlfriend," Elbert laughed.

"Shut up and listen," said Milt.

Over the ridge there was a sound of horses running. Or being run.

Gladiolia Shelton came hurtling from the ranch house, where the dogs were in an uproar. Her husband Garland had taken a wagon to Weatherford that morning. She wore the dungarees and long shirt of a man; all the women on the farms and ranches did that when their husbands were away, under the assumption the savages were always close by, watching. Mrs. Shelton tended to throw back her head, turn red, and puff up like a toad at the least excitement, and she looked explosive now. "We heard the shooting," she said. "Is anybody hurt?"

"No, ma'am," answered Milt. "There might be a damaged horse."

"Me and Emma was out front," she said, trying to catch her breath. "Cleon Hallsey had just rode off. He said there was Comanches all around here last night. They ran off a bunch of horses over on Sanchez Creek. Tried to grab a little girl off one of them Swede farms, but she got away."

The peelers stared at the fading noise and the higher ground.

"There's your evidence, your honor," Milt said to Elbert.

"Somebody's gonna pay for that saddle," promised Bose.

Quanah hadn't actually tried to steal that little girl. He didn't want to have to carry her, share his food, watch her at night, and drive horses hard three days, too.

And because his mother had come among the Comanches as one of these taken ones, and she and his baby sister disappeared forever when the whites stole her back, his attitudes toward the practice were complicated. They never would have seen this girl at all if the horses hadn't panicked her out of the brush near a privy where she was hiding with a calico cat. In a cloud of blinking fireflies she took off running one way, the whitish cat bounding and scampering another, her nightshirt and braided blond hair luminescent in the moonlight. Quanah just rode her down and leaned over to touch the back of her head. He was counting coup, lightly.

The act required no great courage, but some part of her spirit was lifted nonetheless. When they got back to the encampment on the plains, there would be a dance celebrating their success and enrichment of the band in horses, and Quanah was already rehearsing the speech conveying the great beauty of this sight, and swearing to the powers that the deed was his. "I now give this gift to my brother, Toes Grown Together," he would say. And his friend would have to reply with the same formality. "I now take this deed. Sun, Father, Moon above, and Earth, Mother, witness that it's mine." Making it harder for him to gloat over the wagered mares and mule and Quanah's inability to kill that nigger.

They pushed the horses west through sandstone and granite canyons, certain they were being chased, and confident if they were overtaken. Their spare horses were trained to keep the stolen ones bunched close and moving until the herding instinct took over, which freed the raiders to send relays of sentries out in crisscrossing loops, maintaining a watch to the rear. Has No Teeth saw the young Tejanos crossing a creek, some grabbing their saddlehorns as the horses drove hard to get up over a loose bank— Comanches had no respect for white ass horsemanship. One of them, he saw, was a nigger on a gray. They were riding hard, in search of their own deaths. To their seven, there were sixteen raiders. The Comanches would either lure them into a blind curve of a high-banked creek, or else get them running out in the open 'til their horses played out. Either way, three days from now there were be even more branded and steel-shod horses driven through the tipis as the elders grinned and children jumped behind their mothers' skirts; and now the raiders would be able greet the whoops of homecoming and celebration whirling six fresh scalps from points of arrows and muzzles of rifles. More than likely, they'd just kill the nigger.

Has No Teeth got his name from a boyhood horse race in what proved to be a gopher field. He was thrown head first and tried to eat a rock. It could have been worse—for a time the elders were calling him Ruins Good Horses and Can't See the Ground. His own riding skill was no better than fair, and now as he reined his bay around to gallop off and inform the others of their good fortune, horse medicine failed him again. Almost stepped upon, a rattlesnake coiled up and rose out of the grass whirring loud and shrill. The bay horse reared up and bolted, bringing the rider, before he could duck, flush into a low oak branch. Has No Teeth sat on the ground for a moment, holding his broken nose and watching blood course through his fingers. Knowing how difficult it would be to walk down that particular horse, he got to his feet, wiped his hands on his leggings, picked up a stick, and took vengeance on the snake.

The youth who made the next loop behind the herd failed to see or hear the Tejanos coming. Consequently Quanah's raiders were the ones surprised. They were coming out of woods in a bluestem meadow when he heard the first gun go off. Coming from two sides, the Tejanos rammed their horses right through the herd. The sound they made in a fight chilled and rattled Quanah like no Ute or Tonkawa cry. It was an ongoing talking snarling scream—as hateful and unhinged as the jabber of a rabid wolf. Quanah heard two bullets sing past him. He kicked his blue roan horse in a circle, analyzing the situation with a quick count of the hats. His gaze froze on the black Tejano—the one he'd tried to kill.

The nigger drove a gray into the side of Toes Grown Together's spotted horse and jarred them hard. Nearly unhorsed, Toes waved backhand at him with his war club and missed him, clumsily. As Toes partially recovered and drew back the axe for a better swing, the nigger spurred again, leaned in from his saddle with a pistol, and shot him where his ribs came together, from less than an arm's length. Quanah knew his friend was dead or dying from the way he flopped off the horse.

Quanah saw two of the Tejanos bearing down on him. With some nimble riding and the cover of a plum tree he got away. Horses were squalling, escaping into the trees; it was a running fight now. Quanah stopped the horse and watched the stampede reach the end of the long meadow. They were going to lose half the herd. He counted at least five of the Comanche horses running free—and not one of the Tejanos'. Ducking branches, he circled his horse back through the trees until he found his friend propped on an elbow in the tall grass. Quanah looked around and didn't see anybody. He stopped the horse and slid off. Toes' belly, breechclout, and leggings were soaked with blood. He groaned when Quanah started to pick him up and raise him to the horse. "Just let me sit," he said. "It hurts too much." His color was all wrong, and his eyes were glazing over.

"Stole those horses," he said.

"Sure did," said Quanah, taking out his knife. Grief-stricken, he started hacking off his left braid. He drew blood from his arm with a slash through the army sleeve. "Toes, I'm sorry. It's my fault—"

Toes looked at him like he was crazy. "You mean you shot me?" he said, making an attempt at humor.

"We were gone, back up on the plains. I never should have made us stop."

"Quanah, someday you're going to be a man with two thousand horses. Pick of wives. Famous war chief, like that other." He was referring, in their way of deferring to the dead, to Quanah's father. That man died pathetic, Quanah thought blackly. Scared of owl sounds at night. Weeping under piles of buffalo robe.

274

"I hung us up," insisted Quanah. "We should have been riding. Crossing rivers."

"Reason more to kill that nigger."

"Have his ugly hair."

The little clearing was a soft and pretty place, abloom with spring's blue and white buffalo clover. There was a nice breeze. "Quanah?" said Toes, after a time.

"Say it."

"Give my mama the mares," he said. "Brother Runs Slow the mule."

And then his spirit left.

The disquietude of shooting that Indian had not gone away. Bose had often fantasized the act, ruining the innards of victims real and faceless, white and savage. But this gun kick still tingled in the bones of his arm. The boom echoed in his mind.

What stayed with him most was the dull, conceding change of expression that had come over the Indian's face as he saw there was nothing to be done. It was the broad, flat, unlined face of a boy no older than himself. Without a blink of hesitation Bose shot to kill him. In a heartbeat his sensations went from anger and fright to elation and gloom. Murdering wasn't how he was raised, slave folks or white owners. And the odd mix of the aftertaste was not something to be desired, just now. Bullets hissed and rifles cracked all around them. Bose rode his tiring gray horse beside a skinny mare that galloped and wheezed with an arrow in her neck.

The peelers were being herded with the stolen broncs they ran among. None of them were down, as far as Bose could see, but they were outnumbered two to one. Outside the range of their shotguns and revolvers, the Indians raced along both sides of the herd, yelling insults and performing stunts. For a time one sat backward on a running paint, thoughtfully firing shots from a lever-action rifle. But the army bluecoat on the blue roan horse was the one who had their attention. He was bigger, taller, than the others. The uniform coat he wore was filthy and torn, but the deck of sergeant stripes afforded it a personal quality. He had one braid on the right side of his head—the left was crudely shorn. The peelers got this close a look because he was on a fast and strong horse, and he looped back and then rode among them as they twisted in their saddles, trying to keep him in sight, and fired off wild blind shots. They were in serious danger of themselves, trying to kill him. He carried a war club, but when he passed a rider he just reached out and rather lightly whopped him, as if with a magic stick. Then he weaved back through the herd and rejoined the others, who cheered him wildly. Twice he did this. Courage medicine.

The third time Bose had a sense that the bluecoat was coming after him. Bose slowed his horse a little and reined him tighter, to control him better. It would be easy enough to cause a horse wreck, but if his horse went down or he got thrown, he was a dead man. He looked back and saw the bluecoat's eyes and knew this time he wasn't planning any love tap. Bose decided he had more faith in a quirt tied to a saddle string than his pistol, under these conditions. The bluecoat closed in, kneeing his horse left and right, trying to stay in the blind spot. But Bose guessed right: as the bluecoat came around on the right, preparing to brain him with that club, Bose lashed out with the quirt and got him good, across the chest. Just then three guns went off one right after another, and Bose's horse jumped a little gully, and it was all he could do just to stay on and absorb the gonad hurt. When he got his presence back, the bluecoat was nowhere around.

"Bose!" yelled Milt Ikard, reining his horse alongside.

"Yeah!"

"You see that son of a bitch?"

"Got the mind of a child. Don't he."

"What?" yelled Milt.

"Stop shooting at him, if you can't hit him!"

The colors of the grasses and wildflowers went by them in a blur, but in fact the horses were slowing almost to a trot. Every breath of wind came out a grunt, and their mouths were smeared with foam.

"We've got to find a place to stop," said Milt.

"Is everybody still with us?"

"Yeah. But the horses are give out."

Bose grabbed his ruined saddlehorn and pulled himself up in the stirrups, so he could see farther. They were nearing the mouth of a short narrowing canyon, eroded from the breaks of a sandstone outcropping, that he knew from running mustangs—it was a natural trap. At the end were successive ledges and boulders that ended in with a cliff and an immense bank of prickly pear. "Quarter mile back in that canyon," he called, "let's get up in the cactus. They can shoot through it, but it'll be hard to see us, and they're not gonna want to come in after us. They've got those horses. I think they'll go on."

The plan moved back through shout and gesture. The Indians saw their intent and tried to head them off, but they discouraged it with pistol fire and kicked the last run out of their horses. When they reached the rocks they jumped off their horses and ran with guns and canteens and bags of cartridge boxes. Bose was seated with his back to a sandstone slab, pulling cactus spines out of his elbow and feeling somewhat hopeful, when Will Gray said, "Oh, no."

A hundred fifty yards out in front of them, Elbert Doss had gotten cut off. His horse was either overheated or shot, for it walked around woozy. On the ground two of the Indians ran between the rider and the cactus bank, aiming rifles at him. Comanches, thought Bose, were a stumpy and bow-legged bunch. Elbert sat stunned as the crowd grew, pointing and jerking the trigger of an empty pistol. He had lost his hat, and he looked about thirteen years old. "God damn it, Elbert, ride!" yelled his best friend, Sam Newberry. "Spur him! Get on through there."

All around Bose the peelers started laying out all the fire they had. Sidearms, shotguns, hysterical and useless. Several Indians walked around Elbert now, yelling insults toward the ones in the rocks and prickly pear. One showed his bare ass to them. Nobody had to say anything; finally the shooting just petered out. They needed the ammunition.

An Indian rode up behind Elbert swinging a lariat and tossed the loop over him. He dragged Elbert off his horse and rode around a bit, tumbling him through stickers and rocks. Then with pokes of arrows the ones on the ground made him get to his feet. The roper kept his horse backing and sidestepping so that Elbert had to work to stay on his feet. The others would fall dead silent, then with a screech one would ride or run past him and slice him with the edge of an arrow—his shoulders, his arms, his chest, the backs of his thighs and neck. Made from whatever rusted iron they could scavenge, the arrows must have stropped sharp as razors, for soon he was drenched red and crying out to God, over and over, the only prayer he knew. "Forgive us of our sins, and deliver us from evil . . ."

This must have gone on ten or fifteen minutes. Through it all, the bluecoat sat on his roan horse well off to the side. Having none of it, Bose considered, but doing nothing to stop it, nor hurry it up. Once when Elbert fell, the roper let him lie still for a minute. Almost gently, the roper backed up his horse and brought Elbert to his feet. He was blinded by all the blood. ". . . On earth as it is in . . ." he went on praying. Suddenly the bluecoat kicked his horse into a gallop and bore down on Elbert from behind. His bowstring was pulled back so far that when he let go, the arrow went all the way through Elbert and skittered across the ground. Elbert arched his back and looked down, vaguely moving his hands, like he was trying to button a shirt. The bluecoat let out a whoop and rode on past him, leaning down from his horse to retrieve the arrow. Elbert tottered and wobbled and finally fell.

Rifle bullets snapped through the cactus, splattering them with gelatin. The bronc peelers laid out their own sheet of fire when the bluecoat slipped off his horse and walked to Elbert's body. He stood looking at the cactus bank, ignoring the skip ricochets. He produced a knife, grabbed a fistful of Elbert's auburn hair, and raised his head. He made one quick circular slash, put a heel on his chest, then with both hands and a hard yank, before their eyes that savage scalped him.

The Comanches had been gone two hours when a ranger party found the bronc peelers. None of the others had suffered a scratch. The fight was recorded in the Palo Pinto country as a considerable defeat of the hostile Indians, as a testament to the bravery of the youth in those frontier communities, and, as time went by, as the first confirmed local sighting of the one who came to be known as Quanah Parker. Bose cast it in a different light. It was easy enough to get over killing that other Indian. But he dwelled for years on the mother's cries when they rode up in the yard of the biggest house in Weatherford late that day and Sam Newberry had to show her Elbert's body. "Horses!" she shrieked at them. "You got this done to him over a bunch of horses!"

In Broad Daylight

Joyce Gibson Roach

It ain't no small thing to be the high sheriff of Caballo County. No, sir-ee. For one thing, it's elected office-ship. But for several years nobody seemed more interested in the job than they ought to be. I suppose it's because we was civilized, even if not modern—not many killings, border incidents or racial strife, as it was called in the city. Our school didn't have no trouble with the integration policy since we only had us one building and the children was all mixed up since I can remember. But in the year of our Lord, 1970, the sheriff's race in Caballo County got real heated. That's what happens when a piece of trash notices an easy spot and sees the easy way.

The only announced candidate said he was going to deal with only two big issues. He was going to try to keep brassieres on all the women—at least that's what he said was his platform when he announced for office.

I can't imagine why he come out with such of a thing. Wasn't nobody not wearing brassieres that we could notice, but he got a-holt of some information out of Chicago—well, somewheres up there—that told about a new lady's movement that was demanding their rights. And one of 'em was to go bare breasted without wearing a foundation if it so pleased them. They was called the women's liberation bunch.

Can you imagine such a thing? Here we got all this trouble in the county just coming of a drought that was the worst since the Biblical seven lean years, cattle stealing, land swindles, bank foreclosings, moonshine mescal troubles, and a tryin' to get us a doctor here permanent. We was even in the midst of building an old folks home. And this here jerk is going to make women without their brassieres—of which there weren't any in this whole county—the first plank in his platform!

"A Bra on Every Woman. Let's Keep Our Women Decent and Strapped Down!"—that's what he was having printed on campaign cards—can you believe it.

It would'na mattered 'cept nobody was running against this idiot. And such nonsense as the bra business was just a shame. He was making the worst kind of fun of our county, of our women, like there wasn't no other important law business so he'd just rub our noses in somethin' nasty. He also knew he was goin' to get elected because nobody would run against him.

His name was Jessie Earl Putty. Putty! That ought to tell you something. He was of the same Putty bunch that thought the only good Indian was a dead 'un, good Mexicanos were on the south side of the border, good colored people lived in some body else's town. Lynching was the best punishment for anybody accused of anything and ought best be applied before a trial. Women belonged on their backs, barefoot and pregnant—excuse me for speaking so plain, but that's what him and all his family thought. Well, he thought it, anyway, and he was always threatening the town with his family's opinions.

And he carried a pistol in his boot top. We knew that too 'cause he told us, and he was always reachin' down for that boot, and smilin' hateful-like.

We decided to have us an unofficial official meetin' down at the Horned Toad Cafe. I reckon that's as close as we come to a political gathering. For one thing everybody come by during the morning sometime—that is, we men did.

The women were coming too this time, maybe to eat something. But us menfolks only drank coffee—a matter that Flora brought to our attention on a regular basis. She's a good ol' girl, though. We reminded her that if we ate out, it looked like we couldn't get a good meal at home.

They wasn't many of us at the first meetin'. I was surprised, but you know that's how it goes. Folks aren't interested as they ought to be in civic affairs, but you'da thought people would have been more concerned about a man who didn't want to accomplish nothin' but bosom control because he heard about some nonsense back east. And you'da also thought people would have been more worried about Jessie Earl's family past and the stuff he told about how his own people handled business vigilante style all these years.

Joe Don Wheelright was sittin' in his usual corner the day we met. Joe Don was the very first person who had nerve enough to criticize Jessie Earl—why, he even made fun of 'im—and we sure wanted him in on the meeting. In fact, we was hopin' he'd run it. Since he practically lived at the cafe, we knew he'd already be there.

He was busy on the ketchup as usual—puttin' it on his eggs. I swear that boy's mother must have put a nipple on the ketchup bottle when he was a baby. He couldn't eat nothin' without ketchup on it. And his manners was awful—wiped his fingers on his pants and such when he wasn't licking stuff off 'em. He had a big ol' belly that kept him away from the table. He sloshed coffee and dropped food all down hisself when he tried to eat.

But other than that, Joe Don was the nearest thing to a educated man we knew. He had an honest-to-God Ag degree from somewheres and he could talk Spanish real good. He was a sage, a regular philosopher, that told good stories and jokes. One thing about him, he seen right through to the truth of a situation and told it with all the bark off.

Joe Don would'a been the perfect man for the sheriff's job 'cept he was an outsider. Moved here twenty years ago from out around Hobbs, New Mexico. In fact, he was a distant cousin to the Puttys—yessir, kinfolks. But to his credit, he never had nothing to do with 'em and he told 'em off whenever he thought they needed it.

And let me tell you one thing, it was dangerous to say anything critical to such as the Puttys. They went armed, too.

I forgot to mention that. Always carried high-powered rifles in the gun racks of their pick-ups when the other ranchers carried .22s—you know, for coyotes, rattlesnakes and the like. The last sheriff, who got clear out of town when his term expired, had dared to mention m-u-r-d-e-r to the Puttys when some folks from across the border were found dead out by Toad Flats close to the Putty ranch.

Well, anyway, when everybody got situated at the cafe, it was Annie Laurie Rogers called us to order. She was important in the big picture of things in the county and in town, too, but she hardly ever come to town and never got involved. Her family had a big ol' house in Toad and it took up a whole block, but she wasn't there very much. She was a loner.

Her family owned half the ranch country in the county and their ranch bordered the Puttys', who didn't have but ten thousand acres or so. The Rogers name was on a lot of the town itself, too.

She was nice enough, but you know, typical ranch woman—bronc buster, roper, shrewd cattle dealer—even rodeoed some. She didn't put a rifle in her pick-up. She kept hers about her at all times. Talked Spanish real good too and hired mostly Mexicans.

Nobody, and I mean nobody, messed with Annie Laurie. Not a lot of people knew her but they knew who she was. She didn't come to town much except when she moved in a herd to the cattle pens by the railroad. Joe Don worked for a livestock company that headquartered there and bought animals of all kinds from several counties and even Mexico. I reckon he bought her stuff too.

Now and again, Annie Laurie brought mules to ship out. Mules were her specialty. Those mules knew to step lively when she cracked that whip. Man alive! Then you saw her sure 'nuff. And heard her too. Loudest woman I ever heard. Could outscream a catamount or a pen of bawling cattle and still make a deal with the men inside the office.

She wasn't much to look at neither—big old tall gal. Naturally, she was single, an old maid.

Annie Laurie heard about the brassiere business and she was hoppin' mad. It wasn't no trouble a'tall to get her to get the womenfolks involved and she was ideal to do the talkin'. She treated us like she was moving cattle and everybody in the cafe didn't have no trouble a-hearin' her.

"Listen up," she screamed. You could a heard a pin drop. "That dirty-little-son-of-a-bitch Jessie Earl is about to be elected sheriff of Caballo County unless one of you sniveling cowards gets some backbone. The very idea, him saying the word brassiere, let alone breasts, in public."

We all like to have got under the table when she said that breast-word, right out loud in front of God and our wives. There's just some words a decent person don't say in public. But nobody criticized. Not one word.

"You're scared, that's what it is. So scared you'd let your womenfolks be ridiculed."

282

"I for one am real scared, Annie Laurie, and not afraid to say why. I don't want to die. I've grown fond of living," offered Ollie Johnson. "B'ziers ain't no big thing. My wife can take a little joshing."

"Yes, first he'll josh, then he'll be having fun lynching Mexicans, and then maybe you. Or maybe he'll just shoot you and cripple a few. What about your little Tony, Consuela? How would you like to see him with only one ear? And he'll use the badge and the office to kid all of us some more!"

Annie Laurie was tellin' it worse than it was gonna be, maybe, but then what she said had a ring a' truth to it considering what all Jessie Earl was suspected of doing.

Joe Don Wheelright was taking it all in. Now and again he'd pause with his fork, look around at all of us and then commence to eat again. But mostly he was looking at Annie Laurie like he'd never seen her before—I mean really staring at her.

This one and that one said something else. Pretty soon we was in a yelling free for all with Annie Laurie and getting into it with one another. Pandemonium reigned. Even Annie Laurie couldn't outscream 'em.

Things went on in such a way for at least fifteen minutes and most of us was ready to walk out when, can you believe it, Joe Don Wheelright put down the ketchup bottle—banged it on the table was more like it—and got up from his booth, and, so help me God, stood up in a chair!

"I would like to speak," and by the time he got to the word, speak, we had come to order. I mean every person in there including Annie Laurie shut their mouths and was ready to give Joe Don their undivided attention.

"I have a plan. We are going to have a political rally and invite Jessie Earl to speak."

"Oh, come on, Joe Don. Jessie Earl would just love that!" It was Ollie speaking again.

"Then you leave it to me. I'm going to call a rally and handle the proceedings. Ya'll are more scared of Jessie Earl than you ought to be. Don't you know he's just talk?"

And with that Joe Don got down off the chair, which was a sight to see, and walked out of the cafe.

We all went at it again then, hip and thigh, hammer and tongs. Some were laughing, some were swearing. Annie Laurie just shook her head.

Everybody swore they wouldn't be at the rally, but nobody was gonna' miss it either.

Several of us had it figured that Joe Don was going to run hisself. And even if he was an outsider, the idea of him a runnin' for sheriff looked mighty inviting. And honestly lookin' at it, he was expendable whereas none of us was. Excuse my speaking so frank.

Naturally, the rally was going to be at the Horned Toad Cafe and since Joe Don had officially announced it in the *Gazette*, there was a crowd coming down every morning—more than the usual bunch—to parley with him, to see what he had in mind. But Joe Don wasn't there. We supposed he was making preparations, but, so far as we could tell, there wasn't nothin' to be done.

"Flora?" asked Luther Lee, "do you know where Joe Don is at?"

Flora just cocked her head this way and that while she was pouring coffee and said, "I don't know anything about Joe Don's business. After all, he does have a job down at the depot."

From the way she talked, we knew she did know something too! Then she added with some sass in her voice, "I sure miss him bein' here as he is my only real paying customer." We got her drift.

Then she asked us what kind of pie we wanted for the rally so's she'd have plenty. Naturally, we said pecan. Didn't she know there wasn't no other kind? She said she figured we'd want pecan, but since it did cost a little bit more, very little, she thought she ought to ask. Meow! Flo was gettin' a sharp tongue.

The gathering had been called for Saturday night which was only reasonable. It didn't matter much to us town folks. We could meet any time, but Saturday was the natural choice for the ranchers and the cowboys. Those folks made the majority when they all got together. And who was sheriff was more important to them than it was for us since they needed the law out on the range worse than we did in town.

Joe Don hadn't been around to talk to, and we were all gettin' anxious. I got the Missus to fix an early supper and we headed for the cafe around six o'clock—a whole hour early. It was a good thing, let me tell you, 'cause there was already a crowd.

The cafe was full inside. It was pretty small. The yard was filling up and it looked to me like everybody had a piece of Flora's pecan pie. I sort'a wished we hadn't already eat peach cobbler at home, but we had and there wasn't nothing to be done about it now. Besides, we had come for other reasons.

Just about a quarter 'til, Annie Laurie drove in. And right behind her, there was all her boys. By five minutes 'til, it looked like all the ranchers, wives, children, cowboys and their families, too, was crowdin' on the lawn and into the street. And they all arrived at about the same time. I expected lots of interest from the ranchers, but nothing like what I saw.

Then it got straight up seven, but neither Joe Don or Jessie Earl had got there. Ollie came over. "I think Joe Don will get here soon, but I'll just bet you that Jessie Earl don't show. I'd be willin' to wager on it!"

"Oh no, Ollie. Jessie Earl will show. He wouldn't miss no chance to look us all in the eye and count every one of us. I jest hope he won't be carrying no rifle," says me.

Fifteen minutes after the appointed time, Joe Don came walking up. He was coming from the opposite end of town where he lived down close to the railroad cattle pens.

He wasn't alone. He had Jessie Earl with him. We didn't know what to make of that. When they got close up and was makin' their way through the crowd to the steps of the cafe, we could all see that Jessie Earl was drunker 'n a skunk.

Joe Don didn't let on like nothing was wrong. He had Jessie Earl shake hands all around, especially to the ranchers and their boys. And he took him by the arm and pulled him from one woman to the next, too. Old Jessie Earl just smiled and bowed and staggered here and there.

Finally, the two got to the steps and it took a little bit for Joe Don to get Jessie Earl turned around to face the crowd and steady on his feet. Joe Don couldn't get the crowd quieted down a'tall, so he motioned for Annie Laurie.

"Listen up!" she screamed. She didn't even have her rifle with her. "Joe Don Wheelright's got something to say. But before he does, let us pledge the flag."

And so we did just like we always do before we do anything in this town. And then we sang the Star Spangled Banner—we always do that too, sometimes even at funerals when the deceased wasn't a church-going person.

Jessie Earl, drunk as he was, both pledged and sang although his hand slipped from his heart to his belt buckle and then even lower by the time we got to "home of the brave and land of the free."

When we got to the very last notes, I noticed something funny was going on in the crowd. There was a lot of movement. Luther Lee side-stepped over to my Missus and whispered something in her ear. Her eyes got wide and she didn't bother to lower her voice when she told me what Luther said.

"Luther said that there must be a hundred guns in the crowd, Weldon!"

I started looking around and so did everybody else from town. Sure enough you could see guns—rifles, shotguns and pistoles—but only the women had 'em! The ranchers and their men just stood quiet as you please, looking interested.

"Oh, Lord. They gonna' shoot Jessie Earl all at one time." It was black Aunt Rosie who said it, but we was already thinking it by the time she had it out of her mouth. What in the world was going on?

"Now good citizens of Toad. Do not be afraid. We are just here for a political gathering and to hear Joe Don Wheelright speak a few words to us. I ask you to keep your places and listen."

Annie Laurie said it just as calm as you please and polite, too. It seemed like Annie Laurie and Joe Don must'a had some get togethers ahead a' time.

Joe Don stepped up to the porch. He stood above Jessie Earl and Annie Laurie. Putting his hands on both of Jessie Earl's shoulders, he spoke. "Friends and neighbors, you know we are about to elect a sheriff next week. Jessie Earl Putty here is the only candidate."

Jessie Earl reached up his hand and swiped it in front of his nose. He was coming around a little. He looked out at the crowd through one eye, raised his head some and zeroed his gaze in on several he knew. That is also when he seen guns. You could hear all the women from town sucking in their breaths.

But we all held and did not run.

Jessie Earl opened his mouth to speak, but Annie Laurie stopped him with a look. He never did close his mouth, but just stood there looking absolutely scared spitless.

286

"I don't know what to say," Jessie Earl finally blubbered out.

Joe Don patted him on the shoulder to reassure him and then went on.

"Yes, this man is going to be your next sheriff. And so in honor of his undisputed election, I would like to say just a few words.

"We have just pledged our allegiance to the flag of the United States of America, and we have sung our national anthem because—even if we do live in this dry, little bitty ol' place—we are still a part of this great nation.

"All of us—brown, black, or white, tall or short, men and women— got rights. Even big mouthed, mean s.o.b's like Jessie Earl Putty's got rights. He aimed to put down women with this bra business, which I suppose is his right. But I doubt he made any woman feel bad, except to take him exactly for the fool he is.

"What he was really puttin' down was the democratic process and our constitutional right to elect a sheriff who is sworn to uphold the law in our behalf.

"I for one don't want a man like him to be in charge of the law of the United States of America in this county. That's all I'm gonna say."

And with that, Joe Don looked right at Annie Laurie and they smiled at one another and left the steps together.

We was stupified but encouraged mightily by what Joe Don and Annie Laurie pulled off. And sort'a quiet like, it seemed to me for such a big crowd, we started breaking up the meetin' and moved out.

Jessie Earl was standing on the steps alone, still trying to figure out what had happened. I met him there and told him to get out of my way, please, because the Missus and me needed to get inside. He just shuffled down the steps and started back down the street toward the depot.

I went up to the cafe counter and asked Flora if she would sell us a whole pecan pie to take home. She said she would and she did.

The next week we all went to the school house to vote and defeated Jessie Earl with a write-in candidate.

Annie Laurie Rogers became the first lady sheriff in Caballo County. She was a good 'un too.

In a few months she and Joe Don got married and they made a fine couple. I said I couldn't understand how such as them two could have married one another. But my wife said at the wedding in her sentimental voice that she figured they both fell in love with the better parts of each other that nobody else could see. Maybe she's right.

Annie told lots of times afterward that she had to marry Joe Don to protect him from Jessie Earl who swore he was gonna murder 'im in cold blood in broad daylight. Joe Don jest smiled at her and said she was right.

NOT THE TRUTH (I JOHN 1:6-9)

"Watch where you're walking brother," Eziquiel hissed. Sensing the rudeness in his own voice, he added, "'Cause there's rattlesnakes hiding in the brush and the nopales." Faustino scanned the cactus patches. The cold, wet sand and stagnant water of San Manuel swallowed their boots. Faustino cursed himself for not buying some waterproof lace-ups like his older brother. His half-top hikers swelled with the deer-lease's muck.

He also regretted having asked his brother to bring him along. It was for the experience, he reminded himself. Although he'd never hunted deer, he wanted to write about having power over the life and death of a creature as majestic as a buck. He also wanted to hear his uncles reminiscing about past hunts. Faustino wanted to absorb their language, their stories and infuse them into a profound narrative of Rio Grande Valley hunting culture.

Tino looked very much like his older brother Zeke. They shared the same caramel complexion, the same round camel eyes. Many of their cousins on the other side had often joked that all of the Fuenteses were made from the same cookie cutter.

In the monte, only Zeke's sure-footed grace set him apart from Faustino's clumsiness. Through years of brush experience, he'd learned to weave through the razor mesquite branches and the nopal patches with ease. With their rifles slung over their backs, they cleared the brush and stepped onto the sendero where the truck was parked.

Camp was many confusing turns away. Faustino had been to the lease on several corn-drops, but had never seemed to get used to its many convolutions. Soon, they reached the familiar sight of the camp's graveyard. Hulls of rusty trucks and ancient trailers littered the clearing. Never sold or repaired, they were casualties of the rancher's apathy and time's corruption. The glossy Fords and Chevys of the other hunters were parked in the center of the wasteland. Faustino saw his uncle Felix and Chemo among the hungry leasers milling around the coal-black barbecue pit. A hollowed blue house sat on a mound, overlooking the hunters and their pickups. Its broken windows were like jagged maws. Its doorless entry was frozen in a silent, eternal howl. Now he understood why the hunters had chosen the wind over the shelter. Faustino was shaken out of his trance by the seasoned aroma of fajitas drifting into the cab. Faustino smiled. "Oh yeah," Zeke said.

The brothers stepped out of the truck and were immediately bombarded by saludos and questions. "You all see anything?" a hunter asked. Tío Chemo turned to an old man, obviously translating. "We didn't see nothing," Zeke explained. Although none of the other hunters had shot anything that morning, some of them reported having seen some spikes and doe.

Moments later, Faustino shivered with the other hunters while trying to absorb every nuance of their language. He watched his uncles closely, admiring and recording their lanky grace. Felix was a head taller than Zeke and Tino. Unlike the Fuentes brothers, Chemo and Felix had been blessed with a tall mother. Felix stared into the pit's embers and spoke, "Nombre bro', when I was a chiquillo, my pop used to tell me cuentos about when they got twelve pointers all the time. He was chingón with that ol' dos veinte y tres. Nowadays, everybody gotta have a cannon that goes for twenty miles before droppin'. Te digo, most of these new hunters would laugh at somebody usin' a two twenty three. Odd-six, ni que odd-six. You don't need to go that big for the pinche venados down here. All you need is a well-placed shot. Don't matter what calibre. Ahora, anyway, we're lucky if we see anything bigger 'en an eight pointer."

A paunchy hunter wearing camouflaged coveralls sucked his teeth and slurred, "Nombre boddy, te voy a decir algo. You oughta use sumpin' that'll knock the deer down quick. Sumpin' like a dos veinte y tres'll only hurt it; cause it don' got no take-down," he paused, swilling from his can of beer. "You don' wanna use a maimer like that. The vena'o'll just run into the monte and die where nobody can find him. Hay se hechara and then you shot it for nothing—you wasted the meat. Me—I use a two seventy. I don't waste time with maimers."

An awkward silence followed the fat man's harangue. Chemo shook his head. Tino looked into his uncle Felix's face, realizing that he wasn't going to press the issue any further. However, Tino knew how his tío felt. At a quinceañera, Faustino had overheard Tío Felix and Zeke talking about alcohólico hunters like this one. Tontos like that—Tío Felix had said—were so borracho when they hunted that the venados in their scopetes were the only ones that were safe. Zeke had then replied by saying that borracho hunters were no better than spotlighters or poachers. To Faustino, this slob was a disappointment. He'd always admired his uncles' hunting code, which was simple. Never hunt drunk and always eat what you kill. Gradually, the subject shifted to the necessity of four-by-fours in the mud. To help ease the tension, Zeke opened the pit, saying, "I hope you boys are hungry cause we got chingos a meat."

"You bet brutha," said a stocky young man wearing gray camouflage.

"Claro que si, mijo," Tío Chemo declared.

Zeke unclipped the serrated pocket-knife from his back pocket and poked the fajitas, cutting them open to check their color: dark brown on the outside, pink-brown on the inside. They were ready. Using his knife, he hooked the beef-skirts and placed them on a large wooden cutting board. He then checked the sweet-bread. They were still too pink. Knowing the mollejas needed more heat than fajitas, he opened the air shaft and closed the lid.

Soon, all the meat was done and the knot of hunters gathered near the barbecue pit. Every man made his own taco. They tossed the tortillas on the grill like frisbees. Soon, all conversation diminished as the hunters became too occupied. Within each of them, Tino knew there was an instinctual need to eat as much as possible. Fear of an empty belly prompted some of them to make as much as five, even six, trips to the pit. After the meat and tortillas were devoured and every man had eaten his fill, the hunters wished each other good-luck and drove off to their allotted acreage.

About five hundred meters away from the nearest blind, Zeke killed the Ford and turned to Faustino. "Okay bro', a tardeada is different from hunting in the morning. You got less time to track in case you don't kill it right away. So don't make any shot you ain't sure about. If you got doubts, don't pop it, cause if you hit a buck and wound it, we're gonna be lookin' for it all night. Remember, aim above and behind the front leg. Don't hit the paleta; you'll just wound it that way. I gotta work tomorrow and I ain't got time for that. 'Ta bueno bro'?"

Faustino nodded and stepped out of the Ford. They took the same path back to their blinds, but were more relaxed than they'd been in the morning. Zeke was even playful. He walked behind Tino and kicked his soles, which made his little brother take comically exaggerated steps. Although he didn't apologize, Eziquiel managed to atone for being rude to Tino earlier. While laying corn in the Ford, Zeke had explained that this would be where they would separate. Faustino would head west toward his ground-level blind, while Zeke would continue north until he reached the fence-line where his high-blind waited for him. With a smile, they separated at the familiar intersection.

A few minutes later, Faustino reached the dull, dwarfish box. Green and brown spray-paint snaked across its green linoleum skin. Over this layer was a wrought-iron mesh, whose purpose he couldn't ascertain. Faustino's need to relieve himself seemed to increase the closer he got to his blind. All the soda he'd drunk at the camp was now pressuring his bladder. He unslung the rifle from his shoulder and leaned it against the blind. As Faustino began to go, he noticed that the .308 was sliding down the wall. He reached to steady it—which made him spray urine across the blind's linoleum shell—but wasn't quick enough. The rifle slammed on one of the hardened logs strewn around the blind. Now panicking, he lifted the rifle and searched for any nicks in the stock. Zeke always got so mad when any of his guns were damaged. He then looked through the scope and thanked God the lenses were not cracked or chipped. Faustino covered his puddle, then threw dirt over the wet patch on the wall. He stepped to the rear of the blind and unlatched its short, narrow door. Discovering that the entry was too narrow for his shoulders, he turned his torso and entered sideways. Once in, Faustino looked at the brown ceiling—like his brother had told him—for wasps. He then searched the ground for the alacrans that inhabited the lease. Amazingly, the cold-front's icy breath was blocked by the thin wall. However, Faustino knew this temporary warmth would escape the blind as soon as he opened its thin, rectangular windows. Confident there was no immediate danger, he set his brother's .308 on the dry ground. He sat on the rusty revolving stool, sighed and checked his blueminescent watch.

The hours were punctuated by gracious, yet fleeting distractions. Although the clearing ahead of him offered no entertainment, rabbits hopped and quail sauntered out onto the sendero for the corn they'd laid. Faustino was glad to see that there was more activity this time. He even saw a jack rabbit. To Faustino, it was a perversion of the cuddly cotton tails he'd seen. It's pointed, evil face reminded him of the bloodthirsty rabbits from the *Watership Down* cartoon. Then, as lethargy began to flood his awareness, he witnessed the impossible. Approximately fifty yards away, anomalous slivers of black and white stirred in the grass between the sendero's tracks. To get a better view, he picked up the .308. After a moment of struggling with the scope's parallax, he finally found the source of color. It was a badger about the size of a cocker spaniel. However, its proportions defied comprehension. Its body was short and wide, while its head was flat like a spoon. The white stripes on his head were slashes of certainty piercing the haziness of the earthy panorama. The badger sat in the road, scratching its neck with its left hind claw. Gratified, it crawled down a hole. Once again, Faustino was alone. He pondered the badger's alien beauty. It didn't belong here.

Despite the privilege of seeing such a beautiful animal, Faustino was disappointed in not seeing a deer. He wanted to see at least a doe. There were no antlers in the brecha ahead of him or on the sendero. Faustino had planned his actions yesterday. He would capture the buck in his field-of-view and then take the gun off of safety. Then he'd place the reticle above and behind the foreleg—like everyone had told him—and squeeze the trigger. The gun would be unloaded of course, but hopefully he'd get buck-fever. Faustino believed the fiebre was symptomatic of the god-like thrill of controlling fate.

Hours passed. The small animals no longer held his interest. The monte dimmed as the sun set behind the trees. As Faustino was debating on walking back to the truck, he saw movement in the brecha. Tino raised the rifle slowly and quietly. He eased the muzzle into the window and placed his shoulder into the butt. Then he witnessed magnificence. The buck's antlers were spread regally—Tino estimated about eighteen inches and seven points. Although it wasn't "El Muy Grande," it was still extraordinary. Its face tapered, reminding Faustino of a patrician's nose. The tan fur melted into the monte. Then he saw the deer's tail. It raised as the buck looked in Faustino's vicinity. Perhaps it smelled death. Zeke had often said: Humans smell like dead meat to the deer. Ironically, this peace-flag of a tail raised when the buck's life was in danger. Feeling secure, the buck lowered its head and tail, then began eating corn near the tree-feeder. Faustino felt nothing. There was no jitter, no adrenalin flooding his brain. Faustino eased the safety off, made sure he saw the red ring and placed the pad of his forefinger on the trigger. He aimed. The cross-hairs danced near the buck's lungs. Tino paused, disappointed by his persistent absence of emotion. Then the idea struck him.

Faustino reached into his breast-pocket, the cold brass shocking him into the fiebre. He pulled the bullets out, feeling the current flow up his fingers, into his chest and back again. The power was now trapped in Tino's hands, making them shake with the urge of release. Faustino rolled the bolt back. Quaking violently now, it was impossible to load the rounds into the magazine. Tino took two deep breaths, which helped to steady his hands. Somewhat calmer now, he loaded the .308 with two shells and quietly rolled the bolt forward. The buck was still eating near the feeder, oblivious to its clumsy predator. Faustino licked his lips and placed his eye behind the scope. Stillness crept into him. Tino found the target and aimed above and just behind the front leg. Safety off—round chambered—fat of finger on trigger—he was now ready to do it. This was the kill-thrill of hunting, the knowledge that beauty was subject to Faustino's will. The hunter could be merciful and kill the animal swiftly or he could let it suffer. Finally, Faustino understood the fiebre and now he didn't have to kill. However, Tino still wanted to have his own hunter's cuento.

Faustino moved the reticle about five feet ahead of the deer, aimed at a nopal and regulated his breathing. Tino paused, making sure the buck would not move into the bullet's path. Faustino exhaled when he was positive the buck was safe. In the pause between breaths, he eased the trigger back and let the recoil surprise him. The .308 roared, making Faustino's head scream, then ring. Tino blinked reflexively and immediately chided himself for not having trained his eyes. He opened them and searched for the buck through the scope. It was gone.

As Tino headed back to the truck, he concocted the cuento of how "El Muy Grande" had gotten away. He opened the door, replaced the rifle in its sleeve, zipped it up and sat inside. It was dark now. Eziquiel would soon be coming along.

Faustino surveyed the landscape. Wind rushed through the sendero, making the trees heave with inhuman malevolence. He turned the headlights on. Their beams swept the narrow dirt road, unmasking the phantoms that had been embraced by darkness. Crimson prickly pears became blood-red eyes on spiny cactus basilisks. Mesquite branches were the pale, emaciated arms of ghouls. The headlights also fell over the moist, ashen logs, revealing them to be fossilized corpses. Faustino realized he'd entered some God-forsaken netherworld. Then there was the moving shadow that devoured the truck's light.

The creature was gliding toward him now, closing the gap between the living and the dead. The arm that had dangled at its side now raised to its head. The shadow's right claw moved to the left side of its neck, pretending to gently slice its own throat. It paused, then continued the macabre mime—this time slashing itself repeatedly and violently. Then, as terror's grip tightened, he realized that it was Eziquiel walking toward the truck, signaling him to kill the lights.

"You don't take a hint so good or what bro'?"

"Sorry man, I just kinda lost it. I guess I'm just tired."

"Hey bro' what'd you shoot at back there?"

"I saw a seven pointer dude," Faustino said. "Yeah, he was about a hundred yards away. I saw him and I aimed just like you told me. I was shaking bad though bro'. Anyways, I pulled the trigger and missed. He ran back into the monte when he heard the shot. I almost had him."

"Are you sure it was a buck?"

"Pues, como no bro'? I saw the antlers and everything. The cuernos had about seven points."

"Well that's good little brother, we just gotta work on your aim. Well hermanito, let's get the hell outta here."

"'Ta bueno bro', as long as you drive."

They drove out and passed the camp. Nothing stirred in the graveyard. The dilapidated trailers and trucks sat silently, still awaiting their demise. Rust would eventually consume them. All of the other hunters had gone

295

home to their families. When they reached the first gate, Faustino got out to unlock the chain. As Tino fumbled with the myriad of keys on Zeke's key-chain, Eziquiel plugged the spotlight into the cigarette lighter and switched it on. Eziquiel flashed the monte, bathing it in effulgence. Faustino gawked at the light's incorruptible beam. Darkness couldn't dilute its brilliance. "Hey, wait a second. What the hell is that?" Zeke said, training the light on the fence. "Hey Tino, hurry up and unlock the gate and get in. I wanna go check this out." Faustino found the key and unlocked the padlock. He swung the gate open and jumped in the truck. Zeke passed through the gate and turned left into the neighbor's lease. Then Eziquiel shone the light on the fence.

At first, recognition eluded Faustino. In his mind, he condemned the hunter who had chosen not to track his kill. The deer's body had not cleared the top wire. The buck was slumped over the fence, which lent it the appearance of a hanging man. The buck's head hung low, its antlers sticking in the mud. Fresh, bright blood painted the tan coat over the ribs.

Eziquiel unholstered his .45 and approached the animal. Tino knew he'd seen wounded deer thrash violently when approached by their killers. Keeping a safe distance away, he walked around it and knelt. "Yup, it's dead. The tongue's practically dragging in the mud." He holstered the pistol and raised the deer's head by its antlers. "Look," he told his brother. Paralysis rode the wave of realization that washed over Faustino. "Hey bro', come out here and check this out," Zeke said. Tino opened the door and stepped out into the quagmire. He smiled stupidly, trying to shroud his horror. "Hey, I shot it after all," he said quietly. "Yeah, I figure you hit it in the lung. It tried to jump the fence and didn't have enough frijoles to clear it. It probably drowned in its own blood hanging here on the fence. Well ayude me bro', let's get it down." Faustino's feet were planted in the ground. Will alone propelled him toward the buck.

"Okay, we're gonna cross the fence and try an' throw him over." Eziquiel moved to the fence and lowered the mid-wire with his foot, creating a gap for his brother to pass through. Faustino bent over and stepped through the aperture. Now on the other side, he held the wire for his older brother. They lifted the buck by its hind legs and threw it over, tearing the skin of its belly. The deer's body slapped on the mud.

"All right bro', this is what we're gonna do. We're gonna hang him up on one o' these trees. Then you're gonna get that knife o' yours and I'm gonna help you field-dress this venado," he paused, searching for understanding in his little brother's eyes. Finding only a veiled sadness, Eziquiel said softly, "It's all right 'manito." He paused again, then gently massaged his brother's shoulder. "You done good brother; you're a hunter now."

Faustino's head was down, his gaze transfixed by the turquoise luminescence of the eye that gleamed even after death. He kneeled, searching for forgiveness. Yes, it was there, but tinged with something else. In a moment, in a twinkling of the eye, the worm-wood of Faustino's sin evanesced, leaving only the warm, blue water of absolution.

Tino stood shakily, then felt the chilling sensation creep back into his feet and up into his legs. Gelid slime swallowed the hunter's hiking-boots, threatening to make him a captive, a native of the monte.

ROCK-OLA

JAMES WARD LEE

It was Friday night, payday night, in Eastis County, Texas, and Mrs. Pearl Farley, like half the housewives in Bodark Springs, was frying a piece of round steak. It was the first piece of meat she and her husband Cleatis had had since Tuesday. And Cleatis could hardly wait. He had taken off his work brogans and sat wiggling his toes and leaning back on two legs of the kitchen chair watching Pearl cook. Suddenly, Pearl said, over her shoulder, "Every slut and whoremonger in Eastis County is gonna be up at that there Moon River Beach whiskey house when it opens tomorrow night."

Startled by the outburst, Cleatis sat forward in the kitchen chair and banged the two front legs down on the linoleum. He had idly mentioned the new honky tonk nearly an hour before and Pearl hadn't said a word. He knew he should have kept his mouth shut. Now he knew. It was about to ruin his supper. It was not that Pearl didn't know about the new honky tonk. Clyde and Meridian Wilson's Moon River Beach was the biggest item of gossip in four counties and part of Oklahoma. But if he hadn't mentioned it, Pearl might not have brought it up just as she was getting the gravy made. Cleatis, a man who always looked guilty even when innocent, hoped he could ride out the brewing storm, so he ducked his head and said, "Well, Pearlie, I guess they will be people there from Fannin and Lamar counties, too—and probably some from over in Oklahoma if the ferry is still running after all this rain."

"Don't you Pearlie me, Cleatis Farley. I know exactly what you are thinking: you wish you was going."

Pearl could always read Cleatis's mind; he not only wished it, but he had a plan to be there as soon as the doors opened.

Feeling guilty about the elaborate lies he would have to tell to make it to the grand opening, Cleatis blushed and said, "Me, no, hon, I don—"

Pearl wheeled around from the stove, waving the skillet full of meat and gravy at Cleatis, and said, "Well, you can just forget it, Mr. Cleatis L. Farley. I know what you think, but I don't aim to be married to no sot drunkard, so don't let it cross your mind again. Do you hear me? You ain't *ever* going up there. Don't you ever even *mention* that honky tonk to me again. Well, I mean, Lord God Almighty—the Moon River Beach! I never heard of such a thing!"

Cleatis never mentioned the Moon River Beach again—at least not to Pearl. But she was right: every slut and whoremonger and cottonchopper and tie hacker and coal miner and iron worker and round-dancer in four counties and part of Oklahoma showed up. And had a good time.

Even Cleatis L. Farley his ownself. Cleatis got Old Man Mike Sharpe to let him take Jim Bagwell's place and haul a big load of lumber over to Denison, then across the bridge to Durant, and back east toward Bokchita. A trip like that would take nearly all day Saturday. And then as soon as he had recrossed the Red back into Texas, he was planning for the old ton-and-a-half Chevy truck to break down. Then he was going to leave the truck and hitchhike east to the Moon River Beach.

And he did. And he had a good time. A glorious time.

Everybody had a good time but Grady Dell, the rural letter carrier from Bodark Springs. And his wife Mamie. And maybe Grady's nephew J. T. and J. T.'s wife Hattie. They all had to leave the grand opening early.

Mamie had been getting ready for a week or so for the Saturday night that Clyde and Meridian Wilson unveiled the finest roadhouse in Northeast Texas in that fall of 1941 when, though Eastis County didn't know it, it was drifting with the rest of Texas and the world toward Pearl Harbor.

On the Monday before the grand opening, Mamie Dell told Dr. Clayton's nurse, Emily Stringer, "I gonna dance my shoe heels as round as apples on Saturday night up at Clyde and Meridian's new place. What about you, Emily? Are you planning to go?"

That was a mean thing to say to Emily, the girl that Grady always called "that little old narrow-assed gal of Bud Stringer's." Emily hadn't had a date in two years, and everybody in Bodark knew it. She hadn't danced a step since Roy Amos went off to join the CC camps and never came back. Emily always used to look wistful and say, "Nobody ever knowed where Roy wound up." Well, one person did. Banty Isbell knew that Roy had gone to Bakersfield, California, to learn to pick a guitar, and wasn't ever coming back. But Banty swore to Roy that he would never tell anybody in Bodark. And he didn't.

Emily smoothed down the white paper on the examining table as Mamie sat in the chair waiting for Dr. Clayton.

Mamie had come in to see to Dr. Clayton about her gall bladder. Mamie Dell was the only person in Bodark Springs except for Dr. Clayton who knew exactly where the gall bladder was located. And how one felt if it got out of whack. Mamie told Doshie McBrier once, "The first time my gall bladder went out on me, hon, all my muscles locked up on me—all the way from my waist up to my shoulders."

Mamie knew visceral organs. She knew more about a person's insides than old Dr. Elgin, the town's other doctor, and nearly as much as Doctor Clayton. Mamie had good reason to be an expert in the medical arts and sciences. She had overcome liver cancer without medical help, had suffered shooting pains in her back, "jumping headaches," clogged sinuses, a misfunctioning spleen, more heart flutters than she could count, both low and high blood pressure (at different times, of course), rheumatism, bursitis in both shoulders, tonsillitis, impacted wisdom teeth—the worst Dr. Powers had ever seen, Mamie always said—spastic colon, some female problems still not reported in the medical literature, and a bad case of pernicious anemia. Mamie bragged that by the age of thirty she had had seven major operations and two of the hardest births ever witnessed in Eastis County, Texas. But no matter how bad the pain was all day—and often in the dark hours of the morning—Mamie always got well enough to go honky tonking at that part of the evening "when whippoorwills called and evening was nigh." And she always, as she said, "danced her shoeheels as round as apples."

Emily said, "You've *been* up to the Moon River Beach, haven't you, Mamie?"

"Oh, Lord God yes, hon, lots of times. Me and Grady nearly built that place we was up there so much. We are close friends to Clyde and Meridian, so we started going up there to see how the place was coming along as soon as they had Leon Cogburn in to grade off the land. Moon River Beach. Clyde wanted to call it Clyde's Place, but Meridian wouldn't have none of that. She wanted to call it the Coconut Grove after that one up in Boston that you hear about on the radio, but after she went to see Madame Ora Lee to have her and Clyde's fortune told and Madame Ora Lee told her not to name it the Coconut Grove because it would be bad luck. Well, anyway, we was up there once and our daughter Jackie looked off the bluff and said, 'Why don't y'all call it the Moon River Beach?' Well, Clyde, he looked down at the Red River, down where all them cottonmouth moccasins live at and like to of puked. I mean he didn't like that name. But Meridian did, and you know who wears the pants in that family. So Meridian told Clyde to call Boyd McLaughlin and get him to paint a sign with a moon on it and have it say Moon River Beach."

Emily waited patiently 'til Mamie paused for breath, then asked, "Have they got anything good to dance to on the Rock-Ola?"

Mamie said, "Oh, Lord God, hon, they've got everything. That Rock-Ola holds twelve records, and they are all fine dance music. They got Lulu Bell and Scottie singing 'Remember Me'—that song that Grady is so crazy about. He won't go near a music machine that don't have 'Remember Me' on it. I'm getting tired of it myself, but I swear I think Grady would play it every time if he was the only one putting nickels in the coin slide. But then I'm glad to say he ain't. And they got that new Ernest Tubbs song 'I'mWalking the Floor Over You,' and another new one 'When My Blue Moon Turns to Gold Again.' Have you heard that song, Emily?" Emily had, but had never danced to it, and so she didn't exactly consider that she had really *heard* it. And though she hadn't yet danced to the song, she at least knew that Ernest's name wasn't Tubbs and that the right title was "Walking the Floor Over You." Emily knew a lot more about what songs were popular than Mamie did, but she hadn't had the first-hand, honky-tonk experience that made Mamie an expert on high life in far Northeast Texas.

Emily said, "I heard there's a jukebox over in Sherman that has twenty-four songs on it."

Mamie took this as a personal affront. "Twenty-four songs? I don't believe it. I don't know where they'd put the records. Somebody must of told you wrong."

Mamie was still denying that there was such a fabulous music machine when Dr. Clayton came into the room, but she shut up quickly and began laying a trap for her internal organs.

By Saturday, all the sluts and whoremongers and heavy drinkers and round dancers had worked themselves to a fever pitch. Grady Dell had finished his mail route and was checking out his money orders as he thought about the Moon River Beach. He and Mamie were going with his nephew J. T. and J. T's wife Hattie. J. T. was Grady's brother's boy, but he had always been closer to Grady than to his own father. J. T. had been running whiskey all through the Depression and had only lately taken over the boat landing up the river from the Moon River Beach and just across from Iron Stob, Oklahoma. J. T. sold a few cans of sardines a week, rented a few boats, and handled a good bit of bootleg whiskey. What he didn't sell, he drank. People in Eastis County used to mention J. T.'s drinking in hushed tones. They would look serious and say, "Well, you know, J. T., he dranks." The tone and language meant that J. T. was putting away about a quart of whiskey a day. And had been for twenty years. Homer Brantley once said to Grady, "J. T. ain't drawed a sober breath in twenty years." Grady might have hit anybody else who had said this, but Homer Brantly was a one-armed man, so Grady just turned and walked off.

Grady was looking forward to Saturday night at the Moon River Beach. He didn't have much excitement in his life. Mamie was always sick, they got in debt and lost their house in 1936, and Grady had had a stroke in '38 and spent nearly six months in the VA Hospital in Waco. He didn't see much to look forward to. Jackie and Tommie Earl were good children, but Jackie would get married any time now and Grady was forty years older than Tommie Earl, so the boy seemed more like a grandson than a son and Grady doubted that he would ever live to see him grown.

On his way to George Moore's Cafe for a couple of bottles of beer before going home, Grady decided that he hadn't ever had but one good year in his life—and that was 1919. Grady's outfit, the First Division, had seen hard service in the Argonne Forest, but when the war was over, Grady spent nine months in the Army of Occupation in Koblenz. They quartered him on a German family named Gerber, and he fell in love with their second daughter, Eva. Grady would have stayed in Germany if the Gerbers hadn't forced Eva to live up to her marriage contract to a butcher from Cologne.

The night before she was to leave for Cologne, she and Grady met at midnight in the outbuilding behind Gerber's house and made love. Eva cried and sang a few verses of an old German folksong, "Vergisst mein nicht." Grady asked what it meant and she said, "It means that I don't want you to forget me. Forget me nicht. 'Remember me,' I guess you would say. Will you remember me, Grady?"

Grady sobbed and said, "Always; for the rest of my life, Eva."

And he always had. Sometimes he remembered Eva in the strangest places.

That Saturday night at the Moon River Beach was one of them.

J. T. and Hattie came to get Mamie and Grady in J. T.'s Uncle Ev Crider's 1936 Buick, borrowed because J. T.'s 1937 Ford 60 had blown a head gasket. J. T. always called his Ford 60 "the worst goddamned Ford that Henry ever made. It won't pull the hat off your goddamned head." And since J. T. and Hattie both weighed about 250 pounds a piece, it was good luck that J. T. had Ev Crider's Buick because J. T's Ford 60 would never have hauled all four of them up Butts Hill, the only steep hill between Bodark Springs and the Red River.

J. T., red in the face, wearing a half-cast/half-bandage on his left hand where Dr. Clayton had cut a wen off, had nearly a full tank of whiskey in him when he wheeled Ev Crider's blue Buick up to the front door of the Moon River Beach. The parking lot was nearly full, but Clyde had thrown Boyd McLaughlin out for trying to whip Edward Hurst, and Boyd had vacated a space right next to the front door.

"I-God, they knowed to save one for me," J. T wheezed as he nearly rammed Burt Moore's '36 Chevrolet Master Deluxe that was parked in the next space.

Inside the din was heartening to Grady. The Rock-Ola was playing "When My Blue Moon Turns to Gold Again," so he took Mamie on a turn around the dance floor before they even tried to find a seat. When the song was over and Ernest Tubb started singing "Walking the Floor over You," J. T. had got a table for four right up near where the dance hall part of the honky tonk joined the barroom. Up near where the waitresses picked up orders and where people went to whisper to Ed Butts to run outside and get them a half pint of whiskey. Ed, the best barbecue man in East Texas, had been stolen by Clyde from a joint over near Bogota where Ed was cooking for a dollar a day and selling whiskey on the halves. At the Moon River Beach, Ed cooked free but had the bootlegging concession all to himself.

On Friday nights, about dark, Ed began hiding half pints all around the back half acre of the Moon River Beach. He put them under slabs left over from the construction, under barrels that had once held coal oil, and all along the back side of the five tourist court cabins that Clyde had built in case anybody at the Moon River Beach met somebody nice and suddenly needed somewhere to go.

Grady asked Ed to get him a half pint of "white whiskey" and was headed back to the table where Mamie and Hattie and J. T. were settling in for a night of it. Half way across the floor, he saw Mamie jump up from where she was sitting and say in a loud voice, "You get the hell away from me, you bastard! Don't you touch me or I'll bust your head open with this Co-Cola bottle!"

The man Mamie was shouting at was a stranger to Grady, but he could tell at a glance that he must be one of the ironworkers helping build the ammunition plant up near Valliant, Oklahoma. Grady could see a table of ironworkers standing up and laughing at Mamie hollering at the man, a man who looked amazingly like that "goddamned fat butcher from Cologne, Germany." The man laughed and grabbed at Mamie's arm again.

As Grady got to the table, Lulu Belle and Scottie started singing "Remember Me" on the Rock-Ola. Suddenly Grady saw Eva's butcher husband as plain as day. He saw Eva Gerber. And he saw the sorry life he was living now, a life that was beginning to shut down all around him. He hardly noticed that he had the ironworker by the shirt collar and his right hand drawn back to hit that "goddamn fat German butcher." Grady came to himself when J. T. grabbed his arm and said, "Let me hit that sumbitch, Unc Grady. You too old to fight."

Mamie, who had been caught up in the excitement, froze. Hattie thought, 'if I didn't weigh so much I might just get under this table.' Cleatis Farley, who had called his next door neighbor and got her to tell Pearl he was "broke down up between Blue and Bokchita" reached his brogan over and kicked the Rock-ola plug out of the wall just as Ed Butts flipped the switch that turned on every light in the place.

Clyde Wilson was scrabbling around behind the beer box trying to find his Browning double barrel twelve gauge. Just in case. Nobody in the house moved or said a word as J. T. and Grady looked all around the dance hall. Far off in the kitchen one of the cooks had the Paris radio station—

KPLT—turned on low; Grady could hear it plain. It was playing "Remember Me."

Grady said, "Well, Goddamn!" and turned the ironworker's shirt collar loose. He turned to J. T and said, "Jate, if these bastards are all too scared to fight, let's go somewhere else." He turned to Mamie and Hattie and said, "Y'all coming?"

By this time J. T. was starting to draw his first sober breath in twenty years. Or was afraid he would. Mamie picked up Grady's hat, got her purse from the chair that was pushed under the table, and motioned for Hattie to move. Hattie was frozen, and Mamie had to shake her by the arm to get her even to blink. Then the four of them backed out of the dance hall, backed across the bar room next to it, backed out the door—Grady last—and got into Ev Crider's 1936 Buick.

J. T., still looking at the front door, said, "I-God, I hope this sumbitch will start." When it did, J. T. put in the clutch, shifted into reverse, and eased out into the parking lot. Just then the lights on the dance floor went off and somebody plugged the Rock-Ola back in. The record, still resting in the circle that slid the records off the pile, started turning and the needle fell back into place with a hum as Lulu Belle and Scottie started "Remember Me" from where they had left off when Cleatis jerked the plug out.

By now, J. T. had calmed down some. He turned to Grady and said , "We coulda whipped them sumbitches. You wanta go back in there?"

Grady had the window down and was listening to the song through the open windows of the Moon River Beach. And thinking of the only exciting years he had ever had. He took a long time to answer. Finally, he turned to J. T. and said, "Naw, let's leave it with them and go on home."

As they rolled off the lot, Grady could hear Lulu Belle and Scotty singing:

> "The sweetest words belong to lovers in the gloaming;
> The sweetest days are the days that used to be.
> The saddest words I ever heard were words of parting,
> When you said 'Sweetheart remember me.'"

Mama Minnie & Me

Phyllis W. Allen

I spent my childhood with the most special woman in the world, my Mama Minnie.

Mrs. Minnie Almetra Lee to everybody else, she was just Mama Minnie to me. Mama Minnie always said, "You got to make sure that people respect you right off. Won't nobody respect somebody without a title in front of their name; therefore I always make sure that people call me 'Miz.' I don't let nobody call me Minnie without some kind of title in front. Just isn't proper."

In Ferrin County, about twenty miles east of Tyler, Texas, where we lived, my Mama Minnie was legendary for her strength. Not only did she demand that everybody, black or white, call her 'Miz' Minnie, she also singlehandedly raised five sons, the youngest of which was my daddy, Thomas Earl. Big Thomas Earl, my granddaddy, had died shortly after my daddy was born, leaving the farm work to Mama Minnie and the boys.

Mama Minnie worked the fields side by side with her sons. Mama says that Mama Minnie could pick more cotton than most men, yet she still had time to cook the best buttermilk biscuits and fried chicken in the county. During the winter months when there were no crops, Mama Minnie worked in private homes as a maid and cook.

Mama Minnie liked to tell the story about the time Mr. Spenser, a local attorney who wanted her to work for him, decided that he was exempt from her rule of only answering to 'Miz' Minnie. Mama Minnie would lean back in her chair and smile real big when she told this one. "Mr. Spenser always was a fine looking man and him and Miz Andie lived in that big old house out on the Ridge highway. They were mighty prosperous what with Mr. Spenser being the lawyer for everybody in the county and Miz Andie's daddy leaving her all that money from the fertilizer plant. Yes, they were quality white folks all right enough."

Mama Minnie would look around the room to satisfy herself that everybody understood that these were not just ordinary "white" folks. When she was certain that everybody was impressed with their status she continued, "When Mr. Spenser called and tried to get me to go to work for him, I was working at the Athertons at the time. The Athertons couldn't hold a candle to the Spensers in society. Mr. Atherton was just a clerk at the bank and his wife worked at a dress shop in town, but they were forward thinking folks and never had no problem with calling me Miss Minnie Lee. In those days only the richest folks had white help and the white help was the only ones that was called with a proper title. Colored help was just Lizzie or James or whatever. Except for me." Her head would nod now, inviting her listener into her tale as easily as if it were her parlor.

"Anyways, when Mr. Spenser called me up at the Athertons and asked me would I come out to his house to help him and his young wife get their house set up, I told him I had to think about it. Told him I was real happy with the Athertons, made right nice money and they was the nicest folks." Mama Minnie would rub her hands together now in anticipation of what was to come.

"Well right away Mr. Spenser went to assuring me that money wasn't no object. Said couldn't nobody treat me nicer than he and his missus could. Now I start to laughing inside cause I been at the Town & Country Market when him and that wife of his comes in. I know that they don't respect the whites much less a colored woman who is paid to clean their toilets. I am a firm believer that you don't never listen to what a person tells you. You watch what that person does. In spite of the bad I knew of them I agreed to go out to their house to talk. Figured couldn't no harm come of just talking."

Mama Minnie would lean in closer to her audience and point. "Knew the minute I walked into that house it wasn't going to work. Not cause of the house. It was perfect. Every room looking like the rooms in those slick page magazines you see on white folks' coffee tables. There was the lady of the house sitting on one of them perfect white couches, barely making a dent in the thick fabric, not one hair out of place, looking perfect. Mr. Spenser standing there with his white suit and blue shirt holding a cigar, whose ash didn't even fall, looking perfect. But in all that perfection wasn't no sense of folks living there. Just that smell of old money. Ever notice how rich folks' houses all got that same smell?" At this point her nose, round on the tip, would wrinkle as if the olfactory memories were flooding it.

"Now Mr. Spenser kept on smiling and bowing from his waist like one of them little Japanese people, head just bobbing up and down. When he took me down the hall to the little room off the kitchen, always known as the 'maid's' room, he began to describe how he was looking for someone to keep that house. 'I demand absolute perfection from those in my employ. Look around; you'll notice that not one thing in this house is out of place.' That what he said, them cold blue eyes burning right through me."

Mama Minnie would settle down into the big blue velvet chair that was a favorite of hers. Her broad shoulders would form a perfect line parallel to the top of the chair. Her head would be slightly tilted to the left. Mama Minnie was deaf in her right ear but was far too vain to ever admit it.

"I could tell that Mr. Spenser was just waiting for me to disagree, but looking around I couldn't challenge him. What I did think was how Mr. Atherton would come in and insist that I stop working to watch a sunset, a bird, or the first duck to land on the pond in the fall. Mr. Spenser wasn't interested in sunsets or ducks. Onliest way he would be is if they disturbed the perfection of his home. Then they'd have to go. I leaned forward and told him that I understood his demand for absolute perfection because I was a woman who believed in absolutes. Things just seem clearer that way."

Leaning forward, keeping her back ramrod straight, Mama Minnie continued, "Mr. Spenser said, 'Well good then, we understand each other, Minnie. When can you start?' Well now honey, when I looked down my nose at that man and told him: 'Mr. Spenser, I can't work for you and by the way I'm Mrs. Lee to you.' All the sputtering and spitting that man did made me think he done choked on that cigar of his. He was turning red, bordering on purple, but I held my ground. My brown eyes locked on his ice cold blue ones until he said, 'No I guess you couldn't. Thank you for coming Min— uh Mrs. Lee, but I don't think that you're quite what we had in mind.' 'No sir I don't think I am.'" Mama Minnie would start to laugh at this point leaning back into the chair and shaking her whole body with memory of her defiance.

After she finished laughing a faraway look would come over her face. "Made my stand that day but I paid for it later. Never thought that Mr. Spenser would be such an unforgiving man. Wasn't until he became Judge Spenser that he was able to get his vengeance and it wasn't me he took it out on. Took away the only thing I loved just 'cause I wanted to be treated with respect, same as him. Just 'cause he wanted to teach me a lesson he went and sentenced your daddy, Thomas, to more than twenty years down in Huntsville for something that everybody in Ferrin County knew that Thomas didn't have no part in. But that's past and can't nothing change it." She would rise slowly out of the chair and head for her bedroom. Her door would remain closed for the rest of the day. Sometimes it stayed closed for several days.

Mama always said when that happened that Mama Minnie was having her "blue" period. I wanted someone to tell what had happened to my daddy. Why was he sent away? Why wasn't he there when I needed him? But I was afraid to ask.

One day I gathered up all my courage and opened the darkened door to Mama Minnie's bedroom.

The shades were drawn, even though it was the middle of the afternoon. I could barely make her out cloaked in the darkness. She sat bent over with her elbows resting on her knees. Her normally carefully combed gray hair hung like tangled clumps of moss draping her paper-thin, wrinkly skin. Raising her head she squinted painfully at the sliver of light from the opened door and as if by reflex used her hand to shoo me away.

"Go," she'd said, her head falling forward as if its weight was too much for her neck to bear.

"Mama Minnie, you all right?" I ventured a step further into the room, the velvet blackness oppressing me like a wool blanket on an August day.

"All right? Strange you should say that. Am I all right? Can a Mama ever be all right after ruining her child?"

"How did you ruin him? What happened to my daddy?"

Before Mama Minnie's tears had been silent trails of wetness down her nutmeg brown cheek, but that day they were torrents accompanied by painful wracking sounds that seemed to come from deep inside. I stepped back because all of a sudden the room seemed too full to hold me.

"Wait child. I always said when you was old enough to ask I was going to tell you about Thomas. Figured then you would be old enough to understand." Slowly she raised her head and beckoned for me to come to her. For the first time I realized that her fingers were gnarled and wrinkled, those of an old woman. Tentatively I approached her until I was close enough to grasp her cool dry hands in mine.

Her grip was strong and urgent. "Sit down child. How old are you now? Almost eleven, 'cause you weren't but days old when Thomas went away. Thomas was my baby, the child God gave me to remember Big Thomas. I never like to admit it but Thomas has always been my most special child. Then they took him away."

"Your mama and Thomas hadn't been married but two years when he got the job at the lumberyard. Mr. Foster, the man who owned the lumberyard, wasn't the type of man that Coloreds had much dealing with. He was strong against the Coloreds. Thomas was the first one to ever do anything other than backbreaking lifting and toting. Mr. Foster's daughter, Amanda, had come home from out in California with them new notions of us all, black and white, living together. Wish to God she had never come back!" Mama Minnie leaned her head back and closed her eyes.

"Your daddy had been going to night school up in Dallas when Miz Amanda come out to the house and asked him about going to work at the lumberyard. First thing Thomas say is he wasn't interested in being no janitor. Say he already making a living from our truck farm. Miz Amanda say she ain't aiming for him to be no janitor. Say that they needs a Yard Foreman. Well, Thomas just about bust a gut. No Colored never been foreman over nothing in Ferrin County. Didn't nobody never figure that Red Foster's would be the place they would start."

Mama Minnie's eyes took on a faraway look as she paused, seeming to gather strength from the slight stroking she was giving my head. Taking a deep breath she continued, "Thomas didn't take the job right away. He thought on it and thought on it. Him and your mama sat many a night at that table in the kitchen just talking about how it was a big step for him and the Coloreds in Ferrin County. Your mama was sure that Thomas deserved this job, said it was payment for all his studying and working so hard. I felt that way too, some, but mostly I was scared about what people do when they find out Thomas, a Colored boy that growed up right here, was gonna be bossing round some White men. I was scared of them rednecks what come right out of the piney woods with no book learning and no toleration for other folks. I didn't know that I shoulda been worrying about the man in the county with more book learning than anybody."

"Things went all right for awhile. The White men wasn't real happy about having Thomas as no boss, but since it was Miz Amanda's play and Mr. Red backing it, they couldn't do nothing. Thomas had some problems but mostly things just moved along."

A smile broke the gloom of the darkness. "I'll never forget the evening that Thomas came in and your mama told him she been to the doctor. Told him he was gonna be a daddy. Well we had to about scrape that man off the ceiling. He was making plans like she say you coming tomorrow. Talking about college and you being a doctor. Child I tell you ain't never been a man more excited about a child."

I had always heard Mama Minnie say how my daddy wanted me to do this or that or how he was proud of me when I did something good, how disappointed when I did bad things, but he never seemed real 'til that minute. I was always thinking that if my daddy cared so much about how I was behaving or how I was he woulda been there with me. It never occurred to me that he might not have had a choice in the matter.

Mama Minnie hugged me tighter under her warm neck and kept on talking, "Your mama and daddy was so happy. We all were, happier than we had ever been. Then the talk started in town. Nasty vicious talk that people shouldn't never say about anybody, specially about a Colored man and a White woman. First time I heard it I made like I didn't know what the person was saying, but I shoulda known that me playing ignorant wasn't gonna stop that freight train. Figured ignoring it would slow it some. It didn't. Fact is, I think that 'cause nobody in the family spoke on the rumors they just got bigger and more vicious. About a month before your mama's due date Thomas come in looking like somebody who done looked into the face of death. In spite of being the color of coffee with no cream he was just about white underneath. Wouldn't talk to nobody at the supper table and after supper he went outside and sat staring down the road. The next morning the High Sheriff, Pete Wilson, was at the door asking if Thomas was at home. I live to be one hundred and thirty I won't never forget the look in Pete Wilson's eyes. He, who I diapered when he was a little one like mine, couldn't look me in the eye. Just said, 'Miz Minnie, I need to talk to Thomas.' Before I can answer he steps into the house and starts looking around. About that time Thomas come out the bedroom. Without saying nothing to Pete Wilson he looked at me and said, 'Mama take care of Mary 'til I come back.' Your daddy ain't set foot in this house from that day to this one."

"But Mama Minnie, how is it your fault?"

"A whole day went by. Mary and me trying to find out what was going on with your daddy. Mary went to Reverend Sharpley, down at the Baptist Church, asked him to go to the High Sheriff's office and try to help Thomas. 'Sister Mary,' he say, 'These things are best left sorted out by the law and the Lord. Probably be best just leave it to them.' Mary, who ain't hardly never said a cross word to nobody, told that man something that is best not repeated by me to you. Suffice to say three months later when the church took a vote whether or not to turn him out after him and Emma Mae Potter was found over in that motel in Greenville, his pleas for your mama's help fell on deaf ears. After Mary took to her bed about to give birth to you I went down and talked to Pete Wilson. 'Pete,' I said, 'you know that Thomas ain't had nothing to do with Amanda Foster or no other woman, certainly not against her will. Him and Mary expecting that baby and there ain't been nothing else on his mind for months. Can't you just let him go? Find out who it was that hurt Miz Amanda?'

"What that man told me still makes my blood stop in my veins. 'I'd sure like to Miz Minnie. But I got marching orders from much higher up than me. Seems that Judge Spenser done taken a personal interest in this case. He concerned that Coloreds get the idea that it's open season on White women Thomas don't get punished. Don't seem to matter none whether he done anything to be punished for or not. Judge Spenser right set on Thomas going to Huntsville.' When he said that name I knew for certain that Thomas had real troubles, troubles that couldn't nobody on this earth straighten out."

"Mama Minnie why that Judge want to send my daddy away? What my daddy do to him?"

312

"Child your daddy didn't do nothing to Ivory Spenser. Didn't nobody else do nothing to him either. He just one of them people that got to be in control of all that he sees and if he ain't somebody got to pay. When they went to him and told him that that Foster girl been assaulted by somebody and she wouldn't say who he saw a chance to do something that he had wanted to do for a long time. Get back at me. Did it too, through what he and everybody else in the county knew that I loved best, your daddy."

"Well I left Pete Wilson's office and went right straight over to that courthouse where Ivory Spenser kept his office. Since the last time I talked to him at his house, both of us is older, but only me is wiser. First off I walk in he says, 'Morning Minnie. What can I do for you?' Pretending like I ain't even heard him I keep standing there in the doorway of his office just looking at him. Finally, I sidestep his outstretched hand and enter that room. It's just full of that man's evil. Seemed like evil just oozing from the mahogany paneled walls. I could feel it seeping up through the polished hardwood floorboards. Looking him right in his tiny pig eyes I straightened myself up to my full height. When I spoke, the words come from deep like I was pulling them out of some forgotten dark place."

"Ivory Spenser, you may scare some folks in this town but not me. I know what you doing to my boy. You and I know why. But the truth be told I rather see him in Huntsville than living in the same town with snakes like you. You couldn't break me then and you can't break me now. Neither me nor my son is going to ask the likes of you to do nothing for us. Whatever you got planned for us, then you do it! But remember this, what goes around Ivory Spenser comes back around and the second time around is much harder than the first. Didn't have to look back to see how red-faced and speechless he was. His silence said it all."

"Two weeks later they had a trial. Judge Ivory Spenser sentenced your daddy to twenty years to life in Huntsville for assaulting Miss Amanda Foster. Two weeks after that the same Judge Ivory Spenser was found in a park up in Dallas with two young boys under twelve years old. Seems he was committing unnatural acts. Wasn't much he could do to defend himself after that rich wife left and took her daddy's money with her. The townspeople voted him out of office. There was a trial up in Dallas and less than a month later he was on a bus heading to the same Huntsville Work Farm they took my Thomas to. Onliest difference my Thomas is a man. He take everything the state have to give and keep his dignity. Judge Ivory Spenser didn't last much more than a month before he was found hanging by his neck one morning in his cell."

Mama Minnie patted me on my head and stood from her chair. She snapped the bottom of the shade and gulped a deep breath of the sun-lightened air. Putting her hands on her hips she leaned back and said, "Won't be long now your daddy be coming home. That new warden done promised that he gonna look into Thomas' case. Be good for you to meet your daddy. You and him got a lot of catching up to do."

Right then Mama came down the hallway and sticking her head in the door she asked, "You bothering Miz Minnie? You know better to come in here when her door is closed."

"No Mary, she ain't bothering me. Fact is, it's time I opened the door and let some light in here. Can't nothing good come out of darkness."

ALL THAT HISTORY

LIANNE ELIZABETH MERCER

There wasn't much left of Friday morning, and still Nick hadn't arrived. Once again I had driven from Houston to meet him in Luling at our favorite bed and breakfast. The interstate was a feast of bluebonnets, grounsel, and Indian Paintbrush, so the drive seemed short. For eighteen months we'd been meeting halfway whenever my schedule at the hospital meshed with his teaching schedule at his college in the hill country. I usually arrived first and sat near the window in the coffee shop across the street. I nursed a cup of tea and a dollop of time while I imagined how the afternoon and evening might go.

My breath still caught each time Nick drove up in his old blue car, got out, stretched his long legs, and smoothed his hair. It was always unruly again by the time he walked inside, sat beside me, and asked, grinning, "What's the last thing you want to do this time?" "Count the bird nests in the old oak in Palmetto Park," I would say, or "Fly a kite through the 'O' in the 'Coffee Shop' sign on the roof."

The last thing. The first thing. The best thing: being together.

I'd had two years alone. My twenty-year marriage existed in photographs and memories and furniture tucked into my crowded apartment. Nick had a shaky twenty-seven-year marriage. We'd celebrated the times when we could get away and written frequently when we couldn't. Yet recently our letters had been divided by weeks, not days. In the last one he'd said he didn't want to change his life—"all that history"—he'd written.

But he and I had a history, too. I hadn't asked him to leave his wife. I hoped that would be a natural progression. Meanwhile, I'd honored his need for discretion though I knew that in addition to the hidden, passionate excitement, I wanted the comfort of being openly close. Of being reachable. Often I wanted to pick up the phone to call him, but I didn't. Either he wasn't in, or he talked so guardedly it emphasized the distance, not the closeness. We couldn't keep on the way we were. We needed to get together to talk.

Restless, I decided to walk. In a couple of blocks, across a shallow ravine beyond the angular black arms of the trees, I glimpsed the old cotton gin hunkering with buttercups and wild iris in the long, new grass. Despite gray clouds threatening the budding trees with rain, the gin had a certain appeal. The brick-red metal roof and streaks of rust on the silver metal walls gave the buildings an earthy, vulnerable air. "No Trespassing" signs were posted every few feet on a sagging wire fence. Nick and I had never gone near.

I walked down the gravel driveway overgrown with clover and stopped where the fence crossed it. At the end of the drive near the gin, I could see a small historical marker. Nick knows I'm a sucker for historical markers. I squeezed between two leaning fenceposts and had only gone a little ways when I heard footsteps behind me.

I turned and saw a couple walking quickly toward me. The woman was middle-aged and solid-looking, as though she sprang from the German people who'd settled the area. The awkward length of her blue, flowered, cotton dress accented her thick calves. The man was her height but thin. He kept pace beside her with a long, rhythmic gait. They looked united in purpose. They looked like owners.

The best excuse my racing thoughts could muster seemed lame. 'Folks, your gin looked so inviting I thought I'd mosey on in for a closer look at the history.'

"You going to look at the gin?" the woman asked.

"I'd like to."

"Me, too. Are you the owner? I'm Annie Maude Fairchild. This is LeRoy." She emphasized the last syllable.

"Pleased," he said. I said I wasn't the owner. He said, "Annie Maude paints. She's good."

Annie Maude bobbed her head. A proud look passed between them. "Come on," Annie Maude said to me. "My son Dave and his wife, Sally, will wonder where we are. He's coming from the other side with the camera. I paint from pictures."

316

The three of us trespassed down the drive toward the gin and the sign.

"I brought cotton here with my daddy when I was twelve years old," LeRoy said.

"You remember exactly how old you were?" I asked.

"First time I ever drove the loaded wagon. I was scared, and I was sitting so high I could see the top of daddy's head. He let me carry the money home."

"LeRoy was a railroad man forty years," Annie Maude said. "A brakeman."

The historical marker named people who had settled on this small bend of the creek and told what they and their descendants had contributed to Luling in the hundred years since. Beyond the sign and a small building that might have been a bunkhouse, the drive curved to the left. The gin sprawled in front of us—five buildings of different heights and shapes that looked as though an artist had painted them, creating optical illusions from shadow and light and form. The windows had no glass. Black-eyed susans waved next to open doors.

"I drove in to unload over there. One of the horses reared, and daddy nearly got crushed against the wall."

"He always said how brave you were to talk the horse down." Annie Maude squeezed LeRoy's hand.

I felt suddenly lonely and for some reason pictured the last time Nick and I'd had coffee. Near our table, a small child had teetered on her toes, grinning her delight in being able to stand. We had smiled at the child and then at each other. I'd been overwhelmed by my desire to touch him and reached for his hand across the table. Our fingers touched for only a few seconds next to the muffin basket and then he pulled away. I knew why; he worried that even far from home someone he knew might see us.

LeRoy held Annie Maude's arm as she stepped over rotting logs near a large door and walked through weeds into the narrow stall where LeRoy had driven the wagon. I followed. Through a doorway I could see holes in the floorboards. The place smelled of decaying wood and earth. LeRoy let go of Annie Maude's arm and walked on into the room. His boots squeaked like mice beneath the floor.

"They sorted the cotton over here," he said.

317

"This would be a good picture, looking from the inside out," Annie Maude said from the doorway and followed LeRoy into the room. She stepped to the window. "Dave!" Annie Maude yelled, then turned to LeRoy. "Would you please tell him to come on in and take some pictures from here?"

As he left, LeRoy glanced toward the stairs. "The beams are still solid if you want to go up."

"I'd be afraid to climb those stairs," Annie Maude said to me. "Let's go toward the river, and I'll show you where the owners lived."

"You've been here before?"

"Last summer, but we didn't get a decent picture of the gin because the leaves were too thick. I wanted to come back to pick up pecans, but I never did. Maybe this year. Look at those trees, would you? Older than me by a hundred years." She laughed.

Against the dark bark of the pecan trees, I could see leaves just beginning to show. Beyond, I heard the river gurgling.

"Past those bushes is where the old house stood. Don't you know someone must have cried when it burned."

I stepped through buttercups into what had once been the house, now carpeted with fox-glove, primroses, and Queen Anne's Lace. Looming against the sky was a brick chimney burned black on one side and overgrown with vines. The place seemed heavy with old conversations. Nick would have liked it. We could have spread a quilt, entwined ourselves, and forgotten our need for words.

Annie Maude kept talking. "I'm an intensive care nurse in Seguin," she said.

I smiled. "I'm a nurse, too."

"Isn't that a coincidence," she said. "What kind?"

"I work with disturbed teenagers."

"Psychiatric." Annie Maude shook her head. "I couldn't do that. You never know if you're getting results. I like to regulate IV flows and adjust monitors. What are you doing here?"

"Meeting a friend."

She waved her arm at the river, barely visible past the chimney, the live oaks, and the pecan grove.

"My great-granddaddy settled near Bastrop on this same river. My granddaddy sold off the land when the water authority dammed the river to make the lake. I don't think it's good to drown growing land like that, but there's folks who like the water. My daddy farmed cotton right here in Caldwell County. My oh my, the stories he knows. You ever want to come by, he'd tell 'em to you. Of course, he gets mad when I fill in what he forgets."

"If he had a tape recorder, he could tell the stories for his grandchildren."

"And his great-grandchildren," Annie Maude said. "I want you to meet Dave and Sally. She's going to have a baby in six months. Dave is a descendant of Sam Houston. We adopted him when he was just a baby. He's an engineer in Houston, but he likes to come home and help me take pictures. Just imagine, this baby will be Sam Houston's five-times-great-grandson."

"From what I've read about Sam Houston, he had an exciting, often mysterious life," I said. "Not many adopted children can read about their ancestors in history books."

"LeRoy and I tried for ten years to have kids. He wanted a girl, so I said 'Let's adopt one,' but the doctor had this boy, and LeRoy saw how much I wanted him, so we just brought him on home."

"You must be proud Dave's an engineer," I said. My words sounded empty next to Annie Maude's. But in my heart, I heard words full of Nick. They left before my mind could capture them. I wanted to leave the rushing sound of Annie Maude's voice and see if they would return. "I think I'll take a look at the river."

Annie Maude walked behind me. "I haven't done near the things I wanted to do in my life," she said.

I stopped beneath a live oak and took a breath. Above me in the darkening sky, an oak limb reached for but did not touch a pecan branch.

I turned around. "What did you want to do?"

Annie Maude wore a look like a photograph of Sam Houston I recalled from somewhere—staring into the camera with his lips forever closed over the stories of the sudden end of his brief marriage to Eliza Allen and his liaison with the Cherokee woman, Tiana Rogers. "Mama had an old quilt from her mama. I used it for years until it frayed, and then I cut it up

319

for bed pads when Uncle Frank got sick. I wish I'd kept it for Dave's child. Something from *my* family. I've read lots of stories about Sam Houston's family. I even found the pecan pie recipe his last wife, Margaret, made for company."

"But your grandfather's stories . . ."

"They seem like so little."

"But they are really so much."

Annie Maude started to answer but didn't. She looked at me, and then looked away. My cheeks were wet. I hadn't noticed until now that the rain had begun.

"I could send you the recipe if you like." She squeezed my hand. "The books say that Sam was happiest with Margaret, but I think he always kept Eliza Allen in his heart." Beyond her, Dave and Sally and LeRoy walked into the stall from the other side of the gin.

"Yes," I said, "Please send the recipe."

I gave her my address. Annie Maude walked toward the stall. I walked back down the driveway. My shoes sank into the wet clover. The rain came down harder.

I sensed the gin crouching behind me, smelled its damp-earth breath, heard whispers, as though Annie Maude were still talking to me. Some are willing to combine histories and create new ones, she said. And some are not. I squeezed between the fence posts and walked back to the coffee shop.

Nick's car wasn't in its usual place. It wasn't anywhere on the block. I looked again at my watch—he was more than two hours late. Long past time for students talking after class to have delayed him. I walked the wet streets with my frustration. Twice I dialed him from a pay phone but hung up before anyone answered. The questions, the words, the sorting out, were not meant for the phone. Maybe they were not meant for us. Just for me. I wondered what Eliza had told her family when she returned home after only three months of marriage. It had been this time of year—April.

I returned past the gin to the blackened chimney. In front of it I stacked fallen bricks and buttercups and primroses. I held an iris in my hands and kept company with the colors while young pecan leaves embraced the rain. On my face and arms raindrops danced their cool dance.

I licked my lips. What was the last thing I wanted to do today? Taste how Nick's and my story was ending.

ANCIENT INFANT

MARISE McDERMOTT

At night, the infant pulls her yucca mat through the museum drawer and drags what is left of it along the reproduction of a creek bed. In her right hand, she holds the lower part of her jaw, with the words, "mandible of an infant," sketched in black along its edges. Infantile and adult molars couple within the mandible, like barnacles along an abandoned ship part. The child stoops to pick up teeth that sometimes fall from the swinging arched bone.

The guards see the mandible first. They tell me about the jaw swinging next to rabbit bones, which wander through the museum and out the back door. The bones scrape the soil away from the kumquat tree and rest on the leaves.

"That's her skull top," I remind the guards. "And she's not a rabbit, she's an infant from the Lower Pecos."

"If she's a baby, you would bury her." They talk about the tapping at the door before sunrise if they forget to let her in on their perimeter rounds.

The drawer where she is stored never budges. She somehow manages to pull the mat through the cracks like my daughter does her blanket on nights she slips in to sleep with me. "How did you get through the door?" I'll ask, and she will hold up her blanket, as if it held the answer.

The parents who buried the baby 1,500 years ago loved her. Her mother wrapped her in red fox fur and a beautifully woven yucca mat. Her head was placed on a pillow of dry grass. She was adorned in shell and squirrel-teeth pendants. The bundle was covered with layers of mats, tightly woven near the body and more loosely near the soil. The outer mats have been eaten long ago by worms that never made it to the bones. The tighter weave had exhausted a thousand generations of insects.

The skull is now dark black, with patches of gray around the eyes. I know it is a female, though a DNA analysis has not yet been done. The top of the skull narrows delicately toward the front and widens as it reaches the hairline where the few remaining strands of hair are red. When she was alive, her hair was straight and black. Colors fade in death. But bones darken. Two white teeth stick prominently from her black mouth. Seven ribs jut from tufts of tissue, once skin, and rest like harp strings under her collar bone. Her knees are bent and her arms crossed. The bundle was buried as a womb, which she had left just fifteen months ago.

In my lab journal, I had written: "Archaic infant. Wrapped in matting. Found under debris, back of cave, near prickly pear. Implements in second mat: broken cradleboard, fur blanket, shell necklace with squirrel-teeth pendants."

Her skeleton was found by a young boy in 1934, beneath the solidified ashes of a cave. Her cradle was found nearby, its back cracked to release the spirit of life. One piece of sotol branch had not been broken through: the fibers held on, twisted, but intact. The almost-broken cradle was placed in a locked case high up in the rock shelter exhibit. The infant couldn't see it on her nightly jaunts through the museum and out the door.

If only she were a corpse and not a skeleton, with more than just hints of leathered tissue. If only she could speak, like my six-year-old daughter on cold mornings.

"It's too cold out there. I have to stay in bed."

"I've made you warm oatmeal."

"What kind?"

"Cinnamon."

"Oh, Mom, I hate cinnamon."

"Strawberry."

"It's the package kind, then. Can't you make the real kind?"

"I'll give you until the count of five to get up."

Get up. Get up. The medical lab report is filed near her drawer: "The infant exhibits at least four radiographically opaque lines on either side of the tibiae. Identical lines were found in other bones. Growth arrest lines occur in stressful environmental situations, such as food shortage."

One night, Carmella, the front desk guard, pulled me toward her. Her round face was shining. She told me that a Karankawa Indian had come to the front door at three A.M. and asked to bury the infant. "The smell of oyster shells and oily hair gave him away. Because Karankawas ate oysters."

"I can't bury her," I told Carmella. "No matter what story you come up with next, the infant cannot leave the drawer. Besides, she is not Karankawa. She is Archaic. Her parents buried her in their garbage pit, for God's sake."

"You know what your problem is? You are in love with that baby."

I'm not sure how we arrived at this point. I had suspected the bones were rummaged through each night. I confronted Carmella before I even knew her very well.

"I never even been to the collections area. I'm a front desk guard. I see the bones when they come down the stairs or walk out the door. The baby's jaw swings next to them."

"How do you know it's a baby's jaw?"

"Because it's got eye sockets in the skull."

"How long have you worked here, Carmella?"

"Too long." She rolled her eyes and looked past me. Her security jacket and tie made her look like a man. She kept her black straight hair short. She wore a diamond in her right ear. The polyester security pants with a black stripe on the side may have fit her once, but since I arrived at the museum five years ago, her pants stretched across her thighs like shark's skin.

A month ago, the Sioux came. Four large men in flannel shirts and Wrangler jeans walked into Collections. They showed me security badges Carmella had issued. One asked, "You know what repatriation is?"

"You want the skeletons of your ancestors. We don't have Sioux skeletons. Just Lower Pecos people."

"You have umbilical cords."

I had forgotten.

When I returned with the jars of cords, I saw the Sioux men had cleared off a portion of my formica work table. They were burning leaves of sage and sweet grass. All I could see was the smoke rising over their heads, with their black hair tied back in rubber bands behind their broad shoulders. I called the guards to shut off the smoke alarm. Carmella had already done it.

"I figured they'd do something like that," she said and hung up.

An hour later they were gone with the jars. I stared at the photocopies of their Native American ancestry papers strewn along the table next to the ashes of tobacco and sage, enough to scorch but not burn the formica. I brushed the remnants into a specimen bottle and filed the paperwork in the now empty drawer.

I was breathing in the smell of sage, worrying that the museum trustees would find out about the repatriation, when the forensic sculptor from the medical school knocked on the door. He must have passed the Sioux on the staircase, but he didn't ask about them. Sam resembled them in a way, with his long pony tail and Wrangler jeans. His eyes, though, were light and not dark and hard.

Sam came so often that we didn't speak. Just nodded. We entered the archeological vault together where hundreds of large drawers are labeled alphabetically. He didn't ask about the smell of sage. The smell caused me to look at the labels in a haze: Aztec Beads . . . Coil Baskets . . . Cranial Base . . . Infant Skeleton . . . Shaman Skull . . . Twilled Mats. Sam stopped at Infant Skeleton, as he did each day, and opened the drawer. I held on to the table. No drawer for Cradle Seekers, Grave Diggers, Lost Spirits . . . The sage made me dizzy, like the incense of high mass.

I stood beside him to make sure he didn't disturb her any more than necessary. He pulled out her skull and placed clay balls along her nose, near her ears and within her eye sockets. He took the mandible in his hand and attached it firmly to the cranium by using clay and cotton to replace the cartilage. Sometimes he paused to toss his pony tail back over his shoulder. He was building a model of the infant's skull, which would become a sculpture.

"Listen, do I have to disconnect the mandible again today?"

I was cleaning a tribal mask nearby. "Yes, I'm afraid so."

"I only have two days to go before it's complete. But I could make it one if I could keep the thing in place just tonight.

"I'm sorry," I lied, "I've found the weight to be too much stress on the cranium."

"Christ. Ok, ok. Could I at least have a tooth? This could be a good one. To see if it had fevers. A dentist at the medical school asked for one."

I didn't answer. Teeth are the fingerprints of the dead. I didn't want him to know any more about her. He returned to work. I could see he was irritated.

"You know, you don't own this skeleton. Do I need to ask the museum director for the damn tooth?"

I pulled the tooth from the back of her jaw and handed it to him. "Be careful with it."

That night I dreamed of body parts floating past me in a muddy river. I reached for them but they jammed against each other forming bodies, part baby, part mammoth, part old woman. I grabbed onto a log, which was, instead, a leg.

The next week, Sam finished the sculpture at the medical school. He told me on the phone that it sculpted itself.

"I'm sorry I lost my temper. There's something odd about this one. I don't know, its stare or something. It gives me the creeps. The tooth is in a box with the sculpture. Oh, and it definitely had fevers—high fevers. Maybe that's why it died."

After the phone call, I gathered my notebooks and her shell necklace. It was time to find her burial spot.

That night, I sat on Jessica's floor and watched her play with her pet mealworms, "The Amys."

"I can't tell them apart, so that's what they'll have to be named," she told me when she brought them home from school. I watched as she tore a large piece of tracing paper from her pad and placed it on the small table in her room. From the jar filled with cream of wheat spilled two pieces of dried apples and the two worms. She spread the cream of wheat out to a thin layer. The worms uncurled and moved toward each other, but Jessica put her forefinger in front of one Amy and it moved toward her.

"They like my heat," she told me.

"Very scientific." I walked into her room and put my finger in front of the other Amy, but it recoiled.

"Maybe you're too cold."

I stretched out along Jessica's bed and watched as she placed freshly cut apples on the paper and threw the dried pieces in her garbage pail. The infant would have thrown her debris in the corner of her cave. She was buried under the debris. The cave was her room, her bed would have been straw. At Jessica's age, she would have been working beside her mother, eating the worms and not dawdling. The infant's mother would have been happy to eat Jessica's hamster, which lives in a three-story wire cage next to Jessica's bed. A plump rat was a nice feast. I leaned over from my daughter's bed to pull out the small beast. The hamster looked warily as I searched its bones for meat.

The next morning, while it was still dark, I reached over the jar of mealworms buried in cream of wheat and kissed Jessica goodbye. She would be taken to school and picked up from school by my mother. She was used to these trips of mine to the caves.

But this trip was different. I drove south for three hours before I began to see the signs--the lime green and white border patrol trucks, the empty stretch of sandy soil pockmarked by thorny brush, the white stucco houses with blue and green doors. I stopped by a fence post with a red ribbon tacked on. I pulled the attached barbed wire from around the post and drove my Blazer into the brush. I parked in a clearing, pulled my backpack over my shoulders and tramped in. The infant's cave is a six-mile hike, near a backwash from the Rio Grande.

The brush was quiet that day. I could hear scampering in the sea of bleached green grass. Birds perched atop the dark ashe junipers. I tripped across a badger hole and stopped to see a tarantula darting. The sculptures of thorn bushes, especially the *tasajillo*, matched the shape of the spider.

Would the infant have watched the spider in wonder?

Everything matched, nothing was alien. Lone yellow flowers the size of thumbs broke the horizon of green and gray.

Near the caves, the earth drops off into a canyon. Sheer walls of limestone covered with black manganese plummet to the green river. Enormous holes of sand-colored limestone have been carved by rushing water.

Another mile and I reached the infant's shelter cave. A badger had recently shoveled out some debris left by the ancient families, perhaps the infant's. I pulled out her shell necklace from my back and buried it in the badger path, gently covering it with the loose soil. *But was this right?*

Along the edges of the shelter, I filled plastic bags with prickly yucca leaves and a stalk from a sotol plant. I stooped to pick up the excrement of a bobcat. I had never seen one, but its musty scent built my idea of the prehistoric. It was so quiet. I could hear the fish jumping in the river, almost a hundred feet below. I set up my battery-run lantern and unrolled my sleeping bag. At some point I fell asleep, but it was a point in a continuum that evades me still, a point among stars and rock ceiling, data and dream, mosquito bites and dry breeze, old voices and the rustling of a desert night.

Most of the infant's life was good. She and her family lived among small bands in the rock shelters. There were no boundary lines. The open caves were cool in the summer and warm in the winter, filled with ash from constant pit fires and debris: fish vertebrae, nut shells, animal bones. The babies learned to wipe ashes from their eyes before they grasped shells.

In the sea of sage-colored brush and sandy soil, the mothers told stories and brushed away the ants and spiders. They pulled their crawling babies from the mountain laurel and coyote bush. The infant, when just born, was wrapped in soft red fox fur and secured into her cradle with rope made of lechuguilla. Her cradle of sotol sticks was propped along the shelter wall near women weaving baskets and grinding mesquite beans. The women wove tiny sandals for their children and gathered plants or small animals for food.

The infant's mother wove a mat for the baby to crawl on when she left her cradle. The mother cut needles and thorns from the yucca and sotol leaves and pulled the strands through her teeth to flatten the fibers. She told stories from morning 'til night. The baby stood by and listened, clinging to her mother's hair. As the baby grew older, she held onto her teeth so they would not drop out as her mother's did while making mats.

The mother worried. She tried to give the baby milk as they huddled in the cave, but soon the cold dried up the grasses and her milk stopped coming. Winter was the most dangerous time to wean a child in the Lower Pecos. It was the child's second winter. Too soon. She gave the child rat meat that she had chewed to make soft, but the baby spit it out. After several days, the child's bones stopped growing. Finally starving, the baby shoved mountain laurel beans into her mouth. The beans were not meant to be eaten. She coughed and became chilled. She clutched her mother's neck. Her mother wrapped her in rabbit pelts and held her near the fire, brushing away the sparks and ashes. Beads of sweat gathered along the infant's forehead. Her skin was hot to touch.

The baby lay curled in fur as her mother began to weave her death mats. She started with the wide weave of the flattened sotol, hoping she would be able to use it for a sitting mat, but as time wore on, the smaller weave mats emerged as yucca strips narrowed through her teeth. Before the infant died, the tiniest weave mat was complete.

The mother placed a corner of the death mat between the baby's clenched fingers and wrapped the flexed body round and round until the wide, flattened weave mats were all that could be seen. She held the mat-covered child for as long as she could. The mother cracked the baby's birth-cradle to release the living spirit, but she was weak from days of kneeling next to the dying child. When she handed it to the baby's father, the largest sotol branch still clung together by the fibers and remained unbroken. No one noticed.

The father took the wrapped infant and the almost-broken cradle and buried them in the back of the cave under layers of ash. The spirit of life was never released.

I raised my head from the hole in the ground where she had been buried. The morning sun had not yet reached into the river canyon. I gazed at the ceiling where a faceless figure with stick arms held a warped club. Days later, I climbed down from the cave with plastic bags of ancient paint and bone chips.

The walk back was quiet, broken only by the shrill motor of a small plane overhead. It was the lime green and white of a border patrol. I could feel his binoculars.

I had penetrated the cave so deeply that when I came home I watched my daughter to see how to open the refrigerator. I looked to my husband to find bowls and spoons. I held my stockings in my hands before I could remember what they were for.

When I arrived at the museum, the sculpture had arrived. I opened the crate and the bronze baby emerged, with her fat cheeks and bowl-cut hair.

328

She looked at me with knowing bronze eyes. Her small fingers clutched something under her chin. The death mat. Jessica's blanket.

Sam created her in bronze, but to me she was flesh and blood with black eyes and hair and a thick red tongue that rolled around her two white teeth and sucked sweet cactus tuna. The red cactus juice stained her mat and flowed along the cement creek bed on the museum floor. The juice formed a red pool at the base of a museum case. High in the case, behind the locked glass doors was the cradle, almost cracked.

That night, Carmella let me in the front door after dark. She asked no questions. I walked upstairs to the glass case and unlocked it. The bronze sculpture watched. I put my foot on the cradle and cracked the stubborn branch in half. The sound echoed through the rock shelter wing of the museum and bounced off the cement floors. I relocked the case.

From the drawer, I took the entire skeleton and put it in my backpack. A snail shell was among the bones. A gift. A bribe.

Jessica could help me bury her. The walk to the cave is long, but we could collect things on the way. Pretty beetles or more grubs.

Carmella didn't look up from her magazine as I left.

Jessica could climb in the Blazer. She'd look straight ahead with her eyes squinting.

"Why am I going this time?"

"I want to show you where the baby was buried. We're going to bury her again."

"Mom, why is this important? I could have gone to Sea World with Erica this weekend."

"We can collect grubs. Maybe even catch a tarantula."

"All right. But only a baby one that I can raise. I like them young."

The walk into the brush with Jessica was not quiet. The canyon was filled with echoes of her laughter and screeches. She found one, then another spider. None were right. For the first mile, she scampered along the sand, creating clouds of dust behind her. For the last several miles, she trudged. We rested every mile.

She slid down the rope ladder to the cave, with her hair fluttering toward the river. I showed her the infant's burial hole, but she was hunting in the corner for empty shells and arrowheads. I set up our camp as she sung and gathered. I knelt by the new burial mound, pressing in the earth over the wrapped skeleton.

I can still hear her scream. A scream so long there were no echoes possible. On her hunt, a scorpion found her. It was low, on her leg. The swelling took over quickly, blowing her leg up to twice its size. The sun was already down, the sky seemed to darken at high speed. In the cave, time had stopped. Jessica cried in my arms and began to sweat.

The scorpion sting was not lethal if treated. But a child the size of Jessica . . .

I could carry her in the dark over the dangerous terrain. Climbing the shelters at the river's edge is difficult in daylight. Nocturnal creatures had already started protecting their turf. I could hear them howl.

Or I could wait out the night and race her to the hospital in the morning.

"Kids die from scorpions. Mrs. Rust told me," Jessica whimpered.

"No, they don't. Only when they're not treated. Tomorrow, I'll take you to the hospital."

"I can't walk," she whispered.

"I'll carry you."

"Will they give me a shot?"

"I don't know. Now you need to sleep."

Jessica whined, "I can't sleep. My leg stings . . ."

I helped her into her sleeping bag as I spoke. "It's important to sleep. Sleep. Sleep." I placed a pillow on my lap for her head. I stroked her hair until she fell asleep. Her forehead began to bead with sweat. She was warm with fever.

Eight hours to go before dawn.

Seven hours.

By lantern light, she seemed too pale. I touched her heart. She was breathing steadily. Her pulse was good. But her fever had risen. She began to murmur in her sleep. I held her hand, gliding my fingers along hers. Then I carefully pushed her head and pillow off my lap.

I knew the lantern batteries would last all night. I crept over to the sotol plant at the edge of the shelter. Without gloves, I pulled the thorn-

covered leaves off the plant. One. Two. Twenty, Thirty. How many would it take?

My hands began to bleed. I found a sharp stone and tore the thorns from the edge of the leaves. I laid them out, side by side, next to the lantern. Jessica slept on the other side, her face dripping with sweat, fighting the poison.

Five more hours.

I sat by Jessica's face and took one, then another, then a third strip of sotol.

And I began to weave.

I buried the infant in the corner of the shelter. No one will miss her more than me.

Jessica brought home white rats this week, thinking they might be smarter than the hamsters or worms. She created a maze for them, but they thwarted her plans. They grabbed the blocks with their little paws and hurled them aside to escape. She returned them to a new wire cage, which already smelled.

I imagined badgers had found the burial spot. I wondered whether the infant would give up her swinging of the mandible after all.

The winter drought has all but emptied the rivers in the Lower Pecos. Even the pale green sage has lost its color. The river hasn't been this low in a century. The cache is so bountiful that archaeologists spend most of their time along the dry river beds pulling out stone tools from the cracked mud. The cave shelters loom overhead, but the excavators are too busy below to climb the now daunting cliffs.

I haven't traveled to the Lower Pecos since I buried the infant. I changed the order of the archeological vault. The infant's empty drawer is filled with painted pebbles and a shaman's pouch of rodent-jaw scarifiers, mesquite beans and rattlesnake vertebrae. They tell a story also, but not as well as she did. I will eventually build a rope ladder long enough to climb to the infant's cave. She could be anywhere, though, in a thousand pieces, scattered along the limestone, returned.

THE RECEPTION

BETSY BERRY

We didn't grow up together, but we might have. This we found out later, when we met in college, where we were roommates and where we learned just how closely our childhoods mirrored each other's—like those twins you read about: *Separated At Birth!* Our mothers used to sing us "Mister Sandman" to lull us to sleep. Our fathers were Air Force pilots. She was shy, serious, even a little melancholy, a dutiful child. And although I was remembered more for my guided tours of the many neighborhoods I inhabited during childhood, lawn productions of little plays I always ended up scripting and directing, I was fearful, like Carling, of nightfall and sudden noises. There was a train near whatever house we had lived in when I was five, roaring past with such ferociousness I thought it might come through my bedroom window. I visited that house some years ago. What had appeared to me then as a mansion was now a smallish two story house, and the train track was a good two blocks away.

When Carling and I were both ten the Beatles crossed the seas, mop topped and shiny suited, swiftly descending from the boarding ramp of a Pan Am Clipper (Flight 101) into the consciousness of every young girl in the country. We sang "I Want to Hold Your Hand" in our raspy, little-girl voices for a few years until we busied ourselves wasting our father's Polaroid film packs making photo after photo of glossy *Teen Beat* pics of Davey Jones.

I was small, olive skinned and dark haired; she was taller, white blonde, reed thin. At fifteen we spent hours in front of the mirror practicing our makeup—light, pastel blue eyeliner was *de rigueur*; we pored over beauty and fashion articles with the same vapid, exclusionary titles as ever: "That Singular Brunette Allure," "The Cool Shades Blondes Alone May Wear," "Only Tall Girls Need Apply."

We burrowed toward college with huge, haunted, raccoon eyes, done with black kohl pencils and close-up stills of Twiggy. We loved everything about the British scene, Picadilly Circus and double-decker buses, striped miniskirts and tight boots, lipstick the color of talcum powder. Only later would we exchange such common stories, but as early as high school—Carling's in Wisconsin and mine in Texas—we anticipated our great friendship to come. In high school, we were each of us outsiders—an unacceptable, even terrifying term that in our revisionist telling was altered to above-the-fray. She and I were not a part of what was at both of our schools a considerably sizable Popular Crowd—though our name for them, "Poppos," was not shared up north in Carling's country, where they were called "The Its." And in our first hormonal blush we did not get to go out with a blue-eyed, blond-haired, tanned guy who had both a nickname and a real one like Austin, or Hunter, or William III. Many of the girls in our class didn't have to read beauty mags; they were photographed for them—with shiny, just ironed hair and real British mod clothes their mothers had brought back for them from England. Girls that smiled like Mona Lisa, they always had secrets, their infrequent laughter never mistaken for giggling.

But Carling and I pretended not to care much anyway; we tried to think of high school as a sorry little roadhouse stop on our way to a four-star hotel. We said we didn't care whether or not we made cheerleader, and when neither of us came even close to that, whether or not we made the drill team that marched behind the cheerleader squad on the field at half time. We'd both pick a guy we knew we could never have and, when we'd gotten our license, find excuses just to drive past where he lived. (In those days the mere seconds we had to feast our eyes on his house, settling for one delicious moment on the window of the room we thought to be his, were such an exhilaration we couldn't have stood anything more.)

She was this willowy girl in bell-bottoms and a gauze shirt when I first met her, where our brothers had gone to college and where we had followed like lambs, in Anthropology 101, Mondays, Wednesdays, and Fridays, at 9 A.M. She had an impossible-to-spell, German last name—Lendersdarff—and I quickly came to call her, simply, Len.

What remarkably similar tastes we had for two girls who had grown up so far from each other! We never fought about anything except guys, for I'd usually be asked for more dates (curvy, and nice to be in college) than Len (a stick, and so nice to be later). Of course we both joined the same sorority, not one of the best and not one of the worst, and later we found our first little home, a shabby apartment in Dallas' Oak Lawn district. It was appropriately seedy, bohemian style, and right off Knox Street, which has long since been done up with expensive little boutiques and wheat micro-breweries. We'd sleep with our windows open, there where car gears ground at all hours, the thumping bass of revved up disco tunes rattling the screens.

In front our building was an alcove lined with metal mailboxes, a shaded meeting place of sorts, which is where we met Mildew. Mildew is what we instantly named him, a scruffy looking guy named Gary Milden who rarely did laundry and said maybe a couple of hundred words altogether in the three years we knew him. "Far out" was what he said most, in the kind of unprompted, wondrous way that made you think he really meant it. Mildew used to visit us a few nights a week, sauntering over from his apartment on the other side of the building, as far away from the pool as he could get. He said that what he liked to do most was smoke pot and watch dust balls gather, but we secretly suspected him of booking it on the sly. Mildew was constantly taking classes at the university, and even still he seemed to actually be progressing toward a degree in—engineering, I think. A mixture of eclectic people and contrary elements made up the Oakview Plaza Apartments, which became Len's and my own little world.

We loved playing house and decorating, especially ourselves. We would talk forever about the "natural" look, the one that, as one cosmetic company put it, "nature gave us." As long as it didn't mean going without eye makeup and giving up shaving our legs. Nature, after all, only took you so far up its tree before it dropped you from a high branch with a thud.

Of course we were careful to buy phosphate-free detergent at Roy's Nutrition Center, but also we'd load up on huge aerosol cans of hairspray from the Piggly Wiggly. We took the vitamins that were later touted as "antioxidants" and fried our skin nuclear brown at the Oakview pool. We talked about leatherjacketed hunks on shiny Harley motorcycles but frequently were found at fraternity mixers with the silly, beer-guzzling boys most of us would end up marrying. Our so-called uniforms were faded bell-bottom jeans (the bigger at the bottom the better); clingy, big-sleeved tops that tied under our breasts; bandannas helmeted around our heads, hair falling straight down our backs like a horse's tail. Len, tall and skinny, was the Jeff to my Mutt, giving peace a chance and taking no prisoners.

One Saturday when Len, a pretty fair cook even then, made dinner, while I, developing ritual habits that would later approach the neurotic, cleaned up, Mildew appeared at the door. He'd always come over Saturday nights when we didn't have dates—which turned out to be an impressive string of Saturday nights—for shots of bourbon and cinnamon rolls. Hot and sweet with melted white icing, those rolls will forever remind me of ear-splitting guitar riffs Mildew had brought over on tapes, of giggling about nothing, of schemes and hijinks concocted well after the first stroke of morning. This night Mildew was sporting a hangover from the day before, his thick glasses falling down on his nose, chemically inspired to create some kind of yarn collage on the wall over the stereo. In one hand was a huge hammer and a filthy leather pouch of nails, and in the other were three skeins of yarn, which he set to stretching in various directions around the nail heads he had poked haphazardly into the wall. The result was a spider web of glorious colors, sienna and gold and hot pink, a grand concoction of student-income invention and apartment art funk.

"Far out," he pronounced it, in awe of his own work.

"Very, very cool, Mildew," assuring him that no one—even those who would live here long after we were gone—would ever even think of taking it down.

"Maybe it's a little too pink?" said Len, but we told her to drink her bourbon and keep quiet.

"Farfucking out," Mildew said. And the rest of the night we didn't say much, losing ourselves in the dizzying depths of geometry and yarn, Mildew holding Marlboro after Marlboro between fingers sticky with icing. They still make those cinnamon rolls in the can, but they don't taste nearly as good as they used to.

And other things, too, would inevitably change. Mildew left one day that summer to go to graduate school back east, announcing that he knew he was selling out but was tired of being a bum. He'd finally got his degree without telling anyone, the fink. Len and I finished school as well; goaded by our parents, we now had to move on. The little space of time we had so lovingly constructed was already dimming, dust on our shoe soles, and one day I said good-bye to this girl who had been my fast friend and my first and last roommate, good-bye to those years in our little Travis Street pad.

As these things are scripted, we wrote at least once a week for the first year or so, and then less frequently. But in the mid-1980s I returned to the city where Len still lived, in an impeccable one-bedroom in north Dallas, one of many complexes in the hip and huge development called The Village *(The Finest Singles Living).* I came back to marry a man I'd once dated—though we had both had to move away before deciding on this precipitous step. In both newspapers the announcement appeared official and intractable and spoke of participants in a whitewashed dream, a bride who *wore a breathtaking gown of white satin and tulle ruffles, hand-beaded and patterned with antique Venetian lace; the maid-of-honor and brides-maids in tea-length dresses of wine watered-silk with satin empire sashes.* In my wedding album is a shot of my maid of honor, Len, arching in mid-air like a basketball player in freeze frame near the hoop, straining to catch the bouquet I tried to throw in her direction from over my shoulder. Later my brother remarked that she might have gotten a pro contract out of the deal as well, but what she did get seemed precious enough to her. A small bouquet of white and peach roses and baby's breath, a hint of promise for what had become her most fervent wish, to marry and have a family of her own. By this time having children had assumed such importance in her life that I thought she might be willing to bypass the "I do" part of the greater picture altogether.

For reasons nobody seemed to pin down, Len had never had much luck with "guys"; even the way she'd say that word put quotation marks around it. But she had spent countless hours talking with me about little girls and maybe a boy, blond and tall like she was, in starched pinafores or a little suit and Buster Browns. I kidded her then about diapers and spit-ups and the whole impossible sound of it all, us as *mothers,* for godsakes. We laughed together a million times, our month-by-month living arrange-ment evolving into a much larger block of time.

Years it had been, years in which we had grown as friends, so close we were inseparable. And strangely now at my wedding I could think of Len only in silhouette. She was a figure out of sync with the present, growing thinner and farther away, memory like a camera that has pulled back too quickly from a close-up to a long shot. Smaller and smaller she grew in real life as I watched her from the back window of the black limousine that took me away from Dallas for good. A man sat beside me, someone I barely knew, so glamorous to me in his black tie and tails it was hard to hold onto the notion, as true as birth and death, that to leave the past in a cream veiled moment is to never really recapture it whole again.

Nor was I to know that some years later I would return once more to Len's Dallas, in a maroon Chanel suit and with a different man by my side, to attend Carling Lendersdarff's own wedding reception. I had seen her only a couple of times since then, once when she visited me in Indianapolis, Indiana, where my husband Will was a resident surgeon. Len, slim as always, now had haunted, more mature beauty, but she retained the sharp-eyed wonder of a single girl in a married kitchen, missing no domestic detail. Most nights of her visit, Will at the hospital, we would drink grocery store champagne out of the lovely silver goblets she had given me as a wedding present. Those times we became roommates again, newly independent in a big world with few boundaries. When her smile would fade and she would turn pensive, I would try to remind her of the actual conditions of modern marriage, try to gently dislodge some of her cherished notions of marital bliss.

"Len, we're in *Indiana,* for godsakes," I would hiss in frustration. "I'm warming up meat loaf for the second time this week, we're out of ketchup, and I hate my job." (I was an office manager for a branch of Monsanto Chemical Company, in a small building literally in the middle of a cornfield.) But all of this fell on ears primed for far less jarring notes.

Then a phone call might come, would come, a nurse letting me know that the Doctor was in the operating theater even as we spoke and didn't know what time he would be home. In one instance when Len was there, a small child had sustained massive burns from a pot of boiling water overturned when his mother had been scurrying to get dinner ready by the time her husband was expected home from work. For Will something like this meant an eight-hour stretch over an anesthetized body (his favorite kind, I already knew by then), but for Len all it meant was that I was hooked up, electronically connected to someone called a husband. The white-coated knight that could save the damsel from a drab dinner and a bad tv show was how she saw it, while I drenched the meat loaf in blue milk—skim, all

I had—to keep it moist enough to serve to Will in the middle of the night. Outside the wind howled and it looked like snow.

"It's yours, you know. You have it all," Len said at the airport as we waited for her plane back to Dallas to board. I took her to the airport alone because Will was on call that day, at home watching the Cowboys and hoping that his beeper wouldn't go off. I remember wishing at that moment that I could have told Len what I already knew would be the real ending of the story she insisted on reading as a fairy tale. I had almost forgotten the beginnings of this particular narrative in my life, but like a cloudless Texas sky, I foresaw the end with a hard-edged blue clarity.

And I did not see her again until the day of her wedding. We had written sporadically after that visit, sending a birthday gift here or a Christmas card there. For me it had been decided one cold, windy night in my tiny apartment kitchen when the umpteenth call came that Will would not come home that night, that when we left Indiana we would leave for separate lives. As it turned out, he went to Houston to set up his practice, and I went to Austin, with few belongings but the matching set of luggage his parents had given me for our marriage and the tiger-striped cat Will had given me in place of it.

I went back to school, started new work and made new friends, licking wounds that initially enormous became just small scratches. And then one day, there it was in the mail, a stiff creamy envelope postmarked Dallas and addressed in Len's familiar, teacher-perfect script. Inside, surrounded by a handwritten hallelujah and lots of exclamation marks were formal, raised letters which announced the wedding of Carling Lendersdarff and Tyler Wesley Warrick III. My first thought was that Len's ship had finally come in, docking regally with a three-pronged name *and* a roman numeral. My invitation was only for the reception following a private church ceremony for, she had written me, "a few friends and family." The reception would be held at a trendy club on the top floor of the Doubletree Inn, Campbell Center, that duo of blinding copper plated structures that overlook Central Expressway and a hay field that comprises the opening shot of the tv show *Dallas*.

Putting together a series of kitchen tools and gourmet foods in a large yellow ceramic basket, I wrapped up a big package to send to Len. A week later, on a whim, I bought a filmy nightgown in soft mint, a great color for her, packed it in leopard print tissue paper and sent that along as well, in case I couldn't attend a bridal shower that might be given in her honor. To the reception I would take a tiny piece of pottery I had been ritually presented years before and cast outside of Santa Fe by Hopi Indians. The prevailing pattern symbolized love, a long union, and above all, the bounty of fertility. Its simple design was rendered so beautifully that for a time I was caught up again in the warmth of the promise—that magic moment we think life owes us, the glossy guarantees of magazine ads and romance novels. It is harder not to believe in such a bright order of things.

For Harry, the man who will accompany me to Len's reception, I choose an Armani suit and tie; for me, a pale blue satin shirt and the black wool skirt that Len had so admired when I bought it years before. I pack two small suitcases while Harry loads a cooler with beer and sandwiches for what he insists on referring to as the "four-hour drive." "I don't care if you stop and spend the night in Waco," Harry assures me, "from Austin to Dallas is *always* a four-hour drive." At this point in my life I am secure being single and happy being attached, and I'm pretty sure Harry feels the same. I'm ready to believe that, despite what they say, you really can come back, walk into a room of old friends and . . . just be back. I am ready to confirm that returning to such a place after having made another life somewhere else is as easy as taking Interstate 35, looping around downtown Dallas, heading north on Central Expressway.

But on the Expressway is the usual mass of cars alternately crawling and stock still, and the drive into the city is edgy from the moment the horizon reveals the sunset-rimmed skyline of Big D. Somewhere in this space of time I remember that this is a city no longer mine and no longer of me; I only sense remote connections. Still, all the old memories come back, only now they are re-scripted. So we drive a little further than our hotel—on the access road of the highway—because I want Harry to pass by Campbell Center, where the next day the reception will be. Even in winter the Texas sun at dusk lights up the copper panes, making the buildings look like huge neon signs. The reflection shows copper in Harry's eyes, and my face too is flushed. We have both assumed a glow and, artificial or not, it is nice, this spot of time before the sky fades black and lights come on and Dallas will look like a tiny planet lit by the moon. This has always been for me the time of day when many things seem possible, when anything might happen.

I crack open a beer, fish around in my bag for the invitation, its calligraphic lettering taking on new importance. I note again that the ceremony is closed to all but a special few, and I am glad for Len that her father, whom I learned from a mutual friend has survived a stroke, will be there to present his only daughter to her new husband. The reception promises luxury: champagne cocktails and live music with a "big band sound." Can my old friend still think of me as the bell-bottomed dynamo I was as a young woman in college, my life stretched before me like a limitless road? Perhaps not, for with my invitation, she has enclosed a short handwritten note to remind me that the women will be in dresses and men in coat and tie. Also included in the note is an itemized list of gift suggestions and the toll-free numbers for Neiman Marcus and Sanger Harris. Tomorrow will be a day for which Len has been waiting thirty-four years.

My friends will see a new version of me, a quieter persona, a reader of books, a thinker rather than a talker. But when I see Len the next day after Harry and I have spent a noisy and restless night at the Hiltop (changed from Hilton) Inn, see her standing just inside the garland draped french doors entrance to the Doubletree club in a frosted beige, tea-length gown and greeting arrivals in the finest *Modern Bride* style, my earlier plan to stand aside and merely watch the performance dissolves at once. I rush forward and hug her until she says she can't breathe. Her tall, thin body is as stiff as an ironing board.

"Carling, you look beautiful," I tell her. Like that, on some sudden impulse, I call her not Len, my name for her, but Carling.

"I'm thrilled for you! Tell me how it came about, how you got together, tell me everything!"

"Great to see you, Jamey," she says. "Thank you both so much for driving up," she adds to Harry. The sense I get from her is not that we haven't seen each other for two whole years but as if I am being greeted by the hostess of a luncheon.

"Get something to drink," she tells us. "We'll talk later. My husband"— she smiles slightly at the newness of this word—"is somewhere over there."

340

She waves toward the other side of the big room. As the bride turns to her next guest, Harry and I move toward a waiter carrying flutes of champagne with a strawberry in each.

As we take a sip, an elaborately coiffed woman in a purple, pleated Mary McFadden dress comes charging up. "Linda Fay!" she exclaims, planting a kiss in the air beside my right cheek. Linda Fay was a running buddy of mine and Len's, and although we look little alike, Linda does have brown hair and brown eyes.

"It's Jamey, Mrs. Lendersdarff," I say, smiling politely. She's beaming at me. Len's mother is the kind of woman who would beam at you if you told her you'd been undergoing chemotherapy.

"Of course, yes, Jamey, yes," she says breathlessly. "It's all just too exciting, darling, isn't it, really, this *incredible* day!" She turns to Harry and extends a jeweled hand. "We're expecting Linda Fay any moment now," she explains as she grabs another champagne from a passing waiter. At long last—her two boys already "gone," as she puts it—she is finishing up what Len called "the plan," and to this she happily lifts her glass in a toast.

"To my daughter, Carling," she says, taking a small sip. "Of whom I could have used the term 'Old Maid' but never did, and now I don't have to!'"

"And what's up with you these days, dear?" she asks me. "And your husband," she adds, turning toward Harry. "What kind of business are you in—medicine of some sort, isn't it?"

"Harry and I aren't married," I say. "My ex-husband is the doctor."

Harry excuses himself and wanders over to the hors d'oeuvres table, and Mrs. Lendersdarff asks me what Harry does. I tell her that he's a writer, an English professor, and she leans over to whisper conspiratorially to me. "Shouldn't have let that other one get away perhaps, right, dear?"

"Actually, I sent him away," I tell her. And to steer her to another subject, I add that following my divorce I went to grad school and now, just like Harry, I am writing and teaching.

"Of course, of course !" she beams. "How silly of me! I remember looking over the guest list and just the other day saying to Carling that Jamey has been in school absolutely forever, hasn't she?" Her face is so pink from the excitement and the champagne that it looks as if it might explode any second.

341

Now she is glancing swiftly about the room, looking for an escape. "Well, dear. That seems like a fine way to use that journalism degree."

Journalism, in point of fact, happened to be one of the few majors, along with Sanskrit Languages, that I *hadn't* pursued as an undergraduate. No need to correct her; instead, I've got to find a way to join back up with Harry.

But there he is, his hand on my arm. Tactful and diplomatic, providing transition, he eases me out of the situation. "Well, congratulations again on this happy day," he says to Carling's mother, lightly guiding me away from the too bright globe of Mrs. Lendersdarff's face.

"Oh yes, happy, happy, happy. Carling's father and I are going to retire in Naples soon. After the dust settles here of course."

"That's lovely," Harry says. Jamey and I love Italy."

"Florida, in fact," she says, walking away, to no one in particular.

"Cath!" I call out to an old friend I recognize coming through the french doors of the club. Cathy Atherton comes over and throws her purse on a barstool. What I remember most about Cathy from college is her long fringe of eyelashes and a makeup routine that included five applications of mascara and separation of each lash with a straight pin. The whole process, only part of her extensive toilette, took a full thirty minutes, and if called upon she was able to do it using only the rear view mirror of a speeding car.

"I'm married five years now," she is telling me. "I have a little boy. We live in Lubbock."

"I'm fairly sure my life isn't as interesting as yours," she laughs.

"Wanna bet?" I laugh. "I'm a university student—back where we all started." I'm glad to be talking to Cathy and away from Carling's mother, but still I seem to be sinking in a room of faces I know but which don't seem all that familiar anymore.

"Len mentioned that cute little boy of yours in a letter," I say. "I'm envious."

"Envious of *me?*" She seems genuinely surprised.

"Sure. Everyone dreams of having a family, don't they?"

"Well, put up the books, babe." She gestures toward Harry. "Get this guy to propose."

Suddenly I am hungry, and I tell her I'm going over to get a bite. The mood today at this post-wedding party is supposed to be light, boozy, this club a place to renew old friendships. But Cathy digs her polished nails into my arm to keep me where I am standing.

"What d'ya *really* think about Carl's new husband, Jamey?" she asks.

"I haven't met him. But whoever he is, I think this whole thing is great for her." And I mean this. Carling looks less nervous than I remember her; on the other side of the room she is talking animatedly to someone whose back is to me. She even looks a little less thin, a big improvement, and I say as much to Cathy.

"She better stop there," Cathy says. "We're not spring chicks anymore; it's harder now to take it off. Of course she'll lose a bit anyway—you know, on the honeymoon!" She gives me a big wink.

"Anyway. Want to the know the whole story, kiddo?"

But I think I don't, not really. I almost never want to hear the whole story about anyone anymore, even though I am here and here I must stay at least for the moment, looking politely into Cathy's exquisitely made-up face, until I have heard the whole story.

"Okay, shoot," I say.

"They've been together for three years, on and off, she and Tyler," Cathy begins. "So about a year ago she says to him, 'Look here, Tyler, this is it in a nutshell: marry me or screw yourself.' Something to that effect, you know. 'I want a family' she tells him. Get off your duff, you know."

"Tyler's not all that long divorced, and *that* was supposed to be mondo-nasty. So he was fearful of marriage in particular, women in general." A loud burst of laughter erupts from the part of the room where the groom is entertaining a group of his old college friends, and Cathy sips from her champagne waiting for the noise to dissipate.

"So Carling, poor thing, goes to one of those video dating services on Greenville and moves into one of those kind of swinging single places in the Village. At a girlfriend's party there was where she met Tyler in the first place. So she picks this guy, from the dating service, from a photo lineup, and after about a month the two of them get engaged.

"A couple of weeks after that, the guy leaves town. Without letting her know. Canceling payment on her engagement ring. Doesn't really have any other friends around town. Just disappears.

343

"Anyway, after a while, and at least one or two serious relationships for him too, I think, Tyler phones her. Or she phones him. Or something. And he says he'd like to see her again, and when they get together, *she* tells him again that it's marriage or nothing. And he says what the hell, okay. And here they are. Kind of romantic in its own way, huh?"

"Hmmm," I say. I'm now starving. "I suppose that plenty of couples have gotten together in more complicated circumstances."

"Maybe," she says. "Maybe." Then I see that she has been waiting for a strategic moment and, as she leans closer to me, that the denouement is about to be delivered.

"Turns out he's got a very young woman he met on a business trip to Houston. He moved her here. Put her up in one of those luxury high-rises downtown."

"She's still there?" I ask.

"Oh yeah. You bet. They're buying new furniture for the bedroom after he gets back from the honeymoon." She leans even closer. "And from what I hear she may not be the *only* other woman in the picture."

"Poor Len. Hopefully she won't find out," I say. I start to add that maybe he'll change, but the kind of smile Cathy has on her face tells me to forget that notion.

"She knows already," Cathy says. "Maybe she doesn't know about the apartment, but she knows this girl's name, found out that Tyler spent the night with her after his bachelor's party."

"Good God."

"Yeah. That's what I said. Told Carl, too, said she better think long and hard before going through with the wedding. But she said, 'Cathy, I want my last name to be Warrick. I want my children's last name to be Warrick.'"

"Does he want kids?" I ask.

"He does. He's on some fast-track job; he's an accountant with some big-time firm. His boss told him a wife and kids would be an asset. The girl he keeps can't have any. Carling thinks he'll give up his old ways. Can you believe it?"

It's quite a story, so much so that I've forgotten about eating. I reach for another champagne. I feel a hand on my shoulder, and it is Linda Fay, the friend whom Carling's mother mistook me for earlier.

"Linda!" I call out in a high voice I don't recognize as mine. "I'm glad you're here."

"I'm glad to see you, too, Jamey. And I'm ready to party. Mike's out of town on business, bless his little soul. And my daughter's with my mother for a few days, bless hers."

"You look great, Linda Fay," I tell her. And she does. She is dressed to perfection in a designer suit the color of eggplant. Her nails, which she had bitten to the quick in college, are neatly manicured, and she's wearing an emerald and diamond bracelet on her left wrist.

"Well I guess it all came together for us finally, didn't it? Hey, look, Jamey, I'm going around the room, say hi to a few people, but why don't you and your—boyfriend, is it?—come have a drink at my house when this is over? I live nearby, in Richardson."

"We'd love to," I say. "Be terrific."

I walk over to say hello to the groom, Tyler, who is still entertaining his group of friends. Although Carling has written me that I have met Tyler once before, I haven't, and now here he stands before me, in his gray morning suit with a cream rose on the lapel. From up this close he looks like he did from across the room, like a thousand other guys in Dallas, blond, clean-cut, a little officious. You can tell he's good with numbers. He goes well with weddings, receptions, a house and a pool in the suburbs—all part of the package.

"Hello, Tyler. I'm Jamey Greene." He shakes my hand and for a long moment he says nothing. "Jamey. Len's—Carling's best friend from college. We lived together for a few years."

"Ah, yes," he says at last, a bulb switching on behind his eyes—one of which, I now notice, is blue, the other brown. Has Carling ever mentioned me to him, I wonder?

Harry comes up and I introduce him to the groom. "Jamey tells me you're buying a house in Carrollton, right?" says Harry. "I was born near there, lived in Carrollton as a child."

"Carrollton?" Tyler says. "Actually, no. Those were the old plans, but we're looking elsewhere. Property values are down in Carrollton at the moment." He turns away as the wedding coordinator tells him it is almost time to throw Carling's garter.

I shrug at Harry, and we both smile. A photograph is being taken, and I catch Harry's arm as we are caught in the wave of guests backing up out of the camera's range. It turns out, though, not to be Harry's arm I have grabbed but Tyler's. He snatches it away from me quickly. "I have to have my picture taken now," he says.

Flashbulbs now begin to pop around us. The bride calls for photos with her mother, with her father, with her brother, with her grandmother, with her in-laws, with Cathy and Linda Fay, with three other girls we went to school with, with teachers from her elementary school, with her neighbors at the Village, with her aunt Kirsten and her cousin Margaret. I know I want to say, need to say, something more to her before Harry and I leave for our drink at Linda Fay's. But I can't come up with anything proper. I cast about for something memorable, suitable to the importance of the occasion, some smooth transition to get us out of the club and into the elevator that will zoom us back to where we are parked far below.

I catch her as she is walking into the powder room to change into her going-away clothes. "I have so many questions," I say to her in a rush. "So many things to talk about, Len!" It comes out unconsciously, a name that no longer suits her, and it hangs in the air hollowly between us.

"But I have to be leaving now, Jamey,"—she gestures toward the throng swirling about the room—"the guests are waiting to throw rice."

"I understand," I answer. "At least tell me where you're going on your honeymoon." I wanted to think about her wherever she would be in the days to follow, picture her finally contented, with this man she had chosen for better or worse, in some place warm and exotic and sweetened with rum.

"The Caribbean," she says hurriedly, already removing the wreath of flowers from her hair. "St. John. Canille Bay, actually it's called. In the Virgin Islands."

"Yes, I know the place." The final moments of the reception are ticking by audibly. "Have a wonderful time, Carling—a wonderful marriage." Canille Bay is where I had gone on my own honeymoon, deciding on it after Len and I had pored over hundreds of vacation brochures.

"Cathy told me it was paradise," she says.

Somewhere behind us a woman, obviously Tyler's mother, says to a guest, "Can you believe it? Another Mrs. Warrick in the family now."

"Will you write me?" I ask her. But Len has pulled away, calling back to me over her shoulder. "Certainly, as soon as we get settled. When things calm down a bit."

People begin to gather at the french doors, everyone wanting their moment with Carling before the couple, hand in hand, runs out through a shower of rice. Good fortune, good children. The door to the powder room tracks automatically behind Carling, a little puff of air-conditioned air dusts my face as it closes.

I think about her last words again, standing with other guests in the foyer outside the club, waiting for the newlyweds to come out. *Cathy told me it was paradise.* I think about these words as the reception winds down, again as the band strikes up one more time in preparation to accompany the couple's exit, above the chill of the muzak-filled elevator on our way down to the lobby, a final time in our car as we wait to watch the bride and groom get into their limousine for the ride to the airport. The last I see of Carling Lendersdarff is her laughing as she struggles with her veil, blowing over her head like a halo by the wind. She has been told it is paradise.

And still Harry and I sit there, as other guests emerge from the hotel, some headed for other clubs or a bite to eat, everyone going in different directions. A few of the bride's newer friends, elementary school teachers like Carling up to two weeks ago, will journey back to their small apartments in the Village to a tv dinner and a glass of wine. Back to feed their cats, catch the evening news, and, like Carling, think about how very perfect the reception turned out to be.

The young woman who caught the bridal bouquet, without a date at the reception and minus a boyfriend at the moment, stands quietly by the main door of the hotel waiting for the valet to bring her car. A few guests remain in the club high above, quietly drinking as hotel employees begin to gather up glasses, napkins, and plates and prepare for tomorrow's reception.

Harry starts the car and we follow Linda Fay's Volvo out of the parking lot. Even she seems subdued now, as if the last thing she wants to do, despite her earlier enthusiasm, is "party." We pull up to a large house about a fifteen-minute drive away, where on a side lawn her husband has installed a putting green. She turns off the house alarm, pulls off her mink jacket, and switches on a brilliant chandelier in the cream-colored entrance hall. This home, she tells us, has exactly the kind of floor plan that Carling and Tyler intend to build when she comes back from the islands. Already Tyler has signed the contractor who designed Linda Fay's elaborate pool.

In this home of vaulted ceilings we drink a quiet toast to the newly-weds and make small talk for half an hour, while Linda and I mention more than once how great it has been to get together another time. Later tonight she is off, she informs us, to meet friends at T.G.I. Friday's, not the Greenville Avenue Friday's where we all used to hang out together in school, but a new Friday's just completed in nearby Addison. "You have to buy a membership to get a drink there," she says, "which does a lot to discourage the riffraff. And we all know each other; it's a tight group."

"Remember some of our nights at the old Friday's?" I ask her as we say our goodbyes on the her front porch.

"Oh, this one's much better," she says. "They've made lots of improvements in the design."

"And the drinks are stronger!" she shouts to us, waving, as we pull away from the house and the pool and the putting green.

"See you again!" I call out of the car. But she is halfway behind her door and probably too far away to hear me anyway. "Things change, don't they, Jamey," she had said, not a question, in those first moments after we saw each other at the reception.

Harry and I begin the long road home in the dark, me driving as he sleeps off the champagne and Linda's husband's expensive scotch. I switch on the radio in the middle of Paul Simon's "Graceland." *But I've reason to believe we both will be received. . . .*

I watch for the turnoff to Waco and Austin as I near the Dallas skyline, but the sign has been moved since I've last been here, and too late I see I am speeding past it.

A Woman at Twenty

Bruce McGinnis

They sat in the shadows on a low wooden bench built into a recess of the park wall about midway, an older man and a much younger women, almost a girl. The wall was of stone and ran beside the walk which separated the small park from the street and from the houses across the way.

The couple sat close but not touching and not looking at one another. Though obviously acquainted, they had not spoken in some time; and in the dull, slow light coming from the tall lamps at each corner of the park, a casual stroller, noting the difference in their ages, might have mistaken them for a father and his daughter.

To the west beyond the trees lay the University tennis courts and the football field, the latter vacant for almost an hour of the thudding echoes of the late afternoon practice. Beyond that, along South Main, stretched the tawdry delis and Quick-Stop grocery stores and all-night laundries that had sprouted up in the last decade to serve the increasing student trade.

From the north, the first glow of the lights from the University spread across the darkness into the park, and in the distance students moved like small dolls along the mall on their way to classes. Out in the street the rush hour had passed, and people were home having their evening meals and maybe already starting fires in the grates. The temperature, which had been unseasonably warm for so late in the fall, had turned cold in only the last week as if in sympathy with the approach of winter. The first weather front of the season had blasted into the Panhandle earlier in the week, and though it had dropped on south the next day a chill hung in the air at evening, and children no longer stayed outside to play in the soft dark as they had done all fall.

The park was deserted and pleasantly quiet, though every few minutes a car came by in the street and then moved on in the night. The wind was calm, and from the trees an occasional leaf fell straight and silent through the bare branches. On the bench the man and the girl sat stilled, staring straight ahead, as if studying the large old homes with their lighted windows. A few already wore their holiday dress, and strings of lights stretched along the roof lines and winked from the shrubbery.

Directly across from where the man and the girl were seated, a young woman opened the door of one of the houses and came out for a moment to stand on the darkened porch. She stood looking down the street toward the University as though she were expecting someone. After watching for some minutes, she stepped off the porch onto the walk and went along it to the street, where she stopped and looked again. For a time she did not move, only stood holding her bare arms against the evening chill and staring through the dark toward the lighted campus. Finally, she turned and went back inside the house and closed the door, though not before switching on the porch light and the small foot lamps that marked the beginning of the walk at the street end. Through the lighted windows on the first floor of the house the girl could see the young woman walking from room to room as if she were looking for something she had lost or misplaced. Only after she passed out of sight into the back part of the house did the girl turn and look at the man.

"I didn't mean you're insensitive," the girl said, breaking the silence. "I meant him—that he was, so don't be tacky with me."

"I'm not being tacky. It's just the irony. It's amusing to me."

"But I didn't mean it that way. I didn't mean any of the other that way either."

"I know," the man said.

"For God's sake, it's only a story. I just meant their ages and how little they understood each other."

"How's that?" the man asked.

"You know—the way she wanted one thing and he wanted something else. Like us. That's all."

"It isn't the same. He didn't love her. He only wanted her because she was young and convenient. When she stopped being convenient, he didn't want her anymore."

"And what of her?" the girl asked. "Was she so different? She was young and naive and alone in a foreign country. She couldn't even speak the language. She needed him, too. Even before the baby, she needed him. It's the same thing, don't you see?"

"Yes, I do. I also see that need is not necessarily love, though it may be a close synonym for convenient."

"You make it all sound so crass!" the girl said. "It's only a story, for God's sake!"

"But it doesn't fit. Even the details are wrong. West Texas is not the valley of the Ebro, no matter how hot and dry it sometimes gets. It doesn't fit any other way either. I don't see why you brought it up to begin with— unless, like in the story, you're trying to tell me that it's over, that it 'isn't ours anymore' and that you don't love me."

The girl was shocked. The man had never spoken to her this abruptly. She felt she had been slapped, and her pride was hurt. She could not go on. Instead, she looked at the house across the street, hoping to catch a glimpse of the young woman in one of the lighted windows. Beside her, the man sat unmoving, silent like a statue.

"But I do love you," the girl said finally. "I just don't think I can in that other way, and it isn't fair."

"But it isn't like I've—"

"Yes, it is," the girl said. "Maybe it wasn't at first, but it is now, and I won't be the cause of it. I just won't."

The girl shifted now, turning toward the man. She had been crying, and her eyes were shining with tears in the soft dark.

"I just can't be what you want me to be," she said.

"It doesn't make any difference," the man said. "It's all right."

The man had his head down, staring at the ground, and the girl could not see his face clearly. It had been a mistake to bring up the story. She saw that now, though in class it had been her favorite. And the Panhandle was too like that other place. At least in her mind it was. It had been a good story, but now he was using it to mock her, wasn't he? She couldn't tell. She did not know how he'd meant what he'd just said, and she was unsure she should continue.

Just then two cars turned south down the quiet street, from somewhere on campus, and came slowly along the park. The girl watched their approach with indifference until the sounds of their tires on the rough brick street forced her to regard them more directly. Now she wished she were in

351

one of the cars—which one did not matter, as long as it would carry her away, beyond this place. Inadvertently, she picked the one in front and then watched, first with amusement and then with increasing dejection as they reached the edge of the park and drew even with the bench. The lead car was an older model sedan, of indeterminate make and vintage; the trailing one, a Porsche. Almost as soon as the sedan passed, it turned into the drive of one of the stately homes and stopped, but the Porsche went on down the street, picking up speed as it moved until the girl could no longer see it. In her mind, however, she followed it on south to the edge of town and then around the cloverleaf to the interstate. She felt it accelerate with every gear change and saw it racing swiftly away into the night.

Rotten choice! she thought. Damn the luck!

Now the girl turned back to regard the man, who was still staring at the ground as if nothing had happened.

"But it isn't all right," the girl said, more softly this time. "It makes you sad. I know it does, and I can't stand that. I'm not being fair to you."

"I don't expect you to be. I never did. I told you that in the beginning. We talked about it, and it was all right."

"But you didn't want me then," the girl said. "Then it was all right, because it was what we agreed. But now you expect me to love you, and I disappoint you. I know I do, and it makes me feel guilty and afraid."

"Guilty of what? Afraid of what? That isn't the issue at all, you know."

Something of impatience came into the man's voice, the girl was sure of it. Now she did think him insensitive, and it made her protective of herself.

"Afraid of hurting you," the girl said. "Don't you understand! I care for you. You're important to me, but I just can't feel about you the way you feel about me. I won't ever be able to! I love you, but I can't love you in that way. I know you want me to, and I can't. I just can't, and I won't!"

As soon as she'd said it, the girl was sorry. She had spoken too harshly, and she had hurt him. She could see she had. All she'd wanted was to step back a little. His feelings for her were oppressive. He must give her room and let her breathe. She felt she was choking even now and wished again she could have been in the Porsche. She could be moving away into the night, away from all this, away from what she knew was coming. He wanted to ask her to marry him. She could tell he did, and the thought frightened her. Things had been so confused lately, and she could not understand them any longer. Now she wanted to back up, to go back to something simple. That was what she had come to tell him, but she was messing it up. She was hurting him, and she could not stand that. She searched her heart for anything that would explain what she wanted to tell him and yet let her be kind.

Everything had seemed so clear earlier when she had called and asked him to meet her. She would merely tell him how she felt and that they should not see each other for a while. But now that she was with him, it was all confused again, and she did not know what to say. Instead, she kept going back to the beginning of summer and the first time she had seen him.

She had been a student enrolled in her first college class—alone, a little afraid and unsure of herself, at twenty already out of place among the younger high school graduates. Then he had walked into the classroom and stopped in front of the lectern, the teacher she supposed, although not what she had expected. He was somewhere in his thirties, dressed in blue jeans, white shirt open at the neck, and no coat. He had started to talk without introduction, not even giving his name, and to talk with little or no enthusiasm. He seemed bored, and she found none of the pleasant formality she had expected and nothing of the warmth and assurance she needed. His manner had alarmed her at first. He was hostile, uncaring, a teacher in name only, but by the second week she had changed her mind. She felt he was special, if to no one but her. Often she found herself rethinking what he'd said about a story or poem, and she was constantly repressing the urge to laugh at the irony spiced into his lectures and at his dry wit. It was all funny to her, though to no one else that she could tell.

By the middle of the term she knew she was special to him, too. Part of it was in the way he looked at her and part in the way he said her name when he called on her in class. The attention made her feel good. She found herself looking forward to days when she would see him, and once when he had not shown up for class, her whole morning was ruined. Gradually, she sensed he wanted to ask her out, but it was a notion too absurd to consider, and she told herself that even if he did, she would not go. Then one day after class he had asked her, and she had said yes, without knowing why.

That's how it started. All he had wanted was someone to talk to. He had told her that straight out. He had not wanted involvement beyond that, and neither had she. Back then it was clear in her mind, and she accepted it. It had seemed so innocent, and for a long time it had been. Now, it had come to this. She did not know any longer. It was confused, and she wanted it back clean and simple the way it had been at the start. Somehow she had to make him see that.

"I'm still going out, you know," she said. "I'm seeing other people."

"I know," the man said. "I've always known."

"I don't plan to stop either."

"I know that, too."

"I want to do it. It makes me happy."

It was hard for the girl to say it like that, but she wanted the man to see her need to be free and without commitment.

"I said it makes me happy," she repeated. "Didn't you hear me?"

"Then by all means do it."

The man did not sound angry or upset, yet the girl heard something in his voice that made her cautious.

"But doesn't it make you jealous? Even a little?"

"No, not that."

"What then?"

"I guess it hurts my feelings," the man said. "I guess I don't want you to do it."

"That's what I'm trying to tell you. That's what I don't want you to do. I can't bear it. You want me to give over my life, but I can't do that!"

The girl looked across at the houses. She did not want to see the man's face just now, and she concentrated on the big lighted house where the young woman waited alone. What is she doing now, the girl wondered? Is she eating? Is she sitting by herself in the dark? And who had she been looking for when she came out on the porch earlier? Her husband? Her lover? Or had she come out of the house only because she could not stand being along anymore?

"You shouldn't feel that way," the man said suddenly, startling her.

He did not look at her directly when he said it, and she wondered if he had been crying. It was so sad to see what he was doing to himself.

"It's nothing you've done," he went on. "You're not to blame for the way I feel. You've only your own feelings to worry about."

"But I let you love me," the girl said. "I knew it was happening, and I didn't stop it. Now I've hurt you, and I—"

But what was the use. He wasn't listening anyway. She saw how desperate the situation was and how far it had gone. If only she had tried to tell him sooner, it would not have come to this. It was going to end badly for both of them. She could tell it was. There was no way to save it.

"I'm sorry," she said. "I'm very sorry."

The girl looked down at her hands clinched in her lap. She thought once again of the houses across the street and how shortly all of them would be strung with Christmas lights that blinked red and green and blue and orange against their brick fronts. She thought of the children inside and of the presents and the smells of Christmas cooking and the sounds of laughter and kisses and friends greeting friends. She wondered if the young woman would be putting up a tree? Would she be buying presents for her children? For anyone?

"Don't worry about it," the man said, almost as if he were talking to himself and she were not there. "It doesn't matter."

This hurt her deeply. It was such a sad thing to say. But what else could she have told him without lying. He simply did not understand. It was not that she did not like to be with him, and it was not that the times with him had not been special. They had been—the times in class and in the restaurant drinking coffee and the times together at his home. It was only that she did not want commitment. She had other friends, and they were important to her, friends nearer her own age. With them she did different things and went to different places and talked a different talk. This had been her life before the man came along, and she did not intend to give it up. She had her balance, and she knew what she wanted and what she did not want—and would not accept.

"You know," the man said, interrupting her thoughts, "I've seen this coming. When you called this afternoon, I knew what you were going to say."

"You knew?" the girl asked, uncertain what her reaction should be. "You knew all along, and you didn't tell me?"

"Yes. I've always known."

So he had. Of all the nerve! The girl felt she had been tricked, and she was humiliated. She had worried about him needlessly. How selfish of him to put her through all this.

"Why didn't you stop it before it got this bad?" she asked him, trying not to sound hysterical. "Because it would have been unpleasant for you? Because you knew that eventually I would do it for you? That's it, isn't it! Well, that's selfish, and it's cruel!"

The girl was angry now. The frustration of the last few weeks came up in her anew. She could not hold back any longer. This was a part of the man she did not know, and it made her sad and angry to see how insensitive he could be. So it was like the story after all, and he was like the man in the story, too. How could he deny it? And after all she had given over for him. She had trusted him and had continued seeing him against the wishes of her parents and the counsel of her friends. She had been such a baby before him. Now for the first time she saw her mistake. He had used her and taken advantage of her. She wanted to strike out at him, to hurt him the way he had hurt her.

"Why, damn you?" she asked, squeezing her fists together more tightly in her lap. "Why?"

The girl was crying openly, and she had to fight the urge to get up and walk away. She felt cold and had started to shake. The lights in the houses across the street seemed cold too and a long way off.

"Nothing ever stays the same," the man replied. "It had to come here before it could go anywhere else. It wasn't something I could show you until you had seen it for yourself. You were killing what we had out of blindness. You're trying to kill it even now, and you're doing it in the name of love."

"I'm here only because of you," the girl replied, angry once more and sorry she had bothered to come at all.

"That's not the point, and you know it. It's never been the point. It's not me you're worried about. It's you. You never intended to love me, and now that it's happened, you can't deal with it."

"What!"

The girl could not believe what she was hearing. How could he even think that? How could he dare to say it when he had let himself go crazy over her, and she had been the one who kept things balanced between them. It had been her level-headed thinking that allowed any kind of a relationship at all. She, in love with him? Why, it was too impossible to consider.

"It's true," he said. "It's in your voice, and it's in your eyes. You can't hide it, though you have tried. I grant you that."

"It is not true!"

"Oh, but it is."

"You're crazy!"

"No, I'm not crazy. I'm not trying to be smart either. But you're a woman, and you're in love."

"I am not in love!"

"Yes, you are, but you're so damned concerned with protecting yourself you can't see what you want."

"And you can, I suppose!" the girl said, biting her lip to keep from crying again.

"Yes, I can, and you can too," the man said. "But you're so afraid of making a mistake that you can't see you're making one anyway."

The girl was dumbfounded and then angry, all over again. What was he saying? Why, he was treating her like a child. No one had spoken to her like this before, and she would not allow it now. She would leave! But no, first she would humiliate him in the way he was doing her. In fact, what she would like to say to him just now would really hit him hard. She would like to tell him, 'You're thirty-seven years old and divorced. When you were my age, I was three years old. My god, that's disgusting!'

She wanted to say it, but she could not. He was making all that up about her loving him. It was vanity and all in his mind. He was only wishing it were so.

"You never had any perspective about yourself," the girl said, as soon as she calmed herself. "You're trying for the impossible one more time because you think you haven't got that long to find it. You believe I'm what you want and that you can use me to salvage all those wasted years. Now that you see your chance slipping away, you don't know how to handle it, and you're being ugly."

The girl had to bite her lip again to keep the tears back, and she was angry at herself because she was weak now that she needed to be strong. She was only making things worse than they were. 'Poor fool! she thought, looking at the man. 'Poor helpless old fool to fall in love with a girl half your age.'

He was like a boy, a sad lost little boy, and part of her wanted to reach out and hold him and love the sadness out of him. But she could not. He had hurt her and made her mad just to save face, and she would not!

For a long while after that, the man and the girl were quiet. The night air was colder now and a little uncomfortable, 'but what to do except bear it,' the girl thought. 'This cannot go on much longer. He must see that!'

Along the way coming from the university, a couple were walking toward them—a boy and a girl, with their arms around each other. For a time they walked in the white glare of the floodlights on the sides of the buildings, and then they came into the shadows thrown by the lights against the trees. Once they were in the dark, they stopped and kissed. They said something to each other and kissed again and then came on. They walked slowly, and were several minutes passing.

Caught up in each other's arms, the boy and the girl did not see the couple on the bench, and just as they passed the girl whispered to the boy, "I don't want anyone but you. I don't ever want anything but this."

Then they kissed again and went on. The sounds of their shoes on the sidewalk hung in the cold air and faded only when they reached the corner of the park and turned out of sight.

'That won't last,' the girl thought. 'That'll burn out and turn to ashes in her mouth. That silly little fool will wish a thousand times over she hadn't said that.'

Where they sat on the bench, close but still not touching, it seemed to the girl that the man and she were strangers. It was as if they were aware only of their individual selves and did not know the other was there. Then as if nothing of discord had come between them, the man began to talk about the people who lived in the houses across the street. He talked about how they made their living and what they did in their time off and the names they gave to their children and to their dogs. Gradually the girl forgot her anger and hurt. Something in the man's voice had calmed her.

He went on to talk about the University and himself as a teacher there and about books and writing and about ideas. He was making the world magic for her in the way he always could. She wanted to listen forever. His words were soft and warm, unlike earlier, and the girl felt warm now. For the first time since she'd arrived, she was settled inside.

But the girl felt herself weakening too, giving in to the man. That, she must not allow herself to do. She would hate herself if she did. Too much was at stake. He was working on her the way he could, trying to get her to change her mind. She saw that. She was not fooled, even for a moment. She must fight with all her strength. Anything less would be a betrayal of the brave girl in the story who had resisted the solicitations of the man she had once trusted in order to save herself and her baby.

Then the girl's attention was drawn back to the house across the street. She saw the young woman coming along through the empty rooms, now in her robe. She came once again to the front door, opened it, and looked out a last time. Turning, she switched off the porch light and the step lamps and closed the door. Now she made her way back through the lower part of the house, moving from empty room to empty room, switching off the lights as she went. Finally, the house was dark, and then a light came on for a few seconds in an upstairs bedroom and then went off again.

Suddenly, the girl was cold once more, and she began to shiver. She tried to stop herself and drew her coat more closely about her, hoping to control the strange chill that was not really the cold but yet had frozen the very blood inside her veins. She tried, but she could not do it. Now she began to shake even more and knew she was in danger of slipping off the bench onto the ground. In panic, she tried to focus her thoughts, looking for something that would bring her back to herself. Desperate, she pressed her fingers against the ragged edge of the bench, feeling the sharp, rough surface cut into her flesh until she almost cried out. Beside her, the man had stopped talking and was watching her, his eyes kind and soft in the dim light from the street lamps. The pain had brought the girl somewhat back, and she tried to meet his look without turning away.

"You do love me," the man said softly, reaching out for her just as she was getting a grip on her heart which only moments before had seemed about to leap out of her chest.

"No, I—" She tried to tell him once more, but she could not finish. The words would not come.

"But you do. Maybe you don't know it, but you do. You're twenty, and you're confused about how you feel. Anyone would be, but you don't know what's best for you because you don't know what you want. I love you, and I want you with me. Maybe I'm wrong, but I think that's what you want too, if you'd only admit it. It is, isn't it?"

"Yes," the girl said.

It just came out of her. She couldn't stop it anymore. She had not wanted to say it, yet she had, and it was like a betrayal. But a betrayal of what she could not say. She was confused, and the tears in her eyes were hot and bitter. She tried to blink them back, but she was no longer in control. Perhaps she had not been for a long time.

"It is what you want, isn't it?" the man asked again.

Without warning, something let go in the girl, something the crying had turned loose.

"Yes, dammit!" she sobbed. "Yes! Yes!"

And it was what she wanted. She knew that now, though no clouds had parted to show her the moon clearly or to reveal to her what was hers and what she had almost thrown away. But like the girl in the story, suddenly she 'knew things,' and nothing else made any difference. Nothing else was possible. It was a strange, helpless, wonderful feeling, but though it made her happy, it scared her too. She started to cry again, and then turning her face to the man, she kissed him full on the mouth, crying through the kiss and holding him around the neck as if she were afraid to let him go.

"There, there," the man said, brushing her hair away from her face, "it's all right now. It'll be okay."

"Damn you!" the girl said. "Damn you!"

Is the Other Man's Ice Really Colder?

Talibah Folami Modupe

Timmy Earl Stephens, Nathan Samuels, and Johnny Mack Williams were sitting on Timmy Earl's front porch one hot muggy day. They talked about what each planned to do when they grew up. Timmy Earl, age eleven, said if he lived to be twenty, he'd be a dentist. Nathan, age ten and a half, said he planned on being a race car driver because he loved the feel of cars and their speed. Johnny Mack, the youngest, age ten, said he wanted to be a bad ass gangsta like the men he saw on television. The three boys laughed at Johnny Mack's choice of occupation. Timmy Earl observed a large Reddy Ice truck slowly drive by them. The truck stopped at Mr. Charlie's, unloading several bags of ice; then ten minutes later the truck driver delivered several bags of ice to Old Man Mitchell's just a few blocks away. In his head Timmy Earl pondered if it was possible that the truck was indeed, delivering the same ice.

"Man whatcha thinkin' 'bout?" Johnny Mack asked.

"Timmy Earl, brang yo narrow black ass in here," his momma Ethel Mae summoned. "I need you to go and buy a bag of ice . . . and hurry up!" She reached into her bosom and pulled out exactly $1.50.

"Auh Momma, can't Marcus go? I'm busy," countered Timmy Earl frowning.

"Boy, get ta steppin' and don't forget to get tha' ice over at Mr. Charlie's; it's colder!"

"Man, we'll go with ya," stated Nathan, looking in Timmy Earl's hand to see how much money his mother pressed down.

As the three young boys started down the street in the direction of Mr. Charlie's grocery store, Nathan started, "Man, if you buy the ice from Ole Man Mitchell, that'll leave us with seventy cents," Nathan's eyes beamed.

"Man that means we can split the extra money three ways with each of us gettin' twenty-three cents!" Nathan spoke so fast as if he could hardly catch his breath. "Shoots man, we can buy candy or—or pool our money together and put down on that blue kite we saw at Levines in the lay-a-way."

"I don't know man, momma done told me ever since I been in the world that white folks' ice is colder," Timmy Earl confessed shrugging his shoulders and bucking his large brown eyes.

The three boys proceeded with their leisurely walk down the street as they observed the old, but colorful wooden houses. Johnny Mack kicked at a small rock as the three boys continued their stroll in the direction of Mr. Charlie. All the while, Nathan and Johnny Mack repeatedly tried convincing Timmy Earl that the ice was the same and that his mother would never find out. As they continued to profess, Timmy Earl slipped into a delightful daydream of firsthand events that his relatives had told him they had witnessed during their lives.

Timmy Earl remembered hearing how decades ago, during the fifties, colored folks were forced to do business among themselves. It wasn't until the government built super highways through their small neighborhoods, thus giving them an avenue to mingle with non-coloreds, that things really began to change. His uncle Marty told him that once shopping malls such as Big Town and North Park were created, colored folks stopped patronizing each other and flocked to the large malls, taking their hard-earned money with them. "Eventually, colored folks started moving away from each other and it soon built an awful wedge between them," Marty told his small nephew. "Those who fled had an awful time being accepted by people who didn't look like 'em, but yet and still, they loved being around their new friends, despite having their homes burned down, their yards set on fire, and repeated mistreatment," Uncle Marty went on.

Sara Jessica, Timmy Earl's aunt, told him of how proud the neighborhoods used to be prior to integration, with each neighbor tryin' to outdo the other neighbor in the upkeeping of their yards. "Discipline wasn't a big problem back then either," she confirmed. "Everyone disciplined everyone else's child and everyone in the community knew each other."

"Timmy Earl, Timmy Earl, we're here," shouted Nathan. "Man, what is wrong with you? We've been tryin' to get you to decide whatcha want to do." Nathan looked at his friend Johnny Mack then back at Timmy Earl.

362

"Hey cats, I'm sorry. I was jus' thanking bout something my family told me a while back," Timmy Earl smiled at his closest friends.

"So, are we gone buy Mr. Charlie's ice or Ole Man Mitchell's?" Nathan anxiously asked. "Man, I promise ya, yo momma ain't gonna know the difference," he swore, trying his best to convince Timmy Earl to walk just a few feet further.

Timmy Earl began to sweat as he looked back up the street to see if his mother was in viewing distance of them. "Well, I guess it'll be all right, let's go on and get Ole Man Mitchell's ice and celebrate. I'll deal with Mom later," he said, sticking his chest out as if he was taking charge.

After greeting Ole Man Mitchell and purchasing a fresh bag of ice, the three friends collected their change and split the difference. Remembering what Ethel Mae had said to her youngest son, he told his two friends they'd better start running before the ice melted. Upon returning home with the ice, Timmy Earl handed his mother the bag of ice and watched her closely for signs of a discovery. He handed her eleven cents which she briefly looked at and placed inside her bosom along with her other money.

"Boy, get rid of those other thugs, take yo nappy head in there and scrub yo grubby hands—dinner is almos' ready!" Ethel Mae snapped at her son without a simple thank you.

Timmy Earl bade his friends good-bye and watched them disappear behind the row of houses. "I didn't thank that ice was any different," he said out loud. "If only I could convince Momma," he said, rushing to the dinner table.

The Bird Girl

Victoria N. Alexander

I collected birds. I hoarded them, and although I sold some, I never did quite give them up really. I kept the two halves of the shell out of which each had fatally and patiently tapped its way. For every bird sold I had saved a feather. I knew every feather by name, kept them in a wooden box on my bookshelf next to my antique copy of *Hymns* and Roger Tory Peterson's *Field Guide for Birds*. Whenever a bird died I couldn't bury it. I still keep all birds, past and present, in my memory that is a crowded cage.

There was that family of mockingbirds that I possessed for one short afternoon. I'd caught the three fledglings first, easily: they were still awkward on their wings, bouncing around the yard, clumsy marionettes yanked by a capricious puppeteer. After I had their young, the parents came with angry shrieks and a sacrificial boldness. Soon they were in the cage as well. I force fed the entire brood till their crops bulged and then while dusk settled, I sang to them lovingly and low. But when I left them I forgot to latch the door and by nightfall they had escaped. It didn't matter; I imagined they were still mine. Ever since then every time I see a mockingbird I smile and greet it familiarly.

When I was growing up in Carrollton, a suburb north of Dallas, I habitually spent my afternoons recounting and remembering such things, sitting on the roof of my mother's house, leaning against the hot chimney brick, always looking out across an old stock pond that we called the lake. My red-wing blackbird sat on my shoulder, flicking his wings nervously then settled his warm breast against my skin. Looking up, up to the lightest part of the light blue sky, I could watch pigeons—specks, soaring high beyond my reach, which then folded their wings and tumbled straight down. Just before they met the ground they would open their wings again and be caught safely upon a draft like kites. These, too, were mine.

I was the "Bird Girl" to the children of the neighborhood, at least I suspected as much. The title was probable enough given the chatter that could be heard from my aviary and the fact that the red-wing accompanied me on my walks around the lake. Often this herald proceeded me onto a scene, then would light upon my head like a tongue of flame, mark me out as a local eccentric, but I didn't really mind; I wanted to be different.

In my old neighborhood, which at the time was a new development of like houses with wax-leaf hedges and lawns of plush carpet augustine, school kids used to take a short cut through our property. My mother's house was on the hill of eroding Texas black gumbo which overlooked Furneaux Creek. Riding their bikes around the hill, the kids bounced violently down the path that had become a deep gully cutting through high millet grass and wild sunflowers. Boat-tail grackles loudly protested the invasion, making a noise like short-wave radios. As the bicyclists raced through, our dogs also barked frantically behind our fence. I saw that the kids peered in between the staggered pickets. If you went quickly enough the gaps merged and you could glimpse the yard inside.

I liked to sit on that roof because I could spy on these kids as they explored what I considered my territory. I could see the entire lake, the road, and Furneaux Creek where it trickled into the lake and formed a stagnant delta. I could listen to my hookbills chattering in the flight pen. And I could keep my eye on black flocks as they ebbed and flowed between the distant mesquite trees and the ragged creek willows near the house.

Beyond the lake distant traffic on Josey Lane went, as if silently, by. Sometimes a carload of kids from the public high school, with a faint radio blaring, would pass, and though no one would likely be able to identify me from such a distance I would suddenly feel conspicuous, perched there on that rooftop, and I would look away, as if by doing so I might not be seen. I often looked to a small island in the west end of the lake.

Once when the lake had dried up in one of our frequent droughts I had walked to that island, one heat-phantomed July across peeling triangles of cracked mud, sharp as glass on my bare feet. I remember the lake bed had been littered with fish bones and ancient shells. Blue herons soared languidly over crooked trees on the island where the red-wing perched, having gone on ahead to wait for my arrival. There on the island, with the bird as witness, I buried a secret message in a box, knowing that after the rains I wouldn't be able to retrieve it until the lake dried up again in late Summer. I buried the message because I wanted to stow some ideal in an unreachable place, for preservation I guess. I half wanted someone to dig it up, though, I realized on my way home. I never went back for it. The message, I couldn't recall a only few months later, but years later I can still remember the heat of that day and the sticky syrup smell it gave my skin.

Now remembering as I looked from the rooftop across the lake, I saw a blue Buick slide noiselessly around the bend. Although at the distance I couldn't be sure, by the square headlights I guessed it was my mother's car. As the car drew closer and crossed the bridge, a clicking loose hub on the rear wheel confirmed my guess. My two dogs, a beautiful slow shepherd-collie and black terrier, also recognized the sound of that hub and ran to the gate without barking. It was Mother who fed them.

I was about fifteen then. That summer stays in my mind because it was my last summer at home, and I didn't want to leave. As I look back now I remember I fully anticipated the lesson I was about to learn, saw its inevitability, even its purpose and opposed it all the more. I rose and my wakened red-wing resumed his nervous flitting. I swung my legs over the side of the roof, placing my toes on the top of a fence post and climbed down easily; I'd done it so many times.

Fluorescent kitchen lights hummed softly. Rod, my mother's new husband, sat at a bright white table which reflected light up onto his blotchy face. He had eyes the color of weak green tea. "Hey, it's the Bird Girl," he said. The red-wing flew to the back of his chair. Rod, smiling, flicked his cigarette in the same nervous way that the bird flicked his wings. I would have rather denied that similarity, but it was there. "He don't never stay still, that bird."

I didn't reply but just looked at his grin noting that Rod had unusually small teeth. We hadn't quite come to blows yet, but then he'd only been in the house a few weeks. I took a container of raw hamburger out of the refrigerator and rolled pieces into little balls. The bird flew to my wrist to grab the food.

"How'd you train him to do that?"

"He figured it out for himself. He's hungry, and I've got the food."

"Ain't there no love in it?"

366

"I don't know." I turned on the water at the sink for the bird to bathe. He ruffled his feathers like a porcupine and with contracted pupils, he jumped into the spray of running water.

"Ha, look at that! He loves water, don't he? Ought to cover that fishtank," laughed Rod. "You staying home with your birds again tonight? It's Friday," Rod cried. "For Christ's sake, call your girlfriends, your boy-friends. You got a boyfriend don't ya? I swear girl you never go out."

The bird flew to the kitchen table, slipped on the smooth formica. He studied Rod's hand and slowly cocked his head then plucked a hang nail from Rod's thumb.

"Damn," said Rod shaking his hand. He looked at me to see if I was smiling.

"I've got a lot of stuff to do," I said.

"I gotta lotta stuff to do," he mimicked. "Broken record. Well, if you were any older I'd take you out."

I started to contradict him when I smelled my mother's soft perfume and then she came, barefoot, into the room.

"Hey, your baby here just said she wouldn't go out with me. My heart's broke." Rod took up his pack of Winstons and shook out a cigarette. My mother hesitated then turned down the hall. Rod laughed to himself. "She don't care."

I followed her, and the red-wing preceded us both into the living room where he waited for us perched on a lamp shade. My mother sat down on the sofa, then swung her legs over the back, letting her head hang upside down. Her black hair fell onto the carpet in silky folds and blood rushed to her face. The living room was my mother's favorite room. It was cool and faced north. The only bird cage it had in it was an empty ornamental one. I suppose I wasn't the nicest kid to live with, my will being strong and hers so malleable. She threw back her arms and let her hands lie limp on the carpet. "Rod probably wants me to get dinner."

"Tell him you don't want to."

She sighed. "Maybe he won't be around long, his diabetes. I'll keep feeding him all that junk food he likes."

"That would be murder," I said dryly.

"Storm tonight," she said after a while.

"Think so?" I looked out the window. The weather had changed. Rod always said Texas weather was like a woman. But I noticed that the sky was now the color of his eyes. "Must be the one they had on the gulf last night," I said as Rod came into the room.

"She's a wicked one," he said with pleasure.

"Funny how we name our storms after women," remarked Mother.

Rod didn't think so. I stared out the window watching the orange reflection of the burning end of Rod's cigarette rising and falling.

The storm hadn't fully run its course by the following afternoon. I looked up at the windy sky and greedily inhaled the rain-washed air. The trees in the thicket groaned. Thinking of the May hatchlings that might have been thrown from their nests, I said aloud, "Down will come baby cradle and all." I had never realized 'til then how menacing that lullaby was. I was glad my mother was good enough never to have sung it to me. Ironically though, I was actually hoping that the storm had been too much for some tattered nest and that there would be some poor bird to save.

As I went down the slope I stepped carefully, folding down the sticker grass under my bare feet. Out of the corner of my eye I noticed something black and I froze, expecting a grackle to spin off into the sky. But this one didn't. It remained for a suspiciously long moment, then only took a lazy hop away.

The bird was dying. I knew. I knew immediately by the powdered dullness of her feathers, which should have been sleek and iridescent. I knew by the frayed edges of her long flights and tail. I knew by the way she slowly blinked.

Too ill, probably, to be frightened, the bird stood still. I stepped closer then stopped and said, "Hello," as though I were giving her a moment to recognize me. I moved my right hand slowly toward her while she balanced precariously on a reed. I almost touched her, but suddenly she fluttered away and flew fifty yards low over a field. I followed, this time neglecting to fold down the prickly grass. I reached the bird, but she flopped away again, less this time, and again with waning energy. Finally, I caught up to her. She stood still panting on the ground. I moved my right hand over her head and scooped her up with my left. I had her.

I sat down in the field, rocking, holding the bird against my throat under my chin. I could feel her pulse against mine.

When she began to calm, I took her down to the creek. There I knelt and squeezed the sides of her beak, forcing it open. I let drops of water roll off my fingertip into her throat. She swallowed one, two, three. Then water bubbled out of her nostrils. Her eyes were black and bold as she stiffened, and then her head went limp.

I sat there for a long while blankly contemplating her. I shouldn't have done that, but she would have been dead by nightfall anyway. At least I had known her. I thought with a little cleaning up she might again be beautiful, large for a female, probably four, five years old. I would save her and eventually have her preserved, like I planned to do with the others. My father had hinted that he would help with the cost. I hadn't gone through with it yet because there were some birds that would not make good "trophies," as the taxidermist had said, some that had died after long illnesses that left them balding or disfigured in some way. What I would do with these, why I kept them, I hadn't quite figured out.

I went to my aviary and for several hours I sat watching a swirl of feathers and dust in a corner, and listening to the chorus drone on. I would remember that grackle. My mother always complained that I loved birds more than people. I wanted them, that's true. I liked to sing to them in my weak off-key voice. But did I love that parakeet with rickets that had been thrown out of its nest? Mother Nature knows best—Rod had said, always ready with his proverbial wisdom—but I wanted to save the bird. I gave him calcium drops and taped his leg to make it grow straight. I remember watching over the bird as he lay on his breast in an incubator box. Lapis lazuli and white shell markings lined his broad wings and his tapering blueblack tail, like a pharaoh's sarcophagus. "Keep still," I had told him and closed the lid to the dark box.

Hours later when I went to check up on him I found that he had chewed off his own toes, tortured, I guess, by the bandage. I had to swallow hard against a rush of nausea. Was it my fault? Why did I have to ask myself questions like that so soon?

369

Dusk had fallen. The sky was deep pink. Suddenly I realized it was late and that outside the dogs were barking. I opened the door and yelled, "Watcha got guys?"

The dogs looked back, whimpered and resumed their barking. I went to the gate and let in a boy of ten or so. "Call off your dogs," demanded the boy. "I found a sick bird." As soon as the boy was inside the fence the dogs began wagging their tails, their slobbery wide-open jaws grinning.

"They'll only lick you to death," I said laughing. "Let me see."

Cupped in his small sweaty hands this boy held a week-old robin with a bright yellow mouth. "A robin," I said happily. "The storm, it must have fallen in the storm."

"You're the girl with the birds, right? Can you help a sick bird?"

I started to say yes positively, but hesitated and admitted that I could only try. I led the boy through the yard to the aviary. He told me his name was Simon. I smiled and sent the dogs back to their patrol, to beat over and over the same path through the yard, criss-crossing around the maple trees. "They seemed so mean," said Simon.

I opened the aviary door. It was crowded dim and dusty. I turned on the light. Feathers were floating in the air like constellations. The birds were chirping quietly as crickets at dusk. Simon let out a small cry. I sat down at a wooden table among a clutter of books, papers and half-empty seed bags. The boy laid his bird on the table. It was shivering and lethargic, slumped back on its tailbone, legs in the air, its delicate feet clutching at nothing like dying spiders.

"Sometimes it's better to leave babies on the ground so the parents can continue to feed them," I said. "Just the shock of a diet change can kill them. But then again there're the snakes."

"How do you know what to do?" asked Simon.

"I'm not sure anymore," I said sadly.

"Why can't we feed him like his parents would?"

"His parents regurgitated worms and blueberries for him or her—I can't tell yet."

The bird gathered its energy to gape wildly for a moment then it fell back again into a lump and began to twitch.

"Can you tame a robin?"

370

"Yes, but who will teach it to sing?" I teased. "I wish I could but I'm awful."

"Oh, he'll know how," replied Simon so assuredly I had to smile.

"Watch this." I tapped the table to rouse the grotesque blind, blue-bulb-eyed bird. Its mouth sprang open and I stuffed a ball of warm mash into its throat. It swallowed with violent spasms, then lay its heavy head again on the table.

As we left the aviary I turned out the light and one last chord rang out. I told Simon that every time the light went out all the birds chimed once in unison. If I turned the light on and off they would do it again. We tried the experiment more than once. Simon guessed that they did it to let each other know they were still there in the dark. "Yes, I suppose they need to do that," I said. I agreed to take care of "Robin" and Simon promised to stop by after school every day to check on its progress.

On the horizon deep evening blue had pressed the magenta into a thin band. One of the dogs was chasing sparrows out of the honeysuckle. The sparrows scampered out of their violated beds and flew right by us in small bursts of wind. "It's late," Simon cried worriedly. I said goodbye to Simon and as I watched him walk away I realized he had not asked my name.

In bed that night the Bird Girl lay in the center of her big bed. I lay in a fetal position with a feather pillow tucked between my legs and against my belly. Without that pillow I could not sleep. It had taken the place of a dirty stuffed raccoon, which had taken the place of my infant blanket. I listened to my heart beating in my ear. I wondered if my heart ever got tired. Did it really rest between beats? Had I left the red-wing out of his cage? That robin should be fed every six hours. Tomorrow I would have to change the corn cobs in the main flight pen. Someday I wanted to see California. Who would take care of the birds? I couldn't get just anybody. Had I set the alarm?

At noon my bedroom was still as dark as midnight, the windows being hung with thick curtains. My poor birds were probably starving, but guiltily I was glad of the sleep. I stumbled into the kitchen where my mother was watering a plant hanging over the fish tank and Rod was eating his lunch. I remember I stood staring at the white table, absently playing with loose birdseed in the pocket of my flannel robe, when I heard my mother scream, "Your bird's dead." I can see myself grabbing the drowned red-wing out of the fish tank and falling to the floor, holding the soggy body to my breast crying, trying not to think about the ludicrous way the bird had looked floating, head curved downward, feet stiff and straight. Rod stood over me with a joke on the tip of his tongue.

"Do you want me to bury him, honey?" he finally asked with a forced frown.

I thought about the frosted dull pastel boxes in the freezer that had once contained perfume, soap or other little birthday gifts. "No, I'll put him with the others."

"You can't anymore," said Rod.

"Why not?"

"Honey, I couldn't have all those birds in my freezer. We...," my mother faltered.

I stood up, tightened my belt and left the room.

"You got to tell her," I heard Rod saying. "If you don't I sure as hell will. She can go live with her father."

I would go. The aviary would be torn down, by Rod himself, with his own hands. I don't think he condescended even to use tools. I would give some birds away to the neighborhood schools. Others I would simply let go.

I kept only the robin because she was too young to desert. I never caged her nor clipped her wings. So she too was eventually lost, making a bold dash out an opened door on a cold night in some place that wasn't home.

I went down the hill holding my drowned bird that had literally fallen from the skies for me. I stopped at the creek. Before all the new houses in the area had been built Furneaux Creek had run fast and straight. But its course was changed. It now ran wide and muddy and flooded the thicket with every rain. The water knitted strands of grass and twigs around the trucks of skinny willows. Brown fringed foam idled about the clumped grass. I wouldn't sit on the roof with a blackbird on my head anymore. They might stop calling me the Bird Girl. I tossed the bird in the water and turned and ran so as not to hear the "plunk."

Joan and Olivia

Sallie Strange

I picked up Mother first. It was her birthday, and my sister and I were taking her out to dinner. That was the night—Mother's birthday—I first noticed that funny thing about Joan. She kind of faded away. It's hard to describe, but I saw it myself. She disappeared as she opened her front door. Of course, I was really surprised.

Joan has always done what I thought were funny things, but never anything like that. I've always thought she was kind of funny—even peculiar—partly, I guess, because she and I are so different. Our names show that. She was named after Joan Fontaine. You know, the blonde, thin, kind of pale actress, who was popular way back when. And I was named after Olivia de Havilland, who was dark-haired with apple cheeks and full lips. They were sisters too, though they were born in China. To a missionary, I think.

Mother used to be a movie freak. Now she's a TV freak. Mother's eighty-one and in one of those senior citizens' homes, where they let you keep your old bedroom suite, including the TV, and fix your meals for you in the dining hall, which is nice.

Anyway, at precisely 5:00 I picked up Mother, and at 5:30 I pulled up in front of Joan's house—she rented it, same little house for twenty years. I went to the front door and rang the bell. Mother waited in the car.

Of course, I stood outside the screen door. I didn't wait long—a minute?—I saw the front door open, but I couldn't see Joan, couldn't see anybody. I knew Joan must have opened the door because her cat sure couldn't have and I had not touched the screen door much less the knob to the wooden one. So I said, "Joan?" just to make sure that everything was all right in there. Then I saw something in the opening of the door, a kind of smudgy, dark line where an artist would have drawn a line if he had been drawing Joan, life-sized. And I could make out a kind of yellow glow around the top and sides of where he would have drawn her head.

I could see right through her. I saw the spindly little table and the old fashioned mirror—she liked antiques—that were in the entryway right inside the house. And in front of those was where I saw the outline of Joan with the halo where her head would have been. I could see over the halo too because Joan was short, about five one. I'm five seven. Big-boned, Mother always said.

"I'm ready," Joan said, and as the screen door opened, I dropped back and she passed through the doorway onto the stoop. I could see her better there, like she had gone from completely see-through to almost real. I saw her lean forward and close the front door before shutting the screen door. As she went ahead of me down the walk and into the sun, I began to see her like you're supposed to see people.

"You looked kind of funny back there when you opened the door," I told her.

Turning her head slightly toward me, she said, "I think I've lost a few pounds."

I started to say that she was going the wrong way where weight was concerned—she was even skinny as a baby—but I didn't want to start that up again, especially on Mother's birthday. So I said, "It was more than that." I didn't know what was going on, but I figured she did. After all, it was her doing it. It was really more than funny. It was weird and kind of irritating. I was sorry she had done it.

"My new dress," she suggested as she opened the car door and got in.

Her dress was light-colored—paler than summer squash, but not as green as winter squash, kind of like the inside of an eggplant. I'm a gardener, vegetable gardener. I always have liked to be outside, so I worked in the yard a lot, and when the children left home, I took gardening up in earnest. I don't have any use for roses and stuff like that. You can eat vegetables, and they come in all colors, so there's no comparison in my mind. And I like vegetable colors, bright colors, especially orange and red. That's another way Joan and I are different.

I was going to push the issue and get some answers from her, but by the time I got around the car and got in, Mother was saying, "— what phones are for. You pick them up and you say, 'Hello.' I thought everybody knew that. They are not for not answering, everybody knows that." Mother was staring out the windshield.

"Yes, Mother." Joan leaned forward and patted Mother on the shoulder.

Joan thinks all you have to do is say, "You're right" or "I'm sorry," then pat you on the shoulder or arm, and everything is just fine. It's not easy being a sister to somebody who thinks like that. That's Joan's problem. She never does anything, just kind of hangs around—sometimes with that innocent Joan Fontaine smile on her face—and thinks she's doing something. And whenever there's any trouble, she pats you.

We ate at the Black-eyed Pea on Winchester. That was my suggestion. It's a family-type restaurant, which I like, and they always have ten vegetables on the menu, and you choose two to go with your chicken and dumplings or whatever meat you're having. And you can have biscuits or cornbread too. Mother likes the Black-eyed Pea. She used to cook like that for us. And I like it, wholesome. I don't know what Joan likes to eat. Air, I guess.

During dinner Mother talked. That's usually been the way with us— Mother talks and we listen. Or at least I think Joan listens. She says, "Uh-hunh" and "Oh" and things like that. I kind of wing out. It's just not interesting to me. It used to be movie stars Mother talked about, now it's TV. And she used to swoon over movies, but now all she does is complain about TV. The soaps are all 'depraved'—that's her word—and the talk-shows are an 'abomination.' Of course, she's right, but I think she just watches so she can gripe about them. And then she doesn't have anything else to do. That's the reason I took up gardening. That's Joan's problem too. She doesn't have anything to do because she doesn't have any interests, never did have unless you consider Harrison Killigrew an interest, and that had been over for more than ten years as far as I could tell.

When Mother paused to take a bite of cornbread, I jumped in. "Which reminds me," I said to Joan, "how's Harrison? I suppose you're still working at his store." Then she started to do it again. She kind of flickered. It's distracting to have someone do that, especially when you don't know when they're going to do it. I wanted her to stop it. Twice is two times too many. When she came back, I saw she was giving me that look. Joan liked to give the impression that she was all honey and sugar, an impression that Mother usually bought, but it's far from the truth. I should know. I grew up with her and had to put up with all those dirty looks. I was her big sister.

Then she said, "How kind of you to ask." Her voice had an edge to it, but then she lowered her head and pushed her green beans around with her fork.

Joan quit her job at the library when she was about thirty and met Harrison. She told Mother she was tired of working in the library and wanted to change careers and work in antiques and had gotten a job at a fancy antique furniture store in the Oak Lawn area. Of course, Harrison Killigrew just happened to be the owner of that store, so I went there to size him up and I sure did. Harrison was one of those smooth charmers, the kind that kisses your hand. He was married. And he had four school-aged children.

You can bet I brought the subject up with Joan, but she put on that innocent look and denied what I knew to be the truth. Then Mother got in on it and tried to defend Joan though I could tell she disapproved too. That's another trouble with Joan—she just lets things happen to her, when she didn't need to. Joan was very pretty—if you like the pale, delicate type—and plenty smart—got her Master's in Library Science. But she didn't do anything about it, didn't use it, didn't act.

For about ten years everything went along all right—if you call having an affair with a married man with four children all right—because they snuck around and business was evidently good. Then some developers bought the old house where Harrison had his store for a fabulous price—at least, it was fabulous according to Joan—so he moved to one of those strip shopping districts in the old raggedy part of East Dallas. Of course, Joan tagged along. That's when she rented that little house, and Harrison gave her that rickety table and mirror in her entryway that she was so proud of.

A couple of years after the move, I went by the store, just to check it out because Joan seemed, well, kind of more listless than usual. I didn't see any need because there's nothing to do about a woman who throws her life away like that on a man, no matter how charming he is, but Mother kept bugging me, so I did. I waited 'til one day when Joan went over to Mother's for lunch because I didn't want to run into Joan while I was doing my detective work.

376

Everything at this store was different from the one in Oak Lawn. Now it was not antiques, but second-hand stuff, stuff you find at garage sales after all the good stuff has been bought. Also Harrison had changed and it wasn't just that he had got old. He looked worn out and dusty, like his merchandise, and his voice— Well, I wouldn't have known it was him except he came out of the back of the store like the owner would. I didn't say anything to him that time. Just looked around and left.

As I watched Joan—she was sitting to my left—push those green beans around with her fork, I got annoyed. I could see what she was doing— avoiding me like she always had, avoiding me like she had everything else. So I posed the question again, "Are you still working for Harrison?"

Joan lifted her fork from her beans and stuck it into the mash potatoes and began making swirls.

My question caught Mother's attention, moved her from the lighted tube world into ours. Mother really does care. It's that she likes the world of make-believe better than the one she happens to live in.

"Of course." Joan glanced briefly at me, and when she did, it happened again. This time she did not flicker. She just went out like a burned out light bulb. I blinked my eyes hard, then could see the smudge and the halo.

"Why shouldn't she?" Mother was challenging me from across the table. I looked at Mother, who was saying, "It's her job. I wish you two girls wouldn't—"

I took a chance and glanced again to my left. Joan was still de-materialized. I took a drink of water and blinked hard again, then picked up on Mother's voice. "What do you expect her to do? Jobs don't grow on trees. Just yesterday on *Oprah*—"

My thoughts went back to my visit to the dingy, dismal store, and to my visit there the next day, when I was determined to make Joan see what she was doing with her life. I didn't even tell Mother what I had found. I just called Joan and told her I was coming to the store to take her to lunch. She tried to put me off, but I would have none of it. So I went that second day into the store and this time met Harrison and shook his hand and told him I was Joan's big sister and looked him straight in the eye to show him I was no pushover, but a person to be reckoned with.

Joan and I ate sandwiches at a greasy-spoon on the corner, and I told her what I thought. "You're past forty-five," I said. "What are you going to do with the rest of your life? Harrison can't be making a living for himself and his wife. What makes you think—"

"His wife divorced him last year," she said.

That took me aback. "Are you going to marry him?" Then the other thought struck me and I gasped. "You have married him."

She shook her head. She had cut her hair quite short. It hung limp around her skull. She had lost weight. Her skin was colorless.

"You need to see a doctor," I said. Then I almost leaned across the table and took her hand, but I didn't. "I'll make an appointment for you with Dr. Kraus. I'll take you."

She shook her head.

"Get another job. Go back to the library." I found myself pleading with her.

She shook her head again, then looked down at her plate.

"Joanie." I took her hand. "Please. Please."

Her hand was limp in mine. She did not look up. I dropped her hand. Joan and I finished our sandwiches in silence. Then I walked her back to the store, told her to call me, and left. When I got home I called Mother and told her that the store did not look prosperous but that it was probably doing all right and told her that Harrison had divorced his wife. Mother was delighted at the news and thought that now Joan would get married. I hated to tell her different, but I did.

"Did you hear me, Olivia?" Mother was speaking from across the table.

I raised my eyes to look at Mother. I was afraid to move, to look anywhere else. I was afraid even to say anything, to do anything. I was afraid that one wrong word, the slightest change in my tone of voice, the blink of my eye might cause Joan to vanish completely so that there was not even a smudge or a halo.

"And you." Mother was looking to my left. "I want you to answer the phone when I call. I don't care about anybody else who calls, but when I call I expect you to answer the phone. And if you don't know whether it's me or somebody else, you pick up the phone anyway, and then if there's somebody else on the line, you can hang up." She looked around the restaurant. "I'm ready for my ice cream and cake—the way it's supposed to be."

I had not taken my eyes off Mother. A hand intruded itself into my line of vision. It was holding a gift-wrapped package. I heard Joan's voice, "Happy birthday, Mother." I watched carefully as Mother took the package and saw quite clearly Joan's hand move out of the frame. My eyes moved to where I thought her hand had gone and saw it, still moving. It collapsed on her lap, bony fingers attached to a bony wrist on a no-color dress. I moved my eyes to her body. I could see nothing but the ridge of her thighs and the ridge of her shoulders. She had no breasts. My eyes moved up. Her hair, longer now, was the same no-color as her dress. She wore no make-up but grey eye-shadow. Her skin was so transparent I could see the throb of a blue vein in her temple, could recognize the bone around the socket of her eye.

"How nice!" Mother was smiling. She lifted the lid of the box and smelled, then looked up. "I wish they wouldn't put cellophane on powder boxes, but," she put the lid back on, "I'm sure I'll like it. I still love body powder." Then she looked at me.

At first I didn't get it because I was thinking about Joan, wondering if she was cold when she disappeared like that. Then Mother said, "Well, Olivia." And I remembered and took the envelope out of my purse and handed it to her.

"It's a year's subscription to *TV Guide*," I explained. She pulled out the card and read it.

"What lovely daughters!" she said, and we ordered ice cream and cake.

When I got home I went straight to the phone to call Mother before *NYPD Blue* came on. It's one of her favorites. She's keeping what she calls a smut-count on it. Every week she writes down the dirty words and describes the dirty scenes. I wanted to talk to her because after I dropped her off it occurred to me that she had kept talking to Joan when she disappeared that third time. So, I figured, Mother didn't notice she was talking to a vacant chair or she could still see Joan. I decided just to hint at it to Mother. I don't like to alarm old ladies if there isn't any reason to.

I began nonchalantly, "Mother, did you notice anything odd about Joan when I asked her if she was still working for Harrison?"

"No," she said, and I heard her yawn. "I wish you girls wouldn't quarrel. Especially on my birthday."

"Did you look at her?" I said.

"What kind of question is that?" Mother said.

"Did she stay there in her chair or fade away?"

"What did you say?"

I raised my voice, "Was she in her chair like she was real?"

"I declare, Olivia, I don't know what you're up to, but Joan and you are both my daughters and I do wish you would try to get along on my birthday. Besides that, it's one minute to nine, and I haven't warmed up the TV yet. I've got to go. Nighty-night." She hung up the phone.

I didn't want to mention the problem to Phil because I knew what he would say and I didn't want to hear it, but I did, hadn't any choice. Who else could I tell about it? He was surfing the Internet, of course. It was after dinner, wasn't it, and before his bedtime. So I pulled a chair up next to him and told him I needed five minutes of his time. He did look at me and I told him what Joan did. He said exactly what I knew he would, "Olivia, you know better than that," and turning back to the computer, clicked the mouse three times. That's Phil for you.

The next morning I knew what I had to do. I had to get to the bottom of this, so after I watered my tomato plants, I got in my car and drove to Harrison's store.

A bell jingled when I opened the door, and about a minute later Harrison appeared from the back of the store. He came down what might be called an aisle through the junk and just looked at me. When I reminded him who I was, he nodded. Skin hung in folds from his chin. He needed a shave.

"I was in the neighborhood and thought I would drop in and see Joan," I said.

"Oh?" He looked confused.

"Joan does still work here, doesn't she?" I was suddenly alarmed.

"Oh, yes," he said. "But sometimes when we aren't busy, she doesn't come in 'til late."

"And you pay her? You make enough to pay her?"

He smiled and for a second I could see the charmer that I had met twenty-five years ago.

"Olivia. It is Olivia, isn't it?"

I nodded.

"I inherited some money. Several years ago. And I invested what I made from the Oak Lawn sale. I gave some to my wife when she told me she wanted a divorce. I don't need much. I give Joan enough. You needn't concern yourself about that, Olivia."

"It's just that—" I shook my head. "Something— I think I'll drop by Joan's house."

"She'd like that," he said and opened the door for me.

I rang Joan's front door bell twice, then walked around the house looking for a window where the blinds were raised or tilted upward. But there were none. The back door was locked. The door to the attached garage was locked. I rang the front door bell again, then turned and looked at the neighboring houses. All renters, I knew, and Joan never mentioned talking to any of them.

I started to go home, then changed my mind and went by Mother's. She was in her rocker, watching TV. I asked her if she had talked to Joan last night or this morning. She sighed, muted the TV, and said, "Don't start in on Joan again; besides, I've started a list on *Carnie*. I think she's the worst." She glanced at the TV.

"Mother." I pulled the occasional chair over and placed it between Mother and the TV and sat on it. "Joan's not at work and not at home. Have you talked to her since the dinner?"

"I called her," Mother said.

"When?"

"Last night after *NYPD Blue*. That detective and his girl friend got it on in somebody's apartment. Nude." She nodded emphatically.

"And what did Joan say?"

"She didn't say anything because I didn't talk to her. Just called her."

"She didn't pick up the receiver," I prodded.

Mother rummaged through some papers on the table beside her rocker, picked up one, and held it toward me. "I wrote it down. I always write it down when I call Joan so I can tell her when she doesn't answer. Well, I wrote it down but it didn't happen the way it usually does. Last night— Here. I'll read it to you. 'Call Joan at 10:02 P.M.' So after I wrote it, I did it. It rang four times, then the ringing stopped. I didn't hear her lift the receiver or anything like that. It just stopped. I was sleepy anyway, so I went to bed."

"Do you have a key to her house?"

"I used to. I used to have a lot of things I don't have any more. After Daddy died—"

I got up. I didn't have time for this. "Then the answer is 'no'."

"Harrison used to have a key. Back when— You know."

"I know."

I moved the chair back against the wall.

"She not answer the phone when you called, or the ringing stop?" Mother said.

"Neither." I was at the door. "I went by her house and tried to rouse her, but I didn't hear anything. Not even the cat."

"Well, you wouldn't hear a cat, would you? A cat's not a dog." Mother turned up the sound on the TV.

I went back by the store and told Harrison what had happened and asked if he had a key. He did, he said, but it was at home. He would close up the store—it was lunchtime, anyway—get the key, and meet me at Joan's.

He drove up to Joan's house in an old car. Most of the paint had worn off the trunk. He had to push against the door with his shoulder to open it. He moved slowly up the walk to the front door, where I was standing, key in his outstretched right hand.

"I've forgotten," he said, "whether it goes in rightside up or upside down."

"I don't think Joan is well," I said. "She's too thin, too pale."

"My wife said she had the Death Virus and infected me with it. That's the reason she divorced me, she said. So she wouldn't catch it."

"Death Virus?"

He nodded, dropping his hand with the key. "I thought Cary Ellen was just jealous. But then— After I moved the shop, it was like nothing went right. The merchandise, the customers. Even had a leak in the roof. For three years, they tried to patch the leak in the roof and couldn't, so I gave up and started using a bucket. Still use it. And Joan— Well, that didn't go right either after the move. Maybe I was asking too much, you know, but there was like a fog between us. Then Cary Ellen got sick. That's when she told me about the Death Virus. She said I had it and she wasn't going to stay around and get more infected that she was. So she divorced me." He held the key out, saying, "You think I got it? The Death Virus?"

I took the key and opened the door.

"That Hepplewhite mirror and Sheraton table are gems, aren't they?" he said. "I gave them to Joan when she moved in here."

We walked through the beige living room, its sofa and coffee table and chairs and TV neat and clean, through the empty dining room and into the kitchen.

"I'll check the garage. Her car," he said, going out the door.

There was nothing on the counters, on the stove, in the sink. I opened the refrigerator and found a carton of milk, bread, margarine, mayonnaise, peanut butter, and a package of cheese slices. In the freezer were two small TV dinners.

Harrison returned to the kitchen. "Nothing there." He closed the door behind him. "I mean, the car's there. Keys on the nail where she always kept them. I checked the trunk."

I went down the hall, Harrison following. I looked in the open door to the guest room and saw Joan's bedroom suite from our childhood, ivory French Provincial. On the other side of the hall was the bathroom. There on one side of the basin were a toothbrush, toothpaste, a brush, and gray eyeshadow. On the other was a bottle of hand lotion.

The door to her bedroom stood ajar. I pushed through it. Her cat, a long-haired, orange tabby, looked up from his nap on the frameless bed. Against the far wall stood his litter box, water bowl and dry-food dispenser. The easy chair was empty, the floor light beside it off. The phone rested, receiver properly cradled, on top of two phone books on the table beside the chair.

I opened the closet. Nothing seemed out of place.

I looked at Harrison, standing just inside the doorway. "I don't know what to think," I said. Out of the corner of my right eye, I saw something move from the bed toward the door. Did it go out behind Harrison and out of the room?

"Maybe my wife was right," he said. "Maybe the Death Virus just disintegrated her so that she disappeared. Vanished. Gone." He raised his hands, then dropped them.

I closed the closet door. "I guess I should call the police," I said.

"I think that's what you're supposed to do." He moved to the bed and petted the cat, who began to purr. "I think I'll take Ralph with me." He hesitated and looked at me. "If you don't want him."

"Take the cat," I said, "but leave a note. If Joan comes home—"

Harrison turned his head and stared at me.

I called the central police station and told the woman that my sister seemed to be missing. She asked me what I supposed were pertinent questions and said she would call me if she had any information about Joan.

Harrison was still standing by the bed, his hand on the cat. "I don't know what else we can do," I told him. "I'll let you know if—" I got the notepad out of my purse, wrote my name and phone number on it, and held it out to him. He picked up the cat and took the piece of paper. "In case you hear anything."

Then I wrote a note to Joan saying that Harrison had Ralph and that she should call me immediately. "I'll put this under the magnet on the refrigerator door," I said. "That's where we left notes when we were children." Something swelled in my throat.

Harrison followed me out the door, down the hall, and into the kitchen. While I put the note on the refrigerator, he opened a cabinet and got down a sack of cat food.

He started toward the door to the living room, carrying the cat and his food. I stopped him. "Your key," I said.

"You keep it," he said, pushing through the swinging door.

"When she comes back—" But I heard Harrison's footsteps already on the tile in the entryway, then the screen door open and shut.

I saw the movement again. Something seemed to slide out through the swinging door. "Joan?" I spoke softly.

Then I pushed through the door, walked through the dining room, through the living room, started out the door and stopped. I turned and spoke into the house. "I'm sorry. I wish I knew what to do."

I closed the door behind me and locked it. I sighed. Was that all it amounted to? All those years? I started down the walk and concentrated on the important question—What was I going to tell Mother?

Yardman

Marshall Terry

He could hear the roar of the traffic on the expressway just blocks to the east, but it was nice to be out in the trim circle driveway and swatch of yard and curb strip of Asian jasmine which seemed a haven, a safe harbor, on this busy street on this spring evening.

Carefully he picked a small volunteer tree sprig out from the creeping jasmine bedded in dark mulch, then was sorry he had, for the tiny one-leaf plant had been ambitious: already it bore a shell-cracked full green acorn. He threw it on the growing pile of leftover leaves, thatch and of the cigarette butts, flattened paper cups, smushed wrappers and other detritus from the careless passersby of the street, now so much more busy than it had been when he first worked out front here just a few years ago. A passing car honked. He waved. He was brown as a nut and wore an ancient shirt and jeans and old cracked work shoes. He did not know if the person in the car recognized him or was just honking at the phenomenon of work being done along the street at this hour of the evening, and it did not matter in the moment, now.

He picked up the rake and began to thatch again the tough St. Augustine sod in the oval of lawn the circular driveway had left of the former large front yard. The pebbly brown and bluish surface of the driveway was pretty, but it had made him sad to see it poured, though he had rescued some of the grass and used it to help resod the back yard whose many tree branches made the grass grow thinly and die out despite the new plastic-headed sprinklers that piped the water to it. So much technology now yet it seemed to have so little helpful effect, to his mind anyway, on growing grass, on solving the problems of streets, of all the people packed together, of the economy, of the city.

He would lower the blades of the Honda mower in the garage, having raked for thatch, and cut this piece of yard in a day or so, or next week, when he could get to it. Then fertilize it. Technically you should fertilize in early spring after the second mowing, but sometimes now he found himself cutting corners, speeding up processes, just doing what he could when he could, with yard and grounds and many other things.

He looked at the trim house, no mansion but a nice one and saw the lady of the house wave to him through the front window, then make gestures in the form of asking if he would like a drink of water. He waved back to her—a nice lady who had been happy to have this circular driveway put in on this busy street for the sake of herself and her friends, and who was right, for it was very practical given the situation—and gestured no, he did not require water.

He took a black plastic trash bag and zipped it open and knelt with it beside the pile of debris. He half-filled it handful by handful, then sat back from it in a squat on his haunches, pushing the straw hat back on his head. He was part Indian, indio, and could sit like this for a very long time, with or without a wall behind him. Sometimes it was better to have a wall behind you, but sometimes it was not. He laughed. Now the cars were jamming up on the street. The traffic signals two blocks down just a block from the expressway often would become mis-timed. If the lady of the house saw the stack-up of cars she would rush to the phone to call and complain to the city. That was a chief pleasure of the people of this great metropolitan area, complaining to the city about problems large and small. And why not, that was still just, in this society. *Res publica*, what was it, *civitas*?

Now the traffic moved, and thinned. A dark blue Cadillac went by, slowed and nearly stopped. He stood up to see if it would stop, but it accelerated and went on: a large Fleetwood Brougham, the automobile no doubt of an important person. He would have to finish here now, and haul this trash to the back and stack the rake and broom in the garage.

If some of the master planners of this city had their way this street would become even more a thoroughfare, leading to the rebuilt expressway. That was inconsequential next to the need for widening the expressway and attempting to run light rail transport north and south along it. There were people who worked downtown in this city who used three or four hours of their lives each day passing slowly twenty or thirty miles north or south along the clogged three- and two-lane artery of the "expressway." And that was inconsequential next to the problem of survival of the poor miserable derelict human beings they left to wander and sleep in the downtown streets at night as they made their slow but comfortable escape north to home. Ah! He was a yardman, doing his best not to think of these things, these terrible and barely solvable problems of people in this bursting city.

Mexico City barely functioned now. When there, he did not know how in the name of God it began each morning: how the water made its way through pipes, how the old cars started up, how the people in shacks and boxes came out and stretched and bathed, or did not, and began the day. They said the streets of London were filled with trash. That was hard to imagine. But he knew that even twenty years ago, when he was young and there, the trees along the beautiful avenues of Madrid were bare and gray and dying of the exhaust pollution. Even Franco had not been able to stop that! He laughed to himself for the second time that evening.

Looking to the sky, very light blue with traceries of cloud, he remembered back then, in Spain, he had wanted to be a poet. No one driving by— and they kept steadily driving by—could imagine that this stiff and disheveled yardman had once had the aspiration to be a poet! Or had we all been poets then, or just crazy, in that selfish, strange Aquarian time? He looked into himself and for a terrible instant saw the image of his mother just after she had died, in the nursing home, ghastly, growing rigid. It had been years and only now sometimes could he come to see her as she had been, smiling, the poet part in him, his young and lovely mother.

As he had sat once on the bank of a river with another woman, a large mottled snake had slid down from the bank into the water across from them, telling them what they knew. Standing up to go she had exclaimed, like a child, at two tiny flowers growing beneath a tree there, and just now he had ripped up the volunteer sprig of oak without even seeing the acorn on it! Well, it is no secret that one's work makes one insensitive to what one once would have been aware of and sensitive to, is that not the truth?

A car honked not a dozen feet from him, startling him, ripping him from his reverie, these images of his inner eye. An Oldsmobile had stopped by the curb. The woman driving let down the window on the passenger side and heaved her bulk across the man beside her and said, "I only live about a mile from here, and I could really use a good yard man. I'm Mrs. Watson. Give him your card, Henry. If you have good references—"

"No hablo ingles," the yardman said, and turned and picked up broom and rake.

"For God's sake, Marian," he heard the man say as the window rolled up. Turning, he smiled to see the white car take off. It was funny to see an automobile look as if it was bobbling forward, like the car itself was embarrassed and upset.

Around behind the house he put the tools in the garage. The lady of the house opened the back door. "Telephone," she said, making a face. He nodded. "Leave your shoes on the porch," she said.

He took them off. It was true they were a little caked on the soles. He did not wish to soil the linoleum of the kitchen floor, for today he had also mopped that. As the lady disappeared into the hallway of the house he took the receiver from the green phone hanging on the wall of the sparkling green, yellow and white kitchen.

"Robert," the voice said, a man's impatient, somewhat upset voice. "I drove by and saw you outside. You know that meeting's in less than an hour. What are you doing, man, my dear friend and leader, Robert? This is a called meeting of the Council. The honkies are yelling at us, we are experiencing slippage among the blacks, Pete punched out Al last week in public, for God's sake, our own people are barely holding tight and hanging in, and all our Jefe can do is work in his yard—"

"Joe, I thank you," he replied. "I truly do, for your concern. Maybe I can think of something to say tonight to bring us back together. I am thinking of that budget as a yard that needs weeding, and of what the grass needs for it to—"

"For God's sake, Robert!"

"Joseph!"

"Sorry. Yes, sir, Mr. Mayor?"

"Don't despair. We'll get through it. Somehow."

"All right. Do you want me to come back and pick you up?"

"No," he said, in the act of hanging up the receiver upon his wall. "Just a quick shower and I'll be there."

"GOODNIGHT, SWEETHEART . . ."

CLAY REYNOLDS

Dating in my hometown was not easily done if for no other reason than there simply wasn't much to do. The movie had burned down when I was in junior high, and the bowling alley went up less than a year later. Occasionally there was a dance held at the Teen Canteen, but ticket prices were high, and the chaperones usually outnumbered the couples on the dance floor two-to-one. There was a drive-in movie, but asking a girl out to a drive-in was, in those days at least, like making an obscene proposition. Besides, it was only open between June and September. So dating, for the most part, was restricted to driving around and around the town's main streets, "The Drag," with an occasional stop at the Dairy Mart for a Lime Coke, and to attending special, school-sponsored events such as banquets and dances.

Not surprisingly, most kids in my home town didn't date very much at all. There were the "steady" couples who logged hour after hour during the early weeks of their courtships, driving around and around the town with an occasional stop at the Dairy Mart for a Lime Coke. But when their romance had progressed beyond the public display stage, they retired to "The Lanes," where they would park for hour after hour of love-locked embraces, pausing only for an occasional tour of "The Drag" so their parents wouldn't get wind of their teens' torrid trysts on rural byways.

But that was for the "steadies." The rest of us mostly hung around the Dairy Mart parking lot after we had used up all of somebody's gas, waiting on the "steadies" to take their dates home and come by with wild, erotic tales—or for midnight, whichever came first.

Frequently, though, an event would occur that would require even the most reluctant among us to seek a female escort for the evening. Events such as the Senior Banquet, the Sports Banquet, the Band Banquet, the

Future Farmers' Banquet, the Future Homemakers' Banquet, the Future Teachers' Banquet, and all kinds of other "feeds" would force even the Levi-clad cowboy to trade in his boots for a pair of dress shoes and a starched shirt for an evening of preordained misery in the company of some "young lady" to whom he wouldn't have spoken three words otherwise and probably wouldn't say more than five anyway.

I personally participated in a number of these affairs during the four years I spent in high school, sitting beside some "young lady" and eating cold creamed-chicken and cherry cobbler and listening to some bore drone on about the marvelous wonders of whatever organization was sponsoring the affair, and I soon developed a theory about teenaged dating in a small town.

There is no way for an individual to have a good time on a date.

The odds are totally against it. In the first place, no small town boy is going to ask out any small town girl he knows well. The only reason why he would know her well is because he sees her every day—in class or some other activity. To be turned down by a person whom one might encounter on a daily basis thereafter would be intolerably embarrassing. In the second place, no normal "young man" is going to ask out any "young lady" who will fail to provide him with the proper social status he thinks he deserves. As a result, he usually finds some girl who is, in his eyes anyway, ravishingly beautiful, markedly intelligent, and who represents almost everything he does not through her personal interests and activities.

Thus, two total strangers embark on an evening which is designed by him to be interesting for her; but because he has probably totally misjudged her, the event will turn out to be boring, confusing, strained. Then, after spending most of his time worrying about whether she *will* enjoy it and whether she *is* enjoying it, he devotes countless hours to worrying about whether she *has* enjoyed it sufficiently to go out with him again, knowing in his heart of hearts that she wouldn't if her life depended on it.

But despite all this anguish and worry, the dating ritual continues throughout adolescence and young adulthood; indeed, it spans generations. For it is firmly established at an early age. Parents expect it, friends encourage it, society demands it. There are only so many years to master the craft, and it's important to establish experience so one can point to a track

390

record at some point and assert himself as a social if not a masculine animal.

My experience was no different. Years later I would find myself still uncertain and insecure over the same problems that beset me when I was fourteen and, as yet, dateless. But every time thereafter when I looked over at my female companion of the moment, I realized that the pattern for disaster was cut long ago.

I was like most boys at "almost 15." My most prized possessions were my Learner's Driving Permit and my limited access to my old man's 1953 Chevy. As most of my older classmates had done, I had been driving with friends providing the licensed driver in the front seat for nearly a year; and while I had logged my share of miles around "The Drag," talking with my buddies about cars, school, music, college, and, of course, girls, I had not yet found the courage or the motivation to venture onto the highway of society with a "young lady."

I *had* maintained a secret crush on a girl named Sherry French for over six years, all the way back to third grade, and as soon as I received my real driving license, I told myself, I would have no hesitation about calling her up and asking her to be my first date.

Unfortunately, a friend of mine, Allen Jenks, who had been driving for almost a year with a real license, had taken advantage of his early start as a motorist by establishing a dating relationship with my intended. This bothered me somewhat, but I took comfort in the fact that his only access to a car was his one-sixth share in a 1948 Rambler—Jenks also had five older brothers of dating and driving age, and a weekend claim on the auto was a coveted premium. As a result of his situation, he used my car to meet Sherry on "The Drag," with my ever-present self behind the wheel. Also, I was sure his general clodishness would be no match for the *savoir faire* I knew I would exude upon receipt of my real driving license.

But suddenly, in the spring of my freshman year in high school, things advanced at a more rapid rate than I had anticipated. The annual Spring Band Dance was upcoming. Normally, I attended such affairs "stag," usually in the company of a whole gang of friends, including Jenks and some other proud but dateless guys, and I had no reason to think that this time would be an exception. Jenks, however, announced that he was going to figure out which of his brothers had "dibs" on the Rambler that evening and ask Sherry to double date.

Now my whole social life didn't depend solely on one friend, and even if it had, Jenks would not have been the one to set any patterns for me. But later the same day, I ran into my best friend, Matt Holcomb, who tilted the scales in a fatal balance.

Every boy in a small town grows up with a "Best Friend," and Holcomb was mine. I don't suppose we did much of anything in our entire lives without discussing it with each other. Naturally, we each felt superior to the other in various and different ways, and I suppose it would be fair to say that our friendship was based as much on squabbling as anything else. But I was sure we knew each other very well. So it came as a tremendous shock when he suggested that we get dates and double in my old man's car.

Holcomb had, like Jenks, been a licensed driver for quite a while, but his parents had better sense than to allow him out on "The Drag" in *their* car, so he logged his hours on the streets behind someone else's wheel, usually mine.

Once he broached the subject of getting dates for the dance, childhood taboos about seriously discussing girls vanished. We spent the rest of the afternoon trying to figure out, ostensibly for each other, who would be best to ask.

Second to finding something original to do, the major problem about dating in a small town is the limited number of "young ladies" a "young man" could choose from. As a freshman, my choices were even more severely limited. In the first place, there were only about thirty girls in the whole class—junior high girls were absolutely forbidden, and to invite an older girl was to invite ridicule from my peers if not a black eye from some junior or senior—upper-classmen were already dating about half the freshmen girls anyway.

A few more were "undatable" owing to physical deformities or socioeconomic family situation that would have—I'm now ashamed to say—scandalized my parents and robbed me of whatever prestige the date was supposed to provide in the first place. Of the remaining fifteen, five were in the band, and the potential discomfort of having to go eventually without a date and face those who turned me down was more than I could stand. Of the ten remaining, five were Church of Christ and did not dance; two were Baptist, and their parents would not let them dance; and one was a Jehovah's Witness and couldn't go out on a Saturday, even if anyone asked her. That left two; and one of those was Linda Fitzpatrick, whose family was so rich that none of my crowd dared even speak to her, let alone consider offering to chauffeur her to something as mundane as a Band Dance in something as common as a '53 Chevy.

The process of elimination took several hours; there had been much teasing, guffawing, and whispered lewd suggestion, but when we finally got done to the magic one—the only *one* remaining—silence prevailed between Holcomb and me. We were both thinking the same name at the same time: Caroline Hauffman.

Caroline was blond—German blond—blue-eyed—German blue-eyed—quiet and shy. My old man, according to family legend, had dated her mother, Elizabeth, when they were in high school. On several occasions I had heard him pronounce whenever Caroline's mother's name was mentioned, "Beautiful woman, but no personality."

I didn't know what he meant, exactly, but I did know that Caroline was as timid a creature as I had ever known. She had her mother's beauty and would, therefore, be a prestige date; best yet, no upper-classman had shown any interest in her at all. In fact, so far as I knew, she had never had a date. As we talked around her name and shifted our eyes and attention to my collection of model movie monsters, I mentally measured Caroline's assets and liabilities and came up with the most important argument in her favor, the one thing that made her a perfect selection for a date:

I hardly knew her.

She was in none of my classes, played no instruments in the band, and we had no special friends in common. I held my breath and prayed that Holcomb would leave quickly without announcing any deliberate intentions of his own.

Some pre-pubescent taboos were thankfully still in force. He made some excuses about errands for his mother and exited in his usual strolling gait, walking down to the corner where, with a quick glance over his shoulder, he broke into a dead run for the remaining two blocks to his house, his telephone, and a date with Caroline.

But it was only ten paces to my own telephone. And within minutes, without thinking at all about the momentous nature of the event, I was calmly asking Caroline Hauffman to go with me to the Spring Band Dance.

I suppose I should have indelibly etched on my mind the exact content of that conversation, but all I remember is that it seemed remarkably easy, even casual, the way I asked and she accepted, not unlike my asking Holcomb or Jenks to join me for a basketball game. The whole process was almost boring. I do remember wondering if there was something I should have said or asked or let her ask, but there didn't seem to be, so I hung up and pranced around my room feeling rather pleased with myself.

Suddenly, a devilish thought struck me: I called Holcomb's number and found it busy; then I quickly dialed Caroline's number again and discovered that my suspicions were true—I had beaten him to it! Now he was going to have to pick between the wealthy Linda Fitzpatrick and Delores Buckman, who had a set of front teeth to match her name. Within an hour he called me, stating that since there obviously weren't two datable girls for the dance, why didn't we simply go stag as always and double date another time. In the ensuing argument, I recall only the names for each other we invented and that we didn't plan to speak to one another for at least twenty years.

Of course, Holcomb's bowing out presented a problem about transportation. But since I had been using the Chevy on my own quite a bit of late, I was confident my old man would make an exception: just to Caroline's house, out to the Country Club, and back home, just for the one evening. Unfortunately, my self-confidence got the better of me. Preparatory to asking him for permission to drive along for the big evening, I began running errands for my mother "solo," proving that I could be trusted without a licensed driver in the seat beside me.

I had never understood that requirement anyway. The theory seems to be that a "learner" would be less likely to plow head-on into a brick wall if someone was in the seat beside him who knew something that the learner supposedly did not. How this miracle of prevention was supposed to come about, I was not too sure, but I demonstrated the wisdom of the policy on Sunday afternoon—not by plowing head-on into a brick wall, but into the side of our garage.

The result was less damage to the car or the wall than to my pride and to my expectations when my mother announced that I would not be permitted to drive at all until my regular license came though. Cruel as this may have been, it was refined from my old man's original sentence, which was to have my right leg amputated at the knee.

It took me almost the whole evening to work up the courage to tell my parents about my date. They were never particularly sensitive to adolescent needs, and while they surprised me by not being in a mood to tease, they disappointed me by not being in a mood to understand either.

"Your father can pick you up and bring you home," my mother offered as she prepared roast beef left-overs, "What time will the dance be over?"

The opening she left almost escaped me in the overwhelming panic I was experiencing as I envisioned *my old man*, in clear view of my friends, carting me and my date to and fro like some junior high kid, but I quickly recovered and answered, "Oh, midnight . . . after midnight!"

Now my old man was a lot of things, but one thing he was *not* was a night owl. He went to bed every night at 10:00 P.M., sharp. The problem with my mother's suggestion was immediately apparent to both of us, but she only said, "We'll see," which in Mother Language means, "You still can't drive the car, but perhaps something can be worked out."

I knew my next move: I went immediately to the phone and called Jenks, who was still working on the Rambler's reservation schedule. He and Sherry, Caroline and I would double date. When I approached my old man with my "reasonable compromise"—Jenks, not I, would drive the Chevy—he nodded and asked who my date was.

My reply elicited exactly the response I expected, "Beautiful girl, but just like her mother, no personality."

The next week progressed through a flurry of anticipation and preparation that rivaled plans for a military operation. On Monday, Jenks and I tuned and worked over the Chevy's engine so she would be running just right. On Tuesday, I bought a new suit, complete with new shirt, tie, socks, and underwear. Jenks and I added "falsies" to the Chevy's wheel rims to give her that "whitewall look."

On Wednesday Caroline found me in study hall and asked me what color my suit would be. I was so delighted to find out that she knew I had bought one, I could only mutter "blue" and stare at her in wondrous silence. On Thursday, Jenks and I put seat covers on the Chevy, and I managed to mention my upcoming date to my dateless buddies who would form the ever-present "stag line."

Friday found me at the barbershop for a haircut and at the drug store where I bought a bottle of English Leather cologne and a new razor. And on Saturday, at 4:00, three-and-one-half hours before the big event, Jenks and I placed on the Chevy the *pièce de résistance*: a chrome suicide knob. We were set.

I laid out my new duds on the bed, careful not to wrinkle any crease or dirty any lapel, and went in to supper. My mother, of course, served what she always served on Saturday nights: liver and onions. I didn't eat much, which caused my mother to smile a lot and my old man to grumble. As she cleared the table for dessert, she asked, "Did you all have that little talk yet?" My old man grumbled even louder, "Right after dinner," and he motioned me to follow him.

All week long he had been taking me aside for "little talks" that never got anywhere. Tuesday, after I bought my suit, he drove me out to the stockyards where we spent the better part of an hour watching a bull and several heifers look bored and hot in the afternoon sun. He chain-smoked Luckys for a while and finally said, "Oh, hell. Let's go." That, plus some even more inconsequential attempts at sex-education, was the extent of my parents' direct approach to the subject. Some months later they gave me a book.

Now he asked me to come outside for a little bit and lit up another Lucky, awkwardly and suddenly thrusting the pack out toward me. Remembering all his warnings against my even thinking about smoking, I took one paper cylinder and set it unprofessionally on my lip. He grumbled as he lit it, obviously embarrassed as much by *his* foolishness in offering me a smoke as by my foolishness in accepting it. All at once, he reached into his pocket and produced a $10.00 bill. "In case you need it," he said.

I didn't know what to say, and the Lucky was making me dizzy, but abruptly he snatched it away from my mouth and ushered me back inside with a nod to my mother who returned a confident and knowing smile and picked up her ongoing lecture on gentlemanly behavior. And this gave rise to another crisis.

At some point—Wednesday I think—I realized two things:

First of all, I was about to attend a dance where I was going to have to *dance*. In spite of her Baptist reservations, my mother had made my twelfth summer intolerable by enrolling me in Miss Billie Rae Wilson's School of Dance. I recall with a convulsive shudder the shame and terror of those four weeks: slinking down alleyways, making up elaborate lies to my friends about where I was, threatening my kid brother with his life if he breathed a word, and, the worst of it, spending all those hot, sticky nights in Miss Billie Rae's unairconditioned studio, hugging her overweight and overly fragrant waist to my short chest.

At the end of the class, all of Miss Billie Rae's students had to perform in a recital. My mother, secure in the knowledge that my social potential was ensured, was doubtlessly pleased with my performance, even if I did risk my immortal soul by the very activity of moving in rhythm to music in the arms of a girl.

But what my mother never could understand was that the Fox-trot, the Waltz, the Tango and Cha-cha-cha were not the kinds of dancing that teenagers did. As a result, except for the two weeks I spent at Miss Billie Rae's, I had never set foot on a dance floor. In fact, I had sworn never to do so.

But now I was going to a dance. With a date. Things change.

I tried to minimize the problem. It wouldn't minimize. I spent some time watching *American Bandstand*, but that didn't help much. The camera wouldn't focus on one couple long enough for me to learn all the intricate movements of the older Bop and the newer Twist. And these were all city kids who already knew the basics and kept putting in extra steps and movements that looked professional. I borrowed some records from Jenks and tried to practice in my room, but my kid brother kept showing up and laughing himself silly.

I would just have to tell Caroline that I sprained my ankle or something. There was no way on earth that I could dance, not in front of all those guys on the "stag line" who would be doing what we always did on the "stag line": making fun of anyone we knew who was trying to dance.

The second thing I realized was that I really didn't want to spend an evening with Caroline. She was nice enough, and she was just as good-looking as any other girl. But I didn't want any other girl—I wanted Sherry, and Sherry was going to be with Jenks. The knowledge that I would have to spend the whole date in Sherry's company but not *with* her began to eat at me. There had been moments of ego inflation—when Caroline asked about my suit, for example—but basically the image of Caroline paled when held up to Sherry, a girl I had held in secret special affection for years.

Further, I understood, the pattern of my being along with her as Jenks's friend was dangerously close to being permanent. Teenage relationships don't change that readily in a small town, and I was slowly coming to the conclusion that if I wasn't careful, things could take a dangerous and unalterable turn. An undercurrent of anxiety about that ate at me all week, and it was still there as I began to prepare for the evening.

Still, I was determined to put as good a face on the whole thing as I could muster. Surely Sherry would see my natural good manners and suave looks were superior to Jenks's. I could make this a demonstration evening, and Caroline might just be the perfect partner to top it off and attract Sherry's attention.

I took a long, long shower, shaved especially close—cutting myself only three times—and lovingly donned my new clothes. By the time I was dressed I had come up to a peak level of excitement. I was almost breathless.

My old man, squatting in front of the TV, fooling as he always did with the mysteries of the fine tuning knob, tossed me the Chevy's keys as I passed by. He didn't even look up. "What color socks you got on?" he asked.

"Black," I replied, checking to make sure.

"Be sure you never wear white socks with a suit," he ordered as if he didn't hear me. "Anytime you go to the trouble of wearing a suit, put on black socks." That one piece of wisdom has meant more to me over the years than all the father-and-son talks we might have had.

My mother met me at the door and positively beamed as she removed the toilet paper from my shaving cuts. Embarrassed, I tried to push past her, but she stopped me cold with a question, "Where's your corsage?"

Corsage!? I had forgotten about it completely. That was why Caroline asked about the color of my suit. It was a hint for me to find out the color of her dress so I could match it with a flower. How could I have been so stupid?

"Here," she said, producing a blue and pink box, "Mothers are good for something." I think that had she asked me to lie down and die right there, I would have. Instead I only muttered that I didn't know what Caroline was wearing.

"It's all right," she smiled through what I later realized were tears, "I called Elizabeth this morning."

"Elizabeth!" My old man growled from in front of the TV. "Beautiful woman, but no—" The rest was lost behind the door as I left for the date. My first.

I would like to report fantastic details about this momentous evening for which I had planned so long and carefully. Alas, the whole affair was remarkably uneventful. My old regrets about being with Caroline rather than Sherry evaporated when Caroline appeared wearing a sleek, black velvet dress, topped off with a real diamond tiara in her golden hair. It wasn't that Sherry ceased to attract me: that unrequited love would continue unabated for the next three years, undaunted by all kinds of adversity. It was only that for the first time I was proud of being with a person who was apparently pleased to be with me. This provided my ego and unflagging sense of romance with a boost.

I recall that I did most of the talking that evening. Jenks said very little since he and Sherry had a fight over his "honking her out" instead of coming to the door. Sherry tried to talk to Caroline, but Caroline said very little to Sherry or to anyone else. I finally realized what my old man had meant about her having "no personality." It wasn't that she was dumb, uncomfortable, or nervous—she just never could think of anything to say. In later years, her dates would arrive at the Dairy Mart parking lot to complain that she hadn't said two words all evening. She later went to graduate school and became a research chemist. Perhaps she found the solitude and silence of the laboratory more her style.

There were some uncomfortable moments at the dance. It was too hot for one thing, and my new shirt wilted immediately. I managed to dance quite a few of the dances, but my new shoes hurt terribly, and I drank enough of the sickly sweet, too warm punch to make me slightly ill. I recall looking more than once over toward the "stag line" and feeling proud and superior to Holcomb and the rest of the guys, but I also remember wondering if they envied me half as much as I did them.

Caroline and I took a couple of walks out by the pool, but she maintained her silence, and I did all the talking. She was so beautiful, I tried to feel confident, to convince myself that things were really going very well. There was a full moon and music and a warm spring night. If only she would *say* something.

When we left the dance, we made the requisite five or six passes around "The Drag" and drank a couple of Lime Cokes, but Caroline blithely ordered a plain Coke, which was more evidence of my father's theory's validity. And she remained mute, speaking only when spoken to, answering questions in polite monosyllables. I was so frustrated and miserable that I wanted to cry.

After a while, Jenks drove out to "The Lanes" and parked. Had I been able to protest *this* particular side-trip I would have, for I knew that Caroline was not of an inclination to spend any amorous moments with me on that evening or, for that matter, any other. If she wouldn't *talk* to me, I reasoned, she sure wasn't going to "make out" with me, full moon or no.

This was all my fault, of course, not Jenks's. All week we had planned, "if things went Okay," to make a stop on "The Lanes." But I had never really believed that Caroline was going to go along with it. Still, I wasn't about to admit to Jenks that I was unwilling to *try*, or that I was going to eliminate the possibility entirely, days before I had to.

I suppose I had two plans: If the "slow dances" were of sufficient number and Caroline and I managed to spark the right amount of "flame" in each other, then a session under the full moon might be right in order. Actually, I didn't expect that any such "flame" would ignite at all. However, I was eager enough to explore the mysteries of "The Lanes" to carry out the plan if circumstances unexpectedly developed along those lines.

Unfortunately, my sweaty, wilted shirt, aching feet, and slight nausea from the punch cancelled any romantic notions I might have conjured; so I should have gone to Plan B, which was simply to tell Jenks to keep driving around and around "The Drag" until time to take the girls home. But I completely forgot about it until he swing the Chevy onto Airport Road, and it was too late to say anything without implying to him, and especially to Sherry, that *I* was some kind of prude or suggesting to the ever-silent Caroline that *I* was reluctant to spend any amount of time embracing, kissing, or whatever else was expected of a parked couple on "The Lanes."

400

But there we were, and I felt totally mystified as to what my next move should be.

I had run out of witty conversation on the second round of Lime Cokes, and Jenks and Sherry were in no mood to carry on a rousing *repartée*: They had some making up to do and went at it hammer and tongs for three-quarters of an hour. Through it all, Caroline and I squatted in the silence of the Chevy's back seat, since the radio only worked when the engine was running. She sat there, prim, proper, and silently beautiful, her hands folded neatly in her lap; I sat there, stiff, clumsy, and unbearably nervous, wondering if I should move closer to her or attempt to hold hands or try to put an arm around her, and whether I could do any of those things without her screaming "rape."

Our silent stillness continued, however, punctuated only by my feeble attempts at conversation which died in my throat and by the slurping noises and heavy breathing coming from the front seat. Caroline only stared straight ahead as if some fascinating message was printed on the seat covers in front of her. She was simply waiting, politely, patiently, waiting.

Finally, I mentioned that it was getting late, and Jenks—thank God— took the hint. We soon delivered Sherry and Caroline to their respective homes, but not without a mini-reprise of the torrid scenes we had just witnessed, passionately played out in Sherry's drive-way. Caroline and I bade each other Goodnight with assurances that we had both had a "real good time," and with promises of "doing it again sometime, real soon," knowing all the time that we never would.

I had held forth hopes of a goodnight kiss, more for Jenks's watchful eye than my amorous expectations. Although I figured the parking episode had diminished any spark of ardor which might otherwise have developed, I still thought that something in the way of a semi-affectionate bussing might be tolerated. So we waited on her porch, facing each other in the brilliance of the porch-light bulb, both wondering what should happen next.

She stood, staring at me, trying to decide, no doubt, what I might try to do and what she should do when I tried it. I stood, staring at her, trying to decide what she might do if I should try anything, and what, if anything, I should try. I began to lean forward, watching carefully for the invitation of the slightest tilt of her chin upward toward my approaching face. But she didn't move: Not an inch. Not a half-inch. My courage flagged, and I straightened up just as I thought I might have perceived the receptive tilt, but it was too late.

"Well," I said, "See ya 'round." And I galloped toward the Chevy and Jenks's questioning look, which I had already planned to answer if it ever became words with the explanation that Caroline told me she thought she was coming down with "mono."

Thus the event for which such complex plans were made, for which I had waited all my post-pubescent life, ended on an ignominious note: a scurrying retreat from a girl who was probably just as uncertain as I about what to do next.

We made our obligatory trip by the Dairy Mart, but most everyone had already gone home. Holcomb, however, was there, and he thwarted any expectations I had about gloating by producing a pair of empty wine bottles and a tale of city girls, who had driven up and found him and some pals right after they left the dance. The next weekend, they all had dates with these mysterious girls for their own dance, which would have a live band and the promise of illicit wine and beer for anyone who was brave enough to sample it.

They had been making "The Drag," drinking wine and planning their party the whole time I was watching Jenks and Sherry set new records for holding kisses, and now they were full of expectations for their trip to the city and sin beyond imagination. No one—particularly not Holcomb—wanted to hear about my first date. No one wanted to hear the lies I was prepared to tell.

After Holcomb and the rest drifted off, I took Jenks home and bravely violated my old man's embargo on my driving and steered the Chevy to my house solo. I pulled into the drive and got out and was surprised to see a figure standing in the shadows by the front porch. I knew who it was from the glow of his cigarette

"Have a good time?" he asked as I came up the walk, hoping he hadn't noticed that I brought the car home alone.

I nodded, walked into the darkness near him. He was still dressed, hadn't been to bed. I don't think I'd ever seen him up and awake this late when there wasn't a tornado alert or someone sick in the family.

"You get that little girl home okay?"

I nodded again, realized it was too dark to see me. "Yeah," I said. "Uh, yessir."

He offered me a cigarette, again. This time I shook my head. He nodded. "You treat a girl with respect," he said. "You don't talk about her to nobody. You don't do or say anything you can't look her in the eye about the next morning." I nodded. "It don't matter if you like her or not. It don't matter if she likes you or not. Don't mean a thing. All that matters is that you treat her with respect. Show some gumption."

For a moment I stood not knowing what to say. My feet hurt. I was embarrassed. "We had fun," I finally said. "It was fun."

He nodded, crushed out his cigarette. "It'll get better. Take my word for it." He coughed, though he didn't need to. "Tomorrow I want that damned garage cleaned out. Hear me?"

"Yessir."

We started up the steps. He put his hand on my shoulder, opened the screen door. Then he stopped, and in the sudden yellow glow of the porch light, I saw something distant cross his eyes. "Caroline, right?"

"Yessir."

"Going to take her out again?"

"Uh, I . . . I don't know."

He nodded, squeezed my shoulder a little too hard. "Just like her mother," he said. "Beautiful girl, but no personality."

ANOTHER MAN'S BET

LAURIE CHAMPION

You Pick

Al's getting the brakes fixed on his car and Marie calls him to say she'll pick him up in the parking lot and take him to lunch. Marie doesn't like to drive, so when Al walks up to her window and says he'll do the driving, she moves to the passenger seat. "We've got to quit meeting like this," she says.

"Why?" he answers.

Jesus Christ, she thinks, it's a joke. They have to quit meeting like this because he doesn't get her jokes. "Because my husband might find out," she says. "Discover our secret."

"I am your husband," he says.

Of course he's her husband. Jesus Christ. "Lighten up," she says. She wants to say because her boyfriend might find out but she's afraid Al might take her seriously. Get suspicious. She's paranoid about real jokes, the kind that tell the truth.

"Where do you want to eat?" she asks.

"I don't care."

"Neither do I. You pick."

"No, really, I don't care," he says.

"Okay, how about Friday's?"

"Friday's. No, how about somewhere else? I don't like Friday's."

"Then you decide," Marie says.

"No, I don't care," he says.

After several rounds of options and counter options, they finally decide on Luby's. Sometimes Marie wishes she lived in a remote small town with only one restaurant, so she wouldn't have to participate in this little ritual every time she goes to lunch with Al. It might be more convenient not to have so many choices. She thinks about saying "Houston's a big city," but she doesn't want to explain her thoughts to Al. He'd probably just ask "How big?" or something serious.

Cheap Entertainment

Al and Marie sit eating, minding their own business, with little conversation, when the man sitting at the table next to them looks at Marie and says, "I bet I can fit inside your glass of tea."

"Excuse me?" Marie asks.

"I bet you twenty bucks I can fit inside your glass."

"Inside my glass?"

"Yeah."

"Excuse us," Al says, "we're trying to eat."

"Wait," Marie says. "How can you fit inside my glass?"

"I bet I can," the man says. He stands up and walks over to Al's and Marie's table. He's wearing a blue Marlboro t-shirt and jeans. He points to Marie's tea. "I can get my whole self in that glass. Twenty bucks."

"Well, I bet you can't," Marie says.

"Excuse us," Al says, "we're not interested. We don't have much time. I have to get back to work."

The man stands there, looking at Marie. "I can."

"Well, I don't know how you're going to get inside my tea glass."

"Twenty bucks," the man says.

"Please let us eat," Al says. He looks at Marie. "Besides," he says, "don't you know not to take another man's bet? Ever. You should know that. He looks at the man. "No, we're not interested." The man walks toward the cashier and leaves.

"I don't know how he was going to win that one," Marie says.

"Believe me, there's some way. He had some trick up his sleeve. Everyone knows you never call another man's bet."

Marie doesn't want to start an argument, so she just says, "Yeah, of course. I guess he had something weird planned. I'm just curious."

Al says he'd better get back to work, so they leave. While Al drives, Marie tries to figure out the man's trick. Was he going to write his name on a piece of paper and put it inside the glass? Was he hiding a picture of himself up his sleeve to drop in the glass? Even if she lost the bet, it would've been worth the money to find out. Cheap entertainment.

It's a Mystery

When Al gets out of the car, Marie drives straight to Jim's office. From the parking lot, she calls him from her car phone. "I've got your number," she says when he answers the phone.

Jim laughs, says, "I've got the time." When he approaches Mari's car, she rolls down the window. "I'm off for the day," he says.

"Really? Great. What do you want to do?"

"What do you think?" Jim says, cutting his eyes toward her. Marie smiles. He says he'll get his car and suggests they meet at his house.

"Okay," Marie says.

Jim stands looking at her. "Wait," he says, "scoot over." Marie moves to the passenger seat, and Jim kisses her. "Let's just ride together. We can get my car later. I want to be next to you. Now."

When they get to Jim's house, Jim takes a bottle of wine from the icebox. They sit on his bed and sip wine. While she unbuttons her blouse, Marie tells Jim about the man who approached her at Luby's.

"Weird," Jim says.

"Yeah, it was strange. I just can't get it off my mind. It bugs me. I can't figure out how he could get himself inside my tea glass?"

"I don't have the vaguest," Jim says.

Marie takes off her blouse, lies on the bed, and sips wine. Jim strokes her hair. "I don't know why I keep thinking about that weirdo," she says.

"It's a mystery," he whispers.

Marie lights a cigarette and tells Jim that the man irritated Al. "It was like he was lecturing me," she says. "I'm not a child, you know. He kept rambling about how you're not supposed to take another man's bet," she said.

"I know, dear, settle down. It's okay." He strokes her back and kisses her cheek.

"I mean, I wasn't even thinking about bets in general. I was just wondering how in God's name that guy was going to do it. I mean, was he going to pour tea all over himself?" Marie takes off her bra and pulls the covers over her chest.

"It doesn't matter," Jim says. "He probably had something up his sleeve."

"Yeah, I'm sure he did. I just wonder what it was."

"Doesn't matter," Jim says. He takes his shirt off and gets under the covers with her. He pours them both another glass of wine. "I bet I can fit inside this glass of wine," he says.

"I bet I can fit this glass of wine in me," Marie says.

Jim laughs. "I bet you can."

Marie quickly drinks the glass of wine as though killing a shot of tequila. "I needed that," she says. "After having to put up with Al this afternoon."

Jim makes love to her, and his gentle movements and soft touches comfort her. When he tells her he loves her, she knows he's not merely repeating a lovemaking cliché. She knows he really means it. She considers telling him she loves him but decides not to. She feels strange, odd thoughts popping in and out of her mind. At a time like this, she knows she should concentrate on physical sensations, but she can't. She imagines herself as someone else, someone above the bed, perhaps on the ceiling. Isn't it weird what human beings do? If we really look at sex objectively, it's really odd. Jesus Christ. She wonders what God thinks when he looks down and sees people "doing it."

Jim pulls the cover up over both of them and smiles at Marie. "You don't believe me, do you?"

"Believe what?" she asks.

"That I love you."

"Yes, I do," she says. She gets up and turns on the TV. She feels nervous, remembers a couple of months ago when Jim asked her when or if she would leave Al. "Unfair question," she'd answered.

Jim even admitted that he thought about giving her the old ultimatum but decided not to. "I was afraid you'd pick Al and then I'd have to stick to my guns," he said. "I guess I just need to do something else."

"Let's don't think about complications," Marie said.

Marie still doesn't want to contemplate complications. She's not even sure why she sees Jim or when and if or why she might or might not leave Al. She knows Jim makes her smile and she has to admit at least once or twice she has had nuptial thoughts about him—imagined him cooking pasta while she tells him stories, thought about how he'd laugh at her jokes and brush her hair at night. But she also knows there's something strange about their affair. It's like it's not real, some kind of optical illusion or trick of the imagination.

When Marie reminds Jim that she has to pick up Al from work, they drive back to Jim's office. She gets out of the car to sit in the driver's seat, and he hugs her gently, whispers, "You know, I really, really do."

Marie pulls Jim closer to her and whispers, "We've got to quit meeting like this." She hopes Jim knows she's serious. Dead serious.

The True Faith, or, Any Old Wind

Donna Walker-Nixon

My husband Elven always said Father would follow any old wind that blows and Mother wouldn't be far behind. My sister Callie was the youngest of eleven children, and she never had any choice, but to do as Father said. My husband Elven never believed me when I told him that. "Callie's got a mind. Tell her to use it," he said when Father joined the Jehovah Witnesses during World War II.

They came to our house first while Elven was working in the fields. I thought they were right nice people. The woman bowed her head, and the man did most of the talking. "We want to talk to you about a new vision," he said. He talked to me like my views meant something, not the way Elven always did as he looked at me sternly and said, "A woman's place is to follow the man."

I had a mind of my own sometimes, but Elven never let me use it, and I liked this man who had a full head of hair and who looked to be about Elven's age. The woman started chattering too about finding the kingdom of God here on this earth, and the man nodded his head up and down as he smiled at her.

I found myself turning almost green with envy for her since I wished Elven would just once look at me and smile. Then the man said, "Sister, I can feel the interest you're generating. Let me give you a tract that will tell you all about our religion and our beliefs. When you read it, you'll come to understand as we have that our Father in Heaven has a plan far greater than any man can make." He smiled peacefully at me, and I'm ashamed to admit it but I found myself practically grabbing the tract from his hand.

I didn't go past the seventh grade in school since during the time I was growing up many families had to take their children out of school to help with the planting in the spring and with the gathering in the fall. So it usually takes me a good long while to get interested in reading, but the man started saying the words with me as I read. And I looked up as he smiled at me and called me sister.

"I can already tell that God is working his way into your life," he said. His wife smiled, and I felt almost swayed by their beliefs.

Then Elven came in from the fields. He was all dirty and mad at the mule for getting stuck in the mud. "God damn, son of a bitch," he muttered as he came into the house. He didn't realize we had company, or he wouldn't have been using that kind of language.

"Elven," I called to him. "We've got guests. Come and meet them."

The man started smiling at Elven and saying, "Glad to meet you, Brother."

Before the man could say another word, Elven sized up that they were Jehovah Witness missionaries by the black suit the man was wearing and by the fact that rumor had been going around the Downs Creek community that those people were afoot trying to pervert the American way of life.

"We don't believe in your gestapo trash," Elven said and almost embarrassed the pea living wad out of me.

The young man in his black hat blushed and said, "Wouldn't you want to know a better way if it was out there?"

"No, I know what you are," Elven said. "Hitler sent you over here to undermine our efforts in the war, and we ain't about to follow suit." Then Elven slammed the door shut behind them, and I felt bad because of Elven's inhospitality, but I thought we had heard the last of them.

At the end of the week Father and Mother came over to the house with Callie. "We have found a better way," Father said and started preaching the same words that the Jehovah Witness missionaries had said at the beginning of the week. Elven was gone into Lindsey to buy feed for the cows, and I was trying to get Saturday dinner cooked before he came home.

Father kept on talking while Mother and Callie stood there smiling, and Father always treated me far better than Elven ever did. "In days of old our God spoke through prophets. Now we've found the true church of the prophecy." He smiled at me again, and he reached his hand out to me. "Your mother and your sister Callie have found the way of the Lord. Our heart's desire is for you to come and follow the true church."

410

Elven came in from town, and he almost blew the roof down. "Out, out, I will not have this perversion in my home," he said and threw my own people out the same way he did the Jehovah Witness missionaries. He saw the tracts that Father gave me to read, and he threw them into the trash. Then he took the trash out to burn. "I burn all trash that comes into my home," he said.

I was afraid he would never allow me to see my family again. Callie's eighteenth birthday was the next day, and I was the birthday cake maker in the family. I had plans to make a big beautiful cake for her just as I had made for all my other sisters when they turned eighteen. I was afraid of what Elven would say, but when I asked him, he told me, "As long as you realize that I will not have my wife going and joining a Nazi plot posing as a church, then you can go. But I won't have any part of it."

I nodded and told Elven that a woman's job is to follow the ways of her husband. "When a woman marries, she becomes part of her husband, not her father," I said. Elven smiled big like he thought he had won some kind of military victory, and I got to bring Callie her cake.

When Elven left me off at the house, he warned me not to go believing in the Nazi plot to demolish our troops abroad. I held the cake carefully in front of me and nodded to let him know that I was in total agreement with him. He pulled out of the driveway, and I knocked on the door as loud as I could. Callie came to the door. When she saw the cake, her face lit up with the biggest smile, but as I look back, it was the last time I ever saw her smile. "Mattie Lou," she said, "what a pretty cake."

"For my youngest sister on her eighteenth birthday," I said and waited for her to tell me to come in.

She didn't say a word, and I thought she was remembering the little row that Father and Elven had the day before. "That was nothing," I said. "You know Father and Elven are just alike—both as hard-headed as a mule—and neither one's liable to admit that fact. That's what we're always saying about the two." I tried to get her to smile again by smiling so big that my jaws began to hurt, but she wouldn't smile.

"Where's Father?" I asked.

"He'll be down in a minute." She started looking out the door, right past me, almost as if she wished I'd never come in the first place.

"You got something to tell me. What is it?" I finally told her.

411

"In our new life, we don't believe in celebrating birthdays. That's a pagan celebration," she said. I knew she didn't want to believe a word that she was saying, but living under Father's roof she became sway to his thinking.

"Callie," I told her, "wasn't it just last year that the Nazarene preacher came to town and held a revival in the orchard behind the school. By the end of the week, Father had us all going every night, even Elven. Father was telling everyone who would listen that he had found the way of the Lord."

She nodded but didn't say anything.

"This will go away. Just like Father's other fool notions," I said, knowing full well that I sounded like Elven.

Father must have come down the stairs without me realizing it because he started to give me a going over like as I had never had before. "This is not another one of your Father's fool notions," he told me. "If you think that, you can leave my house and never come back."

"No, sir," I mumbled to him. "I'm sorry to make you think that that's what I believe." Then I looked down at the cake and said, "I brought this cake for you to have for supper tonight."

"Not for your sister's birthday?" he asked.

"No, Sir," I said and stuffed the candles deep into my sweater pocket. "No, Sir," I said again.

"In that case, we accept," he spoke much more sternly than I had ever known him to speak. Then he started saying the same words that the Jehovah Witness missionary had said. "We want you there with us," he said after he told me that only 144,000 people would be among those assured of a place in Christ's kingdom. "Sometimes we have to forsake our families in order to do the will of our God," he told me, and I knew he had to be talking about Elven.

If it had just been Father, Mother, and Callie, I would have become a Jehovah Witness in a minute, but I had Elven to think of, as well as my four children. And I had just found out the week before that another was on the way. Besides, there was a strange glint in Father's eyes, and Callie was sitting there with her head bowed in prayer. "Callie, here, has made her decision," Father said, trying to persuade me to go along with them. "This coming week she's going to tell that young Perkins boy that she has found

412

a better way and that, in order for them to continue their relationship, he has to follow suit."

I knew that Clyde Perkins would have none of the Jehovah Witnesses since his father was the Baptist preacher, and I knew I had to talk some sense into Father for Callie's sake. "Father, let Callie make up her own mind about being a Jehovah Witness," I finally worked up my courage to say.

"She has," he said and looked over at Callie to back him up.

"Yes, I have made up my own mind. I am following the ways of the true Church," she said, but I could tell she was being held sway by what Father wanted her to do. Even as a little girl, if Father told her to do something, she never questioned his authority, not like my sister Faye Dean or my brother Carlton who ran away from home before they reached the age of eighteen and moved out of state.

I wanted to cry on the spot because I could see that Father would remain in this church just long enough for it to keep Callie from marrying her sweetheart since she was old enough to have a boyfriend, and then Father would move on to some other religion, but Callie's life would be in shambles. I pushed back the tears from my eyes, and I told Father I had to be getting back to Elven and the children. I left and walked the five miles to our house.

When I got home, Elven was after me again. "He didn't try to convert you, did he?"

"No," I lied because I didn't want Elven knowing just how bad things had gotten.

"Good," he said and told me ten more times at the very least that the Jehovah Witnesses were part of a Nazi conspiracy. Inside, I was torn all to pieces. And Callie was caught in the middle of it all.

The next time I saw Father, Mother, and Callie was at the community supper on Friday night. People in the community were staring at them, and I wanted to sink into the floor like the little man did in the fairy tale that my boys liked for me to read to them. Father had Mother and Callie going around to people trying to give out tracts. Mother and Callie wore long black dresses that looked much more severe than the flour sacks that all the other women's dresses were made out of. I would have been more ashamed than I already was, except for the fact that everyone in Downs

Creek knew all about Father and people were always saying he'd follow any old wind that blows. I was used to that. What I wasn't used to was the raw energy with which Callie was chasing men, women, children around the room and saying, "We have found a new, more perfect way."

People were snickering at her behind her back, and Clyde Perkins wasn't there. When I finally was able to take Callie aside and have a few words in private with her, she tried to duck out of my reach. But I was much stronger than she's ever been since Father started me working in the fields when I was just a little one, and Callie, being the youngest and the apple of Father's life, never had to work 'til she thought her fingers would turn to blood. So, I kept her from getting away from me. "What's happened between you and Clyde?" I asked her directly. "He's not here. That much I can tell."

"I did as the Lord would have me do," she said.

She acted like she had said everything there was to say on the subject. And I knew that she had done as Father told her to, but I wanted to find out what was going on, so I didn't say that to her. "What did you do?" I asked her. "Tell me."

"I told Clyde Perkins about the true Church, and I told him I wanted him to be there too. I said I would never be truly happy without him."

She stopped talking, and I knew that I would have to prod her to get any more information out of her. "So what did he say?"

"He told me he loved me, but he could never believe in a Gestapo plot. He said everyone knows that's what the Jehovah Witnesses are up to, and he said I had a fool for a father."

Again she acted as if she had said everything there was to say, and I thought she would be crying over the loss of what everyone in Downs Creek called her one true love. Her face remained unmoved, almost as if she had lost all human feelings.

"What happened next?" I asked again, determined to get her to tell me the whole story.

"He said he was moving to Waco to start college. He said he had planned to leave at the end of the summer, but that he was leaving now and he didn't want to see me ever again."

In the past, she would have cried and pitched a fit, but now when she talked her voice trailed off, and I wanted my sister back. I was mad at

Father for taking her away, and I turned around and went back into the community center.

Father was still trying to give out tracts, and Elven was following close behind Father and telling everyone to beware of the Nazi conspiracy. Father turned around suddenly and said, "It's not a Nazi conspiracy. It's the true Church."

I grabbed Elven by the arm and told him we had to be going. "He's telling lies to everyone here," Elven said. For once I insisted that we leave, and he agreed.

Not six months later, Clyde Perkins came home from college for Christmas vacation, and he brought a girl with him. I was in church that Sunday with Elven when Clyde introduced her to everyone in church as the love of his life. "We're going to be married this summer," he announced to the whole congregation. He smiled real big, and she beamed up at him in the same way Callie used to do.

By that time, Father had found a new religion. He and Mother had started going to the Pentecostal Church that was being formed in the community, but Callie drew more and more into herself. She'd spend every day sitting by the window seat, seeming to stare out the window, without saying a word to anyone. Father and Mother could barely get her to eat, much less talk to anyone. On the day Clyde came and announced his engagement, I knew someone had to tell Callie. Mother and Father wouldn't, and Elven said, "She's a big girl now. You can't go protecting her all of her life through."

In some strange way, I hoped that if I told her about Clyde, I might be able to get some sort of reaction out of her. I went to the house, right after church, and I remember looking at her lost, sad, blue eyes and her long brown hair that she hadn't run a comb through in at least a month. I remember wishing for the sparkle that had been in her eyes before Father went and joined the Jehovah Witnesses. "Callie," I said. It was like I was talking to a stone wall. She didn't even seem to recognize me. "Clyde was in church today. With a girl he met at Baylor."

I waited for her to do something that would let me know that she heard what I was saying. Nothing came. Not even a look, or a turn of her head. So I took a deep breath and continued, "He's engaged to this girl. They're getting married come summer."

I wanted her head to jerk. I wanted her to cry and pitch a fit like she used to, but she just sat there, staring out into space, like nothing meant anything to her and like nothing would mean anything to her ever again.

"Callie, do you realize what I'm telling you? Please, please," I cried to her and pitched the fit for her. I couldn't keep from crying as I walked away, and I couldn't stop from blaming Father for everything bad that had ever happened to Callie. I wanted to cuss him out like he had never been cussed out before, but it was the 1940s and women didn't talk back to their fathers back then.

By the end of that month, Father and Mother decided they couldn't handle Callie on their own any more. "We're getting on in years, and we just can't meet all her needs," they told me one Saturday when I came to visit.

I knew they were hinting for me and Elven to take her in, but we had already had that discussion, and he had told me, "We ain't taking her in. We've got four children of our own and one on the way. There's no way in God's blue blazes that we can take on another mouth to feed."

I waited for them to say something, and I prayed they wouldn't say what I thought they had in mind. "We're going to send her to the home in Rusk," Father said. He never called it what Elven always called it, the loonie bin.

"We've done all he can for her," Mother said and waited for me to volunteer to take Callie in.

I started mentioning all my other brothers and sisters. "What about Lavinia or Alvie and Winnie?" I asked as they nodded and waited for me to stop naming names.

"You're the one she's always trusted," they said.

I wanted more than anything to take Callie in, to give her a home, but I could hear in my mind Elven saying like he always did when I mentioned Callie to him, "She belongs in the loonie bin, not in a proper home. It's her own fault that it's all come to this. You tried to warn her. You did your part."

But I knew that Elven was right. With four children and one on the way, we could not afford to bring her to our house to live. In the next room I saw Callie sitting at the window seat, staring out into the unknown, and I knew that I had to let her go into the unknown. But still I blamed Father for everything, and I had myself thinking that he was just making up excuses to get Callie off his hands.

"We've done all we can. We can't afford her upkeep much longer," he said, trying to get me to agree with him, which I wouldn't do.

"We thought maybe you and Elven could lend a hand," Mother said.

They were putting the pressure on me, and I wanted to be a good daughter and sister and say that Callie could come to live with Elven, me, and the children, but all I could do was nod and speak to Mother, not Father, "Elven won't let her come."

The next week Father and Mother took Callie all the way to Rusk, and that was where she stayed for over forty years until she passed away in 1985 when she got pneumonia. Five years before she passed, the officials at the home called me one day and said,"She could be released if you could find a place for her to stay."

By that time, Elven had died of cancer two years back, and I was a widow living on a fixed income. All my children had grown up and moved out of state. I had a bad back, and there was no one to help me take care of Callie. I barely made it from one social security check to the next.

I couldn't help remembering how I was as mad as a wet hen when Father and Mother told me they were getting on in years and couldn't take care of Callie. I thought they were making up excuses for not doing right by her. Always in the back of my mind, though, I blamed Elven for not letting her come to live with us. If he'd let me do what I knew to be right, I told myself her life would have turned around and she would have been happy again.

When the man from the state home called, I wished that I had a million dollars so I could afford to hire around-the-clock help to take care of Callie, but I didn't have a million dollars, so I told the man, "I'm sorry. I just don't have the finances."

"Ma'am," he drawled in a young voice that sounded almost like Clyde Perkins. "Your sister'll be drawing a social security check, and a social worker will come by once a week to see how she's doing. We can send the home health care lady over to your house every day to bathe her and to help you out."

I was Callie's only living relative, and I could tell by the way he was talking that he thought I should take her in, but the home health care lady couldn't be there twenty-four hours a day, and I wouldn't know what to do if Callie went berserk and tried to kill someone. There was no telling what she would be like after spending all those years in the state home, and in my mind I could hear Father and Mother saying, "We're getting on in years." And I remembered Elven saying, "She belongs in the loonie bin, not here with us."

I wanted to tell the man that I'd take Callie in, but I couldn't. With tears in my eyes, I told him, "I'm an old lady, and the burden would be too much for me." As I hung up the phone, I couldn't help thinking that I'd done the same thing to Callie that I blamed Father, Mother, and Elven for doing. I had made up an excuse for not doing right by her, but I was afraid of what the future would hold in store, and maybe they had been too.

Massacre

Camilla Carr

It was the worst sight she'd ever seen.

Her breath turned to short choppy gasps. Her hands reached out wildly, frantically, in complete conflict, not knowing whether to try to stifle the scream she felt coming from the bottom of her throat or to plunge into the massacre she saw before her.

The light seemed to go right out of the Texas-humid, still-as-death March day, and like a hailstorm, her head felt black and thick, invaded by huge, heavy relentless pounding.

And then the air seemed to go right out of her head. She could see her own head like a lost balloon, shooting straight up off its string, floating, floating, and then, purged, falling flat and graceless, a rubbery, empty mass, in the midst of the countless torn dismembered, now unrecognizable faces of her family, their arms and legs, heads, torsos, fluttering in a senseless heap, shredded forever into oblivion.

For a long long while she lay still there, hoping none of it had really happened, that her mind had just gone crazed and cracked from the heat, parched and broken from six nights and days of one hundred and fifteen degree white hot heat, and still not even the first day of spring.

Well, no, nights it's went down to ninety-two degrees onct or twict, she reminded herself in her mother's voice. And hearing her mother's voice in her head is what opened her eyes and brought her to her feet and made her look at the monstrous mess and know it was real.

"Oh, I hate you, Mama," she said out loud to the scattered crowd on the floor. "I really do."

She reached for the end of the iron bedstead, and bracing herself for balance, pulling her weight to her feet, she stepped carefully, as carefully as she could, making herself look up, not down, as she started out the screen door that was standing half opened.

"Of course you're half open," she said to the door. "You're green and ugly and open just like you always are!"

She kicked the door as hard as she could. The screen split five more inches at the bottom, and she heard her toe crack, but she didn't feel a thing. She just walked past the open screen door (why close it now?) and down the steps and across the hard brown grass. She stayed off the old red brick path.

It'll blister them feet, she heard her mother's voice say.

"You don't care," she said. "You never cared and now it's too late."

She hit the splitting wooden gate with her palm; it flew right open, no one ever shut the latch. And along the alley, honeysuckle and sweet rotting kitchen scraps lured bees and flies and trails of red ants.

She picked up a board and slammed it into an ant hill. Giant red ants turned upside down and sideways, the thin crooked busy line momentarily disrupted.

"You don't get to live either," she said. "I'm goin' to kill ever one of you when I come back." And then she carefully placed the board right on top of their mound, wondering how long it would take all of them to suffocate.

At first she thought some must have bitten her when the stinging started. She was already inside the back gate of her aunt's house, inside the gate and almost about to step upon the back porch, when she saw her toe was bleeding and turning dark. Then the pain shot through her foot. Her whole foot.

And the next thing she knew she was screaming a long, terrifying, parched-hollow scream.

No one came out of the house.

"I know you're in there, Mama, so come on out!" she screamed.

When no one came, she started to scream again.

This time the door flew open, and the whole frame was filled with a large lumpy woman wiping her dark mustache with the hem of her dress. It was white with red carnations printed all over it.

"Packard, what's got into you, girl? She ain't here and the Academy Awards is gettin' ready to come on, so whatever it is will have to wait." Closing the door, the fat woman turned to go back inside.

"It's a tragedy, Aunt Izzy!" A new scream commenced.

"Not now it inn't. Not at Oscar time, Packard."

"Yes! Yes! Yes! They're dead! Ever single one of 'em! They're lyin' on the floor in a heap all over the floor! Ever thing that means a thing to me is scattered! My whole life is scattered ever place in the back room, torn to pieces, arms, legs, hands, feet and it's *her* fault, Aunt Izzy! *Utter destruction!*"

Izabel Foster's back door flew open and flattened itself against the gray rusty house shingles. One shingle dropped from the force of the door hitting it, another drooped, holding on by one nail.

"Who's dead, Packard?"

Izzy pulled her weight out on the steps, the big red carnations on her muumuu making waves over her flesh as she made her way toward the girl.

"Who's dead?"

"Ever body, all of 'em, they're all just lyin' there . . ."

"Oh, Gawd, oh Lord, I knew this would happen," Izzy moaned, reaching out for the girl. She caught her arm and dragged her toward the gate, down the alley, past the red ant hill covered with a board, through the honeysuckle and garbage pails.

"Was it the dawgs?" Izzy asked.

The girl nodded silently. She was crying now.

"Oh, Law, oh Law, oh Law," Izzy murmured, trying to hurry. "Gate's open, door's broke," she said to herself as she went up the brick path and approached the house. "You stay out here, Packard."

The girl stopped in a patch of brown grass. The sun, greedily eating up the whole sky, washed out the clouds. The girl blinked and waited. And watched her aunt lumber cautiously into the house.

"*Goddammit!*" Izzy bellowed from inside.

Packard walked slowly toward the house and stepped up on the porch, and inside the screen door.

She looked down and pointed. "There . . ."

Izzy just stared at her. When she yelled her face burst with red, contorted rage. "Nobody's dead here!!! Them is paper dolls, girl!"

"Ever single one of 'em! Torn to shreds! Dead! Dead! Dead!" the girl cried. She fell in the heap and sobbed. "My whole life-long family! Dead! Dead! Dead!"

Izzy swallowed uncomfortably and said something about wishing she'd had a child so she'd know how to treat one when it got upset. "You like to have scared the life out of me, Packard." Rolls of fat swam over her huge body, like ocean tide, as the woman breathed in and out, trying to calm herself down. She couldn't stop thinking of her sister, who didn't seem to care how she treated *anything*. Izzy reached out tentatively and gave two short soft yanks to one of the girl's long pigtails. "Bury 'em tomorrow, honey," Izzy said quietly. Then, in a more firm voice she continued. "Right *now* we're missin' the show. I don't want to miss the cars driving up and the stars getting out. I need to see what Faye Dunaway's wearing. She's nominated for *Network*. I'm just torn between her and Sissy Spacek in *Carrie*."

"What about Jodie Foster in *Taxi Driver*?" the little girl sniffed. "She's my age. My own age."

"Well, you don't want to miss seeing *her*. She's not the star, though. Robert DeNiro's the star."

"What makes a star, Aunt Iz?"

"They're the ones you pay the most attention to," Iz said. "They set the styles. Give the rest of us something to aspire to. In England, they have kings and queens. Here in America, we have cinema royalty. Look," Iz offered, "I'll give you my brand new Sears catalog, you can get a new bunch of paper people together and we can have a little funeral here in the back yard for these folks tomorrow."

"No, we cain't. Not in this back yard," Packard sniffed. "She's got it filled. I think I broke my toe."

"It cain't be full of dead dawgs," Izzy said.

"It is."

"Then use a spot in my yard," Izzy replied. "Not in the petunia patch or the corn and beans. Somewhere where nothin's growin'." She was trying to think of where that could be. She didn't like grass, so she planted other things, any other thing, and where things wouldn't grow, she placed rocks and pebbles. "Come on now." She tried to stare down at the girl's foot, all the way over her own stomach. "Maybe you just stumped it."

"I'm goin' to dig them dogs up."

"Good," Izzy nodded absently. "I hope we're not missin' the cars drivin' up and the stars gettin' out and talkin' to each other. How could you forgive yourself if you missed Sylvester Stallone?"

"I'm killin' Highway," Packard said as she reached for a paper head with blonde hair wearing a black-veiled hat.

"What?"

"Highway. That's who did this. That ole chow dog with the black tongue she found out on the highway and named Highway."

"Oh, him . . ." Izzy had located the black-suited torso that went with the blonde's head. "Looky here, honey!"

Packard took the piece and placed it beside its head. "Why don't she name things names?"

"It's that ole Indian custom she picked up from that Indian-man boyfriend she claims was your daddy. Wherever she is when she gets something, that's what she names it."

"I don't look like a Indian. I'm *not* a Indian." Packard started to cry again. "Am I a Indian, Aunt Izzy?"

"I don't know, honey. Oh, look! Are these the feet and shoes?"

"Yes, yes, yes!" Packard grabbed the pieces from Izzy's fingers and lined them up next to the matching legs. "I could have been called Mercury or Cadillac or Thunderbird or even *Rambler* if she'd a been in one when I was made! I guess I'm lucky it was a Packard, even if it does sound like a boy. People don't know me, they expect a boy."

"Once they see you though, they know you're a girl," Izzy offered. "Now listen. I got tape. You can see you can fix them back together. Get that shoe box over yonder and gather these up and bring 'em on over to the Oscars."

Packard nodded and smiled. "She's together onct I get me your tape."

"Honey, please come on," Izzy pleaded.

"I guess I'll kill Highway tomorrow," Packard said. "And I'm stealing his bed."

"I would if I was you," Izzy said, almost breaking out in a sweat from the effort of trying to bend down to yank an old tattered quilt from the bottom of an old wicker basket. Izabel finally attached one finger and her thumb around the handle of the basket. Straightening, she pulled both the basket and the quilt up with her with a heave and a groan. "The only thing I can depend on your mama to do is never pass on a thing that was give to her. She keeps ever last thing for herself until it dies or leaves and in between she just flat-out forgets she's got it." Dust fell from the quilt. "Shake it out later. We're missing the show." She stuffed the quilt down into the basket. "That's a double-wedding-band quilt design and far too few bands for Mrs. Cordelia Franklin-Jackson-McGhee-Jordan-Whitehall-Oates. She's married everything but a decent man at least once, but who knows? If one Mr. Judge Dewey Gammill don't get a-hold of hisself, your mama may surpass herself and bring Mr. Judge Gammill down to her own level."

Packard placed the remains of her paper people on top of the quilt and moved slowly to the screen door with the basket. "She goin' to marry Judge Gammill?"

"Or somebody," Izzy replied. "Come on."

Packard followed her aunt back along the alley carrying her paper people in Highway's old bed. Packard looked at the faded soiled quilt, still lovely in spite of the dirty marks and torn places spotting the delicate curves of the wedding bands, pieced with patches of pale greens, lavenders, and blues, duplicated again and again and again, a continuous pattern broken only by the exposed cotton stuffing where the quilt had ripped. Just as she was vowing to hand-wash the quilt herself, three fleas crawled out from under the black-veiled hat of the rescued blonde Packard had placed on top of the pile.

"This quilt has fleas, Auntie Iz," Packard said. "We should have waited and washed it."

Izabel kept walking. "It'll just fall apart. Why do you think I give it to you?" She waddled on toward her house.

Packard stopped and stood in the staleness of the alley. Before her and a little to the right was the board she had used to cover the ant hill. She sat down the basket and moved the board to one side.

Izabel was almost inside her own gate when she heard Packard's scream.

"SNAKE BITE!" the girl cried. "I put down that board to kill them ants and then I was tryin' to save them, but that snake was under the board and it bit me!"

424

Izabel looked frantically around, hoping the snake had gone and wasn't standing anywhere underneath her muumuu where she couldn't see it.

"There it is!" Packard screamed. "In my basket! On my *people!*"

"It's a grass snake, thank you, God," Izabel sighed. "It just stung you. You won't die."

"No, I won't," Packard cried. "I just won't die! Nothin' can kill me today! Snakes, flies, fleas, ole mean messy chow dogs, four or five or six or seven daddies, who knows? *I may even be a Indian!* And now a sorry shitty green grass snake! I'm *beyond* death!" She looked up at the sky and wailed. She took the board and hit the hole again and again and again.

"They're still comin' out," Izabel murmured, staring at the ants.

"That's the way ants do!" Packard screamed.

Izabel looked over at the snake in the basket. She picked up a sharp stick and in the next instant, the snake lay in two pieces, its insides oozing out over the bottom of the paper people collection and soiling the already damaged quilt.

"Oh, no," Packard whispered, dropping the board. She stared dully into the basket. "That's it. *The End.*"

Izabel stood helplessly holding the stick. She couldn't think of a thing to say.

Packard walked over to the basket, picked it up, along with the quilt, and dumped the two pieces of the snake and all her entire life-long collected paper doll family into the tin trash can.

She took her paper-cutting scissors out of her pocket and chopped off both her pigtails before Fat Izzy could move her weight to stop her.

"What are you doin' child?" Izzy cried.

"It's over," Packard said. "I'm just not going to be a girl no more. From this minute on, you can treat me like a man."

Izabel stared at her niece, irritably. "What'll I tell your mother? That's no hairdo for a little lady—"

"I'm not no lady. I'm not no weakling little lady," Packard said. "I always heard God was a man. And from now on I'm just goin' to give up and be one, too."

"Fine, Miss Ridiculous." Izabel hurried down the path, alone, calling back, "I just hope you hadn't made me miss those Oscars!"

Packard went back to her own porch and sat down and tried to imagine her life as a man. President. Pope. Astronaut. Dallas Cowboy. She didn't get up for an hour.

By the time she finally went into her aunt's house, Izabel didn't even look away from the TV screen. And her mother, half drunk on the couch, snuggled up to next to her favorite dog, Highway, giving him sips of her bourbon and 7UP, real pissed off that Judge Gammill was having to watch the Oscars with his one and only wife.

Packard waited for her mama to stop fondling that dog and complaining about Judge Gammill and notice her new bad haircut. But she didn't.

The TV screen was announcing Best Actor and showing clips of *Taxi Driver*. Packard Jordan took one look at Robert De Niro, went into the bathroom and shaved the rest of her hair off into a mohawk. She painted streaks of red down her cheeks with *Make Me Red* Revlon lipstick. She went into the living room, holding a gun from the bedside table in one hand and a knife from the kitchen drawer in the other and when Izabel saw her, she was so frightened she could hardly even scream. But her Mama screamed. She screamed good.

"You talkin' to me?" Packard asked, in her best Robert De Niro voice. "Who you talkin' to? You talkin' to *me?*"

That did it. That got their attention.

"Oh Yeah, Texas: A Journal Entry"

Saturday, July 8, 1967

Last night Johnny stayed over for the first time. I still haven't been to his place. If I was at home, Buddy and me'd probably be sleeping over two or three times a week, but people don't seem to do it much down here. Jared, of course, made a bunch of stupid cracks about the two of us sleeping together, and I really think—if Grandpa hadn't been standing right there—that I would've told him he was the one always talking about boys screwing, so the way I figured it he must be the one always thinking about it. And then I guess he would've pounded my face into the Coke machine, and I'd be trying to write this with two black eyes. Oh, well.

It was neat having Johnny over, though, because we had the whole second floor to ourselves, and we didn't have to worry about Ellie barging in, and when we were doing stuff we weren't supposed to, like looking at Jared's *Playboys*, we knew we wouldn't get caught because we could hear Grandma and Grandpa coming up the stairs. Which they didn't do anyway.

We had one of Grandma's enormous suppers—chicken fried steak, mashed potatoes, green beans (she calls 'em string beans), gravy and biscuits. And apple pie. Mama never cooks that much, but then maybe that's because we don't have so much money. Or maybe huge meals are just the old way.

Johnny didn't say much. He talks plenty when it's just us, or just kids, but adults make him nervous, I guess.

It was about seven when we got through eating.

"All right if we go down to the swimming hole now?" I asked.

"On a full stomach?" Grandma asked.

"We won't go into the water for thirty minutes," I said.

"An hour," Grandma said.

"Forty-five minutes?" I felt like I was buying a car with Dad.

"Papa?" she said to Grandpa.

He swished some iced tea around his mouth. "I reckon forty-five minutes'll be long enough."

"Thanks, Grandma, Grandpa." I got up.

"You're excused," Grandpa said.

"Oh, sorry."

Johnny stood up then. "It was really good, Mrs. McKamey. Thanks for having me over."

"Oh, you're certainly welcome. We're glad to have you," Grandma said. "Willy's been a little lonely—"

"Grandma," I said. I couldn't believe she was embarrassing me in front of Johnny. Well, actually, I could believe it. She sure did a good job at the Gibson's store.

"Well, it's true, Willy."

"Grandma!"

She sighed. Made a lot of noise under her breath.

"Come on, Johnny," I said.

He looked as embarrassed as I was.

We went out and headed along the southern edge of Grandpa's garden. The corn's getting pretty high now, almost to my shoulders.

"You wanna hike over to Mills' Pond?" I asked. "Walk off some of this food?"

Johnny shook his head.

"Why not?"

"Jared and his friends'll probably be there. Drinking."

"Maybe they'll give us some." I was joking, but Johnny didn't catch it.

"No, thanks," he said. "He's puked enough for both of us."

"I was joking. You really think we could get beerbreath past my grandma?"

He shrugged.

"Is he always out there on Fridays?"

"Most of the time, unless— Hey, that's right. There's a dance at the park tonight. He might be there."

"The city park?"

He shook his head. "No, at Garner."

"So—"

"Okay. It's a great place to swim. Rocks all around the edge to jump and dive off." He looked at the sun. "You think we can get back before dark?"

"There's a moon, isn't there?"

"Yeah. Okay. But let's not stay long. I wanna show you the books I brought."

"Who?"

"Arthur Clarke. Robert Heinlein."

I stared at him. "You read those guys too?"

"I told you I liked to read."

"But I figured—" I stopped, afraid to make him mad.

"What?" he asked, kind of like he was challenging me.

"Well—I thought maybe—Louis L'Amour. Like my dad reads."

"Shit. I live in the country, not in the nineteenth century."

"Sorry."

We skirted the picnic pasture, the one field Grandpa keeps all mown down, and turned almost straight north. We had to watch the ground, going around clumps of prickly pear cactus and yucca plants and jumbles of rock. I unbuttoned my shirt and pushed the flaps open. There were just a few clouds in the west, and it was hot as hell. Thick air, just like in Dallas. Does no good to dry off when you get out of the shower.

Johnny looked at me. "That don't tan?"

I glanced down at my scar. "No."

"I guess mine wouldn't either, but it doesn't have much of a chance."

I laughed. "Yeah, I can just see you strolling around Oh Yeah naked."

Johnny shook his head at my tone of voice. "It's not so bad, Will. I know everybody. I got all these creeks and hills and stuff to mess around in."

I spit through my teeth. "Johnny, it's— You're right. Oh Yeah's not so bad. I mean, I miss getting to look for records and P&J's, and books at the dime store, but—Mostly I just miss—people."

For a while he didn't say anything. We scrambled down a narrow dry creekbed and climbed up the other side. He got to the top first and turned around to give me a hand up. "I know. After my mom died—"

429

Made me feel pretty dumb to be whining about missing everybody. At least I can still see them, sooner or later.

"Jared," he said, "Jared's really pretty good to me. I mean, he gives me lots of shit, and I hate it when he's drunk, but he wouldn't let anybody mess with me."

"I don't really know him." I felt kind of guilty about all the rotten cracks I'd made about Jared.

"Oh, you know him the way most people do, the way he wants people to know him—a hard-ass." He pulled up the tail of his T-shirt, smeared his face, then pulled the shirt over his head. "He even does the laundry about half the time."

"Yeah? Who does it the rest of the time?"

"What do you think? Me."

We came up over the rise at the edge of Grandpa's land. There's the fence there, then a long slope down to the old quarry. Mills' Pond is down there. It was quiet, and we couldn't see anybody.

"Hey," Johnny said, "I guess they're all at the park." Like he hadn't really believed it when he said it before. He got a little kind of half-grin on his face that made him look a lot happier. Not that he usually looked sad— he just didn't look happy either.

"So let's hit it."

We tried to be good and sit on the shore for a while and let our dinner settle, but the air was so warm and the water looked so cool that, pretty soon, we were out of our clothes and into the pond. It's a lot deeper than Grandpa's swimming hole, partly, I guess, because of the chunks taken out of the ground by the old quarrymen; partly, maybe, just because it's so much bigger. The swimming hole's bigger than a backyard pool but not as big as a city park pool. But the pond covers—according to Johnny—at least half an acre. In the shallow parts the water's completely clear. We stood there for a while, watching little fish come up to nip at our feet, then our legs, but when one made a run at my balls, I jerked my legs up and started swimming. Johnny fell in beside me, and we raced to a big platform-looking rock on the north side, closest to the old quarry cliffs that are still above the water. We pulled ourselves up onto the rock to catch our breath and looked back west at the sky.

430

Some clouds had started to roll in, and the sun was already turning the edges of the clouds orange and pink. "I'm not so sure about that," Johnny said.

"What do you mean?" I asked.

He motioned toward a thick clump of cloud not much over the horizon. "See the color there? That looks like hail."

"Really? Soon? Should we go back already?"

"Nah, not yet. It'll take at least an hour to blow in."

"Good." I pointed at the big rocks around us. "Which is the best for jumping off of?"

"You wanna jump or dive?"

"Jump mostly."

"Then we wanna be high." He twisted around on his butt. "That one"— a big rounded boulder on the southeast (I think) corner—"is the tallest, but there's a lotta mud and stuff that's washed in over there. So you almost always hit bottom, unless you do a really good cannonball. This one"—he patted the rock we sat on—"is best for diving, because it's real deep right here in front. The high school guys do most of their jumping off that one." He pointed at a wedge-shaped rock back almost halfway to the other shore. "It's easy to walk up to the top, and when you jump there, it's at least twenty feet deep. At least that's what Jared says. I've never touched bottom there."

"You wanna do it?" I asked.

"Sure."

So we dove in and swam over. We jumped and screamed and acted goofy for fifteen minutes or so, maybe longer. The sky was getting darker, but slowly, because the sun had just gone down, and the wind was getting up enough to almost be cold when we first climbed out of the water. I had just come up the backside of the wedge and was getting ready to sprint up and out, when I heard a voice yell, "Hey, pretty boy." It was a girl's voice.

For a second I just froze, then I put my hands down to my dick and started backing down the wedge. I could see two people under one of the trees, but it was shadowy and I couldn't tell who they were.

Then the same girl yelled, "Too late, stud! I've already seen your jewels."

"Shit," I said and kept backing. Johnny had heard her and was waiting for me at the bottom of the rock. "Shit," I said again, "what are we gonna do?"

"That's Laurie Pence," Johnny said. "I recognize her voice. She's the high school whore."

"What?" I said. "You mean she takes money for—"

He shook his head. "Okay, I should've said slut. She—puts it out for free."

Shit! And Mama thinks Dallas is wild.

"So what do we do?" I asked. "Our clothes are over there."

Johnny shrugged. "It depends on who she's with. If it's one of Jared's buddies, he'll probably throw 'em in the pond."

"You're kidding."

He shook his head.

"Grandma'll kill me if—"

But then Laurie solved the problem. Sort of. She yelled, "I know there's two of you. Two sets of clothes. You might as well come get 'em."

"What does she mean?" I asked.

"What she says. Come get 'em." Johnny spit into the water and kind of shivered. "It's getting dark. We better do it." He turned, like he meant to just dive into the water, swim around the rock, and walk buck naked up the shore and get his clothes.

"What the hell are you talking about?" I grabbed his arm. "I'm not shaking my dick up there for some girl."

"You got a better idea? You wanna walk a mile back to your grandparents', naked, barefoot?"

"I can't just walk up there with my—"

"Hell, you can't. I know what she's like. She bugs Jared sometimes. Hanging on to a couple of kids' clothes 'til they come to get 'em is right up her line."

"God." I rubbed my hands against my forehead. It was starting to get chilly. "Johnny, she's a girl. I'll start out of the water, and I'll get a hard-on just thinking about her looking at—"

"So she'll have one more thing to laugh at us about."

I stared at him. "Don't you care?"

432

"Fuck, yes, I care! What do you think? But I'll be damned if I'll rip my feet to pieces walking back to your place." He made fists then, although I don't think he really meant to.

I shivered. I was humiliated at the thought of coming up out of that water with some slut standing there. It was a billion times worse than the first time I'd had to strip down and shower at school. That, at least, was just guys, and they already knew what dicks were. Of course, according to Johnny, so did Laurie.

"Well?" he said finally. "You want me to get yours too? And bring 'em around to where we came down? Then she'll only see your butt."

I thought about it. I thought about it hard. Then I realized it wasn't fair to Johnny. He'd be in Oh Yeah 'til he graduated at least. People could make fun of him about this for years. With any luck, I would be gone by the time school started. And I didn't have to live with Jared, who for sure would hear about this. Besides I didn't want Johnny—or even Laurie and whoever her boyfriend was—thinking I was a complete pussy. If I got a hard-on—I decided—then she could just get an eyeful.

"No," I said finally, "but—will you go first?"

He laughed then. "Yeah. Come on. Let's get it over with."

All our talking had one good effect—by the time we'd swam around to the shore, it was a little darker. Laurie's "date" was sprawled on the ground, leaning up on one elbow, smoking a cigarette.

"That's Bo Mitler," Johnny whispered. We were walking up now, only rib-deep in the water.

"Come on, little boys," Laurie said. She was laughing. She had Johnny's underwear dangling off one finger. The finger was stuck into the fly.

"Who's he?" I whispered back.

"In Jared's class. Football player."

"Great."

Now we were only waist-deep, and Johnny glanced over at me. "I thought you—"

"Just keep going." I gritted my teeth. "If we both come out at the same time, she can only look half as much."

Johnny almost laughed.

"Oowee!" Laurie squealed. "A couple of big wieners. Hair and everything."

The air hit my dick and, since the wind was cool, I started shriveling instead of growing. Thank you, God!

We kept walking.

"All right, Laurie," Bo called then. "You've seen their little peckers. Give 'em their clothes."

"Jealous?" she asked. She turned to look at him.

He snorted. "Yeah, right."

Johnny grabbed his shorts while she wasn't looking and stepped around her to the rock where our clothes were. I followed him.

"You're not bad," she said to me. "I haven't seen you before. Maybe we—"

"Laurie!" Bo called.

She turned to him again.

"Get your clothes, fool!" Johnny whispered.

I bent, trying to stand sideways to her, to hide my dick and butt both.

"You're no fun, Bo," Laurie whined.

"Naked little boys ain't my idea of fun," he said.

"C'mon," Johnny said to me. He had all his stuff in his arms, held low enough to shield his crotch.

"Let's put our underwear—" I started to say.

"Not here. Come on."

"Hey, Johnny!" Bo said.

"Yeah?" Johnny stopped, but didn't turn around.

"Tell Jared I'll call him in the morning."

"I'm not going home tonight."

"Oh," Laurie said. "The naked bunnies are having a sleepover."

"Shut up, Laurie," Bo said.

I followed Johnny, still not believing I was walking down the little bank of a pond, stark naked, with a high school slut staring at my butt. "How the hell far are we going?" I hissed.

"Behind that rock," he said.

We dried off as good as we could with our shirts, then got dressed. I leaned back against the rock—it was still warm from the sun—and put one foot on the other knee to tie my shoe. "I guess they're having a good laugh," I said.

434

Johnny frowned at me. "You kidding? He's already on top of her by now."

"You mean it?" I bent down, hiding my blushing, and tied my other shoe.

"She's fast," Johnny said. "Ready?"

"Yeah."

The whole western half of the sky was clouds now, but the moon was up in the east, and we could see all right. Now that we were walking, and back into our clothes, the chilly wind felt good.

"Well, Johnny," I said, "I don't think that's one I'll write home about."

He laughed. "Know what you mean. Save it for the grandchildren."

The whole thing didn't really seem to bother him too much. So I thought I'd take a little poke at him. "Of course, you were so cool about it, I'd've reckoned you prance around naked for girls all the time."

He spit, which I'd figured out by now was his way of saying, Like hell. "Shit, I've had to stand up to Jared ever since I could walk. He still smashes me, but at least he can't call me a cunt."

That is the first time in my life anybody ever said that word to me. God, me and Buddy think we're crude saying pussy.

"But, Johnny, if they tell—"

"No if."

"Well, then, my grandparents are going to hear—"

He put his hand on my shoulder. "Willy, they're gonna tell—Jared and everybody else at school. But nobody's going to tell your grandparents."

"Not even Jared?" I couldn't believe it.

"Not even Jared's gonna tell your grandpa Laurie Pence saw you wagging your wienie in the air."

"Swear?"

He laughed. "If your grandparents ever say a word to you about this, I'll stick my hands in my back pockets and let you beat the crap out of me."

"Why would I wanna do that?"

He shrugged. Then a big crack of lightning shattered about half the sky, and we started to run.

435

After popcorn and Cokes with Grandpa and Grandma, Johnny and I went upstairs. We sat on the floor in front of the big windows in Dad's old room and watched the storm let loose. Big wads of lightning exploded over the house, reaching down like snakes' tongues. Then the hail hit. It was dark, except for the lightning every minute or so. Easy to talk.

"Johnny?"

"Yeah?" He said it real slow, not sleepylike, but just real calm.

"About Laurie—"

He turned to me then, but I couldn't see more than the two dark sockets of his eyes. "Yeah?"

"Does she really—just—do it with—"

"Anybody. Yeah." I couldn't tell if he thought it was exciting or disgusting.

"Don't she—you know—worry about—getting pregnant?"

He shook his head. Then he said, "I mean, I don't really know, you know, but Jared said— He said she got pregnant last year, and her parents took her to Acuna—"

"What's that?"

"City in Mexico. And they had it—taken care of."

"Meaning?" I felt so stupid, really out of my league.

"Abortion."

"Sheesh."

"Yeah," he said. "And the doctor screwed it up. Now she can't get pregnant." It was quiet for a few seconds, not even any thunder.

"Johnny?"

"You sure like to talk."

"And you don't?"

He shrugged.

"Well, listen, do you think—Jared's ever—" I stopped.

"Done it?" His voice was low, like he was getting a cold.

"Done it with her."

Another big flash of lightning, and we both looked back out the window in time to see a hailstone smash into it.

"Damn!" I shouted, and we jumped back.

"I heard that, William McKamey!" Grandma yelled from downstairs.

436

Johnny and I laughed. I stretched out on my belly and rested my head in my hands.

"Jared's as scared of girls as I am," Johnny said.

"Huh?"

"Sure," Johnny said. "I figured it out last year. He always talks about the girls, but he always goes drinking with his friends. I think—"

"Yeah?"

"I think maybe that's why he drinks."

"Wow."

Johnny stood up then and leaned against the window.

"How does he, you know, keep your dad from finding out?"

Johnny let out a long breath. "Will, half the time Dad gets drunk with him." His fingers tapped on the windowpane.

"Oh. Sorry."

"Why?" He kept looking out the window, even though I couldn't have seen his face anyway.

"Asking so many dumb questions."

"You're not dumb," he said. "Just new. Everybody else already knows all this stuff."

It was a scary thought, everybody knowing everything about you. You'd have to be mighty good, or just not give a shit. I mean, when Stephen conned the guy at the drugstore into letting him buy a *Playboy*, he knew that guy would never remember him. Had no idea who he was. Wouldn't tell Stephen's dad next time he came in the store because he didn't know him. But in Oh Yeah— Shit, I'm Hub's boy.

And then Johnny really surprised me. He said, "Besides, you're probably the best friend I've had in five years."

I didn't know what to say. So I just laid there for a while 'til it got uncomfortable, then I reached over and slapped Johnny's ankle and said, "Hey, let's look at those books you brought over. And listen to the Byrds."

"Sounds good."

And he gave me a hand up.

Sheesh, I'm bushed.

Ex Libris

LYN FRASER

Grace peered through her lookout position between 581.5264 *Deciduous Forests of North America* and 581.65 *Just Weeds*. She could see the regulars arriving. Enid Slack, Head Librarian, opened right on time today at 8:30. Yesterday's opening had occurred at 8:32. Grace always felt better when Enid opened on time. It gave her a sense of confidence about the day.

She circled behind 614.317 *Textbook of Meat Hygiene* and headed toward the card catalog. By 8:47 the activity in the library was at a level sufficient to cover Grace's emerging from the stacks rather than entering through the front door. Grace had a thin frame and frizzy gray hair, and her visible clothing was muted—khaki slacks, light blue permanent press blouse, and gray walking shoes. The slacks covered her purple and gold striped socks. Grace had once overheard her boss remark, "Grace looks like she lives in a library." Now she did. She had moved in six weeks ago. And it was working out fine, so far.

Grace felt safe in the library. She also felt safe in the bathtub. She missed her bathtub, but it was better to feel safe most of the time, living in the library, than just some of the time, in her tub. She couldn't stay in her tub all of the time because the water wrinkled her skin, even with the bubbling bath oil, and she eventually got clammy. So she had moved into the library. Rarely did she get hot and clammy in the library. The library thermostats maintained a constant temperature and humidity. And odor. Grace liked the way the library smelled, its special library smell of books and dust and mildew in an enclosed space. It was the books and the smell and the quiet, especially at night, that she liked. And not talking to anyone.

Not talking to anyone was definitely a plus. Especially not talking to anyone in groups and not talking to anyone standing up. Her pit mode of interpersonal relating was talking to groups of people in a large room occupied by many other people talking to each other in groups. Grace could handle, for brief periods, conversations with one person. Or talking to more than one person if she and the more-than-ones were seated. Something about standing and talking annihilated what limited oral communication skills and self confidence she possessed. Eventually, whether the conversation was with one or more than one, seated or standing, large room or small, the outcome was the same. Their eyes would shift as the she, he, it, or they sought escape from her to another person—or even to a place. Apparently leaning against a wall was preferable to conversation with Grace, she had observed. And occasional anyones had even stared at wallpaper while Grace talked, not even waiting to shift.

Grace was relieved from worry about the un-lasting of relationships in the library. Not that living in the library didn't present its own set of potential unpleasantries. Where to sleep, for example. Grace didn't like Current Periodicals because of the cold formica floor. The offices had carpets but they were locked at night. There was too much open space in Reference. The area behind the Service and Information desks was too cramped, and that was the first place the staff came in the morning. If she overslept they'd find her there, first thing, and then she wouldn't get to live in the library anymore. She had finally settled on the Children's Room, which was isolated and had a carpeted area surrounded by bean bag chairs. The cleaning crew vacuumed the carpet every evening, eliminating any worry Grace might have about sleeping on or near the day's dirt. And the children's space felt cozy, enclosed by the bean bag chairs and picture books.

Possibilities for relating were endless in the library, and there was no danger of rejection here. None whatsoever. She had yet to be abandoned by a book or current periodical or learned journal. And she treated them with equal respect.

Each day Grace worked on a new topic, building a reservoir for when she was ready to live outside—a reservoir of facts and insights and solutions and scintillating conversational topics and perhaps even a strategy for life. A strategy that would involve something besides being alone all of the time.

Today's new topic was anthropology, which fit all of the criteria including the strategy because Grace thought she might like to be an anthropologist. It was a lifelong dream, or at least one she'd had since college, not having heard of anthropology before college. People in Sublime, Texas, hadn't talked much about five-syllable academic disciplines.

Last spring, in a frivolous and perhaps anticipatory mood, Grace had bought a Bombay pith helmet at the Banana Republic store on a trip to Dallas. The helmet looked especially nice with her khaki slacks and it made her feel adventuresome, transporting her out to the field, where she could imagine herself not talking to anyone except an occasional tribal chief.

Grace kept her library wardrobe in the large walk-in staff closet that also served as a lost and found center, so there was no problem hiding her clothes in it. She had been careful about what she brought and hadn't brought, no cotton garments, for example, because they would require ironing. Her selections included three permanent press blouses (light blue short sleeve, dark blue short sleeve, and a light blue long sleeve with button-down collar), a yellow T-Shirt with little blue running shoes in the shape of musical notes that she'd gotten in a 5-K run/walk she entered to support the local symphony, blue running shorts, an assortment of white and beige underwear, a gray London Fog rain coat with a zip-in lining, and a pink thermal blanket. The Bombay pith helmet had presented the greatest challenge, but she had finally solved the problem by hiding it under the bottom layer in a box of toilet paper. Each evening she restocked the top three layers to be sure that the helmet remained safely covered.

She had nine pairs of socks in a variety of textures and colors. Having plenty of socks was important to Grace. She kept most of the garments overlapping on two hangers, wedging the socks and underwear into the middle of the jumbled lost and found box in a plastic bag, which doubled as a laundry bag, and she put the extra shoes and slippers loose in the box.

Grace always began on her day's selected topic at the card catalog, a hard-copy catalog at this library, mercifully. Computerized and microfilm files, encountered at other libraries, intimated her so much that she roamed stacks for hours rather than look up a title. Grace's mornings were spent with a serious book on her day's subject, followed in the afternoon with a scholarly journal, and she ended the day—after the library closed—with a fun book, usually a novel, related to the topic.

On the anthropology morning she had trouble choosing the serious book. So many titles. She rejected the basics: *Anthropology, Principles of*

Anthropology, An Introduction to Anthropology (four copies of that one; it must be boring), and *A History of Anthropological Thought*. The active approaches tempted her: *Figuring Anthropology, Living Anthropology, Reinventing Anthropology*, and *Anthropologists Do It in the Ruins*. Grace looked up from the cards and noticed Marsha Pendleton and Bubba Joe Smith, two of the younger members of the library staff, huddled together in the 301's. Marsha appeared to be helping Bubba Joe with his belt or something. Grace thought it incongruous that anyone named Bubba Joe Smith worked in a library. Clearly, equal opportunity employment was available in Texas. And she couldn't imagine what they were doing in the 301's since Marsha worked in Reference and Bubba Joe at the Service Desk.

Grace had enjoyed tracking the "Bubba controversy" in the Texas Senatorial election. She allotted twenty-three minutes to daily newspapers, sacrificing learned journal time, to keep abreast of current issues, especially those that might contribute to the scintillating topics category, like "Bubba." One senatorial candidate, male, was accused of appealing to the "Bubba vote." The accused responded that he was a Bubba. The female candidate said thank God her parents hadn't named her Bubba. The male candidate said he was taking Spanish lessons in order to address the Mexican American population in its native tongue. The female candidate evaluated her opponent's educational pursuit: "Bubba has become bi-ignorant." A female newspaper columnist from Ft. Worth provided a definition of Bubbas for people from the East Coast, having to do with gender, language use, type of vehicles driven, and location of beverages and weapons within said vehicles.

Bubbas, especially political candidate Bubbas, could produce a lot of negative energy, but some produced other kinds as well. Grace had had a crush on Bubba Bob Conrad her sophomore year in high school, and he'd danced with her once during a Paul Jones, though he'd first tried to cross over in a diagonal move to Sallie Sue Davenport. Suspecting his eyes were shifting the entire dance, Grace held on tightly to his middle belt loop in the back. He'd never had political aspirations that she knew of, or the rifle. He did have the pickup, a green Chevy. Her fantasy had been to steam up those Chevy windows, but he only steamed with the lead twirler, Lila Lee Thornton.

Resuming her search, Grace found some more intriguing-sounding titles: *Celebration of Life, Women in the Field, Anthropological Experiences,* and *Beyond Kinship, Sex, and the Tribe.* She finally selected *Notes on an Undirected Life: As One Anthropologist Tells It* by Esther S. Goldfrank. Grace thought she would enjoy a personal perspective.

En route to getting her book via the 301's, now unoccupied, she spotted 301.426 *Release from Sexual Tensions* on the shelf where Marsha and Bubba Joe had been leaning. She sat at a table in Reference to keep an eye on Marsha and to read about Esther's undirected life, which turned out to be such an interesting book that she almost read past 11:40 lunch-leaving time. Fortunately she finished just in time. It was imperative to arrive at Threadbelle's Cafeteria by 11:50 in order to beat the noon line, and Threadbelle's from the library was a seven-minute walk plus the bathroom stop.

By 11:50 all the food was out at Threadbelle's but nothing had been standing too long. Once Grace had made the mistake of going back to the cafeteria for dinner on a night when the library stayed open late, and she encountered the same eggplant casserole that had been served at lunch. She recognized it because of the piece of broccoli, spilled from a lunch serving, in the southwest corner of the eggplant casserole pan. Grace sometimes developed abdominal cramps and even diarrhea from food that had sat out a long time. Since the unfortunate broccoli-spotting, she had limited her meals at Threadbelle's to lunch.

For the entree she had chicken fried steak with cream gravy or broiled fish, which was a difficult choice because the chicken fried steak and cream gravy tasted better, but the broiled fish made her feel virtuous. She always had either cole slaw or carrot and raisin salad to work in something raw, fresh, and fibrous. She liked macaroni and cheese with the fish and mashed potatoes with the chicken fried steak. If she were really in the mood for macaroni and cheese, then for the vegetable she'd have broccoli, green beans, okra gumbo, or squash casserole. Some days she gave up the fish and the chicken fried steak and had both macaroni and cheese and eggplant casserole with another vegetable, but then the vegetable couldn't be the squash casserole because there wouldn't be any green unless she got cole slaw instead of carrot and raisin salad.

For dessert Grace had either pie or cake. Threadbelle's offered a wide variety of both. She really liked the strawberry pie, but when she had strawberry pie at lunch she burped strawberries the rest of the day. So she had strawberry pie only a couple of times a week. A couple of times a week it was worth it to burp strawberries.

After finishing lunch, she went back through the line to buy her dinner and the next morning's breakfast to carry out. For dinner she got mixed fruit, cheese wedges in plastic wrap, packets of melba thins and rye crisps, cake or pie (the opposite of what she'd had for lunch), and a carafe of white wine. For the next day's breakfast it was a carton of orange juice, a bran or blueberry muffin, and two envelopes of coffee powder. All of that would fit into Grace's large maroon purse/case.

Fortunately for Grace, Threadbelle's was open every day of the year except Christmas. She hadn't decided yet what she would do about Christmas Day.

Grace arrived back at the library shortly after one, and didn't leave again except on Tuesdays, when she gave up the afternoon's learned journal to go to the bank, post office, and laundromat. Before moving into the library six weeks before, she had closed her apartment and locked her blue Volvo in the parking garage. A lawyer was handling her routine bill payments and other business affairs, and there was rarely anything in her post office box except correspondence from him or an occasional letter from Aunt Arrow, her only living relative. Before moving into the library, Grace told Aunt Arrow she was going on an extended vacation in the western U.S., and she regularly mailed her aunt postcards from pretend locations, mostly national park ones she saved from real trips. With Aunt Arrow's eyesight, or lack thereof, she wouldn't notice the postmarks, but the diminishing supply of post cards worried Grace mildly.

At her weekly bank stop Grace withdrew a week's amount of cash and checked her balance. Grace figured she had enough in her savings account to last another seventy-one years (when she'd be 122) at her current rate of spending and adjusting for inflation at a seven per cent rate.

How long would she be here? Not seventy-one years, Grace hoped. Something less. The library wasn't a permanent solution, she realized that. So how long? When the post cards ran out? When the reservoir was big enough? How big was enough? Would there ever be enough facts and insights and scintillating topics for her to cope? When she had a definite strategy?

Polly said there weren't any quick fixes. But then psychotherapists, even Polly, didn't know everything. Grace's apartment would turn to dust if she stayed forever. And the Volvo's battery would need charging. And Aunt Arrow would miss her. Or someone like Enid would catch on to Grace's permanent residence in her domain. Enid had shrew eyes.

No, she couldn't live here forever, not forever and ever amen, even though she felt good here, most of the time. She believed she would find a way out. When the time was right.

The awfulness had overtaken her only once, in the night, when she awoke from a series of recurring nightmares, dreamed that night in disoriented, relentless segments: standing outside a circle of girls wearing striped shirts and waving knives; not making it to the final exam she needed to pass for college graduation; sinking into deeper and deeper water, submerged and suffocating; and in the last part of the dream, being pulled in her little red wagon by the neighborhood boys and trying to make them slow down, but they pulled her faster and faster until the wagon crashed over the curb and she was thrown out, ruining the little red wagon that she and her dad had picked out together at the Western Auto store in Sublime.

The darkness she had felt almost all the time before moving into the library came back after the dream. She re-entered the dark hole of depression and hopelessness, chanting her litany. *I hate myself, I hate myself, Kyrie eleison* intermingled with sweat from the nightmares.

"Why am I here?" she asked the bean bag chair. "Why am I here if it's just as bad in the library?" Having the feeling return, in the safety of the library, was scary.

An antidote to the blackness surfaced unexpectedly in the following day's topic: dream interpretation. She found it in the day's serious book, 154.63 *Dreamwork: Stepping Stones To Metaphoric Processing* by Hester Sliferstein-Thorton, which she had selected in a close call over 154.6339 *Dream Interpretation: A Walk Through Landscapes of the Night* by Fuller J. Montrose. Initially Grace thought the idea proposed by Sliferstein-Thorton—to pick a symbol from a dream and pretend to be that symbol—was silly. But Sliferstein-Thorton was quite persuasive about the importance of that step if one wanted to deal with multi-level issue dreams, which Grace did.

The book unfortunately provided no guidance on how to select a symbol or instructions about how to pretend to be a symbol, leaving Grace on her own with those aspects.

She mentally reviewed the inventory of potential symbols from the night before's dream series: striped shirt, knife, exam, mortar board, water, red wagon. Unable to choose, she wrote each item on a slip of paper and jumbled them in an open space between 978.412 *The Buffalo Runners* and 978.792 *We Pointed Them North: Recollections of a Cowpuncher.* Out came "knife."

'Knife,' she imaged intensely. 'How do I be a knife?' Standing straight, Grace raised her arms stiffly and folded her hands together holding a nail file above her head. 'Now what? The book said to carry the symbol back in time.' She tiptoed through the stacks, maintaining her knife posture, through Current Periodicals to the Children's Library room, making slices and cuts, ignoring stares.

"Take that, blackness," swath, swath. Grace swung and slivered, providing no insight into the interpretation of her dream but shocking her dark mood into retreat. Temporarily. Swath, swath.

Fortunately the library's staff blamed the hole in the bean bag chair on Bobby Ellis who had run away from his mother shouting "puff, puff, chug, chug," during the children's story hour, a reading of *The Little Engine That Could*.

Since today was Thursday, Grace did not have to leave the library again after returning from Threadbelle's. She put her food (except for the coffee and crackers that she kept in her purse/case) in the staff refrigerator to stay chilled. The library had a staff of fifteen and a rotation of volunteers each day, so there was plenty of activity in the staff kitchen and foodstuffs in the refrigerator to camouflage Grace's storage.

The volunteers wore a yellow plastic card that read "Ask Me" attached to a nine-inch green ribbon with "Volunteer" printed vertically and "Women's Service League" horizontally across the bottom. Grace confiscated one of the volunteer badges early on in her library residence and always wore it when she went into the staff kitchen. The badge-wearing occasionally resulted in her being asked to fill in at the Information Desk, a task she accepted willingly because Grace did not mind talking to anyones when she had a function to fulfill. And she had lots of information about the library. So far she had disseminated only a miniscule portion of it. Today Grace got in and out of the staff kitchen without incident.

Having selected her journal, *Historical Anthropologist*, Grace settled into a favorite chair between 574.19 *Dynamic Aspects of Biochemistry* and 606.9 *National Plumbing Code Handbook*. She liked to start with the book reviews to get a feel for what was being published in a particular field. Grace had worked in publishing for twenty-six years as a copy editor for Scorpio Press. She mostly edited "How To" books, some of which were in this library: *How To Be Your Own Travel Agent, How To Start an Organic Garden, How To Run In Place: An Inside View of the U.S. Senate* (her all-time favorite), *How To Reduce Your Thighs in Thirty Days* which wouldn't be necessary if one had read *How To Cook in a Wok*.

Flipping to the end of *Historical Anthropologist*, Grace noticed the review of a book, *Choice of Barbed Wire and Its Implications for Social Behavior As Manifested by Ranchers In Texas*. How would anyone even conceive of such a topic, much less execute the research? She read the review with a keen interest and uncharacteristic optimism.

The field research had involved interviews with 437 ranchers selected at random from the 2,352 who had responded to a questionnaire sent to 37,886 participants in the screwworm eradication program from records provided by the U.S. Department of Agriculture. The book's author, William Winston Davidson IV, had traveled to each of the 437 ranches, interviewed the ranchers, and photographed and categorized the ranch's barbed wire fence(s) according to number of wire strands (single, double, triple), design (left twist, right twist, oval twist, zigzag, kinked, split diamond, coils, forked tongue, open wrap, parallel variation, humped) and number of barbed points (two or four). Separate sociological categories were established for ranchers who used more than one type of barbed wire.

A rancher's social behavior was measured by such variables as marital status (married, single, divorced, widowed, remarried ____ of times); religious affiliation (Protestant, Roman Catholic, Eastern Orthodox, Judaism,

Islam, Hinduism, Buddhism, Confucianism, Shinto, Taoism, None); political party preference (Democrat, Republican, Independent, Libertarian,
None); dancing type (square, two-step, cotton-eyed Joe, put your little foot,
other_____); most frequented early-morning gathering place (cafe,
barber shop, domino parlor, other _____); favorite beverage (beer, light
beer, bourbon, other alcoholic, soda, diet soda, iced tea, lemonade, juice,
other _____); and primary source of news (newspaper, magazine, television, early-morning gathering place).

The review left out important information. Was there really a relationship between the number of barbed points and how a rancher danced,
whether the wire were twisted or kinked and how a rancher voted? Well,
she could see the point on the voting. Was any rancher in Texas a Taoist?
Or a Buddhist? Or a Libertarian? Grace was sure that none drank diet
Coke or light beer. The review described the study but presented none of
the author's conclusions, stating only that William Winston Davidson IV
had found statistically significant relationships. Although the reviewer assessed the book as a valid and significant contribution, Grace doubted that
anyone with a name ending in IV could relate—in any real and meaningful
way—to barbed wire.

But she could sure relate to barbed wire. And the climbing over fences
made thereof. Grace quit her reading of the review in mid-skepticism, overwhelmed by childhood memories of climbing over barbed wire fences,
which she did whenever visiting friends who lived on ranches outside of
Sublime. Climbing over a barbed wire fence in those adventures was the
necessary prerequisite to getting to any of the good places. Never an easy
task, the climbing-over involved stepping gingerly and slowly, with the
constant danger of intense prick and tetanus shot. But the rewards—when
the climbing-over succeeded—were rich. Jumping into the Frio River and
swimming in waters that were so clear she could see all the way to its rock
bottom, even in the deepest holes; watching the first nursing of a newborn
Hereford calf; playing hide-and-seek and an occasional more interesting
game in the mesquite brush with Jake Parker. Yes, climbing over a barbed
wire fence was worth the risk. At least it was when she was a child.

I took those risks when I was ten years old, she thought. Why not now?
Yes, why not now? Is there any difference between the pricks I got from

barbed wire and the ones I talk to Polly about? Is there really any difference?

Grace whispered, "That's it," looking around quickly to ensure no one was in hearing range. "That's it," she said in a normal tone.

Barbed wire, Grace thought. That's the answer, that's my way out. Barbed wire is my way out. Kinks and twists. And Polly tried to make it so complicated, to talk ad nauseam about family dynamics and the critical inner voices, when it was really quite simple. Quite. The clue I needed was right here in the library. In a book. Well, a review of a book. That's close enough. I knew it all the time, I knew I'd find it. Something besides pretending to be a knife. She blushed.

"Barbed wire," Grace said aloud.

"Shh," from a table beside the 600's.

I just needed to see my problems as barbed wire, as a challenging fence to climb over, she thought, sensing release. Release from the library, a reason to leave. She had her strategy. Yes, I can have a new beginning. I can start over. Like a newborn calf.

Suck, suck, Grace pursed her lips. What happened last year doesn't matter, she thought. Or even when I was in junior high school or college or when I was thirty-seven. Or five. *Suck, suck.* Doesn't count. Or when I was four months. I can be free of them. Who didn't talk to me or who did and shifted. They're all just types of barbed wire. Coils and forked tongues and parallel variations. I just needed to see them as barbed wire. Twisted and prickly.

"That's it," Grace nodded, then corrected, "that's them."

"Shh," from the 600's table, and pencil-rapping from the 500's.

The hiding was over. Grace smiled for the first time since Monday when server number three at Threadbelle's had given her an extra portion of banana pudding with meringue by mistake. She set down *Historical Anthropology* unfinished, a rare act. Leaving a book or learned journal unfinished was on par with an unmade bed or unwashed dishes. In this case, having what she needed justified the unfinishing, and she hadn't rejected the book, definitely not. She patted its beige cover gently as she imagined herself skinny dipping with Jake Parker in the Frio. If I can start over, she thought, like a newborn calf, what shall I do? Besides swim. And suck. Of course I don't look like a baby or a calf, I'm just a baby symboli-cally, Grace clarified quickly to herself, a new beginning, symbolically.

Grace was stumped, momentarily, searching for the appropriate forum to implement her strategy. Where and how she would begin to take the risks. She didn't want to waste them on just anyone(s), anywhere. Not that she hadn't already given the matter considerable thought . . . and desire. Even before she had the strategy. Memories of her 'university catalog-reading' day erupted simultaneously with the years of thought/desire, over-taking the stumpedness.

Shortly before five o'clock, Grace began her evening routine, slipping over to the stacks to wait between 251.01 *English Pulpit Oratory* and 251.09 *The Heeded Voice* as the staff made preparations to close the library for the day. In the six weeks she had lived in the library, Grace had never seen anyone in the 251's. The staff cleared out fast, and she was in the staff closet by 5:20, well ahead of the cleaning crew's arrival at 5:45. She waited in the closet for the forty-five cleaning minutes, and then the library was hers from 6:30 on.

Grace immediately changed into her running shorts, T-shirt, and run-ning shoes. Running up and down every aisle in the open stacks four times took twenty-three minutes and elevated her heartbeat to the desired 145 beats/minute level. Next she had her sponge bath using the double sink in the staff kitchen, one side for soapy water and one side for clean water. That night her spirits were so high that she actually climbed up on the counter and dipped herself into each side, singing from 784.4 *Swedish Emigrant Ballads* and boldly using three of the staff's clean cup towels instead of the usual one.

"Thank God for white wine," Grace said, blessing her evening meal.

Finally, she snuggled into a bean bag chair to read Margaret Atwood's *The Robber Bride* and fell asleep, smiling over Roz's twin daughters in-sisting that all the male pronouns in stories be changed to female—Peter Rabbit, Winnie the Pooh, the Big Bad Wolf. It's amazing the difference the pronouns make: burned her fur, *her* fur.

The next morning Grace waited by 598.2734 *Birds of the Peloponneus.* Enid opened the door at 8:34. Wearing her pith helmet and carrying her maroon purse/case packed with items retrieved from the closet (except for the trench coat and thermal blanket, which she tucked under her arm), Grace walked to the front desk. She had abandoned much of her library wardrobe to the lost and found box, packing only the necessities (eight pairs of socks; she was wearing the yellow ones).

"I'm turning in my library card," Grace announced.

The sight of Grace in her pith helmet with a pink thermal blanket under her left arm and a gray trench coat under her right rendered Bubba Joe speechless.

Before Enid could get to the desk to help Bubba Joe, Grace left.

She had practiced several times early that morning marching out of the library triumphantly. Instead, when the moment came, Grace *skipped* to and through the main entrance, tripping slightly as she went down the library's front steps.

A Straw in the Wind, a Rooster in a Bottle

PATRICK BENNETT

Eyes still shut, Chick Patterson grimaced and stretched, half turned in the leather-cushioned chair and thought: "I'm not in Heaven. If I were dead, I wouldn't have a crick in my neck."

Opening his good eye, he discovered four other men sleeping in the sunlit hotel lobby's chairs. They had given the one couch to an old woman, had also given her the lone all-weather coat to cover her skinny old bottom.

Patterson closed his right eye and opened his gimpy left. The lobby dissolved into soft-edged shimmers. He then concentrated on opening both eyes, to restore form to the world.

Pulling the curtain aside ten inches to peer between the slats of the venetian blind, he saw a new automobile with its windshield smashed. Behind the car loomed the courthouse with the dignity of a senile statesman. It had sheltered him during the worst of the previous night. At the bottom of the steps mounting to its west entrance was a sign, "Unsafe, Do Not Enter." On its lawn lay scattered boards, scraps of cloth, tree limbs.

"I must phone Abby," he thought. Abby Dean would be at work now; he pictured her hustling behind the counter at the Cozy Cafe. Then he felt a stab of guilt: "I must call Mums too and tell her I'm alive." He phoned Mums daily after breakfast.

Patterson got up and walked back past the registry desk and into the little room behind. A stout woman in a print dress was pouring herself a cup of coffee.

"Is there a phone I can use?"

"If there is a phone in ten miles that works, I'd be flabbergasted," she said. "The lines must be tangled up like spaghetti. No telling how much property was destroyed. I hear the Davis boy and his wife were killed and no telling how many others." She poured a second cup of coffee and handed it to him. "They already got the National Guard over from Wichita Falls, and some Red Cross people. You're one of the ones from the courthouse, ain't you?"

"That's where I took cover. You know, my father was killed in a tornado like this one when I was a kid."

"No joke?" She eyed this thirty-eight-year-old stranger with more interest. "A twister blowed your daddy away?"

"Mama has a neurotic fear some disaster will grab me too."

Thirty miles to the west in Belplain's Cozy Cafe, the twister was the main topic among the morning coffee drinkers. They filled the stools at the L-shaped counter, filled the chairs at the two tables that crammed the small native-stone building.

A low partition between the cooking and serving areas left plenty of room for the bald man who was the Cozy's fry cook-owner to joke with the coffee drinkers. Abby Dean, happy that her late-thirties figure still made it necessary to parry occasional flirtations, took orders and replenished coffee cups.

Each newcomer when he entered was taxed for any yarn he had heard about the big Dunlop tornado the previous night, and then was given the corporate knowledge the crowd had collected.

No one, however, bothered to pump Jessy Guthrie when he came through the door. A sixteen-year-old clad in blue jeans and T-shirt, Jessy obviously would not know anything. Jessy said hello to those who looked up and then seated himself on the stool just left of Mack Beall, fifty-eight, owner of Belplain's shoe repair shop. Gus Hill, thirty-five, the bootmaker who worked for Beall, sat on the other side.

"Did you hear about the big Dunlop twister, Mr. Beall?"

"We were just talking about it."

"Down at Clowers' station just now, a one arm fellow, smoking a big cigar, he told me it blew a rooster into a milk bottle. Just left his head sticking out so it could crow a little."

"I heard it blew a straw through a telephone pole," said Abby Dean. Her wit was lost on the newcomer.

"Man, there must have been some weird things going on over there," said Jessy.

"I'm a good mind to just drive over to Dunlop to see what did happen," said Mack.

"Might not have been any storm at all," said Hill.

Behind his grill, the fry cook had a thought: "Didn't Chick Patterson leave here yesterday for Dunlop, Mack?"

Mack pushed back the plate he had cleaned of eggs. "Yeah, but he drove over to Dunlop early, and was going on to Vernon before dark."

"He would have been gone long before it hit," said Abby. Then she blushed and emptied an ash tray.

Mack and Gus rose from their stools, and on the way out stopped to pay Abby at the cash register (on which hung the sign: "You have an honest face, but we can't get it in the cash drawer"). In the alley, shallow pools of water lingered.

"Is Chick still sparking Abby?" Gus asked.

"You seen her turn red back there when his name come up."

"Think they'll tie the knot?"

"I doubt it." Mack wagged his head gravely.

"Maybe he's the kind of traveling salesman with a gal in every town."

"Chick's not that kind. But he takes care of his widowed mama in Fort Worth."

A shout came from behind them: "Hey, Mr. Beall."

They turned to see Jessy, newly emerged from the door of the Cozy. He hurried to catch them.

"Are you two really going over to Dunlop?"

"Thinking about it," said Gus.

"That sounds like a great idea to me. Reckon I could tag along sort of."

"If we go," said Gus.

"Oh, we might as well go as stand here and speculate on it all morning," said Mack.

They walked on past two empty store fronts with their windows still soaped full of words and streaks from Halloween several months previously. The sun shone clearly now.

"Y'all get in the car, said Mack, indicating a cream colored Ford; "I'd better go tell them at the shoe shop where I'm going."

453

The Ford was streaked and spattered with dark brown clay.

"Must be a little muddy up your way, Mr. Beall," said Jessy.

"I may just buy me a Dalmatian dog to go with my car," Mack said.

When he returned from the shop, Mack started his engine, and without allowing it to warm, backed away from the curb. He followed an elderly lady driving an elderly car around two sides of the courthouse square before he could turn onto the highway.

"I wonder if they've ever broke that bottle to let that rooster out," Jessy said. "I heard he was just crowing to beat the band."

"I think somebody has been pulling your leg, Jess," Gus said. "I've heard about that rooster after just about every other storm too, but I haven't seen him yet."

"What about that soda straw in the telephone post?"

"Not a soda straw, a broom straw. No, I think it really does that, although come to think of it, I never seen one."

"It's the strong wind," Mack said, in the tones of Dr. Einstein explaining the bending of space. "They say the wind opens up the pores of the wood while it bends the pole, and the straw goes right in. That's the way I've heard it explained."

The car sped along, splashing occasionally through a low place where the ditch water covered the highway.

"Did y'all go to the storm house last night?" Mack asked.

"Papa made us all go," said Jessy, "and that wasn't easy, because Mama nearly squashed a centipede by sitting on him when we went during that storm we had in March. I guess y'all went."

"No." Mack said it ruefully. "Lottie hears something blowing up, and she gets me up to watch it. Then she goes back to bed. It's like she thinks the weather can't do anything bad as long as I have my eye on it."

"Women!" Gus was divorced and living alone.

"Well, I've always had a horror of being blown away with my pants off. With Lottie around, at least that won't happen."

After five minutes, Mack emerged from a reverie: "Lottie got me up when we had that big twister two years ago and then popped back into bed as usual. Well, I was watching and things got worser and worser. So I got Lottie up again and got her as far as our screened-in back porch on the way across the alley to Waller's cellar. Then she said, 'Oh Mack, I don't think

454

anything is going to happen.' I said, 'Yes it is.' But she just stood there and argued. I was getting pretty aggravated when whomp, it blew down that big Chinese elm tree in our back yard. She said, 'Let's go to the cellar,' and I just said, 'Too late now,' and walked back into the kitchen."

"Women can sure be hard headed," Gus said.

In Dunlop, Chick Patterson walked out of the hotel lobby onto the sidewalk. He walked along the mashed shop fronts on the west side of the courthouse square, the most prosperous part of Dunlop's small commercial section. The crick in his neck caused him to twist his whole torso when he looked around him. A large sign, "Matthews Men's Clothing," swung crazily on one hinge; a giant tree limb stuck out of Dill Pharmacy's door.

Patterson glanced down in time to step around a sparrow's small feathered corpse. He thought of Abby Dean's parakeet, an amiable bird that liked to perch on the frame of his glasses to peck at his eyebrows. Then with a spurt of guilt: "I've got to phone Fort Worth to talk to Mums."

In the street a squad of young men in green fatigues was picking up the polyglot of litter. At midblock a deputy sheriff in sunglasses stood talking to a National Guard officer. In Mason Jewelry, its display windows smashed, a middle-aged man and wife carefully packed crystal glasses in a box.

Patterson felt a tug of suspense: What had happened to his car? Down the side street he saw the narrow old red-brick building that housed Charlie Blaine's shoe shop, weedy vacant lots on both sides, his green Chevy parked in front. The car's roof was caved in, and an odd, elongated shape stuck out of the car's roof, as though a heavenly archer had driven an arrow shaft into the top on the driver's side.

Stepping closer for examination, he found the wind had torn loose the brick façade that rimmed the top of the shoe shop and dumped it on his car top. The elongated shape was the little flagpole which stuck out, usually naked of any flag, from the façade. Curiously, the front display windows of the shop were intact, as was the windshield of Patterson's car.

Peering through the windshield of Mack's car when they rolled into the outskirts of Dunlop, the three Belplain men at first found little evidence of anything more than a heavy rain. Jessy examined the first few telephone poles as well as he could at thirty miles an hour but could detect no straws sticking in.

Damage grew as they drove. The overhanging roof of a gas station twisted grotesquely and rested one eave on the concrete drive. Houses without roofs, a pickup jammed into the side of a two-story residence, trees down, a house with only two walls.

"Wasn't that a church?" asked Gus. He stared at a huge pile of yellow bricks on which a squad of Guardsmen and a half dozen civilians dug doggedly.

"It was First Baptist. Reckon somebody's under there?"

A guardsman stood in the middle of the street, rifle at present arms. Mack pulled up.

"Cars not allowed downtown, sir. Do you have relatives or friends downtown?"

"Yes, we thought we'd better check on them."

"You'll have to park and proceed on foot, sir."

"Is somebody buried in that church?"

"We don't know yet, sir."

They parked on a muddy vacant lot fifty yards back down the street. A number of cars also stood on the lot, which was overgrown with weeds and had an abandoned well in the center. Dismounted, they sloshed back to the sidewalk and started walking downtown through the jetsam of the storm.

"Who do you need to see about?" asked Jessy.

"I need to see about that rooster in the bottle," said Mack.

"We can't drive all this way without seeing what there is to see," said Gus.

Chick Patterson, now that he had seen what there was to be seen, left his car to walk back to the windowless jewelry store.

"I hate to bother you, but has anybody seen Charlie Blaine around his shop?"

The middle-aged man stood up from his packing task and turned his attention to Patterson.

"Charlie was around maybe a half hour ago. He was asking about his kids' dog. The dog has disappeared."

"Have you heard how many people were killed in this thing?"

"I just don't know. Somebody said the undertaker has a full house, but I haven't heard any names. You can hear anything. . . ."

Patterson again asked about a telephone and got the same answer before walking back to his crushed car. As he began to pull chunks of brickwork off the roof, he wondered if he ought to ask the Guardsmen about using any radio they might have. Now and then he felt a twinge in his neck, but motion had loosened it.

As Chick Patterson pulled the last of the bricks off his crumpled auto, his earlier frenzy was replaced by a depression. With heavy steps he walked back to the corner. He watched the jewelry-store couple, now loading their car trunk with figurines.

Turning with a neck twinge, he saw three men walking toward the square. Two looked familiar. Recognition gave him a surge of energy, and he hurried past a wrecked neon sign toward them.

"Mack! Gus! I knew you'd remember me!" he shouted as they came within a half block of one another. Soon they were shaking hands all round and introducing Jessy.

"How d you get through the blow, Chick?" Mack asked.

"My poor old bucket of bolts is a goner. All I got was a crick in the neck from having to sleep in a chair. I got quite a scare though my dad was killed in a storm like this, you know."

"I knew that," said Mack. He frowned and looked away because he had forgotten.

"I knew you'd remember me over here," Patterson said again. "Man, I wish I'd stayed in Belplain after I called on you."

"I told you ought to," Mack said. "I thought you were going on to Vernon last night."

"I fooled around and didn't get off before dark."

Patterson did not feel it necessary to explain that he was running behind schedule because he had left Belplain late yesterday because he was out late with Abby the night before.

"Where were you when it hit?"

"I was eating supper at Green's Cafe when it began to storm. My car was in front of Blaine's shop, and I intended to drive on to Vernon. Then it got to raining real hard, and the sheriff came driving like crazy through town honking his horn. All us fellows at the cafe half swam and half waded over to the courthouse. It sounded like a great big freight train when it

457

came. And I'll tell you something: I was watching out a basement window when some fellow started to try to run across Main Street. He got about halfway and then just went straight up. After it was all gone, they got us out-of-towners to go to that little hotel around the corner. It ripped the roof off the motel. The hotel had run out of beds by the time some of us got there, so I slept in the lobby."

"How's your car?"

"Flat as a pancake. Bunch of bricks and a flagpole from the shoe shop building landed right smack dab on top of her."

Patterson led them back around the corner and down the side street to the car. They examined it with curiosity.

"Good thing you wadn't in it," said Gus. "That would have given you a serious scalp problem."

"I need to get to a phone some place to call Mama," Patterson said, hesitating before adding, "and some other people." Mack and Gus glanced at one another.

Mack studied the damage. He said, "Chick, you might be able to crawl behind the wheel if you scrunched down a little."

The door on the passenger side squeaked when Patterson opened it, but it closed firmly behind him, and sure enough, he squeezed behind the wheel. Despite a pang from his crick, he leaned a little to one side, stuck his head out through the roof hole, and said, "It can be done."

"Try cranking it," Gus suggested.

The second time Patterson pressed the starter, the engine started, hummed in a normal manner. Patterson backed out, drove fifteen feet down the street, backed up the same distance, and reparked. He wormed his way out on the passenger side again.

"I believe I might just be able to drive it back."

"Ab Beauchamp could probably straighten that tin can out somewhat if you could get to his garage in Belplain," said Mack.

Mack, Gus, and Jessy walked back to their own car on the muddy vacant lot. Mack had started the engine and driven to the edge of the street, when Jessy said, "Looky yonder." Gus and Mack turned in the direction he pointed, the direction of the collapsed church fifty yards away, where two covered bodies were being borne on stretchers to a waiting van.

Patterson came down the litter-strewn street moments later.

458

"He's wanting to get back to phone Abby Dean," Gus said. "Reckon there's a chance in the world those two will get hitched and start manufacturing engines for tricycles?"

"Not a chance with his mama around his neck," said Mack. "Chick's a only child. Too bad too, Chick and Abby have about reached cutoff age in tricycle-engine manufacturing."

Once out of town, Patterson sailed off at a leisurely forty miles per hour, afraid to drive faster in his cramped position. Every few miles, he would stick his head through the roof-hole to reassure himself that Mack's crew was still behind.

"Chick looks kind of like that rooster in the bottle," said Jessy, and he laughed. All three laughed.

HIDDEN TREASURE

GUIDA JACKSON

On the way home from work, he often drove out to the canyon's rim, twenty minutes away down a back road that promised nothing more than the same monotonous flatness until the moment of the breathtaking drop-off. This day as he passed a clutch of poor whites' shacks on the edge of town, Paul noticed a teenage girl bouncing on a mattress in one bare-dirt back yard situated on a corner lot. Her flat, dismal surroundings would be unbearable, he thought, except for the nearby canyon, not visible on that broad landscape from even a few yards away: the majestic, heart-thudding beauty of the sheer coppery bluffs carved by the clear running trickle hundreds of feet below were completely out of sight, existing only in memory of the people in the dusty little town. Perhaps her squalor was ameliorated by the secret awareness of such hidden splendor.

While he watched the canyon reds turn to purples with the waning sun, the girl hovered in the back of his mind, bouncing, bouncing, and he felt a welling power. He fantasized filling the vast canyon with his seed, spewing it in a mighty unending stream, watching it roll in great thick eddies against the darkening walls, fertilizing everything in its path.

To his amusement, despite the gloom of twilight, she was still jumping on the mattress as he returned to town. The sight filled him with inordinate pleasure and warmth which he elected not to analyze. Back home, in the great cheerless bungalow that he had shared with his mother and his aunts since his divorce, she existed in his mind, alongside the canyon.

He drove by occasionally and saw her several times—always doing the same thing, her slender bare feet sinking deep into the old tufted mattress with each bounce, despite the fact that she was very thin. Once, when the wind caught her skirt, he glimpsed the roundness of her thigh and it occurred to him that she was quite pretty and perhaps older than he thought.

One day while having a burger at the Tastee Freeze, he saw her outside, hands and forehead pressed against the glass, eyeing a chocolate-covered cone through the window. He was struck by her fragile beauty. She looked almost breakable to him, and when her glance flickered over his for an instant, his breath was sucked away. He noticed that she wore a cheap ring with the stone missing that had turned her small finger green.

On impulse he assumed a false bravado, bought a cone, took it outside and offered it to her almost as a joke, if she would tell him why she was always bouncing on the mattress. But from her stricken look and the sudden flush on her cheeks, he knew it had been a mistake to ask: bouncing on the mattress must be her only entertainment, he realized at once with a pang both painful and sweet. He thrust the cone at her stammering, *just kidding*, and fled, ashamed.

Stunned by the thought of such poverty, he wanted to do something for her. He invented reasons to drive by: taking the elderly women for a breath of air after an interminable dust storm, for a trip to the cemetery to freshen fading flowers in crumbling urns, for a look at the canyon—hardly daring to cast a quick glance toward the little hovel where the girl lived for fear she would recognize him.

He got out the old bike, telling himself he needed more exercise. The first trip to her house left him winded and disappointed; by the time he got there, dusk had settled in and she was inside. The next time he started earlier and saw from a block away that he was in luck. He stopped by her side yard, on the pretense of adjusting his bike chain, feigning surprise to see her. As if it had just occurred to him, he offered her a "pass" to the movie (which he had bought), saying he won it and couldn't use it. She stopped her bouncing and looked at him warily before she ran over and took the ticket, then rushed into the house, banging the screen door without a word.

He haunted the movie house until he saw her go in, then he bought a ticket and sat across the aisle—just so he could watch her rapt face. He wished he had thought of popcorn.

He fantasized buying her a pretty dress, bringing her home for a nice meal, introducing her to his mother and his aunts. But that, of course, was impossible. The difference in their ages or economic station had little to do with it—some of his people were poor, too. There was a line no one

461

crossed in the town, and everyone on both sides knew where it was as if it were eight feet tall and made of Texas granite. It had to do with *ancestors*, he thought, although he couldn't be sure. In his mind she was there, on the other side of the wall, bouncing, the carefree folds of the shapeless dress swelling out from the calculated puffs of King Tantalus himself.

Still, he longed to bring her some new joy. He wanted her to have a proper ring—became obsessed with giving her a ring with a stone. Finally he bought a silver one with a small onyx, telling the jeweler that it was a graduation gift for a niece. The jeweler wrapped it in gold paper and stuck a mortar board on the bow, which Paul removed as soon as he left the shop. He pictured her delight as she tore off the foil paper and found the black velvet box.

But before he could figure out how to give it to her, she had taken up with a rough-looking biker. On Main Street he watched her on the back of the Harley, hugging the man's bare chest, slender arms sliding easily beneath his leather vest, skirts flying above her thigh, ecstasy coloring her face, flashing in her eyes. He should be happy for her, but he knew something bad would happen, and he imagined that it would happen on the mattress. He saw her occasionally in town after that, once with a bruise on her chin, later with a protruding belly.

He remained obsessed with giving her the ring, concealing it under roadmaps in his glove box for weeks, months, before he could bring himself to drive by again. As the days lengthened into summer, he replayed the scene of *bestowing the gift*, embellishing details, until on sultry nights, lying damp atop wrinkled sheets, he could hear her papery voice saying *my darling*, could feel her press her lips to his and lean her slender body— he dismissed the protruding belly—against his. The vision remained with him even during dreary mealtimes, as his mother and his aunts clucked over his poor appetite. The vision was like the canyon: it lingered just out of sight in the back of his mind no matter what else he was doing. He could almost believe that she shared it with him.

Finally he gathered courage enough to stop one day as she hung out wash on the line. He gave a quick gasp as he noticed the new baby lying on the mattress nearby, but he had already braked the car. As he fumbled in the glove box, she looked up, puzzled at first. Recognition lit her eyes in a momentary glimmer, but quickly the light receded and she returned to her clothes pins.

He examined the shiny package, now wrinkled, the bow mashed and shoddy, and hurriedly tore off the paper, even removing the ring from its box to make the whole thing seem more informal. He got out and stumbled forward—on nothing: slippery pebbles perhaps—he hardly knew where to put his feet. Confused by her indifference—so unlike her behavior in his vision—he stopped several feet away and addressed her profile, making an awkward speech about a gift for the new mother. She stopped working and, head down, sidled nearer until she could see what lay in his damp outstretched palm—he felt stupid, thoughtless, for not having left it in the velvet box, at least.

From this proximity the deep sockets of her eyes were like gray smudges, the listless eyes themselves fringed with almost colorless lashes at once abhorrent and appealing, as if their very lack of pigment implied lack of substance—or perhaps lack of defense. He could see that she wanted the ring but seemed afraid to take it. The shadow of a bruise showed on her bare shoulder; he felt sudden fear for her and wished he hadn't come.

All at once she reached out for the ring, almost snatching it, so that her nails scraped across his palm and sent tingles up his neck. She put it on briefly, holding her thin hand up to the wind, which watered her pale eyes. Then she hurried to the corner of the house where the hoe stood, scratched a hole in the hard baked dirt, and placed the ring lovingly in the hole. She patted the dirt in place and remained squatting beside it, not looking up.

I'll always know it's there, she told him.

He looked at his palm, half expecting to find evidence of the momentous miracle of her touch. It stung, like an indelible stigmata that would always be there.

WHEELMEN

JO LECOEUR

I drink to Saturday night. And to song, never mind the singer crashed my party. I drink to the South Texas wind, soft as fingertips sliding up my neck. And to the view from up here on the third floor terrace. High above this city of woe, my troubles all filtered down to street level, absorbed by the neon sleaze. Only two bummers left at this altitude: the beer is warm and I got to share it.

Hilltop allows us one beer with supper. I save mine up all week and the occasional extra that falls into my lap—enough for a Sunday morning too hungover to shave. Tonight though, this new guy caught me palming the beer off his supper tray, made a big deal about me sort of being staff. I didn't so much talk him out of turning me in as he blackmailed me into sneaking him and his buddy out here after bed check to cut in on my fun. Here's to one-man parties. Still, unwelcome guests do not change the fact that it is Saturday night. And still alive!

I drink to the factual chunk-chunk sound of the lawn sprinkler system far below. And when it cuts off, I drink to the cut clover smell carried up here by the breeze. A dense sexy smell, wet clover. I drink to next month. To the fact of my twenty-third birthday. To the smell of wet clover.

The blackmailer is not such bad company, gazing up shit-faced at the moon, singing his heart out. Nothing wrong with his lungs. His song has a beat to it. I snap my fingers, sway in my chair, dancing from the waist up, a little bump and grind with my head, my shoulders oogah, oogah. Choo choo choo with my chin.

My real bitch is with the buddy. The blackmailing singer's buddy of the blank expression. You'd've thought he was doing me a favor letting me haul his skinny ass out of bed, getting him dressed and mobile. Which is not as easy as it sounds. I drink to things that sound easy. My sports chair sounds easy—custom-built to allow me maximum upper body mobility. Still, it is a work-out dressing two grown boys. Think about it: rib belts, back braces, sweat pants, button shirts and shoes. I was sweating like a pig at an orgy by the time I got them strapped into their chairs and ready to rock 'n roll, leave out the rock.

I drink to rock. To upper body mobility. To beer. I'm on my last one now, and trying to make it last. My two guests've been putting them away too, sucking on their long plastic fluid straws like hound puppies on a bitch too weak to wean 'em. No drinking experience. Well, they've got an excuse now. Troubles to drown.

They're better off than some quads. Singer's cord damage is not as high as his buddy's. And they've both got high-dollar, power chairs with state of the art computer equipment. For maximum independence, reads the ad. Singer's got enough lateral movement in one arm to maneuver his chair with the joystick on his armrest. And he certainly has not lost any lung capacity, as has been noted. A strong baritone that kind of goes with his factual jaw. He is really getting into his song. He rocks his head at me, inches his chair forward, stops, inches back, then pivots to the left and circles right, doing his own chair-dance.

The bored buddy has the use of his shoulders and sufficient lung capacity to power his own chair. It's run by a Sip 'n Puff motor control system. He sucks and blows codes into a small plastic tube hooked up to a tiny computer mounted behind his chair. The Sip 'n Puff tube is firm enough to stay in place within his head reach, so he does not *have* to stay parked back by the fire escape. He could move out here with us and take in the view. He *could* join in the dancing. But he just sits back there under the light, looking bored as a Baptist preacher's wife.

He sees me looking back over my shoulder at him, unmouths his fluid straw and starts in on that tired refrain that every new guy thinks so original. He groans how he wants to die, but all he can do is hold his breath until he blacks out.

Singer makes no comment on his buddy's lament, just stops chair-dancing, sucks an empty-can noise with his fluid straw. I've got a dead soldier too. The wind's picked up and lost its softness. It's the kind of wind that'll whip a cedar fire around in your face, so the fire you're chasing starts chasing you.

465

Way up in the next block on the other side of the street I spot the neon sign I'm looking for. "Time for a beer run!"—my words barreling out of the chute before I think. Sounds so good I don't know why it never came up before. Except before, I didn't have to share. *"Texas Liquors* is just up the street."

Singer likes the idea. He is nodding like a ventriloquist's dummy, eyebrows dancing. His brain still thinks body language, so his facial expressions come out too large; while his buddy's face is frozen in don't-give-a-damn.

Sneaking back in through the building now after lights out would be risky. I roll over to the fire escape to scope it out. We haven't had a fire drill in the months I've been here. But it looks easy—there are landings every half floor. The ramp is pretty severe; an inch of grade for a foot's descent is government code now, but this one was built awhile back. Still, not even dangerous enough to be exciting. "No need in us all going," I say magnanimously, intending to volunteer. But they ignore me. Singer is belting out the chorus to "Margaritaville," the buddy absorbed in boredom. It hasn't taken these two long to get used to service. They take it for granted that I am their designated gofer. I never cared for the attitude of privilege and learned a long time ago the best way to handle it. "How about we draw straws," I say, "to see who goes?" The bored one is good, does not even look up. And Singer is busy selling his song.

I roll over to one of the big clay pots where somebody tried to grow palms. The wind has dried them out, beat them to death, left palm stubs sticking up in big clay pot ashtrays. I find two filter cigarette butts and one nothing but filter. I roll over and stick them in Singer's face. He has stopped singing and is looking at me like I'm crazy. He says he's got no money. I tell him I've got enough for a six pack. He works his Adam's apple, his energy for physical confrontation reduced to eyes of purpose and a hard swallow. Brain signals to clench fists and puff out chest get translated to chin-set, his neck an arm reaching out. His teeth snatch one of the long ones from my grip. I show him the two left. He sighs relief, but his eyes look disappointed. I feel like I am watching a Grade B movie at the old South San Theater. And when it is over I will stand up and walk home.

466

About. Face. I wheel around, suddenly conscious how the legs' instinct for flight has transferred to my arms. The bored one is sucking on his long tube straw, eyeing the beer can I'd left wedged between his knees. I park in his face and begin unwrapping his fluid straw from the stiff tube that holds it in mouth-reach. I roll it into a ball, stow it in my side tote. There is nothing he can do to stop me. I reach between his knees, lift his beer and hold it up in a mock toast to him. Then I finish it off. He does not react. Ex-Singer has rolled up to watch. I lean across the bored one's lap, stick two filters in his face. His muscles do not flicker. He thinks I'm kidding. He's the kind whose mama still made his bed even before he got work-exempt. I touch the filters to his lips. A good man would bite my finger off, but his face stays stone. I pull out, leaving the short filter hanging on his bottom lip, letting the long filter roll out on my palm.

"This is crazy," says Ex-Singer.

"I'm not the logical one to go," says his buddy. I pantomime playing a violin with accompanying sounds. For the first time the buddy looks directly at me. His eyes reflect the moon white and blank. "Have *you* ever driven a truck," he asks, "with no steering wheel and no brakes?"

Hazing him just for the devilment of it, I stick beer money in his shirt pocket. "So the cashier can get to it."

He surprises me then—maybe you do get drunker with a straw—he reaches out with his neck, takes his Sip 'n Puff tube in his mouth. Blowing computer codes to his chair motor, he rolls to the fire escape. Probably thinks I'll stop him.

He enters the shadows of the landing, his hulking silhouette blocking out city lights in the distance, then begins a slow descent, in control of the chair's speed and direction with his sucking and puffing. His brakes are automatic. If he stops blowing, they'll lock, slowly enough not to jolt. It may skid a foot or two given the ramp's incline, but that's it.

I roll out onto the landing and park. I am craning my neck trying to see him when he hollers up that he's made it down to the second floor landing. He adds an unoriginal idea involving my ass and Ex-Singer's joystick. He sounds winded. He'll have to stay put awhile, I figure, to catch his breath.

I reach under my knee and lift one leg. Funny how natural it seems now to do that. I thought I'd never get used to the feeling of picking up my legs and putting down my legs like sacks of chicken feed. I am still readjusting leg position for circulation so the blood won't pool in my butt when I hear a thud, an oomph and a squeal. I lean out over the railing just in time to see him go scooting out across the ground floor patio toward the back lawn. And then I can see him on the ground. That is, I can see his chair on the ground behind the hedge, on its side, one wheel in the air spinning silver in the moonlight.

Things are happening too fast. I holler down at him and realize when I hear my voice that I am cold sober. He is not, because he yells back, "Hey Baby, save the last dance for me."

"Only if it's an old-fashioned waltz," Ex-Singer has rolled up behind me, "you know how I hate dance fads." Maybe they're not such friends as I thought.

I start rolling down the escape, deliberately not using the handrails. Wind rushes past my face. A hundred fifty miles from the Gulf, I swear it smells salt. I brake at the half floor landing and holler down is he hurt.

"Not at all," he yells up at me. "Great fun. Just a little motor trouble is all. Come gimme a hand with this chair."

He could not have had motor trouble. And he does not sound hurt. Chairs do not malfunction. You can trust your chair. He had to have been blowing full speed ahead the whole time, or his brakes would've locked. I hope he's happy. He sounds happy, down there yammering about his broken chair and how he's going to pull himself back up the escape with his jaws so he can do it again.

Suddenly he gets quiet. Freerolling down to the second floor landing, I glimpse a pedestrian walking down the street way out beyond the lawn. I want to yell at him to come lend us a hand. But I am coming in for a landing. I brake too fast, pitch forward a little, catch myself on the railing, bounce back hard, but manage to keep my chair underneath me. I catch a breath and yell, "Help." The ped turns toward my voice. He hurries down across the lawn toward the patio looking for me at ground level. I lean out over the railing. "Hey Man, how about helping my friend down there?" The ped looks up at me. "On the ground," I yell. "Behind the hedge." The ped takes a peek behind the hedge and jumps back. "Come on, Man, he won't bite." I push off from the railing, don't stop for the last landing, just guide the wheels through the turns and let her roll. The momentum takes me clear out to the edge of the patio.

It does not take the ped and me long to get the quad and his chair upright, just a matter of leverage. He couldn't've been going fast when he rammed the hedge—all the velcro held. He's still chest-strapped in and seems to have been well protected by the chair's construction. It's got a high sturdy back and a neck-supporting head cradle. Given the motor's weight, low center of gravity and anti-tippers, I'm surprised it turned over, but runoff from the sprinkler system has the ground behind the hedge pretty soft. Crash due to pilot error with contributing ground conditions I'd say; equipment sound.

Soon as the ped gets most of the mud off the quad with his pocket handkerchief, I whip out my wallet. "Much obliged," I say and hand him a dollar. He doesn't want to take it, but I get real indignant with my don't-want-your-pity act, which always works with pedestrians. He takes it and takes off.

The quad's leg bag has burst so he's peed all over himself, has a cut on his nose and a good start on a shiner. But there is a look of mild interest on his face. His chair is o.k. The Sip 'n Puff system still works, though the tube is a bit chewed. He sits looking to me for direction. Since he is working on a personality and I have already come this far, I figure I might as well go along too and keep him out of further trouble. I holler up at Ex-Singer to see if he wants in on the fun.

"No, y'all go on," he calls, then starts a drum roll with his voice. So we take off like Don Quixote and Sancho Panza on wheels.

The harder he blows the faster he goes, but his lungpower activated motor is no match for my arms. Most of us are athletes, most of us male, between seventeen and twenty-five, prime for adventure and physical fun. Twenty-six is the age people start slowing down. I mean if you got a choice. We stop briefly halfway to the liquor store to let the quad catch his breath, but soon as he starts trying to make conversation, I figure if he's got air to talk, he's got air to travel.

Besides, conversation always leads to two questions: number one, How did it happen? Number two, Can you still . . . you know? Answer number one, It's nobody's business how I got my butt stuck in this chair. Number

two, I got a constitutionally guaranteed right to a private life. What I want
to know is what about the normal questions. Whatever happened to Hello,
what do y'do? Sancho does not know I'm trying to line up a job making
videos for national distribution. I'll demonstrate making chair adjustments,
how to change the wheel camber, adjust the center of gravity. I'll show
viewers how to scuba dive, maybe stick in a little commercial for web-
fingered gloves. I'll demonstrate golf swings, javelin throws and difficult
shots at the pool table. All Sancho knows is I'm sort of staff. I get room
and board for helping out with the new guys. I organize games, chair football, computer war. I suggest ways to handle peds who go on and on about
our courage, and how we're not handicapped, just physically challenged. I
give pep talks and tell what a full life I lead. I leave out a lot. It's an unwrit-
ten clause in every disabled job description to leave out a lot.

We get to *Texas Liquors* without further incident except that I'm sober
as a virgin at a Sunday School picnic. Sancho's still drunk or else high on
oxygen. He plays with the automatic door while I browse. The *Wild Turkey*
is up too high on the shelf, but I hold a fifth of *Jack Daniels Black Label* to
my chest and dream. We buy a cold six pack, go out and park ourselves in
the shadows of a closed shoe store. Sancho's still kind of muddy, so I pour
half a beer over him to wash him off. Then I wedge the can between his
knees, get his straw out of my side tote and wrap it around his Sip 'n Puff
tube so he can get to it. Then I open my beer. Been so long since I've had
a cold one, I can't believe how good it tastes. I've got to start getting out.

Sancho starts talking. Mr. Quiet before, he's the flipside now. Got a
two-beer story—all predictable stuff—Mr. Rodeo-Champ or Most-Likely-
To-Succeed or Olympic-Contender. Begins a ride, a jump, a back flip. Ends
up dead in the water. Would have choked, been trampled, or drowned, if
not for the lifeguard, best friend, rodeo clown, or stranger. Gets detailed
about the lifeguard, best friend, or stranger who rides along in the ambu-
lance, comes every day to the hospital to visit. Next—the girlfriend: Miss
Personality, Most Beautiful, Most-Likely-To-Be-Sexy. Sticks by him.
Camps out in the intensive care waiting room. *Until* she leaves with the
lifeguard, best friend, stranger. He thinks he is the first person that any of
this ever happened to.

He gets quiet, the self-pity thick and smelly as bedsore cream. After a
bit he clears his throat, asks me the number one question, "What happened

470

to you?" I tell him I didn't swipe my grandmother's car keys while she was sleeping one off, and she didn't wake up and plug me in the spine with her silver-plated pearl-handled .45. Then I laugh and laugh, 'cause we've killed the six pack. Now there's only one thing we need. And that's another six pack. We pool our assets; he's got zero and I've got enough to buy a post-age stamp on credit. So we roll on down the street hunting for a pool hall to increase our cash flow.

The cold beers've got me feeling up again. I pop a wheelie and check out Sancho's reaction. His jaw drops, and he rolls to a stop. His chair works perfectly I notice. Buy good equipment—you can count on it. That'll be my lead-off when I move from videos into commercials.

I roll a couple of tight circles around him. Fast. Showing off a little just 'cause it's Saturday night and still alive. Out on the town. Just a couple of guys out on the town. I tell Sancho about my chair, point out its design, tailored down to allow for maximum upper body mobility. The convertible of wheelchairs. Small back rest. No arm rests. Titanium frame. Low to the ground. Pneumatic tires. Sixteen pounds total.

I tell him one of my career goals is to make chair commercials: Ultra-luxury limos, Mountain climbers, Workhorses, Featherlight sports mod-els, Lightning-bolt racers. I tell him about the SPITFIRE! A three-wheel racer. Gutsy excitement on wheels. Hybrid of *grace* and speed. Plastic frame. Racing tires. Aluminum rims. Eleven pounds total. "So light," I tell him, "I can pick it up in the air—with me in it—and I'm working on levi-tation in case my arms ever get tired."

"What really happened?" he asks. He has stopped rolling. I keep go-ing. This is what is wrong with people. Nobody listens. Nobody cares what you want to say, only what they want to hear. Me, me, me. Satisfy *my* curiosity or shut up.

He catches up with me. We roll along side by side. It is hot. No breeze moving around down here at street level. His skin is red with exertion, shining sweaty under the streetlight. Written on his face are the only things he wants from me: What happened? And can you still . . .?

"I was a biker," I tell him, "a *Bandito*. One Saturday night riding alone out on this Hill Country hairpin road when a pretty little doe, breath smell-ing of fermented berries, picked my headlight to play chicken. But God had a purpose for my life," I say, moving on to question two, "So instead of swinging today on pearly gates, sopping biscuits in milk and honey, and twanging on a golden harp, I'm rolling my rocks around town and like to beat off while talking to young girls on the telephone." I laugh just to confuse him. And then I'm laughing for real at what a full life I have. I don't stop until we get to Fatso's Pool Hall.

No steps and the door open wide, Fatso's looks ripe: dark, almost empty, no nasal *Tejano* on the juke box. I roll in and head toward two big-boned girls in tight jeans sitting with their backs to the bar. They are watching two guys strike poses with cue sticks while pretending to play pool. One girl is barefoot and swinging her long foot, toenails polished. Under her barstool are a pair of high heel red sandals that ought to be illegal, they are *that* good. I park in front of her.

She looks down at me like she's trying not to look down at me. Then she goes back to watching the guys. I talk to her knee. I tell it, "I'm an alcoholic on the wagon and can't nobody suck pussy like an alcoholic on the wagon." I look up at her. She blinks, shakes her head like she does not trust her hearing.

"Unless maybe it's a Sip 'n Puffer," says my loyal sidekick cutting in.

One of the pool guys says, "Hey," lays the tip of his cue on my shoulder like he thinks he's my father. I grip the cue and invite his belt buckle to step outside. He tries to wimp out.

"Don't cut the bacon if you can't get it in the pan," I tell him, still holding the tip of his cue. I lunge, using the stick to push him off balance, ram him with my chair, jerking the stick out of his hand, wedging it between my knees. I roll over his leg turning my chair around, and head for the open door.

Soon as I'm outside, I pivot around behind the door and get a good grip about halfway up the cue stick. He steps out. I wallop the back of his head, then get him again in the kidney before he hits the sidewalk. The barefoot girl has come outside screaming HELP BLOODY MURDER. I look her in the eye and start to swing the stick over my head. She tries to run back inside, but Sancho's got the door blocked. Keys fly out of her hand when he rams her. Her guy's still down. I roll over and scoop up the keys.

There're three cars in front of Fatso's. I don't even try the two newer ones. The key fits the old two-door Malibu. I toss the cue stick on the seat and lift myself in. It feels real good, sitting squarely behind one wheel instead of sandwiched in between two. I lose some time leaning out and folding my chair, but it has become a part of me, like Ruth in the Bible— where I go it goes. I slide it in behind the car seat. Then I crank the Malibu, use the pool cue to give her the gas, back her up, and then take off. Burn rubber.

I do not believe what I am seeing in the rearview mirror. Out in the middle of the street, chasing after me—the quad! Suddenly the impossibility of his dream touches me. I hit the brake with the cue stick and back up. I put her in park right there in the middle of the street, lean over across the passenger seat and open the door for Sancho. Then the impossibility of *my* dream hits me—Did I think he'd just hop in? Or was I going to slide over, unstrap him, grab him up by the scruff of his neck and haul him into the car for a clean getaway? Did I really think we could just ride out in all directions looking for wrongs to make right?

And that's when I register the sirens all around us. They have appeared out of nowhere, and we are surrounded by cherry tops flashing like the Fourth of July. I should not have come back for the quad. I guess old Fatso dropped the nickel on us. If we were hardened criminals instead of a couple of crips out on the town, the cops wouldn't be here yet.

Through the windshield I see half a dozen uniforms walking toward me, all sworn to enforce the law through heat, rain storm, flash flood, tornado. Closing in, their fire-chasing faces, not expecting the fire to turn around and chase them. I roll the car window down with one hand, grab the cue stick with the other, use my arms to pull myself half out the window, start swinging the stick like a club, yelling "KILL."

Me and Sancho in his Chair from Hell give the cops so much factual shit right out there in the middle of the street they have to haul us in, the quad for assault with a deadly weapon, insulting an officer, and driving a wheelchair while intoxicated. Me, they charge with assault and battery with a cue stick, resisting arrest, D.W.I., and car theft.

They take us down to the jail, fingerprint us and take mug shots. I fake a pervert-voice and ask aren't they going to strip-search us. But they are reluctant. No doubt put off by the smell.

In the holding cell I look over at the quad. This is probably the least bored-looking that I have seen him. His eye is almost swollen shut, his nose is probably broken, and he has a couple of cuts I hadn't noticed earlier. But he's wearing a size-Texas grin.

Until he stops gawking at the cell-scenery and looks over at me. Then his face clouds up like rain coming, hooked on sympathy the way an Olympic contender gets hooked on applause. If I hadn't felt sorry for him and gone back, I could've been in the next county by now. I could've been out on some Hill Country hairpin road.

I roll over to him. "Hey, Man," I say, "it's Saturday night and still alive!" I punch him on the shoulder.

His eyes watch while my fist lands another one, a good one this time, solid. He works his cheeks for a minute like a squirrel with a nut. Then he spits at me. While I'm wiping my eye, he rams his chair into mine, but he's so close it doesn't count. Still, looking at the fireworks going off in his eyes, I can almost feel the impact.

HEARTBEAT

TERENCE A. DALRYMPLE

When my father died, I lived in Long Beach in a small renthouse with a first-hand view of San Pedro Bay. After my mother called from Dallas with the news, I wandered out onto the covered but unscreened porch and sat staring out to where I knew the horizon should be. When I closed my eyes, my grandfather's face, not my father's, came to mind. I opened my eyes, tried to think of my father as I stared out across the bay.

The early March day was perfect: seventy degrees or so, with a mild breeze, a brilliant silver sun, and a cloudless blue sky. Small clusters of sea gulls, shiny white and graceful, hovered and dipped, hovered and swooped above sailboats gliding over the shimmering bay water. I squinted against the sun's silver glimmer on the water and tried to distinguish the horizon. The farther out I looked, the harder it was to perceive any difference between the water and the sky. Where I thought they met, they did so without a visible seam, like perfectly matched wallpaper, forming one solid, massive cerulean wall haphazardly patterned with little flocks of gulls and bright white, yellow, green, red, and rainbow triangles of the boats' sails.

My father would have liked it there. He had always loved beaches and ocean water. As a child, I never knew any vacation spots but Galveston or Port Aransas on the Texas coast. At least once every summer, sometimes twice, we visited one place or the other for a week. My mother spent her time lying on the beach, cooling off in front of the television in an air-conditioned motel room, poking around in nearby shops, and touring various historical sites.

My father could fish contentedly for hours. Easily bored if the fishing were slow, I never tired of running up and down the pier, feeling the heat of the weathered wooden slats my feet slapped against, counting the seemingly lifeless jellyfish that floated listlessly just beneath the surface of the murky green water, picking up discarded chunks of bait and throwing them to the gulls hovering and squawking above the pier, running back to my father with news of some odd looking fish someone had caught. Especially impressive were hammerhead sharks whose heads, I thought, really looked as if you could hammer nails with them; croakers that grunted louder than the fat, shirtless men who caught them; angelfish whose black and gray, laterally compressed bodies made them look much too pretty and too skinny to eat.

Occasionally, one of my bare feet would find a splinter or a carelessly discarded fish hook, and I would hobble back to my father, crying all the way. He would dig the splinter or hook out, dab the wound with the Mercurochrome always in his tackle box, wrap the orange-stained foot in a tattered hand towel, and then hold me in his lap, pressing me against his sweaty, hairy chest and telling me everything he knew about the fish I had seen. My arms tightly around him, I listened intently and felt the soothing strong beat of his heart where my cheek pressed against his chest. When I felt better, he would go back to fishing while I sat nearby and watched the tail of his unbuttoned Hawaiian shirt flap in the salty sea breeze. I would study his broad, sweat-shiny chest, his hard looking jaw, his squinting eyes, and his thick hair, curling wildly in the sticky coastal air.

My mother always complained that we stayed in the sun too long, and we always winked at each other and told her about all the beautiful girls in bikinis we had seen. She would laugh and brush our comments away with a sunburned arm.

Sitting on the porch of my small rent-house in Long Beach, I closed my eyes and tried to remember what he looked like the last time I saw him. I had not seen him for two years. I did well just to pay for rent, groceries, and child support and simply could not afford a trip to Dallas. My mother had flown out to see me twice, but my father's emphysema left him too weak for long-distance travel. While she was away, he stayed at the V.A. hospital.

I wondered what that hospital was like, wondered if it had the same pale green hallways and purple-tinged soft white lights as the hospital where my grandfather died thirty-two years before. I had stood in one of those hallways feeling dizzy, feeling bodiless and breathless, feeling as if I were about to be sucked down the length of that pale green tunnel and smashed against the emergency exit doors at its end. I had watched my father comfort my sobbing mother there in that hallway. That was the only face I could remember: my father's face, not two years before, but thirty-two years before, my father's thirty-four-year-old face.

My mother had cried pitifully. He had said nothing, simply held her against his broad chest, his thick arms wrapped tightly around her, his jaw taut, the flesh at the outside corner of each eye wrinkled more than I had ever before noticed. He leaned slightly backwards, and I wondered if he strained against something, wondered if he felt what I felt, wondered if he knew what it was. Silently, he held my mother for fifteen or twenty minutes, held her until she slowly, slowly, slowly stopped crying. Then he kissed her forehead and took us home.

I had hardly known my grandfather. He was the tall, wrinkle-faced, deep-voiced man who came to visit from Oklahoma every Christmas and every Fourth of July before I turned ten. He was the gruff old man who frequently cursed, who occasionally belched without excusing himself, and who rarely had more than three or four words to say to me on any given day. Beyond that, I knew him only as the man whose wife brought him to our house one year in the middle of September, the man whose bedridden presence there for almost a month was somehow responsible for my developing insomnia, the man who later died while I hugged him in a hospital with long pale green hallways and cream-white doors.

Every night after he arrived, I lay sleepless in bed, feeling some vague and frightening force pull and strain and tug at me. Rigid, I would clutch the sheets, feel nothing, clutch again, and still again, until finally my damp palms felt the damp sheets. I would lie motionless, trying to focus on something familiar in my room, which seemed increasingly foreign.

One night the strange tugging force felt worse than usual. Trembling, I reached for the bedside lamp, squinted against its brightness, found nothing familiar in my room. I shivered, slipped out of bed, intended to creep into my parents' room and crawl up beside them. Instead, without knowing why, I stopped at my grandparents' room and eased into bed beside my grandfather.

He seemed barely to be breathing at all. He lay on his side, facing the edge of the bed. Next to him, my grandmother stirred slightly, sighed, but did not waken as I carefully slipped one arm under my grandfather's side and folded my other arm over him. His ribs felt like little more than brittle sticks wrapped in tissue paper. I pressed my cheek and ear against his chest, closed my eyes, listened to the *thump-thump thump-thump* of his seemingly strong, steady heart. I not only heard it, but felt it too: against my ear and cheek, in my arms, in my legs, in my own chest. His heartbeat, my heartbeat, one and the same.

It felt comfortable, familiar. I had felt it hundreds of times, probably thousands of times before, times when I ran a splinter or a fishhook into my bare foot, times when I fell on the sidewalk or crashed my bicycle or fell from a tree, times when I felt sad or frightened or lonely. Those were the times when my mother would gently clutch me against her softness or my father would wrap a thick, hard arm around me and squeeze me against his broad, firm chest. My mother's blouses always seemed smooth and silky as I pressed my cheek and ear against her, felt the fleshy softness of her breasts beneath her blouse, smelled the candy sweetness of her perfume, felt the beat of her heart run through my own body. My father was much harder, his shirts scratchy with starch, his smell usually a vague reminder of the damp earth of the garden where we sometimes searched for fishing worms. But the effect was the same; his heartbeat felt the same.

And it felt the same with my grandfather, even though I hardly knew him, even though he was sick and dying. I felt the *thump-thump* and smiled. The force straining against me diminished.

Every night after that I tried to stay in my own room, tried to fight the tugging sensation alone. But every night I ended up sneaking to my grandfather's room and snuggling against his chest. I didn't sleep, always lay awake waiting until I heard my mother or father in the bathroom. Then I would sneak back to my own room.

When I flew in from Long Beach, my mother met me at the Dallas-Fort Worth Regional Airport. She wore dark glasses and I knew she had been crying ever since my father died. We spoke quietly on the way home.

"We both knew it was coming," she said, looking out the car window instead of at me. "I think he accepted it."

"I don't see how anyone can," I said.

"One learns."

"I can't remember him, Mother."

"Don't be ridiculous." Her voice cracked.

"You should have moved to Long Beach when I asked you." That was after my divorce.

"I'm sure the air there is no better than it is here," my mother said, still looking out the window.

"He'd have liked it there," I said. "Right on the ocean."

"He liked it here." She cried quietly.

"You should have come."

"Leslie," she said, suddenly turning to face me and removing her dark glasses. Her eyes were bloodshot, their lids puffy. "Your grandfather came to us when he was sick. Do you remember? It didn't help. It doesn't help."

She had prepared the larger spare room for me, but I chose to stay in my old bedroom. In bed that night, I tried not to think about my grandfather, tried to think of my father, tried to remember our vacations at the coast, tried to remember what he had been like the last time I saw him. But I could think only of my grandfather. I felt ten years old again, lying in that bed and wishing my grandfather weren't in the hospital where I could not get at him.

He had stayed in the hospital for three days before dying. For the first two days, I was not allowed to see him, was not even allowed to go to the hospital. But on Saturday when I had no school, my parents took me with them. On the sixteenth floor, they left me near the nurses' station, despite my pleading to follow them. I watched them walk halfway down the long, pale green hallway before they entered a room on the left. Then I wandered across to the lobby and knelt backwards in one of the steel-framed, orange-cushioned chairs.

Although it was early October, the day outside the gray-tinted window was clear and hot. The Dallas buildings and Dallas streets and Dallas people sixteen floors below looked busy but lifeless as I watched them through heat-wave ripples. That vague force tugged at me and I suddenly feared that it might jerk me through the gray-tinted window and suck me down until I splattered against the street below. I turned around, sat stiffly in the chair, clutched the seat edge with both hands, studied others in the lobby.

A young Mexican woman sat staring into her lap, her dark hands squeezing, releasing, knuckling a loose fold of her purple knit skirt as if she were kneading dough. She tilted her head and spoke harshly to the little boy who tugged at her sleeve and whined in Spanish.

In a corner opposite them, an old man sat with his head thrown back and his mouth open. He snored. Every few seconds his pointed jaw moved slightly and he uttered a half-formed no. I wondered if he were a patient or a visitor.

When my parents and grandmother finally returned, a doctor walked with them. They stood together in the lobby while the doctor talked. My father nodded gravely; my mother cried; my grandmother fidgeted with her handkerchief.

Another doctor in a long white coat approached the Mexican woman and sat next to her, leaning in to speak quietly. Without looking up from the fold of purple knit skirt she kneaded, she began to moan, deeply and quietly at first, but gradually shriller and louder. The doctor took her by the elbow, helped her up, and slowly led her down the hallway. "*Ay, Dios mio,*" she wailed. "*Ay, Dios mio, Dios mio, Dios mio.*" The words echoed through the long green hallway, and the little boy added his screams as he clung to her purple knit skirt.

As my parents and grandmother listened intently to my grandfather's doctor, I walked slowly down the hallway to the cream white door through which they had passed earlier. His eyes closed, his mouth slightly open, my grandfather lay in the electronically controlled bed, the polished steel crib sides pulled up so he would not roll out. He looked as brittle and as hollow as the cicada shells I sometimes found stuck to the trunk of our tall pecan tree. Only his knees, propped up with small pillows, gave any contour to the sheet.

I felt the persistent tug. I climbed up over one of the steel crib sides and hugged him, pressing my cheek and ear against his chest. I listened to his shallow breathing. I felt his heartbeat in my own chest.

After a time his shallow breathing stopped. I still felt the heartbeat in my own chest. I climbed out of the bed, walked to where my parents and grandmother stood in the lobby.

"I think he's dead," I said.

"My God," said my mother, and she collapsed against my father's chest, crying loudly.

My grandmother began crying too. "I want to see him," she said. The doctor led her down the hall.

I did not sleep at all the night before my father's funeral. Weary and dazed from the night of sleeplessness, I went through the funeral feeling numb. At the graveyard, my mother squeezed my hand. After everyone had left, I put my arm around her shoulders as she cried, and when she stopped I walked her slowly to the car.

That night, she was calm. We talked about some of her memories and some of mine. I reminded her of the beautiful girls in bikinis. She smiled and waved my reminder away with a pale arm.

After she went to bed, I sat outside in the fenced back yard and stared up at the stars. I remembered walking down that long pale green hallway to tell my parents and my grandmother that my grandfather was dead. I remembered fearing that my father would scold me for having gone to my grandfather's room. But he had said nothing. He had simply squeezed my mother with his thick arms and pressed one of his broad hands against the back of her head as she pressed her face against his chest. He had leaned slightly backwards. I had studied the little wrinkles around his eyes and felt dizzy and so physically light that I could not fight the force tugging at me. I had felt the heartbeat in my own chest.

Sitting in my mother's back yard, I closed my eyes and finally saw my father's face as it had been two years before—his pale, wrinkled, aging face, so much like my grandfather's face had been.

Later, I lay in bed, one hand splayed across my chest feeling my steady heartbeat.

La Llorona of Leon Creek

Susan San Miguel

Green and brown glass shattered in the parking lot of Shopper's City Mall on Military Drive. The sun, just before descending for the day, touched pieces of the glass here and there and each piece flashed brilliantly in a sort of scattered rhythm to the screech of Iron Maiden on a passing car's stereo, "Do you enjoy your lay or is it the pay. . ."

Jo Jo ran his fingers through his slicked back black hair, stomped out his cigarette under his steel toes, and sauntered over to a newly parked pick-up to place a beer bottle beneath the back tire before the owner, who just went into the E-Z Rental Furniture, returned. Later, when the guy backed up, and the bottle sprayed glittery sparks at his tailgate like a soaring comet, Jo Jo and his friends Ramón and Tony didn't even glance in his direction. They didn't notice, couldn't have cared less when he shot the finger at them. They had moved on to other things, lying back on the hood of Jo Jo's black and gold Chevy Camaro, smoking cigarettes, checking out the view. From there they could see over the six lanes of Military Drive's impending traffic to the girls on the roof of a long red Oldsmobile parked carelessly in the Sears parking lot. Those girls were definitely striking seductive poses meant just for them.

The girls wore denim miniskirts and tight striped midriff T-shirts scooped low at the neck, and their faces were painted with dark make-up so that their lips were very red and full and their eyes dark and vivid, and the guys could read their sultry expressions even from across the street, mouths pursing like kissing baby dolls, eyebrows arching in upside down Ws. One of them lay on her stomach, propping herself up with her elbows so that her breasts spilled from her low clinging shirt. She pretended to flip through a magazine even though there was hardly enough light left for reading with the sky already deep violet with streaks of scarlet in the west trailing up from Military, like a drive into the sky. Another of them pointed her strong well-toned legs in the direction of the guys across the street and the oncoming traffic. She tapped her black leather pumps lightly on the windshield and made faces at herself in her compact mirror as she brushed on more lipstick.

Cars passed and blew their horns and someone yelled out the window, "Hey, what's your number?" but the girls just smiled at themselves in their compact mirrors and that was all.

Jo Jo, Ramón, and Tony had cruised by that same couple of girls ten times at least earlier in the evening. "Join us for a little ride, that's all, Chicas." They would turn into the undertow of slow traffic, other guys cruising for girls.

"Just a little ride. That's the plan, nothing else, down Military and back."

Stuck up bitches. Jo Jo decided it was time to make a run to the Taco Cabana to order a large coke to mix with the Jack Daniel's so that it would last longer between them. They had been saving it long enough. He stuck his head out the car window as he pulled out of the parking lot and said, "So long. Catch you later. This place is going nowhere fast." The girls glanced up from under their thick eyelashes. Those guys'll be back.

But for now they sped away from the red and white car lights and Metallica's guitar solo wailing over car engines to where all they could hear was their own car sputtering its exhaust, and their own voices that seemed to ring clearly out the window. And they laughed and passed around their large paper Taco Cabana cup, drinking Jack Daniel's and coke from a straw.

The early spring wind blew cold on the bridge of the Leon Creek where Anita stood gazing out into the black rushing water. The wind brought with it the scent of car exhaust and desert cactus, sweet grass and early corn. A light shone in the south across the fields where cattle grazed. So brightly it shone that she was drawn to it even when she tried to focus on something else, the dark trees rising up from the bank below, the water rushing across slate and gritty earth.

It is like a spotlight seeking me out, damn light. I will not go there. There is no telling what my father has already told them about me.

It must have been at least ten years ago when Aunt Idalia had called the city of San Antonio and requested a street light on the grounds of the ranch house "to discourage vandals from preying on we three helpless old women."

Helpless? Amusing. Aunt Idalia would have drawn blood with her fingernails if anyone had tried to harm anything that was theirs. But now the aunties were asleep in the old stone ranch house beneath that thick veil of trees, certainly not expecting their great niece Anita to knock on their door.

Besides, what in the world would she say to them?

"You see, it's like this," she would explain to the trembling old women, come to the door in their flannel night dresses holding a candle to light the way as if from another time. And she would be trembling too because the sight of them always inspired such awe. Such respect, they demanded. That was what it was. "My father," she would begin, "he said just get the hell out of the car and so I did and here I am."

No, no, she couldn't say that. That's not how it happened exactly. This afternoon as he steered the car out of the driveway, putting an end to the Sunday afternoon visit with the aunties he glared into the rear view mirror where he could see his two daughters expecting to be driven home, and his eyes rested on Anita. "Why do you always have to try to shock people with your questions?"

She had asked Aunt Lucia why she hadn't had children. What's wrong with asking. "I was just curious. What's there to hide?" she answered her father.

"God damn it. Haven't I taught you anything?"

And she said, "Stop the car. I want to get out."

And he pulled over. "Fine. Get the hell out of the car."

And she did. The dust puffed in a cloud around her as she watched the old station wagon pull away, her younger sister Madeline hanging out the window, her mouth, a slash of grimness across her face, her eyes refusing even to look at her.

Well, of all the tumultuous moments between Anita and her father since her mother died, her father had never just left her on the side of the road before. That was hours ago, when it was still daylight. He wasn't coming back.

She closed her eyes but still the blue white light glared at her through her eyelids. She listened to the water gurgling over rocks, in a loud whisper, talking to her. "I'm getting the hell out of here," it said. "I'm going somewhere fast."

When she heard male voices nearby, the rumble of a car's engine drawing closer, raucous laughter, too drunk, too filled with male comradery for her heartbeat not to quicken, she was afraid. "Be careful what you say. Be careful how you act. You know what they're interested in," her father's stern warnings rang in her ears even though she had always told herself she wasn't listening.

Ramón was the first to see her slight figure standing alone on the bridge. His spine tingled and his hair prickled on his scalp. La Llorona, the crying woman is searching the dark rushing waters of the Leon Creek for the children she drowned. He had never seen her before but he had friends who had. He jostled Jo Jo on the shoulder and pointed.

Jo Jo's reflexes were quick. He saw a girl on the bridge and already smoothly started a conversation as he pulled over. "Hey baby, Whatcha doin'? Lookin' at somethin' special?"

His words flowed together smoothly, like water. To Anita, still lost in her own thoughts, his voice was the voice of the creek, urging her. She stared blankly at the faces in the car, causing even Jo Jo to become a little uncomfortable. He looked uncertainly at his friends for help. Something about her, her glassy brown eyes, looked past you far away. Maybe she wasn't real.

"I don't know man. Maybe she didn't hear you," Ramón and Tony encouraged him to try again.

"Que estás haciendo aqui?" he tried in Spanish, which to Anita was the language of the water exactly. This time she managed a weak smile and answered his question just so that her voice didn't shake.

"I was just taking a walk."

He dangled his arm coolly out the window while he checked her out, stroking his slight mustache sensually with his finger. He liked her sad scared face and that she was dark and unsmiling, maybe unfriendly. She seemed to be a white girl, at least from the other side of town. No girl wore baggy white shorts where he came from. He thought that she must be about fifteen or sixteen, at least five years younger than himself. Her hair was too short though. Girls should wear their hair long so you could run your fingers through it. At least she wasn't wearing all that make-up that rubs off when you touch it like the girls he knew wore.

He nodded as if he didn't believe that she was taking a walk but it's okay with him that she's lying.

Ramón tapped Jo Jo on the shoulder and asked him what she said. Anita turned and pretended to look up at the moon, a pale sliver enveloped by a pitch black sky, while Jo Jo told Ramón what she just said. Then they laughed and mumbled something and Jo Jo reached out and touched her arm lightly, familiarly, as if they were already friends.

"There's a dance at Mission County Park right now. Wanta come?" He grinned. "It'll be fun."

Anita glanced over his shoulder and got a good look at Ramón sitting next to him and Tony in the back seat sipping from the cup. Ramón stretched his arm across the seat and nodded just enough to acknowledge her presence, the way the popular guys did in high school. She decided he looked a little like Luis Miguel who sings slow love songs in Spanish. Luis Miguel, the most romantic singer in the world with his light brown hair flecked with gold and skin the same brown gold color, deep blue eyes and heavy sleepy eyelids. This boy had black hair and brown eyes but somehow he looked the same to Anita. Women always quivered and squealed and threw roses at Luis Miguel while he sang. She watched television in Spanish just to see him and now here he was. In the back seat Tony sucked on a straw like a child slurping down a milk shake and smiled at her mischievously with quick black eyes. He was shorter and stockier than the other two. She could tell even though he was sitting. Probably someone's little brother. Then he struck a match in one quick motion that caught her off guard, letting it burn down to his fingertips without a flinch. The tiny fire flickered in soft undulating waves so that the inside of the whole car looked as if it were under water, casting a strangely warm glow onto their eyes and faces. Then he lit a cigarette and passed the box of Winstons around. He even offered her one, pushing the box in her face and motioning for her to take one. She shook her head no but had second thoughts. She could seem superior and disinterested with a cigarette in her hand but then she didn't know how to smoke and would probably cough embarrassingly. She decided the one in the back seat was maybe a little older than she had thought at first.

The lights of their cigarettes shone like sparks from a campfire inside their dark car. It was probably warm in there. She wasn't supposed to get into the car. That would be a really stupid thing to do. Her little sister Madeline would shake her head at her and say how could you have been so stupid. Her father would shut the door to the reporters' knocking when they found her dead, dumped like a stray dog in a ditch on the side of the road. Of course Madeline might also ask what they looked like. They looked fine, slick dark hair that shone silver blue even on this black night, white T-shirts that glowed fluorescent in the darkness like the white lights that light up a baseball field, and blue jeans faded the softest, lightest blue.

Anita had never been to a dance at Mission County Park. She had never even been to a dance. She wondered if that was really where they would take her or if they would take her further down this dark road. She got in the car.

She walked around to the passenger's side already decided that she wanted to sit in the front, in the middle between Jo Jo and Ramón.

"Wanta drink?" Tony handed her the cup from the back seat and she drained the last gulp, without bothering to taste it. She passed it back to him and he filled it almost to the top and passed it over the front seat. Ramón took a sip and gave it to her. They introduced themselves in monosyllables and she sat looking straight ahead clutching the cup with both hands and every once in awhile drinking from it hungrily so that she could believe where she was. Noncommittal, refusing to say anything just yet.

Ramón and Jo Jo took turns glancing at her and then at each other. Finally Ramón stretched his arm out across the seat again and around her shoulders. She looked up at him with her scared eyes and sucked hard on the straw. In this darkness she could not even see the cows or the trees or the bushes that she knew were on the side of the road. Just road being swallowed by car, that's all there was. Another sip. Jo Jo drove faster. The hood of the car vibrated; the doors squeaked and rattled.

She wanted to rest her head on Ramón's shoulder and pretend that she was still in the car with her father and Madeline, driving home where she could eat leftovers from lunch and watch the Sunday night movie on television if it wasn't too late. She drank straight whiskey—they had run out of coke a long time ago—and she lay her head on Ramón's shoulder. Her eyes began to close half way. Jo Jo and Ramón exchanged knowing glances and grinned. Jo Jo's foot hit the accelerator, the car whizzing down the road like a roller coaster ride.

Then she saw it, the blur up ahead, a deer in the middle of the road? Deer crossing, wasn't that what the sign just said? She opened her eyes wider and could see a white figure bent over in the road. She pointed but they weren't paying attention to her.

"Stop," she gasped. "Don't hurt it."

This took Jo Jo so much by surprise that he slammed on the brakes causing them to screech sideways onto the side of the road, just missing the girl who seemed to be caught in a perpetual pause still bent over in the middle of the road, oblivious to their approaching car.

Jo Jo winked at Ramón. "This is the place, man, the place to pick up girls. Next weekend I ain't even gonna bother with the strip. Know what I mean."

"Yea, they're behind every tree, seems like."

Jo Jo dangled his arm out the window and spoke smoothly, as if he hadn't just almost wrecked the car. "Taking a walk by yourself tonight? We're going to the dance at Mission County Park. Wanta come?"

The girl peered inside the car uncertainly. Her eyes met Anita's. They asked is this a good idea. Are these your friends? The look on her face was so trusting and pure that Anita turned away, pretending she hadn't seen. The girl thought Anita's eyes said come with me and do what I do. It'll be fun. She stepped into the back seat next to Tony.

And then she began to talk. She said she lived two miles away and was just out taking a walk the night was so lovely and she had seen these pretty stones mixed in with the gravel on the road and she thought they looked like they could be jewels and that she could make a necklace out of them somehow to wear with her pretty dress. Anita noticed that she was wearing a soft pink dress made out of some gauzy type of fabric and that the dress had artificial rose buds with little green leaves that bordered the neckline which slipped slightly off her thin pale shoulders. Anita liked the dress a lot. She wished she were wearing something else besides her shorts and T-shirt. The girl held up her pebbles for Anita to see and the pebbles along with some dust from the road spilled through the girl's long thin fingers onto Anita's lap.

"I've lost my pebbles," she exclaimed tragically.

Anita thought she was overreacting. They were only little bits of gravel and dirt. "Don't worry. I'll help you look for them later."

Now her white shorts were dirty.

The girl continued to talk to Anita all the way to the dance, as if she were the only other person in the car. Anita couldn't tell if the girl was ignoring the boys just to be aloof and get their attention or if she really didn't notice them. The boys all stared at her with great respect, no longer aware of Anita's presence it seemed.

The girl said her name was Charlotte. She asked do you like my hair. It was long and chocolate brown. "I know it looks brown at night but during the day it's auburn. Really it is. And in the middle of the summer when the sun shines on it, it's red."

She said English was her favorite subject in school, especially the stories by Mr. Edgar Allan Poe. She said her sister had a pet turtle and that her father owned lots of horses and she loved to ride them. And she talked and talked about herself in what seemed to be the most interesting way even though no one had even asked her a question. The boys continued to stare, easily impressed. Anita nodded politely and sipped from the cup.

And Charlotte danced with just about everyone at the dance. As soon as she arrived she leapt from the car and began swaying to the beat of the cumbia, tapping her foot lightly on the trampled earth. The crowds of people dancing beneath the pavilion parted to let her through and watched curiously at first as her lithe body swayed to the accordion's rhythm, the way the limbs of trees sway and show off the silvery leaves in the wind before a storm. She twirled in circles, her pink tiered skirt fluttering around her long legs and she laughed as she danced from one partner to another, her voice jingling like a tambourine filling the night with her own music.

Why, she was just standing out there on the side of the road waiting for them to drive by and take her to this dance, or so it seemed to Anita who hung back self-consciously and watched her in awe.

Finally Jo Jo, who had not even come to the dance to dance but to stand back and watch other people dance, flung his jacket to the ground, took Charlotte by the arm, and glided along the dance floor following expertly her every move. Anita looked at his jacket longingly. She was cold, but she didn't dare pick it up. Maybe he had a bad temper and would get angry. Ramón still stood by her side and eventually asked her if she wanted to dance. No thank you.

They looked like little puppets, the people dancing with their cowboy hats bobbing up and down to Mexican polka music and their pointed black boots tapping, raising little puffs of dust. She liked the way the men swayed their hips and the women raised their skirts a little with one hand and held their man's waist with the other. She liked that some couples had brought their children, even their babies, and were dancing with them. When the music stopped she could hear the soft gurgling of the San Antonio River slinking slowly by, just down the slope from where they were dancing; it drifted through the park and away from the city.

Ramón left her standing there and went to dance with Charlotte. He held her closely, securely, as if he were trying to protect her from a giant meteor shower that could burst from the dark sky at any moment. Anita walked sleepily away to sit in the car. She passed a couple of girls wearing short denim skirts. They were yelling Jo Jo's name.

"Have you seen Jo Jo?" One of them grabbed her brusquely by the shoulder and asked her in Spanish, too quickly. Anita looked at them dumbly. "Leave her alone. She doesn't understand Spanish."

Anita pointed out to the dance floor. "He's probably with Charlotte," she answered.

"Who's Charlotte?" they wanted to know.

"There, in the pink dress." She felt like she had just sacrificed Charlotte to them but she didn't care. She watched as they marched out to the dance floor as if they already had plans to beat up the skinny pale white girl who clearly, they could see from where they were standing, had captured the attention of everyone there.

The wind tingled icy cold on Anita's bare legs. It touched her beneath her light cotton T-shirt and gave her chills. She turned and stumbled onto the car where she sat shivering in the back seat, a little dizzy. The sliver of moon kept bobbing up and down when she opened and closed her eyes and she thought someone must be shooting fire crackers because her ears kept popping and ringing. Ramón knocked on the window, bang, bang, like a firecracker and he smiled. She rolled down the window.

"Estás boracha, no?" You're drunk, aren't you? And he laughed like that was the funniest thing in the world.

"Maybe just a little."

"Can I come in?" It's no fun out here." He shrugged his shoulders and shivered, hugging himself as if he wanted Anita to keep him warm. Anita pretended to sigh. She opened the door.

"Where do you go to school?" he asked, curiously, friendly enough.

"The University of Texas."

"No way man. You can't be in college. You look like you're just a little kid. You ain't no more than sixteen at least."

"I'm twenty-one."

"For real?"

Then he became quiet as if he didn't know what to say next. Anita guessed she was older than he was so she decided not to ask his age. He looked out the window interestedly. He seemed to be searching for somebody over the maze of cars.

"That Charlotte girl your friend?"

"No. I've never seen her before."

"She acts like she knows you."

"I've never seen her before."

"She sure can dance."

He looked out the window again. Anita did too, to see what he found so interesting. She could see the lights from the Mission Four drive-in, which when the screen flashed brightly, lit up the domed roof of the Mission of San José just beyond it. A family was sitting on the hood of their car two cars away where they probably had a pretty good view of the movie. They were having a midnight picnic. The smell of chicken and rice and boiled eggs wafted through the crack in the car window. Anita felt like throwing up. Ramón turned all at once and swung his arm around her neck; his hand dove between her legs. He kissed her.

"Not now." She tried to push him away but he pushed her down on the car seat. "Just open the window at least," she gasped. "I can't breathe in here."

He let her up to get some fresh air. The window let in an accordion and laughter and shivering wind and the strong smell of baked chicken. She inhaled a few breaths. She was hungry. She felt much better.

"Can you sing?" she wanted to know.

"No." He waited restlessly, impatiently tapping his fingers on the car seat. She lay back down on the seat and began to take off her clothes, pulling her T-shirt over her head.

"Put a blanket over me at least. There's a family outside, children running by the windows."

"They can't see anything. The window's all foggy. Besides there ain't no blanket."

She took his shirt which he had removed while she was getting her breath of air, and she draped it over his head which was already pressed between her legs.

"You're all slippery like a fish."

"Do I taste like a fish?"

"No, you taste like a woman," and he looked up at her greedily and then dove into her again.

Outside the car window, she heard a little girl laughing and talking to herself which caused her to flinch. The little girl could bounce her ball in this direction and what would she think if she saw us? He doesn't seem to notice the little girl outside. I'm a fish and I'm wet like the ocean and he is very thirsty. She resigned herself to staring out the window at the stars. She couldn't see the moon from that angle but she could just make out the big dipper. You could always see the big dipper when you came this far south of town on a clear night. She remembered all those drives with her family. What she wanted to know was what does she have that he seemed to be enjoying so much. At least she was wanted. Just come inside me and give me some strength. All his boyish self-confidence could fill her up, maybe, for a while, like medicine. A tap on the window, the little girl. She flinched again.

"Hey man what you doing in there?" It was only Jo Jo.

"Later," Ramón raised his head and panted.

The window was rolled down enough to where Jo Jo could see. She heard his boot crunch to only a few steps away. She knew he was standing somewhere in the shadows waiting.

Ten minutes later when it was all over and Ramón lay back on the seat limp, spent, with a weak smile on his face as if he were about to go to sleep

and dream some wonderful dream that maybe she would be a part of, Jo Jo
came back.

"Get out of the car. I want to see the senorita." It was that grin again.
She could hear it in his voice. He was happy to see her. They wanted her,
not Charlotte.

Ramón opened the door exposing her to the world outside but no one
saw except Jo Jo. She lay there with Ramón's shirt wrapped around her,
naked and shivering from the wind that had grown stronger and colder,
sprinkled with drops of rain that felt like glass scraping her skin. It was
going to storm.

"Can I have my shirt?" Ramón asked. She gave it to him and now she
had nothing to cover her. Her own clothes were trampled somewhere on
the floor of the car. He didn't seem to notice. It's okay, he just wasn't
thinking she told herself as she watched him stumble sleepily away.

Jo Jo began with a kiss, a violent one. He thrust his tongue in her
mouth so hard that she couldn't kiss back. She wanted to.

He said just lie back and do as I say. But she was lying back.

She said, "Uh, sure."

He pressed his body against hers. It was hot and damp and slippery
with rain drops and sweat. He was warm.

"Why didn't you clean yourself up? You're all sticky."

"I didn't have time. How could I?" He glared at her, annoyed as if she
were making excuses. And he thrust himself into her in the same violent
way he kissed with his tongue and she thought maybe she could be as
strong as he was if she'd just shut up and quit asking so many questions as
she knew he wanted her to do.

Outside the window the stars had disappeared and purple and pink
lightening streaks flickered across the sky like the veins in someone's eye.
He heaved against her, back and forth creating warm friction that burned
her skin. Thunder crashed so close that she thought it might have hit one of
the oak trees in the park and started a fire. Jo Jo looked up for a second and
then let out a long slow sigh. She lay still because she didn't know whether
or not he wanted her to move.

Outside women shrieked and laughed as they ran to their cars; she
imagined the men holding their coats over the women's heads so they
wouldn't get wet. She heard their feet pattering against the muddy earth,

the sounds of their feet blending with the splattering of the rain that poured from the sky in hard drops, banging against the hood of the car like millions of rubber balls.

"Sounds like maybe it's hailing out there," Jo Jo said.

That was sort of a friendly comment she decided. She wondered if this was a good time to ask for more whiskey. She wanted it badly enough to try.

"Is there anything left to drink?"

He looked around. "Maybe so." And he found the bottle lying underneath the passenger's seat still one fourth full. He watched without comment as she drank from the bottle as if it were water she was drinking and then he said let's do it again.

"Again? Okay."

She lay back down and noticed that the car's interior was red like her own car and that it looked brown in the darkness when the lightning flashed on it, brown like the color of dried blood. When he touched her breasts his hand slipped with the sweat that had dripped from his body to hers. His fingers skidded roughly across her nipple causing her to moan so he did it some more. This time she didn't notice when a lightning bolt reached out from the sky and flicked its long wicked finger against the branches of the old oak tree as if that streak of lightning were an old woman spindly shaking finger.

Outside the people, who were scattered here and there on the way to their cars, stopped and exclaim, "Ahhh" together in one long slow breath. The tree had split in two pieces right down the middle, exposing its tender pale insides.

"Cuantos años tiene este árbol?" Many people in the crowd asked each other the same question.

"One hundred years at least," someone said.

"It was probably here, a big strong tree in its prime, before the Spaniards even arrived. Now it's dead and they'll have to send someone out tomorrow to cut it down. Too bad."

Jo Jo looked up and said the tree's dead. "You liked that, didn't you?"

"Yes."

Now Charlotte and Ramón and Tony all tapped against the windows at once. Charlotte's laughter jingled with the rain against the window.

494

"Está lluvia. We're drenched," they giggled in unison.

Anita felt dizzy again. Their voices kept circling her head whizzing away and then flying back like an annoying mosquito. She grabbed Jo Jo's arm desperately just as he was about to open the door.

"Don't. Just help me find my clothes at least," she pleaded.

"Hurry up. They're getting wet out there." Charlotte began to sing "De Colores" and Ramón and Tony joined in. Their voices warbled in the rain. They forgot the words and then laughed some more.

When she opened the door she saw that she had her shirt on backwards and wrong side out. Tony, took hold of her wrist and said hey man, what about my turn. She smiled weakly. "Maybe another time," she answered.

"My jewels," Charlotte exclaimed after they had gotten settled in the car. "You said you'd help me find them."

Anita got down on her hands and knees and searched the floor of the front seat. She was able to come up with four little pebbles that were beginning to look a little bit like beads to her. They were translucent, purple or blue. Maybe they really were jewels. She wondered how Charlotte would make a necklace out of them. How could she string them? Anita wanted to ask but she was too tired.

"You can only find four?" Charlotte asked, disappointed.

Anita lifted her head from where she was bent over in the front seat, and looked straight at Charlotte, exasperated. She felt a tear roll down her cheek. She really didn't want to cry.

"Yes. I can only find four. I'm sorry." Her voice was so small and meek that they could hardly hear it.

Everyone in the car grew silent and Charlotte stared at Anita intently for a moment, the innocent look on her face changing to one of understanding. She asked if she could sit in the back seat with Anita because they had things to discuss. The boys groaned and Tony and Ramón got out of the back seat to trade places with Anita.

"What's the matter, honey?" Charlotte asked after the car had started.

Anita shook her head. "Nothing," she said, while tears flowed freely from her eyes leaving dirty brown streaks down her dust-caked face.

"Don't you worry. They'll be other dances."

Anita hoped not. Finally she asked, because she didn't want to talk about herself, "Did you have fun?"

"Oh yes," Charlotte answered. "I'd never been to a dance before. Can you believe it? And I've always wanted to go to one too." She tapped Jo Jo on the shoulder and said, "Just drop me off where you found me."

"I'll have to walk home and sneak in," she whispered confidentially to Anita.

Jo Jo pulled over to the side of the road and let her out next to a fence covered with honeysuckle. "Is this it?" he turned and asked politely as if he were her very own personal chauffeur.

"This is perfect. And thank you so much gentlemen for a wonderful evening." She curtsied and bowed her head which would have made Anita want to roll her eyes and snicker but she just couldn't. At first after Charlotte got out of the car, she just stood there waiting, with the sun rising behind her, showing itself in the soft auburn glow of her hair. As they sped away Anita turned back to see Charlotte's lithe figure moving southward, her neck curved downward as she searched the ground for more pebbles. Anita decided she liked Charlotte and waved at her one last time even though Charlotte couldn't possibly have seen her.

"Man, that's some girl," the guys all exclaimed. And then they started talking about how Charlotte had befriended everyone at the dance, even Jo Jo's grandmother who had asked to be introduced to her.

"Abuelita will be asking me when we're going to get married when I see her at church next Sunday." Anita noticed that Jo Jo seemed to like that idea.

Charlotte had even made friends with the girls from the South Side. They had danced together, to some old song from the fifties.

Anita wondered what they would say about her after they had dropped her off.

"Where do we drop you?" Jo Jo asked abruptly. Anita stuttered that she lived on the other side of town.

"That's just what I thought. I ain't got enough gas to get to the other side of town."

Anita thought about how it would take forty-five minutes for them to drive to her house and how angry Jo Jo would be and how she didn't want them to know where she lived anyway and how she would ring the door bell and stand there waiting with those three guys waiting in the car annoyed and daylight coming on and her dad answering the door because he refused to give her a key and him seeing her all dirty with tears streaked down her muddy brown face and the guys over her shoulder in the car thinking they're doing the right thing but not wanting to and her dad slamming the door in her face. "What the hell have you been up to?" That's what he would say. Then what would she do?

"That's okay," she said. She asked Jo Jo to please just drop her off at the bus stop on Military Drive.

"Good. 'Cause there ain't no way I was gonna drive all the way to the north side. I'm tired."

Whatever. She couldn't wait to get out of the car. Her eye caught on something sparkling beneath the seat and she bent down to pick it up. One of Charlotte's jewels. With the sun coming up now, she could see it better. It certainly was a jewel, an amethyst, she decided. Charlotte had left this for her especially, as a gift, she was sure. She held it tight in the palm of her hand. She would keep it and try to make a pendant out of it so she could wear it on a chain around her neck like Charlotte.

Jo Jo pulled over. "Hurry. Get out. There's cars behind us. When can we see you again?" he yelled out the window as he drove away.

Anita managed to smile and wave. They hadn't asked Charlotte when they could see her again.

THUNDERBIRD

CHUCK ETHERIDGE

I was in El Paso to take care of my Dad, who's just had his second triple bypass, and I was driving along Mesa Street looking up at Mt. Franklin when it hit me: I've climbed every peak and major rock formation on it except for the Thunderbird. Right then, I knew I was gonna try.

That's how I wound up where I am now, which is flat on my back in an ocatillo, its spines digging into my back and butt. I'm actually kind of grateful I fell into it, on account of how it broke my fall when I got to the top of an escarpment and surprised a mule deer and her two fawns and she got startled and I got startled and went over backward. If the ocatillo hadn't caught me, I would have fallen five hundred feet.

The only thing more painful than falling into a spiny thing like an ocatillo is trying to climb out of one, so I just kind of lie there, in moderate pain, watching the muledeer scoot nimbly down the mountain, its two young scrambling after it. I'm wondering how I'm gonna get myself out of the situation until Lisa's blonde, Texas-Ranger-ballcapped head pokes back out over the escarpment I've just fallen off of and says, brightly, "So, did you see the deer?"

"Yes," I say, as calmly as I can, expecting her to come back down and help me.

"I've lived in El Paso nearly my whole life and have never seen one in the wild." She doesn't make a move to climb down.

"Me either," I reply, managing to roll out of the bush and onto a rock without falling farther. Then I sit up and begin pulling barbed needles out of my calf muscles, which hurts whole lot, let me tell you.

"And she had twin fawns. That's really rare."

"You don't say," I grumble, and begin to scramble back up to her.

Lisa is not one of your solicitous, "Oooh Fred Are You Okay Let Me Get You Something to Make You Feel Better" type females, but I'm a little surprised she doesn't comment on the spill I took. Then I decide that she's ignoring it 'cause she thinks I'd be embarrassed if I thought she'd seen me fall, which I was, so I decide I'm grateful she didn't say anything after all.

I reach her and stand next to her on a large rock, pretending to watch the damned deer but really catching my breath. Then I really begin to look around, because we've climbed up far enough that there's beginning to be a view. It's been raining recently, something that rarely happens in El Paso, especially in July, so the rock-and-caliche mountains are bathed with a green sheen because the cautious desert plants have unsheathed their leaves a little.

"God," I hear myself saying, "I love it up here," and the way it comes out it's more like a prayer than a swear.

"Me, too." So we both just stand there, looking down past the city to the desert which is so huge and big and empty that it's obvious the city doesn't belong there.

I'm not sure why I'm with Lisa McAdams on the slopes of Mt. Franklin climbing toward the Thunderbird. When I got my bolt of inspiration and decided to scale the 'Bird, I decided to call one of my college buddies, Manuel, and ask him to come with me. Sort of like I automatically thought of the climb as a Guy Thing, something to be done with a male friend I'd done other Guy Things with in my life, like play City League basketball against superior talent. I guess I'd kinda assumed that, since Manuel and I had played defense against some ex-NBA players, he wouldn't be afraid to confront a mountain that hadn't moved in the last millennium.

But when I called Manuel with this great idea, he actually laughed. At me, his best friend from college. Began with a chortle, then busted into a full-fledged belly laugh, then, sobbing tears of mirth into the phone, he said, "You want me to do WHAT?"

"Climb Thunderbird."

"Like, the mountain?"

"Yeah," I replied, defensively.

"Freddie, you're thirty-four years old; you are, excuse me, fat; you don't live in El Paso any more, which, I must remind you, is four thousand feet above sea level. If you don't have a heart attack, you'll pass out from lack of oxygen, and I'm not going to carry your lard butt back down the hill."

So just like that, Manny punches me below the belt and turns this into a macho contest, which, I'm embarrassed to admit, is a fairly easy thing to get me to engage in.

"Manny, I've been playing hoop four times a week. Full court." This is actually true, by the way.

"What about the altitude?"

"I've been here three weeks taking care of Pop. I've had time to adjust."

"Okay, Fred, I've got to admit it. You haven't seen me for a while. I've put on a few pounds. My back hurts most of the time. I'm two years older than you. Even if you can make it, *I can't.*"

Embarrassed silence. Manny started a macho contest and let me win. Dirty trick. "So," I said, pleading, "I can't even get you to try?"

"No way, buddy. But the Coronas are on me if you make it. If you don't, give me your folks' number."

"Why?"

"'Cause my Tío Juan is a stonecutter, and he'll give them a headstone cheap because you were kind of like family to me." Manny was already referring to me in the past tense.

Lisa is all raring to go again. "Ready?"

"Sure," I reply, and begin to methodically pick my way up the constantly shifting rocks and pebbles as she darts nimbly up. I'm huffing again before I've climbed fifty feet.

Part of me feels like I should be bothered because she's breaking the trail, but I'm not. Any latent chauvinism I might have had bled out of my butt and into the ocatillo thorns. She's younger, she's in better shape, and I have, gallantly I tell myself, agreed to carry the pack which contains, among other things, several quarts of fluid, and is getting heavy. I plod along deliberately, content to follow.

Her voice drifts down from above, saying "Uh-oh." I secretly hope that she, too, has fallen into an ocatillo bush, but am ashamed of myself for thinking it.

"What's wrong?"

"Spanish daggers." She points to her right, and there is, in fact, a huge patch of short, very thorny, plants that do, in fact, look like little green blades growing out of the ground.

"Girl," I ask, "Where do you think you're going?"

"To the Thunderbird." She points back toward Ranger Peak.

I cover my face with my hands, trying not to let her see me laugh. Lisa is this strange mixture of competence and dinginess. This is a case in point—she's clearly the better climber, but she's got us going in the wrong direction.

"What?"

"Thunderbird is right there." I point up, but you can't see it from where we are. Mt. Franklin is kind of like a huge staircase, a series of sheer rock faces with relatively smooth slopes between them. Once you are on the side of the mountain and are standing near one of the rock faces, as we were, the formation blocks your view so you can't see the top.

Lisa looks skeptically at me. "Are you sure?"

"Yeah. Thunderbird is the northernmost formation on the west side of the mountain. You've gotten us headed back south."

"Oh," she says, and then she laughs, at herself. You can't help but like a person who can laugh at her own mistakes. "I've lived here nearly my whole life and didn't know that."

I take the lead for a second. "I'll show you. Look up when we get to the top of this face." The stones here are getting larger, more secure, with no smaller pebbles that can come loose under your feet and send you back down the mountain, plus there aren't too many plants to avoid, so it doesn't take me long to climb up to the crest.

The top of the Thunderbird is visible, like a granite version of the Rock of Gibraltar growing out of the forehead of the mountain, a huge formation that juts out like of the northwest face of Franklin at about a forty-five degree angle. I find a rock that looks like it's big enough to accommodate my butt, hop up on it, open the backpack and break out some purple Gatorade, which I swill, my legs dangling over the edge, waiting for Lisa to catch up.

Lisa and I are old, old friends, high school buddies who've know each other for nearly twenty years. Our lives have taken very different paths and this trek is something like a reunion for us. I'm married and have two kids and live in Abilene now. She's back in El Paso, trying to put her life back together after a crappy marriage and an abortive attempt to live in Houston. As I sit there sipping Gatorade, it dawns on me that the biggest difference between the two people we married is that Ana, my wife, trusts me and couldn't care less who I'm up on a mountain with, while Lisa's ex, Edmund, would, if they were still married, be insanely jealous and would probably be stalking us both with a high-powered rifle right about now.

It's kind of weird, but just last night I'd decided that my friendship with Lisa was more a thing of the past than a current, in-practice, living and breathing friendship. The last couple of times I've seen her, we've made plans to go out and do something, and I've always wound up going out with her and a bunch of her current friends I don't know and I kind of wind up feeling like a fifth wheel. I know it probably sounds like I'm jealous but I'm not; it's just that most of the time I don't know what or who she was talking about. Anyway, I'd decided that I was just going to appreciate the friendship I remember us having but I wasn't going to make the effort to call anymore whenever I am in El Paso, which is not often, anyhow.

And the dinner conversation was weird, too. I mean, we'd driven up to Las Cruces to see some art flick with some people Lisa teaches with. And, even though I felt like a fifth wheel, I'm really good at talking with people I don't know, so I was telling Life in Abilene with the Fundamentalists stories to these people 'cause I'd promised myself I wasn't going to let Lisa know I was having a lousy time, and I mentioned that one of the things wrong with Abilene was that it doesn't have a really good Ma and Pa Japanese restaurant, when, out of the blue, Lisa butted in and said, "Didn't you take me to some Japanese restaurant on a date once?"

Well, to me the words just kind of hung there, 'cause honest and for true I had forgotten that Lisa and I had ever dated. We've been friends for so long, and what feelings I have for her are more along the lines of the way I feel toward my little sister, Veronica, that it just slipped my mind that yes, once, for a period of a couple of months in the late '70s, we had in fact been romantically entangled.

Well, I just picked up the conversation without missing a beat and continued on with a story about how, at one of the colleges in Abilene, they used to patrol the bars looking for student stickers from that particular school on account of how they made all their students sign a no-drinking pledge but then kids always find ways to drink anyhow. Lisa's friends thought that was pretty funny and we all laughed and they told me that they couldn't take living in Abilene but I told them I felt that way when I first moved there but now Ana and I have kids and that changes how your feel about a place.

Lisa's hand appears over the crest and I reach down and help her up. She plops down on a rock besides me and asks for some water, so I hand her one of the Evians she has thrown into the back pack. I note with insane glee that she, too, is puffing, but I don't say anything.

"Look," I say, "We can see the Rio pretty clearly now." I point down and, sure enough, you can see it. The Rio Grande is usually like one of the dirt washes on the side of Mt. Franklin, but today it's full of water, a byproduct of the rain we've had, and from this distance it looks like a crooked, slate gray ribbon that shoots off to the north.

"It's full," she says. People in other cities talk about the weather; El Pasoans talk about the water level in the river. Here, it's always hot and sunny, so the only thing you can comment about in idle conversation is the amount of H_2O in the Rio.

"I love how there's a band of green on either side of the river for about fifty feet. It looks so different—kind of like someone made a mistake and transplanted a piece of Kansas into the desert." Right away, I'm embarrassed I said it, 'cause I never tell people how much I love the desert on account of how they look at me like I'm crazy, even good friends like Manny.

But Lisa just nods her head and gazes out at the river with this dreamy glance. Then she says, "Freddie, I've reached one decision. If I can't live here, I'm going to at least live in the Southwest. I love the desert and the mountains, too."

All the years I've known her and I didn't know that the desert makes her heart sing, too.

I don't say anything for quite a while. This is actually why I climbed the mountain, so I could sit and look down and enjoy staring at the empty space and thinking about how big it is and kind of just getting off on the feeling I get. I'm getting high, I think to myself, then laugh at my own joke.

Lisa looks wounded, like I've laughed at her, so I explain, and she laughs, too. "So, we're getting high together, Freddie."

I smile and nod, but what I'm really thinking is that I could kill Edmund for what he's done to her. Before she got married, she wasn't the kind of person who got her feelings hurt at every little thing, but afterward she was really sensitive even with old friends like me, taking lots of things the wrong way, kind of like she was criticized so often that she kind of expected everything that was said to be another criticism. She's gotten a lot better than she was just after the divorce, but still has moments when she lapses, like she just did when I laughed.

"So," I say, "Why are you thinking about leaving the Southwest?"

"Well," she says, then pauses to pick up a rock and flings it at a barrel cactus that had been sneaking up on her, "I really love teaching but I don't think I can take being in high school for the rest of my life."

"I don't think I could do it for as long as you already have," I say.

"Yeah. A lot of the time, I feel more like a cop than a teacher. Anyway, I've been thinking about going off to grad school and getting another degree so I could teach college."

"Great. Why don't you go for it?"

"I'd miss the mountain too much," she says, smiling.

I laugh, 'cause I know just how she feels. "You could come back and visit it, like I do."

"Yeah, I suppose so." She pauses, then continues, sounding more serious. "I guess I'm more afraid to leave because of my parents. Dad's starting to lose his eyesight, and Mom needs help some days."

"It's kind of weird when they get older, isn't it. I mean, like this thing with my Dad and his heart. This time has been nothing like when he had bypass fifteen years ago. Then, he bounced right back, but not this time. He's getting a lot better, but for a while it was like taking care of a baby, and I was thinking that some people have to take care of their children and their parents at the same time."

She nods, understanding. One thing we do have in common is that our parents were a bit older when we were born, so they are all getting up there.

"Did you know I free climbed Ranger Peak the last time Pops was having triple bypass?" I ask.

504

"During the operation?"

"Yeah."

"Why?"

It's a good question. I think it made my family mad when I did it, but I couldn't just sit in the hospital for hours and wait and reassure Mom that everything was gonna be all right, because I didn't know if it was gonna be or not. I've never thought about *why* I went before.

"I dunno. I guess—Look, you know how thc mountain is kind of like an old friend?"

"Yeah," she says, placing a hand on a rock like she was caressing it.

"Maybe I thought that if I did something really dangerous, like climbing the east face of Ranger without equipment, it would take care of me, and—and it'd take care of Pops, too, or something."

When I put it into words, it doesn't make any sense, but Lisa nods like she knows just what I'm talking about.

There doesn't seem to be much more for either one of us to say. Our parents are getting old, period.

I break open a candy bar on account of how I'm feeling light headed from all the exertion and I need some quick energy. Either that or I'm just addicted to Reece's Nutrageous. I scarf the whole thing in about three bites, put the wrapper in the back pack, and empty the Gatorade, which is still about half full, in one swallow.

Lisa daintily takes another sip of the Evian, which is still three-quarters full.

So last night when we get done watching this art flick, which I really enjoyed and really wish they showed films like that in Abilene, Lisa and I and one of her friends piled into Lisa's truck and started riding back down to El Paso, which took about forty minutes. About the time you hit the Texas/New Mexico border, you can see the city lights, which are, like, unique. I've never seen anything like them anywhere in the world. The mountains in Texas on one side and the mountains in Mexico on the other side form this kind-of-like bowl, and it's all full of lights of every color you can think of and some you can't, and it's heartbreakingly beautiful and looks like a Fairy Land, which is what I used to call it when I was eight years old, before I learned that the word "Fairy" also meant something else.

"Look at the mountains," said Lisa,

"Yeah," I said, just to fill the space in the conversation.

"We ought to go mountain climbing some time," she said, like she'd been reading my mind or talking to Manuel or something.

For a long time, I didn't say a word, biting my tongue because I've decided that I was going to let the friendship slip into the past, but then I thought maybe it's like a sign that you maybe ought to hold onto that friendship a little harder than you'd planned, so finally I just blurted it out:

"I've been up every peak on Franklin but Thunderbird. Let's climb it tomorrow."

"Okay," she said, and it was settled. And I felt kind of good, because I'd given up on the idea of getting up to Thunderbird on account of what Manny said, but BOOM, like that, we were going.

So Lisa is now sipping her Evian and I'm thinking that says something about her, that she's sipping mineral water on the side of a mountain. And at first I think she looks out of place, because she's one of those people who's always neat and now, even after about 1500 feet of free climbing, she looks like she's enjoying a refreshment at an afternoon tea party. But then I look again, a little closer, and I see that she's getting little tiny crow's feet, like I've already got, and that she's sweating, and that she had the sense to wear a long sleeve shirt in the blazing sun instead of a tank top the way she would have done if she really had been a tea-party-lady, and it dawns on me that she belongs here on the side of the mountain, that, despite the fact that she's what you might call a petite woman and very artsy looking, she's iron tough and she's a desert rat, just like I am.

And it dawns on me that I've been underestimating her for twenty years.

"So," she says, "Show me this Thunderbird."

We spin around on our stone perches and I point out the right formation, and she says, "Oh, I see."

"What?"

"There are its wings," she says, pointing back in the direction of Ranger Peak, "and its tail," pointing to another formation below us to the south, "And that," she says, pointing toward the granite, "is its head."

"I'll be damned," I say, after looking for a moment. "It really does look like a bird."

506

"I think it's the Tigua or the Mescalero who say that the Thunderbird is was flying along and crashed. Its soul inhabits the mountain now."

"I didn't know that," I say, impressed.

Her turn to laugh at me. "You've lived here your whole life and you've never heard that story?"

"Nope." I laugh at myself, too.

"Well, let's go," she says, tossing her bottle of mineral water back at me. I snatch it out of the air and flip it into the pack in one fluid motion, then I start up after her, climbing easy and free, like my muscles are remembering what it feels like to be on the mountain and are enjoying feeling that way again.

She's climbing faster now. The vegetation is sparse and there are virtually no little pebbles, so I'm keeping up, beginning to feel the excitement build, wondering what the view on top of the old 'Bird's head will be like.

Climbing is pretty repetitive while you're doing it—look for a steady place above you to put your hand or your foot, put it there, test it to make sure it'll hold your weight, pull yourself up, and repeat the process again. In a strange way, it keeps you so busy it gives you time to think.

What I think about it the conversation we'd had the night before, about having dated, a fact that seems odd, now, like a curiosity. Although she was younger in years it was me who was the one involved in a boyfriend/girlfriend relationship for the first time; she always seemed more wise and mature than I was. When we broke up, I felt like I ought to hate her because we'd broken up, after all, but in my weird, teenage way that didn't sound right, 'cause I really liked her as a person and it had seemed a shame to cut yourself off from a good person just 'cause you weren't dating anymore.

It was Lisa who had taught me, a macho, chauvinistic male, that men and women could be friends, that I could be buddies or pals with a woman, just like I was with Manuel. Since then, some of my best friends have been women, so, it suddenly dawns on me, that Lisa has taught me one of the most important lessons of my life.

We're near the crest of the last escarpment before the Thunderbird when I look down and see blood. A lot of it. My right sock is drenched, and when I pull it off and look at my heel, all of the sudden I remember that I cut it open a couple of days ago and that it hasn't healed. The days-old bandage I put on it has shriveled up and is offering no protection against the rubbing of my shoe. I guess climbing had made it numb, but when we stopped that last time, the feeling came back. It hurts. Bad.

Like an idiot, I also remember that I meant to put Band-Aids in the pack but forgot.

"Damn," I say, out loud.

"What?" This time Lisa stops and starts working her way back down toward me. Why couldn't she have done that when I was in the evil clutches of an ocatillo?

"Look," I say, and hold up my foot.

"Appetizing," she says, making a face. I just sit there for a moment 'cause I can't believe I'm a couple of hundred feet below the Thunderbird and have done the equivalent of had a blowout in a car and have been caught one the side of the mountain without a spare. Then, I kind of stretch the old Band-Aid out so it sort of covers the wound, shove my foot back in my shoe, and stand up, saying, "Let's go."

She looks at me real close, actual honest-to-God concern in her face. "Are you sure?"

"Why weren't you this worried when I fell into a damned cactus?"

"Because I knew you could handle *that*. You have a thick hide."

I look down at my ankle. "Not thick enough. But look," I say, pointing back up at the Thunderbird, "Look how close we are."

And it is close, agonizingly close, like I could just reach out and touch it with my hand, but I stumble a few more steps and realize that it might as well be another thousand feet up, 'cause there's no way I'm gonna make it today. I stop.

"Look, Lisa. You've gotta go on up. We're so close."

"No," she says.

"Just another couple of hundred feet."

"No, let's just go back now. You better be able to make it, because I'm not going to carry you."

Well, I feel terrible because my stupidity is keeping her from making it up to the top, like I've held her back or something. I can't believe I didn't re-wrap my ankle before we left, and I really can't believe I forgot the Band-Aids, which I had put out on my parents' kitchen table the night before so I wouldn't forget.

I use the wrapper from the Nutrageous to make a kind of shield between the wound on my ankle and my heel, walk a few steps, and realize I'll be able to make it down, because it's harder on your ankles going up than it is on the descent.

I turn back around and look at the Thunderbird one last time, 'cause this is the closest I've ever been to it. At first I thought it looked like Gibraltar, a fortress, forbidding, mocking me, daring me to try and make one last attempt to storm it. But then I saw the bird, and it looked friendly, cautioning me to take care of my foot this time but inviting me back for another visit.

"Lisa, I'm sorry," I say one more time, aware I'm saying it too much.

"What for?" she asks, smiling. "We'll make it the next time." She says this with absolute certainty.

I feel a big grin spread across my face and I know she's right. "Yeah," I say, "We will."

She takes the pack from me, and we slowly head back down the mountain.

SUE ELLEN LEARNS TO DANCE

JUDY ALTER

"Sue Ellen!" He cut the engine on the clattering Model A truck, in 1934 some ten years old and threatening always to fall apart. When he raised his voice again, impatience rang in it. "Sue Ellen!" He stayed in the car and waited.

She came to the door carrying a child on her hip, though the child was plainly old enough to walk on his own. Still, his arms encircled his mother's neck with a tenacity that indicated he would not easily be put down. Sue Ellen Flett was a lean woman with lank hair, faded to the pale yellow of corn silk. She wore a shapeless cotton dress and over it, an apron that clearly said "Burrus Flour Mills" across the front. With her free hand, she pushed her hair behind her ear. The other hand held tight to the child.

"What is it, Alvis?" Her voice was soft and tired, lacking the life of his impatience.

"Ma says Grammy's dyin' and we got to go to Kaufman."

"Go to Kaufman?" she echoed. From where she stood, on the slanted porch of a rough board and batten shack near Eden in South Central Texas, Kaufman, beyond Dallas, deep in East Texas, might as well be as far as the moon. Then, though, she said softly, "Your grammy's dying?"

He scoffed. "She won't die. That woman's got too much sin stored up in her. She'd go straight to hell, and she's knows it."

"She's not a sinful woman," Sue Ellen said mildly. She looked at him. He was thirty, looked fifty and, she often thought, acted sixty. When she married him, he was twenty-two and stood straight and tall, his eyes sparkling with laughter. But that was before the rain stopped and all of West Texas turned to dust that blew away if you looked at it and the bank took their farm up to Kaufman, where they'd both been raised. Now they share-cropped a tiny, worthless piece of land. Konrad Schwartz, the German farmer who owned the land, provided a tractor, fuel and seed, and they farmed on halves. The parcel of blown-away land was all mesquite stumps and rattlesnakes, and they made a poor crop. She worried about the children, who went too many days without meat and milk, and she worried about Alvis and herself, who were cross, tired, and hopeless most of the time.

At least, she told herself ten times a day, they lived in a house. Not much of one—a shack some would call it, with slanted floors and cracks so large between the siding boards that she could look out at night from her bed and watch the stars. But there were folks in this region, she knew, who'd lived in half dugouts not more than ten years ago. No, Sue Ellen counted herself lucky to have a house.

"Well," she said, looking at him, "I reckon Grammy Flett can't put it off forever. If it's her time, it's her time." She barely got the words out before a young girl of six banged through the screen door, letting it slam behind her and ignoring the precarious way it bounced on its hinges.

"Don't slam the door," Sue Ellen said automatically, while the girl asked, "Who's got sin in their soul, Papa?"

Sue Ellen gave him a long, hard look and then said to the girl, "No one, Marisue. Your papa didn't mean that."

"My grandmother's dyin'," he told the child, ignoring that he had made his wife unhappy and that the child would instantly know it was his grandmother who had sin in her soul.

"Is she goin' to Hell when she dies, Papa?" Marisue asked.

He opened his mouth, but Sue Ellen spoke too quickly for him. "Of course she's not goin' to Hell, Marisue. How you do talk. You remember Grammy Flett. She always gave you candy, and you used to like to sit on her lap when you was little."

"I disremember," Marisue said.

"Well," Sue Ellen said, turning her back on her husband and leading the children inside, "it's been a long while since you saw her. Grammy Flett's old, near ninety I think."

"Are we going to see her?"

Sue Ellen sighed. "I guess we'll have to." Turning, she asked over her shoulder, "Where's Albert?"

"I left him in town, swamping out Tubbs' store. He'll walk home."

She turned without another word. It was, she knew, a long walk for a child of eight to make alone, but no harm would come to him. And she'd save back a potato for his supper.

That night, to Alvis' back, because now he always turned away from her in bed, she said, "I hope to heaven that rickety truck will make it to Kaufman."

"It'll have to," he muttered.

She wanted to reach out and touch him, rub his back, riffle his hair, but she knew he would flinch and pull away. "Can't feed no more babies," he'd told her the last time she'd tried to touch him in his privates. Instead, she asked,

"Why do you say she's so sinful her soul's goin' to Hell?"

He groaned, a sure sign he didn't want to talk about it. At last, after a long moment, he spoke. "Ma told me. She . . . she was . . . you know . . . one of those women, back when cowboys were the law in West Texas. She . . . ." It was obviously hard for him to bring the words out. "She . . . danced in saloons in Fort Worth, that kind of thing."

"Grammy Flett?" Sue Ellen sat straight up in bed, barely remembering to pull the covers up to hide herself. She thought this was surely the most astounding news she'd ever heard . . . and the very thought of Grammy Flett dancing in a saloon somehow lightened and lifted Sue Ellen's mood. But she could never tell Alvis that.

"Family's been ashamed ever since," he said stiffly. "We don't talk about it."

"Your family's still ashamed about something that happened . . . what? fifty, sixty years ago?" She could never give voice to the thought that was really on her mind, for it was almost envy . . . envy of Grammy Flett and the good times she must have known.

"Don't do to have bad blood," he said, muffling his voice in the pillow.

"Well, I'll be!" And with that, Sue Ellen lay back down in the bed, pulled the covers to her chin, and lay with wide open eyes half the night.

The truck ground to a stop short of Fort Worth. From Eden, they'd gone north to Ballinger, then angled over to Brownwood, on to Comanche, and finally to Cleburne, all the while bouncing over rutted roads so rough

that Sue Ellen ached in every bone in her back and bottom. Dust blew in at them, but Sue Ellen had been covered by dust for so long now she paid it no mind. Her skin had turned a nut-brown color, and fleetingly she sometimes thought of her mother's admonition to always wear a poke bonnet, lest your skin acquire an unbecoming darkness. Hers had, and it was too late to worry about it.

The baby in her arms cried, and in the back, supposedly resting on a pallet, Marisue whined about needin' to use the restroom and wantin' to sleep and when were they gonna' get there. Albert sat stoic, staring over the boards of the pickup bed at the passing dry land.

Sue Ellen looked at her children, their faces wary and unsmiling, their clothes soiled with ground-in grime that would not come out no matter how hard she scrubbed, their feet bare and dirty. She sighed and turned back to stare sightlessly at the road before them.

When the children finally slept, Sue Ellen said, "She wasn't sinful, you know. Grammy Flett's one of the best persons I ever met. I wouldn't have a problem lettin' my soul follow hers."

He gripped the wheel tightly and stared straight ahead at the rutted road. "You can send your soul wherever you want. I know I'm obeying the Good Book."

"It says," she whispered, "love thy brother . . . and that means thy sister . . . and thy grandmother too."

Alvis didn't answer.

They were just beyond Cleburne, some thirty miles from Fort Worth, when they hit a deep rut in the road, bounced badly, and heard a clattering sound. In seconds, the car died.

"What'd you do?" Sue Ellen asked.

"I didn't do nothin'," he said angrily. "The thing just stopped." He got out to study around the car. Finally, at a loss to do anything else, he crawled under it. After what seemed forever to Sue Ellen, Alvis emerged, holding up a squarish metal pan—something, she thought, she might have baked in if she ever could bake again.

"Oil pan," he said. "Guess it got bounced off."

"What's that mean?"

"Means the engine ain't got no oil, and it's froze up. Probably ruined."

"We might just as well walk back to that last town," Sue Ellen said, "get something for the children to eat." Her own stomach gnawed at her, but she would not eat.

"What you gonna buy it with?" he asked. "Your good looks?"

She wanted to tell him there was no call to be mean, but she kept quiet.

"No sense goin' backward," he declared. "We'll hitch to Fort Worth."

Leaving the car that much farther behind, she thought.

Hot and dusty, they waited by the side of the road for a ride, the baby crying all the louder when Alvis took him to relieve her and Marisue whining all the more, saying she'd just sit in the shade and wait for them to come back for the car.

"What shade?" Albert asked, scorn in his voice.

Finally a farmer in a Model A stopped for them. Alvis sat in the front, while Sue Ellen and the youngsters crowded into the back. The farmer made laconic conversation about car trouble and having a passel of kids, and it was plain to see he was glad he was not part of this pitiful family. In Fort Worth, he let them out at a garage where he, personally, recommended the honesty of the owner.

"Lost the oil pan?" The man snorted. "Ain't no use to go look at it. Bet you ruined the motor."

Alvis nodded sagely. He thought so too.

Sue Ellen protested. "Can't you at least go see if you can fix it?"

"Lady, you want me to charge you $30 for telling you what I already know? The engine's burnt out, running with no oil, even for a little bit."

Sue Ellen stared off at the concrete around her and clutched Marisue to her.

The mechanic took them to a church with a soup kitchen for the homeless, and they were fed the best hot meal they'd had in months—soup, corn, potatoes and fresh homemade bread—and Sue Ellen tried to ignore Alvis' mutterings, "We ain't like these people. Don't need no charity."

Finally, she poked him hard in the ribs and said, "Without it, we wouldn't be eatin'. I ain't too proud to feed my children on charity if I got to."

When their plight was made known to the pastor of the church, bus tickets to Kaufman shortly appeared.

"Don't know when I can repay you," Alvis muttered.

514

"No matter," the pastor said. "It is our mission to help those in need. Go with God."

They rode to Kaufman, Sue Ellen holding the baby, Albert staring out the window, and Marisue dozing in her seat.

"You gonna' be nice to Grammy Flett?" Sue Ellen asked him.

"'Course I'll be nice. She's my grandmother, ain't she?"

"You think she's sinful . . . and I, well, I just think it's sinful you feel that way."

"Who's sinful?" Marisue asked shrilly. "Are you talking about Grammy Flett again. What'd she do?"

"Hush and go to sleep," her father told her. "Don't be tellin' everyone on this bus our family business."

There were three other passengers, none of whom appeared to have heard the outburst.

From Kaufman, it was no trick to find a ride to the Flett family farm.

Mama Flett greeted them at the door, hugging the children and telling Alvis, "It's good you got here, son."

"Thought you might need me," he muttered, and that was as close to affection as the two of them came.

But Sue Ellen got a hug and a murmured "I am glad to see you, child. You're lookin' thin. I got chicken and dumplings on the stove."

Sue Ellen knew that, from the smell that filled the rambly old white clapboard house that had belonged to Alvis' grandparents and had stayed in the family by hook or by crook all these years. Alvis' father was gone now, some five years—just up and left he did one day, Mama Flett had told them. Nobody knew if he'd run off, though that seemed unlikely, or if he'd hurt himself back in the wilds of the piney woods, hunting alone in some place so remote that nobody had yet stumbled on his body. His huntin' dog had come home three days later, but he hadn't been real communicative about what had happened to his master.

Sue Ellen didn't understand—and never would—how Mama and Grammy lived, beyond that truck garden in the back of the house, but they survived nicely, much more nicely than she and Alvis and the children.

While Marisue clamored for dinner and Albert stood staring hungrily at the stove, Mama Flett reached for the baby. "She's in there," she said to Alvis, motioning with her head toward a room off the kitchen that had apparently been turned into a sickroom. "But she's outa' her head, talkin' strange, she is."

With a finger to the lips to caution the children to be quiet, Alvis led his family into the sickroom. Grammy Flett barely made a bump under the thin coverlet spread over her. She lay on her back, eyes wide open and staring at the ceiling, hands folded over her chest as though she were anticipating death and willing to save the undertaker at least the chore of arranging those hands with their paper-thin skin.

"She's singing," Marisue stage-whispered, and Alvis drew back a hand as though to cuff her.

But Marisue was right. A weak, high, reedy sound came from the bed, and looking close, Sue Ellen could see the thin chest rise a little and the pinched mouth moving ever so slightly.

Alvis was clearly disconcerted. "How're you doin', Grammy Flett?" he asked in a voice so loud and hearty that even Albert jumped a little.

Her eyes turned slowly, as though making an effort to focus on this new person. Then, smiling ever so slightly, she said, "I been dancin'. You know, at Uncle Windy's in Fort Worth . . . in the Acre." Her voice was whispery.

"Hush, now," he said too harshly. "We don't want to be hearin' about that."

She paid him no mind and what back to her singing.

Back in the kitchen, Albert carefully asked, "What was she talkin' about? Uncle Windy's and the acre?"

"Nothin' for you to know," his father told him harshly, and Albert subsided, but not before Sue Ellen saw the resentment in his eyes. Had it been up to her, she'd have filled Albert with the little knowledge she had: Grammy Flett had been a dancehall girl in Fort Worth before the turn of the century, when Hell's Half Acre was the flourishing sin district in that town. Oh, Grammy had never been a whore—Alvis had made that point clear and Sue Ellen chose to believe it. But Alvis did not want his son to know even the varnished truth.

They ate mightily of chicken and dumplings, fresh tomatoes off the vine, green beans that had cooked their way to mushiness the whole day, and a blueberry pie. "I'm sorry I ain't got no cream for the pie," Mama Flett apologized.

"Is she all right at night?" Sue Ellen asked as she dried the dishes for her mother-in-law.

Mama sighed. "I been mostly sleeping in that chair in her room. Don't sleep too good, but if I was to come and find her gone some morning, I couldn't live with myself."

"I'll sit with her tonight," the younger woman volunteered.

"Land's sake, you had that hard trip. I'll hear no such thing."

"I want to, I really want to." And Sue Ellen found that she did want to, indeed was almost desperate for time alone with Grammy.

"You sure?"

"I'm sure."

And so, by ten o'clock, they were all packed off to bed, even the baby whom Mama Flett took to sleep with her. Albert, feeling big and manly, took a blanket and went to the loft in the barn, and Marisue curled into a big double bed all by herself. Alvis chose to sleep on the sofa, lest he be needed in the night, so he said, but Sue Ellen knew after that big dinner she wouldn't be able to rouse him if she needed him.

She took a last cup of coffee and went to sit by Grammy's bed in a big old rocker. Setting her coffee down, she reached for one of those thin, frail hands that were all bone and no flesh and held it in her own browned and roughened hand. "Sing to me again, Grammy."

Grammy had been dozing, but she roused now, turning her head ever so slightly toward Sue Ellen and staring at her. Then the thin voice raised in a song Sue Ellen knew was not a hymn. Sue Ellen closed her eyes and let her mind drift, holding that hand and listening to the weird music.

"We danced, you know," Grammy said, suddenly stopping her singing.

The sound of her talking voice startled Sue Ellen awake. "Yes . . . yes, Grammy, I know you danced. . . . I . . . I think it must have been wonderful."

"Not always," she said, "but sometimes . . . not when you were dancing for pay with men you didn't like. But when we'd dance for ourselves

517

. . . and the music made you feel free and alive . . . and I wasn't beholden to no one then . . . no parents, no husband, no children, just me!" She paused to catch her breath.

"I was young . . . and pretty"—it seemed not to shame her to admit that openly—"and I had lots of young men courtin' me. I've carried those memories all my life."

"Were you . . . Grammy . . . did you do anything sinful?" Sue Ellen bit her lip, knowing she'd overstepped the bounds with the question.

Grammy snorted. "Sinful? Not on your life. I was raised Baptist and dancing was sin enough . . . but no, I was never wicked."

And they both knew what she meant.

"Tell me," Sue Ellen said, "about the music again and how you've heard it all your life."

And so, late into the night, Grammy Flett—spurred by an energy nobody thought she had any longer—talked about life in the city. And sometimes she'd stop talking to sing awhile. And then she'd talked again.

Listening, her eyes closed, Grammy's hand still clutched in hers, Sue Ellen ever so briefly felt that she too heard the music and that she was free and young and beautiful and happy. And she knew that Grammy was giving her a dream that she would carry through her life.

In the morning, Mama Flett found Sue Ellen sound asleep in the rocker. Grammy Flett had gone to her reward, her hand still clutched in Sue Ellen's and the corners of her mouth lifted as though she were smiling . . . or singing.

Sue Ellen and Alvis never went back to Eden. Abandoning the car outside Fort Worth and the furniture and clothes in their shack at Eden, they stayed in Kaufman, where Alvis farmed and eventually, when the Depression wore itself out, became a man of some small means, free of debt at least, though he never lost his dour and pessimistic streak . . . and he never liked to talk about Grammy Flett. Sue Ellen fixed chicken and dumplings and blueberry pie for her children and grandchildren and tended the truck garden and kept the house . . . but sometimes, they'd find her staring off out the window, singing a strange song none of them recognized. And when they'd call her back to the present moment, she always had a smile.

I Just Can't Bear It

Carmen Tafolla

(from the series *Muertos pero Muertitos*: Dead but Really DEAD Dead)

Jimmy Lopez was the kind of man everybody knew would have lots of people at his funeral, and you knew there were gonna be lots of nice things said about him from the altar and all. In fact, you knew that the people would start showing up in large bunches even at the "Visitation" at Angeles Funeral Home. So his wife made sure to get her hair dyed even before the "viewing" at the funeral home, and her sister-in-law helped her put cold cucumber slices over her eyes that morning, so the puffiness would go down a little, though, that day, it didn't seem to help much.

And sure enough, just as expected, people who'd voted for him as well as those who'd voted against started showing up to shake their heads, cover their mouths, whisper a few complimentary stories to the people beside them and, of course, work their way slowly to the widow's side, at an available moment, and offer an *abrazo,* a handshake or a *"pésame."*

"Le doy mi pésame,"(I offer to you that I share your pain) said several of the *comadres.* "What a tragedy for us all," said several of the important business people. "He was a model citizen . . . a pride to our race," whispered Mike Gomez, who hoped to replace him in the next election for school board. "Mr. Low-pezz will be hard to replace," pontificated the Anglo school board president who had been shocked at the rumor two years ago that a SECOND Mexican-American might run for and be part of the ten-member board.

One by one they would float toward the front pew, where Jimmy's wife sat, eyes dazed and makeup odd and clownlike, she had concluded this morning as she stared blankly at the mirror. The sounds of praise and mourning seemed to rise and wane, like gentle ocean waves in the distance, rolling gently forward in "Ohs" and "Ahs" and then receding in quiet, respectful whispers, punctuated by the seafoam of sniffles.

Visitors also whispered to each other, each paying their dues for their living presence. "He was so well respected. . . . Even the one-armed man who sells apples in front of the courthouse came, and sat quietly in the back row for almost twenty minutes! They say Jimmy once gave him money for medicine."

Sometimes their stories built on each other's, each trying to be more complimentary than the preceding.

"If Jimmy hadn't been Mexican," the mechanic whispered, "he'd a probably been a City Councilman!"

"No, compadre," whispered back the owner of El Sombrero Mexican Restaurant, his eyebrows raising in self-importance and his eyes assuming that hunt-for-a-big-enough-exaggeration look they all recognized, "if Jimmy hadn't been Mexican, he'd a made it all the way to Mayor!"

There was not a soul in the room who did not shake his head and express sorrow at Jimmy's passing. Occasionally, someone would sob, more often they would just sigh, but it was a very, very nice gathering.

"AY, I JUST CAN'T BEAR IT!" the shout cut the room. "I CAN'T BEAR TO SEE HIM!" screamed the inconsolable bawler in the back row.

Somehow the rhythm of ocean waves was broken.

"NO! NO! NO! HE JUST CAN'T BE DEAD!"

Every eye was trying to strain their peripheral vision backward, while the torsos were frozen in polite postures. Neck muscles strained, and a few uninhibited souls turned clear around to study the face of the woman who was in such pain. People blinked their eyes, lowered their heads, and tried to keep their thoughts, or at least their body language, focused on their mourning, but the sobbing screams of the woman made it hard to maintain even a façade.

"I CAN'T BELIEVE IT! I CAN'T BELIEVE IT! NO, THIS IS TOO MUCH TO BEAR! THIS IS JUST—"

Within seconds, a chain of questions had been passed through them, via eyebrows and wide eyes, clenched jaw muscles and twisted mouths, but no one seemed to know who she was. They scanned their memories, trying to place a distant niece or a cousin's child, perhaps even a loyal worker whose crisis he'd resolved, but no one came to mind. No one even faintly recognized her, and they could not even pretend to pretend that she was a distant cousin.

"—TERRIBLE! I CAN'T BEAR TO SEE HIM LIKE THIS."

By now, even the widow had turned around to study the face, with her lips all screwed together and an out-of-patience look in her dead-serious eyebrows.

"—TAKE IT. I JUST CAN'T GO ON!—"

The out-of-patience look had been replaced by an I'm-gonna-kill-her look.

"AY. AY!! QUE TRISTEZA! SE ME QUIEBRA EL—"

Most of the faces at the funeral were easily familiar, but some had taken a while to identify, as information was passed from one person to the next. People assumed most of the unfamiliar ones were business associates of his, or friends from different circles, perhaps even different towns. Mr. Lopez often traveled to nearby burgs for what he always said were "very important meetings," although some had whispered that he could more easily enjoy the bars where he was not as well known or as quickly recognized. "He did like his cups," said one man, with a half-smile. "Have to admit he knew how to enjoy life," said another, "and had a great eye for women . . . ."

"—CORAZÓN! TELL ME IT'S NOT TRUE!"

"There was one time we crossed over to Piedras Negras, when we were young, just into our forties, and—" the man was cut off by a jab from his wife.

"AY, NO PUEDO! NO PUEDO CON ESTE—"

The bawler didn't even stop for breath, but just ran one scream into another, each one louder and more dramatic than the previous. There WERE a few *comadres* in town that were heavy criers at the funerals (one had even threatened to throw herself in the grave when her first husband passed away), but this lady surpassed anything they had ever witnessed from a non-spouse, non— "Well," they thought, "we'd better not even say it."

"DOLOR! I JUST CANNOT BEAR IT! I JUST CANNOT BEAR IT."

The school board president had already scooted out, mumbling something about an important meeting, and Mike Gomez was casting nervous glances at the door, trying to figure how to exit gracefully. The El Sombrero owner just shook his eyes and his head rapidly and mumbled, "Well, some secrets never come out 'til the grave . . ."

The lady who did his wife's hair every Saturday was whispering to her neighbor, "You know, one time I saw him driving out of town and I just KNEW that something susp—"

The widow had had enough. She stood in a motion so slow and power-ful it drew an unintended gasp from the crowd. She moved to the front of the room, body slanted only partially to the coffin, but eyes focused in a threatening slant to the back of the room, and she addressed the dearly beloved slowly, word by carefully chosen word, in a voice both calm and booming:

"Our. sorrow. is . . . overwhelming. Our words . . . cannot. express. We cannot bear . . . the sad farewell. But—"

"GOODBYE, JIMMY," she announced loudly as she slammed down the lid of the coffin.

The ears of the mourners were blasted with a sound louder than the coffin closing: the ringing sound of sudden silence. The bawler had stopped her crying. The bawler, her eyes spread to two long ovals, had dropped open her mouth.

"Jimmy?" she asked blankly.

"This is Jimmy? You mean this is not Chemo? Chemo Carrizales? I was positive she said yes when I asked at the door if this was for Chemo."

Then she rose from her seat, saying simply, "It's not Chemo," and walked out. Only the people in the back two rows heard the mumble as she moved down the hall, "Who the hell is Jimmy?"

Everyone stared at each other openly, the corners of their eyes not quite yet ready to crinkle in the asking of permission to giggle.

In fact, the giggling had only begun to spill forth when from down the hall in a different "Visitation" room came the familiar wailing:

"AY, I JUST CAN'T BEAR IT! I CAN'T BEAR TO SEE HIM!"

The volcano of laughter had begun to erupt, but everyone, even Jimmy, knew that Jimmy's "Visitation" for that day was over.

BURIED HORSES

PAUL CHRISTENSEN

My friend Ted bought a small farm near Stephenville, in northeast Texas. It was a quiet little place with lots of gray hills and a few dry creeks meandering among the hackberries and scrub oak. There was a little shotgun house on the knoll, so-called because you could shoot a gun from front to back door and not even hit a door knob. All the rooms ran off a central corridor which led you out to a wooden stoop over the chicken house. In summer the heat drifted through the hall bearing the tangy aroma of weeds and parched earth.

When I saw him a few weeks back he took me for a walk down to a hollow where a creek used to spill into a pond. The ground lay scorched and rusty from iron in the rock; a few bones lay about from squirrels and moles. It was a peculiar place, scooped out of the prairie clay as if someone had dug a big hole there a long time ago. The country around it fell away in soft undulating mounds, and the horizon rose out of the summer haze like a brush fire. Nothing precise or firm, just heat waves and dust.

But it was good land and there had once been cotton crops, and sorghum, milo, even corn fields here. A corn crib poked out of the mesquite bushes, and the barn used to hold great quantities of hay for the cattle ranches. Now the cattle are further north, and the land lies fallow.

Strangers moved in, all sorts of people from the cities and from vague places known only as the West and East. Broken down salesmen, retired teachers, oddballs who needed lots of space to store their antique cars or airplanes. And the scattered religious ranches full of fanatics and cult leaders. Their hymn singing would drift across the prairies on a windy night; the thump of their tambourines could be heard faintly on Sunday mornings when the air was thin and sharp.

In the little market town down the road, a string of honky tonks and a truck diner made up the tourist end of town; in the center was a courthouse painted white, marble pillars and all, glinting like an iceberg in the noon sun. Around it were the forlorn shops that had withstood time and change, and still peddled a few old-fashioned suits on rickety manikins, assorted pieces of jewelry draped over bits of fly-specked velvet, a faded poster of a beach with swim towels folded beside it.

A hardware store next to the depot sold barbed wire from a wooden spool, sacks of feed grain, and leather harnesses; mainly it sold little plastic bottles of tacks and screws, glazing points and other useful items to a new wave of settlers coming in.

The new settlers were not remarkable for much but their sallow cheeks and worried looks. They were fussy, urban people fleeing from the city who wanted a hammer or a door hinge and off they went again. They were fixing up old farmhouses and righting fence posts, digging out mailboxes smothered in dewberry vines. The driveways were rutted paths winding up the hills to little dwellings under an elm or a clump of cedars.

I helped Ted move in, lugging over sofas and chairs in my pick-up. Ted was done in after his marriage broke up. His wife took off with the two kids and went home to Baltimore after he lost his job at the university. It seems he had become too friendly with a graduate student which led to accusations of favoritism and then sexual misconduct. The faculty lived under a kind of frontier justice, and the judges were all hanging judges when it came to morals.

Whether he did or didn't sleep with his student was never resolved. The taint on his character was reason enough to gather a lynch mob from the ranks of underpaid, drudging instructors who turned their bitterness against each other for lack of access to those higher up. After a few panel reviews in which he was deemed guilty, his office lock was changed and he was given notice that a warrant stood against him should he return to campus for any reason. His files and effects were delivered to him in a small crate and that was the end of his career.

Ted sulked for a long time and drank a few liquor stores dry, and then went on the wagon, turned pious briefly, and finally landed on his feet again. He was living in a shabby little complex off the airport highway, in the flight path. Jets came down low over his house spewing kerosene vapors and rattling his window panes. The little topless bar across the way, the Jet Stream, did a noisy business down to the wee hours, and Ted slowly dwindled away from lack of sleep, lack of interest, lack of anything much to live for.

He would drift back to his old haunts in East Dallas, where he had grown up on a crumbling little street of bungalows with porches shaded by tattered awnings. Now the drug trade had crept closer and his mother reported drive-by shootings on the weekends. A crack house set up a few doors down in a dilapidated building that was once a laundry. Furtive eyes would stare out of its black windowless holes, and young black girls would saunter in on afternoons and not come out again until after dark. Men and boys would drift around in the shadows and skulk in and out through the night. The edges of the city were collapsing, and all the life in the streets was swirling into an abyss.

Ted began dating an older woman who quickly took charge of his life. I stopped calling the apartment after a few tedious rounds with her on the phone. She had established herself as nurse, secretary, and now bossy mother, and it was impossible to get Ted to come to the phone without her permission. I dropped Ted for a few months and then began to worry about him.

One blistering afternoon in July, I found him hunched over a salad in one of the health food bars near the museum. He was staring into the sun with a piece of lettuce hanging from his fork. He looked like a mental patient on furlough, lank, disheveled, empty. I sat down and ordered a coffee and tried to cheer him up, but everything I said made him look away and fade out again.

All around our little table were cheerful young business couples and pretty women chatting over tea and croissants. It was a nice little place, full of expensive salads and macrobiotic dishes. Ted was still handsome and youthful under the pale skin and vague looks; I saw a woman giving him the once over and go back to her magazine. He might have struck up a little crosstable chat with her, changed his life, gotten rid of the harridan waiting in cold fury for his key in the door. He was a beaten male, and there was little he could do to recover himself.

That was that, I thought. We drove out to the countryside north of town and went up and down the hills looking at the heaving sea of prairie fading away to the vague horizon. It was a great open space, the wild, unconquerable grasslands of America that have endured bison herds, scorching heat, blizzards and droughts, tornados and brush fires, the coming of the sod busters, ranchers, oil men and wheat farmers, and still stands there in impassive grandeur, vast and unchanging. Kansas wheat and Illinois corn may have striped its surface, and great sprawling suburbs nibbled at its edges, but it is still the gray belly of America, an immensity that is like a dry ocean, an inland Pacific of waving, tumbling grass where a few early navigators traveled on foot, later in prairie schooners, but mainly on the backs of pintos or on moccasins, with a few dogs trailing along pulling a *travois*. No matter that long streaks of asphalt scar the boundless haze; only an occasional truck or dusty sedan goes meekly through the expanses and disappears.

Here and there a ranch went wild again, bristling with mesquite and prickly pear, a few buildings turned silver in the sun slowly sinking to the ground. An old tractor lay in a gulch brown with rust, its disk hanging from the end of a frame that had snapped thirty years before, when a farmer spit, kicked the dust, and walked away to thumb a ride to California, or to shoot himself in the barn.

The farms are dead, and along the edges of certain hills are blackened grave stones marking the remains of prairie wives broken by heat, child rearing, wood chopping, canning, bills, religion, the steady crush of life between land and sky. They lay in somber repose under the ceaseless whispering of the wind, accompanied by children struck down by fever or a tractor, or a hand applied with too much fury.

We drove in silence and as night fell I turned around to go home, but he stopped me. He wanted to stay the night somewhere among the gray hills. I found a motel along a stretch of desolate farm road and rented rooms. We were the only tenants for the night. I sat with him awhile among the crickets and the gusts of a few trucks racing by and finally went to bed, but I heard him leave his room and walk into the night. I dressed and followed, and found him wandering over the hills, walking into the great expanding void before him. He walked for an hour or more, sat down on a little rise of ground and rocked on his haunches, staring up at the stars. Then he came back again, went to bed and was up early, eating breakfast in the diner across the highway.

He was cheerful and flirted with the waitress, a highschool girl with pigtails and bright eyes. He seemed his old self; he was very jaunty and wanted to go hiking a while before returning to the city. We roamed around the warm fields until it was too hot to go on and came back to the car, which was shimmering in a blind rage of sunlight at the parking lot. We drove home in friendly silence.

The next week he ran off his girlfriend and began cashing in his stocks and bonds. He was buying some land, he said shyly, then he told me about it over beers in his packed up living room. He had bought a small ranch, he said. I must come out and see it. Then he asked if I would help him move. Of course I agreed; I wanted to see what he was up to.

When we entered the dusty path leading to his house on the knoll, I felt sorry for him. It was just a sliver of fenced land under the endless sky; there was nothing to temper the isolation, the dry gulches and grassy swells, the broad, unyielding emptiness that had driven people to worship an unforgiving god. The only sign of humanity was the brittle house with its leaning porch. The barn stood in the distance, shrunken and hollow against the powers of the sun. The wind blew softly through the thistles, rattling a few weed stalks that had pierced the tough prairie skin and endured.

There I left him after a day of tacking up curtain rods, gluing down shelf paper, sweeping the sandy dust from corners of rooms, pulling down the rotting paper from the walls and exposing the rough pine shiplap beneath. There, scored into the dry wood, stood numberless small nails among bits of cheesecloth backing, the ears of a thousand nights of wind and children's voices, crying and anger, and remorse. The wood was splintered and bore a few holes where someone had hung a calendar from the feed store or reverenced the dim photograph of a relative for awhile, until something else took its place.

When I came back a month later, I was surprised to find a few shrubs newly planted and thriving at the cattle guard; along the road were boulders daubed with white wash marking the way up. More green shrubs appeared around the porch, which had been neatly repaired and trimmed with molding. Inside were bare, dark walls of wood that had been stained and oiled, with only a tuft of feathers tied up and hung from a rawhide cord. It bore the colors of the weeds and dry earth, and fit. A rough table stood in the center, with a jug and a wooden bowl. The kitchen was tidy

527

and painted a soft green color; a few pots stood on the drainboard, and a smell of fresh thyme and parsley hung in the air.

"You're in time for soup," he said, pulling a clay pot out of the oven. "I've been keeping it warm until you came," he said, smiling. He was pleased with my reaction to everything. I was amazed at all the work that had been done. The place was simple, sturdy, immaculate.

We ate black bread and vegetable soup, and drank delicious coffee after the meal. The bedroom held a narrow bed and rocking chair, and a small dresser of crude pine covered with a strip of woven cloth. The floor was made of wide planking that had been painted dark blue; a knotted rug stood by the bed. A vase stood on the floor filled with thistle flowers. There was a bible on his night stand, and a notebook.

"So," I said, sitting back on an old armchair in the living room. "This is what you've been up to all this while, playing house."

"Yes," he said, handing me a glass of warm whiskey. "It's been a lot of work. I'm knocked out, but I love the place. You can't imagine the silence out here at night. It's absolutely pure. Nothing but the stars, and a little puff of wind now and then."

"Don't you miss Dallas," I asked.

"Never. I remember nothing. I am only here."

We went down the path in back of his house and followed an arroyo as it wound around aimlessly between the brown slopes. It seemed to have nowhere to go, ambling along like a snake with its distant memory of bearing water. There was no sign of it now; it was arid land, hard-pan, with only a few ugly tufts of gray shoots emerging from the lifeless soil. It went on forever, inching forward among the little rises and falls of earth, searching for some place to end its life. But there was no indication that it found it; in the far distance one could see the undulating ground creased by the creek bed, until the hills went off in customary vagueness.

A farm house stood on the next rise and we walked toward it. A dog barked along a wire fence, and sniffed our shoes as we approached the gate. It seemed odd that anyone should still live in the place; it was an old clapboard building with a shingle roof, with scraps of tar paper tacked on around chimney and dormers. The door hung on a hinge and there was a hole where the lock had been. A piece of baling wire held it shut when no one was home. The soiled curtain lifted and a face appeared and then the door dragged open.

"Yes?" a man asked, staring down at us. He was quite tall, about seventy years of age, handsome and solidly built.

"I'm your neighbor," Ted said, smiling. "Thought I should introduce myself."

"In the Grigson place, are you?" he asked.

"Yes, that's right. Bought it a couple of months ago."

"Fixing her up, eh? Come on in," he said, standing aside.

The room was warm and smelled of leather and dogs. It was clean but shabby inside. A woman's voice spoke softly from the other room. He looked up and excused himself, then came back with a tray and glasses.

We sat down on the odd chairs in the room and smelled dust. A clock ticked; there were cobwebs on the window shades, and a layer of dust on sills and table tops. A piano stood in the corner with a hymn book on the stand, with family pictures arranged along the top. It was a room at the end of the world, where nothing could escape the loneliness and silence. What kept this man and woman from madness was beyond me. The clock was an unbearable reminder of lost time. Everything in the room was old, tired, battered and repaired, and had witnessed the desolation of the years.

"Iced tea in a moment; the missus is fixing it," he said, sitting down in a way that indicated this was his particular chair. He faced us with the light falling on him through the gauze curtain. He looked fit but at a point where aging would no longer visibly alter him; he was a timeless aspect of the countryside, like one of those silvery planks hanging by a nail from the barn. His eyes were clear and wreathed in crinkles from a life in the sun.

"You folks from Dallas?" he asked, warming to us.

"Yes," I said. "I still live there. I'm a lawyer for the government."

"Federal," he asked.

"I handle interstate regulations, very boring and technical."

"My son's in that line," he said, rubbing his knees. He knew more than I gave him credit for. He was quite comfortable in this conversation.

"And you," he asked Ted, "are you a farmer now?"

"A gentleman farmer. I'm enjoying the peace and quiet. I have a little garden, and I might put out a few goats and make some cheese," Ted said.

"Goat cheese. The French like it, don't they. There was a man here years ago used to raise sheep. He made a kind of cheese out of the milk, but no one bought it. Too funny tasting, I guess. He went away again. Never heard of any goats though. Suppose it could be done."

"What was your business, if you don't mind my asking."

"Cattle. I had a couple of feed lots. Never did like messing with cows; they wanted to break out and graze on the range, but you'd catch all kinds of hell from neighbors. I gave up. You couldn't raise your head in church some days people'd be so cross at you for one thing or other. Then the oil men came around poking holes in the ground; told me I was going to be richer than a sheik. Now they draw out a few barrels a week and give me my allowance, which doesn't buy enough bread to put the butter on. But it's something. Most folks around here live off their children."

"It's hard country," I said.

"Hard? Don't tell 'em that in town. They think we're living like kings out here, nothing to do but shoo flies off the sugar bowl and cash our oil checks. This ain't hard country; it's just country. People got so used to doing things the easy way they don't know what work is any more."

Iced tea was brought in by a wraith-like woman in her late sixties. Her hair was pulled back in a knot, and the flesh of her face seemed drawn back with it. Her eyebrows were raised in a permanent look of surprise. She told us we were an item of gossip in town. Newcomers always are, she said.

"How long does it take to become old hat," Ted asked.

"About a year," she said. "After that, you need a good scandal to get your name around. Are you famous?" she asked.

"No, I'm quite obscure, actually. But I have a somewhat shady past," he said, "I'm divorced."

"Even the crickets get divorced out here," Henry, the old man, said.

"Are you ever bored out here," I asked them.

They looked at each other and smiled. "You start to realize you're not alone," Henry said solemnly.

"You mean you start believing in God?" I asked.

"I mean, you begin to see you aren't alone; you forget all about being an individual; that's for city folks. You talk to yourself a lot; Angie's always talkin' to someone around here I've never seen. I'm always feelin'

I'm two people, maybe more. You forget all about being the center of things and start livin' more humbly. I think maybe I'm just a flea, a bit of life hanging onto the prairie, sucking its blood."

"Well, *I* don't think like that. The Lord's looking after me, but let's me do the hard work. That's as far as I take it, but Henry's educated and likes deep thoughts. He's always making people scratch their heads trying to keep up with him. They think he's more a pagan than a Christian."

"Maybe I am," Henry said. "I believe in lots of gods, one for every tree and bush. The Comanches thought their gods were everywhere; you can't find a hill or a bit of rock that wasn't sacred for something in their world. That's the only way to relate to the ground you live on, if you ask me. If we'd change our faith, maybe the river gods would come back and we'd have good water again. But folks think if you holler a few hymns up at the ceiling, you'll be saved and that's all you need to worry about."

We got up finally and went back to the house; it was eight o'clock and the sun was a deep orange color. The shadows were long and a cool breeze was blowing down from the hills. A blue flame stood in the grass; Ted saw it first and put out his hand to stop me. We stood in the front yard, on the wiry tufts of grass, with the hill sloping up before us. The house seemed like a small boat trying to climb the earth-colored wave forming over it. Midway up in the curl of this murky wave was the flame, a delicate pointed blue shape wavering in the darkness. He went on alone and came close to it. I could hear his voice speaking to it. Then, just as eerily, the flame thinned out and disappeared.

When Ted came back, he was elated. He bounded into the house and pulled down a bottle of wine and we sat at the little wooden table drinking from mugs. He eyed me carefully.

"Do you know what that was?"

"Up on the hill? No, but I'm waiting for you to tell me. Please don't say it was the Virgin Mary on her nightly visitation to you."

"No, she's much older than the Virgin Mary. Mary is a mere child compared to some of the great ones."

"Ted, it's been a tough year. Now you're out here in the prairies and it's getting to you. You're going soft."

"Not soft enough. That's it," he said, pulling up his chair. "Soft is the precise term for it. I was . . . I was *hard*, Frank. A hardened skeptic. I had put it all away from me, everything all the pleasures, all the contentments, the *mysteries*! They were nothing to me. The only thing that mattered was me, I was the center of the whole thing. Everything, wife, kids, job, people, America, planet Earth turned around me. And I couldn't be bothered with the fussy little monkeys chattering away inside me. I kept telling myself, I am the one who decides, only I get to sing my own beautiful lullabies at night."

I was being careful with my expression; I had the habit of putting on my father's sardonic little smile when things got personal. I decided I would sit there quietly, not looking up but not looking away either. I sipped from my mug.

"I wasn't having a fling with my student. That was all crap; I'd gotten a big grant and had to do a little shoving to get it. It pissed off a lot of people who thought I didn't deserve it. Then they waved a deanship at me and that was that. A cabal in the department got a scandal circulating about me and Pringer, my research assistant, and it was all over. I couldn't stop it. But Joan kept saying, it wasn't Pringer, who did come on to me occasionally, and I must say I didn't mind it. I played it up, just to prove I still had it. Anyway, Joan sat up one night and turned on the light and said it was done, finished. She said I was a stone. I was no longer any good for her. She was trying to live in some kind of relation to the world, and I was the obstacle to it. I poisoned her life and it had nothing to do with any shenanigans with Pringer. She couldn't have cared less about it. She said she was leaving me so she could begin to grow and open herself. She was crying out for something to believe, something to pray to. I thought it was all bullshit and some counselor we went to took me aside and said Joan was going through menopause and was all screwed up. He said women at middle age hate the changes in their bodies and go looking for spiritual replacements for the men they married. There was nothing to do but be patient and caring. I let her go. She went like a flash, a streak across the sky, a *meteorite*."

He paused and sipped his wine. A silence dropped over us like a soft breeze. The light was a pale sliver of warmth against the silence, which was immutable and solid.

"She hardly knows me now. The kids struggle with it, but she's so convinced of her happiness that they can't entirely mourn the old life.

They've adapted and are doing great in school. There is a curious lack of problems from this decision, as if it were ordained. My children accept me as the distant man who once controlled their lives. And who now calls and sends small amounts of money to them and writes occasionally."

"And you? Are you happy as well? Or are you going off the end talking to ghosts?"

"You heard what the old geezer said: you're never alone out here. He was right about the Comanches; they were like the aborigines. They even had their own song lines, their sacred maps. You couldn't cross a foot of ground in these hills without feeling you moved through a crowd of gods. Imagine that, Frank. A world crowded with gods all running around turning on the rain and the winter frost, and pulling up the corn, sending death to this person and life to that one, filling a woman with seed and giving some boy courage, and so on and so on. Joan was trying to imagine all this on her own, trying to invent some kind of Indian religion for herself. She was stumbling, but god knows, she couldn't do it with me going around with Calvin in my head, trying to prove I was among the chosen few."

We finished the bottle of Bandol he had opened, and I suddenly felt numb and tired. I excused myself and went to bed. In the morning I woke to hear Ted out in the back yard standing with his hands in his pockets, chanting some little phrase over and over. He had lit a little fire of kindling and leaves and stood before it; it was just past dawn. I doubt he had gone to bed at all.

When I came down, he wore the same animated expression from the night before.

"Sleep well?" he asked, handing me a cup of coffee.

"Pretty well. I'm a bit hung over," I said.

"Eat mint. That always works for me." He found a clump of it in the yard and gave it to me. It was gritty with sand, and I rinsed it off under the tap. I sat there chewing a leaf waiting for the coffee to cool. My head cleared. I felt light and refreshed. The coffee was wonderful. He sat down and watched me a moment.

"Did I scare you last night, Frank?"

"No. I just think you should take things slowly; don't try to catch up to Joan or force some new religion on yourself."

"I knew you'd say something like that; reminds me of your father, a bit. You're better, more human than he was, but you got his habits. I want to break through this suicidal country, Frank. It teaches us to doubt everything that can't be sold, and to distrust every kind of fellowship and love to keep us lonely, groping, hungry for America's candy food and candy television. We're a doomed race if we go on living like this much longer. Nothing really works, nothing matters, nothing is permanent or different. It's all human affairs day and night, everything is cash registers and money in the bank. I couldn't go back to that way. I'd rather die out here in my rocking chair thinking about spirits than go back and teach some business majors how to write their goddamn reports. The prairie is God's body, Frank; it's alive; it moves at night. It's a great pile of little gods all pushing together, a sea of them, crazy gods in all forms. And the one I speak to, the little woman god who keeps coming to the edge of the yard, is like the mother of some very old sea bed, some slab of granite or limestone in which all the fossils were her creations once. She is the voice of something holy and impossibly old, and she tells me I am changing. I am going to make it, I am going to save myself."

He had dark bags under his eyes, and his hands trembled as he spoke. I would have drawn the sum there and considered calling a hospital, except that I half believed him. Something good *was* happening in him. He was better off half-mad than he was groveling in the snake pit with his colleagues. Except for a lack of sleep, he seemed very fit.

"Come and see my garden," he said.

We went out to a patch of ground that had been fenced off with chicken wire. Inside were little mounds of earth with green shoots poking out. He dribbled water on them from a perforated hose. He was growing spinach, egg plant, artichokes, garlic, onions, parsley, and there was even a bit of clover with a bee in it. To make a prairie takes "one clover, and a bee, and revery. The revery alone will do, if bees are few."

"Your altar?" I asked, pointing to some field stone.

"My kneeling pads," he said simply. "I pray for the garden, and thank the spirits for helping me."

"You really are mad, aren't you," I said.

"Yes, but I need to be crazier before it all makes sense. I need to crack this egg and let it flow down into my spine and my liver," he said, pointing to his head. "My visions aren't strong enough. Henry is a very powerful guru, and the things he says are full of healing. But everyone likes to pretend it's too deep to understand. His wife understands what he talks about, she just pretends it's all silly. She believes him. The ground out here is so strong, Frank, it breaks everyone down, it just breaks them down cell by cell until you are totally changed. If they didn't believe in the meanest possible god down there at the church," he said, pointing toward town, "they'd never have the guts to keep fighting the land. They've got to believe that their god would come along and beat them all to death and fling them into hell if they should change one inch of their ways. They just go along fucking up the rivers, pouring asphalt over everything, poisoning the fields because if they didn't do it, progress would stop. They would begin to turn things around, and flow back into families and communities and stop trying so hard to perfect themselves. They'd start living on the simple rules of the land, and it would just kill them to lose their culture in that single change of mind. It would all go, Frank, it would go like that!" he said, snapping his finger.

I'd had enough of the Gospel according to Ted, who was bent over his bean stalks in the back when I drove away. He was talking them into good health. I was in a bad mood the whole way back. When I got into town, the streets seemed dreary to me. I walked down to the park and watched a few of the old men play tennis. Women were out walking their dogs for the evening. Houses were all lit up for supper and things had settled down to another evening of television. I kept thinking about Ted walking around talking to his ghost, and Henry sitting in his rocker in the stuffy little living room thinking up new ways to call the river gods back.

It was all a dreary fantasy to think that living out there on the desolate hills was a spiritual rebirth. Poor Henry had deluded himself into becoming a pagan again; and Ted could cover up all his woes and failures with a bean stalk and a lettuce shoot. It was ridiculous.

> Nine bean rows will I grow there
> And a hive for the honey bee,
> And live alone in the bee-loud glade.

With the wasps and the rattlers about your feet, and the hard ice-honed northers beating at your tin roof. Sure enough. And the fire ants biting you

535

until your ankle swelled like a water melon. Yes. And the dust storms blew over and took another inch of precious top soil away, leaving the yellow clay to harden and crumple the last bit of bean stalk withering in the garden. Poor Ted—he was unhinged, having a nervous breakdown and mistaking it for a divine revelation. I had to give Joan some credit; she knew when to quit. The aftermath was a messy spectacle, a man putting on his rope sandals and hair shirt and going about with his begging bowl, talking to the weeds and greeting the marsh gas as a visitation of angels.

I made another pilgrimage out to Ted's shrine and we stood for a long revery among the curlicues and loops of his bean row, which festooned a trellis he had erected. His corn was high, and his artichoke plants looked like a row of spiked land mines. It was an impressive piece of jungle wriggling in its tiny square of black earth against all that sea of gray hills.

Inside he had hung wild bouquets from his rafters and begun caning his own chairs. He had woven a rug out of bits of yarn and yellow grass and seeds and other things he found on his nightly prowls. It was done with a certain tentativeness from hands and eyes that had never done these things before. A loose bit of straw hung from what was supposed to be a certain intricate curling in of leaves. I noticed the flaw more than the intent, I suppose. My eyes dwelled on the little imprecisions that crept into the process of turning from one vision to another.

We ate a "field salad," as he called it, wild herbs and grass, and a few leafy weeds, and he poured his own bit of sunflower oil on it all and tossed a few pepper grains over it. It was mild, chewy, satisfying in an odd way. A remote feeling came into me as I ate the food; something about its sources puzzled me. It hadn't come from the ordinary places, a store, someone's roadside stall. He had found it lying out there on the breast of some dull, mouse-gray hillside, as if it were growing there as part of his philosophy. The sun left its nutty aromas in the food, and something of the dusty wild earth remained in its blunt texture. I could taste midnight and cold starlight as I ate. It was not a satisfying taste, but foreign to anything I accepted as food. I felt lost, as if he were speaking to me in a strange tongue, something halting and guttural that came with living out here under the fierce weather and loneliness.

Anything could happen to a man who gave himself too willingly to this unbending earth. It seemed to claim you the moment you agreed to take food from it. And here, in the wooden bowl with its rough greens and glistening sunflower oil, were ingredients that seemed to undo the civilization you came from. I felt foolish picking at clover stems and whatever else his hand had found digging through the hard little tufts around his house. I should defend my beliefs more vigorously, I thought, while he gave me those cheerful looks and forgot even to wipe the oil away from his mouth.

There we sat, as dusk lowered over the house and erased all sense of time. A smoky light lingered on the edge of the hills, and beneath it moved a silence that was as deep as an ocean current, and as cold. The hooves of invisible animals went close by the house, and in the gold fog of sunset I could almost believe I saw riders moving into the hills behind the great bison herds.

In the evening he led me back down to his little dry pond and stood there for a long while. I saw a shape in it, a kind of circle with the tail leading off into the arroyo that once fed it.

"You know what that was, Frank? Henry told me a few days ago. It wasn't always a pond. The Comanches dug it out once and buried their horses there, the bravest ones. This is sacred ground. He told me the man who owned this place wouldn't touch it, wouldn't even let them drill a test hole for oil. When the world changes, Henry says, there will be water in it, and the souls of these horses will rise and run free. Nice, isn't it? A good dream to have."

ABOUT THE AUTHORS

Victoria N. Alexander, who was born in Carrollton, Texas, began raising birds at age ten. She graduated from Walden Preparatory in Dallas before moving to New York to attend Hunter College. Her first novel, *Smoking Hopes* (The Permanent Press), won The Washington Prize for Fiction. She is currently working on her Ph.D. at The City University, New York, and writing her third novel, *The Bird Girl*.

Phyllis W. Allen, a Fort Worth businesswoman and author, is a promising new voice in African-American literature. Her stories have been anthologized by Guild Press (University of Minnesota) and the Center for Texas Studies (University of North Texas). She received the 1994 *KenteCloth* Short Fiction Award, judged by Layne Heath, for "The Shopping Trip." In 1996, Ms. Allen attended the Iowa Writers Workshop where she refined her novel in progress about a family who endures racial injustice in North Texas.

Judy Alter has been Director of TCU Press since 1987. She holds a Ph.D. in English, with a special interest in the literature of the American West, from Texas Christian University. Before that, she earned an M.Ed. in English from Northeast Missouri State University and a B.A. from the University of Chicago. The Fort Worth author and publisher is a past president of Western Writers of America. Also a novelist, Alter won a Spur Award from Western Writers of America for *Mattie* (1987), the Best Juvenile Award from the Texas Institute of Letters for *Luke and the Van Zandt County War* (1984), and a Western Heritage Award from the National Cowboy Hall of Fame for "Fool Girl," a 1991 short story. Her most recent novels are *Libbie*, *Jessie*, and *Cherokee Rose*, which form a series of historical works about women in the Old West.

Rhonda Austin returned to college after raising a family. She is a graduate student in Alpine where she edits *The Sage*, the literary magazine of Sul Ross State University. She has had her nonfiction in newspapers and business publications, although "Kyla Gene's Wedding" is her first work of fiction to appear in wide release.

Patrick Bennett has published fiction in *Sou'wester*, *Small Pond*, *Concho River Review*, and in other literary journals. His short story in *New Texas '93*, "Winifred and the Wolf Man," won the 1993 Betty Greene Award from the Center for Texas

Studies. Texas A&M Press published his nonfiction books *Talking with Texas Authors* (1980) and *Rough and Rowdy Ways* (1988). *Talking with Texas Authors* offers twelve interviews with Francis Mossiker, Tom Lea, Larry McMurtry, and others. Recently, Abilene Public Library published a chapbook by Pat and Shay W. Bennett, *Culture on the Catclaw: A List of Published Books and Produced Plays by Abilene Authors*. Bennett teaches creative writing at McMurry University.

Betsy Berry, an assistant professor of English at Southwestern University, is presently grinding out her first novel, *The Buried Life*. She has written nonfiction for a variety of publications and was once a ghost writer for Tex Schramm, generating public relation blurbs for the Cowboys. Berry's literary writings have appeared in *Texas in Poetry*, *New Texas '95*, and *The Texas Observer*. She describes herself as "a writer from Texas rather than a Texas writer." The Austin author says that *The Buried Life* is set in a Houston that is "like Mars, only with traffic."

Jerry Bradley is a professor of English at West Texas A&M and recipient of a Boswell Poetry Prize. He earned his B.A. at Midwestern University and M.A. and Ph.D. at Texas Christian University. As a critic, reviewer, poet, and short story writer, Bradley has had his work appear in *Western American Literature*, *Studies in American Humor*, *Small Press Review*, and *Texas Review*. In 1991, his book-length collection of poetry, *Simple Versions of Disaster*, was published by UNT Press. He was the editor of *New Mexico Humanities Review*. Born in Jacksboro and raised in Mineral Wells, Bradley lives in Canyon.

Mark Busby, who was born and raised in Ennis, graduated from East Texas State University and the University of Colorado. He is Director of the Center for the Study of the Southwest at Southwest Texas State University, where he also serves as a member of the English faculty. Busby has authored a number of book-length studies, including critical analyses of Preston Jones, Lanford Wilson, and Ralph Ellison. He edited the 1993 anthology, *New Growth 2: Contemporary Short Stories by Texas Writers* (Corona Press). In addition, he coedited *The Frontier Experience and the American Dream* and now, with Dick Heaberlin, he edits the periodicals *Southwestern American Literature* and *Texas Books in Review*.

Camilla Carr is a resident of Venice, California; however, she returns as often as possible to her Texas hometown of Chillicothe to visit family and continue writing where she first began. Carr is the author of the novel, *Topsy Dingo Wild Dog*. Her fifth motion picture for television, an adaptation of Pulitzer-prize-winning Edna Buchanan's novel *Nobody Lives Forever*, will soon air on ABC. She coproduced the original Los Angeles award-winning production of Jane Chambers's play, *Last Summer at Bluefish Cove*. Carr is currently working on her second novel, *Packard Jordan's Final Appeal to the Texas State Parole Board,* along with a teleplay for Dolly Parton.

Pat Carr, this year, is working on literary projects on an Arkansas farm. She does have deep Texas roots. Carr lived in south Houston while becoming a summa cum laude at Rice. After earning a Ph.D. from Tulane, she taught at Rice, then Texas Southern and the University of Texas at El Paso. Her work has appeared in *Texas Monthly* and *Yale Review*, as well as in the anthologies *Her Work: Stories by Texas Women* (Shearer) and *Common Bonds* (SMU Press). In *The New Handbook of Texas* (TSHA Press), Don Graham recommends one of Carr's short story collections: "Pat Carr's *Night of the Luminaries* (1986) spoke in spare rhythms of modern themes." Carr's novella *Bluebird* was in the 1993 SMU Press anthology *Careless Weeds*, and her ten books include a collection of Civil War stories, *Our Brother's War*, and a novel, *The Grass Creek Chronicle*.

Laurie Champion, whose Texas hometown is Princeton, has had her work included in such publications as *The Explicator, New Texas '93, North Texas Review, Southern Literary Journal, Texas Short Fiction II,* and *American Literature*. The author of "The Other Man's Bet" has lived in a variety of locales in Texas and in the United States. Champion is an assistant professor of composition and literature at Sul Ross State University in Alpine.

Paul Christensen, poet, editor, and Texas A&M English professor, received an NEA poetry grant in 1991. An American literary critic, his studies include *Charles Olson: Call Him Ishmael* and *Minding the Underworld: Clayton Eshleman and Late Postmodernism*. He is also the author of a memoir, *An American in Provence*, and a novel, *A Freak of Nature*. His story "Water" won the 1995 Short Fiction award from the Texas Institute of Letters. His poetry collections include *Old and Lost Rivers, Gulfsongs, The Vectory, Weights & Measures*, and *Signs of the Whelming*. Christensen is currently teaching on an NEA Fellowship in Oslo, Norway, a change of pace from his professorial duties in College Station.

Lawrence Clayton has authored or edited fifteen books, most on Texas and Southwestern subjects, and more than a hundred articles and reviews. In 1990, UNT Press published his critical biography, *Benjamin Capps and the South Plains: A Literary Relationship*. In 1994, Eakin Press released Clayton's *Watkins Reynolds Matthews: Biography of a Texas Rancher*. Clayton is a member of the Western Writers of America and the Texas Folklore Society. He is also a professor of English at Hardin-Simmons University and co-editor of HSU Press.

Jerry Craven, a Corpus Christi native, has published his poetry, fiction, and drama in such places as *Concho River Review, REAL, Texas Short Fiction* II, Isaac Asimov's *Science Fiction Magazine, Analog*, and *The Texas Anthology*. His books of poetry are *The Last Running, My Own Choric Song*, and *Oleander Wine*. Craven is also an editor of literary anthologies and a co-editor of language textbooks. Selections from his *Amarillo Daily News* column will soon be released in book

540

form by Texas Tech University Press. For many years a professor of English at West Texas A&M, Craven is currently teaching in Azerbaijan, although he is expected to return to Amarillo.

Carol Cullar, along with being a poet, short story writer, visual artist, and a high-school art teacher, is editor and owner of The Maverick Press. Cullar publishes the journal *Alacrán*, along with the annual winning manuscript of the Southwest Poets Series contest. She graduated from Hardin-Simmons University and Instituto Allende, San Miguel de Allende, Mexico. One can find her writing in such publications as *Southwestern American Literature*, *New Texas '93*, *Texas Short Fiction II*, *Grasslands Review*, *Texas in Poetry*, and *Concho River Review*. Her books of poetry are *Haiku, The Hunger, Life & Death, Mostly*, and *Inexplicable Burnings*. Cullar teaches and creates in Eagle Pass.

Terence A. Dalrymple is a professor at Angelo State University. Dalrymple was the editor of *Concho River Review* and has served in various capacities with the Texas Commission on the Arts. He has had short stories, articles, and reviews included in such publications as *The American Literary Review*, *RiverSedge*, *Modern Short Stories*, *Red Neck Review of Literature*, *Writer's Digest*, *New Mexico Humanities Review*, *and Western American Literature*. The San Angelo writer had his story "The Last Time I Saw Lynn" anthologized in *New Growth 2*. Dalrymple's novel for young readers, *Fishing for Trouble*, was released in 1992 by New Win Publishing.

Ruben Degollado has an English degree from the University of Texas Pan American. He teaches English/Language Arts at Mission Junior High School in McAllen. Degollado has been published in *Gallery*, UTPA's literary magazine and *Delusion*, a chapbook distributed in Austin. The author of "Not the Truth: (John 1:6–9)" has a story forthcoming in *Bilingual Review* of Arizona State University.

El Paso native **Chuck Etheridge**'s literary highlights include having served as a Rent-A-Poet for the old Monnig's Department Stores in Fort Worth and having written catalog descriptions of staplers for an office supplier. Along with appearing in a variety of scholarly and literary journals, his work has been included in such anthologies as *A Measured Response* and *A Loving Voice II*. Etheridge is an administrator and professor at McMurry University in Abilene.

Lyn Fraser spent a West Texas childhood in Uvalde. She is author of *Water from the Rock* and *Finding Grace in Time of Grief* (Paulist Press 1994). Her articles have appeared in a variety of magazines and journals, including *The Writer*, *Walking*, *Texas Highways*, *Colorado Outdoors*, *Country Woman*, and *Baseball American*. The author of "Ex Libris" now teaches English at Mesa State College in Colorado.

Greg Garrett was born in Oklahoma and has lived throughout the South and Southwest. He received his Ph.D. in English from Oklahoma State University, where he studied with Gordon Weaver. The author of "Black and White" now lives with wife Tina and his son Jake in Waco. An award-winning professor at Baylor University, Garrett has had his short fiction appear in the *South Dakota Review*, *High Plains Review*, *Grain*, *Texas Short Fiction II*, and *Writers' Forum* as well as in a number of other Canadian and American magazines and journals. In 1993, Garrett won the Pirate's Alley Faulkner Prize for Fiction for his novella *Minuet*. *Cycling*, his forthcoming novel, is set in Waco.

Albert Haley is the author of *Home Ground: Stories of Two Families and the Land* and *Exotic*, the 1982 winner of the John Irving First Novel Prize. His stories have appeared in *The New Yorker*, *Atlantic*, *Rolling Stone*, and in many literary journals. Originally from Duncan, Oklahoma, Haley grew up in Alaska, earned an economics degree at Yale, and returned to his northern home to be "steeped in the oil industry, writing, and the politics of wilderness." Haley is now in Houston, teaching creative writing at the University of Houston and at the University of St. Thomas.

H. Palmer Hall directs the library and teaches writing at St. Mary's University in San Antonio. He has published poems, stories, and essays in little magazines throughout the country and on the internet. His story "Night with Tim" appeared in *New Texas '93*. Hall is co-director of Pecan Grove Press and co-editor of the *Texas Writers Newsletter*. His books include *The Librarian in the University* and *From the Periphery: Poems and Essays*. Hall also edited *A Measured Response*, an anthology of poems about Vietnam and the Gulf War.

Jack O. Hazlerig has spent most of his adult life as an English professor, with some time off to run a business and work as a salesman. Prior to college (degrees from the University of North Texas and Texas Tech), he worked at diverse jobs, including farming. Hazlerig served in the infantry during the Korean War, where he was awarded a Bronze Star. He has taught at the two universities mentioned and at Central Missouri State University. He teaches Shakespeare as well as South-western literature at Texas A&M International University. His fiction has appeared in *Texas Short Fiction* and *RiverSedge*, and the Laredo writer's reviews have been published in *English in Texas*.

The author of nine books, **James Hoggard** has degrees from Southern Methodist University (B.A.) and the University of Kansas (M.A.). In 1990, Hoggard won the Texas Institute of Letters Award in Short Story for "The Scapegoat." The Wichita Falls author and educator has been a former N.E.A. Fellow, and presently he is President of the Texas Institute of Letters. Hoggard has published a nonfiction book, *Elevator Man*, and a novel, *Trotter Ross*. His poetry and prose appeared in

Texas Stories and Poems, *Travois*, *The New Breed*, and *New Growth 2*, and *New and Experimental Literature*. In 1994, Northwestern University Press released Hoggard's collection of English translations from the poetry of Tino Villanueva, *Chronicle of My Worst Years*. Hoggard has been a professor at Midwestern State University since 1966.

John Irsfeld, of Mineral Wells, is the author of many novels, including *Coming Through* (1975), *Little Kingdoms* (1976; reprinted in 1989), and *Rats Alley* (1987). Soon after the publication of *Little Kingdoms*, Boston University's Dr. Howard Gotlieb asked Irsfeld to name that institution's Mugan Memorial Library the repository of his papers, where they are now being collected. Irsfeld characterizes himself now as a recovering writer, who has recently returned to classroom teaching at the University of Nevada, Las Vegas, after a decade in central administration.

Guida Jackson, an author of fiction, nonfiction, and plays, grew up in Amarillo and received her B.A. in journalism from Texas Tech. After raising four children, she returned to school for an M.A. in Third World Literature and a Ph.D. in Comparative Literature. Among Jackson's thirteen books are the novels *A Common Valor* (Hamlyn Press) and *Passing Through* (Simon and Schuster). Her short story "The Evil Eye" appeared in *New Growth*, "The Umbilical Cord" was selected for inclusion in *New Texas '91*, and "The Hired Girl" was in *New Texas '92*. With her husband William Laufer, Jackson edits the literary journal *Touchstone*. Recently, she published *Traditional Epic: A Literary Companion* (Oxford University Press) and her *Encyclopedia of Literary Epic* (ABC Clio) is forthcoming.

Jo LeCoeur, a native of rural Mississippi, grew up without a television; she had a Ph.D. from L.S.U. and a job at Loyola University before she got one. She recently declared that she "has a grandson too good to be True, but that's his name." LeCoeur, a professor at the University of the Incarnate Word in San Antonio, has had essays in *The Southern Review* and *Louisiana Literature*; fiction in *Jessamyn West Review*, *Pompa*, and *Palo Alto Review*; and poetry in *Borderlands*, *The Sow's Ear*, *The Raven Chronicles*, and *New Orleans Review*. In 1994 Pecan Press published her book of monologues, *Choc'lit Milk and Whiskey Voices*. The winner of The Maverick Press's 1996 Southwest Poet's Series award was LeCoeur's *Blues in a Red-Eye Glass*.

James Ward Lee, a former President of the Texas Folklore Society, is author of scholarly articles, editorships, essays, and short fiction as well as editor or co-editor of numerous books and journals. His writing has appeared in *Concho River Review*, *Southwestern Historical Quarterly*, *Range Wars*, and in the publications of the Texas Folklore Society. The Denton author and educator founded the *Southwest Writers Series* and coedited *Southwestern American Literature* and *The Texas Tradition*. He also wrote a study on the life and works of William Humphrey as

543

well as the annotated bibliography *Classics of Texas Fiction*. His 1993 collection of essays, *Texas, My Texas*, was published by UNT Press. Lee teaches in the English Department of the University of North Texas.

Ernestine Sewell Linck, Commerce Texas, is a former professor of English at the University of Texas at Arlington. Linck contributed a study on Loula Grace Erdman to the *Southwest Writers* series and has published widely in the areas of literary criticism, rhetorical studies, and folklore in addition to her reviews for *Texas Books in Review* and *Review of Texas Books*. She is a member of the Austin Writers' Guild, Women Writing the West, and Western Writers of America. She co-authored the 1989 winner of the Texas Institute of Letters' Best Nonfiction book, *Eats: A Folk History of Texas Foods*. Two of Linck's books of nonfiction were released in 1996: *How the Cimarron River Got Its Name and Other Stories About Coffee* and *The Amazing Etta Booth Mayo*.

Pat LittleDog (formerly Pat Ellis Taylor) wrote *Afoot in a Field of Men*, short fiction originally published by Slough Press and republished by Atlantic Monthly Press. Also among her books are *The God Chaser*, a collection of fiction and poetry (Slough Press), *Border Healing Woman: the Story of Jewel Babb*, an award-winning nonfiction work (University of Texas Press), *Tonic, Teas, Roots, & Remedies*, a poetry collection (Slough Press), and *In Search of the Holy Mother of Jobs*, another work of fiction (Cinco Puntos Press). Her short fiction has been anthologized in *Common Bonds*, *Her Work*, *South by Southwest*, and *New Growth*. A former recipient of NEA and Dobie-Paisano fellowships, LittleDog has several children and one grandchild. The Bryan native now lives in Austin, Texas.

Marise McDermott received her B.A. from Queens College, and in 1966, an M.F.A. from Southwest Texas State University. She has been Director of the Humanities Center, The Witte Museum in San Antonio, has served on the Texas Committee for the Humanities, and was editor of *The Texas Humanist*. Her writings on the arts have appeared in various magazines and newspapers, and her stories and essays have been included in *The Guadalupe Review*, *Popular Writing in America*, and other publications.

Bruce McGinnis, who has three published novels, grew up on a small farm in Comanche County. He received his B.A. and M.A. degrees from Hardin-Simmons University. His novels have been favorably reviewed in *Publishers Weekly*, the *New York Times*, and *Booklist*. His first novel, *The Fence* (Vanguard), was praised by Larry L. King and other critics, and his second novel was *Sweet Cane*. McGinnis has a newly released historical novel, *Reflections in Dark Glass: The Life and Times of John Wesley Hardin* (UNT Press), a literary work based on the life of the legendary gunslinger.

544

Joy-Ellis McLemore, whose hometown is Longview, has had her essays, stories, and poems appear in a variety of publications. Her award-winning story, "The Seduction," was published in *Texas Short Fiction II*. She has taught college English for twenty-two years in five different states. McLemore is a faculty member of the Department of Humanities at UT Tyler, having returned to her native East Texas.

Ann McVay is a nurse and free-lance writer who lives in Allen in Collin County. A graduate of Centenary College in Louisiana, she has had her nonfiction appear in *Dallas Life*, *The Dallas Morning News*, and in other publications. Her fiction has appeared in *Concho River Review* and *Southwestern American Literature*. One of McVay's stories received the first-place prose award at the 1995 University of Houston at Clear Lake Literary Festival.

Lianne Elizabeth Mercer's poetry has appeared in *RiverSedge*, *Concho River Review*, *Texas Short Fiction II*, and *Negative Capability*. Her short story "The Legacy" was included in *Common Bonds*, and "Waiting for Eddie" was anthologized in *New Texas '93*. Her 1994 poetry collection is *No Limit but Light* (Chili Verde Press). Mercer, a psychiatric nurse, has taught both writing and nursing courses. In 1994, she moved from San Antonio to Fredericksburg, where she is closing in on a book-length collection of short fiction.

D. R. Meredith, author of thirteen novels, has had her award-winning work published in twenty-one different editions, including large print and in French. She has over a million books in print and has won two Oppie Awards for *The Sheriff and the Panhandle Murders* and *The Sheriff and the Branding Iron Murders*. She is a regional director and on the national Board of Directors of Mystery Writers of America. She is an editor for *Western Books in Review* and for *Roundup Magazine*, published by the Western Writers of America, and a contributing editor for *Kirkus Reviews*. Meredith also writes reviews for *The Amarillo Globe News*. "Retrospective" is the author's reply to those who wish to know the eventual fate of Mattie Jo Hunter and Jesse McDade, protagonists from Meredith's historical novels.

Talibah Folami Modupe received her B.S. from North Texas State University. She has published three collections of short stories: *Talibah, Can We Talk?*, *Let's Be Frank*, and *The Grapevine Still Alive & Workin'*. Her story "The Right Reverend James" appeared in *New Texas '94*, "Inmate 93274" in *Texas Short Fiction II*, and she had two stories and an essay in *KenteCloth*. The Dallas author is working on a novel, *Recruit*, and a children's book, *Won't You Be My Friend*.

Violette Newton has published ten books of poetry, including her Texas Poet Laureate collection, *The Proxy*. Among her other titles are *The Scandal and Other*

Poems, The Shamrock Cross, and *Jason's Journey*. Her poetry has been anthologized in the yearbooks of the Poetry Society of Texas as well as in *Travois, Texas Stories and Poems, New Texas '92*, and *New Texas '95*. Newton's short stories have appeared in *Stone Drum* and *Fiction and Poetry by Texas Women*. She is working on a book of poetry, *Morning Tide*, which concerns the death of a friend. The poet and short story writer has long taught creative writing in Beaumont.

Keddy Ann Outlaw is a Houston librarian and writer. A native of New York, she jokes about coming to Texas because of her surname. Her poems, stories, and book reviews have appeared in *Borderlands, Grasslands Review, Lilliput Review, Exit 13, Karamu, Library Journal, Houston Chronicle*, and *Sulphur River Literary Review*. One of her poems was included in the 1995 American Book Award-winning anthology, *I Am Becoming the Woman I've Wanted* (Papier-Mache Press). Outlaw's selection in *Texas Short Stories*, "Pink Walls," features characters first introduced in the story "Total Darkness," published in *i.e.*

Jill Patterson serves as Assistant Professor in the Creative Writing Program at Texas Tech University. Her work has appeared in *Concho River Review* and *Cimarron Review*, and she currently serves as fiction editor for *Windhover*, a new journal of Christian literature. She also continues to serve on the Board of Directors for the Texas Association of Creative Writing Teachers.

A lifelong Texan, **Jan Reid** has had his work appear in a variety of publications including *Texas Monthly, Inside Sports*, and *Esquire*. He received a Dobie-Paisano fellowship in 1977, the Texas Writer Recognition Award from the Texas Commission on the Arts in 1981, and an NEA grant in 1984. Among Reid's book-length publications are the 1974 nonfictional *The Improbable Rise of Redneck Rock* (Heidelberg), a 1985 novel, *Deerinwater* (Texas Monthly Press), and the 1986 nonfiction *Vain Glory* (Shearer Publishing). Reid's story in this anthology, "Second Saddle," is part of a novel in progress.

Charlotte Renk, a native East Texan, is an English professor at Trinity Valley Community College. She has had her poetry and prose appear in *Sow's Ear, Atelier, El Locofoco, Concho River Review, Southwestern American Literature, Texas in Poetry, New Texas '93, New Texas '95, REAL, RiverSedge, Culebra*, and in other literary publications. Renk writes and teaches in Athens.

Stephen Renner lives in El Paso. His story in this collection is a section from an epistolary/journal novel, *Oh Yeah, Texas*, a work being circulated for publication. His poetry, usually published under the name Cooper Esteban Renner, has appeared in *The Quarterly* (New York/Toronto), *Chelsea*, and *Fine Madness*, and online in *elimae* and *Gutter*. His poem "Creation" is being featured in a special exhibit at The Berg Collection of the New York Public Library and will appear in a publication of that institution.

Ivanov Y. Reyez was born in McAllen, Texas. He received his Master's in English from the University of Texas, Permian Basin. His short fiction has appeared in *Nebula* (Canada), *Notebook: A Literary Journal*, and *El Locofoco*. He has a short story forthcoming in *Out of the Margins: Two Hundred Years of Sephardic American Writing* (University Press of New England). His poetry has appeared in *New Texas '95*, *Pinyon Poetry*, *Aileron*, *Afterthoughts* (Canada), and in other literary magazines. Reyez is currently working on a novel, *Cosima*. Since 1978 he has taught at Odessa College.

Clay Reynolds, a native West Texan, holds degrees from the University of Texas and Trinity University; he received his doctorate from the University of Tulsa. Among many publications, Reynolds has written three novels: *The Vigil*, *Agatite*, and *Franklin's Crossing*. *Franklin's Crossing* was selected for the Violet Crown Award in 1992 and was entered into Pulitzer Prize competition in that year. *Agatite* has been reissued under the title *Rage*. Reynolds is an N.E.A. Fellow and a member of the Texas Institute of Letters. His short stories have been anthologized, with "A Better Class of People" appearing in *New Growth* and "Etta's Pond" in *Higher Elevation* (Swallow). Reynolds' forthcoming publications are a nonfictional book, *Twenty Questions: A Guide for the Aspiring Writer*, and a new novel, *Players*. He lives with his wife and two children in Denton, Texas.

Joyce Gibson Roach, who grew up in Jacksboro, co-authored the award-winning *Eats: A Folk History of Texas Foods*. Her story "Just As I Am" was anthologized in *Women of the West*. She is a two-time winner of the Spur Award from the Western Writers of America. Novelist Benjamin Capps comments on *Cowgirls*, one of Roach's Spur-Award-winning works: "Cowboys have always had more attention than their female counterparts, but in fact the Old West never was, nor is today, totally a man's world. Joyce is the ideal writer to set the record straight." Roach edited the 1992 *This Place of Memory: A Texas Perspective*, and she has in recent release *Wild Rose: A Folk History of a Cross Timbers Settlement*, as well as *Collective Heart, Texans in World War II: A Literary Portrait*. Roach is helping Disney Incorporated with the design of a National Cowgirl Hall of Fame.

Paul Ruffin has a B.S. and an M.A. from Mississippi State University and a Ph.D. from the University of Southern Mississippi. He is Director of Creative Writing at Sam Houston State University and Editor of *The Texas Review*, one of the state's foremost literary journals. His prose and poetry have appeared in such publications as *Contemporary Southern Fiction*, *Best of the West*, *Texas Stories and Poems*, and *New Growth 2*. Ruffin has authored, co-authored, edited, or coedited twelve books, among them the notable anthologies *The Texas Anthology* and *That's What I Like About the South*. In 1993, SMU Press released Ruffin's short story collection, *The Man Who Would Be God*, which was favorably reviewed by the *New York Times*. In 1996, Browder Springs Publishing released Ruffin's most recent poetry collection, *Circling*, and he has recently completed a novel.

Jan Epton Seale graduated from Waxahachie High before earning her B.A. from the University of Louisville and an M.A. from the University of North Texas. She has been the recipient of an N.E.A. Fellowship, participated in seven P.E.N. fiction projects, and has taught in the Writers-In-Education Program. Her stories have been broadcast on NPR and published in many literary magazine. Her poetry books are *Bonds* and *Sharing the House*, and she was one of four featured poets in *Texas Poets In Concert*. Individual pieces of her prose and poetry can be found in such collections as *Common Bonds*, *New Texas '91*, *New Growth 2*, and *This Place of Memory*. Seale's well-received short fiction collection, *Airlift*, was published in 1993 by TCU Press. In 1995, New Santander Press released her nonfiction *Homeland: Essays Beside and Beyond the Rio Grande*. Seale teaches creative writing in the Rio Grande Valley.

Susan San Miguel, the author of "La Llorena of Leon Creek," holds a B.A. and M.A. in English from the University of Texas at San Antonio and teaches writing at San Antonio College. She co-founded and edited *Midtown*, a literary and arts journal in Houston and is the editor of *Xeriscapes*, an annual anthology of poetry and prose by San Antonio youth. Another of her stories is to appear in the anthology *Southwestern Women: New Voices*. She is currently writing a novel, *The Snake Woman*.

Sallie Strange taught at SMU for over twenty years. Her work has appeared in *Stone Drum*, *Concho River Review*, and *i.e.* Strange's story "The Smartest Man in the World" was included in *New Growth 2*. She won the prose performance award at the Fort Concho Literary Festival in 1992 and had an essay in *Texas Goes to War* (UNT Press). She has a story forthcoming in the anthology *Other Voices* (University of Illinois Press). The Dallas native now lives in Flower Mound.

Carmen Tafolla has authored three books of poetry, seven television screenplays, one nonfiction volume on Chicana women, and numerous short stories, articles, and children's works. Her latest book of poetry, *Sonnets to Human Beings and Other Selected Works by Carmen Tafolla*, has just been released in second edition by McGraw-Hill. Her poetry has appeared in such journals as *RiverSedge*, *the Pawn Review*, and *The International Journal for Humanities and Peace*. Her short stories have been anthologized in *Common Bonds*, *New Growth 2*, and *Southern Exposure*. A native of the West Side of San Antonio, Tafolla received her bachelor's and master's degrees from Austin College and a Ph.D. from the University of

Texas at Austin. She now lives in McAllen, where she is at work on an autobiography, *Between the Borders*, and has just completed a movie script, a feature-length comedy entitled *REAL MEN . . . and other miracles*, co-authored with Sylvia Morales.

Chuck Taylor has been a Texas A&M English professor at College Station and at Korijama, Japan. He has also taught at the University of Texas, managed a bookstore, been an editor at Cedar Rock Press and Slough Press, along with holding down a variety of jobs, including graveyard-shift house parent for the Texas School for the Deaf. Taylor has published essays, short stories, poetry, a novel, and a play. His poetry has been included in *Travois*, *Texas Review*, *Concho River Review*, *Texas Quarterly*, *Texas in Poetry*, and *RiverSedge*. His poetry collection, *What Do You Want, Blood?* received a 1988 Austin Book Award. He has a new book, *Poet in Jail*, which fuses poetry with personal essay.

Marshall Terry is an award-winning author of five novels and a collection of short stories, as well as historian, newspaper book critic, essayist, and educator. In 1986 Terry published the collection *Dallas Stories* (SMU Press) and the novel *Ringer* (Corona Press). Terry's "The Antichrist" won the 1972 Best Story award from the Texas Institute of Letters. His first novel, *Old Liberty*, was published in 1961 (Viking Press) and republished in 1992 (Texas Tech University). Terry's novel *Tom Northway* (Harcourt, Brace) was a co-winner of the 1968 award from the Texas Institute of Letters for best work of fiction and has also been republished. *My Father's Hands* (Texas Tech), the next in the "Northway" series, was published in 1992 and received the PEN-Dallas/Fort Worth Golden Pen Award. The third novel in the series, *Land of Hope and Glory*, was published by University of North Texas Press in 1996. Terry is a teacher and administrator at Southern Methodist University.

Michael Verde grew up in East Texas where he has worked as a pig farmer, a youth preacher, and a cab driver, but now teaches English at Lamar University. He graduated from the University of Texas with a degree in Plan II, then earned his M.A. from the University of Iowa. His first short story was selected first-place of 5,000 entries in *Guideposts* magazine's National Youth Writing Contest in 1985. He now lives in Hamshire, commuting to Beaumont to teach.

Donna Walker-Nixon is a professor of English at the University of Mary Hardin-Baylor in Belton. She sponsors the *Baylorian*, the student literary journal at UMHB. Walker-Nixon has had her fiction appear in a number of journals, with "And Nothing But the Truth" appearing in *New Texas '93*. An earlier version of "The True Faith, Or Any Old Wind," the story in this edition, was published in *Echoes*. The central Texas author is busily establishing a new literary magazine, *Windhover: A Journal of Christian Literature*.